Come What May

FOUR CHRISTIAN ROMANTIC SUSPENSE NOVELS

SUMMER HEAT 2023
BOOK THREE

EMILIE HANEY   CARA PUTMAN   KATY LEE

CHAUTONA HAVIG

TWO DOGS PUBLISHING, LLC.

eBook ISBN: 979-8-88552-223-6

Paperback ISBN: 979-8-88552-226-7

Published by: Two Dogs Publishing, LLC. Idaho, USA

Cover Design by: EAH Creative, Emilie Haney, eahcreative.com

Serial Heat

EMILIE HANEY

Chapter One

Clancy

ANNA MAE STEVENS HAD BEEN MISSING FOR TWO WEEKS, FOUR days, and seventeen hours, and former cop turned private investigator, Clancy Sullivan, was out of leads.

His strides ate up the sunbaked sidewalk, and he yanked open the door to the small local grocery store with more force than necessary. Bells clanged a warning as he stormed inside and made a beeline for the produce section.

The scent of overripe bananas assaulted his senses, and he tried to clear the dark thoughts from his mind as his eyes swept over the bins full of colorful fruit. It was no use. Anna's mother's plea haunted his dreams and now took over his waking hours.

Find my baby. Please. You have to find her before it's too late.

He grabbed a bag of apples and spun in a half circle looking for a basket. That's when he saw her and froze.

Same long blonde hair with a slight wave to it. Same height. Same weight. Same—

Clancy shook his head. No, that wasn't Laura Zuker from his last case. That was just some woman from town.

She spun around as if she'd sensed his attention and boldly held his stare. Golden hair framed an oval face with soft features and parted pink lips. Her dark eye makeup accentuated silver-like eyes, and he saw she wore a retro band t-shirt and flared jeans she'd paired with chunky silver bracelets. He caught sight of a delicate flower tattoo on the inside of her wrist.

He couldn't look away. It wasn't just her beauty, though that was obvious, but the way she didn't back down. Didn't even blush like most girls would.

"You know how the saying goes, right?"

He blinked. When had she stepped closer? And was that floral scent coming from her? "What saying?"

"Take a picture. It'll last longer." Her eyebrows rose as if in challenge.

"Right." He gave his head a little shake and a lock of his chin length hair fell into his eyes. He brushed it away. "Sorry. You look like someone..."

"You know?"

"Knew." His mouth was dry.

"Oh." She took a breath. "You new in town?"

Perpetually. How many times had he heard that question? "Yeah. Been here a few weeks." He clamped his mouth closed so fast his teeth snapped.

"What brings you to Chamberlin?"

And there it was. The question he liked to avoid. Coming to Washington had been the right call. He was ninety-eight percent sure of that, but it didn't make the reason any easier.

"Well, I—" His phone went off, and he checked the screen. "Sorry. Got to take this."

"Right." She snatched an orange from the stand next to them. "Don't stare at me on the way out."

He barely caught her last words but couldn't help the tug at his lips. He forced it down with the reality of why he'd come to Chamberlin and answered. "Sullivan here."

"Hey there, Clancy. Good time to talk?"

Clancy scanned the surrounding store. Aside from the young woman shopping her way to the front, it was empty. "Sure."

4

"I've got a tip for you from the Riversong brothers."

Numbness flooded through him. "What kind of tip?"

"Hopefully, a useful one, but I can't be sure."

"Yeah, I know." He pictured the old man on the other end of the line with his wispy white hair, oversized t-shirt and jeans, and the carved wooden cane with the head of a rattlesnake he leaned heavily on. He'd met Eddie McFadden at the local diner and found him to be both helpful and a bit of a talker. "Let's hear it."

"They were hiking a day or two ago, and I could tell somethin' was off when they came back to the trailer park. You know, set my senses tingling. Anyway, I went over to see Old Jim—you remember that's their dad?"

Clancy's foot tapped the shiny linoleum. "Yep, I remember."

"Good. Yeah, well, he was out there smoking a pipe, and I sat and talked with him for a while until his sons joined. Didn't want to be suspicious." He said it with an accent on "picious" and Clancy fought a smile. "Asked them what was happening, and that's when Daniel—he's the older brother—said they'd seen something disturbing on their hike that morning."

"Disturbing?" Clancy's back straightened. "What did they mean?"

"Hold yer horses, boy. I'm getting there."

Clancy took a calming breath and paced to the pasta aisle so he wouldn't press the man to go faster.

"I asked them what they meant, and at first, it was real hard to get them to talk. They don't trust anyone, 'specially not most towns people, but they know me. I think I wore them down with questions, because he finally said he thought it could have been a body."

Everything in Clancy vibrated to a crescendo then stopped. His heartbeat. His breath. All movement. He was stone but also fury. This couldn't be how things ended. Again.

"Where?"

"Now hold on before you get your knickers in a twist. I don't know if they really thought it was that. They get spooked real easy. But then they mentioned a place up on Coal Ridge that's also got bad vibes. Don't know what that means, just the word Darren used—that's the younger brother."

Clancy thought he heard his phone crack, his grip was so tight on the device. He took in several deep breaths before he could calmly ask, "Where did they think the body was, Eddie? I need to know."

"I know you do. I just wanted to warn you it could be nothing—or a deer, for all I know. Don't want to get your hopes up."

"I know." It was too late for that. He needed a lead, even if it wasn't the lead he wanted.

"I'll send over the map with the spots marked. The...whatever it was they saw was at the old Crenshaw sawmill, long abandoned, and then there's a cabin up Coal Ridge. You sure you know the area enough to get up there without help?"

A stab of annoyance hit him at the words, but he was an outsider to the locals. It didn't matter that he knew his way around the outdoors and topographical maps. No one expected him to make it without a guide.

"I'll be good. Thanks, Eddie."

"Sure, sure. But Clancy," Eddie's usually congenial attitude slipped, "it's probably nothin'—or so I hope, for her mama's sake."

"Me, too, Eddie."

Clancy hung up, and the next moment, his phone dinged with two photos. He saved them to his image album and headed for the door. He'd get food later, but right now, he had a lead.

That was all that mattered.

Chapter Two

Willa

WILLA MARTIN TOLD HERSELF NOT TO WATCH THE HANDSOME man walk out of the grocery store, but she couldn't help it. It wasn't often that anyone new came to Chamberlin and stayed longer than a few days, but he'd said he was going on three weeks now.

"Willa?"

"Sorry, Mr. King. How much did you say it was?" She reached into her oversized purse for her wallet.

"Five sixty two. Paying in cash today?" Mr. King flashed a kind smile at her from behind the counter, and she pulled out a five and some change with a nod. "You keeping busy while your dad is away?"

"Always." She flashed a confident grin back and accepted her change. "Speaking of, I need to get in to work."

"Have a good day, Willa." His nose scrunched up. "I guess I mean I hope it's a slow day for ya."

"I get it," she said on a laugh.

The heat hit her like a tidal wave when she stepped outside of the air-conditioned grocery store. Fanning herself with the receipt and making little impact, she rushed down the street toward her office. Her knock-off

7

Birkenstocks threatened to melt to the pavement, but she rushed on, checking the time on her phone. Five minutes before she was officially late.

Her fingers tingled as she grasped the handle of the door to the dispatch office. It felt like coming home.

"Hey ya, Willa. You're cutting it close," Marilee said from behind the reception desk.

"I know, I know." Willa rushed past and picked up her pace toward the break room they shared with the Sheriff's Department that was also housed in the same building. Two sides of the same coin, as her father liked to say.

She plucked the pre-made salad, orange, and herbal tea from her cloth shopping bag and stuck them in the fridge, though she took a moment to let the cool air wash over her sweaty skin.

Standing up, she closed the door and turned to head to her desk when blue eyes slammed into her like a battering ram.

It was foolish, really. After almost three weeks, Willa knew better than to let the pictures of her best friend Anna Stevens get to her. They were everywhere, and she couldn't stop functioning just because she saw the missing poster Anna's mother had made. But as logical as that all sounded, it didn't sink deep enough to make an impact.

Anna was still missing, and it was still her fault.

"Willa, are you planning to working today?" Barney popped his head into the kitchen and drilled her with a gaze that could turn a person into a pillar of ice despite the heat.

"Yeah. Sorry." She swallowed, her gaze traveling back to the poster. To the picture she'd taken of Anna from a hike earlier that spring. Anna had insisted it become her social media profile image. It highlighted the rich color of her auburn hair, her carefree smile, and her expertly done makeup. Willa could never understand how she got her eyeliner to look so perfect and—

She stifled a sob, thankful Barney hadn't waited for her. How was she supposed to go on with her life like nothing had happened? Like her best friend had been there one day and was gone the next?

"Willa!" Barney's call came from down the hall.

"Coming!" She had to pull it together.

Wiping a finger under her eyes, she sniffed and brushed her hair back over her shoulders. She could do this. It was her job, and she was good at it.

The dispatch room was expertly controlled chaos. Computer monitors took up all available space on desks, and as Julie slipped out from behind a desk, Willa took the headset with a whispered apology.

"You're on time," Julie said with a light chuckle. "It's just Barney who thinks being on time is being late."

Willa slid into the chair, and the tumultuous feelings she'd had ebbed. Working dispatch was stressful, but less so when you'd worked the job over five years.

"Thank you for joining us," Barney said. He was in a mood. "Here are the notices for today." He slid a paper over to her.

Nothing stood out, but she'd go through it more carefully once her boss had filled her in on the rest of the day.

"Also, it could be a busy shift."

She frowned. "How so?"

"Weather reports a storm rolling in from the west. It's picking up speed and should hit in an hour or so. And you know what that means."

"Lightning."

"Exactly. And with this drought we're having, you also know what that means."

"Fire." She knew it all too well. Every summer, it was a race against the clock before the first fire would hit. Barring arson, lightning fires were the most common cause of the blazes that had taken over the Pacific Northwest for the last several summers. "Thanks for the update."

"Hey." Barney's voice dropped low. "You okay?"

It was odd to see the middle-aged man out of his boss-mode, but he'd known her all her life, and occasionally, he let his softer side show.

"I'm fine." She tapped a few keys, hoping he'd go away before she burst into tears. It had happened in the office only once, the day after Anna had gone missing, and she'd promised herself she'd leave the crying to her bedroom at home.

"Should I take down the poster in the break room?"

"No." She met his dark brown eyes. "It's important that it's there. It's just...hard."

"You doing okay with your dad out of town?"

9

Another stab to her gut. "I'm twenty-eight, Barney. I can be home on my own."

"I know, but he had to leave right after…"

"He offered to come home, but *I* told him to stay. You know he loves the chance to do national dispatch every summer, and I will not take that away from him. Besides, Glenn and his guys are on it. We're going to find her." Was she trying to convince herself?

"You're right. Okay, I'll leave you alone. Let me know about any lightning strike calls. That'll shift our night for sure."

Nodding, Willa refocused on her computer screen, willing the tears back.

She was tired of this. Tired of waking up every morning wanting to hear news about Anna but dreading it, too. The odds weren't good—not after almost three weeks—but Willa still had hope. She had to.

A call came in, and she switched off her emotions, trapping them in a box deep inside. It's how she did the job so well. Nothing ever truly touched her. Though, she couldn't say the same for feelings about her best friend. That was a persistent, dull ache she couldn't move past.

Chapter Three

Clancy

CLANCY FORCED HIS JEEP TO SPEED UP THE STEEP MOUNTAIN roads. Faster. He needed to get there now.

Although the roads were paved, he could easily imagine he was the only one out there. Towering pine, cedar, and fir trees lined the steep slope to his right and jutted up despite the drop off to his left. While his AC fought to keep up with the heat outside and the speed he demanded of the Jeep as the elevation climbed, Clancy felt a drop of sweat race down his back.

He'd waited for a tip like this, going back to witnesses and questioning them for anything they could remember. Even while talking to Anna's mother, the woman who had convinced him to come search for her daughter, his hope had waned.

Three weeks was a long time—too long—for a young woman to be missing.

Clancy flexed his fingers on the steering wheel and checked the GPS. He twitched his foot back from the gas. He was almost on top of the location. His eyes searched the right side where Eddie had pointed out a logging road that would lead further into the forest.

It crept into view, and he turned in, his tires crunching on loose rocks. The GPS tracked him until he was right on top of the spot. He pulled to the side of the road, though he assumed no one would be coming up behind him, and climbed out.

Heat radiated off of the packed dirt road but abated some when he stepped into the shade of a nearby pine. Its tangy scent greeted him as his boots crunched over cones, dried needles, and sticks. He scuffed at the forest floor detritus, or slash, and shook his head.

This place was a tinderbox waiting for a spark.

His gaze scanned the sky and landed on fast-moving clouds. "And there's the match."

Growing up in Washington, though further south than Chamberlin, he knew the signs of trouble. The dark storm rolling in from the west could mean lightning, which would spell disaster. He needed to pick up the pace.

With a hand to the gun at the small of his back to check that it was secured, he pulled out his phone and set off toward the spot Eddie had typed out instructions to. It wasn't too far off the logging road, but it was just far enough that someone driving by wouldn't have seen anything.

Birds chirped and animals skittered out of his way—never seen, only heard in the movement of tree limbs or brush. Shadows fell around him as he moved further into the trees and an unnerving feeling landed in the spot between his shoulder blades. He rolled his neck to dispel the tension.

That's when the scent hit him.

Clancy picked up his pace, cursing the fact the Riversong brothers had been right and hadn't called it in. They were likely wary of getting involved with local authorities, but it didn't make it right.

He hopped over a log, dodged a low hanging tree branch, and stepped between two enormous trunks before he saw it. The body was in the middle of a clearing. The scene was almost reverent but for the unbearable stench that wafted to him. Death and decay.

He pulled out his phone and dialed Max Long's number. He'd befriended the Deputy Sheriff upon first coming to town and had found the man to be receptive to information sharing—to a point. He had told Clancy to call at the first sign of anything, though, and Clancy knew better than to get on the wrong side of law enforcement.

The phone rang and rang but kicked over to Max's voicemail. "Hey, call me back. I found something."

Clancy ended the call and took a few tentative steps toward the body, willing himself to breathe through his mouth, not his nose. It was in a state of decomposition consistent with when Anna was taken, but was it her? Was this the end of yet another case he'd worked without success?

He knew it was next to impossible to know until the medical examiner could investigate, seeing as the decomp was so advanced, but the need to know ate away at him.

He checked his phone again. "Enough. Stop stalling." If Max couldn't get back to him, he had a duty to call it in.

He typed in 911 and put the phone to his ear, taking several steps back from the body and the stench.

"911—Please state the nature of your emergency." The voice on the other end of the line was calm.

"Hi. My name is Clancy Sullivan, and I'm a private investigator in the area. I'm in the mountains north of town near Coal Ridge and have found the body of a young woman."

"What?" The calm voice suddenly took on a frantic tone. "I mean, is there a way for you to give me your exact location?" She sounded like she was barely holding it together. A far cry from the professional who had answered the phone.

"Sure. I've got GPS. Hold on." He pulled up the app on his phone and read out the coordinates to her. "You'd better send a team up quickly. The storm is rolling in, and I'm not sure if those clouds hold rain or just lightning."

"I—I will. Dispatching them now. But...can you see any distinguishing markings on the body?" Her voice broke on the last word.

Clancy's frown deepened. "I'm sorry—what?"

"A tattoo. On her wrist? Is there a tattoo on her wrist?"

Then it clicked. This woman knew Anna Stevens. He recognized her description of the distinguishing mark Anna's mother had told him about as well and chided himself that *he* hadn't thought of that first. "I'm sorry, but..."

His phone rang, and he saw it was Max calling.

"Please, can you just—"

"I've got to take this call. It's the sheriff's office."

"But—"

A twinge of guilt nudged his conscience as he hung up. He'd worked with enough dispatchers to know what the woman had done was not okay and outside of protocol, but could he blame her? If it was his friend, wouldn't he do the same?

He racked his mind for any familiarity with the voice he'd heard. He had interviewed all the friends Hillary Stevens had included on her list, but the dispatcher didn't sound like any of those women. Though if he thought hard enough about it, he could recognize something familiar in the timbre of her voice.

His thumb jammed the answer button. "Max, I found a body."

"I just heard over the radio and saw the missed call. You went up there without me?" Frustration edged the man's deep voice.

"I honestly didn't think I would find anything. It was a tip from Eddie that led me here, and he made it clear he had no confidence in it."

Then again, how many tips had Clancy followed up on that had proved useful? Things no one thought were important that ended up solving the case? He'd learned long ago to take everything seriously and follow it to the end, no matter what.

This body was just another example, albeit a gruesome one.

"I'm on my way. I don't think I have to tell you not to touch anything."

Clancy rolled his eyes but forced the annoyance from his tone. "You got it."

Silence hung between them. Then Max said, "You think it's her?"

He roughed a hand over his face. What *did* he think? All signs pointed to the fact that it was Anna. He'd seen the clothing on the body, and it was consistent with something she would wear, but even Anna's mother hadn't known what she was wearing the day she disappeared.

"Honestly, Max? I don't know." His gaze traveled to the body centered perfectly in the clearing. "But it could be."

Max exhaled loudly over the phone. "We're about fifteen minutes out —maybe less if I push it."

"Got it." Clancy hung up, and the silence pressed on him again.

Another dead girl. Another body on his conscience. Even if it wasn't Anna, Clancy felt the weight all the same.

Chapter Four

Willa

WILLA PULLED HARD ON THE WHEEL OF HER HONDA CIVIC, heart pounding as she hugged the curve at breakneck speed. Tears blurred her eyes, and she tried to blink them away. If they fell, she wouldn't be able to wipe them, not at the pace she was driving and especially not on this dangerous, curvy road.

She'd known a call like this would come in. That someone would find something, and she'd assume it was Anna. She just hadn't expected it today.

"Please, God, don't let it be Anna." The plea tumbled from her lips yet again. It had become her mantra since the call came in.

Her phone rang, and she jolted, nearly going off the road. One glance told her it was Sloane calling. She'd heard about the body. It was the only explanation.

Willa jammed the answer button followed by the speaker button before reclaiming her grip on the wheel.

"Willa?" Sloane's voice came out hollow. It was hard to hear her over the full blast of the weak AC, but Willa couldn't afford the hand to hold it closer.

"Speak up. I'm in the car."

"Where are you?"

Willa ground her teeth.

"Please tell me you aren't headed up to Coal Ridge." Sloane sounded anxious rather than frustrated. "Willa?"

"I have to be there, Sloane." She fought back the fresh wave of tears. "I —I have to know if it's her."

The constant noise of the air coming through the vents filled the silence until Sloane spoke again. "You shouldn't see her like that—if it's her." She rushed the last past as if she realized what she'd said too late.

"I need to know. I—" Willa's voice broke.

"What did Barney say?" Sloane shifted topics, perhaps to give her space. She was like that. Compassionate to a fault, but with a backbone stronger than iron. She had to be firm working as an ER nurse, but she hadn't let it affect her soft heart.

"He was *not* happy." Willa surprised herself with a hoarse laugh. "I think he turned three shades of red, but I kind of didn't give him a choice."

"Girl, you are calling in every favor."

"It's important for me. I think he knows that." Willa imagined the look of frustration mingled with disbelief when she'd requested to leave early for the day. She'd never done that—it was almost impossible to fill a shift on such short notice—but somehow, Barney knew she was going no matter what. He'd agreed to step in for her, but his warning was clear. If she did this again, she was out, no matter how much clout her father held.

Sloane blew out a breath. "Okay, well, if you're set on going up there, then all I can say is I'm praying, and I'll be here if you need me."

"Thanks, Sloane. Pray it's not her."

"I am. And Willa?"

"Yeah?" Willa slowed as she caught sight of the turnoff and the line of deputy cars filing the logging road.

"Be careful."

"Always." Willa hung up and pulled in at the end of the line, leaving enough space so she wouldn't block anyone in.

She turned off the car, grabbed her satchel, and stepped out, but she couldn't make her legs move. This was her nightmare come to life. The reality she'd prayed wouldn't come to be.

But she knew the facts. The statistics. She knew it was unlikely Anna had gone off on her own, like the sheriff seemed to think. Or that she'd just moved back to Seattle and not told anyone.

The sun beat down on her back and was finally the push Willa needed to move. She stepped onto the logging road and followed it up the incline, going deeper and deeper into the trees.

The forest surrounding her was familiar, like slipping on your favorite pair of worn-in tennis shoes. Comfortable to her in a way most things weren't.

She knew the way twigs cracked underfoot. The scent of musty, deciduous leaves mingled with the yearly fall of needles that created a blanket of softness on the forest floor. And she also knew the scent of death—at once, foreign and familiar—as she drew closer to the epicenter of chaos in front of her.

As a kid, she'd once come across a deer carcass in the wilderness. It had smelled similar to this, but this was a thousand times worse.

Willa pulled the neck of her t-shirt up over her nose, fighting back the feeling of nausea. She'd have to battle the scent, but that was nothing if it meant knowing the truth.

She caught sight of the deputies as she came around the last bend. Like a football huddle of tan and green, they stood in a circle, Sheriff Glenn Harding gesturing toward the clearing and back. He was the coach, and they were the players in this macabre game of death.

Instinctively, Willa hung back and waited. She knew Sheriff Harding would send her packing the first moment he saw her, but if she could slip past when he was distracted, maybe she could get close enough to see.

Her stomach turned at the thought. She didn't *want* to see a dead body, but she had to know if it was Anna. Willa wasn't going to sit behind her computer screens wondering. She was going to get her answer now, and that was the only way she'd have any rest. Any peace.

The huddle broke up, and she watched from behind a tree as Sheriff Harding and Deputy Max Long walked toward the body. Max was tall and lean, with reddish blonde curls that were covered by his campaign hat.

His height made Sheriff Harding's shorter, stocky frame look even smaller, though the man made up for it with his commanding presence.

The two men approached the body and began circling, Max making notes as the sheriff gestured.

Her gaze shifted to the two other deputies. Jase Duncan was like a brother to her. He was as tall as Max with dark brown hair but boasted broad shoulders and thickly muscled arms and legs that spoke of hours in the gym. She enjoyed teasing him about his annoyingly regimented attitude toward working out, but she knew it was about more than just looks for him.

As she watched, Jase walked around the outer perimeter of the clearing. His focus was on the ground, and she assumed he was looking for evidence.

The newest edition to the sheriff's department was left to stand guard. Quentin Klein, or Q as they all called him, was harder to figure out. She hadn't interacted with him as much as the other guys, but he seemed more of the shy type. His reddish, strawberry blonde hair and freckles added to his boyish appearance even though, according to Jase, he was older than the other two deputies by several years.

Jase called out something Willa couldn't make out, and she saw Sheriff Harding split off from Max just as another man entered the clearing. He'd come from the woods opposite Jase, and he—

"What?" She clamped a sweaty hand over her mouth, thankful Quentin hadn't heard her.

The surprise at seeing the man from the grocery store here—in the clearing with a dead body—was too much of a jolt to her system. Why was he here?

Her numbed mind slipped a fact to the front, helpfully supplying the answer. This man had to be the caller—the private investigator. She could see his name typed out on her screen by her own fingers. Clancy Sullivan.

Willa ground her teeth. It wasn't fair. Just because he was a PI and apparently friendly with Max shouldn't mean she had to wait by the wayside to find out if the body was her friend or not.

Coupling together her will and determination, Willa moved out from behind the tree. Chin down and fists clenched, she charged toward the clearing. Her footsteps were light from years of walking in the forests surrounding her hometown, but even the stealthiest of people couldn't have gotten far in broad daylight.

Willa had almost made it to the clearing when powerful arms wrapped around her, barring her path. She appreciated the effort, but there was no way they could keep her from the truth.

Chapter Five

Clancy

THE STENCH WAS ALMOST UNBEARABLE. NOW THAT THE sheriff and his deputies were here, Clancy could get closer to the body, but that didn't mean he liked it. He surpassed the urge to vomit and focused on what Max was saying about the location and how he'd need to talk to the Riversong brothers.

Clancy was only half listening, though. Now that he was closer, he could see what he hadn't from the tree line. She'd been posed.

"Max." Clancy took a step to the right.

"What?" The man met his gaze over the body.

"This was intentional." He gestured to the surrounding trees. "This is like a stage, and she's the center of the focus. Set up on display."

Max's eyes narrowed. "Tell me you're *not* saying what I think you are."

"Remember the other girl fifteen miles south? Remember your words in the report?"

Max's jaw flexed. "Why do you have to have such a good memory?"

"You wrote, and I quote, 'It's like she was on display'." Clancy's gaze drilled into the deputy. "That was, what? Two months ago? And now this, with Anna still missing."

"Don't." Max shook his head and crossed his arms over his chest, shifting the star of his badge higher. "Don't go there. You're only going to create a stir and—"

"A stir? You've got to be kidding me." Clancy roughed a hand through his sweat dampened hair. "It's not a stir if it's the truth."

Max closed his eyes and took a deep breath before remembering they were feet from a corpse. He coughed instead and shook his head. "No. Let's not go making wild assumptions. Even if—and I do mean *if*—this poor girl is connected to the body down in North Bank, it wouldn't mean what you're thinking."

"It would if Anna is the next victim." Clancy knew why the man was worried. The accusation he was throwing out was rash and gut-founded. That wasn't how he liked to operate, being a man of facts and clues, but sometimes, you had to trust yourself.

"There's no evidence of that, Clancy, and you know it." Max leveled his gaze at him, but Clancy thought he caught a flicker of hesitation. Or had he wanted to see that?

"Dare I list out the facts?" Clancy looked down at the sunbaked ground to order his thoughts. "One, a girl goes missing from a church function in North Bank. Isn't found until two months ago—dead in the woods and posed much like this. Two, we know Anna went missing two, almost three, weeks ago. Three, another young woman is found dead in the woods. *Posed*. It's time to stop making excuses and own up to the facts. It's likely you have a serial killer on your hands, and the sooner you face up to that, the—"

Clancy's words died on his lips when he looked up to meet Max's gaze. But Max wasn't looking at him, he was looking behind him, eyes wide.

Clancy turned slowly and came face to face with the woman from the grocery store. Same blonde hair, though sweat now dampened stray pieces to her forehead. Same wide, silvery eyes. Same pink lips. But her expression was nothing like the bold, devil may care look she'd worn then.

Tears made her silver eyes swim, and her red cheeks spoke of the heat and emotion boiling inside of her. He caught the fisted hands at her sides just as the scent of decomp hit her full on. She gagged and stepped back a few paces, but her boot snared on a fallen log, and she tripped.

He stepped forward and caught her arm in time to save her from falling, but she yanked herself free the next moment. Wiping furiously at her eyes, she spun to face the deputy.

"Is he right, Max?" Her lip trembled. "Is this Anna? Was she... murdered by a serial killer?"

"You shouldn't be here, Willa." Max looked behind her, and Clancy saw the other deputy they all called Q. He shrugged as if to say he'd tried his best to stop her, but it hadn't worked.

"Shouldn't—she was my friend! And I'm the only one who thinks she didn't run away." She whispered the last part, more to herself than the deputy.

"Tell her," Clancy said, meeting Max's gaze.

Max's expression hardened, but he turned to Willa. "It's not her, Willa."

"Wh-what?" She looked between Clancy and Max, casting only a brief glance at the body feet from them. "But you said..."

Clancy regretted his bold words but not their truth. "We don't know who this is, but it's not Anna. This victim has a prominent gold tooth."

The young woman—Willa, Max had called her—nodded. She pressed a hand to her lips, and he wasn't sure if it was to keep from getting sick or to press the emotion back.

"Why don't you go back to the truck, Wills? There's nothing you can do here."

Clancy shot the deputy a glance. It was clear he knew her enough to use a nickname, but he wasn't offering her much comfort.

"But—"

"Willa."

Clancy recognized the deputy's tone as one that left no room for argument. Her shoulders slumped, and it looked so wrong on her that he spoke before he could stop himself. "I'll come with you."

She cast him a look but stalked off toward the road and out of the sun.

"She's too invested in this," Max said before Clancy followed her. "Be careful what you tell her."

"What? Like the fact that I think this is the work of a serial murderer?"

"Especially that." Max ran a hand along his jaw.

"A little too late, don't you think?"

Max rolled his eyes skyward, flinching when they met bright sunlight. "No good comes from ramping up the already tightly wound tension of Chamberlin. Without corroborating evidence—or a third body, I might add—there's no telling what this is."

"You and I both know waiting for another body is no way to do our jobs." Clancy's anger made his jaw ache.

"That's not what I meant, and you know it."

"Maybe not, but it's about time someone started connecting the clues." Clancy stalked off after the young woman, wondering what he was going to tell her.

She stood with her back to the scene, shoulders slumped with arms wrapped around her middle like armor.

"Hey." He circled around her so she wouldn't have to face the body again. "You okay?"

"Not really." She blinked rapidly. Her dark makeup smudged thick lines under her eyes and looked out of place with her delicate features.

"I'm sorry I just blurted all that out. I...I didn't know anyone else was around."

"It's not that." She sniffed and met his gaze. Eyes impossibly bright with profound depth stared back. "It's the fact that Max and everyone else think that Anna ran away. It's ridiculous."

His gaze narrowed. "You were friends with Anna?"

"I was. Good friends. We were really close."

He frowned, and she caught it.

"What?" she demanded. Her arm dropped to her side, and he caught some of the fire he'd seen at the grocery store returning.

"Don't take this the wrong way, but Hillary Stevens gave me a list of Anna's friends to interview. You weren't on it." *I'd remember you.*

She shook her head and shrugged. "Of course, she wouldn't know about me."

"What do you mean?" His senses tingled in a way that told him he was about to get a piece of vital information.

"Anna came to Chamberlin to get away from her mother." She shrugged. "But it was more than that. Anna found faith in God, and from what she told me, she couldn't live the life she wanted to by staying in

Seattle. She's struggled with drugs and alcohol for a long time, and being around her mother didn't help with that."

Clancy nodded slowly. He'd recognized the effects of drug use when he'd met with Hillary, but those things didn't play into him finding a person. "You befriended her," he guessed.

"She came to my church, and my friend Sloane and I invited her out to coffee. It was clear she didn't know anyone in town, and we wanted her to know she was welcome. Anna and I became really close after that." The woman looked away and drew in a deep breath.

"I'm sorry." He meant the words and hoped she saw that in his expression.

She wiped another tear away and pulled her shoulders back. "Me too, but that doesn't change this." She motioned toward the body. "And it doesn't change what you said."

His jaw clenched. "It's a theory, as Max was good enough to remind me." *But it wouldn't be for long.*

"I think you're right." Determination ignited a fire behind her pale eyes. "Anna wouldn't have left on her own. She didn't want to go back to her old life, and she didn't run away. I may not have known her that long, but I know those things to be true of her."

"Knowing and proving are two different things." He felt the need to temper her enthusiasm. "I'm working the case as best I can. I'll get to the bottom of this, no matter what the truth is."

"I can help you."

"No." Clancy didn't need to think about the reply, it was automatic. He worked best alone.

"But—"

"Look." He let the full weight of his stare bore into her. "I get that you want to find your friend. I want that, too. The best way for that to happen is to let the deputies do their job and me to do mine." He didn't add that he had no time to devote to babysitting some woman who wanted to play at true crime solving. She'd only get in the way.

"I'd be an asset." She stood taller, as if her slight frame could match his six-foot height. "I grew up in these woods. I know them better than the back of my hand. You're clearly not from around here, so don't be stupid. Let me help."

Her words grated. She had no idea where he was from or what he was capable of. He tried to let her bluntness roll off him, reminding himself she was worried and afraid for her friend, but he couldn't keep the frustration from his tone. "No, thanks." He spun back toward the clearing but paused, turning to say, "Besides, I don't need some wide-eyed girl throwing up at a crime scene and contaminating evidence."

Chapter Six

Willa

"I'VE GOT A STRONG STOMACH." WILLA FORCED HER GAG reflex to obey as she stepped up next to Clancy where he observed the corpse. The look of surprise on his face was almost worth the mental battle she waged against the stench of putrefaction. Almost.

"Max know you're here?"

She shrugged. "Q let me come back."

"Used to getting your way?" he asked with a raised eyebrow.

She couldn't help the smirk. "Always."

He shook his head and refocused on the crime scene, and she followed suit. It was one thing for Willa to know this wasn't her friend, but another for her to will her mind to take in the details in front of her in an evaluative manner. She'd have to get used to this, and now was as good a time as any.

Her hand slipped into her satchel and pulled out the sketchbook and three gradients of graphite pencils. She flipped past the other drawings she'd done and attacked the fresh page with detached gusto.

"What are you doing?"

"Baking a cake." She didn't look up but heard his grunted chuckle.

"Charming, aren't you?"

Willa began a deep inhale through her nose but quickly switched to her mouth before replying. "We haven't met, officially. I'm Willa Martin."

"Clancy Sullivan."

"PI, right?"

His grunt was the only reply.

"I was your dispatcher." She felt his eyes on her. "I'm sorry for how that call went." She refocused on the scene. "I've never broken down like that before."

"It's dangerous to care in this line of work."

She had a feeling he meant the comment for them both, and she agreed even if she wasn't going to give him the satisfaction. She'd seen her father come home from his toughest shifts a shell of a man. Every morning, he was back to his usual self, but those calls took a toll. She knew it firsthand now.

She heard the sound of tires on dirt but kept her focus on the body, the area, the position. Every detail that would matter. She had to get it down before Max kicked her out.

"CSI is here," Clancy said. "You'll probably have to leave."

She knew a few of the people on the crime scene investigation team, namely her friend Delaney Price who took photographs for several counties in the area. "They'll let me stay."

"Hey," he reached out and plucked her pencil from her grasp.

"Excuse me." Her eyes flashed back at him. "Give that back."

She watched his eyes scan over her second drawing, this one narrowed in on the skull itself, bringing life from decomposing flesh and bones. Her chest felt tight as she waited for his next words.

"You're good."

The tension relaxed, and she tried to grab the pencil from him. He lifted it out of reach, and she crashed against his chest, surprised at the solidness there. His dark green t-shirt hid more than just his pit stains; it hid a wall of solid muscle.

She huffed a breath. *"Please,* may I have my pencil back? I need it for the detail."

He looked from her back to the sketchbook and then to the nearing clouds. She followed his gaze and knew what he was thinking. They had to work fast because the storm would be on them before long.

"If I give it back, will you take your gruesome drawings and leave all of this alone?"

"No." She turned to face him. "What I said before was true. I'm not just some girl who's going to mess up the investigation." She cast a glance at the corpse—which was how she saw it now. Not a dead girl, just a decomposing body in need of identification. "I know this area, and I can be an asset."

"That you, Willa?" The soft voice came from behind them, and she turned to see Delaney.

"Hey, Dee. Yeah, it's me."

"Oh, no. Is it—"

"No." Willa cut her friend off. "It's not Anna."

"Good. I mean," Delaney made a face. "Not good. Uh, you know what I mean."

"I do." Willa swallowed. "We're almost out of here."

"No problem." Delaney's gaze took in Clancy appreciatively before she turned back to the crime scene. "I'll start with closeups first."

Willa spun to Clancy. "See? I know this town. These people. I can help you."

"It's not a good idea." With a glance, he stepped past Delaney and moved toward where Quentin and Jase stood.

"He's cute," Delaney said, never removing her camera from her eye. "Just saying."

"Whatever." Willa went back to her drawing, despite the fact she had to use the wrong pencil to capture the detail of the bowline. The lines were too thick, and she paused to take one more look at the man.

She tried to see what her friend did in a furtive glance. Clancy was towered above her at over six feet, if she had to guess, and had a mop of dark brown hair naturally highlighted by prolonged time in the sun. It was long enough to curl at the nape of his neck, but she could tell he didn't do much more than run a hand through to style it. He also had a close-cropped beard and intense dark brown eyes.

Her artist's eye could objectively admit how he cut an impressive figure with broad, muscled shoulders, a narrow waist, and a strong jawline. Less objectively, his unwillingness to let her help—and the pencil theft—clouded his handsomeness.

She turned to steal another look, but this time Jase caught her attention and motioned for her to come over. Frowning, she pointed to the pad in her hands. His forceful head shake and the set of his jaw told her any leeway her familiarity with law enforcement had gotten her was gone.

"I'll see you at church, Dee."

"Bye, Wills." Delaney kept her focus on the scene, and Willa folded up her sketch book, returning it to her bag. She'd gotten through two sketches of the overall body and area and a third close-up of the face that was still very rough, but she was sure she could finish it from memory.

The more challenging—and more important—task would be convincing Clancy he needed to let her tag along. She had a few days off work coming up anyway, and she wasn't going to sit by if there was something she could do to help find Anna before it was too late.

She'd tried begging Jase to fill her in, but he stayed tightlipped for the sake of the investigation. Those restrictions didn't rest on Clancy. She wasn't sure what he knew, but it had to be more than her, and that's what mattered.

"Wills, what are you doing here?" Jase asked as she joined the group of men. She felt more than saw Clancy's eyes on her.

"I got the call and had to know." She willed the emotion from her voice.

"I would have told you as soon as we knew," he said.

"Would you, though?"

Jase looked affronted. "I said I would, didn't I?"

She looked from him to Quentin who squirmed beneath her gaze. Then she faced Clancy. Of all of them, he looked at her like he was trying to figure her out, not like she was an annoying fly he wanted to swat away.

The sound of thunder interrupted her brooding, and they all turned to the darkened sky. Willa had been so focused on her drawing and then her anger at the men in front of her that she'd missed the shift from bright sun to muted light. The reprieve as the temperature dipped felt amazing, but worry replaced the heat.

"Not what we needed right now," Jase muttered to himself. "Q, let's go. We'll help CSI. Gotta bag this evidence before the storm hits full force."

The two men headed to the CSI vehicle parked close to the clearing, and Willa turned back to Clancy. He held out her pencil with a raised eyebrow, and she snatched it back. She was about to redouble her efforts to make him see that she would be valuable to him when another truck pulled up.

Chapter Seven

Clancy

"WHAT IS THIS? GRAND CENTRAL STATION?" CLANCY muttered to himself as he took in the two officers that climbed out of the white truck. From the way it was parked he couldn't make out the emblem, but there was definitely something on the side of the truck.

"Hardly. We're in their territory," Willa said.

He shot her a glance, but one of the men walked right up to them. "Willa, what are you doing here?"

"Could say the same about you, Kendrick." Willa had one hand propped on her hip and a defensive slant to her chin.

"We were coming back from Bakers Peak. Just got a call from Callahan Lookout where they spotted a lightning fire."

"Already?" Some of the fierceness left the woman, which was the first thing that gave him pause. If she was worried, he had the feeling he should be, too.

"Hi. Clancy Sullivan." He burst into the conversation when the older of the two men joined them.

"Morrison Conway, and this is Kendrick Fischer. We're LEOs with the Forest Service."

"Nice to meet you." He accepted the handshakes from the law enforcement officers responsible for the United States Forest Service land they stood on. Now, he knew the symbol on the truck was USFS.

"You think there's a fire threat here?" Clancy asked.

Kendrick looked at Morrison and shrugged. "It's possible," he finally said. "It's been a dry summer—too dry if you ask me—and that spells danger for this entire area. You see the forest floor," He kicked a mound of pine needles and leaves. "This'll ignite if you look at it wrong."

"What my cheery friend means is that fire is always a possibility in the summer," Kendrick said. Clancy confirmed what he'd first picked up. Kendrick was British or spoke with a British accent. Clancy had questions —like how he'd joined the USFS, but now wasn't the time.

"I should probably get going." Clancy pulled out his phone and tabbed to the next location Eddie had given him. "Either of you guys know where Coal Ridge is on this map?"

"Coal Ridge isn't on the map." Morrison sent a pointed look to Willa. "But you should ask her. These woods are like her playground."

The look she gave him was overflowing with triumph and a good helping of *I told you so.*

"Of course, it is."

"But be careful," Morrison said, leveling his gaze at them both. "That storm is bringing danger with it. I'd say it's about time to get off the mountain."

Willa nodded as the two officers moved toward the clearing, and Clancy decided it was time to be the bigger person. "Looks like I'm in need of some help."

"I thought you'd never ask." She had the nerve to wink. "Let's go."

"Go?"

"I have to direct you there. It's tricky, and there are a few turns you won't see coming. Trust me, you don't want to go without someone who's been there."

Clancy roughed a hand over his jaw. He was going to regret this.

He worked alone for a reason, and although she could be a good guide, he didn't want to be responsible for her. "You sure you can't just point me in the right direction?"

She stood there, arms crossed, and waited for him to arrive at the right conclusion.

"Fine. You can show me the way." He took a step toward the road.

"What do you drive?" she asked.

"Jeep."

"We'll take your car." She turned around. "Jase, drive Sally home?"

The deputy rolled his eyes but held out his hand for the keys. She tossed them and turned, her hair fanning out behind her like a blonde cape. "Now, we can go."

He led the way to his Jeep. The minute Willa got inside, and he turned on the car, she flipped the vents straight at her and stuck her face in the cool air.

"Hot?" Amusement tuged at his lips.

"It's got to be close to ninety out there." She made a disdainful face. "I hate the heat."

Another loud clap of thunder rattled the SUV, sending the cross attached to a leather cord on his rearview mirror swinging.

"We'd better get going. Morrison was right about this storm." She leaned forward, looking toward the mountains around them as he pulled out onto the road. "Take a left."

He followed her instruction and headed back down the mountain. The AC blasted them both, helping to take the edge off of Clancy's already frayed nerves, but it also carried something with it on the breeze. The perfumed scent of lavender.

Willa leaned forward, still taking in the surrounding mountains, no doubt looking for lightning fires, but it meant her neck was close to the vent. Whatever perfume or body wash she used was filling the car, and Clancy wasn't sure what to make of it.

"Sally, huh?"

She turned to look at him. "You didn't name your Jeep?"

"No." He flexed his fingers on the steering wheel.

"Sally the Civic. I thought it had a nice ring to it." She bent forward and pulled out her sketchbook, flipping to the last page. "You're going to go about another three miles, and then we'll be making a left turn."

"Okay." He glanced at the drawing. It was good. Really good. In fact, it was so good he wasn't sure how she'd managed to pull it off in the span of time she'd spent at the crime scene. "How'd you learn to draw?"

She added detail to the victim's right eye with the pencil he'd stolen. "I've always liked to draw things. Everyday household stuff, you know? I've got a nice collection of fruit still lifes." She laughed, the sound bright and so at odds with the gruesome scene on the page in front of her.

"And you just thought, 'wow, it would be fun to draw a dead girl'?" Her cutting look told him his words came out more harshly than he'd intended. "Sorry, that came out wrong."

"Actually," some of her usual bravado waned. "I'm taking classes to become a forensic artist."

"Oh." He was an idiot. *Open mouth, insert booted foot.*

"I guess it would look odd, me going out there to draw, but my teacher says that the best way to learn is to practice, and while I hate that practice means drawing the dead..." she paused. "I guess it's like my job. *Usually,* I'm very professional, and the only way to do that is to dissociate myself from the call. It's information, and I'm relaying it. The same thing has to be true of my art. Things like bone structure and brow ridges are information, and I'm just capturing that on the page."

He nodded and tried to swallow past the lump stuck in his throat. "Forensic artists are crucial to cases. I know that." He felt her eyes on him.

"What exactly do you do as a PI, Mr. Sullivan?"

"Please, call me Clancy." He slowed as they came to the three-mile mark. "Turn here?"

"Yeah. You're going to go for about another five miles, and then we'll see a dirt road to the right."

"Logging road?"

"Yep."

Silence descended again, but she didn't let it last. "Well, Clancy?"

"You're persistent," he said on a chuckle.

"And you're avoiding the question."

She had him there. "I investigate."

"Missing persons?"

"At the moment."

"You're looking for Anna for a paycheck?"

It was his turn to give her a look that said she'd crossed the line. "I'm

35

not taking a dime from Mrs. Stevens. I'm looking for Anna because..." He swallowed again. "Because her story spoke to me, and after my last case... well, I needed to get out of Montana."

"What happened with the last case?"

"You're like a dog with a bone. You sure you're not the PI?"

"Sorry," she grinned. "My dad says I let my intuition get the best of me. It just seems like there's more you're not saying."

If only she knew. "Aren't there always things people don't say?"

"Yeah." Her voice was small, and it tugged at the part of Clancy he tried to suppress.

She went back to shading, and he watched the road, but visions of Laura Zucker flooded his mind. The grisly scene in the warehouse he'd traced her killer to. Her mother crying when the truth came out. The feeling of complete failure and his need to leave. To go to the next thing.

"I didn't find who I was looking for in time." The words slipped free. A means for Clancy to cleanse his soul, or maybe just admit his defeat.

Her pencil stilled. "I'm sorry." When she looked over, her pale gray eyes were filled with compassion. Her gaze shifted, and she fingered the hanging cross. It was a reminder and a prayer wrapped in one.

"Here." She released the cross and pointed to a small dirt road. He slowed, and they turned off and began to climb the slow slope into the forest.

"Sometimes, all we can do is our best, you know?" She spoke the words with conviction.

It sounded nice, but what if his best wasn't good enough?

Chapter Eight

Willa

CLANCY WAS AN ENIGMA TO HER. HIS STOIC SILENCE FILLED the cab of the Jeep, but his vulnerability spoke even louder with his humble admission. She had a feeling that he was running from something —or maybe himself—but she knew that observation would cross a line.

Still, she wanted to know more. They had another five minutes of a drive before they reached the old sawmill that filled the clearing on Coal Ridge, so she went for it. "How did you pick Anna?"

He shot her a look. "What do you mean?"

"There are hundreds, maybe thousands, of girls who go missing. Why Anna? Why Chamberlin?" Willa chewed on her bottom lip.

"I guess there were several factors."

She waited, his answer holding her captive. Why it mattered, she wasn't sure, but motivation was important, and she wanted to know Clancy's. Was he the type that would give up after a month of her friend being gone? Or was he in it for the long haul?

"I grew up in Washington, for one."

He'd chosen the safe answer, but she shouldn't be surprised. "Where?"

"Outside of Olympia."

"And you wanted to come home?"

"No."

This answer came so fast it was telling. "What then? Why Anna?"

"Why does it matter?" He swerved around a branch in the middle of the road.

"She's my friend, and I guess I want to know if you're here for some sort of publicity or—"

"It was something her mother said." He cut her off, his fingers flexing out and then wrapping around the steering wheel again. "She said Anna had made mistakes, but that it was time for her to come home. And that spoke to me."

Willa could sense there was more to his answer he hadn't revealed, but they pulled into the clearing of the old sawmill, and she saw her chance vanish as Clancy shifted into PI mode.

"What is this place?" he asked, climbing out of the Jeep.

"The old Blanken sawmill. It's been abandoned for a long time and is basically adjacent to USFS land." She stepped out of the car and pulled her satchel across her body.

"Forest Service land?" he confirmed.

"Yeah. That's Coal Ridge," she pointed in front of them behind the mill. "It's privately owned along with this land, but over there," she shifted and pointed to the left, "is where federal land begins."

"But anyone has access to this. That logging road wasn't blocked off."

"Since the mill isn't in working order anymore, I don't think the owners care. Last I heard, they live in Seattle and hold on to this land because it was in the family."

"Got it." He headed toward the ramshackle buildings covered in weathered gray wood with rusted tin roofs. "Seems out of the way for a sawmill."

"Guess they would log up here, cut the boards down, and take the lumber out on trucks to the railroad depot in town. Had a good thing going for a while back in the early 1900s."

"You know a lot about this area. Are you secretly a lumberjack?"

She laughed and stepped over a small pile of old wooden planks, wishing she'd worn shoes instead of sandals. "No. I just pay attention when the old timers talk."

"Looks like it's chained up." Clancy indicated the two large sliding doors.

"Let's try around back." Willa moved toward the corner of the biggest building, ducking a support beam.

"You've been up here before?"

"Not here specifically, but I've hiked Coal Ridge. There's a trail that starts further down the mountain and takes you up along the ridgeline. The view is incredible, but it's a tough hike. Driving was much easier."

She caught his responding smile as she turned the corner and saw the door. It sat halfway open on rusted hinges.

"Good instincts," he said.

His praise tugged at her, but she pushed the feelings down. Instincts were only as good as the information backing them up—or so her father always said.

"You coming?" Clancy paused at the door to look back at her.

"Right behind you."

They stepped into the pitch black, and a rush of goosebumps raced up Willa's arms. There was something off about the space. What should have smelled like moldy wood and dust carried an unnatural human scent to it. Willa couldn't put her finger on what that was exactly, but it unnerved her.

"Teens come up here sometimes," she said, more to herself than for Clancy's benefit. "Party and whatever."

She trailed off as Clancy knelt down and let out a soft curse.

"What is it?" She rushed to his side.

He held up the light from his phone, and she gasped. Metal cuffs hung attached to an old pipe that went below ground. There was dried blood on them.

"Someone was held here." Clancy took a step back and swung his light around. "Could have been recent, but it's hard to tell."

Willa's hope ignited. Had Anna been held here? If so, where was she now?

There was an old ratty blanket next to the cuffs as well as food wrappers and a foul-smelling bucket a little further back. Willa didn't have to guess what the bucket was for.

"Who would do something like this?" Her voice wavered, and she swallowed hard.

"A very bad man." Clancy pursed his lips in thought. "This is looking a lot like I was right."

"You mean about it being a serial killer?"

The full weight of Clancy's brown eyes met hers. "I'm sorry you had to hear that like you did."

Willa was drowning. The weight of her worry over Anna pressed down on her, added to by her own guilt. She couldn't alleviate her responsibility, and now, faced with the visible reality that her friend could have been taken by a serial killer, her vision started to go black.

"Hey, you okay?" Clancy stepped close, his palms warm against her sweaty skin as he steadied her.

"I—I'm fine." She fought nausea, but her instincts kicked in. She stepped back from him and pulled out her tablet.

"You don't have to—"

"I know." She met his gaze. "But it helps me process."

He nodded. "Do you have a light?"

"Yeah." She pulled out her phone and set it up on an old saw table, illuminating the area. Her pencil flashed across the clean page, and she tried to distance herself from what she was seeing.

"Don't touch anything." He put his palms up, face out. "Sorry. It's a habit from when I was a cop."

She searched his eyes, there was more to him than she'd first thought. A deeper story that went beyond a bad case he was trying to escape.

"I'm going to check outside. You sketch, and then we'll call for CSI to get up here."

She nodded, refocusing on the tragic scene in front of her as he stepped past and moved around the back of the building. Drawings weren't important in a situation like this when there were no bones to interpret, but she needed the focus her art gave her.

The darkness was oppressive without him nearby, but she fixated on capturing details. She took a few photos with her phone, too, just in case she missed something, but she was almost done with the wide-angle view of the scene when her attention snagged on a wrapper.

She knelt down to get closer to it, holding her phone higher. The wrapper was on top of the rest, as if it had been discarded most recently, but there was something familiar about it. The purple coloring on the back—

Willa gasped. It was from Lois's Market. Now that she realized what it was, she felt stupid that she hadn't recognized it before. Then her hope plummeted. The purple wrapping meant that it was blackberry, and this late in the summer, Willa knew they hadn't been sold for over a month.

No one had been here for over a month—long before Anna was taken.

Despair wrapped around Willa's shoulders, as oppressive as the heat, and she fought back the returning nausea. She hated this. Hated the thought of anyone captured like this. She forced herself to look over the scene again to make sure she hadn't missed any other important detail.

Taking a hesitant step toward the bucket, she held her breath and leaned close to look around it. Her assumption was that whoever had been cuffed here would have wanted to be far from it due to the stench, but some instinct in Willa made her go closer.

She breathed shallowly through her mouth and used the light to look around. Nothing out of the ordinary. But her gut told her to keep looking. There was nowhere else...but under the bucket.

Wrinkling her nose, she used her toe to push the empty bucket over. She'd been right. There, laying in the indentation of the soil beneath the metal bucket, lay a leather cord.

Willa pulled a tissue from her satchel and picked it up. There were no distinguishing markings on it, but it struck a chord with her. What was it about this that felt familiar?

She was holding it up, shining her light on it when she heard footsteps pounding outside followed by a shout from Clancy. "Fire!"

Willa wrapped the cord up and shoved it in her satchel before turning to meet Clancy at the door. He all but barreled into her, gasping and out of breath.

"Fire," he said on an exhale.

"Where?"

"Up on the ridge." He pointed north, and she nodded, racing outside. The ridge north of them blazed with flames.

Willa rushed back in. "We need to go."

He knelt down by the blanket, a plastic bag in one gloved hand, while

41

he gingerly picked up wrappers. "We need to take some evidence. If there's a chance this place burns down, I am not letting this get away."

"We don't have much time."

"I know." He reached into his backpack and took out a pair of gloves. "Take these and unlock the cuffs."

She took the gloves and the key from him and set to work collecting as much as they could before racing back to the Jeep. By that time, the flames had reached the clearing and billowing smoke rose in a great plume behind them. Willa could already feel the heat.

"Are we going to make it out of here?" She threw herself into the front seat.

Clancy took a second to meet her gaze, and she was surprised to see a wild grin on his face. "You bet we are."

Chapter Nine

Clancy

AN INFERNO CONSUMED THE TREES BEHIND THEM. CLANCY pressed the gas pedal harder as they careened down the narrow logging road. Willa's knuckles had gone white where they held the door handle and edge of the seat, but he couldn't care about her comfort. Her safety was more important.

"Look!" The tension in her voice radiated through the cab, and Clancy yanked his gaze from the rearview mirror to the road in front of them.

It was on fire.

"We're going through."

"Are you crazy?"

He sensed her eyes on him, but there was no time for second guessing. He gunned it and headed straight for the wall of flames.

Everything inside of him said this was a stupid idea. Probably the worst he'd ever had. Still, he barreled forward toward the line of burning slash that covered the unused road.

Clancy's only thought was their freedom as glowing embers swirled in front of them and ash rained down. They reached the burning line, and he shot through it like a bullet from a gun.

The flames were surrounding them one second and gone the next.

"How—" Willa turned around to look behind them and then slumped against the seat. "Wow."

His white-knuckled grip on the wheel relaxed some, but his concern shifted. Had he melted the tires? Would they burst and leave them in a worse position on a burning mountain with no way out?

"I'm going to check the tires. Give me a minute."

He maneuvered toward a pullout area where cars could move to the side to let faster drivers pass on the narrow two-lane road. Checking behind them before he got out, he saw the flames coming, though they were still far enough away that they weren't in immediate danger. Yet.

The heat that greeted him outside the jeep felt supercharged by the dark, thunderous clouds above and the wall of flames and smoke behind. He started with the tires on his side when he heard the passenger door open. He'd wanted Willa inside in case they had to make a mad dash again, but he watched as she walked to the edge that overlooked the valley and bent over. Hands on knees.

Circling the Jeep, he checked the other tires. Surprisingly—mercifully —nothing was melted, and the contact with fire had been brief enough that nothing had been damaged.

A choked sob drew his attention back to Willa.

"Willa, what is it? Are you hurt?"

He visually checked her but didn't see any signs of injury. Her shoulders shook, and she heaved in great draughts of air, bursting into a fit of coughs due to the smoke, he assumed. Approaching her like he would a wounded animal, Clancy gently rested a hand on her back.

It acted like a spring mechanism, and she popped upright. Tears coursed down her cheeks, and her eyes were red rimmed, the black makeup almost washed away.

"Willa?" he tried again.

She shook her head, as if she couldn't bear to talk, and wrapped her arms around herself, turning away from him. It was the way she looked though. Frail, almost. It broke him, and he stepped close, wrapping an arm around her.

It was hot. Too hot for an embrace, really, but she let him hold her, and her sobs increased. Great, body-shuddering cries that wracked through her. She was a woman in pain, and he had no idea how to help her.

He let her cry it out, though he kept his attention on the fire behind them. They needed to leave, but he wasn't sure what she needed. Time? A listing ear? Silence?

Finally, after she'd quieted down, he said, "Are you okay?"

"I'm sorry." She stepped back from him, and he found he missed the connection to her. It made no sense because it was a lot cooler to stand apart, but he didn't let his mind linger on the reason.

"Don't apologize. You've been through a lot today."

"It's old." More tears slid down her cheeks.

"What's old?" He was lost.

"Back there. What we found. It—it can't be where Anna was. The wrappers are from a specialty hand pie that Lois makes. She hasn't sold them for over a month. It couldn't have been Anna that was held there, which means we're not any closer to finding her."

Clancy angled to look down at her. "You noticed all of that in the few minutes I left?" He couldn't keep the surprise from his words.

"Yeah," she sounded hesitant. "I just...it seems hopeless to me. We're no closer to finding her, and it's been so long and—"

He wasn't sure what made him do it, but he moved forward and brushed a lock of hair to the side with a knuckle. The contact stole her words, and he became acutely aware of just how close they were standing.

Forcing a tightlipped smile, he stepped away. "We should get going. Come on."

Her fragrance filled the Jeep again, and he directed his vent to blow air in his face. The smoky scent invaded the space despite keeping the air circulating inside, but it helped clear his head.

"I know it's a lot to take, Willa, but we're going to figure this out. What we bagged from the scene, the photos we took, and your drawings—it's all going to help."

He caught her nod from the corner of his eye, but she didn't reply. The silence grew awkward. That, or he was just hyper aware of it.

Searching for something to say, he saw the corner of her sketchbook protruding from her bag.

"How long have you been interested in forensic art?" It felt like a lame, work-related question, but she seemed to take it in stride.

"A few years now, I guess? I was visiting a friend on the campus of the community college in North Bank. She knew I was interested in art and that I worked in dispatch, so she suggested I check out a class. It sounded interesting so I took it."

"Looking to change careers?" He braked for a sharp curve, and some of the tension he'd held seeped away.

"No. Well, maybe?"

"What's that mean?"

She shifted, taking in a deep breath. "My dad has been in dispatch since I was young. I guess you could say I kind of inherited a position there, and while I do enjoy the work, I'm passionate about art..." She trailed off.

"And you'd rather do something you're passionate about," he finished for her.

"Yeah." She kept her gaze focused on the trees as they flew past them. "I don't know how my dad will take that, though."

Clancy's eyebrows rose. "He doesn't know?"

Willa was quiet for so long he almost changed the subject, but she finally spoke up. "I've debated telling him about the class but haven't pulled the trigger yet."

"Where does he think you go when you take the class?"

"Yoga." Her laugh was short and mostly without humor. "I know. I should tell him, but with Anna missing, and well, everything, there hasn't been a good time. He's in Washington, DC right now working as a fire information officer, and I don't want to ruin that for him. He loves that summer assignment."

Clancy slowed as the twisty mountain road gave way to a thoroughfare that led toward town. "Sounds like you guys are close."

"We are." Her voice brightened some. "It's just been us for a long time now, but he made my childhood pretty great. He was always home waiting for me after school, took me hiking on the weekends, and encouraged me in pretty much any sport I wanted to play."

Clancy's gut twisted at the memories she shared. He didn't know what it was like to experience a home like that. Family like that.

They stopped at one of the town's three stoplights, and he looked over at her. "I'm heading to the sheriff's office with the evidence. Where can I drop you?"

Surprise at his curt tone registered on her soft features. "I, um, I could go with you."

It was on the tip of his tongue to disagree, but he shrugged instead. "Okay."

He needed to clear his head after the gruesome scene he'd uncovered that morning, but Clancy wasn't sure that distance from the enigmatic woman with a talent for art and a happy home life was going to give that to him. In fact, the more time he spent with her, the more he wondered if he'd be able to walk away when all this was said and done.

And that thought scared him the most.

Chapter Ten

Willa

SHE'D SHARED TOO MUCH. OR HAD SHE PUT HIM OFF BY HER stupid tears? Clancy was more closed off now than he'd been before with that muscle in his jaw working overtime.

Willa was angry at herself and a little embarrassed about breaking down on the mountain over a package wrapper. She'd worked dispatch for five years now, and she'd never once cried in public. Clancy wasn't exactly public, but he also wasn't like Jase or Max—brother figures—or like her father who had wiped her tears as a child.

He was...different.

They were several blocks away from the sheriff's office now, and she surreptitiously snuck glances of his profile. *As an artist, of course.*

She saw a faint scar above his right eyebrow and caught a few gray hairs in his beard. How old was he?

"Are you staring at me?" He looked her way, and she met his gaze.

"Payback."

A deep chuckle rumbled in his chest, and while Anna was still missing, and they'd found the dead body of another girl just that morning, a

48

glimmer of peace pierced her heart. It was a strange reaction to the mysterious man next to her, but she couldn't ignore it.

Just like when he'd brushed the hair from her eyes on the mountain.

She looked away at the same time he returned his eyes to the road. Was she blushing?

Growing up with just a dad who'd himself had four brothers and only one sister, Willa was used to being around men of all ages. She'd joined sports rather than play with dolls, and she'd always preferred jeans to dresses. In all that time, she'd learned how to be confident and self-assured, and that had always served her well in her friendships with men.

This was different. Her reaction to Clancy scared her. Awakened things she'd pushed aside as her career kept her busy, and the town left her with few options for dating. There was just no way she could see the men she'd known as brothers as anything else.

They pulled up in front of the sheriff's office and headed inside where Marilee greeted her. "And who's this handsome fellow?"

Willa felt the heat of another blush threaten to surface so she ushered him past the older woman's reception desk with a muttered word about helping with an investigation. They turned down a long hall toward the side of the building the sheriff's office occupied.

"She's a little nosy," Willa explained. Clancy didn't respond, and she took a deep breath to focus. "I'm not sure if Sheriff Harding is back yet."

The hall ended at a door next to a plexiglass talk-through window. The man behind the safety glass looked bored, but that was nothing new.

"Hey, Nelson," she said, leaning against the counter and flashing her dispatch badge out of habit. "We're here to see Sheriff Harding."

"He's not back yet." Nelson looked from her to Clancy. "Who's he?"

"I'm Clancy Sullivan, Private Investigator."

Nelson's eyebrows rose. "Fancy."

"Is Jase back?" she tried.

"Yeah. He just got in. You, uh, both want to see him?"

"Please." Willa looked back to Clancy as he pulled something from his wallet.

She couldn't see what it was as he slipped it through the narrow opening at the bottom of the window, but Nelson took one look at it and slid it back saying, "Come on in."

"What was that?" she asked.

"Credentials," was his simple reply.

The door buzzed, and Clancy opened it, allowing Willa to enter first.

"You know where he is," Nelson said, already back to the game he was playing on his phone.

"Charming," Clancy muttered, and she stifled a laugh.

She took the lead and headed down a gray hallway—gray walls, gray carpet, light gray ceiling tiles—and then angled toward the main shared office space.

"That's Glenn—uh, Sheriff Harding's office," she said, pointing to the closed door across the room. "And the rest of the guys have desks out here."

The desks stood in neat rows, though papers and folders crowded the tops of most except for Quentin's desk. She knew the guys gave him a hard time about his tidy ways, but she appreciated it.

Jase stepped out from a hallway at the back of the office, the one that connected with dispatch on the other side and sent her a narrow-eyed look. "Where've you been?"

"Up at the old Blanken sawmill."

"Coal Ridge?" He shifted focus to Clancy then back at her. "It's on fire."

"We know," Clancy said, holding up a paper bag. "And we were there just before the fire started. Got some things of note."

Jase's eyes lit with interest. "What do you mean?"

"Got a lab?"

"Yeah, come on back. But Wills," Jase nailed her with a stern look. "You need to talk to Barney."

She cringed and met Clancy's gaze. "I guess this is the end of the road. My boss is next door."

"Thanks for your help." He spoke so matter-of-factly that all she could do was blink before he spun on his heel and followed Jase toward the lab.

No goodbye. No parting hope to see her again. Just thanks.

Willa clenched her teeth and set off down the hall toward dispatch and Barney's wrath, but her thoughts remained fixed on the evidence in the bag Clancy held. She had no doubt it was connected to the dead girls that had been found in both North Bank and now here, but how? Was it one of the existing victims? Another victim they knew nothing about? It couldn't have been Anna, at least Willa was fairly certain of that, but that didn't mean Anna wasn't being held like that somewhere else.

Her heart ached at the thought of her friend held captive and fearing for her life. If Clancy was right, and there was still time to find her, Willa needed to do everything she could. Even if that meant bugging Clancy until she convinced him to let her help. Then again, with the way they'd parted, she had a feeling she'd just seen the last of him.

"There you are." Barney's voice held an edge of anger she'd never heard from the man.

"I'm sorry, but—"

"I don't want to hear it. I just need you to put your butt in that chair and answer the phone like you're paid to do."

She blinked, stunned into silence.

Barney's shoulders fell. "Look, I'm sorry. That was too far. But honestly, Willa, what were you thinking?"

"I was thinking about Anna. That's what."

His lips pursed. "And did you find anything?"

She relayed what they'd come across at the old sawmill and how the fire had likely destroyed the rest of the evidence. His facade cracked, and she saw his relief that they'd saved what they could.

"I get it," he said, reaching out and gripping her shoulder with a comforting squeeze. "We all want her back safely, but I've also got a dispatch to run. I called in Tessa to take over for you, but she could only stay for a few hours. I—*we*—need you here."

She nodded. She knew he was right and was being more than generous about her running out on her duties. Any other workplace and she'd be looking for a new job, but her long-standing career there had helped—as well as her father's influence.

"You've got it. I'll just—"

"Willa?"

The sound of her name on Clancy's lips caused a strange sensation to snake down her spine. She turned to see him at the entryway, uncertainty on every plane of his handsome face.

"You have a few minutes?" he asked.

She looked up at Barney and winced.

"For the love—" He huffed a breath. "Go. But you've got five minutes before I drag you back to your desk."

"Thank you," she said, giving him a quick hug and rushing toward Clancy.

Her heart did a happy little dance that she squelched as quickly as possible. This wasn't a time for celebration. Or was it?

The bright light in Clancy's dark brown eyes spoke of hope. "There's good news."

Chapter Eleven

Clancy

"THERE'S A SOURCE OF DNA." CLANCY RUBBED HIS JAW. "Well, there *probably* is."

"What does that mean?" Willa wrapped her arms around her middle and leaned against the wall in the small break room. He saw traces of fatigue on her soft features, but it was overshadowed by the spark in her eyes. Hope.

Was that why he'd sought her out? The news was insignificant, and he could have had Jase tell her, but he'd selfishly felt the need to be the one that shared it with her.

Dangerous territory, man. Watch yourself.

"Yeah. So." He ran a hand through his hair and caught the whiff of smoke on him. Today had been too close for comfort. It rarely bothered him, but that's when it was just *his* life he was endangering. Not someone like Willa.

"Clancy?"

He jerked back to reality with her gentle use of his name. "Sorry, spaced out for a second there. It means that there is a source of DNA on those cuffs. They tested it, and it's human blood. As long as it's not degraded too much, it could prove useful."

She bit her lip, and he watched the movement before he looked away straight into the eyes of a young woman. Anna. She smiled back from a missing poster, and he flinched. He needed to update her mother.

"How long will that take?"

"Weeks." He shrugged. "If there're connections to the crime lab in Seattle, and your sheriff can pull some strings, it could be sooner."

"Okay, good." She nodded and paced back and forth in the small space. "That's good, right?"

"It's a lead." He wouldn't qualify it. "And it's more than we had before."

Her gaze shifted up and behind him, recognition alighting there. "Hey, Q. Thanks for what you said earlier."

Clancy turned to see the deputy. He looked between them, but his gaze rested on Willa. Clancy caught the nervous tick his thumb made against this thigh and wondered what the guy had said to her. Was that interest he saw behind the man's dark eyes?

"Sure thing. I, uh, heard you guys did some investigating." Quentin eyed him. "Kind of dangerous, don't you think?"

"No more than any other part of my job." Clancy wanted to throw off the guy's idea of him and list his credentials, but this wasn't a contest, no matter Quentin's calculating stare. "And we made it out just fine."

"Barely, from what I heard."

Was he issuing a challenge? Clancy took a step forward, but Willa filled the space between them. "We're all trying to accomplish the same thing, right Q? I mean, we just want to see Anna found and safe. That's what matters."

Clancy saw the shift in the deputy's eyes. "You're right. Sorry, Wills."

She flinched, the movement so imperceptible he was positive the deputy hadn't seen it. "I, uh, need to get back to work." She turned toward Clancy, and he kept himself from smiling as she easily dismissed Quentin.

"I'd better go fill in Anna's mother. I'll be at my motel later if you need anything." The words slipped free from thought, but after they were out, Clancy wondered why he'd said it.

If she needed anything? What could she need? This was her home-town. and he was the visitor.

"Thanks. And thanks for everything." She flashed a tentative smile and then spun on her heel back to the dispatch space. The constant sound of phones ringing greeted him as she slipped through the door and was gone.

His eyes rested on the door for a moment longer before he pulled his attention away.

"Hey, PI."

Clancy turned around to see Jase. He'd seen the man around but had kept his contact with the sheriff's office limited to Max. It always worked better if he could find one guy who trusted him and stick with that.

"It's Clancy. Or Sullivan." He knew men like Jase. Solid, hardwork-ing, and territorial. He wasn't sure if there was anything between him and Willa, but his bet was on no by the way she'd interacted with him at the crime scene.

"All right. Sullivan then." Jase stepped up to Clancy, and they met eye to eye, though Jase had a good thirty pounds on him and all in solid muscle. "What you did today, it was stupid."

Clancy's eyes narrowed, but he didn't speak.

"Taking Wills to that sawmill with the weather like it is? Reckless, man. Do I need to worry about you?"

Clancy waited to see if the kid would pound his chest, too but then took a steadying breath and used a more civil approach. "I thought it would be a quick trip, and I never would have taken Willa if I'd thought there would be danger."

Jase's eyes narrowed. "But there was."

"We all make mistakes." He dipped his chin. "But it won't happen again."

"Wills is like a sister to me—to a lot of guys here—and we don't want to see her hurt. By anyone or anything." His point was obvious. He didn't trust Clancy, and he especially didn't trust him with her. "Besides, she's got a big heart under all that bravado. I'm worried it's going to get her into trouble."

Clancy bristled at the man's words. He knew the kid cared about her, maybe like a sister, or maybe secretly more. But although she'd broken down in tears on the mountain, he could tell that Willa could handle herself. Besides, it was her life and her choices to make.

"I hear you." Clancy took a step to move past the man, but Jase purposely blocked him.

"Do you?"

"Loud and clear. But know this..." Clancy leaned in. "Willa's a smart, capable woman. Smart enough to make her own decisions. I think you should respect that."

Clancy sidestepped the man without another word and headed for the exit. The testosterone in the office was a little too overwhelming.

The super-heated air that greeted him was tainted by smoke, but he drew in a deep breath. He knew what it was like to have a team that supported you and looked out for you. Or at least, he had known that once. That's all Jase was doing. Looking out for his teammate against him —the outsider.

Clancy fisted his hands. That's all he was here. Someone who didn't belong.

He took the main road through town, stopping at the remaining two stop lights, before the vintage motel sign came into view. The Blackbird Motel was a squat, two story building with pull-up parking spaces in a courtyard area and a pool that looked just off enough to dissuade Clancy from taking a dip.

A few other cars filled the otherwise empty lot, and as Clancy passed the motel office, he saw the young woman working the desk wave to him. He offered a tight-lipped smile and a dip of his head before pulling up in front of room 102. He'd specifically requested a bottom floor room, and the young woman had been more than happy to fulfill his request.

He climbed out of the Jeep and hauled his backpack from the back seat before fishing the plastic keycard from his wallet. He paused at his door and looked around out of habit. A mother and child sat in the pool area, the young boy splashing in the kids' pool. An older man walked past the motel, bare chested in shorts. On the other side of the parking lot, a couple emerged from their room in shorts and t-shirts, heading toward their small SUV.

Everything looked ordinary.

He huffed a breath and opened the door to his room. Two queen beds sat to the right, their thin, cheap bedspreads neatly tucked in. The small black refrigerator, television, and dresser took up the remaining space to the left. It smelled like disinfectant with a trace of cigarette smoke. The office clerk had assured him the room was non-smoking, but he figured, in a place as old as this, the smoke had seeped into the walls long ago, leaving the odor a faint but ever-present note in the background.

He flipped on the wall-mounted AC unit. It spluttered to life and spewed out damp but semi-cool air. Then he pulled out his laptop and opened it on the small round table near the front window.

Clancy knew he looked rough and desperately needed a shower, but updating Anna's mother was his top priority. He untangled a set of headphones from his bag, connected to the complimentary wi-fi, and sent a text to Hillary Stevens.

It only took four minutes for the woman to respond and agree to a video call.

"Hi, Mrs. Stevens," he said when the blurry video image crystallized into clarity.

"Is there news? Have you found her?"

Clancy had specifically used the word *update* in hopes of dispelling any false hope she might have had, but the wording hadn't done its job.

"I'm sorry, but no. I have some things to tell you though."

"Okay." Hillary ran a hand over her face and took in a shuddering breath. "What have you found?"

Clancy slipped into a routine update he'd perfected over years working with the families of victims and then clients after that. He explained the tip he'd gotten and what it had led him to, though, aside from assuring her that the dead girl had not been Anna, he didn't share his thoughts about the serial killer theory.

"That's it?" Hillary asked when he'd finished. Her already-thin cheeks looked hollow, and dark circles accented the area beneath her eyes, but she looked hungry for more.

He'd felt like the news was good—movement after weeks of unrest—but she wanted more, and he couldn't blame her.

"I'm afraid so, Mrs. Stevens."

She nodded and leaned back against a bright red velvet sofa. The shift showed him the other side of the couch where several empty beer and wine bottles lay scattered.

Hillary was a study of contrasts. She had overly pale skin and dark hair threaded through with silver. Each time they'd spoken Clancy noticed she dressed in black with understated makeup though she always had dark burgundy lipstick on. But despite the outward image of composure, she was fraying at the edges. Worry did that. Hard living did that, too.

He'd caught her at home today, the large modern art piece behind her tipping him off. He recognized it from his one trip to her house before making his way to Chamberlin. She was an artist with a thriving community in Seattle, but her success hadn't seemed to ensure her happiness. At least, not from Clancy's few encounters with the woman.

She sought mind-numbing activities instead. The same ones Willa said Anna was trying to escape from.

"What's next?" Her voice was barely above a whisper, but it broke into his thoughts all the same.

Clancy felt the urge to lie to her. To say that a breakthrough was right around the corner. That Anna would be all right. That she didn't need to worry.

But the statistics spoke another truth.

"Honestly, I'm not sure. I'm not giving up," he rushed to add. "I just want you to know the realities here."

Hillary's chin quivered. "I understand. Thank you for keeping me updated."

He nodded. "I'm doing everything I can."

"I know you are. Thank you, Clancy." Hillary ended the call, and Clancy stayed staring at the black screen.

He'd chosen to work this case in hopes of a better conclusion. While the setting had changed, the grief was the same. The displaced hope was the same. His fear was the same.

He just wished the outcome would be different this time.

Chapter Twelve

Willa

"SEE THAT?" PROFESSOR SCOTT USED THE RUBBER COATED TIP of his metal pointer to tap at the screen where an oversized image of a skull stared at them. "That's the point of impact. We have to consider how the injury will affect the rest of the skull structure when we're working on a reconstruction."

Willa tapped her pen against the blank piece of notebook paper in front of her. Try as she might, she couldn't find anything to write notes about. As much as she *wanted* to keep her attention focused on her forensic arts class, she couldn't convince her mind to pay attention.

"Now," Professor Scott clapped his hands together and turned to them. "I've got a crate of damaged human skulls"—he pointed to the back of the classroom—"for you all to practice on. One per station. I want to see you home in on those details and their rippling effects. These skulls are in mostly good condition, but the real challenge comes next semester when we have to work on reconstructed ones with parts missing."

Willa watched as one student at her station got up to retrieve their skull and then set it on the slowly rotating platform in the middle of their unit of desks. It was harder to draw like this, with the subject always moving, but it gave them each a brief view every few seconds. Their professor liked to say that it also helped them to sketch faster, like a real-life setting, but Willa knew differently.

She picked up her pencil and opened her sketch book but stalled on the pieces she'd drawn earlier that day. Her gaze traveled over the dark lines and then the more detailed area around the dead young woman.

There hadn't been time to truly process what she'd seen earlier that day. Not while calls about lightning fires flooded the dispatch lines along with their regular calls for assistance. Barney had been in a mood as well, which meant he'd circled their desks like a vulture looking for weakened prey, barking reprimands and nitpicking every detail.

The twenty-minute drive south to North Bank for class that night had been her one chance to destress, but instead she'd put on a rom-com audiobook and shut off her emotions.

Now though, with the gruesome images staring back at her, she wondered if she should have worked through how she felt in the privacy of her car instead of in the middle of a public class.

She flipped the page to the next section of images she'd done at the Blanken sawmill. At least there wasn't a body there, but the scene was nonetheless terrible. Her eyes traced the angry lines of the metal cuffs and over to the wrappers that had clued her in to the fact that this hadn't been a step in the right direction to finding Anna.

"Is that Gibbons mine?" Willa jerked back from the voice at her elbow, and Professor Scott held up his hands. "Did I startle you?"

Willa knew her cheeks had to show her embarrassment, so she looked down at the image. "Uh, no. Sorry. I was lost in thought. This is the Blanken sawmill."

"Huh." Professor Scott leaned over, and without touching the page, pointed. "This is really well done, Willa. You've brought attention to what I can assume are important elements, giving them context but without too much distracting detail."

"Thanks." Feeling calmer, she looked up into the face of her professor.

He was in his early fifties, with short-cropped brown hair with chunks of gray at his temples, dark-rimmed glasses, and a bit of a paunch. She knew he had worked for most of the local departments as a forensic artist over the years but made his home in North Bank. He liked to say he taught his class so he'd be able to retire, hoping to find someone to replace him, but she had a feeling he enjoyed teaching.

"You're sure this isn't Gibbons mine though?" He gestured to her hasty sketch of the exterior. She'd done it from memory but felt like it was relatively accurate. "See that ridge there? Looks just like where the mine is set. And then here," he gestured to the small clearing to the left. "That's the road leading back to town."

"Nope. I'm positive. That's Coal Ridge." She pointed to the area he'd indicated, and he nodded.

"I see. Well, either way, these are fantastic. You have talent, young lady." He offered her a fatherly smile but then motioned to the skull. "How about turning it to the assignment?"

She smiled and nodded, flipping to a blank page. "Sorry. Will do."

He moved to the next grouping of desks, and she caught muttered observations and gentle suggestions as she began to sketch the skull in front of her. She could tell from first glance that it had been a head wound with the point of impact being the right temple. Cracks spider webbed out from the location, and she did her best to imagine the area whole, but her mind continued to wander.

She'd been to Gibbons mine a few times. It was on another mountain ridge almost parallel to Coal Ridge, but she couldn't remember the name of it. It wasn't accessible from the side of the mountain they had been on, but she knew the road that went up to the mine.

Her pencil stalled.

Gibbons mine was isolated, set in much the same type of location as the Blanken sawmill, and was another place that wasn't frequented by anyone. As far as she knew, one of the old-timers in town owned the mine but never went up there.

She pushed a strand of hair behind her ear and tried to sketch the shadow of the Zygomatic bone accurately. If she made it too deep, it could throw off the starkness of the cheek bones once flesh was approximated over it.

Her pencil stilled again. Two girls had been found dead. One here in North Bank. One today on the USFS land. Then she and Clancy had found the remains of captivity at the sawmill.

Willa's mouth went dry, and she reached for her metal water bottle, swigging deeply from it. Was it possible that whoever was hurting these young women was using deserted property structures to hide them? If so, Gibbons mine would be the perfect place to hold someone captive.

Willa shot to her feet, drawing the attention of most of the class. She flushed again and began shoving her pencils and erasers into her bag.

"Is everything okay, Willa?" Professor Scott asked, weaving through chairs and desks toward her.

"Yeah. I—it was a hard day at work. Do you mind if I leave early?" She snapped a quick photo of the skull and then pointed to her in-progress sketch. "I can do the rest at home and scan a picture to send to you."

He met her gaze with softness. "Sure thing. You take care of yourself, all right?"

"I will. Thanks, Mr. S."

She ducked her head and raced out the door. There was only one person she could think of who *might* believe her, and he might just be crazy enough to go with her, but it was a risk.

Clancy had taken the time to tell her that the evidence they'd collected would be useful, but she hadn't been able to figure out *why*. The fact that it could take weeks to process dampened some of her hope, which had left her wondering why he'd bothered to seek her out.

She remembered his long look at the door once she'd passed through, obviously not able to see through the tinted glass as she could. Her eyes had traced the hard lines on his face and the inscrutable look he'd worn until Jase had confronted him.

What she wouldn't have given to be a fly on the wall for that conversation, but Barney had herded her to her desk, and she'd put those thoughts out of her mind. Until now.

The drive back to Chamberlin seemed to take forever, but Willa left the audiobook off and focused on hacking through her raw emotions with the sword of prayer. It's what she should have done in the first place, but sometimes, zoning out was so much easier.

By the time she pulled into one of two motels in Chamberlin and saw the dusty Jeep, Willa was ready to do her best convincing.

After a quick stop in to see Fatima to find out Clancy's room number, she took a breath and knocked loudly three times on the door.

She heard the chain being pulled back, and the door opened to reveal Clancy in gym shorts. Shirtless.

Instant heat flooded Willa's cheeks. It was a ridiculous reaction, seeing as she'd seen her fair share of men shirtless, but there was something about seeing Clancy this way that made it nothing like seeing Jase or Max.

"Willa?" Clancy yawned and rolled his shoulders.

The motion drew her attention to well-muscled biceps that led to strong pecs and down to defined abs and—

Willa jerked her eyes back to his. Thankfully, he seemed ignorant of her reaction to him, the fact she stood backlit hopefully helping to hide her pinked cheeks.

"What are you doing here?" He propped his forearm against the door jamb and leaned forward, yawning again.

"I'm..." Words failed. The scent of fresh soap enveloped her as it rushed out on AC cooled air. Her eyes trailed back to his chest before she commanded them to stay on his face. "I'm here to see you."

His eyes narrowed, and she thought she caught the slightest tilt at the corner of his lips before he sobered. "How'd you find my room?"

"Fatima is a friend of mine."

"So much for privacy," he said, shifting back and crossing his arms over his chest.

Somehow, that was worse. Or better? Now all she could see was his bulging biceps on display and how his waist narrowed and—where was his shirt?

She met the dark brown pools of his eyes. "I thought of something at class tonight, and I need your help. It's about Anna."

An eyebrow quirked, but his gaze trailed behind her and over the parking lot. "Come on in."

She hesitated. She didn't really know him, not more than the time she'd spent with him earlier that day, and now he was inviting her into his room. Where she expected to hear warning bells, she only sensed peace.

"Willa?" He half turned back to her, curiosity in his gaze.

She stepped inside and watched as he—mercifully—pulled on a shirt and sagged onto the unmade bed.

"Did I wake you?" She checked her watch to confirm it was only six thirty.

"I just dozed off. What's up?"

Willa tried to clear her head of the jumble of thoughts, but being in Clancy's space was worse. He'd clearly taken a shower as evidenced by the wet towel draped over a chair back, and the scent of his soap—or was that deodorant—permeated the room like fresh spring rain with a masculine edge.

Then there was Clancy himself.

Earlier, she'd seen him dressed in jeans and a t-shirt but now in shorts and a t-shirt, barefoot, he looked relaxed. He was propped up against the head of the unmade bed, and Willa felt like an outsider. Her usual bravado in the face of all things faltered, and she was suddenly hyper-aware of how attractively masculine he was. From the mess of his small suitcase to the damp, disheveled curls of his brown hair.

"Are we going to play some type of guessing game? Or are you going to tell me what you need help with?"

Willa flushed again and bit the inside of her cheek wishing she could will the heat away. This was about Anna, not some ridiculous crush—

Rather than let that thought out completely, she focused on pulling out her notebook from her bag. She flipped a few pages then turned it toward him. She had taken a hasty moment to sketch the image in the car before leaving the community college, but she was curious what he would say.

"Okay, so we *are* playing games. Pictionary, apparently."

She gave him a piercing look and pointed to the image. "What do you see?"

"Is this a trick question?" He frowned but then seemed to decide to humor her. "The sawmill we were at today. The one that is likely nothing more than ash at this point." He added the last part more to himself and ran a hand through his chin-length hair, the curls tugging straight before bouncing back.

"But that's just it. This isn't the Blanken sawmill. This is Gibbons mine on a completely different range."

He leaned forward, elbows on his knees. "You sure?"

"Positive. This is the sawmill." She flipped back to her earlier image. "The ridges are slightly different."

"What are you saying?" He leveled his gaze at her, and while he now wore a shirt and she should be completely fine, she couldn't help the reaction of warmth that pooled in the pit of her stomach at her body's reaction to him. One she couldn't seem to stop.

"That if there is a serial killer out there preying on young women, this would be the perfect place to hide someone." Clancy opened his mouth. but she held up a hand. "And if he was willing to use a place like the Blanken sawmill, he might also use a place like the Gibbons mine."

"And you what? Want to go out there?"

"Yes."

He didn't look away, but she caught his furrowing brow. "The sheriff—"

"Can't do anything. It's just a hunch, but," she turned, biting her lip to keep the tears back, "I don't think I can sleep if I don't go and see for myself."

"Willa, it'll be dark in a few hours and—"

"Forget I said anything." She stood, flipping her notepad closed. "I'm sorry to have bothered you."

She was almost to the door when warm skin brushed her arm and gentle fingers closed around her forearm. Willa didn't move, frozen in place by his touch.

"I'm sorry." The heat of his hand fell away as he let go. "I didn't mean to make you think I wouldn't help. I just don't want you getting into anything...dangerous."

She spun to face him. "This isn't about me. It's about Anna."

The shift in Clancy's features was subtle, but she saw the moment he gave in. His resolve hardened, and the 'take charge' attitude was back.

"Let me change, and we can go."

Chapter Thirteen

Clancy

CLANCY TOLD HIMSELF TO FOCUS ON THE ROAD, THE TWISTS and turns demanding all of his attention, but he couldn't help but sneak a glance at Willa. She'd changed out of the jeans and T-shirt he'd seen her in earlier and now wore a flowy yellow tank top over light colored jean shorts that showed off shapely legs.

He redirected his attention to the yellow double line in the road and told himself not to think about Willa's legs. She was beautiful, he could have been half-blind and seen that, but the determination she showed when it came to finding Anna was almost more attractive than her legs. Almost.

The lavender scent permeated the Jeep again, but stronger this time, and he guessed she'd grabbed a shower before her class as well.

His mind supplied the ever-deepening blush on her cheeks when he'd answered the door shirtless. In a very uncharacteristic move, he hadn't even checked to see who it was before he'd answered the door. It was either a product of too little sleep, or he was starting to feel comfortable in Chamberlin.

Either way, he couldn't quell the fire her reaction to him had flamed to life. His grip tightened on the steering wheel. Beautiful women flirted with him all the time, but their attention turned him away rather than drew him near.

But Willa....

She had the opposite effect. She'd been trying and failing not to look at his bare chest, and it had stirred a long dead urge in him. The desire to see if her lips felt as soft as they looked.

He forced out a breath and sensed her gaze on him. He flashed a tight-lipped smile at her to reassure her before looking back to the road.

Calm down, Sullivan.

This wasn't the time for these thoughts. They were drawing close to the place she'd marked on the map, and he again asked himself if he crazy to have given in to her request to go up to check out the mine that night. Maybe he should have convinced her that the first thing in the morning would be best. But he knew that was a lie.

He knew the statistics. The faster they could check out the location, the better. But did that mean he was bringing her into a dangerous situation?

The thought doused all others like a bucket of ice water. He had to be on his game in all aspects if he was going to keep them safe. No matter how much he might be attracted to her, he would only bring chaos into her already settled life, and that was a fact.

"We're almost there," she said, pointing to a small road partially obstructed by branches. "Do you think you can make it?"

"Yeah." He didn't say more—couldn't with the swirl of emotions in his gut—but then a sobering observation caught him center mass.

Broken branches. Some lay on the ground and others hung limply from the branches they'd once been attached to. Someone had come this way and recently, judging by the fact that the downed evergreen boughs were still green.

He didn't point out the branches, but one look at Willa told him he didn't have to. She'd seen them, too, and she knew what they meant. His gut clenched and only tightened further when they pulled out into the open in front of the old building.

Willa was out of the car before he'd put it into park. Thankfully, she waited at the front of the Jeep while he checked his Glock 19 and placed it in the holster at the small of his back, making sure his shirt wasn't covering it for easy access. He also picked up his pack with evidence collection materials and a flashlight. If they came across anything they'd need to call it in, but he always carried it with him.

"Ready?" He met her eyes fully for the first time since they'd left his hotel room.

"Yes." Her voice wavered, but she held his gaze, and he saw the steel-like strength that seemed to run through her veins.

As one, they turned toward the building. He caught sight of the opening of a mine off to the right, set into the side of the mountain. The structure itself was in a worse state than the sawmill had been in. Boards were missing, making the building look like it flashed them a gap-toothed smile, but there were still parts that looked solid.

"That door looks like it would open," she said, pointing to the right side of the building.

He'd seen it, too. "Yeah, let's go in through there."

They turned toward that side of the building and began picking their way through the detritus of old railroad ties, mining bins, and indeterminate metal objects that littered the yard.

"Wait." Clancy's hand reached out and gripped Willa by the shoulder. Her skin was soft and warm, hotter than the air around them, and he released her like she'd burned him.

"What is it?" She hadn't seemed to notice his odd reaction.

"That." He pointed to a piece of trash. It didn't look like anything they'd found at the sawmill, but he still pulled his phone out and took a picture. "Okay."

They reached the door, and Clancy stepped in front of her. His hand went reflexively to the Glock at his back, and he pulled it out, keeping the safety on with his finger running alongside the trigger.

Willa shrank back behind him, and he pushed the door in, training his light in front of them.

Dust motes took to life in the illuminated beam of his flashlight, but beyond scattered and fallen boards, he didn't see anything of note.

"Come on." He stepped inside, putting his gun away, and felt more than saw Willa follow him.

They picked their way across old floorboards and through a maze of partially fallen support beams toward the back of the building where it was darkest. He reasoned if anyone had used this to hide someone—or was doing it still—they would want a spot in the most stable area of the building.

Above them, boards creaked, and bits and pieces of sawdust and debris continued to fall. They hardly made a sound with their steps, but it was as if the building knew they were trespassing.

"Do you see anything?" Willa whispered.

He felt the urge to tell her to be quiet, but there had been nothing that made it seem necessary. Aside from the trash outside, which could have come from teens partying, there was nothing in the building that looked disturbed.

"Not yet," he finally replied.

They side-stepped around an old, broken-down conveyor belt. A loud clattering sound caused him to whirl around, though he dropped his hand so only the light shone on Willa. She stood in the beam, leaning against a wooden rafter. A long, rusted iron wrench lay on the ground at her feet.

"Sorry." She let out a held breath and slumped against a nearby wooden support.

He shook his head. "Not a good idea to—"

A loud, groaning creek echoed from overhead, and the beam Willa leaned against shifted. She jumped away, and Clancy's eyes went wide as the beam began to move as if in slow motion. He jerked his gaze upward, and with sickening realization, knew that things had just gone from not great to terrible.

"Willa, we have to—"

The beam split in two with an echoing snap.

Clancy didn't take time to explain. He reached for Willa's hand and raced back the way they'd come. The light bounced with his gait, making it nearly impossible to see, and he nearly tripped two times as they neared the door they'd came in through.

Suddenly, Willa was dead weight dragging him down. He skidded to a stop to see she'd fallen. One leg stuck through the floorboards up to her thigh with angry red scratches showing the impact of her fall. Her palm was bloody and racked with splinters where she'd tried to catch herself.

"Can you move your leg?"

"Just get me out." She clasped his arms, and he pulled up. She wasn't heavy, but the angle of her leg made his efforts precarious.

Another crash followed by more ominous groans caused Clancy to pause and look up. The whole building shifted from side to side, the motion becoming more and more dramatic.

"Hold on, Willa." He shoved the flashlight into his belt and moved behind her. Reaching under her arms, he pulled back instead of forward, and her leg came free along with a soft cry of pain.

"Can you walk?" He shouted into her ear to make himself heard over the sound of falling boards.

"Yes," she said, hobbling forward.

"Here." He put an arm around her, and they limp-shuffled toward the exit door. They were almost there when Willa screamed.

With more force than he would have expected, she shoved him forward. He half-tripped, half-fell through the door as another resounding crash echoed behind him. Pushing up onto all fours, he turned. The door was blocked by a pile of rubble.

Willa was nowhere in sight.

"Willa? Willa!" He threw his backpack away from the building and plunged back into the half-darkness. "Willa, where are you?"

Heart pounding, Clancy knew she'd been caught by the falling beam. Knew she had to be under the rubble in front of him. He willed it not to be true but—

Then he saw it. The barest hint of yellow to his right.

He rushed in, careful of the falling debris, and fell to his knees next to Willa. She wasn't moving, and her blonde hair covered her head as she lay face up. His gut clenched as he gingerly moved the hair away. Blood oozed from a nasty gash near her temple, but he found a pulse when he felt for it.

His heart hammered to life again, and he took in his surroundings. It seemed the worst of the building's shifting had ceased, but he couldn't take the chance. He had to move her, though he knew it was risky without knowing if she had sustained any other injuries.

"Willa, can you hear me?"

Everything in him begged God for her to be okay. Pleaded that he couldn't lose another young woman.

Please God, no more death. Not Willa.

He felt her head, then her neck, and on down in an evaluative way. Feeling no other injuries, he tried one more time, cupping her cheek. "Willa?"

Her eyelids fluttered open, but he didn't see understanding there. Only confusion.

"I'm going to move you. I've got to get you out of this building. I'm sorry." He didn't know why he apologized, but as her eyelids fluttered closed, she gave the barest of nods.

Taking that as his cue, he picked her up and rushed out the door just as another loud crash interrupted the calm of the descending night. Clancy rested her on a patch of ground covered with soft pine needles and made sure her airway was open. He checked her vitals again and was reassured with a strong pulse.

Then, for the second time that day, Clancy called 911.

After explaining what had happened, the dispatcher said she would send an ambulance out to them immediately. She was starting to ask more pressing questions when Clancy's phone lit up with Max's contact.

He groaned, knowing he shouldn't hang up on the dispatcher but also knowing Max wouldn't stop calling.

He switched the call. "Yeah."

"What in the name of all that is good were you thinking?"

"Guess you heard my call."

"Clancy," Max said his name like a curse. "If she's hurt..."

Clancy couldn't bring himself to speak. Didn't know what to say.

"Need I remind you you're *just* a PI here? You have no jurisdiction. You have no authority. You shouldn't be out breaking into private property on any account, but bringing Willa with you... What were you thinking?"

He had no reply. He'd let her passion convince him that it would be fine. That he was helping *her* by going with her. Part of him had thought she might have gone by herself if he hadn't gone with her, but was that justification?

And Max was right. He was an outsider. He didn't belong here, and he'd stuck his nose in deep this time.

Clancy's gaze trailed over Willa, willing her injuries to be less severe than they looked. Head injuries always bled a lot, but the gauze he'd pulled from his pack was already soaked through. His chest constricted as he traced the soft lines of her face.

This was his fault.

But then he looked back to the building. There might not have been anyone held hostage here, but there had been someone at the sawmill. Willa's instincts were spot-on even if they were misguided this time. And he couldn't discount that.

He hung up on Max. There was nothing else he could say to quell the man's anger, but there was a woman right in front of him demanding his attention. And that was more important than anything else.

Chapter Fourteen

Willa

Soft beeps worked their way into her dream. Was she being attacked by angry robots? What was—

Her eyes fluttered open, and she took in the stark room. At TV hung high up on the opposite wall, and something that looked like a tall shower curtain hung to her left. Her hand hurt, and she looked down to see the IV poking into the thin flesh there.

Realization crystallized. She was in the hospital.

Willa fought her memory. She'd been with Clancy. They'd been at the abandoned Gibbons mine, and they'd gone inside and—

She gasped in realization. She'd seen the shift in the massive rafter right above the door, and before she could think about it, she'd shoved Clancy out while she dodged to the left. Clearly, she hadn't been fast enough.

Her fingers traced over the gauze that wrapped around her aching forehead until she touched a tender part. Wincing, she dropped her hand, also wrapped in gauze, and looked around. Something that looked like a remote lay next to her on the bed. One button said Call Nurse under it, so she pressed it. Maybe they'd be able to get her some water. Her mouth was so dry she could hardly swallow.

Less than a minute later, a familiar form rushed through the door. "Oh, my goodness, you're awake. Girl, how are you feeling?"

"Sloane!" she rasped.

"I'm not your nurse, but I convinced them to let me come see you first. Here, have some water." She picked up a beige cup with a ridged straw and held it out for her. Willa drank long and deep, and finally feeling somewhat refreshed, leaned back.

"What happened?" Willa asked.

"You don't remember?"

"Some parts of it. But how am I here?"

"Wait." Sloane leaned in conspiratorially. "Please tell me you remember that hottie in the hall."

"Hottie?"

Sloane nodded in the direction of the small window that offered a view into the hall, and Willa looked up to see Clancy pacing back and forth, cell phone plastered to his ear.

"That's Clancy." Willa's face flushed, and she knew her friend saw it.

"Oh, my gosh. You *do* know him. We were taking bets he was just some guy who found you. Though, to be honest, he seemed a little *too* concerned about you."

Willa watched as he spun on his heel and paced the other way, a bandage on his hand. So, he'd been injured, too—and it was her fault.

Guilt washed through her at the thought that yet another person had gotten hurt because of her. She mentally shook herself. They still didn't know if Anna was hurt or not.

"Wills?"

"What?" She realized her friend had been talking, but she'd tuned her out.

"I asked if he's single." Sloane winked.

"I—I don't—"

"Sorry, I'm just giving you a hard time. How are you feeling?" Sloane switched into nurse-mode and checked her chart and vitals.

"Just have a bit of a headache. Otherwise, I feel okay." Willa was surprised to find that it was true. While her head hurt and her neck was sore, the rest of her appeared to be fully functioning.

"Good. I don't know if they'll want to keep you overnight or not. You have a mild concussion, but everything else looks good."

"I'm not staying." Willa reached for the IV, but Sloane stopped her by resting a calming hand over hers.

"I'll talk with your doctor."

"Please do. I can't stay—I'll just take up space for someone who really needs it."

Sloane met her eyes. "Are you really okay? I told you to be careful, and yet it was like you ran head first into danger."

Willa searched the room as if looking for the answer. "You know Anna and I had grown close."

"You guys were inseparable whenever you weren't at work." Sloane crossed her arms and added a smile. "I was getting jealous."

"You're busier than I am."

"True," Sloane agreed.

"We spent a lot of time together because she was hungry for truth. Sloane, I've never known someone so lost before." Willa's mind slipped back into all of the questions Anna had asked. How she'd genuinely wanted to know their answers and had been willing to put in the work to find them. "Our friendship was about more than just being friends. It was about introducing her to Jesus."

Sloane's eyes turned glossy, and she sniffed. "That's really good to hear, Wills."

"I know, which is why *I know* she didn't run away. I know Sheriff Harding wants to believe me, but he's got years of police work and statistics that tell him she's just like any number of girls who you think are changing but never do."

"That's why you went to see if the body was her." Sloane gave a nod. "You think it's more likely she's been kidnapped or killed rather than being off somewhere living it up."

Willa wouldn't have put it like that, but her friend got the gist of it. "She's been taken by someone bad. It's the only explanation."

The weight of her words landed between them, and tension took up residence in the room with them like it was a live thing. Willa wanted to shoo it out the door but knew better. There was no getting past hard truths. Willa had learned that when her mother left her and her dad when Willa was nine, and she'd never forgotten that lesson.

"I'll talk to your doctor. See what I can do, okay? But you—call your dad. He's worried."

Willa groaned. "Tell me you did *not* call him, Lo!"

Sloane shrugged. "He's your emergency contact, and we felt he needed to know."

"He's probably already on a plane back. I did *not* want to ruin this trip for him."

"Just call him. It's better than guessing." Sloane handed Willa's phone to her from a pocket in her scrubs and left, closing the door most of the way.

Willa tapped the contact button for her father and waited. It barely rang when her father's deep, gruff voice answered. "Willa Rose, is that you?"

"Yeah, Dad, it's me."

"Thank God! Are you okay? Sloane called and said you were in the hospital, and I thought—"

"I'm fine, Dad. Promise. Just a bump on the head." She bit her lip knowing that was over-simplifying things by a lot.

"Honey, I'm going to come back. I was just searching ticket sites and—"

"No, Dad. Please don't do that." The ache of guilt settled deeper in the pit of her stomach. "I would never forgive myself if I made you come home because I got a mild concussion."

"It's more than that, and you know it." Her father took a breath. "Sloane said they found a body."

"It wasn't Anna."

"But leaving work to go to a crime scene? Willa Rose, what were you thinking?"

"Barney called you." Willa dropped her head against her palm, carefully avoiding the injured side.

"More like I called him to see what was going on. What you did was...rash."

That was putting it mildly.

"But I think I understand." Her father's words softened. "Honey, what you've been through over the last few weeks breaks my heart. It's taking a toll on you. I think I should come back just so I can be there. We can talk and—"

"Dad, I'm fine. Really. I made an impulsive decision, and things got out of hand, but I'm okay. Please don't make me feel like I'm the reason you're leaving a job you love. I couldn't handle that on top of all of this."

"I hear you, but you're not making wise choices. Why were you out at Gibbons mine in the first place?"

Willa bit her lip. She knew her father would be adamantly against her involvement in the case in any form or fashion, but she had to give him some explanation. "I met a guy." She winced. This was dangerously close to lying to her father.

"I—oh."

"I mean, he's new to the area and I decided to show him around." She frowned. Her not-lie was going to fall apart very quickly.

"And he wanted to see the mine?"

"He needed a guide." She closed her eyes, an embarrassed flush flooding her cheeks despite the fact they were on the phone. "And he's cute."

"Oh." Her father let the awkward pause linger. He'd never been good at talking about emotions and feelings with her. "Well, that's good then. Will you see him again?"

Bless his heart, her father was trying. Fresh shame washed through her. "I hope so."

"Well," he cleared his throat, and she waited three breaths until he finally exhaled. "Okay. I guess you're doing all right and don't need your old man interfering. But if I hear anything else has happened I'm on a plane back. You hear me?"

"Yeah, Dad."

"All right, sweetie. Text me and let me know when you're home."

"I will."

"And, uh, I hope the guy asks you out. If, um, that's something you want."

"Thanks, Dad," she said, covering her eyes with her free hand.

"Bye, honey."

She hung up but kept her hand in place. Had she really just used Clancy to get out of telling her father the truth?

"Cute, huh?"

Willa's eyes popped open. "Clancy."

He leaned in the doorway with his arms crossed, and enigmatic look on his handsome features.

"Have—" Her voice rasped. She took a sip of the water and tried again. "Have you been there long?"

The corner of his mouth seemed to wage a valiant battle against his willpower, but in the end won out, tipping up into an amused half-smile. The sight brought all sorts of warm feelings to Willa's clenched stomach.

"Long enough. That was your father, I gather?"

Willa wished the hospital bed would swallow her whole, but when it didn't comply to her pleading, she nodded. "Yeah. He's in DC right now, and I was trying to convince him not to come back for a little bump on the head."

"I see." Clancy studied her, his eyes tracing over her bandaged head and down to her hand. "How do you feel?"

Relief that he wasn't going to bring up what she said coursed through her. "Fine. Good. I mean, it hurts a little, but I think they'll let me go soon." She nervously tried to push a strand of hair behind her ear only to run into the bandage.

"Look." He stood and took a few steps into the room. "I'm sorry for what happened. I shouldn't have let you come with me and—"

"What are you talking about?" His eyes narrowed, but she pushed on. "It was *my* lead, and you didn't *let* me do anything. Besides, neither of us could have known the building was ready to come down." Was she trying to convince him or herself? Or both? Maybe they could have—should have—guessed the outcome based on looks alone, but she'd seen rundown buildings before, and it didn't mean they *would* topple, just that they could.

"Right." He rolled his neck and reached up as if to massage a sore part. That's when she saw his bandaged hand again.

"Are *you* all right?"

"This?" He looked at his left hand like he'd forgotten it was there. "Yeah. This is nothing. You got the worst of it."

They held a weighted gaze, and Willa tried to read whatever it was Clancy wasn't saying. His eyes flickered over her head bandage again, and she saw the shadow he tried to hide. It brought clarity and she knew what he was thinking.

"This wasn't your fault, Clancy." He blamed himself, which was ridiculous. "We were both at risk going in there and both agreed to it. If anything, this is my fault."

He crossed his arms again making his biceps and shoulders bulge in the light gray T-shirt. "Your fault? How do you figure?"

"I came up with the idea. I begged you to come with me. I went in when I should have known better. See? *My* fault."

He raised a questioning eyebrow. "Are you sure you're not just saying that because I needed a guide, and I'm cute?"

Willa groaned, pulling the pillow up to bury her face in it. So, he *hadn't* decided to let that slide. "Can we pretend that I never said that?"

"What, you don't think I'm cute?"

Willa stilled as Clancy's deep voice spoke just above a whisper from beside her bed. His sudden nearness did funny things to her stomach, and she considered the fact that the pillow in her hands might combust due to the heat flaming from her face.

"Well?" He gently pulled the pillow down until she was forced to look up at him.

His smile was full of delicious teasing that made his eyes sparkle, and Willa forgot to breathe. Forgot the pain in her head and the reason they had been at the mine in the first place. All she could think of was the scent of strong soap and warmed forest coming from the man beside her.

Every nerve tingled to life as she felt the heat radiating off him through her thin hospital gown. It reminded her that she was cold—too cold—in this antiseptic room.

"What was the question?" She blushed further at the breathlessness in her voice.

He licked his lips, the motion drawing her attention. He had good lips, though they were hard to see with the scruff that lined the lower half of his face. She had the urge to reach up and run her thumb across the sharp line of his jaw.

"Willa." Clancy said her name, and she drew her eyes up to meet his. Had she really just been staring at his lips?

"What?" She blinked and ran a hand over her head though she hit the sore spot and winced.

"Are you really okay?" Concern melted his brown eyes. She only then noticed the darker brown that rimmed his iris.

"Yes. Really."

"Good." He stepped back suddenly, clearing his throat. "I—I just wanted to make sure. You should probably get some rest." He turned to go.

Willa wanted to ask him to stay, but she had no reason to. She didn't even know if she'd see him again or if—

"Clancy." His name slipped free of lips, and he stopped, half turning back to her. "Will you let me know if you have any more leads?"

He frowned. "I'm not sure that I can."

"She's my friend. Please." Tears flooded Willa's eyes, but she willed them back.

"I'll...try."

He spun and left, taking with him the hope she'd tried so desperately to hold on to.

Chapter Fifteen

Clancy

HE LOVED LIBRARIES. NOT ONLY WERE THEY FREE TO THE public, but they were cool, usually quiet, and chock-full of books. He'd shown up at the Chamberlin Public Library at eight o'clock when they opened and had been there for two hours already.

The kindly older woman who said her name was Ethel had greeted him at the front desk and had shown him to the historical section. He'd been there ever since combing through local history. He'd found the two locations he'd already visited as well as a dozen more. After narrowing in on what he could only assume was part of the killer's MO, Clancy had to agree with Willa. The mine would have been a likely spot for another woman to be hidden.

He clenched his fist at the fact that he hadn't been able to fully clear the building before the fall-in. It was possible there was evidence there that they'd missed, but he wasn't sure he could convince the deputies to check into it without any kind of proof. He needed to establish the pattern, and one location wasn't enough for that. The young woman he'd found in the clearing could have been held at the sawmill and that was that.

But his gut said otherwise.

"How are you doing, Clancy?" Ethel asked. She stood at the entryway to the row he'd taken up residence in, a stack of four books in her thin, sweater-clad arms.

"Good." He offered a sheepish grin from the floor. His bag sat next to him, a notebook on one knee and a history book in the other.

"There are chairs or desks if you'd rather use them," she said, looking helpful without a hint of censure.

"Here's good." He shrugged.

"Well, if you're sure..." She trailed off, her head tilting to one side. "You know, we've got an updated edition of that book if it would help your research."

He held up the one he'd been reading, *Chamberlin: A History of Places and People.* "Really?"

"Yes, the author is a local man, and he just put out the new edition, oh," she tapped her chin with a finger, "a few months back?"

"I'd love to see it."

"Come with me." Her smile widened, and he sensed it was the look she got when she helped someone find the perfect book.

He shoved his notebook into his bag and reshelved the other books he'd been looking at, making sure to check that they were put back in the right slots. Then he stepped out into the main library space and looked for the woman with her gray bun and frameless glasses.

She stood near the front door where a display had been set up. He'd glanced at it when he went inside, but he hadn't stayed to look.

"This is our local history feature. It was my idea," she said with pride. "I thought it would be nice to show folks all the history that rests in and around Chamberlin. It goes all the way back to before Washington was even a territory."

"Impressive." He took in the categories of books both non-fiction and fiction with a smattering of children's books on the area or the wider Washington State.

"Here it is," she said, picking up a tome that looked similar to the one he'd been looking through.

Clancy accepted the book with a smile and nodded toward the desks. "I think I'll use a chair this time."

Her smile grew, and she nodded as he turned toward the study section.

He'd been close to flipping the original book closed and calling it all a loss, but the fact that this book about historical people *and* places in the area had been updated recently gave him courage.

The previous book was published in the late eighties, and while informative, hadn't been up-to-date enough to truly help him narrow in on locations that might be of use to the killer.

If that was even what was happening here.

Clancy ran a hand over this face and sighed. He wondered if he was grasping at straws, but he flipped open to the "places" section, pulled out his notebook, and began to jot down areas of interest.

Twenty minutes later, he had a plan.

His eyes flicked to his phone. The nurse, Sloane, who seemed to be good friends with Willa, had exchanged numbers with him the day before so she could update him on how her friend was doing—something he was pretty sure *wasn't* legal. He was tempted to call her and ask after Willa since he still didn't have her number, but was it better if he left things as they were?

He remembered their conversation from the evening before. Seeing her in a hospital bed had caused an overly emotional reaction in him. One that still concerned him. He'd been angry, mostly at himself, for how he'd let her get hurt, but other emotions had swirled through him, too. Like how vulnerable she'd looked and how the fire was missing from her eyes, which worried him more than anything else.

Teasing her about the overheard conversation had brought some of that fire back, but it had also affected him more than he'd wanted to acknowledge. Her lavender scent haunted his thoughts, and worry over her safety chased him through his dreams.

The smart thing for him to do was follow up on the leads he'd found himself. It was easiest to keep himself safe without the anxiety that she'd get hurt again. But the look on her face when she'd told him that Anna was her friend wouldn't leave him.

What would he have done if it had been his best friend Trae? Or his brother?

Clancy shot off a text instead of a call, and the reply set his course for the rest of the day.

Fifteen minutes later, he was at the address Sloane had forwarded. He pulled at his T-shirt in the middle of his chest, letting the material fall back in place with the hint of a cooling breeze before he pressed the doorbell.

Less than a minute later, he heard something on the other side of the door followed by the *click* of the deadbolt set free. Then the door opened to reveal Willa in a black tank top and cotton shorts. Her bare legs seemed to go on for miles, and Clancy had to yank his gaze from following their descent with more attention than the situation warranted.

"Hi."

Willa looked surprised and then, somewhat nervous, wrapping her arm around her midsection. "Clancy. I—how did you get my address?"

"Sloane."

The word was all Willa needed to hear. "You, uh, wanna come inside?" She looked up at him through her lashes.

"Sure."

She stepped back, and he passed her into the cozy living room of the modest sized house. The couch was a dark, worn leather, but colorful throw pillows added softness, as did a fuzzy throw and a few side tables with framed photos and a few books.

Each one held an image of Willa and a man Clancy thought had to be her father. No sign of a mother in any of the images.

"You want anything to drink? Or...are you hungry?"

He spun back to her, chiding himself for looking at the space with his PI eyes instead of focusing on the reason he'd come.

"No. Well, yeah. I'll take some water or something."

"Come on back to the kitchen. I was just making some breakfast."

He followed her down the hall lined with more images, these held other family members like grandparents, cousins, and aunts and uncles. Then, a row of awards for a Shawn Martin—likely Willa's father.

The hallway opened up to a warm kitchen in tones of cream and olive green with a small nook that looked out over a postage stamp backyard with patchy green grass sheltered by a towering oak tree.

"Have a seat," she said, pointing to the nook before she went back to the oven and bent down to pull something out.

Clancy looked away, the temptation to trace her curves so foreign to him it was shocking. What was this? Attraction?

He snuck another glance as she set a square dish on a wire cooling rack. Her blonde hair hung loose in wavy kinks around her shoulders, and his eyes traced her profile. As he watched, she bit her lip in concentration as she cut into whatever was in the pan and used a spatula to bring it out and onto a plate.

"Want a slice of homemade coffee cake?" She caught him staring and familiar pink pools highlighted her cheeks.

"Sure." He couldn't bring himself to say anything more. Instead, he continued to watch as she reached for another small plate and proceeded to pull another slice out.

Her movements were graceful, and it unlocked desire deep in his chest. The desire for a home like this. To wake up each morning and spend it lazing around, reading the paper, and eating homemade coffee cake.

Oblivious to his internal thoughts, Willa brought the cake over and then returned with two cups of coffee. She set everything in front of them and slid onto the bench seat across from him. She'd taken off the over-large white bandage that had wrapped her head wound from the day before, and now, two butterfly bandages covered the spot, blue and purple bruising just visible beyond their reach.

"Everything okay?" she asked.

He pulled his gaze from her injuries to take in the cake and then the cup of black coffee. The sense of *rightness* came back to him. It invaded his thoughts and made it hard to get past the overwhelming want of making this his morning routine for the rest of his life.

"Clancy?"

"Sorry. I..." What could he say? That this case was supposed to be like all the rest—get in, do what he could, then leave. But that this strange desire for a place to call home was so foreign to him, he didn't even know how to process it. That he found himself wondering if it was better than wherever could be on the horizon. "I didn't sleep well last night."

"I'm sorry to hear that." Willa dug a fork into her cake and savored her first bite. "They gave me some medication for the pain, and it put me out fast."

Her smile warmed his frozen thoughts, and he followed suit, taking a bite of the coffee cake. It melted on his tongue. Sweet vanilla cake. Spicy cinnamon. Warm brown sugar. The ultimate comfort food.

"Wow." He took another bite and moaned at how good it was. He couldn't help it.

"You like it?"

"This is *so* good. Seriously. You made it?" The blush that touched her nose and cheeks entranced him, and he forced his eyes back to the cake.

"I did. It's an old family recipe."

"Your mom's?" The question slipped out before he could stop himself.

"Nah." He caught her reaction—a mix of anger and resignation. "Mom left when I was nine, but she was gone a lot before that. It's my grandma's recipe. My dad's family is from here so I'm pretty close with them. My Aunt Janet taught me how to cook and bake."

He caught the flash of pain that crossed Willa's expression. "Sounds like you were close to your aunt."

"I was." Willa shot him a probing look. "Until she died."

There was a world packed into Willa's explanation, but Clancy sensed she didn't want to talk about it.

Instead, he focused on the coffee cake and let his thoughts be tricked into thinking that this was his life all the time.

Chapter Sixteen

Willa

WILLA FORKED ANOTHER BITE OF HER GRANDMOTHER'S COFFEE cake and tried to shake out the mental fog that came from having Clancy sitting across the table from her. In her home. While she was still in her pajamas.

She ducked her head for another bite and to hide the resounding flush that threatened to flood her cheeks. At least she was wearing a sports bra and had thrown on a tank top before answering the door.

It was ridiculous. She wouldn't have thought twice about it had it been any of the boys she'd grown up with. They'd seen her work out in a sports bra and shorts so many times she'd lost count, and it had never been an issue.

But Clancy...

She peeked at him through the fringe of hair that had fallen in front of her eyes. He looked a little tired, as he'd said, but lacking sleep or not, he still cut an impressive figure. Broad shoulders that pulled his dark green T-shirt tight, muscled forearms that rested on the plaid tablecloth, and long, dexterous fingers.

She forced her gaze back to the coffee cake. Why was he here? He'd hardly said anything to her, and she couldn't stop her knee from bouncing at the lack of answers.

Willa took a tentative sip of the hot coffee and then forced herself to look directly at him. "Not that I don't like sharing breakfast with you..." She cringed. Was that too flirty? "But why are you here?"

His smile tucked into the corner of his mouth, and he leaned back, also sipping from one of her father's favorite mugs. "I think I know a few other places to check. Ones that are like the sawmill and cabin we went to. I wanted to see if you were up to coming with me."

Her eyebrows hiked up in surprise. "Really?"

"I know you're injured, but I asked Sloane, and she said you were cleared as long as we're not doing anything too strenuous. But if your head hurts and you'd rather not, I understand." He dipped his head, hands cupping the mug in front of him. "I wanted to give you the option."

A surge of confidence bolstered her at his words. The simple fact he'd asked her what *she* wanted to do, not assumed he knew best, flooded her with warmth.

"Thank you."

He looked up. "What?"

"Thank you for asking me. For taking the time to see what *I* want." She took in a deep breath. "I'm going."

She saw his hesitation, the desire to ask her if she was up to it, but he didn't speak. Merely nodded once.

Clancy took another bite of his coffee cake, the obvious pleasure on his face filling Willa in a different way. She threw caution to the wind. "What about you? Your family?"

His head snapped up, and she caught the widening of his eyes like she'd accused him of something. "My family?"

"I told you my history. Your turn." She flashed a quick smile and ate the last bite of her cake.

"I, uh, there's not much to tell. Mom was a bit crazy, but she passed a few years ago. Didn't get along with my dad, and spent most of my time with my grandpa."

He turned to look out the window, offering her a view of his profile. A muscle worked in his jaw, and Willa knew she'd touched a sore spot.

"Sorry. I didn't mean to pry."

"You didn't." He turned back to her. "My home wasn't much of a home growing up, and I had to find my own way."

"That must have been tough."

"It's all I knew." He swallowed the last of his coffee. "Would you be up for going out to one place today? Or do you need another day of rest?"

She felt his eyes on the cut on her forehead. "Today is good. I know time is important. Let me go change."

He didn't respond, but she stood and took their plates to the sink. She'd have a mound of dishes to clean when they got back, but if going today got them even one step closer to Anna, it would be worth it.

Willa rushed up the stairs though slowed near the top to catch her breath. Her head pounded in time with her rushing blood, and she wondered if she'd done the right thing by deciding to go with Clancy. She could use more sleep, and her doctor had told her to take it easy, but if Sloane told him she would be all right, Willa trusted that.

She dressed in a dark blue tank top and ripped jean shorts, pulling on a pair of old tennis shoes. She reached for a baseball cap but paused with her hand hovering over it. Was it likely to press on her stitches? Probably.

She left the hat and ran her fingers through her hair before weaving it back into a loose braid to get it off her neck. After brushing her teeth and swiping on some Chapstick, Willa was ready to go. Though perhaps not ready to be back in Clancy's overwhelming—and distracting—presence.

He was, at once, an enigma and someone she felt drawn to. There was a world behind his simple statements about his family, a world she wanted to unravel, but there was also the natural hesitance of polite distance between them.

They hardly knew one another and had only come together because of her missing friend, but Willa couldn't help but think she didn't want their time together to end.

She covered her face with her hands. That was a horrible thing to think of because it meant prolonging finding Anna. It wasn't that Willa didn't want to find her friend—the opposite was true—but she didn't want Clancy to leave as a result.

Fighting off her tumultuous feelings and knowing that they had no place in her mind for that day, she took the stairs down, but slower this time.

As she neared the kitchen, she heard running water and...singing?

She slowed, drawing closer to the open doorway. It was definitely the sink running and what sounded like an old Eagles song. Willa peered around the corner and caught sight of Clancy. His back was to her, arms elbow deep in soapy water, and he was singing *Take it Easy*. And he didn't have a bad voice. Not bad at all.

Rather than stop the miracle that was a man doing her dishes in her kitchen, Willa folded her arms and watched for a few minutes before he seemed to sense her presence and peeked over his shoulder.

His grin melted Willa's insides like a flame to wax.

"You do dishes, too? Where have you been all my life?" The words slipped out easy and free on a laugh, but only after they landed did she think about what she'd implied.

He seemed not to notice—or chose not to—and instead rinsed his hands and wiped them on her green and yellow plaid hand towel hanging from the oven like it was the most natural thing in the world.

"You cooked, I cleaned. Only seems fair."

Be still her heart—Willa could fall for this man with words like that. "Thank you."

"Sure." He pointed to the counter. "Can we fill these?"

Two refillable water bottles sat drying, and she nodded. "Definitely."

She did, and once the bottles and a few snacks were in a tote bag, she grabbed her satchel and turned to face him. "Ready."

"Let's go."

She fell into step behind him. "Where are we going?"

He paused at the front door just as she reached for the handle. He towered over her, but the effect didn't make her feel weak but delicate. Protected. Especially with the way he was looking at her now.

"Are you sure you're up for it?" His eyes traced her features, and she felt oddly exposed before him. Then he reached up and thumbed the spot where the beam had impacted her. His touch was so light she almost didn't feel it, but the gesture was intimate. So much so she stopped breathing until he spoke again. "Willa?"

"Ye—yeah. Yes. I'm good." Though she was about to dissolve into a puddle of nothing on the floor. How did one look of concern have the power to do that to her? She was the walking cliché of an infatuated woman.

"Positive?" That teasing smile was back, and she wanted to drink it in. Scrap that, she wanted to taste it. Her eyes dipped to his lips, and she licked her own in response. Had she imagined it, or did he take in a breath?

"Yes." Her eyes flickered up to his and saw her own want reflected there.

"Okay then." He moved so she could open the door, and she jerked back into her body from wherever her mind had gone. Cursing her weakness in the presence of a handsome man, Willa yanked the door open and stormed past.

Was she really so pathetic that one look from a handsome man turned her to mush? Sure, it was more than that—he'd washed her dishes for goodness' sake. There wasn't anything sexier than that in her mind, but that's *not* what this was about.

She had to erase the notion that he saw her as she saw him. Had to forget the feelings that were growing toward the puzzle that was Clancy Sullivan. Had to keep her distance.

More than anything, Willa knew the one thing she should be focusing on. Anna.

Nothing else mattered.

Chapter Seventeen

Clancy

WHERE WAS A BUCKET OF ICE WHEN A GUY NEEDED IT? NOT only was it hot outside, the temperatures reaching ninety at only eleven a.m., but the look in Willa's eyes rivaled the sun in intensity.

She was like lava, and Clancy felt her slowly burning away everything that held him back from taking her in his arms and kissing her senseless.

He gripped the steering wheel more tightly as they took the road out of town that led to the western mountain range. She felt it, too. He knew she did by the way she stole glances at his lips and how her cheeks had flushed at his nearness, but he knew dangerous territory when he saw it.

There was a job to do. More than that, there was a missing woman to find, and he felt sick at the mere thought that he'd wanted to kiss Willa when there was a lead to follow.

This wasn't how he lived. He wasn't some Casanova who sought out a cheap facsimile of love in every town. Heck, he hadn't had a girlfriend in five years and hadn't gone on more than three dates since then. All of them had been with nice girls who did nothing more than remind him of the fact that he'd need someone special to love him if there was ever to be a relationship in his future.

Most women couldn't understand his dogged focus on the job. They hadn't when he was a cop, and they couldn't now that he was a PI. There was more to it than going to work at nine and coming home at five. It was late nights and working weekends and being so obsessed with a case you lived and breathed it. That left little room for anything else.

But Willa...

He glanced at her, catching the swift movement as she dropped her hand from where she'd traced the lines of her stitches.

Perhaps he should have left her behind, no matter what she'd said. It was a risk bringing her, but he had to admit, it helped having someone who knew the area. Or was that just him justifying her presence?

"How did you find these leads?" She'd asked before, but he'd made it clear he wanted to be on the road before he told her anything. Not that he was all that worried about being overheard. Time was of the essence. Enjoying breakfast with Willa had set him back, and yet, he couldn't find it within himself to regret the meal. If anything, it was the opposite.

He dove into the story of how he'd holed up at the library and how the new edition of the book showed revised locations of places that were still standing.

"I've seen that book," she said, bracing herself as he took a turn a little too sharply. "My dad knows the author."

Clancy wasn't surprised. She'd said her family was from here, and it seemed as if the author was a long-time resident. "I noticed that at least five of the places he'd listed in the first edition have since either burned or been taken down, but that left four other locations."

"And you think, what? The killer is using them?"

He sneaked a look at her. "Maybe?" He grimaced, turning his eyes back to the road. "I know it's a long shot, but I couldn't help but think that there might have been something in that building that collapsed, and we just didn't see it in time."

"So, all we know of is the sawmill where we found the evidence."

"Yeah, but on the off chance I'm correct..."

"There are at least four places Anna could be." He heard Willa take in a breath.

"There's no evidence she's in the wilderness at all, Willa. It's just a hunch." He thought back to what he'd texted Max before coming to see

Willa. He'd filled the deputy in on his suspicions for the same reason he was telling her. It was better to know and be wrong than to never investigate at all.

"How long have you been a PI?"

Her question caught him off guard, and his mind raced through the years. How he'd left home at eighteen determined to join the military, but his grandfather had convinced him to go to community college first. "I majored in criminal justice and became a cop in L.A. out of college. I worked the job ten years then decided to go into business for myself."

"Ten years? Why'd you leave?"

He felt Willa's eyes on him. "I could have stayed in, but half-way through my career, my grandfather died and left my brother and me an inheritance." Clancy couldn't believe he was telling her this. "I thought I could stay and work the job, but I got burned out. Decided I wanted to go into business for myself so I could help others with no avenue left to them.

"I take on cases that have run the gamut of what law enforcement can offer but haven't quite gone cold yet." His mind filled in the blanks with his last case. "I do what I can."

"That's incredible, Clancy."

"It's just a job."

"But it's not." Willa rested her hand on his arm as he took on another curve of the mountain road. "You give people hope. You give me hope."

Cold dread snaked through him. There was no guarantee that they'd find Anna, and even if they did, no telling what state she'd be in. Had he just given Willa false hope?

"No. I do a job. Sometimes, I'm successful. Sometimes, I'm not."

She seemed to understand the dark turn his thoughts had taken, and her hand slipped away, but her words stayed with him.

You give people hope.

That's what he'd wanted, but things didn't always work out that way. They hadn't for him, and they may not for Willa. The sooner she realized that, the better.

Chapter Eighteen

Willa

WILLA SENSED THE DARK PLACE CLANCY'S THOUGHTS HAD just traveled to. She didn't want to press him, but she wanted him to see that, no matter what happened, it was his actions that offered the hope, not the outcome.

They took a few more turns, and Willa consulted the map that was part of the library book Clancy had checked out. Horse Creek Mine sat adjacent to USFS land, just like the other two places had, and was a gold mine established in the mid eighteen hundreds. It had gone out of use as late as the 1940s, but the property had been kept in the family's name since then, passing from generation to generation.

She'd never gone to this particular mine, but she'd seen several others like it while on hikes in the past. They were typically cut into a mountain side and usually unstable so many years later, but the image of this one showed a few buildings on the property.

"The photos are new," she said, noticing the copyright to a local photographer she'd heard of in the area.

"I'd noticed that." Clancy slowed when she pointed to the narrow logging-type road that shot off to the right of the main road they were on.

"It's why I picked this one first. The others have buildings, but they aren't in as good a shape as this one. Not to mention the mine."

Willa wrinkled her nose. "There's no way someone would go far into those mines. They're unsafe."

"Maybe."

She heard what he didn't say. A killer may not care about safety if he were merely stashing his victims there.

They drove down the road, tires crunching over rocks and loose gravel as low branches scraped across the sides of his jeep. The air conditioning kept them cool, but she knew the minute they stepped outside, she'd be drenched in sweat despite the dryness of the heat.

The road curved and then widened to a clearing overgrown with knee-high weeds and brush. Jutting up through it all was a wooden building with a slanting roof. The grey-white boards boasted the corrosion of time but were surprisingly mostly intact on the side facing them. To the right Willa caught sight of the mine opening, the thick railroad type beams that framed the opening sagging under the weight of the mountain.

She shuddered at the mere thought of stepping inside, knowing that at any moment, the tunnel itself could come crashing down.

The rest of the space was cluttered by rusted out pieces of equipment, broken down mining carts, and stacks of old and rotting wood.

Clancy pulled to a stop, and Willa automatically opened the door just as he turned the Jeep off. Hot, dry heat hit her like a parched tidal wave, bringing with it the scent of sagebrush and dirt. She immediately began fanning herself, but her hand did little good. She'd just have to suck it up and take the heat, glad she'd chosen a dark colored tank top to conceal the sweat that was already tracing salty lines down her back.

Clancy came out of the Jeep, his hand going to the small of his back where she saw the butt of his gun sticking out. He pulled his shirt up so it rested behind the gun for easy access, she assumed. His forehead was creased in concentration, and he searched the area with trained eyes.

She turned in a slow circle and did the same, shielding her eyes from the sun. Something felt off. The typical sounds of birds or the rustling of forest creatures through the underbrush were absent. Even the breeze, slight as it was, slowed then ceased.

It was still, and Willa knew it was wrong.

"Clancy—"

A gun shot rang out into the stillness, the sound like a tree splitting in two.

Willa knew the force of gravity as she was pulled to the ground, cushioned by Clancy's hand on the back of her head. They rolled, and suddenly, his muscled bulk was on top of her, sheltering her by the Jeep. He'd taken care not to jostle her too hard, but the swift motion still caused her vision to swim.

His breaths came in short gasps that she felt against her chest. One hand still rested under her, supporting her, but his other moved up to aim his handgun at the mountains around them.

"Cla—"

"Shh." His warning tickled her ear, but all Willa could think of was another shot piercing through Clancy.

"Clan—"

"Quiet." She followed his gaze from her awkward position under him and saw that he was searching the mountain where she'd thought the shot had come from.

Another shot rang out and pinged off of the top of the Jeep with a metallic *shink*. Clancy's jaw clenched, but she saw the look of triumph enter his eyes and assumed he had a better idea where the shooter was.

"Clancy." Bolstered by getting his whole name out she rushed on, "Do you have another gun?"

He glanced at her quickly before looking back down the sight of his Glock. "What?"

"Gun. Do you have another? I'm a really good shot." She wouldn't go into how good a shot just then, knowing they didn't have the time, but she'd taken first place all four years on the high school rifle team and kept up with regular visits to the range. She wasn't going to sit by and be helpless if she could do something. Anything.

"I...uh, yeah. Hold on." Keeping his gaze trained on the location he'd spotted, he gently slid over her until they were side by side. "Ankle holster."

Without sitting up, Willa angled down and reached the gun at his ankle. It was another Glock, but subcompact to fit his ankle holster. It was light but effective. After checking the magazine, she chambered a round and flipped the safety off. Then she flipped over to her stomach. "What's the plan?"

Willa sensed Clancy's quick glance at her, but she kept her focus on the woods, eyes searching for any sign of movement.

"Not sure. I thought I saw a reflection about five yards to the left of that stump."

She saw which one he was looking at, aimed to the left of it, and zeroed in. "Are we going on the offensive or staying on defense?"

"Uh." He seemed at a loss for words at her question, or maybe he was considering all options, but when he spoke, she could tell he was hesitant. "That's up to you."

"I say—"

Another shot rang off, but this time, Willa was watching and caught sight of the movement Clancy must have seen. Or this time the guy was making his move. She wasn't sure, but either way, she had a target.

Finger moving from the outside of the trigger to curl around it, she took aim and squeezed. The gun had a slight kick and she quickly adjusted her grip to match the kickback and took another careful shot.

They both heard a yell, and Willa jumped to her feet. "Come on, I think I got him."

"Willa!" Clancy called after her, but she was tired of waiting. Tired of not knowing whether her friend was dead or alive. The shooter, whoever he was, had to be the killer. There was no other reason someone would be out here *and* taking shots at them. They were nervous because she and Clancy were too close to the truth, and he was trying to take them out. It was the only thing that made sense.

All of these thoughts filtered through her mind in a haze of rage and acted to focus her on one goal and one goal only. Find the guy and make him tell them where Anna was.

She burst through the tree line, vaguely aware of Clancy on her heels, but she didn't care. She was born for this. She'd run through these mountains since she was old enough to walk. They were like her second home, and she would use that to her advantage to find this creep.

She passed a tree with a splatter of blood and knew she'd hit her target, though she didn't know *how* wounded they would be. Up ahead, branches fell back in place and gave her the path to follow. She crashed through, gun at the ready, and searched for the next clue to the assailant's path.

The crunch of broken limbs directed her even as she heard Clancy whisper shout for her to wait. She didn't.

Racing through on a deer trail, she caught sight of movement up ahead. She was gaining on him when another shot rang out. Then two more.

Nothing was close enough to her, and she didn't slow her pace, no matter how foolish she knew it was. Whoever had shot at them, whoever *she'd* shot, was not only wounded but running for their life. They weren't going to stop and aim. The shots were merely a deflection, poorly done as they were, and she wasn't going to let that scare her.

She burst from a thicket of branches to a semi-clearing when she saw him. He looked about as tall as Clancy—maybe a few inches taller—and was wearing jeans and a dark hoodie with the hood up. He had to be dying of heat, but she assumed it was to mask his identity. She couldn't see where she'd shot him, but he was running fine. Perhaps in the arm then.

"Stop!" She paused to level the gun. "Stop, or I'll shoot!"

He hesitated. His back to her. A rifle was gripped in one hand while the other dangled loose. Was that blood just below his shoulder? She was still too far away to gain much detail into the man.

He took a step.

"I said stop, and I mean it." She was tempted to show him just how much she meant business and snipe the tree branch next to his head, but she held back. This wasn't her gun, and she didn't want to accidentally hit him where it could be fatal. Where was Clancy? She'd cover this guy, and he could go and apprehend him then—

"Willa." Clancy burst into the clearing next to her distracting her, and the man took it as his exit. He banked a hard left and disappeared around a clump of three trees that had grown closely together.

"No!" Willa rushed forward just as Clancy reached for her, but the next second, she was falling forward. Her shoe had caught on a root she'd been too preoccupied to see, and she was going down.

Bracing herself, she landed with her forearms to the ground in a hard thud, but the next second, dirt and debris gave away, and she went head-first into a black hole.

Chapter Nineteen

Clancy

ONE MINUTE WILLA WAS FALLING TO THE FOREST FLOOR, AND the next she was being eaten by the ground.

"Willa," Clancy gasped, his breaths coming in pants.

He clenched his fist but took a moment to look around the clearing. He'd twisted his ankle—like an idiot—following after her through the forest, and then by the time he'd hit the clearing, he saw the second he distracted her from her shot with the perp.

He'd played right into the guy getting away, and now, Willa had disappeared. Things were going from bad to worse.

Sure that the shooter was gone, Clancy rushed into the opening and to the edge of the gaping maw Willa had fallen into. She lay sprawled out at the bottom, and Clancy's stomach ached like he'd been gut punched.

"Willa," he cried out, his voice raspy from the dirt still in the air. "Willa, are you okay?"

He leaned further but sensed the ground slipping beneath his grasp. He skittered back on his stomach to safety. When he was far enough away, he pounded a fist into the soft dirt cursing the clumsiness that had kept him from being the one to get trapped in the hole.

He considered jumping down—he had to know if she was all right—but he knew he'd be stuck, and they'd both be worse off. Instead, he pushed up and raced to the Jeep. Grabbing one of the water bottles, he rushed back, and careful not to lean too far out, dropped a cap full of water as close to her face as he could.

Willa gasped, sat up, and burst into a fit of coughing. The sound of it was sweet relief to Clancy, but that didn't end their problems by a long shot.

"Willa, are you injured?"

She coughed a few more times then pushed to standing. That simple act alone relaxed Clancy even more, but he caught the moment she swayed, and worry gripped his throat again.

"I'm okay." More coughing. "I just got the wind knocked out of me."

He knew it was more than that. She'd been knocked unconscious, after having a previous head injury, but he was loath to bring that up now.

"Take stock. Are you hurt?"

She looked down at herself, doing a visual check along with what he guessed was a mental one, and then she looked up at him. From the light filtering into the hole, he could see streaks of dirt across her cheeks and neck, but he saw no signs of blood.

"No, really, I'm okay. I'm not bleeding. My wrist and shoulder hurt a little, but I think the soft dirt and debris down here broke my fall." She began circling the small space. He held back the urge to caution her to be careful, knowing she was just as capable as he was.

"Do you see a way out down there?" He gauged the distance to her as more than ten feet, maybe even twelve. If the edge was sturdier, he'd consider bending down to reach her, but as it was, he couldn't get close to the edge without it crumbling away. It truly was a miracle she hadn't broken anything.

"Nothing. It looks like this was a mine shaft that caved in on both sides long ago. I just happened to run across a weak spot." She pressed a hand to her head.

"Does your head hurt?"

"No. Well, yes, but not because of the fall. Or not *only* because of the fall. I'm just mad at myself. I let him get away and—wait, Clancy, is he still up there?" Concern flooded her silvery eyes.

"He's gone." He was mostly positive about that. "Nice shooting back there, by the way."

"Yeah?" She stopped directly below where he leaned over to look down at her. The pleasure that shone in her eyes made him want to compliment her again, but that would have to wait.

"Look, I can't get to you from up here, and I don't have any rope in my Jeep. I'm going to have to call 911."

"No, you can't." She shook her head, and bits of leaves and pine needles fell away. "This is so dumb. I should have been more careful." The last words were directed to herself, but he caught them anyway.

"Willa, I'm not leaving you in a hole. What are you going to do, climb out?"

She made a face. "Um, no. Okay, what about this—call Kendrick and Morrison. They're always patrolling up here on Forest Service land. They'll have something to get me out."

"I don't have their numbers."

She grimaced. "Me either. Um, call Max?"

That was the last thing Clancy wanted to do, but he knew she made a valid point. "Okay. Let me go get my phone. What do you need?"

"Water and maybe one of those granola bars I threw in my bag?"

"Got it." He stood up, careful not to put too much weight on his ankle.

"And Clancy?"

He leaned over as carefully as possible. "Think of something else?"

"My sketch book and pencils?"

He shook his head. "Really?"

"I saw him." Everything in Clancy froze. "I mean, not his face, but I saw him standing, and if we take measurements of the tree, it could get us an approximation of his height."

"Good thinking." Clancy turned to go but paused. "Willa, I think you'd make an incredible forensic artist."

She bit her lip as she craned her neck to look up at him. "Yeah?"

"Yeah. I think you should tell your dad. He'd be proud." It was hard to tell from the distance, but Clancy thought he saw her blush.

"Uh, I'll think about it." He turned to go, but she called out again. "Can I get a sweater or something, too?"

He leaned back over. "You're not in shock or something, are you?"

"No, it's just a lot cooler down here." She shrugged, and he had to laugh. Only Willa could want a sweater in the middle of a heat wave.

"Be right back."

He rushed through the woods toward his Jeep, his ankle barking at him with every step, but he pushed the pain to the back of his mind. It wasn't bad, probably hardly sprained, but it hurt enough to make him notice and want to take a pain killer.

He reached the Jeep and paused with his eyes on her bag. He could look in it for the things she'd asked for, but even he knew better than to dig through a woman's purse or bag—whatever. He shouldered the bag and rustled through the cargo area for something warm. All he found was a slightly musty smelling flannel that would have to do. Taking that, his phone, and the other water, he rushed back to the hole.

After delivering her items to her, he stepped away to call Max.

"Long."

"Hey, Max. Clancy here. Uh, do you happen to have a number for Kendrick or Morrison? The USFS guys?"

"Why?" Suspicions laced the deputy's words.

"There was a bit of a cave in, and we need some help."

"We? So help me—Clancy, are you talking about Willa?"

Clancy deserved the man's anger. He really did. It should be him in the hole. "Yes."

Max muttered something Clancy was glad he couldn't make out. "Where?"

"You know where."

Max paused. "What are you talking about?"

"I texted you about it earlier today. I told you where I was going."

"I don't know what you're talking about." Max's voice held a note of suspicion. "I have no idea where you are."

Clancy frowned and pulled the phone back from his ear. He navigated to his messaging app and searched for their latest conversation. The one where he'd told Max about his idea and where he was going with Willa.

The messages were gone.

"Clancy, where are you? What is going on?" Max's voice came back loudly to him as he held the phone up to his ear.

"I—I messaged you earlier today. Told you we were going up to Saddle Creek mine to look around. You said it was a good idea."

"I have no idea what you're talking about."

Clancy let the silence hang there for a moment. Either Max was messing with him or...or what? What was the alternative? Clancy's mind began to chew on the problem, but he willed it to the back of his thoughts. It was a puzzle he needed to piece together, but that wasn't what was most important right now.

"Look, I don't know what's going on. I had a conversation with *someone* at this number earlier today, and then Willa and I showed up to the mine and got shot at and—"

"Wait, shots were fired? Why didn't you lead with that?"

"What's most important right now," Clancy stressed, "is the fact that Willa fell in a mine shaft hole, and I can't get her out. She doesn't want me to call 911 and suggested the USFS guys could help. Either you give me their number, or I start calling around town. I'll find it one way or the other, but I need that number, Max. I need to get her out." Desperation leeched into his tone, but he didn't care. It was more important that he help Willa over appearing in control at the moment.

"Okay. Got it. I'll send it over ASAP. But when you get back, we're talking about this supposed conversation we had."

"Deal." Clancy hung up, and the next second, his phone dinged with their numbers. After a quick call, it went through to Kendrick who knew exactly where they were and promised they'd be over in twenty to thirty minutes.

"Rescue's on the way," Clancy said, coming to sit at the edge of the hole. One glance down, and he saw Willa propped up against the wall wearing his flannel and sketching like mad.

She paused to look up at him, and her face hit a shaft of light giving her blonde hair an otherworldly glow. Her smile shot flaming arrows of warmth through him. "Thanks for not calling 911. My boss would freak out."

"You do realize you're stuck in a hole after someone tried to shoot at you, right?"

She shrugged. "Yeah, but my boss is pretty scary when he's unhappy."

Clancy couldn't help it. He laughed. The feeling rumbled deep in his chest and bubbled out in a release he hadn't known he needed. Willa soon joined him, and they laughed until she wiped tears from her eyes.

"You have a good laugh, Clancy. And a nice smile."

Even from the distance, her words struck a soft place in his heart and landed with a resounding impact. "Thanks. There's not been a lot to laugh about in my line of work." *Or my life.*

"That's got to be hard." She stared up at him, and though she was over ten feet from him, he'd never felt this close to a woman before.

"It hasn't been easy."

She bit her lip. "Can I ask you something?"

"Yeah, I think you've earned a question."

She grinned and tapped her chin. "Just one? I'd better make it good then."

He didn't say it, but he was pretty sure he'd tell her anything if she asked.

"What did you mean when you said your mom was a bit crazy?"

Anything but that. He blew out a breath and rubbed a hand over his face, wiping the sweat away on his lightweight hiking pants. "You really go for the jugular, don't you?"

"I'm sorry. Too personal? You can just forget I asked." She looked back down at her drawing, but she didn't put pencil to paper.

Was he really going to do this? Open up to someone who was basically a stranger? Then again, he was starting to know Willa. She was head-strong, willing to run head-first into danger, and a great shot. But more than that, she was compassionate and brave. And...so much more.

"My mom was an alcoholic." The words themselves weren't that big of a deal, but it was the emotions behind them he didn't like. "When I was a kid, I thought I solved my first case as a detective. Jewelry and money started to go missing, and one day, I was positive I caught the housekeeper taking the items. I told my dad and got her fired—I felt so vindicated. I knew there was right and wrong, and I had helped stop a wrong." He forced himself to relive the moment that he overheard his mother yelling at his dad. "Turns out, I wasn't that great of a detective. My mom was making the housekeeper sell her items so she could buy alcohol without Dad knowing. I'd gotten the woman fired and outed my mom, but I didn't even have the whole truth."

"I'm sorry, Clancy."

He shrugged. "It was just one way my mom was dysfunctional. She let the lust for drink overrule everything. I despised her for that and what it did to our family. It put a wedge between her and my father, and I could never fully shake the feeling that I'd done that. I'd outed her, and if I hadn't, things could have gone back to normal."

He let the weight of his words settle between them. He hadn't admitted that to many, not even to his brother, though he had told Trae in a weak moment.

"What happened?" Willa's words were so soft he almost missed them.

"She eventually died of liver failure because of the one thing she loved. I tried so many times to warn her, to get her to change, but it was never enough. I don't know that I ever forgave her for picking her vice over my brother and me."

Chapter Twenty

Willa

AN ACHE FORMED IN WILLA'S STOMACH AS CLANCY SHARED the story of his mother and how her obsession had ruined their family. She wished she wasn't stuck in the musty hole and could put her arms around him. Comfort him in the midst of the memory she'd forced him to relive.

"That was more than you asked for. Sorry." He cleared his throat and looked out over the rim of the pit as if he couldn't bear to make eye contact again.

The urge to share about her aunt rose up in Willa like a growing tidal wave. The need to connect with him, even if it was only through tragedy, too strong to ignore.

"I know what it's like to feel guilty." Willa dropped her head, the tail end of her braid falling over her shoulder where she twisted it back and forth. "I feel responsible for my aunt's death."

She finally looked up and saw that his gaze was on her, the full force of his dark eyes boring into her. His silence invited her to say more, and while she would rather keep the dark thoughts to herself, she thought of his openness and forged ahead.

"I've always prided myself on my intuition. It's been like that ever since I was a kid. Knowing when someone is hurting or hiding something. I always thought it was a good thing to know someone would want something *before* they actually wanted it." She bit her lip and twisted the tail of her braid again. "But it got me into trouble, too. I did things too adult for being ten years old. When I knew my dad was too tired to cook, I'd try to and then end up burning something. Or I'd tell my aunt something about my dad only to have it blow up in my face."

"Seems like you were just a smart kid who had to grow up too soon." Clancy's words were soft, but they still reached her.

"Some of that was true, but it got to a point where I was getting in trouble more often than not and started to distrust myself." She remembered the first day she noticed that something was wrong with her Aunt Julie. "I knew that Aunt Julie was sick—or I thought I did. She wasn't her usually bubbly self, but we had a big family reunion coming up, and she pushed herself to get things done. I was so close to telling my dad about my suspicions, but what if I was wrong? I didn't want to get in trouble and not be able to go with my cousins to the movies the next weekend so I kept it to myself."

Tears came back to her even now, even eighteen years later.

"She was sick?" Clancy's question held hesitation.

"She had a brain tumor. She died six weeks later." Willa dropped her head into her hands though she didn't let the tears fall. "If I would have said something, they could have operated, and maybe, she'd still be here today."

"Willa, there's no way you could have known. Besides, you were a kid."

"I know, but it's worse than that."

Clancy shifted, sending a small avalanche of rocks tumbling into the hole. "What is it, Willa?" She sensed the shift in Clancy's tone. He saw that it was more than just a years-old pain.

"It's Anna." Willa took in a shuddering breath. "I didn't trust my intuition and look what happened." She let the tears fall freely now, streaking down her cheeks through the dirt and grime. She hoped they were hidden in the darkness—she hated crying in front of others—but it was too much. A weight she'd been carrying ever since Anna's disappearance.

"What are you talking about, Willa?"

She took in a shuddering breath. "Anna said she'd met a guy."

"What guy?" Clancy's question snapped her frayed nerves.

"I don't know. She wouldn't tell me anything about him, but the day she disappeared, she was supposed to be going on a date. I had a bad feeling about him from the start because she said he didn't want their relationship to be public yet, and that just felt off, but she was so happy."

Clancy was alert now, on his knees at the edge of the hole. "And you didn't tell anyone this?"

"No, of course I did. I told Max. I mean, I thought it was important, but they couldn't find anything in her phone—no messages with her and any mysterious guy. He told me he thought she had made it up as a way for her to leave without suspicion, but I never believed that. I really think she liked the guy, which is why I didn't say anything. I should have." Willa dropped her head into her hand. "It's my fault she's gone."

"Willa." Clancy's sharp reply was just short of a demand, and she looked up. "It's not your fault. You were trying to be a good friend, encouraging her in a new relationship she seemed happy in. You couldn't have foreseen any of this. You can't own the blame."

"It's easier said than done," she said.

He dropped his head, though his gaze still rested on her. "We can't take on the guilt of situations that ultimately had nothing to do with us. I can't blame myself for my broken family any more than you can blame yourself for Anna going missing. What matters is what we do about it now."

Willa wanted to believe him. Wanted to see her part in all of this as passive. but if she'd said something sooner, wasn't it possible her friend wouldn't be missing? That none of this would have happened?

As she looked up through the dusty haze the thin shafts of light created she saw Clancy's profile and wondered what that would mean for them. Would it have been better if they hadn't met?

The sound of voices reached her, and Clancy jumped to his feet. She saw his hand reach for the gun at the small of his back and then watched as his shoulders relaxed. It had to be Kendrick and Morrison. They were here to help.

Soon, a rope ladder dropped into the hole, and she stashed the hastily drawn sketch of the back of the shooter in her bag along with the water bottle, gun, and snack wrapper. No use leaving trash if she could carry it out.

It took a few tries to get all the way to the top and over the side, but when she was finally pulled to safety, she collapsed on the ground cushioned against the poky pine needles by Clancy's jacket. It smelled like him, even if it was a little musty. Sitting up, she pulled it off as the heat of the day hit her now that she was out of the hole.

She took in a few deep breaths only then noticing that Jase was there.

"What are you doing here?" She directed the question at the deputy and instantly knew something was wrong by the way he avoided her gaze. "Jase, what is it?"

"We found something. I—I think you should come."

Clancy turned toward him. "What is it?"

Jase merely shook his head, refusing to share more.

"I'll come, too," Clancy said. He stepped over to her and extended a hand to help her up. The look in his eyes was deeper, more intense than she'd seen it, and sudden dread coursed through her.

This couldn't be what she thought it was. But there was only one way to know.

"Let's go."

Chapter Twenty-One

Clancy

CLANCY'S VISION CLOUDED WITH THE MEMORY OF WILLA'S tears as he followed Jase's sheriff's SUV up a narrow two-lane road higher into the mountains. Willa had chosen to ride with the deputy, and Clancy tried to tell himself it was because of her familiarity with the man. Not anything more than that.

His mind replayed the last several hours. He'd gone from an impromptu breakfast with Willa, to being the object of someone's nefarious target practice, to the news that there *was* news with the case. His stomach clenched at the thought. It couldn't be good, not with the way Jase looked at Willa—every line on his already stoic face an apology.

Clancy fisted a hand and hit the steering wheel. It had to be about Anna, and that bothered him the most. With Willa's admission about a secret boyfriend in the picture, he had almost started to think it was the next lead he needed. First, the book with the locations and then this—new information! But he had the sinking sensation that it was going to be too little, too late.

The line of cars turned, and he braked as he saw Jase's brake lights up ahead. They were close now. No matter how much new information he'd been given, it wouldn't be enough to save the young woman if this was her burial site.

How had he missed the boyfriend aspect? Yeah, sure, Hillary didn't know about any men Anna's life, but not all mothers knew things like that about their children. He'd done his due diligence to ask the friends Hillary had listed, but he should have asked Willa. She hadn't been on Hillary's list, and he should have treated her like a piece of the puzzle, not a distraction.

The thing that bugged him was the fact that she *had* told Max, and Max hadn't told him. Yes, Clancy knew that there were certain things that the deputy couldn't share, even with a PI, but he'd felt like their working relationship had been good thus far. It felt like a clue Clancy would have needed to know.

And something else bothered him. The text messages that were suddenly gone—the ones that told Max exactly where he and Willa were going to be. Pieces of the earlier puzzle clicked into place, and unease settled on Clancy's shoulders.

Was he seeing something that wasn't there, or was he seeing clearly for the first time?

The line of cars slowed, and Clancy pulled over. His dark thoughts about the man he'd assumed was his friend spiraled deeper in his gut, but he'd need more evidence than what he had so far.

The heat hit him like an anvil to the gut as Clancy stepped out and slammed the Jeep door behind him. He saw the ambulance followed by the coroner's van and knew it was bad. Like dead body bad. He saw Willa climb out of Jase's vehicle and had the strange urge to go to her.

Jase turned around and motioned him forward in a heads-up gesture. He steeled himself and picked up the pace. His boots crunched on the uneven ground, and his ankle twinged with each step, but he willed himself not to limp. Or at least not too noticeably.

Clancy followed them past the line of cars and up a small deer path until he saw a circle of men ahead of them. It was another clearing, much like the one where they'd found the other young woman. If there was a hope—a prayer—that this wasn't Anna, Clancy prayed it then, but the looks on the faces of the men that turned toward them told him differently.

Sheriff Harding broke away from the group and approached Willa. She stopped in front of him, and Clancy took the last few steps to come even with her and Jase.

"Wills, I'm sorry to have to tell you this, but we've found Anna." The sheriff's mouth turned into a thin line of regret. "She's gone, Willa."

"No!" Willa's strangled cry shattered something inside of Clancy, and he took a step forward, but the sheriff continued.

"I know this is hard, but I also know you were close with her. Her mother has been called, but she's in Seattle and can't get here in time. Will you...could you identify her?"

"Are you kidding?" Clancy took another step. "Surely, there's someone else who could identify her."

Sheriff Harding sent a sharp look at Clancy. "I wouldn't have asked if there was anyone else."

"We've all seen her photos. Any number of your men must have known her as well. Why couldn't—"

"I'll do it." Willa's voice was a whisper, but it broke through Clancy's tirade all the same.

"Willa, you don't have to—"

"I do. She was my friend, and I knew her really well. I—I can do this."

Clancy wanted to protest. He knew what it was like when a body was left out in nature for days on end. Clearly, she hadn't been there that long, or they wouldn't have asked Willa for an ident, but that didn't mean Anna would be pleasant to look at. It wasn't the type of image you wanted as your last memory of a friend. He saw no way of changing Willa's mind though.

"Are you sure?" Jase seemed to share Clancy's concern. "It's not easy to see."

"I can do it." Her words were steel tipped.

"Do you want me to go with you?" Clancy rested a hand on her elbow. She paused, and the sheriff and Jase moved toward the body, giving them privacy. "It won't be easy."

She shook off his touch, the motion surprising him. "I thought you could find her."

Her words shocked him as did the fact she couldn't look him in the eye. Defeat rested on every line of her slumped posture and was at odds with the woman he'd gotten to know so far. He wanted to take the pain from her, but he didn't know how.

"I thought..." She swallowed and shook her head before finally looking up at him. "I really thought she was alive."

"I'd hoped she was, too," he admitted, though he also knew enough to have prepared himself for the inevitability of her death. It didn't help the blow hit any less hard, but it landed on calloused hopes rather than fragile ones.

"But she's gone. I—I didn't think..." Tears trailed down her eyes.

Clancy fought the urge to reach for her. He couldn't read her emotions, what she was thinking. "I'm sorry, Willa."

"This is my fault." She pressed a hand over her eyes, drawing in deep breaths.

"Don't do that to yourself." Clancy fought the urge to grip her shoulders and shake sense into her. "You had absolutely nothing to do with this. Some sick monster is out to get women, and he happened across your friend. You couldn't have known."

"But I did." She dropped her hand and looked up at him. "I *knew* something was wrong, and I kept it to myself."

Clancy fought for the right words, the ones that would reach through to her. "I've been looking for lost people for a year now. You know how many I've found alive?" His voice cracked, unwelcome emotions clogging the truth that he wrestled to free. "None. I haven't had a successful case since I started."

Her eyes blurred with more tears. "Why do you do it?"

"Because it's better to know the truth—even if it hurts you." It had slowly become his life's motto. "It's better to know that she's gone than to always wonder. I know it doesn't feel that way, but you can heal now. I think it's my mission to bring that healing, even if it makes me the bad guy."

She shook her head, wiping under her eyes. "You have a sad way of looking at things, Clancy. It's like you expect the worst and then aren't surprised when you get it. But what about hope? Just because you learned to let your mom disappoint you doesn't mean that everything in life always will."

Her words were like an icepick to his conscience. Had he let his jaded

view of the world seep into his PI work? Had it made him work less dili-
gently? He didn't think so, but he knew that the news of Anna's death,
while tragic, didn't surprise him. And maybe that bothered him more
than he wanted to realize.

"I don't know what to tell you."

"You don't have to tell me anything, Clancy." And with that, Willa
turned and walked woodenly toward the middle of the clearing and the
body covered by a sheet.

Chapter Twenty-Two

Willa

THERE WAS A HOLLOWNESS IN WILLA. THE DEPTH AND vastness of her emotions frightened her, as did the fact that she couldn't push them aside. Usually, especially working her job, she was able to shelve traumatic things until she had solitude to process them, but she couldn't stop the rising tide. Maybe it was talking with Clancy while in the pit, or perhaps it was just how tired she was, but Willa couldn't seem to handle the fact that they'd found Anna and that she was dead.

She knew better than to blame Clancy for the fact her friend hadn't been found alive, but there was such a deadness in the way he approached his job it had rubbed her the wrong way. She was usually an optimist, and for some reason, she'd expected Clancy to have more of a reaction to everything.

It was stupid to be mad at him for not breaking down. He hadn't known Anna, and most guys she knew wouldn't show much emotion anyway. But it still stung.

"Wills, you really don't have to do this." Jase walked up to the body with her, his solid presence a familiar comfort next to her.

"I do." She started to take a deep breath, but the potent sent of decay came at her in full force, and she gagged. "Just pull back the sheet."

He did, and she took a moment to let her eyes trail over her friend's face for the last time. There were things she'd never unsee, but the dainty, dangling earrings and the cross necklace Anna always wore, as well as the blue shirt she'd left the house in, were untouched by death.

"It's her."

Willa turned away, holding in the desire to run away and throw up. Anna deserved her respect, and she'd keep calm to honor her in the only way she could now.

"Can you confirm her identity?" Sheriff Harding asked, the compassion in his fatherly expression making her want a hug from her dad.

"Yes. It's her. I—that's the shirt she left the house in."

He nodded once. "We figured it was her, but this helps the process go faster. Thank you for being willing to do it, Wills. I know it wasn't easy."

"What happens now?"

The sheriff looked behind her for a moment before his gaze came to rest on her again. She glanced back the way he'd looked and saw Clancy there, hands in his pockets, wearing a concentrated expression.

"I can't share much, but you're like part of the family, Wills, so I'll tell you this. That PI wasn't wrong in his assessment. This is the third body, and that means we're dealing with a serial killer."

Willa pressed a hand to her roiling stomach. "How do you know?"

"Most things I can't share, but seeing as you've been to the last two crime scenes, that there is something familiar about the placement of each young woman. It's what we call a signature. He likes to display the women in the same way each time."

She took in the clearing and saw what he meant. The trees created a natural near-perfect circle, and Anna was at the center of it all. It spoke of a sick type of reverence.

"We also think that based on what you and that PI found at the sawmill, he likes to keep them for a while. We don't know what goes on during that time—perhaps a grooming of sorts. But then something triggers the, uh, death." The sheriff swallowed as if only now realizing all of what he'd told her.

"I see." Willa heard the frailty in her voice, but she resisted the urge to break down into more tears. "Has there been any information on the things we brought in from the sawmill?"

"Not yet. I've got a friend at the lab in Seattle who is rushing the processing, but that still means about a week or so."

Willa nodded, looking back at Clancy now. He was deep in conversation with Jase, and she realized she didn't want to talk about all of this with him. She didn't want to face her own failure in helping Anna, nor did she think she could mask her sadness much longer. As comfortable as she'd grown with Clancy in the last few days, she also realized that he was still a stranger. He was likely going to move on to the next case just like the previous one he'd left to come here. It was how he worked, and as much as she'd started to see him as something more than just a PI looking for her best friend, she couldn't see him as anything else now.

Her heart couldn't take any more disappointment.

"I—I need a ride home."

Sheriff Harding looked down at her with compassion. "I really am sorry about all of this, Willa. Why don't you ask Q for a ride? I'm sending him back with the evidence we've collected so far. I need Jase to stick around to continue to process, and Max should be here by now, but he hasn't answered his phone." The sheriff made a show of looking around, but the deputy wasn't in the clearing.

"I'll see if Q will take me. Thanks, Glenn." She turned and looked for the newest hire to the sheriff's department.

Quentin wasn't her first choice to ride with due to the spark of interest she'd caught in his glances when he thought she wasn't looking, but he was better than riding with Clancy. She didn't want to face the ugly fact that they had failed, and at the end of it all, she was nothing more to him than a guide through the mountains. Just another person to help him on his quest to bring closure to hurting families, nothing more.

She spotted Q at the other side of the crime scene and broke off toward him. He wore gloves and baseball cap that wasn't part of his uniform. She guessed that for work like this, the sheriff didn't mind the lapse in uniform.

"Uh, Q?" She walked toward him and noticed his red face, sweat beading down his neck and changing his uniform from olive to forest green. He had to be hot in it since his uniform top had long sleeves.

"Could I catch a ride back to town? Glenn said you were headed back that way."

He looked up, blue eyes wide in surprise. "Uh. Yeah, sure."

She tried to ignore the hopeful look on his face. She'd seen it before when boys had a crush on her, but he was the last man she'd be interested in. Her gaze shifted back to Clancy where he still stood talking with Jase. As if he sensed her attention, Clancy looked up and met her gaze. There was something sad that rested behind his eyes, but she didn't have the emotional energy to uncover what that was.

She turned away and found Q beside her. "Let's go."

"Yeah." Willa forced a half-hearted smile and followed the deputy to his SUV.

"Mind sitting in the back?" He flashed an apologetic grimace her way. "I've got a bunch of gear up front."

"Uh, sure. As long as the AC works back there."

"Definitely." He grinned, and it helped to transform his usually blocky features a little, but she still wouldn't classify the man as handsome. He had a boyish look with pock marks on his cheeks she guessed were from acne. He was well built though, but not like Jase. Then again, no one she knew was built like Jase.

The interior of the car was stuffy and hot, but Q slid in and revved the engine to life, immediately turning the AC on. "Better?"

"Yes. Thanks." The cool air blew in from vents in the front as well as two in the center console, and Willa leaned back, clipping her seatbelt in place.

Anna was dead.

Willa pressed her forehead to the window, eyes closed, as she tried to hold her grief in. She'd go home, take a cold shower, and cry herself into a well-deserved nap. Her wrist and shoulder still hurt from how she'd fallen, and her head pounded, either from the tumble or the earlier concussion, but more than anything, her heart hurt.

"You doing okay?" Q asked as he slowly maneuvered his SUV into a three-point turn to head back down the dirt road.

How was she supposed to answer that? "I don't know."

Q maneuvered out of the turn and picked up speed, though as they passed where Clancy and Jase still stood talking, Clancy followed the car with narrowed eyes. His gaze connected with her, and she tried not to see his look of abandonment.

Rather than face him or anything else, Willa pulled out her sketch book. She didn't want to draw Anna, not as she'd seen her, but maybe she could create her friend's happy, life-filled expression from memory.

She flipped past the other crime scene drawings, the skull recreation she was half-finished with for class, and then to the quick sketch she'd made of the shooter back at the Gibbons mine. The drawing made her pause. There was something...familiar in the set of shoulders. What was it?

Willa closed her eyes, remembering the image of the man. He was comparable in height to most of the men she knew from the sheriff's department. He seemed well-built, but not to Jase's standard. But it was something else—perhaps the proportions between legs and torso?

She flipped past the image and focused on the blank page. It called to her to make something beautiful now, something to redeem the image burned into her mind of her dead friend.

Willa started to draw Anna, as full of life as she could remember.

Chapter Twenty-Three

Clancy

CLANCY WATCHED JASE WALK BACK TOWARD THE SPACE where Anna lay covered by a sheet. The coroner would remove her from the scene soon now that she'd been identified, and the deputies were finishing up their work. He briefly wondered where Max was, but then he'd watched Q drive off with Willa, and his thoughts scattered like birds from a thicket.

Was she so mad at him she couldn't stand to have him drive her home?

The thought ate away at him, and he fought the urge to ask Jase what to do. He hardly knew the man though. They'd talked work-related things regarding other serial killer cases he'd dealt with, and he'd offered tips where he could, but nothing more than that.

"You doing okay, mate?" Kendrick walked over, his expression grim.

"I...yeah." There weren't enough words to describe all the things Clancy felt in that moment.

"Poor choice of words on my part. Anything I can do for you?"

This caused Clancy to turn toward the man, pulling his gaze away from the grim scene before them. "Thanks, but I don't think so. I just hate to see another case go this way." He clenched his jaw.

"You see a lot like this?" Kendrick folded his arms over his chest. He looked like he spent a considerable amount of time in the gym, which was something Clancy respected.

"Unfortunately, yes." He thought of how he'd thrown statistics at Willa. As if telling her the number of his cases that had ended badly could make her—or him, for that matter—feel better.

"Look, I do a very different kind of law keeping here, so I'm not saying I get it, but don't be too hard on yourself. I heard the coroner estimate five to seven days, and if the signs of binding were any indication, he'd held her for a good two weeks before he killed her. Ever since she went missing."

"And the sheriff's office wasted that time by convincing themselves she was a runaway." Clancy ran a hand through his hair. "Sorry. That was out of line, but that's why I came. Hillary Stevens didn't think her daughter had run away, but no one would listen. They were out of leads after the first forty-eight hours, and I stepped in, but I'm getting sick and tired of being a last resort." The words flowed out of him, and Clancy couldn't seem to stop them. "For once, I'd like to step into something I had a hope of solving."

"I hear you, mate," Kendrick said, after a moment. "But I wonder how much of that is on the case, and how much of that is on you."

"What's that supposed to mean?" Clancy sent a sharp glance at the LEO.

"What cases do you take on?" Kendrick leveled his gaze at him, but Clancy saw his point. "You expect to fail. In fact, I'd say you set yourself up for it, and that's what I can't get. I looked you up after we met at the other crime scene. You're the patron saint of lost causes, and I would have guessed you like it that way."

"I pursue every case as if I could find them alive."

"I don't doubt that. Really, I don't, but maybe deep down, you don't put too much hope in—just in case." Kendrick tilted his head to the side. "Except for this one. Our Willa made you care, didn't she?"

Clancy looked away, rubbing his chin with his hand.

"She's convincing, that one. All I'm saying is it's not bad to get invested. Sure, it'll open you up to more hurt, but maybe you're here for a different reason."

"Like what?" Clancy finally found his voice.

"There's a serial killer on the loose, isn't there?" He nodded toward Jase. "I heard you giving away all that information. Sounds like you know what you're talking about, so why don't you put that knowledge to use rather than skip town to the next lost cause?"

Clancy wanted to punch the kid almost as much as he wanted to shake his hand. He settled for a silent nod.

"You're welcome, mate," Kendrick said, walking past him to meet up with Morrison.

The kid was right. If he was going to care, he shouldn't stop now.

He thought of Willa. She was the reason this was different. He hadn't lied to the LEO, he mourned every death, but he had started to expect it. The hope he'd started his PI firm with had faded quickly in the light of devastating circumstances, and he'd found it was easier to stop caring than it was to invest his emotions in each case.

He thought of Laura, the last young woman he'd found dead in the Montana mountains, and how he'd felt empty after it all. The locket she'd held clutched in her fingers that held a photo of her and her family. Her mother's cries. The sullen, blank look her father wore once they'd received the news.

It was, at once, all too much and not enough.

Clancy broke out of his staring contest with the trees and strode toward his Jeep. He didn't know where he was going, but he needed to run through the clues again. There were now three bodies, all connected by location similarities and the signature of how they were posed as well as the fact that they each had been held captive. It spoke to a killer who liked to take his time. Possibly of someone who needed to spend time with them before he killed them.

The thought cast a shiver up Clancy's spine despite the pounding heat. This man was sick and, regardless of the fact that his job was technically done, Kendrick was right. He couldn't stop there. There was a killer on the loose, and he had to stop them.

He entered the outskirts of town going too fast and had to brake fast to stop at the first light leading into town. He didn't know where to start. The first victim had been found south of Chamberlin and was likely to be a missing student from the community college. His gut clenched at the thought knowing that Willa went to classes there. Was it another student? A teacher preying on his students?

But then the other two women had been found north of Chamberlin. First, the young woman who was still unidentified, and now, Anna. They were in similar areas but on different mountains accessed by different roads.

Without knowing much about the backgrounds of the other young women yet, Clancy wasn't sure he could do much. All he had was information about Anna. Though he had a new clue thanks to Willa—Anna had been seeing a guy.

Was it possible the other young women had been as well?

Clancy slowed even more as he came into the main part of town. He passed the Post Office, a local credit union, and the diner—

He pulled into the diner so fast his tires squealed in protest. He'd questioned the owner and the staff who had worked with Anna, but he'd never asked about a boyfriend. As far as he knew—as far as anyone knew, except for Willa—she'd been single. He'd asked a few friends, but their answers had all been no.

But the diner was one place they might have risked being together. Couples shared meals, and in a town as small as Chamberlin, perhaps they'd felt comfortable enough to eat together without it looking like a date.

It was a weak hope, but it was all he had.

Clancy climbed out of the Jeep and rushed toward the side door. The bell chimed above him as he walked into the cool restaurant that smelled like greasy French fries and hamburgers. His stomach growled, and he realized he hadn't had anything since the piece of coffee cake Willa had made.

The thought made him ache. Would he be able to clear the air with her? Then again, should he? If he was just going to leave, what would be the point?

"Howdy, stranger," and older woman said, coming from the kitchen through two bright red swinging doors. "Looking for some lunch?"

He sought his memory for her name. Geraldine Fisher, he was pretty certain. "Geraldine?"

SERIAL HEAT

"That's me." She grinned wider, showing off a gold capped tooth on her right side. "What can I do for you?"

"I may want something to go, but I've got a few questions first."

"That's right. You're that PI. Shoot, Gumbo."

He offered a half smile before slipping onto a round barstool and propping his elbows on the speckled Formica counter. "I know we talked about Anna Stevens before, but I have a few more questions. That okay?"

"'Course, hun. She's a sweet girl. I hope they find her soon."

He fought a reaction and instead rushed to his first question. "Do you know if she was dating anyone?"

"Not that I knew of." The older woman seemed to be searching her memory. "I got the impression she'd had a hard life but then found Jesus. Isn't that what they say?"

Clancy nodded. While her mother hadn't known much of this, Willa had filled him in on Anna's life-altering choice. "Yes, ma'am. I've heard it said that way."

"Either way, it seemed to stick. She's a sweet thing and worked real hard. I never had a worry about her stealing or anything like that. Never saw her come in with a guy though."

Clancy fought back the disappointment. "No one comes to mind at all? Even a customer who flirted with her, and she seemed not to mind?"

Geraldine pursed her lips for a moment. "Nope. No one I can think of...wait a second."

"What?" Clancy dared to hope.

"I do remember something about one afternoon not too long before she went missing."

"What was it?"

"She was getting off work a little early and seemed real happy about it. I asked her what she was up to, but she was vague about it. Usually, she'd tell me her weekend plans or things like that. Anyway, I saw her dash outside and get into a car with some guy in the driver's seat."

Clancy's heart hammered in his chest. This was it. The missing link. It might have very well been the man Anna was seeing. "Did you see him?"

"Not well, I'm afraid. He was out there," she pointed to the front row of windows. "Pulled up to the curb, and she jumped in. I did see the back of his head though."

"What did you see?" Clancy held his breath.

"Strawberry blonde hair. A good head of it."

Clancy's stomach dropped. "Did you see what kind of car it was?"

"Not really. Like I said, I just got a glimpse. Looked like a black SUV."

Clancy gauged the distance from the back of the diner to the front, his worry settling in the pit of his stomach. He pushed off the bar stool and thanked her. He was halfway toward the door when she asked if he wanted any food.

As hungry as he was, his worry superseded his hunger. If he was right in putting the pieces together, there was only one person who could have been dating Anna with a reason to keep it secret.

Max Long.

Chapter Twenty-Four

Willa

THE SKETCH OF ANNA WAS TAKING SHAPE. IT WAS A MEMORY Willa had from a few days before Anna disappeared. She'd been sitting at the small kitchen nook where Willa had just been this morning. Willa had made another one of her family's recipes—an egg quiche dish she'd always loved—and she'd invited Anna over for breakfast and coffee.

Willa could see her friend so clearly, sitting at the nook, looking out the back window at their nonexistent yard. She'd been dressed up, more so than Willa usually saw her, and Willa had teased about her going on a date. That's when Anna had told her about the mysterious man she'd been seeing.

Willa shadowed the lines of her friend's long fingers as they curved around the mug, one of Willa's favorites from a long-ago trip to Disneyland her father had taken her on. Even as Willa drew her now, she remembered the taut lines of Anna's posture as Willa tried to coax more information out of her. But Anna resisted. Said that she'd been praying about it, and she'd agreed to keep the man's identity secret for the time being so as not to get him in trouble.

That had sounded ridiculous to Willa, but she'd chalked it up to the fact she'd never really dated anyone. She'd have liked to think she'd be proud to talk about a man in her life, but Anna seemed hesitant. Was it that she was afraid Willa wouldn't approve? She'd hoped to be a better friend than that, but perhaps she'd made Anna think she would be judgmental.

Willa yanked her gaze up from the drawing. The ache in her chest had grown so large she thought it might separate itself from her, taking a chunk of her with it. Drawing in air quietly, she refocused on her surroundings to pull herself from the memories—and the self-loathing—she was falling into.

They were nearing the base of the mountain, and she saw that Q had taken a moment to roll up his sleeves.

Good for him. He must be hot.

Her gaze stilled on the tattoo on the back of his forearm. It was a curving snake that started up his arm and wove its way down to his wrist—

A preternatural calm settled over Willa. Her body stilled while her heart continued to race. There, just above Q's smart watch, sat a thin leather cord bracelet.

How had she forgotten?

Slowly, so as not to draw attention to herself, Willa slipped her hand into the outer pocket of her messenger bag. Her fingers closed around the tissue, and she edged it out just far enough that she could pull the end of it back. There, nestled in the pocket of her bag, forgotten from that first fateful day with Clancy on the mountain, sat a leather thong bracelet exactly like the one Q wore.

Her body went numb. She shoved the tissue back in her bag and grabbed the image she'd drawn from memory of her friend. Latched to her left wrist right above where her fingers encircled the mug sat the same leather bracelet. Willa had drawn it because Anna had been wearing it in her memory. She hadn't given it a second thought. Anna had always worn bracelets, but that was a new addition to the silver charm one she'd gotten from her mother as a birthday gift at sixteen.

But what did it mean?

Her gaze unconsciously traced the line of Q's bracelet before she forced herself to stop. She couldn't draw attention to the fact she'd noticed it. She looked up as they turned, but this time, Willa knew something was wrong. Instead of taking the road back to town, he'd turned onto a lane that bisected the mountain they had been on and would take them to the next range over.

"Wh—where are we going?" She licked her cracked lips and tried to swallow past the dryness in her throat. Was it getting warmer? "I mean, do you have to run an errand?"

She didn't want him to know what she did, but what was that? That Q was Anna's killer? Or was he just her secret boyfriend? But no, that made no sense. The place she and Clancy had found hadn't been the right time for Anna to be held there due to the food wrappers she'd seen. But that's where she'd found—and forgotten— the bracelet she kept in her bag.

Willa thought she might be sick. There were bottles of water in the cup holders for anyone the deputies arrested. She grabbed one and took a sip. It was cold and went down smoothly.

"Little detour. Nothing to worry about." Willa caught sight of the hard lines on Q's face from the rearview mirror. Gone were the timid glances as if he were considering flirting with her. In their place sat determination and something darker.

"I—I really need to get home. My dad, he's coming back." She didn't regret the lie if it made him reconsider taking her home. Her throat felt drier. She took another sip.

"I didn't think he got back for a few more weeks." Q flicked his gaze to meet hers, and his eyes had shifted to mirror the depths of a dark sea. His look sent slivers of ice to her heart, and she began to panic.

"I really need to get back. Can I get out here and call Clancy? He'll come get me so you can do your errand."

"That doesn't sound safe. Haven't you heard? There's a serial killer loose." Q's voice had changed. He no longer sounded timid or at all like the deputy she'd gotten to know over the last few months. No, he sounded cold. His words measured. Calculating.

Willa reached for the door handle. She didn't care if she had to break a bone or two by jumping out, anything would be better than being in this car with a killer.

The doors were locked. Of course, they were. She turned back to him, but her vision swam. What was going on?

"It's all right, Willa. Calm down."

"Calm—calm down?" She blinked fast, her head swimming. "What—"

"Take another sip of water."

Her stomach plummeted. The water. He'd spiked the water. "Who... are you...?"

"I think that's the wrong question, don't you?"

"What...?"

"The better question is what kind of death is most befitting you?" Q's ice-cold gaze landed on her, and she looked away, the motion sending her slumping against the car door.

She was going to be sick. No, she didn't even have the energy for that. "Why—"

"Why?" Q laughed, the sound grating like nails on a chalk board. "Because nice, sweet girls like Anna deserve to be loved by men like me. Anna was perfect—so good and kind." Something like a sick agony took over his features. "But it never lasts. She wanted to go—wanted to leave—and I couldn't let that happen."

Tears streamed down Willa's cheeks at the thought of her friend captured by this man. She opened her mouth to yell at him, but no words emerged.

"You don't deserve my kindness, Willa. You're too bold—too straight forward. You'll have a fitting pyre, and you should be thankful for that. Then it's on to the next stop. I think I've outgrown Chamberlin." He laughed again, and this time, the sound echoed in her head like a death knell.

Her eyes closed of their own accord, but all she could think of was the fact that she was trapped in the car with the man who had killed her friend.

And he was going to kill her next.

Chapter Twenty-Five

Clancy

CLANCY BURST THROUGH THE DOOR TO THE SHERIFF'S department like a man possessed. He'd flashed his creds to get past the lazy guy at the window, but now that he was in, he wasn't stopping until he had his man.

"Max!" Clancy's voice thundered through the empty space. He guessed that the other deputies were still up on the mountain, but of course, Max wasn't. Was he planning his getaway? Was he planning on taking another woman before he went?

"Whoa, Clancy, what's wrong?" Max's eyes flew wide, and his cheeks flushed, bringing out the smattering of freckles that dotted his nose and cheeks.

"What's wrong?" Clancy barreled into the man as he stepped forward. Gripped his uniform with one hand and hauled him against a wall while he pulled his gun out in the same motion.

Max's eyes blazed, and he clung to Clancy's wrists, though he shied away from the gun. "You'd better have a good reason for pulling gun on me."

Clancy leaned in. "I know your deadly little secret."

Max's eyes went wide and then narrowed in confusion. "What in the world are you talking about?"

Clancy had expected the man to respond differently, but faking innocence wasn't how this was going to play out. Fine. He'd get the truth one way or another.

"Give it up, Long. You were dating Anna. You knew exactly where Willa and I were when we were *conveniently* shot at. You've been messing up this investigation from the start, and it ends here. Turn yourself in, and maybe I won't shoot you."

Max dropped his hands. "I have absolutely no clue what you're talking about. Look at me, Clancy. Am I lying?"

Clancy had known liars. It started with his mother and had followed him into his former job as a cop. He'd learned how to spot the tells. Either Max was the best actor in the world, or he was telling the truth.

"Say it again," Clancy growled. "Say you it wasn't you."

"It. Wasn't. Me." Max held Clancy's gaze and didn't resist.

Clancy let him go and stepped back. If there had been other officers in the station at that moment, he knew he would have had every gun pulled on him, but as it was, Max was the only one at the office.

"I'm going to put my gun in my holster."

"I'd rather take it from you," Max said. The hard lines of his jaw betrayed the anger he was keeping in check.

Clancy held Max's gaze.

"But as a sign of good faith, I'll let you keep it." Max didn't blink. Didn't waver.

Clancy returned the gun to his holster. "Something's wrong."

"You think?" Max visibly relaxed though not in total relief. He looked just as amped as Clancy. "Where is everyone anyway?"

"Up the mountain. The sheriff said he contacted you."

"I've gotten no messages all day."

Clancy huffed out a breath. Someone was messing with their communication. Deleting messages and now blocking calls. If it wasn't Max, then who?

"What made you think it was me?" Max cut into his thoughts. "You said something about dating Anna? What are you talking about?"

Clancy filled him in on what Willa had said and how she'd told him about Anna's boyfriend. He looked bewildered.

"First, you tell me we were texting earlier today, and now you say that she told me about a boyfriend, but I have zero clue what you're talking about. Willa never told me that."

"She told someone. She would have no reason to lie to me about that."

"I agree, but who?"

"And how..." Clancy spoke more to himself than the deputy and began pacing back and forth.

His texts with Max had been erased. Had they also been intercepted? Was it possible Willa had texted with someone she thought was Max but really wasn't?

"Do you text with Willa ever?"

"Yeah. I mean, she's like my little sister."

"Check your messages."

Max pulled out his phone and navigated to his messages. His brow furrowed. "That's weird. They're all gone."

"Like the whole thread?"

"Yeah."

Clancy ran a hand over this face. "We've been played by someone who knows how to cover their tracks." He whirled to face Max. "Wait a second. Red hair."

Max's brow furrowed. "What—"

"Q—Quentin. He's got red hair too."

"Yeah, so—"

Clancy told Max about what the diner owner had said about Anna, but the next revelation lodged in his throat.

"Oh, no."

"Clancy, what is it? What's wrong?"

"She's with him. Right now. He was supposed to take her home."

"Let's go." Max rushed to his desk and strapped on his side arm before following Clancy back outside.

The heat still struck him like a superheated pillow to the face, but he pushed past the discomfort. Nothing but finding Willa mattered.

"Call her," Clancy said as he went around to the driver's side door of his Jeep. "And call the sheriff. Can you track his car?"

"I—I'll call the sheriff and see what he says. What are you going to do?"

"I'll go by her house and see if, by some miracle, he dropped her there."

"If not?"

"I don't know."

"I'll go to his apartment. I've got the address on file. I think I have probable cause to break in—if not, oh well. If he's got Willa, it doesn't matter."

Clancy nodded. "Call me when you get there."

Max nodded, and Clancy floored it out of the sheriff's department parking lot toward Willa's house. Fifteen minutes later, he'd assured himself she wasn't there and was racing to meet Max at Q's apartment.

He parked at an awkward angle and jogged up to the door where Max had kicked it in.

"Find anything?" Clancy asked, gasping for breath.

"Not specifically about Willa but look." He beckoned Clancy in and opened the door to the pantry. Inside was a wall of photos. It started at the top with a beautiful woman with brown hair and black-rimmed glasses. There were candid shots and ones Clancy guessed Q had pulled from social media sites. Then the next line of photos was a young woman with black hair and a big smile. She looked carefree and happy, but Clancy also noticed one of the photos that showed her in a shirt he recognized.

"The second body."

"Yes. And there's Anna." Max pointed to the third line which was filled with a face that would haunt Clancy's nightmares, reminding him of his failure.

He forced himself to look lower, and his blood chilled. "Willa." Her name sounded like a plea on his lips even as everything inside of him turned to burning fury. It was just one picture, her and Clancy standing in the clearing of the building that had collapsed on her. Q had been there. Had he caused the collapse?

It was too much information to process. He stepped back.

"Okay, so it's definitely him. How do we find her?" Clancy ran a hand through his hair.

"So far, this is the only other thing I found." Max pointed to the small round table in the kitchen that was filled with maps. So many—too many —locations were marked. It would take them months to check them all, but they didn't have months. They barely had hours.

Clancy stepped up to the table and began shuffling through the maps, using a pen to move them. He recognized some of them. He shifted one of the large maps over, and his eyes landed on the book.

"I know this book." He turned to look at Max. "Willa and I were checking off places where there might have been buildings standing that the killer—that Q—would use to hide the women so he could take his time with them." The words were bitter in his mouth, and Clancy wanted to spit.

"What's left of the ones you'd checked?"

"You got gloves?"

The deputy nodded and fished out a pair of black disposable gloves. Clancy slipped them on and turned to the now familiar page of locations. As he did, he checked them off verbally for the deputy.

"Blanken sawmill was where we found the first items. Gibbons mine is where the cave in happened. I texted you about going to Horse Creek mine, but it's clear that Q intercepted those messages. He shot at us, like I told you on the phone, so we can rule that out. It doesn't make sense he'd go back there, maybe thinking that it's tainted."

"That place is near where the girl was found today." He pointed to one of the three locations left.

"That leaves JT mine and Charles Gorge mill." Clancy met Max's gaze. "We've got to split up."

Max grimaced. "I called Glenn on the way here, and he says he'll provide backup, but he needs to know where."

Clancy looked at the overall area map. "The body—and the rest of the sheriff's department—is here." He pointed to one ridge. "The other two places are pretty far from that. One is here," he pointed to one closest to where the body had been located, "and one here." The last location was farther away and would take almost forty-five minutes to drive to.

"You take JT mine—it's the one closest to backup. I'll go to Charles Gorge. We'll keep in contact."

Clancy hesitated. He wanted to be the one to find Willa, and he sensed that Q would go as far from the mass of sheriff's deputies at the crime scene as possible, but Max had a good point. He was outfitted for more than what Clancy could handle.

"Deal."

Max held his gaze. "You see anything, you radio it in. Don't go being a hero, Sullivan."

Clancy smirked. "I've never been accused of that before."

On silent mutual agreement, they both turned and sprinted from the apartment to their vehicles.

Clancy prayed he was going to be the one to find Willa. Not because he wanted to be a hero, but because for the first time in a long time, he wanted to have hope. Hope that she was still alive, and that he would be able to stop the evil that was trying to take over.

As he pressed the gas pedal down, he held tightly to that hope because without it, he had nothing.

Chapter Twenty-Six

Willa

WILLA'S HEAD POUNDED IN RHYTHM TO HER HEART.

Boom. Boom. Boom.

Thud. Thud. Thud.

The throbbing hurt. Maybe she could take some pills and go back to sleep. She forced her eyes open, but her vision didn't want to cooperate. It was fuzzy and a little distorted. She blinked more, and rather than seeing the dark green of the accent wall in her bedroom, she saw darkened gray boards.

She blinked again, and the space around her came into sickening clarity, as did the fact that her hands and feet were tied.

Panic seized her chest, and she tried to sit up, but the room swam, and she fell back against the dirt. Gasping for breath, she realized her mouth was cottony and dry.

That's when it came back to her. The spiked water that had knocked her out. The dread that had overtaken her with the realization Q had killed Anna and the other women. The certainty that he was going to kill her.

She forced her breathing to calm and took stock of where she was. She was tied up, but she didn't see Q. He wasn't there holding a knife to her or some other kind of nightmare-inducing thing he could be doing. She was alone in....

She looked around. Another old sawmill? Seeing as it was Washington, the state of trees, she wasn't surprised. Was this one of the locations on Clancy's list?

Her chest tightened at the thought of Clancy. She was an idiot. She wouldn't be in this position if she'd gone with him. If she hadn't pushed him away in her anger and sorrow at finding out her friend was dead. She'd all but accused him of not caring, which was the last thing he did.

If anything, she could see now that he cared too much and was trying to protect himself.

Willa let tears fall, feeling the heat of them crawl down her already hot skin. The sawmill, or whatever this place was, had no air flow, and she was melting into a puddle on the floor.

She shook her head. She still wasn't thinking clearly. What was the plan?

Taking her time, Willa slowly sat up and allowed the spinning to settle. She stilled and waited, expecting to hear Q any moment, but it was silent. No movement in the big empty space and nothing outside.

She tried pulling her hands out of the ropes, but they only cut more deeply into her hands. She could reach her feet, but the ropes had been tied from behind, and the knots were equally tight. If only there was something to cut them with.

Willa let her gaze wander over the old building. It was clear of most things, the floor covered in a layer of dirt. An old table stood to one side, opposite which was what would have passed for a window back in the 1800s, the glass broken and long gone years ago.

Maybe she could climb out that way? It would require the use of her hands and feet, or at least her feet.

Moving onto her knees, Willa pushed to standing and took a look around from the new vantage point. A door met her gaze. She hop-shuffled to it and tried the round handle. It was surprisingly solid, and it didn't budge. She tried pulling, pushing, and even throwing herself into it, but all she got was a dull ache in her shoulder added to her existing injuries.

Turning her back to the door, she looked around the rest of the space.

Nothing new stood out to her except...she could see that what she'd thought of as a table wasn't. It was a table saw—or circular saw.

There had been a brief period of time where she had thought she might go into woodworking, and she'd studied under a man in town who had pushed the importance of knowledge, too much for Willa's liking, but she praised his over-enthusiasm about all things wood working in that moment.

The table would have looked normal to most, especially if someone mistook this for a miner's cabin, but it was actually a woodworking shop of some sort. She hopped over toward the table and could see that the blade had been broken long ago.

Her hopes plummeted. Of course, Q wouldn't leave her in a room with a saw.

She sank to her knees. The edges of the table were too soft to use against the ropes. There was no glass in the window. There was nothing.

God, help me.

The prayer felt like a last resort, but that's not how she wanted to treat her faith. She knew God cared about her, and she knew He heard her prayers. It had just gotten harder to believe.

Anna hadn't lived. Willa had begged and pleaded, but it had done no good.

And yet, Anna's own words came back to her in that moment. *Wills, if God is who He says He is, shouldn't we live every moment with confidence knowing that what's happening is supposed to happen?*

They'd been talking about Willa telling her father that she wanted to pursue being a forensic artist instead of a dispatcher. She'd shared that every time she'd started to tell him, something had come up, and she'd lost her nerve.

If you haven't told him yet, it's because it wasn't the right time. That time will come, just trust.

Tears rained down Willa's cheeks at the memory of her friend's young but strong faith. Anna had seen God in a way Willa hadn't, like a child and with a deep sense of wonder. Watching Anna grow closer to God had made Willa want to see Him like Anna did.

"God, I'm here for a reason. I...I can't think of a good reason right now, but I know that You're bigger than these ropes, and You're bigger than my fear. Help me." She fell forward on her knees, hands fisting the dirt as she prayed. She asked for forgiveness for her unbelief and thanked Him for the time she'd gotten to know Anna. It wasn't enough, it never could be, but she had to be okay with that.

When her tears were spent, she took a deep breath and moved to sit up. Her tied hands shifted on the soft dirt and slid forward several inches until they met the edge of something.

Something sharp.

Breath held, Willa dug in and uncovered a broken saw blade. It rested at the base of the table, covered in layers of dirt and dust, but it was still sharp. More tears flooded her eyes. This broken piece of metal was the answer to her prayers.

Thanking the Lord and taking extra care so as not to cut herself, Willa braced the saw blade between her knees and began cutting. It took less than five minutes for her bonds to break and another five for her to cut away the rope around her ankles. When she stood, the room still swam before her eyes, but she quickly regained her balance.

She was getting out of here.

She raced to the window and pulled herself up only to be met with a wall of flames.

Chapter Twenty-Seven

Clancy

THE ROAD TOOK A SHARP CURVE TO THE RIGHT, AND CLANCY braked hard, gritting his teeth against his squealing tires. There was tension in every muscle in his body. He was wrung so tight, he imagined himself snapping like a rubber band pulled taut.

He'd consulted the map and put the coordinates in his phone's GPS, but he wasn't sure he could trust it. Not up here in the mountains where the signal faded in and out with every bend of the road. At least it was paved—for now. It made his increased speed possible, though still unwise.

A sharp glance at the GPS showed a small logging road coming up on his right. When this was over, and Willa was safe, Clancy hoped he wouldn't see another logging road for a good long while.

He used the love the mountains—and still did, in all honesty—but right now, he wished he could be on a beach somewhere. Preferably with Willa.

The image struck him. Them together. Side by side on the beach enjoying the sunset.

It was so out of place but stuck with him all the same. Pushed him on to find her. To end this.

His radio crackled to life. "Long to Sullivan. Status report. Over."

"Sullivan here." He keyed the radio but almost dropped it on another turn. "Nearly to the turnoff road. You? Over."

"I'm still about a good fifteen or twenty minutes out. Do you see anything? Over."

Clancy took a second to look. He slowed down, seeing that the road wasn't too far ahead, but he sensed the need to be careful. If this was where Q had gone, he didn't want his haste to blind him to obvious dangers.

"I see the road. Hold on." He pulled to the side and stepped out, standing between the door and his Jeep. His eyes took in the thick forest of trees that jutted up to the right on the mountain slope. To the left, he saw that the road dropped off dramatically. "Everything looks normal. I'm going to proceed up the road. Over."

"Copy. Be careful, Sullivan. Over."

He didn't feel the need to reply. The warning was obvious, but in a situation like this, Clancy valued efficiency over caution. He knew the stakes. He knew the timeline. If Willa really had been taken by Q, which was the most likely outcome, then she was running on borrowed time in the hands of a skilled killer.

They weren't talking the usual forty-eight hours to recover her. It was more like minutes at this point, and Clancy wouldn't let slow driving keep him from his objective. He hoped Max wouldn't either.

Back in the car, Clancy cranked up the AC. It was fleeting relief when the heat index was so high, but he'd take what he could get as long as his Jeep didn't overheat. He threw the vehicle in drive and barreled toward the entrance of the logging road. As he thundered up the narrow, one-lane dirt and rock strewn ground, he passed his first clue. Perhaps a good sign.

A few hundred feet up the road, he saw a gate that normally would have been closed to bar access to the road. It was thrown wide, and from Clancy's hurried glance, it looked like the chain and lock had been opened by a pair of bolt cutters, not a key.

This was it. Q had taken her this way, Clancy knew it in his bones.

His pulse thundered through him like a drumbeat leading the way to battle. He was going to put a stop to Q, but more than that, he was going to get Willa to safety. Nothing else mattered.

His tires spun on loose gravel as he gunned it through the gated section and ascended the mountain. Trees and brush lined the road with a few broken branches that showed another vehicle had come this way not too long ago. It was like a repeat of their trip to Horse Creek mine.

Clancy's mind took in his surroundings, but in the background, his thoughts swirled. How had Q gotten away with this? Clancy knew the process to become a sheriff's deputy wasn't an easy one. There were tests to pass, evaluations, and even a polygraph. All of that was to weed out guys just like Q.

The only thing Clancy could come up with was a transfer. If Q had somehow worked in another department, or had faked something like that, he could get transfer papers.

Bright light indicated the tunnel of trees was coming to an end, and Clancy wondered if it would end in a clearing like the other building sites. Was this going to be the place where Q stashed Willa? Was he still there, or had he sensed them closing in on him?

He'd made sure that he and Max use a special channel for their updates so as not to warn Q, but there was no telling what kind of information Q had gotten before going off the grid.

Clancy slowed the Jeep. He wanted to be ready when he did drive into the open. Q had shot at them in the clearing with a rifle. Thankfully the man wasn't a particularly good shot, not like Willa, but that didn't mean he couldn't hit a target given enough time.

Clancy let the Jeep roll forward but soon saw that it wasn't a clearing like he'd thought. It was a landing. Clancy gave the Jeep gas and moved into the open. His skin crawled at the exposure, but he soon saw there was nothing. No buildings, no sign of Q's vehicle, and no Willa.

He did a repeat of before, stepping out of the Jeep but staying between the door and the vehicle. He scanned behind him, but there was nothing but trees. Then he craned his neck backward and took in the top of the ridge, and his breath caught. There was movement up there.

Cursing himself for not having binoculars handy, Clancy used his phone to zoom in. It was inefficient but somewhat effective. He could make out the outline of a man, and beyond him behind some new growth trees, a black truck he'd never seen before.

Clancy didn't have to guess. He knew it was Q by the way the man moved. And he hadn't seen Clancy—yet.

Jumping back in the Jeep, Clancy scanned the landing until he found the road that led up to the ridge. It was even narrower than the first one and covered in dense foliage, but that was a blessing. It meant Q wouldn't see him coming.

He took the road as quickly as he dared, but there were several areas that had been washed out with deep depressions he had to navigate around. It was slow going, and more than once, he considered getting out and running the rest of the way, but he wasn't sure what he'd be walking into. The Jeep would provide solid cover, unlike the narrow tree trunks of this young forest section, so he pushed on.

The last part of the road before he reached the ridge was unbelievably steep, and he fought for every foot the Jeep took, praying that it wouldn't spin out and slide back down the mountain, but he finally crested it. Then he saw the black truck parked above.

He almost laughed. Q had gotten his truck high-centered on a sharp protruding rock, and it looked like he was trying to maneuver it free. Served him right. But it also meant the man was distracted, and Clancy had the upper hand.

Slipping silently from the Jeep, Clancy pulled out his gun, checking that there was a round chambered, before he circled through the forest toward the truck. When he'd thought he might be entering a shootout, it had been more advantageous to be near his vehicle, but now, he saw that he'd need to catch Q off guard in order to stop him.

Clancy's steps whispered through the forest floor of pine needles and debris, edging ever closer to Q, who was bent over with a shovel, tossing dirt behind the back rear tire. Clancy scanned the truck for signs of Willa, but the windows were too tinted. Was it possible Q had her in the back? Was he using this neglected mountain road to get to the other side and evade capture? But what about Willa?

Everything Clancy had learned about the killer thus far—albeit very little—focused on the fact that he liked to take time with his victims. He wasn't one to race to the finish...unless he didn't see Willa as one of his, but more just a victim of opportunity?

She'd made his wall of victims—but only one picture. Did that have significance?

Clancy took another few steps closer, maneuvering behind a collection of smaller trees. He was now within ten or twelve feet of Q, and the urge to shoot first and ask questions later overwhelmed him. It was wrong, and Clancy wouldn't give in, but he recognized the temptation. Then again, if he killed Q, and Willa wasn't in the truck, he may not get to her in time.

Taking in a deep breath, Clancy stepped into the clearing, gun drawn. "Hands up, Q."

Q's movements stilled. He paused, bent over with the shovel six inches from the ground. "So, you found me."

His voice was different, effused with confidence and hinting at sarcasm. He turned then, dropping the tip of the shovel to the ground but not releasing it.

"Drop it," Clancy said, using a nod of his head to motion to the shovel.

"And what if I don't?" The Q from before was transformed. He still looked the same, but even his facial features had hardened. Taken on a darker bent. His brow dipped low and accentuated the hollow depths of his eyes. "What will you do?"

I'll gladly shoot you.

"Drop it." Clancy overrode his gut response.

Q didn't move. He just waited. And then, as the wind kicked up, he closed his eyes and drew in a deep, reveling breath.

Clancy was about to demand he drop the shovel again when he realized what was happening. The scent was frighteningly familiar.

Smoke.

"What did you do?" he barked.

"She will go down in flames as is fitting one so fiery."

Clancy's gut clenched. *She.* He was talking about Willa. "Where is she?"

Q took another deep breath and then opened his eyes. He motioned over his right shoulder with a nod, his smile growing wider. "JT mine. Although, I'm guessing you already knew that. You *are* here, after all. And alone, it would seem."

Clancy clenched his jaw. "Is she dead?"

"O death, where is your sting?" Amusement danced in Q's eyes. "She didn't deserve my attention. Willa is far too bold and entirely too willful for her own good. I will let the fire cleanse her of that."

Clancy's heart stuttered. Beneath the rhetoric Q was spouting as if he were some benevolent god, there was a thread of hope that Willa was still alive.

Clancy advanced several feet, gun still trained on Q's center mass. "I'm going to tell you one more time. Drop the shovel."

The scent of burning brush and thick smoke assaulted Clancy as the flames hit the sap of living trees. Q had started a fire to kill Willa, and her time was running out. He needed to secure Q and—

Q struck like a cobra. He swung the shovel at Clancy in a movement so fast, he only had a moment to turn aside. The metal head of the shovel connected solidly with Clancy's left shoulder in a resounding thud and threw him off balance. He took the hit in stride and went to ground, rolling with the momentum to come up closer to Q.

Clancy aimed the gun, but Q anticipated the movement and kicked it away. The Glock skittered across dirt and rocks to land several feet from them, but Clancy didn't have time to consider it as Q brought the shovel down at him, point first like he was trying to behead him.

There was a mad glint of euphoria in Q's eyes that sickened Clancy. The pure evil he saw there only acted to spur Clancy faster. He rolled closer to Q instead of further away and took him down at the legs.

Q landed with a thump, his head smacking a rock with a sickening crunch. But he wasn't out. He rolled onto his stomach, blood gushing from the head wound, as he reached to his side and pulled out a knife.

Clancy had taken the moment to get closer and used that to his advantage. He got a solid grip on the hand where Q held the knife and used his free hand to land a solid punch to Q's temple opposite the bloody wound.

Q groaned and spat blood, but he redoubled his efforts, trying to bring the knife to bear against Clancy's throat. They were equally matched, muscle to muscle, will to will, but Clancy had something Q didn't.

Hope.

It surged to life in his chest even as the scent of smoke intensified. Hope infused him with a supernatural strength, and he threw the man off with a kick followed by a striking blow to the ribs. The resulting grunt of pain meant he'd connected with something vital.

Clancy didn't pause, he rolled over two times and reached for his gun. He almost had it when Q was on top of him again. He straddled Clancy, the knife in one hand aimed at his chest as his other fought to hold Clancy down.

Clancy regretted giving his ankle holster gun to Willa, but the location of where his other firearm had fallen was cemented into his mind. He knew just how far he had to reach to get it, he only needed a window.

"I'm going to end you," Q said, blood and spittle dripping from his lips.

Clancy's grip shook with effort as he worked to push the knife away from his chest with one hand as the other used what strength remained to keep Q from choking him out. His vision tunneled, but he mentally waged a war against his weakening muscles. He couldn't give in—

On a wave of clarity, Clancy knew what to do.

Sucking in what little air he could, Clancy let go of Q's hand at his throat and reached out. He connected with cold metal. It was the sensation of life at his fingertips. Life and chaos.

He reached for the gun, his vision spotting to black. Just when he thought he couldn't hold off the knife in Q's hand any longer, his fingers found purchase. In one swift motion, he dislodged Q and brought the gun to bear.

A shot rang out.

Q's eyes went wide and then dulled as he slumped to the side.

Clancy drew in deep lungfuls of air, shoving Q off of him even as he crab walked backward from the scene.

Tears pooled behind his eyes. He hadn't wanted to kill the man, no matter the things he'd done. Clancy wanted justice, and it was hard to feel that was served when Q got off so easily.

A sense of urgency overtook him as he rolled over to his hands and knees. The following burst of adrenaline pushed him to his feet.

He needed to get to Willa. Had to find where Q had hidden her before it was too late.

Chapter Twenty-Eight

Willa

WILLA JUMPED AWAY FROM THE WINDOW AND THE SLOWLY approaching line of fire, panic causing her hands to shake. What was she going to do? That psycho had started a fire, and she was basically inside a box of kindling, ready to ignite at the first ember.

Her stomach churned at the thought. She had mere seconds to figure something out.

She took in the space again. The glassless window was on the same wall as the door—and the fire—and there was nothing at the back. Or was there?

Now that she was fully standing, she had a better perspective. There, hidden by a half-fallen beam from the ceiling, she caught the outline of another door opposite the one she'd just tried. Her heart surged, and she rushed toward it. Using her shoulder, she shifted the beam to the floor. It went down with a thud followed by clouds of dust but uncovered the door behind it. She lightly tapped the rusted metal handle, but it felt cool to the touch.

Praying with everything in her, she yanked the door open and was greeted with blessedly smoke-free air. She tripped outside, her legs still numb from having been tied up for so long, and ran to one side of the shack and then the other. The hope that had surged through her died like water on coals.

The cabin had been built up against a steep mountain side for access to a broken down mine shaft. Q had started the fire accordingly. It blazed like a half-moon of destruction coming ever closer to her. The only escape was up, but she knew her chances of making it very far up the shale-covered slope were minimal. Besides, even if she could make it to where the mountain leveled out, she wouldn't know where to go.

"God, show me the way." Her faith, bolstered by the broken saw blade, surged back into her.

There had to be another way.

Her eyes fell to the mine shaft. "No." Willa shook her head as if to enforce the idea that she was *not* going into a mine shaft, especially not one that looked like it had already fallen down.

She stepped to the side of the building but had to rush back. The flames were closer, and the roof of the dilapidated cabin was already on fire. The heat billowed toward her in waves and pricked her skin with heat.

Willa reluctantly moved toward the shaft.

Everything about it said *bad idea*. The support beams that were supposed to keep the entrance clear were both broken, causing the top beam to rest at a tilted angle. Piles of dirt littered the front of the entrance and as she drew closer, rested inside the opening as well.

Willa knew she would die if she went in there. But when she looked back at the cabin, now almost completely engulfed in flames, she knew she would die if she didn't.

She moved closer to the entrance and looked inside. There was a path, but it was interrupted by fallen beams and loose rock. It was a death trap. But so was the fire behind her.

Praying for strength and safety, Willa ducked under the leaning beam and entered the mine.

Chapter Twenty-Nine

Clancy

GRIPPING HIS SIDE, CLANCY RACED TO THE OVERLOOK. BELOW, he could see exactly what Q had done. There was a small cabin—a shack, really—that butted up against a steep wall. Q had set the fire around it in a half-circle and let the eastern wind do the rest.

Panic gripped his chest, and he struggled to draw in a breath through his bruised throat. Willa was in that cabin, and any second, she could burn up.

Clancy turned and ran back to his Jeep, not bothering to give Q's body a second glance. He jammed the gear shift to drive and burst into the clearing where Q's truck had stalled. He sideswiped it with a rasping, metallic sound and burst onto the narrow road that led down toward the building.

Clancy reached for the radio as some of his mental fog cleared. "This is —" He swallowed and tried again. "This is Sullivan. Found Q. He's dead. Going after Willa. He started a fire. Get a team up here ASAP. Over."

The radio crackled but nothing happened.

He repeated the message two more times and waited. Nothing.

He was on his own.

The Jeep rocketed into the clearing behind the fire, and he skidded to a stop. Jumping out, he called out at the top of his lungs. "Willa! Willa are you in there?"

The sound of flames devouring the tinder-like wood of the cabin was the only sound to greet him. He knew it would be nearly impossible for her to hear him over the roaring, but he tried again until his voice gave out. Then he circled the cabin.

It was set far back in the clearing, and the fire had already eaten what dry vegetation had surrounded it. The flames narrowed their hungry focus on the house. It was the perfect, devastating blaze, and Q had known it would be.

Defeat hunched him over. Hands on his knees, Clancy drew in air, but it only made him cough. This was his fault. Somehow, it was his fault. The one case he'd had a fighting chance to solve with good results was over.

Willa's flirty smile that day in the grocery store came back to him. Her confidence to confront him about staring. The way she'd teased him. He hadn't really known her then. Didn't really know her *that* well now, but he knew enough.

She was incredible. Brave. Strong. Vibrant. And talented. She had a future and....

He slipped to a knee, the overwhelming weight of knowing there was nothing he could do to save Willa engulfed him just as the flames did the structure in front of him. He forced himself to watch. Forced his attention on the building and the agony in the pit of his stomach. He'd been too late.

Too late to save her and too late to tell her how he felt.

A strong gust of wind *whooshed* through the trees and half of the building toppled, sending up a geyser of orange sparks into the air. Heat crashed into him, and he flinched, but he caught sight of something across the burning rubble he hadn't been able to see before. A gaping hole dug into the mountain.

A mine entrance!

Clancy shot to his feet. Was it possible...did he dare to hope that Willa had gotten out?

He rushed to the side for a better view where some of the flames had died down, and now, he could see that there was a door opened at the back

—one of the only things that remained standing of the building. It infused him with renewed focus.

What had Willa said about mines in the area after she'd fallen into the pit? That there were some that had been dug from one side of the mountain to the other. Was it possible this was one such a mine?

There was only one way to find out.

Chapter Thirty

Willa

SHE STUMBLED AND WENT DOWN, HER KNEE LANDING ON A sharp rock which caused her to cry out. Wracking coughs seized her, and she paused, leaning against the side of the mine that hadn't caved in.

The heat and the smoke followed after her, hot on her heels and almost as dangerous as being caught in the blaze. It didn't matter if there were flames or not if she couldn't breathe. She pulled up the bottom of her tank top and covered her mouth with the thin fabric. It didn't do much, but it was something.

She stumbled forward again, the darkness growing ever deeper. It was oppressive. Stifling.

If only she had a light or her phone—anything to tell her where she was and if she was making progress.

Her tentative steps slowed her down, but she didn't want to fall again. Besides, without sight, she wasn't sure what she'd be walking into. The pitch of the floor felt level to her, but that could be wishful thinking. If this was a mini adit, it would only go in so far, but if it was a tunnel that connected thin points on the mountain, it could open to another side.

After a few more hesitant steps, the toe of her shoe connected with something. She reached forward, keeping a hand on the rough rock of the wall to her right, and felt for what she'd hit. Her fingers brushed stone.

She searched and found more stone and soft dirt. A cave in.

She tried to breathe more deeply to calm herself, but the air was hot and stifling. She'd reached a dead end. This was it.

Willa slid down to the floor. It was possible she could wait out the fire and exit from the entrance she'd come in through, but that was if the fire didn't start to burn the wooden support beams in search of more fuel.

She'd heard tales from the older men in town whose fathers had mined in the late fifties when a boom of mining had streaked through Chamberlin. She'd heard the horror stories of wooden supports burning and trapping miners. Oxygen being at a premium, Willa wasn't sure if she'd make it if the fire did leap into the tunnel.

Her head pressed back against the wall. It was one thing to reach a cave in and know the there was an open space to crawl through, but she couldn't see any of that. All she knew was the wall she'd met and the seeming impossibility of getting through.

Perhaps that meant she was just supposed to wait. To trust.

Peace flooded over her at the thought. This wasn't the dead end she thought it was. It was her escape. She just had to have hope and—

Rocks tumbled to the ground next to her, making her jump. Was the tunnel caving in?

She rushed to stand as more rocks came down, and then a faint light played over the ceiling. *What's going on?*

"Willa?" Her name came to her along with a brighter flash of light that showed open space at the top of the cave in. Soft rocks and dirt fell away as the space grew wider. "Willa, are you there?"

"Clancy?" Her voice came out in a rasp, and she attacked the pile of dirt, digging her fingers into the space he was making. "I'm here."

"Willa!" His voice thundered so loud she was afraid he'd cause a cave in himself. She laughed, tears streaming down her cheeks.

"You found me." Her voice broke, and suddenly, the weight of her exhaustion coursed through her. She wanted to see him. Wanted to make sure he was okay. And she wanted to get off this mountain.

"I'm almost there. Just hold on." He dug more frantically, and she helped, breaking fingernails in the process and not caring. She'd do anything to get out of this tunnel.

Finally, a space big enough for his whole arm opened up, and he stuck it through along with his head. His face was covered in fine dust, and dirt clung to his hair, but she threw herself against the pile and cupped his cheeks.

"You came for me." She could barely make out his features beneath the grime and through the dim light of his flashlight, but it didn't matter. His expression radiated what she felt. Relief and something more.

"Let's get you out of here." The words. His confidence. Everything about him spoke of the fact she was safe.

He pulled back and dug more, the dirt and rock falling to the side as she did the same on her side until the hole was big enough for her to fit through. She went in headfirst, her arms over her head. He gently pulled her through, all but cradling her in his arms until she could gain her feet, and then he tugged her toward the exit.

They neared the light—the most beautiful sight to her—but she pulled back on his hand that hadn't let hers go. "Wait."

"What is it?" He pulled up short, and she crashed against him. He steadied her with a hand to her arm and peered down at her.

"Q—he—he killed Anna and—"

"He's gone." Clancy spoke in such a matter-of-fact way all she could do was stare mutely back at him. "I found him up on the ridge, and we fought."

Only now, closer to the light, she saw the signs of their altercation. The angry red welts on Clancy's neck that would likely turn dark purple. The cut on his cheek seeping blood. Even the way he stood told of the pain he was in.

"Are you—you're all right?"

He nodded. "Come on."

His hand gently squeezed hers and pulled her toward the light. Toward freedom.

The first taste of fresh air was glorious as were her next several lungfuls. There was smoke climbing the ridge behind them, but it wouldn't reach them—at least not yet.

He tugged her toward the Jeep he'd wisely parked in the shade and propped her up against the side as he dug in the back for water and what she thought was one of his clean shirts.

"Here." He doused the shirt with a water bottle and then instructed her to drink the rest. She did, and then he wiped at her face, gentle around the cut on her forehead that still hurt. "Did he...hurt you?"

The gravelly nature of Clancy's voice forced her eyes up. To really look at him. He was shaken to the core. She could see it in the hard lines of his face and the way he couldn't take his gaze from her. He searched over her form, looking for injuries, desperate to put things right—or so it seemed.

She stilled him by reaching out and taking his hand in hers. "I'm all right, Clancy."

"Are you sure? Your knee." He pointed to the scrape on her knee from where she'd fallen in the tunnel.

"It'll be fine. It's just a scrape." He stared at the spot as if the sight of her blood had him transfixed. She bent over to look up at him. "I'm okay."

"I thought you were in the building. He said..." Clancy drew in a sharp breath.

"He tied me up in there, but I got out. I escaped. And you saved me." She wanted to impress that on him. To make him see that *he* was the one who had saved her because something in her knew he needed to hear that. Internalize it. "*You* saved me."

His shoulders slumped, and he let out a grunt. Was he in pain? "Are *you* all right?" She stepped closer, looking up into his eyes.

"I am now." His hand reached up to cup her face, and his thumb traced the line of her cheek bone. A doorway opened when his gaze met hers. He was letting her in. "You were right. I lost sight of what hope is. I've been so caught up in disappointment, I couldn't see that there are still good things in this world. Really good things." His gaze shifted to her lips.

"Remember what I said before?"

He frowned and met her gaze. "Which time?"

"To take a picture. It would last longer."

His laugh blossomed in his chest, and she took a step closer to him, relishing the feeling of his hands as they slid into her hair. "I remember."

"Well, I think I was wrong."

"Oh yeah?"

"I think you deserve more than a photo." Her lips tilted up in a flirtatious smile.

"Do you have something in mind?" His forehead gently rested against hers. Their breath mingled, and despite the heat of the day, she wanted to be closer. Wanted him to encircle her in his arms.

"I think so," she whispered right before her lips met his.

The kiss was filled with the passion of hope that reached out and surrounded them both, drawing them together. Their bodies met in heat and connection and security. Clancy dug his fingers deeper into her hair, his other hand snaking around her waist and drawing her closer. She slipped her arms up and over his shoulders, pulling his head down for better access.

He groaned in pain, pulling back for a moment. "Sorry," he rasped, his breaths coming in short and fast.

"Are you all right?" She pulled back.

"Got hit in the shoulder with a shovel." He grunted a laugh, but she could see the pain radiating through him.

"Clancy." His name came out on a worried breath.

"I'll be fine." Her fingers played with the hair at the nape of his neck.

"I'm so sorry for all of this." Willa felt the pressure of tears.

"It wasn't the outcome anyone wanted, but we stopped a killer. He's no longer a threat. And you're safe." The weight of emotion in Clancy's gaze nearly melted Willa on the spot.

She knew they hadn't known one another very long, but when you went through literal fire together, it changed you—for good or bad. They had been fortunate enough for it to be the former.

His head bent low, and she tilted her lips up to meet his. This time, his kiss was less frantic. Almost reverent in his attentiveness. He filled her senses with his clean scent marred only by the smoke in the air.

The warmth of him everywhere their bodies touched filled her with comfort and a sense of security. Clancy had risked everything to come after her, and she could tell by the way he kissed her that it wasn't for temporary pleasure.

She pulled back and met his gaze. Her thumb trailed a circle over the scruff on his jaw, and he momentary closed his eyes, taking in a shuddering breath. "You drive me crazy, Willa Martin."

"I hope that's a good thing," she quipped.

He pressed a kiss to her lips then a light one on her nose. "A very good thing."

She searched his eyes, and though this was something new for them both, she sensed it was something lasting. Her gut told her so, and this time, she was going to trust that.

Chapter Thirty-One

Clancy

A WEEK HAD PASSED SINCE HE'D FOUND WILLA IN THE TUNNEL, but to Clancy, it felt like a minute. A second. Whenever he was with Willa, there was never enough time. She'd gone back to work a few days later, and Clancy had spent his time working up his final report to Hillary, one he hadn't wanted to give. She'd been gracious, despite her grief, but he still hated the outcome.

Then he'd turned back to his usual channels, looking for his next case, but he hadn't found one. Every time he thought he had it, he pictured Willa and then heard her words. Not everything in his life had to disappoint him.

The cases he usually took on did have an element of the impossible, and while Clancy had convinced himself it was just his way of offering hope in the darkest of circumstances, he'd started to become jaded, and that wasn't the way to approach any case.

He checked the time. He needed to get to the sheriff's office for his meeting with Glenn, and then he was having lunch with Willa and her father afterward.

The fact that he'd stayed in Chamberlin this long after a case was unique, but agreeing to lunch with Willa's father was even more surprising. It was a step. One of many, but certainly the first in a long line he wasn't sure he was ready to take.

Or was he?

He pulled out his wallet and the small photo he always kept there. It was wrinkled from the curvature of his back pocket and faded with time, but the smiling faces of him, his brother, and his parents stared back at him, daring him to remember the times when things had been good.

He traced the image of his mom with her frizzy 90s hairstyle and confident smile. He didn't know what had changed her from that loving image of what a mom should be to a shell of her former self, but he was old enough now to know it hadn't been as simple as before and after like he'd made it out to be.

There had been times of transition, and he'd been there for it all. As unfortunate as it was for a child to see his mother go through that, it didn't have to shape how he spent the rest of his life.

"You would like Willa, Mom." He spoke to the quiet of his hotel room, needing to swallow past the tightness in his throat. "She's beautiful and smart and just a little sassy."

His laugh warmed the impersonal space, and he took a deep breath. It felt like the first step toward healing, and he embraced it. Slapping his hands on his knees, he stood. It was time to go make decisions for the future that didn't include his past.

The now-familiar sight of downtown Chamberlin came into view, and Clancy allowed a small smile. It felt like his hometown not too many miles south, and for the first time, the association didn't bother him.

He drove past the diner. An image of Geraldine winking at him while trying to sell him a second piece of pie made him grin. And then there was the grocery store where he'd first seen Willa. His chest tightened at the memory and the subsequent ones that filled him with joy and fear as he relived the last few days.

Then the sheriff's office shared with dispatch. A place he was quickly coming to know well, thanks to his daily visits to Willa.

Marilee grinned at him as he entered the air conditioned space and took off his sunglasses, shoving them into his hair. He really needed a haircut, but Willa insisted she liked it longer.

"Hi-ya, stranger," the receptionist grinned. Her round cheeks pinked, and she tilted her head toward dispatch. "Here to see our Willa?"

"Soon, but first, I'm meeting with Sheriff Harding, actually."

"Oh." Her lips formed a perfect oh. "How nice. He should be in. Just head on back, and Nelson will let you through."

"Thanks." He nodded at her and walked past, the feeling of familiarity extending as he approached the talk-through window. "Hey, Nelson. Here to see the sheriff."

"Yeah, yeah, go on through, Mr. PI." Nelson went back to his phone, but he held a smile at the corner of his lips.

Clancy pushed through the door as it unlocked for him, moved silently through the hall, and then wound through desks to the back door where the sheriff's office sat. There was a window that looked into the office to show the man bent over paperwork. The door was ajar, so Clancy knocked.

"Come in," the sheriff called out. He looked up from behind his desk. "Ah, Clancy. Right on time. Have a seat."

He did, and the sheriff closed a file folder and placed it on top of a growing stack to the right of his desk. "Busy day, Sheriff?"

"Call me Glenn, and yes. There are still many reports to go over after the events of last week."

Clancy shifted uncomfortably in his chair. He'd given his statement multiple times but knew that he'd been involved in the shooting and subsequent death of a deputy. There would be legal ramifications, but he wasn't sure what they would be. Even if he'd been in the right.

"I called you down because I wanted to fill you in on some things."

"Okay." Clancy couldn't keep the edge of worry from his voice as he leaned forward and rested his elbows on his knees. "Shoot."

"First off, I didn't get a chance to tell you thank you for what you did."

Clancy's eyes widened. "Uh, me?"

"Son, you singlehandedly took on a serial killer and lived to tell about it. *And* you rescued our Willa, so there's lots of things to be thankful for."

Clancy was tempted to say he'd just been doing his job, but it had been more than that. "He had to be stopped, sir."

"I know. And that's why I wanted to talk with you. I'm sure you've wondered what will come of all of this, but you don't need to worry. Some things have come to light, and while I'm not technically authorized to tell you, I'm going to anyway. What are the perks of being sheriff if I can't exercise some discretion, right?"

Clancy couldn't help his grin. He liked this guy. "I think you've got to do what you think is right."

"Exactly. Let me give it to you straight. Q—uh, Quentin—lied to us all, and not just in the way you think." Glenn leaned back in his leather desk chair and steepled his fingers. "When I got the request for him to transfer in, frankly, I was overjoyed. We don't get much new help being such a small community, but we've got a wide territory and—well, you don't need to hear about my woes as a county sheriff. His papers looked good, and when I called his boss, I was pleasantly surprised at the praise he was willing to give Quentin. That should have been my first clue."

"How do you mean?" Clancy asked.

"We struck a deal. I'm not proud to say it, because it was a lapse in judgment on my part, but hindsight and all that. The sheriff in his county in southern Washington assured me that Quentin was a new hire and a promising deputy who had just gone through all his evals and had passed with flying colors. He explained that Quentin's grandmother lived in North Bank and was sick. The sheriff said Quentin needed to transfer to take care of her for a time."

"Sounds reasonable."

"I thought so, too. I agreed to let him do a lateral transfer here, and then we'd reevaluate after six months. I guess that's all the time he was supposed to need." Glenn rubbed his jaw. "Turns out that, while his tests were completed, he photoshopped them to show better scores, and there was one instance where he may have bribed someone. We're still trying to figure that out. And the boss I talked to? It had to be him. The sheriff at his old department had never heard of me."

"I'm guessing there was no grandma," Clancy said.

"None that we could find. I've got my suspicions—namely, that these women are not the first ones he's killed—but it will take more investigation to know for sure."

Clancy nodded, recalling Quentin's words to him. "It sounded to me as if he had a fascination with power and control over the women he fixated on."

"From what we've gathered so far, he found them at churches or small groups, convinced them to date him secretly, and then abducted them and placed them in a controlled environment, which fits what you're saying. I should have seen it." Glenn rubbed a hand over his face.

"I'm sorry, sir. I know it must be hard." Clancy felt for the man in a difficult position in a small community doing the best he could for them.

"I played into his hand, and I have to come to terms with that, but all of that to say, you didn't actually shoot a legitimate deputy. None of that matters due to the evidence we have against him. The items you and Willa brought in can be linked to him with video footage from the store as well as DNA and fingerprint matches. He wasn't very careful, though we suppose he planned on burning up the evidence from the beginning. Anyway, it was clearly self-defense on your part, so you've got nothing to worry about."

"I'm glad to hear it."

Glenn leaned back and leveled his gaze on Clancy. "I know you were a cop before becoming a PI, but it's never easy to shoot someone in the line of duty. Make sure you talk to someone about this. Got it?"

"Yes, sir," Clancy said. Warmth from the man's caring words washed through him, and he clenched his hands together in his lap. He could tell Glenn was someone who cared about his officers.

"And, speaking of being a cop, I've got a proposition for you."

"What's that, sir?"

"I'd like to offer you a job."

Clancy laughed. "Really?"

"You bet. I could use a smart, resourceful, and clearly brave man on my team. Chamberlin isn't much, but it's what we've got, and I like to keep it as safe for residents as possible."

Clancy opened his mouth to turn the man down, but the words wouldn't come.

"Why don't you think about it? The offer stands so don't feel pressure. Sure would like to see you stick around for a while. I think someone else would as well." He nodded his head toward the window into his office, and Clancy turned to see Willa standing there talking to Max and Jase, an older man with the same color of blonde hair standing next to her.

Just the sight of her did funny things to Clancy's insides, and he turned back to the sheriff, knowing he was wearing a ridiculous grin. "I've, uh, got to go. Lunch date." He stood but paused at the door. "Thank you for the offer. I'll consider it."

"That's all I ask. But Clancy" —the sheriff leveled a look at him— "you be good to our Willa, you hear?"

"Absolutely, sir." He planned to do that and more.

Chapter Thirty-Two

Willa

WILLA KNEW THE MOMENT THAT CLANCY ENTERED THE OFFICE space. She couldn't see him, but the scent of fresh soap and the outdoors clung to him like the most perfect cologne, and she inhaled a little more deeply before turning.

He'd just exited the sheriff's office but slowed when she met his gaze. Her smile grew wide, and his matched. He was so handsome with his rugged, chin-length hair and scruffy beard he'd trimmed just for their lunch, or so she guessed. And his eyes, brown and darker brown, were so familiar to her now she couldn't imagine *not* looking into them.

This man had burst into her life and turned things upside down, but she didn't want to remember what they'd been like right side up.

"Hey," she said, coming to greet him as her father talked with Jase and Max about some fishing spot he was going to check out that weekend.

"Hey yourself." He took in her outfit and met her gaze again. "You look incredible."

She laughed, heat flooding into her cheeks. "I'm wearing a tank top and shorts, not a ball gown," she said.

"You make them look good." His appreciation twisted his lips up, and she so desperately wanted to kiss him right then and there in the middle of the sheriff's office, but she held back. Not only would Jase and Max tease her for eternity, her father hadn't even met Clancy yet.

"How about you tell me how good I look later?"

His knowing grin warmed her insides and flooded her veins with heat. Maybe just one kiss—

"Hello, sir. You must be Willa's father. I'm Clancy Sullivan."

Willa spun to see her father had come up next to her. Good thing she hadn't given in. "Clancy, this is my dad, Shawn."

"That's Mr. Martin," he said, extending a hand with a serious face before he burst out laughing. "Kidding. Please, call me Martin."

The two shared a laugh as Willa shot eye-daggers at her father. Taking a deep breath, she turned to Clancy. "You can still do lunch, right?"

"Right." He nodded, looking between them. "Anywhere you two want to go?"

"The deli," her father said with a decisive head nod.

She rolled her eyes. "Couldn't we go somewhere nicer? Even the diner would be a step up from that place."

"Nope. I've missed Hal's sandwiches."

She sent Clancy an apologetic glance. "It's nothing fancy."

"I love a good sandwich," he said.

"Then it's settled." Her dad clapped his hands together and rubbed. "And you're paying," he directed to Clancy.

Willa just groaned.

"This may be the best sandwich I've had in my life." Clancy took another massive bite and closed his eyes, clearly in sandwich heaven.

"I told you," Willa's dad said. "It's something about the way Hal cuts the meat so thin and—"

"Mixes it in between the cheese," Clancy added, his excitement showing. "I agree."

Willa rolled her eyes as she dug into her market salad. So far, lunch had gone far better than she'd anticipated, and it seemed as if Clancy and her father were hitting it off better than she could have hoped for.

As she watched them interact, she smiled, but doubts threatened her inner peace. Not only had she not told her father about the next set of forensic art classes, she also didn't know what Clancy was up to next. He had always had the air of a wanderer about him, but what did that mean for them?

There was only way to alleviate one of her worries. "Dad, I've got something to share with you."

Both her father and Clancy turned to look at her. She blushed under the weight of their combined gaze but willed herself to push through what she needed to say.

"What is it, Wills?" Dad asked.

"I want to be a forensic artist." The words tumbled out without preamble or much thought. They just were. One glance at Clancy, and she saw his approving smile, but it was her father she had to convince. "I've been taking classes in North Bank at the community college, but my professor says I'm really good and need to increase my studies. And...I want to. There's a set of classes next semester, and I want to take them, but it will mean cutting back at work."

Her father blinked a few times, clearly composing what he would say. "All right. Is this something you enjoy?"

"Yeah, Dad. It means giving faces to faceless people. It also means seeing things from a different standpoint and being able to help the police. It's important—just like dispatch, but it's more...me."

Her father's confusion softened into an encouraging smile. "I always knew you were good at art. I just didn't think...this is great, honey. You need to do what *you* want to do, not something just because your old man did it."

"I just didn't want to disappoint you." Willa sucked in a breath as tears threatened. At the same moment, Clancy reached out under the table and took her hand in his, giving it a gentle squeeze.

"Oh, Willa, you could never do that. I am so proud of the woman you've become. You're a good dispatcher—very detailed—and I think that'll make you good at this, too."

"Thanks, Dad," Willa said, her voice cracking.

Her father looked a little uncomfortable with the emotional aspects of their conversation, but she could tell he was trying. "I just wanted you to know. I'll work my schedule out with Barney."

"Whatever you need, you just let me know."

"I will." She cast a glance at Clancy. "Would you mind if Clancy and I took a walk?"

"Of course not." Her father beamed at her and then turned to Clancy. "It was an honor to meet you, Clancy. I hope I see you around—a lot." He grinned, and Clancy sent her a shy look.

"I think you will, sir. In whatever amount Willa can stand me."

Both men laughed, and they stood, leaving her father to finish his sandwich. Outside, the sun beat down on them, though clouds moved in swiftly to intercept the worst of it. She directed them to a narrow path behind the deli that followed the curve of the creek.

"Did you mean what you said?" she asked, turning to look up at him in the shade of the tall evergreen.

"That really was the best sandwich I've ever had."

Willa laughed. "Not about that." He grinned down at her, and she had the feeling he'd known what she meant. "About coming around more."

"Oh, that," he pretended to be surprised. "What do you think?"

She pulled him to a roughhewn bench the Boy Scouts had put up a few years before and sat, turning to look at him. "I'd like it, but I don't know if you're the kind of man who knows how to settle."

"Who says I would be?"

She frowned. "I just mean...before you came here, you said you'd worked a case in Montana. It doesn't sound like you stay in any one place very long."

Clancy rested his arm along the back of the bench but leaned forward, peering into her eyes. "I don't. Or, I haven't. Not in a long time. I told you my grandfather left my brother and me money. What I didn't say was that I could live off of that for the rest of my life and never have to work." He pushed a strand of her hair behind her ear. "I was chasing something before. Looking for meaning, I think. Or maybe I was just looking for something to believe in. Something that wouldn't disappoint me."

"And what about now?"

"Well, there's this girl with wild blonde hair who makes some killer coffee cake and can draw better than anyone I've never known. She's smart and beautiful and tells it like it is." He leaned forward and pressed a gentle kiss to her left cheek. Then her right. "I never wanted to stay anywhere before because there was nothing worth staying for." He shifted to press the lightest of kisses to her forehead where the cut was nearly healed. "But now, I think I've found something worth staying for. *Someone* worth putting down roots with."

Love for this man welled and bubbled over in the pit of Willa's stomach. It surged through her every limb and drew her closer to him. Closer still. Her lips hovered centimeters from his, waiting for him to close the distance.

"But I meant what I said," he whispered against her lips.

"What's that?" She reached up and fingered a lock of his hair, his breath catching at the motion.

"I'll only stay if you want me to." His nose nuzzled hers, and he leaned back to look into her eyes. "Do you, Willa? Do you want me to?"

Heat flushed through her at the huskiness in his voice, and she gripped the back of his neck, drawing him close again. "I do."

This time, she waited, not willing to close the gap unless he wanted to, but it was clear when his lips met hers that theirs was a mutual want. A sparking desire that coursed through the connection their lips made. It surged through her and wrapped around her in the shape of Clancy's arms.

He kissed her thoroughly but pulled back too soon, catching his breath with his head nestled next to hers. "Willa, it's more than just this need I have to kiss you."

She laughed, feeling weak at the nearness of him. "Oh?"

"Yes." He shifted to look her squarely in the eyes. "I meant every word I said. You are something special, and I don't want to mess this up. I—I haven't been in a relationship for a long time, and I—"

She stopped his worries with a quick kiss. "None of that matters. This isn't like the cases you've worked. This doesn't have to fail. It doesn't have to end. You can hope—in us."

Her words hit their intended mark as she saw the softening behind his eyes. "You're right," he leaned in again, though this time his kiss was sweet and tender. The desire still lingered, but it wasn't what they needed now. No, what they needed was a foundation to build on.

And that started with hope.

About Emilie Haney

Emilie grew up in the Pacific Northwest and has a love for the outdoors that matches her love for the written word. She turned her passion for stories toward writing at an early age, finding entertainment and adventure in made-up worlds fed by the books her parents read to her as a child. Now, she's still getting lost in those worlds but they are of her own making.

Emilie writes contemporary fiction with strong themes of romance and suspense and believes that--no matter what--love fights for what's right.

Website: www.emiliehaney.com

 twitter.com/emhaneyauthor
 instagram.com/emiliehaney_author
 tiktok.com/@emiliehaneyauthor

The Art of Deception

CARA PUTMAN

Janyre Tromp, thank you for catching the vision for my next legal suspense series and for seeing what this book could be as a lead-in book for that series. You came into my writing life at a time professionally when I needed the encouragement. Thank you!

Acknowledgments

Readers, thank you for making the time to read this book. You wouldn't hold it in your hands or on your e-reader without the commitment and dedication of my dear writing friend Beth Vogel. For reasons that sometime I might explain, I had to reshuffle the order of books in this series at literally the last second. That meant this book was written in April rather than given to Beth to edit in April. Then she kicked it back to me with a key point about the heroine. You have to understand, I really like Charlotte. And she's Charlotte to me. Her son Drew is key in Book One of my next series and that book was already written...and macro edited. So there were constraints...big constraints. But Beth was right. I won't say more because I don't want to spoil that story or this one, but let me just say that Beth once again worked her magic and helped me make this book and these characters much stronger. Thank you, Beth! I cherish your sharp eye. But even more I cherish our friendship. You are a gift to me!

Thanks to Liz Bradford for asking if I'd consider being part of this collection and Lisa Phillips for enthusiastically welcoming me. This has been so much fun!

And always, thank you to my family for accepting this crazy life I lead and take them on. Having an author for a wife and mom is not for the weak at heart, y'all!

Chapter One

As she adjusted her nameplate that said *Marie Montgomery* on the reception desk at Hunter & Associates in a suburb of Indianapolis, Charlotte Montgomery wondered if she could reclaim her true identity yet. She shook her head reminding herself she had to be Marie to keep her son safe, even if that meant hiding from the fullness of who she was. She longed to push back the boredom at the firm, the ever-present longing for something more. Her job paid the bills but didn't feed her soul. Pigments and canvas had filled her dreams as a young adult—not the endless columns of numbers that surrounded her as oh-so-serious employees in the cubicles and small offices forced them into ordered rows.

Circumstances had required her to abandon her dreams in the hills of Tuscany. For eight long years, she'd looked back over her shoulder. Was she truly safe? With each year of quiet, she wondered if she needed to remain within the strict lines of hiding. Of separation. No one had appeared from those dreadful last days in Italy, so maybe . . . maybe she could return to her family.

She'd left her life in Italy behind. Now she was ready to abandon her shadowed, shallow existence.

The phone rang, jerking her from her thoughts. Marie hit the button to accept the call. "Hunter & Associates."

"Thayer Jackson, please."

Marie recognized the deep voice of the man who called a couple times a month for Thayer, one of the staff accountants. She'd noticed the quiet, shy man who had a good way with clients. Thayer kept to himself except for the times this person pulled him from his small office. Then Thayer would disappear for a couple days. She hadn't quite figured out the rhythm of it, but she should remember that wasn't her job. Keep her head down and do the mindless work that covered her bills.

That's what she needed to do as a single mom—pay the bills.

Maybe someday she could allow herself to breathe life into dormant dreams, but not now.

No matter how much her fingers itched to pick up a paintbrush. Or how many times she took Drew to a Hobby Lobby or Michaels just to look at canvases, oils, and sketchpads. It was a slow form of torture. But one she'd endure.

"Ma'am?" The clear voice brought her focus back.

"Sorry. Let me get Thayer for you." With a few quick clicks, she connected the call to Thayer's extension, and then dropped her forehead onto her crossed arms on the desk with a long sigh. She had to keep her attention right here, right now, no matter how boring. Maybe she could allow herself a few minutes on the design website. It wasn't like anyone would notice, and five or ten minutes of adding layers and dimension would quiet her mind.

That's what she needed. What she could do.

Just a few minutes.

~

Thayer Jackson had to admit his friend FBI agent Johnson Paarlberg knew how to sell him on an emergency request. "All you need to do is go to the gallery and keep your eyes open. See if anyone looks out of place."

Thayer rubbed his forehead. "How will I know?"

"They won't belong." Johnson said the words like the people would be wearing a sign stating, "I don't belong here."

"If we hadn't been friends for years, I'd hang up right now and go back to my clients who pay prevailing market wages."

"But you wouldn't get the satisfaction of helping your government."

"I'm not sure serving as a consultant counts."

"Oh, it does. Especially when you agree to help with things like tonight's gallery show."

Going to the 42nd Street Art Gallery show didn't make sense. Thayer wasn't an undercover agent. He didn't have the necessary skills—wasn't even sure what those were. He had the nagging suspicion that one day Johnson would put him in a situation that could get him killed. The thought wouldn't leave Thayer as he stared at the art show invitation Johnson had forwarded to his email. "Remind me why I should do this again."

"Because I need an extra set of eyes and you don't look like an agent. Everyone else is wrapping up the drug bust. You're the best qualified." Thayer could hear the grin in Johnson's voice. "Print the invite off and go have a great night. After all you earned an A in art appreciation."

"A-." Thayer muttered, not admitting it was the class that damaged his 4.0. "You know I don't do field work. I work the computer."

"You'll be fine. Just pretend you don't know me. Bring a date and enjoy the art while billing us for your time."

Thayer glanced at the invitation again. "Bring a date? I can't snap my fingers and walk in with a beautiful woman." Though there was a woman he'd tried to work up the nerve to invite to coffee for a few months. Maybe this would work to test the waters.

"Ask the receptionist. What's her name? Clara?"

"Marie."

Johnson chuckled. "See. Ask her. What's the worst that could happen?"

"I don't want to answer that." But after he hung up, Thayer squared his shoulders and pushed from his desk. This was the kind of request he'd make in person. Face to face. Where he could see her reaction and the micro expressions that would flit across her pixie features.

When he crossed the hall and reached the reception area at the front of the office, she sat at her large desk, some sort of software pulled up on her monitor. It didn't look anything like the basic excel worksheets the prior receptionist worked on as he'd prepped for the CPA exam. Instead, it looked like she'd doodled, only it was no casual drawing. She was good, the "doodle" a recognizable rendition of some hillside, maybe Italy or Spain, but before he could fully identify it, she clicked the site closed and smiled up at him. "Mr. Johnson, how can I help you?"

"It's Jackson."

"Isn't that what I said?" She smiled in a way that suggested she really believed she'd said his last name.

It was enough to kill the bit of confidence he'd collected and make him decide to go to the art gallery solo, but then her gaze trailed to the invitation he'd printed and now twisted in his hands and a wistful softness stole over her face.

"Are you going to the opening?"

"I was considering it, but the invitation is for two."

"I'm sure you have no problem finding someone to accompany you to events." She gave him a polite smile that did nothing to inspire great courage.

He cleared his throat. "Would you go with me?"

"You really don't need to ask me

"I'd like you to come . . . if you're free."

She glanced at her watch. "Much as I'd enjoy it, I can't. I have a little boy, and that means I need to get home." It was like a wall she kept carefully erected snapped back into place, but there was a crack. Something that let him see past the coolness of her blue eyes.

"Are you sure? We could go for an hour. Right after work. Stay as long as you're able, and then leave." He held up his hands trying to signal there was no pressure. "I promise I'll take you home the moment you need to go."

She glanced down at her outfit, a beautiful robin blue sweater that emphasized her eyes topping a skirt that exploded in bright color that he'd noticed swirled around her calves as she'd delivered a bouquet of flowers earlier in the day. "Are you sure? I'd need to make a call. And I'd drive myself."

"You look perfect." He hadn't meant to say the words out loud, but she looked up at him, a glow warming her face.

"I don't do things like this, but it would be nice to go for a few minutes." She gave a quick nod.

"I need to see one person and enjoy some art. It doesn't have to take long." He wouldn't waste this opportunity.

~

"I'll make a quick call." The moment felt reckless, but not risky, like she might try to live for the first time in almost a decade. Indulge her dream, for what? An hour? It was time. Well past time. She could do this and relax into the moment. She'd watched Thayer and knew he was a good guy. One who treated others with kindness and respect.

But if she really believed that she wouldn't close the app with her art the moment he came near.

She'd lived an undetected existence ever since she left the beautiful Italian hills, the ones she's been sketching when Thayer arrived with his unexpected invitation. So why was she even entertaining the idea of going with Thayer Jackson, a man who seemed to see her when she needed to stay hidden.

Eight long, lonely years. Surely that had been enough time. And a single hour on one night should be fine. She had to believe it could be.

It only took a conversation of a few minutes to confirm the high school student who stayed with Drew would be delighted to have an extra two hours with him that night. And Marie would get an hour or two to pretend her life was normal.

"It's all set." She looked at the small digital clock on her desk. "I can be ready in twenty minutes. Does that work?"

"It's perfect."

"Great. I'll follow you. That way if I need to leave, you can stay." She needed to know she wouldn't be trapped. That she could escape the moment she needed to even though there was nothing frightening about Thayer with his floppy hair and relaxed grin.

He nodded, the slightest droop of disappointment around his eyes. "Of course. I understand."

"Thank you for inviting me. It means a lot."

He nodded, then stumbled backward into a chair, and she bit back a grin as he hurried down the hall to his small office.

Time dragged as she waited for five o'clock. As soon as it did, she switched the phones to voicemail and hurried to the bathroom to touch up her makeup. Since returning to the States, she'd become a minimalist by nature and necessity. She didn't have the resources to maintain the more elaborate habits she'd cultivated as the pampered girlfriend of a rich Italian playboy. And then she'd learned he wasn't at all who she'd thought. She stared into the mirror and shook off the shadows the memories brought to the foreground.

Was it safe to go back to the world of art? Even in the small periphery in a city like Indianapolis?

One hour at a small gallery show would be fine.

Maybe for sixty short minutes she could imagine what her life would have been like if she'd never stumbled into a certain coffee bar in Roma and locked eyes with the man who smiled a bad boy smirk and who'd captured her heart with every James Dean movie fantasy she'd ever giggled over with her grandma.

She gave a slow nod. "Here's to the future. One small step at a time. You can do this, Marie."

And she could.

Why?

Because she wanted her life back.

She wanted to stop hiding and start living. She'd start tonight, and she'd make it wonderful, because she wanted to live for Drew.

Chapter Two

THAYER HAD WALKED MARIE TO HER CAR AND THEN followed her until a red light had separated them a few blocks from the gallery. Then he'd circled the block hunting for parking. Had she already entered the gallery or should he wait outside? He shot his cuffs and strolled to the front door of the 42nd Street Art Gallery. He was on loan to the FBI, but first he needed to find Marie.

How could he get this right when he wasn't even sure what exactly Johnson needed him to do other than ignore him? How did the art gallery with a Salvador Dali and other lesser works by local artists play into the complex cases he consulted on?

Wait. Marie's car was in the lot, so maybe she'd slipped inside to wait for him, but he didn't want her to be stranded if she needed his invitation to access the show. Thayer shook his head and pasted on what he hoped looked like a solemn, interested smile as he followed a well-dressed couple into the brightly lit gallery. Inside, the hard wood floors gleamed while clean white walls served as a blank easel for the art that lined walls covered with wood on the lower half that matched the tone of the floors. Small sculptures sat atop dark pedestals. The overall impression was one of wealth, excellence, and impeccable taste.

He did not belong.

But here he was.

He squared his shoulders and scanned the space for Marie. She should be easy to spot with her blonde waves that fell to her shoulders and youthful wistfulness. Her colorful clothes and small smile always made him think of a free spirit who flitted about the world in a creative fugue. The space was deep but it wasn't that large. He should spot her easily.

As he worked his way around clusters of chatting people, he passed paintings on easels interspersed with others hung on the walls. All had a similarity to their color schemes even as the styles transitioned from impressionist to more classical and similar to Leonardo da Vinci.

He stepped closer to one, noticing the brush strokes on the piece that paid homage to Monet. Only instead of haystacks or lilies, its subject was a cat sitting in a field of daisies.

"Do you like it?" He turned toward the familiar voice, and found himself staring into the bluest eyes, clear and innocent—the eyes of the woman he'd sought.

~

Marie bit back a smile at the way Thayer froze as if he'd been struck mute. What was it that caused that reaction? "So what do you think?"

He gave his head a tiny shake, but she caught it. That's what artists did. Noticed the details about the world around them.

"I appreciate the artist's interpretation of Monet's style."

"I do too. But Monet didn't paint cats . . ."

"That we know." She froze after they spoke the words in harmony. "That's odd."

"What?" He almost whispered the words as he studied her.

"I'm not usually synced in thoughts with anyone else." That was the part of having an artist's perspective that she didn't appreciate. No one saw the world the way she did—not even close. She was always on the outside. Desperate to be seen—or even better, to be welcomed in. Rather than keep trying, she'd built a careful life for her seven-year-old son Drew. He didn't disappoint her, unlike his father who had lied to her. She shook off the dark thoughts. Time to move back to the light. "If the rest of the art is similar, it will be an interesting show."

"Could be." He turned his attention from the painting to her. "Sorry I lost you on the drive over."

"Sorry I didn't wait in the car for you to collect me."

"You didn't need to." A small smile curved the corner of his well-shaped lips, and then he offered her his arm. "Want to wander with me?"

Her peasant skirt created a swirled rainbow of color in a sea of suits and sheaths. She knew she stood out—was different—and it was okay. It was part of her identity, but she didn't love all the side glances she felt as she glided among the attendees next to Thayer to the middle of the first floor and then climbed to the second floor. A nineteenth century bar that approximated the age of the building filled the middle of the space.

"Did you know the owners had this bar shipped from Boston when they renovated?" Thayer tapped the wood with his free hand, sharing the detail he'd learned on the website.

"That's an elaborate expense."

"Fits this space well." Thayer glanced around as if looking for someone and then stilled.

"You okay?"

"Do you mind if I step away for a minute?"

"I'll get something here."

"Sure?" A small V formed between his eyebrows as he glanced from her then back toward the stairs.

"I'll stay right here and be easy to find."

"Thanks." He squeezed her hand and stepped away.

The bartender greeted her with a bright smile. "What can I get you?"

"Sparkling water with a slice of lime." She settled on one of the stools and gave it a quick spin.

His grin turned to a smirk. "Drinks are on the house."

"I know." But she had a son to get home to.

"You're different from many here tonight, who seem to enjoy the besotted image." He reached under the counter and pulled out a pure La Croix. "This work?"

"Perfect." She gave him her sunniest smile and then watched as he filled a glass with ice, the sparkling water, and then the lime. She could almost pretend she was back in Italy. Almost. She accepted the drink and turned to take in the people who had wandered upstairs. The second floor

187

wasn't as active as the first, but that would change as people realized where the bar was located. She took a sip and let the bubbles tickle her throat.

A man settled onto the stool next to her, but she ignored him, enjoying the moment. In her early 20s she'd imagined this would be her life. Her art displayed for the public. Her own successful gallery showing. It had been the dream that chased to her to Italy. Then she'd fled, and her aspirations had morphed into staying alive.

Smaller could be better if you were alive.

But survival wasn't enough anymore.

She finished her drink and looked at her watch. It had been fifteen minutes, so it was time to find Thayer or head home before her defenses lowered and the tendrils of her old dream wrapped around her heart again.

Thayer watched the patrons from his position next to a painting. He wasn't sure who he was looking for, but he'd caught the impression of a man he'd seen in a photo array for an Italian company Johnson had him digging into. Now the man had disappeared, so he pretended to appreciate the art in front of him as he waited to see if the man reappeared. Thayer considered the imagination and depth that hinted at something joyful in the lines and colors.

Then he glanced at the price tag and winced.

Fifty thousand dollars for a piece that fit inside an eight by twelve picture frame? That was too much per square inch for his bank account even if he loved every centimeter of the way the light danced along the waves and the boat's sails played in the pull of the invisible wind.

He stepped to the next painting. This one was priced at the princely sum of seventy-five thousand dollars.

He let out a low whistle. "Do people actually pay these prices?"

"They do and the artist is grateful." Marie's soft voice was easygoing with a touch of southern and alerted him that she'd rejoined him. "The gallery keeps forty percent. The agent takes a percentage of the remaining sixty. You might be surprised how little artists actually live on."

"Even half isn't shabby." He'd have to work a lot of hours to equal the same.

"True, but maybe the gallery will sell three or four tonight and the artist won't sell another painting all year. Supplies are also expensive." She shrugged.

"You know a lot about this process."

"I guess I do." She gave him a small smile and then kept strolling. "Did you find who you were looking for?"

"I'm not sure." He shook his head. "I might have imagined it."

"Then I'll wander while you take another look."

"Thanks." Thayer watched her walk away and then headed back toward the stairs. This wasn't how he wanted to spend the time, but he owed it to Johnson to give the gallery one more quick search. He wasn't going to learn much by mooning after Marie like a middle-schooler.

This time he passed behind the stairs toward the back of the gallery and the parts near the back he hadn't explored yet. Raised voices caught his attention, so he slowed his steps and perused each piece as he reached it.

The gallery owner stood in conversation with a man who had a full head of styled silver hair, a smarmy smile, and was dressed like he'd recently visited his personal tailor somewhere in Europe. He looked like every rich person standing in the room only taken to another level of poshness. Then Thayer noticed the rings decorating the man's hands as he used them to punctuate his words.

"Julian, I need to buy the right painting." The man waved his hand as if to encompass every piece hanging from the walls. "None of these are right. You have to get me something different. Something more." The man's voice echoed in the space enough to start pulling all attention his direction. Was that his intent?

It was an interesting strategy, but why?

Thayer took a few steps closer as he examined the next painting. This was another of the exhibiting artist's, but it had the air of a van Gogh. The artist had a gift for mimicking others' styles. Only her subject matter was a field of butterflies dancing over irises. It was stunning. The colors vibrant and the subject gliding on the canvas. The piece exuded joy. How did she accomplish that?

"Stop speaking so loudly." The words were hissed with authority and

189

pulled Thayer back to the reason he stood in that gallery rather than watching a basketball game at home.

"No. I need a painting, and my client will pay top dollar for the right one." Something about the way the man said the words had Thayer edging ever closer to the two men.

Julian grabbed his arm and sidled him toward the back wall. "Keep quiet, you fool. I know you think your galleries make you an art connoisseur, but you're a hack."

"I'm a hack with clients prepared to spend a lot of money on good art. We can make this a strong partnership that pays each of us well. I'm also on the board of the Elliott Museum at Monroe College, and we're looking for a few paintings to round out our collection. I'd like to see your Salvador Dalis."

Julian tugged him toward the back. "You're a fool to think I'll pull those out of storage because you asked."

"You should."

"No." Julian kept them moving, their conversation getting softer with each step.

Thayer glanced around and then decided to follow. Maybe this was what Johnson had hoped he'd overhear. It was better than eavesdropping on the other attendees' random gossip. Then again, he wasn't an FBI agent. He was merely a consultant who sat at a computer and scanned data when he wasn't serving his corporate clients.

He took a few steps after the two men but a large man in a suit with white shirt that was unbuttoned at the collar stepped in front of him. "Where are you going?"

Thayer glanced around and pointed at the paintings behind the man. "Back there to look at the other work."

"It's closed right now."

Thayer made a show of looking around and then took a step to the side, only to have the man match his step. He held his hands up but stood his ground. He'd never liked bullies. "Why can't I go over there? I don't see any signs or anything."

"It's a private conversation."

"Then someone needs to tell that man, because he talks loud."

The man smirked. "That's what I thought."

That's when Thayer realized his misstep. He'd just admitted he was more interested in the men than the art.

The glass sweated in Marie's hand as she made her way back down the stairs after collecting a refill. This should be a princess moment, but no one noticed her, even with the brightly colored skirt swirling around her. She shouldn't be surprised, but part of her longed for someone, anyone, to notice her. It would be so freeing to be herself tonight.

She hadn't anticipated how hard it would be to walk among the evidence of her dream. She'd stay a few more minutes, then thank Thayer for the invitation and slip home. It had been a nice idea, but she should stick to coffeeshops and science museums. Those didn't hit so close to her hopes and remind her of everything her naivety had cost her. Her steps took her near a painting and she froze.

It was hers.

No.

It couldn't be.

She'd left all of them behind when she'd fled.

She took a step closer.

Examined the canvas with its swirl of blues, the sky merging with the river, separated only by the white of the bridge spanning the river and the grey of the building. Looking at it cause her heart to yearn for Venice and the soft sway of the gondolas along the canals. The painting had been a challenge because the blues had told a story of depth in the river and brightness in the sky.

Her fingers reached out involuntarily, as if she could reach for the bottom side of the frame where she'd slipped the extra copy of the flash drive.

It couldn't still be there.

Not after eight years.

"You can't touch the art." The woman's voice was stern as she hurried toward Marie, her high heels clicking against the floor.

"Of course." Marie stepped back, lowered her arm to her side. "I'm so sorry. It's beautiful. Who painted it?"

The woman frowned at Marie. "It's listed in the catalog, but not for sale tonight. It's part of a private collection. The owner is displaying it tonight to add some variety at Julian's request."

"Julian?"

"Bond. The gallery owner." The woman looked at Marie like she wasn't very impressed by her lack of knowledge. Still, she handed over a catalog. "There's more information in here if anything catches your interest."

"Thank you." Marie took another step back. "I'll just find my friend now." As she worked her way around the room to the back of the staircase, her mind spun. How could her painting be in Indianapolis?

She set her glass on a tray. Where was Thayer? She spotted him being manhandled by a large man who looked like some sort of security though it seemed like overkill. It wasn't like the gallery held seventy-million-dollar paintings in a community with a large crime problem.

Her dad had always told her to stay small and out of the way. That was the best way to not get hurt.

Well, her father had been wrong about a lot in her life.

She advanced on the large man and tapped him on the shoulder. "Thanks for finding my date. I lost him in the crowd." She ran her arm through Thayer's and smiled up at him. "Where did you go?"

He stared at her with a befuddled expression in his face as his long bangs flopped into his eyes.

She bumped into his side with a playful giggle. "I've missed you." She glanced around. "There are so many people here that I don't know." She gave a little wave to the big man. "Thanks again for finding him." Then she pivoted. "Let's get a drink." She waved her glass, letting the ice clink against the sides.

The man stumbled after her. "What are you doing?"

"Saving you."

"What?"

"That guy looks like the kind that hurts people." She gave a slight shudder.

"How would you know that?"

"Trust me, you don't want to know." There was something dangerous about the man's aura, but she didn't want to explain it. Marie pasted on a smile. "About that drink." Then she noted the man following them. "No, not a good idea. You should leave. You've caught his attention and I'm not sure why."

She led him to the front door. Leaned into give him a light kiss on the cheek. "Be careful."

"I'm not leaving without you." Thayer touched his cheek where she'd kissed him. It was the sweetest gesture, maybe more so because she could tell he didn't know he'd done it.

As Thayer walked her to her car, she tried to forget about her painting, but she couldn't. Something strange was happening. Her art should be buried in a villa in Tuscany, not hanging on the walls of a gallery halfway around the world. How had it gotten here? And why?

Thayer held the door for her just a moment longer than he needed to. "Thanks for coming with me tonight."

"You're welcome. I hope you got what you needed." Because all she got was questions. And they were the kind that could shatter the cautious, small world she'd created for herself and Drew.

She couldn't allow that to be destroyed.

Not now.

Chapter Three

FRIDAY MORNING, THE SOUND OF CONVERSATION PUSHED through the soundtracks playing through his earbuds as Thayer clicked from cell to cell of the million plus records in the spreadsheet checking for inconsistencies. The chase required precision and discipline, the pursuit of details that could get lost in millions of digits. He might not be Abby from *NCIS*, but he found his own way to track down criminals through his work as a consultant for the white-collar section of the Indianapolis office of the FBI.

He was supposed to be hard at work, but he could barely focus.

Last night kept spinning through his mind.

It had been a simple trip to an art gallery.

Nothing to it.

But then this morning, he thought he saw the same sedan multiple times on the drive to the FBI office. Maybe he'd imagined it like he'd imagined the sweet smell of Marie's lemon shampoo. She'd glowed like a ray of sunshine as she'd walked him out of the gallery, and then she'd slipped into an old VW bug and disappeared into the night, leaving him watching her like an abandoned puppy.

The night had been magical, even if it had ended faster than he'd hoped.

It had been close to a date. And it had been everything he'd imagined.

He'd wanted to race back to Hunter & Associates first thing that morning, so he had an excuse to see Marie, but instead, he'd kept to his preplanned schedule and headed to the Indianapolis FBI office to work with some of the data Johnson had for him to analyze.

Unlike the agents who spent their days and nights behind the desks in this building, he didn't aspire to take down criminals. Instead, with the strains of the Piano Guys colliding with Michael Jackson and Vivaldi filling his ears, he was an artist who painstakingly weeded through the data. Line by line. Entry by entry. Looking for the anomaly that others knew existed but couldn't quite identify.

All in pursuit of the data that revealed the action that led to the takedown.

Without him the action didn't happen.

But he got to stay in the background.

It was perfect.

It was also safe.

There. He'd admitted it. Doing the right thing safely mattered. But last night had been . . . interesting.

Was that what fieldwork was like? Maybe he should apply for the academy before he aged out.

Then he shook his head. What was he thinking? Nothing serious, that was for sure. He was an accountant. He made numbers tell a story when other people wanted to run screaming in the other direction. He'd see patterns and understand what those represented.

And it's what he needed to get back to because he was way out of his element last night. If Marie hadn't come along in her whirl of skirts and sunshine, he would have been pounded into the gallery's wood floor.

He wasn't trained to handle muscle and yet that man had clearly seen him as a threat.

Little did he know.

Thayer shook his head and forced himself to focus on the spreadsheet.

The numbers started to swim into alignment as a slow pattern formed. He stood and looked around for Johnson. A quick scan didn't show his friend's lanky frame hunched over his computer or walking the aisle, so

Thayer locked his computer. Now would be a good time for a mug of what passed for coffee in this office.

Thayer kept running with the numbers as he passed the bank of cubicles and outer offices for the break room. He found Johnson in front of the coffeemaker. It was one of those one-shot espresso makers, fancy enough to make a college-aged barista proud, while challenging enough to make the agent behind a multi-million-dollar methamphetamine drug bust look forlorn and lost as he considered the buttons on the gadget.

Thayer came alongside Johnson. "How exactly did you graduate with honors from Wabash?"

"The bigger question is how I made it through the academy." Johnson didn't budge.

"Clearly skated through on your looks."

Johnson snorted. "Clearly. Whatever happened to the simple coffeepots? The kind where you measure coffee grounds and water and voila! Coffee."

"They still exist."

"Just not here."

"Nope." Thayer grabbed a clean mug, set it on the tray, hit a couple buttons and a few seconds later handed his friend a fresh hit of caffeine. "Here you go. And I think I found something."

"Great. Show me when you know for sure."

"That's harsh."

Johnson inhaled the fresh aroma, his smile growing. "Not at all. We've got a meeting in ten to review the bust. I have to stay focused. By the time you know you have something, I can give you my full attention." He paused and considered Thayer. "Unless you're already there? I can connect you with someone else."

He had inklings. Suspicions. Enough to go on a field trip. Check some thoughts. But nothing concrete. Not yet. That would come, if his gut was right, and it usually was. "When you get back, I should be ready." And until then, he'd make himself a cup of coffee and go back and play with the numbers some more. All from the safety of his computer screen where nothing went wrong, and no one got hurt.

~

Usually, the rhythm of incoming calls could keep Marie engaged or at least keep her mind semi-occupied during the work hours. But the day after the gallery showing, her thoughts spiraled back to her painting hanging on the walls like a magnet attracted to its opposing pole.

What had it been doing there?

Maybe she needed to back up.

There could be a chance it wasn't one she had painted that year in Italy.

After all, the odds it had survived, let alone traveled across the ocean and made it to the same city she now called home, was infinitesimal.

Italy had been the culmination of her art education. She was supposed to return from Italy ready to launch her art career. She'd spent hours in the great museums, copying the works of the masters. She'd never imagined one of her reproductions would hang on the walls of a gallery. Those canvases were destined for the trash. She'd worked hard on them, perfected the styles of the artists she copied, but that didn't mean they were designed for display or sale.

She couldn't let that happen.

When her Italian boyfriend—she still couldn't bring herself to think his name—started asking her to forge the masters, she'd known she had to distance herself from him. He'd ignored her insistence that she could not agree to become part of the family business. All the riches in the world didn't make it okay to deceive buyers into believing they were buying a real master's art.

No, she needed to take a field trip over her lunch hour and return to the gallery.

Only then could she confirm whether the painting was hers or another person's copy.

She also didn't like that each time she heard steps, she looked up to see if those steps belonged to Thayer. She shouldn't care that he hadn't stopped by to say good morning, but she was bothered by his absence. Had he decided he didn't want to spend time with her after last night?

She'd thought their time together went well, but maybe she'd misread his interest.

The phone rang and she picked up the call. "Hunter & Associates."

Five calls later, she'd connected clients and prospective clients with the correct accountant, but she felt like her soul would shrivel and die. The boredom of sitting at the reception desk vibrated through Marie in a way she couldn't press aside.

She missed the days that dance moves swayed through her as she studied a canvas, the colors swirling through her in rhythm with the music. She would close her eyes as she imagined what color to place next. Then she started singing along about dancing making her happy, ad libbing lyrics about painting and dancing making her come alive.

The ding of the alert jerked her mid-memory.

She blinked once. Then again.

Why would she have an alert now?

She rotated her wrist and looked at the face of her watch, then her eyes widened as she read the reminder. Lunch time.

One thing hadn't changed. Where before she would throw brushes in a Mason jar with two inches of murky turpentine, then toss a cover over her palette of paints, now she hit a button on her computer and stood from her desk. Now, instead of tripping her way out of her studio over the drop clothes covering the cement floor, she gathered her purse and pulled her keys free. She had an hour to try to get to the gallery and back. But the thing that hadn't changed was the way she could forget simple things like taking a break to eat. The need to leave on a schedule to pick up her son from his after-school care in a timely fashion.

She loved that boy, but parts of her struggled with the dailyness of single mom life. She would have thought in seven years she would have found her rhythm, but saying she was an artist only carried so far.

She needed to go.

She spun in a tight circle searching for her keys and purse. Why couldn't she keep the simplest system in place?

~

Something tapped on his headphones, and Thayer startled. He blinked a couple times and glanced up. "Yes?"

Johnson stared at him. "Have you moved?"

Thayer rubbed his hands over his face and rolled his shoulders. "Just did. What's up?"

"Meeting is over, and I'm ready to hear what you have."

"Another ghost for you to trap."

The man raised an eyebrow. How did he do that? "Can you be more precise?"

"Steven Gershkovich. He's the president of that company you asked me to look into. RJ Imports. Specializes in items from the Silk Road and the *stan* countries."

"Like?"

"Uzbekistan. Kazakhstan. Azerbaijan. Wait. That one's not a *stan*, but you get the idea. Only there's not much of anything to import from there. I think it's a front."

"For what?"

"Your typical organized crime." He rubbed his eyes for real this time. "I'm not sure, but I think there's money laundering occurring. Still trying to figure out how."

Johnson rolled his eyes. "Well, I need you to take a break from this fascinating research and fill me in on what you learned last night."

"Where were you?"

"Got called in for backup for the bust." He pulled a chair around the corner. "So, what happened?"

"Not much. There was a guy there who kept me from getting closer to a couple men who were talking."

"What do you mean kept you away?"

"He physically stopped me and then was taking me out front. But Marie, my date, came and I'm not sure if she was worried or thought I needed help, but she got me out of the situation."

"How?"

"What's with all the questions?"

Johnson gave a quick one-shouldered shrug. "Just making sure I understand what's at stake."

"I don't know."

"Why were you following the men?"

That was the key question. Explaining there was something about them that bugged him didn't seem like a great way to articulate what had happened. He'd acted on instinct. Not something he should do as a consultant. He needed to remember his role. Stay in his lane.

199

"Never mind. It was crazy. Guess I wanted to pretend I was you. Silly, huh?"

"Not a word I would ever use to describe anything you do." Johnson studied him. "But you'll tell me if there's something more."

Sure. Because Thayer always did what was expected of him. Even when it didn't always make the most sense.

Johnson walked away, assuming Thayer would do as asked. And why wouldn't he? Thayer's mission in life was to do the right thing in all circumstances and help everyone else accomplish the same goal.

Thayer grabbed his laptop and keys. He needed fresh air and a change of scenery—something other than the walls of the cubicle. He'd head back to Hunter & Associates after a quick stop for coffee on the way.

By the time she reached the gallery, Marie had ten minutes before she had to turn around and return to work. She couldn't afford to be late. Was this nothing more than some crazy idea that she hadn't even invested enough time into to confirm the gallery was open before she made the drive?

So foolish.

She knew how to adult, but sometimes she was still the twenty-five-year-old who jetted off to Italy on a whim. She had gained Drew, but had lost her family and her career because she now had to stay hidden. To keep Drew safe. She'd even lost her name, changing it from her given name *Charlotte* that appeared on her birth certificate to her grandma's middle name, *Marie.*

How could she even think of reclaiming her life if she couldn't remember the basics?

Sitting in her car and staring at the door wouldn't tell her whether she'd created that Italian landscape in the gallery. If she had, she would know by the little tell she'd painted into most of her copies. It had been her little secret, the thing she hid to keep them from being used as forgeries when she realized how good she was at reproducing other artists. She'd wanted to create a reputation for her own work, not for mimicking others.

She opened the door and crossed the street. The gallery's interior looked dark with only a few lights on, but when she tried the door, it opened.

"Hello?" Her voice echoed against the wood floors and walls. She stepped further inside, letting the door close behind her as her eyes adjusted to the dusk. "Is anyone here?"

There had to be, because the art hanging on the walls had value, too much to leave the door unlocked and the art unattended.

She took a few more steps into the space, then headed back toward the area that housed the offices. Maybe whoever worked there just hadn't heard her.

Then she stopped.

This was her chance to see the painting without anyone interfering.

She redirected her steps toward the gallery.

Chapter Four

HER LOW HEELS SOUNDED AGAINST THE STAIRS AS SHE TRIED to slip up them.

Slip up, peek at the art, and leave. No one will know you were here.

Then she could reframe what she'd seen, get back to work, and forget about this foray into art.

It's what she needed to do.

Maybe then she could take Drew to meet his grandparents. It was past time for a visit home. Mom and Dad didn't understand why she hadn't come home. That she kept away to keep them safe.

She shook her head and tried to remember where she'd seen the painting in the gallery. There had been so many people and the chaos that came with a busy space.

Her Italian boyfriend was the one who had extended the dare to her. He'd made it sound like a challenge she wasn't capable of performing. He didn't believe she could copy one of Frencesco Guardi's paintings of Venice. If he'd asked her to reproduce one that included hundreds of people like the one of the Piazzetta San Marco with the Festival of Giovedi Grasso, she wouldn't have succeeded, but Emilio had made the mistake of leaving the selection to her. She'd chosen one of his many Venice paintings, but this one had swirls of blue sky and river, with a few people, but only a handful. Emilio hadn't believed she could paint a convincing copy, but when an art historian came to his family's villa and Emilio showed off the family's latest acquisition, the man hadn't questioned it.

Emilio had been thrilled. He'd celebrated her success, crowing that it took true skill to convincingly copy the great Italian masters.

He'd been right.

Time slipped away as she circled upstairs. The painting wasn't there.

She spun again.

Had she missed it? Imagined it?

No, it had been here. She was certain.

As she walked down the stairs, a tall man with the build of a linebacker stared at her from the bottom. She froze and swallowed. "Hello."

"What are you doing here?"

"I attended the opening last night and was back to look at a painting." She closed her mouth before she started babbling as she considered him. He looked familiar. More than just from the opening. "Have we met?"

He scrutinized her in a way that made her wish she could retract the question. "You should leave."

"You aren't good at selling paintings. The purpose of a show like last night's is to sell art. I'm back because of a piece I saw then. That should have you eager to show me around and sell me on the wonders of your collection."

"That's not my job." He didn't crack a smile but did crack his knuckles.

"I'll just take a quick peek around the first floor. I'm clearly not remembering where the painting was."

"Wait."

"It's fine. I don't need you to help. I'll find it." She started moving again. "The painting may have sold, and then I've lost my chance and made this trip back here for nothing." If that was the case, she'd have to evaluate her next steps. If it wasn't her painting, it was no loss, but if it was and it was in the same frame, then she needed to see if the small drive was still tucked inside it. And she'd want to discover how a painting that should have been forgotten or thrown away in Italy instead resurfaced in Indianapolis.

The towering man glowered at her and as she neared him, Marie had the uncomfortable sensation she did know him but couldn't think how. She knew she didn't want to stop to identify how.

He seemed a foot taller than her, and he clamped his hand on her arm as she stepped next to him on the steps. "You shouldn't be here. Julian will not like it."

"I'm not sure who Julian is, but if he owns the gallery, he'll love it if I decide I want to purchase the painting." She tugged her arm free and brushed past him. "It must be this way."

Time was ticking by, but she considered the door. Maybe it would be smarter to leave and forget the painting. After all, she'd done that for eight years.

~

Why was Marie back at the gallery?

Thayer hadn't intended to follow her, but she'd brushed past him as he'd arrived back at the office, her focus intense as she muttered about a painting and the gallery. When he'd greeted her, she hadn't heard. Instead, she'd had a singular focus on her errand. But why she needed to see a painting was a mystery.

Concern ricocheted through him—he didn't know why the FBI focused on the 42nd Street Gallery, but it had. However, he knew Marie wouldn't have returned there if he hadn't taken her the prior night.

Now she was rushing back into a situation that he didn't understand, so she couldn't fathom it either.

He trailed her to the garage and watched her climb into her classic VW bug. Then he'd followed her to the gallery, hoping she wouldn't think he stalked her. When she slipped inside the gallery, he wasn't sure if he should follow her. Should he wait? Go in? Either way she'd consider it odd he happened to be there.

There was no good way around it.

He'd have to explain he'd followed her for no reason other than he was curious about why she'd returned less than twenty-four hours after the show.

The best way to learn the answer was to go inside the gallery rather than wait in his car.

The lights were dim when he entered, and Marie stood on the stairs with the hulking man who hadn't liked his presence the night before. Seeing him almost had Thayer spinning around to leave, but maybe the man wouldn't remember him.

"Marie, did you find it?"

She startled and turned her attention to him. "Thayer?"

"Sorry it took me a few minutes to find a good parking space," he ad libbed as he turned to the man. "We're back to look at the art."

The man crossed his arms and frowned as he stared through Thayer. "I'll get Julian."

As soon as he moved away, Marie spun on him. "What are you doing here?"

"I'm ..."

"Following me." She crossed her arms.

"I was concerned."

"Why?" She tapped her foot in a sharp staccato.

"There are things going on here." He clamped his teeth together before he said something he really shouldn't.

She raised her eyebrows as she leaned toward him. "Like what?"

"I don't know."

"Don't know or can't say?"

"Maybe both."

"Then don't waste my time. And I don't need a CPA I can't trust for a bodyguard. This is an art gallery. I'm fine."

"Have you noticed that man you were talking to? He could play in the NFL."

"Maybe." She shrugged, then glanced at her watch. "I have two minutes to find a painting and then head back to work." She started to follow the large man. "The painting has to be this direction." Then she glanced at Thayer. "How did you know I was coming here?"

"You muttered to yourself as you passed me at work."

She frowned at him. "You weren't at work today."

"I'd just arrived." So she noticed when he wasn't there.

Marie seemed to read his thoughts. "I have to know how to direct your calls." Her mouth slumped down. "Even so why would you come here? Were you following me?"

He sputtered a moment. "I was concerned."

"Really? That's what you're going with? So you decided to join me?" She rolled her eyes. "I don't have time for this right now."

~

"Wait. There's a reason to be concerned."

"There always is." She sighed but kept moving. "I really have to leave in two minutes. First, I need to know if that painting is here."

"Why?"

"Just like you don't tell me what you do for the FBI, there are things I can't tell you."

He couldn't tell her that he and Johnson were convinced this Carmel art gallery was a front for money laundering of some sort. Set in a charming location, it seemed an unlikely space, but wasn't that the best cover? "Maybe we could talk more?"

There was an innocence yet experience to her that was compelling. Was it all an act, or did she see life through a unique lens?

She glanced at her watch again as if she was concerned about another meeting. "I have to get back to work."

"If now isn't a good time, we could arrange a different time. Maybe after work."

Her arms remained crossed her arms as she studied him. "I don't know what you're up to, Thayer, but you need to understand there is only one man in my life, and he is seven years old. He is my world, and that's not changing any time soon." She puffed out a breath. "I really have to get back or I'll lose my job. I'm going to look for that painting and then I'm leaving. Don't do any more of this." She waved a hand between them. "I don't know what this has been other than weird."

He wanted to cut through her resistance but got a sense that only would come with the truth. Maybe that would give her a willingness to talk and, more important, listen to what he wanted to share. No, what he *could* share. He wasn't cut out for cloak and dagger, not when he was wired for finding truth and exposing lies. It's what made him so good at audits, but wasn't working in this more clandestine role. Johnson had been crazy to send him here. And he'd been crazy to follow Marie back here today.

Marie shook her head and stomped off. Then she circled back, her shoulders slumped and defeat in her posture. "I can't find it, and that man won't leave me alone." She shuddered as her watch vibrated. Groaned as she tapped the face to make it stop. "Out of time. See you back at work."

Then she walked away without a backward glance. But when Thayer looked up, he spotted the linebacker of a man watching from the shadows. There was an intense focus to the way he watched Marie that caused Thayer to spin and follow her out if for no other reason than to block the man's view.

Something wasn't right in the way he focused on Marie.

When she walked through the door, Thayer turned and marched back to the hall where the man lurked. He'd disappeared, but Thayer continued, looking in each alcove he passed. The office door was open, and the man's deep voice rumbled from it. He slowed to listen, surprised they hadn't heard him.

"It's her." The voice held an accent he couldn't identify.

"How can you be sure?" This voice might belong to the gallery owner.

"She is unforgettable. I need to make a call." Steps came toward the door and Thayer took a couple steps forward making as much noise as possible. The large man burst through the door. "Why are you here again?"

Thayer puffed up his chest, hoping this didn't get him hurt. "Leave Marie alone. I don't know why you keep watching her, but she isn't someone to be ogled." He looked around the man to the owner. "You might want to find an employee who's better at selling the art you have here. She wanted to find a painting she saw last night, but he didn't take the time to help her." He nodded at them both, then spun on his heel, their gazes pressing against his back.

What had they meant?

MARIE FLEW INTO HUNTER & ASSOCIATES AND THEN HURRIED
to the reception desk. "Sorry I'm late."

Angelina, the secretary who filled in over lunch, shrugged. "It was
pretty quiet. See you in at three for your break."

A couple calls came in and Marie pulled up the office supply order,
but had barely started entering in people's requests when Thayer
hurried up.

"We need to talk." His gaze flitted around as if searching for trouble,
and he bounced on the balls of his feet.

"Why? You just saw me at the gallery."

"You left before I overheard a conversation."

"You were right behind me."

"I went back in because I didn't like how that man kept looking at
you. I informed him that he should respect women."

Her jaw dropped as she considered what could have happened to
Thayer if the other man didn't like the words. "He's twice your size."

"Doesn't mean he can say and do whatever he wants."

"It kind of does."

"That's not what matters." He took a deep breath as if fortifying himself. "Marie, he knows you. And he was going to tell someone he'd found you."

She collapsed against her chair. "Oh."

"That's it? How does he know you?" Thayer's brows lowered and a thundercloud covered his face. "That man is dangerous."

"I know." She held up her hands defensively in front of her. "Don't ask me how because I'm not sure. But it sounds like I need to figure it out."

The phone rang, providing a welcome escape from this conversation. What could she tell Thayer about her story—if anything?

Marie probably didn't notice the way her hands trembled as she hit the button to take the call, but Thayer did. She was far more rattled by the fact that man claimed to know her than he would have anticipated. What if she was somehow embroiled in the illegal mess brewing at the Gallery? If that was possible, then he had to determine how she factored into the financial mess there.

She patched the call through, and then seemed surprised to see him still standing in front of her desk. Or was it just an act?

"Look, we can't talk here. What if I can find someone to cover your desk for an hour? I'll tell Mr. Hunter that I need your help with a client."

"But you don't."

"Actually, I do."

That sentence caused her eyebrows to disappear into her bangs. "Really?"

"I think so. But the only way to find out for sure is to go someplace we can have a conversation."

She tilted her chin like she did when she focused on someone. "Okay."

He forced a grin. "It won't take longer than necessary."

Marie pushed some hair behind her ears. "If you can find someone around four, they can cover the last hour. That would be less disruptive than the middle of the afternoon."

"Done."

A few hours later, he was back at her desk with the assistant who supported him and a couple other CPAs, who seemed to welcome the change of pace. Marie gave her a quick primer then stood. "Thanks for the help."

"Glad to do it." Then the woman winked at Thayer. "Remember I want a venti tomorrow."

"Got it." He linked his hands behind his back as he walked to the door then held it open for Marie. "Where to?"

"I know just the place." When she reached the sidewalk, she didn't stop to see if he was behind her, but kept walking. Thayer hurried to catch up with her, and she jumped when he touched her shoulder. "There's a little coffee shop I like around the corner this way."

"Lead the way."

"I am."

"So you are." He'd thought the line might garner a laugh, but she was focused on getting this over and done with. "Can you tell me why that man knows you?"

"Maybe." Her steps slowed and she turned to study him. "Can I trust you? If my son's life was at stake, should I?"

Her words were heavy, and he didn't want to rush past them. Yet at the same time, he'd been raised to always do the right thing, even when no one was looking. "Yes. Absolutely."

Except, it didn't feel like he was being truly honest with her. Not when he didn't admit the real reason he'd been at the gallery. Maybe it made him a fraud in the ways that mattered. He needed to get back to his spreadsheets and computer—where he was competent and could ferret what was right and wrong. He was swimming in deep waters.

At last, the coffee shop came into view. Marie desperately wanted to relax, but there was something about Thayer Jackson right now that set her on edge. What did he mean that the man at the gallery knew her?

She was trying to pull him from the depths of her subconscious and couldn't. That was a terrifying reality, because that meant they could have interacted in Italy. If so, he was part of her past that she had fought so hard to forget and move beyond.

It had stayed buried for eight years.

Why was it now catching up to her?

What had changed?

She waited for him to hold the door open for her, then stepped into the cozy brightness of the Lemon Bar, a place Marie visited when she needed a reminder life could be bright and include a delicious slice of cake. Thayer would stand out in the eclectic, artistic vibe, which was fine with her.

"Ms. Montgomery." Anna at the front counter smiled when she saw Marie. "Are you celebrating another beautiful day?"

"I am." She turned to Thayer. "Isn't it nice to be known? To walk in somewhere and realize the people there really see you. You're more than a credit card or a tip." He had a quizzical look on his face, like he wasn't quite sure what to make of her. "Didn't you ever watch *Cheers*? It was a sitcom. One of the famous lines was that it was a bar where everybody knows your name."

"How old were you when it aired?"

She waved a hand in the air, not willing to tell him she was six when it stopped airing. "That's not important. Ever heard of streaming services? It's a nice idea and I've found it here." She scanned the cake display case, wishing she could make a meal of each delicious slice, Instead, she asked, "Which cake do you recommend today, Anna?"

"I'm partial to the lavender lemon, but you know that." She giggled. "If you want to be adventuresome, try the white chocolate raspberry with homemade chocolate ganache on top. I could eat the ganache by the spoonful. It's worth every extra step you have to add to your daily count."

Marie eyed the chocolatey delight in the case noting the plumpness of the raspberries dotting the top. Then she shook her head. "I'll take a cafe latte in your prettiest mug."

Thayer cocked his head. "Prettiest mug?"

"You could ask for the ugliest. I'm sure it gets lonely on the shelf because no one wants it." She reached for her credit card, but Thayer stopped her.

"I've got this."

"I'm not sure you should, since we work together."

"That didn't bother you last night."

"Last night had a Cinderella element, and you didn't buy anything. Right now, we're a couple blocks from work, and anyone could walk in and see us."

"Marie, this isn't a date. You'll know when it is."

Her breath hitched at his words. Would it be unkind to say she wanted to be something more than colleagues? That she wanted to know if he could see her that way? Instead, she jerked her chin down. "So, you're a gentleman who doesn't make the women around him wonder. You're making it hard for me not to like you."

"Good." He grinned at her and asked for a black coffee in the ugliest mug possible along with a slice of the lemon lavender cake and another of the white chocolate raspberry. After they settled at one of the bistro tables, she tried not to laugh while he frowned at her. "What?"

"You look slightly ridiculous poised on the edge of that chair."

"What can I say?" He waggled his eyebrows. "I'm too much for this place."

She nodded. "You might very well be." After blowing across the top of her Bubble of Happiness mug, she checked her watch again. "All right, Mr. Thayer, you have my full attention for thirty minutes. What do you need to ask me?"

Could the man skirt around that kind of directness?

There was a reason he'd insisted on having coffee with her, and it had nothing to do with spending time with her. The fact he was on some kind of a mission was written all over his face. Did he know he was that transparent? It was an interesting question, and one she thought she could answer.

He glanced around the half empty space.

"Despite what I said a moment ago, I don't know anyone here." She settled back then decided to take a taste of each piece of cake. "Can you tell me more about what you overheard?"

"Just that the security guy was telling the owner that he knew you and had to tell someone he'd found you."

Marie's blood chilled. "Security?"

"Isn't that what you'd call him? He's lurking in the shadows and bounced us from the building."

"I guess." Her mind started racing through a photo collage of people from Italy, one that she'd repressed for years. Could it be? *No.* Not when she feared the harm he could do. "Rahul."

"Who?"

"If he's who I'm remembering, then that's his name." She felt herself sway and then Thayer's cool hand pressed on top of hers, anchoring her in place. He might not be able to stop Rahul if the man barged into the restaurant, but Thayer was here.

She wasn't alone.

"What do you need? Some water?"

"I'll be okay." She blinked and noted the concern etched in the lines on his face. "Sorry."

"I have friends who can help."

"At the FBI?"

He blinked. Nodded.

"Your friend calls a few times a month. It didn't take much time to figure out the number he left was a government one."

"So who is this Rahul?"

"He worked for a man I dated in Italy."

"Italy?" Thayer sat taller and his hand slipped from hers. She wanted to reach for him and hold on but resisted. "How long were you there?"

"Several years."

"Wow. There has to be a story."

"It's nothing special. Typical story of someone who thinks they excel at art and can transform their talent into a livelihood. So I went to Italy to study after college."

"I'm a numbers guy, so there's nothing typical about it." He leaned closer and took a forkful of the lemon cake. "But you're a receptionist, not an artist."

One simple sentence to tell her anything but simple story.

"I got my bachelor's in art and, about the time I was convinced it had killed any creativity in me, I got an internship at an art gallery in Rome. I hated the work that summer, but I fell in love with the country, so much so, I stayed. I took art classes when I could afford them, travelled, painted every free moment. Visited every museum I could find. Studied the art in those museums. It was wonderful."

"How did you come back here?"

"The money ran out the first time." She smiled at the reminder of the first time she came home. "My dad was convinced I'd finally learned my lesson and would settle into something 'worthwhile'." She put little air quotes around the words. "But I worked hard waiting tables, and the moment I had enough, I was back. Italy gets in your blood, you know?"

"I don't. I've been a homebody most of my life."

The way he said it so matter-of-factly made her sad for him. "Then you need to create a list of places and experiences your soul longs for. There's something special and expanding about seeing corners of the world that are different from ours. I expand when I'm in Italy. And something new fills me. Maybe its perspective or experience. But it's amazing." She sighed and took another sip of her latte to slow her thoughts. "I used to love travel."

"It's contagious."

"In a good way." She smiled. "I stayed in Italy for five years that time."

"What brought you home?"

She hesitated. This was a part of her life that people either glossed over or judged. There was no in between. "I became pregnant and came home."

Thayer studied her a moment. "You've mentioned your son before, but not his father. Is he here?"

"Italy." She gave a small smile. "But Drew and I have a good life."

"But no art?"

"None."

He let her word linger as if waiting for her to fill in the reason why, but she didn't. She couldn't.

"I can help."

"If I say too much, he'll show up." She swallowed against the fear that wanted to bubble up in her throat and overwhelm her. "Drew's father was my biggest mistake, but Drew is a gift."

"And this Rahul has something to do with Drew's father?"

"Maybe."

"That scares you."

"Terrifies me."

"Why?"

"Because when I left, I took something from him that I thought would be my insurance policy—but . . . but it might have only insured he'd never stop looking for me." She clenched and unclenched her hands, trying to get blood flowing back to her fingers.

"My friends can help."

"Keep me safe from an Italian crime family?" She exhaled a sharp breath. "I'm sure that won't be a problem."

Chapter Six

How could Marie Montgomery be involved with an Italian crime family?

It didn't make sense.

In fact, the conversation seemed to have acquired a life of its own. Thayer needed to call Johnson and get some direction because right now he felt like a sailboat on a lake being buffeted by a strong wind without a skilled captain to steer a smooth course. "We need to determine who this Rahul is and if he has ties to Italy."

"Not me. You or your friends. I have to keep Drew safe. I'll do whatever that takes."

"Whatever?"

"Yes." She met his gaze with a steely determination that had him looking away and up into a frilly green and pink light fixture of some sort. He was not this restaurant's target market.

"What can you tell me about him?"

"Nothing, really. All I remember right now is his first name. Rahul. It's been eight years, and I've intentionally tried to forget as much of that last year as I could."

He frowned as he considered her words. "Why only the last year?"

"Because it wasn't all bad. Parts were magical. It was Italy." She met his gaze, but he could sense her reluctance, like she expected judgment. "Have you ever been?"

"No. It's on my bucket list though."

"Move it to the top of your list. It's wonderful, and I'll never return."

"Why?" Then he thought about what she had said. "Your ex?"

"Yes."

"Is he why you gave up art?"

"In part, though maybe that will change." A softness stole over her features. He sensed it was a deep desire of hers to return to her art, yet it was chased by some dark fear.

"Maybe you could copy a painting. I could make it worth your while. Say ten, fifteen thousand dollars."

She blinked at him as the words reverberated in the space between them.

"Maybe twenty thousand?" He felt heat crawl up his neck. "Sorry. Don't know where that came from. Forget I said anything."

The directness in her gaze and words left him little wiggle room. Anyone would have introduced the topic better than he had. Anyone. His approach was awkward, but he needed to get to the crux of why they were in the middle of this ridiculous dance. See how she took the bait. If he was right, if her art was being used as part of a money laundering scheme, then she either knew or was an unwitting pawn.

Based on their few interactions, he had a hope, but hope wasn't enough. How she responded would give them actionable data. And that's what he needed. No, that's what the FBI needed. He didn't need anything other than to get back to his comfortable computers.

"I'm not sure I heard you right." She blinked a few more times, eyes wide and mouth in a bit of an O. "You want me to copy something?"

He needed to back pedal fast. "For my home. I'd like to build a personal collection, but don't make enough for the real pieces. Who does, really?"

"Paul Allen."

He blinked. "Who?"

"You asked who made enough." She waved a hand through the air as if it was nothing. "The Microsoft co-founder. His art collection sold for *a lot* after he died. Think of some zeroes. Add a few more. A lot."

Did she understand how adorable she was when she thought like that? He could sit here all day listening to her, but instead he took a bite of cake and forced himself back to the script. "Well, I don't have that many zeroes in my account, so as you talked about your art training, I had the crazy idea I could hire you to copy a few paintings for me." He shook his head. "Forget about it, I'll go online and get some cheap prints."

She still looked skeptical. "Why would you think I would do that?"

"I could go online and purchase one or . . ." He gestured toward her with his fork. "It was a silly idea."

"You don't know me."

"We work together." He leaned forward, carefully to put his elbows on either side of the cake plate. "I also guess you don't tell everyone your story."

"Just those who ask."

"Not too many, right?"

She looked away and he knew he'd nailed it. Then she glanced at her watch, a gesture he'd seen her do repeatedly.

"Everything all right? You keep looking at your watch."

"This?" She held up her wrist as if to show him her smart watch. "I get easily distracted, so I've set lots of timers to help me stay on task and avoid going so far down a rabbit hole that I forget to come back. Well, come back in time to get Drew."

"Your son?"

She smiled slowly, but there was a cautious edge to it, like she didn't want to give him too much information. Didn't she realize she'd already shared incredibly personal information with him?

She was easy to read in so many ways, displaying her emotions for others to see if they cared to take the time.

He did. More than he should. "So will you paint for me?"

"I'm not an artist, not anymore. I can't be and keep Drew safe."

"What if we could give that back to you?"

She turned back to him and there was such longing in her gaze, it hurt to see. "You can't."

"But what if we could?"

"If Rahul is here and if he's who I think he is, then Drew and I probably aren't safe anymore. I'll need to change that."

"What if you didn't need to hide?" The words slipped out, but based on her gasp, he'd hit a nerve.

"What do you mean?"

"What if you could be fully the person God created? What if?" He stopped as tears filled her eyes.

Marie blinked rapidly and then stood and hiked her purse on her shoulder. "I have to go."

Marie froze as her gaze traveled to a table in the corner, and the man she recognized. She sank back down. "What is going on?"

"What do you mean?"

"The man from the gallery is over there. He'd better not have followed us because he can't know where I live or work." But what other explanation could there be? She wanted to groan as her alarm went off again. "I have to go, or I'll be late collecting Drew and then I'll be fined. Again. Did you know daycare will charge you extra for each minute you're late? I understand why, but it gets expensive."

She returned to her feet. "Thank you for the coffee, but do not let that man follow me. I don't care what you do, but use some of that FBI hocus pocus to distract him while I leave." She leaned into the table. "I have a son. Remember that tidbit. That man over there," She pointed to Rahul, "makes me nervous. I've learned to listen to my instincts, and I won't ignore them now. That means I'm not playing whatever this is." She gestured between them. "Protecting Drew has no price tag. Goodbye."

Then Marie stiffened her spine and decided to try the direct approach and set the man back a bit. She had little to lose as she plopped into the chair across from him. "I don't know who you are, but if you follow me, I'm calling the police. See that man over there?" She pointed at Thayer. "His best friend is an FBI agent, and I will take advantage of that. Leave. Me. Alone."

"You have no idea, do you?" The man looked so smug. Why did men act like that around her?

"Stay away from me."

"Even if I stay away from you, you have a son."

The hair on her arms stood, and she knew his words were no idle threat. She couldn't show weakness, not in front of him, but she wanted to melt into a puddle right there on the floor of the Lemon Bar. Instead, she straightened her spine and tried to pretend she was as powerful as Wonder Woman. Instead, she felt like Barbara Ann Minerva before she became Cheetah, but she had to pretend no one could push her around. "Do not mess with my son."

The man scoffed. "What could you do if I did anything?" He settled back and somehow that was more terrifying than if he'd risen to his towering height.

As he crossed his arms, she noted a small tattoo on the inside of his wrist. Everything inside her froze.

He seemed to misinterpret her silence as some kind of strength. "Be careful what you do. It will haunt you."

She refused to look away from his arrogant gaze for a minute, though it took all of her will power. It was that or bolt, and that would only give him more control. She had to be strong. Just a little longer. But she also had to leave, as soon as she could, before he realized she knew.

Seconds later, she strode from the Lemon Bar trying to ignore the stares boring into her back.

Trying to walk, when she longed to run as if her very life depended on it.

Because it just might.

She listened hard for footsteps behind her. Nothing. As soon as she was outside, she picked up her phone and pretended she was on a call. She needed a best friend, someone who would know if she disappeared. Instead, isolation wrapped around her like a heavy cloak.

As she hurried down the block her thoughts spiraled. She needed to see Drew, make sure he was safe. Then she could figure out what to do next.

Thayer and his words had struck a nerve. Sharp. Electric.

Was it even possible to step back into her identity?

To reclaim her family?

To be the person God had created her to be?

Walking away from her art had been penance for allowing Emilio to seduce her away from what she knew was right and wrong. She would never regret Drew, but guilt laced her choices for entwining her life with a man who had evil embedded into the fiber of his being. If she could undo that, she would.

Art couldn't be part of her life. It didn't matter how much she longed to walk away from being a receptionist and back to who she'd been created to be, if her past was in Indianapolis, she couldn't risk embracing her passion.

Why had she confronted Rahul?

Should she take the risk of slipping back into the gallery and trying to locate her painting again?

Or did she need to pack up and flee as fast as she could? Take Drew and disappear?

So many questions.

Rahul acted like he recognized her, but right now he wouldn't know her new name or anything else about her. All he had was her appearance at the gallery and that wasn't enough to locate her. He'd need a name or place she worked to truly find her. More than a million and a half people lived in the Indianapolis metropolitan area, which was why it had always felt large enough to safely disappear.

Had that changed with Rahul's appearance?

She didn't think so, but she needed to be smart and make a plan for a quick exit.

As far as she knew Emilio had no idea yet that he had a child and she intended to keep him in the dark. But that could change quickly. She had to act as if Rahul would tell Emilio Rahul had found her. And that she had a child, but how he knew that baffled her.

Her sweet son would not be raised to be the heir of an Italian crime family.

As she continued walking, she tried to stay aware of her surroundings.

When she'd first returned to the States from Italy, she'd been scared of everything, convinced that Emilio or one of his people would find her and drag her back to Italy. That hadn't happened, but part of her had never stopped watching.

Now Marie wanted to return to her apartment and hide, but not just from Emilio. No, Thayer saw her—and that reality terrified her. She didn't let people see the real her. Every time she had, that person let her know she wasn't living up to their expectations. She hadn't conformed. She didn't fit the proper mold. Not that she wanted to, but it meant she constantly heard she was the wrong fit. But Thayer didn't say that. Instead, he seemed to lean into her uniqueness and embrace it.

She didn't want to run from it.

In fact, she wanted to run to it. Which meant she should run away.

As fast as she could, because this wasn't good.

It wouldn't end well.

He would betray her whether he knew it or not. But she knew it. Because it always happened.

Chapter Seven

THE TREMBLING STARTED AS SOON AS SHE SANK INTO THE front seat of her car. Marie's hands and arms shook so much she couldn't fasten her seatbelt. Somehow, she had to pull it together and go get Drew, but she couldn't drive like this, and she also couldn't show up hysterical at Drew's school. And there was no way she could go anywhere with Rahul on her tail or whatever they called it in the movies. She had to keep her son safe.

Images of her Italian boyfriend and his family flooded her mind.

She had always made it sound like she left Italy willingly.

That wasn't true.

She had fled to protect her unborn child.

Emilio had suspected she was pregnant, and while she hadn't necessarily expected handsprings, she hadn't anticipated coldness. Then her fears had been confirmed when she learned a couple days later, he'd killed a man, solidifying the whispered worries in her mind that she'd tried so hard to ignore. She couldn't stay, so she'd disappeared in the middle of the night. Just leaving Florence wasn't safe enough. Not when she knew her boyfriend's family could have people watching her and be poised to grab or harm her. She'd only started breathing when her plane had taken off from Rome's Fiumicino Leonardo da Vinci Airport.

All the money in the world wasn't worth the tradeoff of greed and destroying others. Yet, that was what she expected over time. There was no path up, only an ever tighter spiral down.

So she'd disappeared, even from her family, desperate to keep them safe too. The only way she'd known to do that was to empty her accounts, change her hair and name, and never go home.

It had worked.

For eight years, her plan had worked.

Now Rahul was here with his tattoo that matched that of the bodyguards employed by Emilio's family.

Had they come looking for her after eight years of relative peace?

Why now?

She prayed for peace and wisdom as she scrambled to strap in. She had to get to Drew. She needed to know he was okay as images of someone showing up to take him filled her mind. It was moments like this that made her wish she could call her mom.

Isolation crowded in.

Someone knocked on her window, and she screamed.

She scrambled for her purse looking for anything she could use to defend herself. The knock came again, and she whimpered as she grabbed her phone and held it up with the SOS button pulled up as she turned. "Stay away."

Thayer?

≈

Marie looked scared out of her mind.

It seemed like a good idea to follow her, make sure she got back to her car. She'd turned so pale, looking like she'd pass out before she made it back to her VW. Then she'd sat in the car for so long, he needed to know she was okay. Maybe it wasn't any of his business. Yeah, it wasn't, but she looked so alone, he couldn't walk away.

He'd knocked and she'd screamed—a sound he'd hear that in his dreams for a long time.

He hadn't thought she could get paler, but when she met his gaze, her skin was practically translucent and her eyes sparked. She threw open the door, and it hit him in the midsection with a *whomp*! His breath pushed from his body and made it an effort to stand.

"What were you thinking? I could have died of fright!"

"Most people don't jump out of their skin at a simple knock."

"There's nothing simple about my life right now." She shoved a finger in his chest. "What are you doing here?"

"I need to get my car too."

She stared at him, mouth opening and closing, before she reached some decision. "Fine. I have to get Drew." She climbed back in her car, cranked the engine and took off, but not before he noticed the way she shook. She was coming off some serious adrenaline high.

There was more going on than a simple receptionist who used to dream of being an artist. Thayer considered going inside to work for a couple hours, but he sensed she was spooked by that man. Maybe Johnson could find out who he was. Then Thayer could use that information to help Marie.

Could he tell her the truth about why he was focused on the 42nd Street Art Gallery?

He knew what Johnson would say.

No way.

But Thayer wanted to.

There was something about that man that had stopped her mid-thought. She'd frozen like a rabbit that had a fox hot on its trail.

The golden question that he couldn't answer was *why*?

He wanted to help Marie, but he needed to get back to his spread-sheets. They at least made sense and didn't jump out of their skin when they interacted with him.

Marie drove in circles for a few minutes, not sure if she'd detect someone following her, then pulled into a parking lot and stared at her phone. After eight years protecting her family, she had to ask for help. Could she do this? She didn't even know if the number still worked.

No, that wasn't true. She'd called it once a year on Sundays when her parents would be at church. It was her way to confirm they still lived where she had grown up. Then she could picture them even if she couldn't visit. It had been enough because it had to be, but now she needed someone who could come get Drew on a moment's notice. It wasn't fair to her parents, who she'd intentionally kept the in the dark about his existence to keep them safe if Emilio had come looking for her.

If she called now was she putting them in danger? Possibly.

For that reason alone, maybe she needed to delay calling them a little longer. This could all blow over and then she would have risked their safety for no reason.

Or she could have reconnected with her parents and taken a chance on introducing them to their grandson. Drew's life would be richer for knowing her parents. She knew that in her heart.

Could she handle this alone?

Not if Emilio showed up.

She had to know that Drew was far away, and since her parents had never made the trip across the ocean, he had to be safe with them while she found a way to use the flash drive to buy her freedom.

How could she frame this conversation in a way that didn't kill her parents with shock?

Father, guide my words. Please let this be the right decision and not lead to harm. I don't know what else to do.

Before she could over-think her response, she clicked the number she'd never deleted from her contacts.

The phone rang so many times she almost hung up. She couldn't leave a message, but then a voice she knew—one she'd missed for eight long years—answered. "Hello?"

"Mom?"

There was a long pause. "Who is this?" Wariness touched with hope.

"Mom, this is . . ." And she said the name she hadn't uttered in eight years. "Charlotte."

There was a shriek, then an audible sigh, as if her mom gathered herself. "Charlotte?"

"Yes."

The call ended with an abrupt click. Marie shuddered as she noticed wetness on her cheeks. She deserved that. She'd abandoned her family and they couldn't understand why. All they knew is she'd walked away for seemingly no reason. Maybe someday she could explain the whys, but even then, it would be hard to accept. She pushed from her car, tears coursing down her cheeks. She needed a minute to collect herself before she finished her drive to get Drew or she'd scare him. He wouldn't understand the raw emotion simmering through her.

Her phone rang, and she glanced at it not sure she could handle anything right now.

She froze as the familiar number flashed.

Then she slid her finger across the screen. "Hello?"

"Charlotte, is it really you?"

"Yes."

"I want to reach through this thing and hug you and throttle you."

Marie smiled. That was her mom. "I know."

"Have you talked to Carter? We have to tell Carter!"

Marie's breath caught and her vision tunneled. "Not yet, Mom. Can we take it slow?"

"All right. Where are you?"

"Indianapolis."

There was a pause. "Why there?"

"It's a long story and someday I promise I'll tell you all of it. But right now I need to ask you for help, even though I know I don't deserve that."

"Do you need money?"

Marie laughed as she cried. "I wish it was that easy."

"Are you in jail?"

"No. Again, that would actually be potentially easier than this." She closed her eyes and rubbed her forehead. There was going to be no easy way to say this. "I have a son, and I don't think we're safe right now. Can you come get him?" Silence. Nothing more for several long, excruciating seconds. "I wouldn't ask, but we're so alone."

"By choice." The words were said softly but were harsh in their honesty.

"Yes." Marie didn't have time to explain or the energy to try to give all the reasons behind her disappearance, not in this moment. "Someday I want to tell you the whole story. For now all I can say is I had a good reason, but I know it hurt you and for that I am sorry. I had to flee dangerous people and I didn't want to put you in harm's way."

Her mother gasped. "You thought that could happen?"

"Yes."

"Charlotte. Are you okay now?"

"At the moment, but I don't know if that will change." She took a deep breath, but there was no easy way to do this. "Are you sitting down?"

"Ye-es." The word was elongated and drawn out.

"Mom, you have a grandson. He's wonderful and delightful. I know you'll love him, and he will be so glad to meet you." Marie took a breath since she was babbling.

"I have a grandson." Her mother's voice held a touch of awe.

"You do. His name is Andrew, but I call him Drew."

"When can we see him?"

"I was hoping he could come stay with you for a few weeks."

In the pause, Marie could almost hear her mom blinking. "I'm sorry, but why?"

"He'll be safer far from here."

"How old is he? I can't believe I don't know how old my own grandson is."

"He's seven."

"Then he's in school."

"He's in second grade. Missing a few days at the very end of the school year won't derail his educational future." But staying here might do much worse than that.

"True, but this feels very sudden. He hasn't even met us. Won't it be upsetting to him?"

"Someone from my time in Italy may be back, and I need to know Drew's safe while I try to figure out what's going on."

"I know you well enough to know there's more to this story." A note of skepticism remained in Mom's voice. "Like you said, you'll need to tell me some time, and I need to check with your dad. If we start driving tonight, we can get to Indianapolis by tomorrow night or the next day. Is that soon enough?"

"Yes."

"Charlotte?"

"Yes?" It was so strange to hear her name on her mother's lips after so many years.

"Are you sure you're okay?"

"We will be."

"Okay, we will call from the road to get your address."

"I'll text it to you." And Marie hung up before her mother could drag the story from her. The one she had kept buried for eight years. Maybe longer depending on where the first page of the story started. Was it when Emilio swept her off her feet? Was it when she realized she loved him and made the terrible choice that led to her pregnancy that became a wonderful choice because it gave her Drew? Was it the moment she realized she would be tying her life to a branch of organized crime?

There were so many moments.

Or did it start when she slipped into Emilio's office and tried to copy his computer onto a flash drive? Instead she'd seen enough to know there was so much more happening than she'd ever understand and she had to flee. Then she'd overheard the conversation where Emilio ordered the killing of a man and she'd fled. She'd used the flash drive to capture everything she knew.

It was her insurance, flimsy as it was.

But that one small tattoo.

It was enough to warn her that a tiny flash drive wouldn't save her if Emilio's family decided to come after her. No, she needed help way above her brain power.

Maybe the TV shows were right, and she could trust the FBI to help her.

But first, she'd get Drew, prep him for his adventure, and then research.

She pulled into the after-school care pick up line. When Drew was strapped into his booster, she took a deep breath.

Everything would be all right.

Now to sell Drew on his adventure.

She pulled into traffic and then headed to his favorite ice cream shop. After they each had an ice cream cone and were seated at a picnic bench, she ruffled his hair. "I've got exciting news for you, buddy."

He took another lick of his ice cream, seemingly unconcerned.

"Don't you want to know what it is?"

"I'm eating ice cream. It's serious." He frowned at her then took another lick, eyes sparkling with fun.

"Ice cream always is." She grinned at him, then sobered. "Know how you've always wanted grandparents like the other kids have?"

His eyes widened and he stopped mid-lick before nodding.

"Well, my parents, your grandma and grandpa are coming for a visit. You might get to go to their house for an adventure too."

That got his attention. "What's an adventure?"

"It just means somewhere but here."

He frowned at her. "But I like it here."

"And I like it when you're here, but this will be a special chance to spend time with your grandparents."

"Why do they want to see me now? They've never come before." His lower lip puckered in a pout, and she hated the pain she saw there.

"It isn't their fault, Drew. They didn't know about you and now that they do, they are hurrying to come meet you. They're excited." At least she hoped her dad would be.

He licked his cone in silence a minute, then blinked a few times "Okay."

"Do you have any questions for me?"

"Not until I meet them. Then I'll have a lot." He looked from her to the picnic table. "What if they don't like me?"

"They'll love you, bud." They had to, but she couldn't let him see her fear. "How was school?"

"Fine. We went to the library after school. A man with a spider on his hand came up to me. You wouldn't have liked it because it was big." He made a motion like the spider had been two feet wide.

Marie swallowed a gasp, but it wasn't because of the idea of a spider that large. Drew's father had worn a tattoo like that. And so did Rahul though his was smaller. Did that mean either was that close to her son? If so, she had to get Drew out of town immediately. "Did he say anything to you?"

"No. But I said I liked the spider."

"Oh, Drew. I'm glad you'll be with Grandma and Grandpa and not have to fight a big, bad spider." She needed him safe while she figured out why Rahul was everywhere. At the thought she scanned the parking lot, though she had no idea who she was looking for other than him.

"Do I get to come home?"

"Of course." She slid around the picnic table to his side. "You'll have a fun adventure. And then when you're all out of fun, you'll come back."

"But I think you're fun."

She couldn't fight the giggle that wanted to erupt at his earnest expression. "I love you too. But this will be fun." She licked her dripping ice cream before she could say fun fifteen more times. What was wrong with her?

"I'll go if that's what makes you happy."

"It doesn't really make me happy because I won't be with you." She kissed his nose, noticing the sweetness of the ice cream speckling his face. "But before you know it, you'll be back home."

"I just need to pack Mr. Bunny."

"Of course. You could take a couple stuffed animals if you want."

The rest of their time at the ice cream shop, he babbled about all the things he would pack. It pained her to think of him leaving, but she knew with him safe she could focus on determining what was going on.

Because something was and she would figure it out, because she wasn't bringing Drew home until it was safe.

That night after Drew was in bed, Marie went into the closet in her small room. In the back buried under hanging coats stood an oversized suitcase where she stored off season clothing. She tugged it free and pulled it into her room, where she set it on the floor and unzipped it. She ran her fingers along the inside lining and then tugged the flash drive free from the tape securing it to the hard shell.

She stood and moved to the bed where her laptop waited and inserted the drive.

Nothing happened.

She frowned and ran her thumb on the mousepad. Nothing.

She flipped over to the search function and clicked on a few folders until she finally found the drive. This was why she should live in the world of art and not pretend she could do anything else.

Opening the file she made herself read the notes.

She had loved Emilio. Believed forever was possible for them. In the process she had ignored the signs that she hadn't wanted to believe.

She'd had her art and Emilio and life had been beautiful perfection.

Then she fled.

And she rebuilt a life that was good.

Now Rahul and possibly Emilio were back, and she needed the reminder of why she had to stand firm.

Chapter Eight

THE HEADPHONES DIDN'T DROWN OUT THE MONDAY MORNING activity all around as Thayer tried to focus on the spreadsheets open on the monitors in front of him. If he could take the data anywhere else, he had a better chance of concentrating, but here everyone watched him as if he was a fraud.

No, the FBI had invited him to consult, and he needed to remember that.

He might not have passed the interview as a college senior, but he'd found an alternate route to make a difference in the battle between right versus wrong. What he did mattered, because digging through all this data wasn't easy. It took focus and determination. A kind of determination he had in abundance.

The challenge was finding the right thread.

This particular data set was being coy.

There were so many records, he struggled to dig deep enough to find the right source.

He'd get started tracking one account and then after spooling through rivers of transactions, he'd find that everything was exactly as it should be. Then he'd backtrack and conduct more queries. A few more and he might find the right current to follow related to the 42nd Street Art Gallery.

Numbers told a story—they didn't lie. Sometimes it took some exhaustive investigation, but the story existed.

Johnson leaned over the partition surrounding the desk Thayer used when at the office. "Got anything?"

"Have I ever hidden anything from you?"

"Not that I know of, but if it's hidden, would I know?" The man's tie hung askew, and he looked like he'd had about three hours of sleep.

"You okay?"

"Hanging in there. The paperwork is enough to kill me." He rubbed his hands over his head, and his normally carefully brushed hair stood in all directions. "I'll be okay. Just need to get a good night's sleep for about a year."

Thayer laughed. "If you figure out how to do that, let me know."

"Sure." He came around dragging a chair with him. "Seriously though, do you have anything?"

"Not yet. What I have is a bunch of research into where the crime isn't happening." Pressure built in his chest as columns of numbers mocked him. "There's real business embedded throughout the data. It's a great cover, or the laundering is happening on a small scale on the side. Either is possible, but it's not easy to pare down to the truth."

"What do you need from me?"

"Just time to keep working through this."

"I can give you some. We're hearing rumbles that something is brewing."

"Anything clear?"

"Nope. That's why I'm hoping you can find something that will give us a lead or two to chase."

"Any direction you can give me?"

"Other than we're almost certain some laundering is happening through the art gallery? No." He leaned back in the chair, and it teetered on the back legs. "The art crime unit called with the query, but they didn't have much to give us either."

"I'll keep digging, but I have to tell you, Marie Montgomery . . ."

"Who?"

"The receptionist from work. Anyway, she recognized one of the men at the gallery. I'll call him the muscle man."

"Who is he?"

"Rahul."

Johnson waited then frowned. "That's it."

"Except that he's got ties to an Italian crime family."

"And how does she know this?"

"The son is the father of her child."

Johnson sat back. "Huh."

"Yeah." Thayer sighed. "She was an artist and spent five years in Italy and somehow got embroiled with the son."

"Who?"

"I don't know."

"We might need to know."

"Understood." But it didn't mean he wanted to know the details. "She's afraid of them. Walked away from art to escape."

"Did she bite on painting for you?"

"Not really. It kind of slipped out and then I tried to cover it up." He didn't need to tell Johnson how awkward he'd been.

Johnson shook his head, a small smile on his face. "What if I told her we need her help?"

"I suppose you could try."

"Let's do that." Johnson glanced at his watch. "Then we can create a story for the gallery owner. . ."

"Julian Bond."

"Yeah, him. . . where you're selling a painting that you uncovered in your grandparents' home, and you grossly undervalue it. We can see if he takes the bait on a painting he can launder while you continue to dig. Your cover can be that you were at the show to gauge whether to approach him. You're not part of that world, which accounts for some of the awkwardness of the interactions."

"We don't know if she can paint."

"She has to be good or one of her paintings wouldn't be in the gallery."

Thayer shook his head. "You haven't been through there lately then. It's a random collection of some really interesting pieces. If we could find her painting, that might be enough to earn her help." He ran a hand along the back of his neck. "She seems really concerned about finding that painting, but I'm not sure why."

"Maybe she just wants it back because she created it."

"Maybe." But there was something more. He just couldn't put his finger on what.

"Ask her to come in and meet with us." Johnson yawned and then rubbed a hand over his face. "Let's see what she's willing to do."

"Okay. If you'd seen the way she turned all mama bear when talking about her son, you'd understand what I mean. You don't mess with a mom who's the only provider for her son." Even one who struck him as free spirited and independent. She probably had to be, and that made him admire her. Did she have anyone she could rely on?

"Something is brewing." Johnson yawned again.

"You need to get some sleep, man."

"Yeah. But first I have some other things to finish." Johnson started moving. "Keep me posted."

"Always." And he would, but first he'd make sure Marie stayed safe.

He might not be able to do anything about the FBI's concerns, but he could stay close to her. Something was going on, and until he knew what it was, he could do his best to keep her safe.

Maybe he didn't know how, but if he stayed near, he could at least try.

And that was better than knowing she could be in trouble and not doing anything.

Marie couldn't sleep and so found herself at the kitchen table, missing the days she had a studio and could throw open the windows bright and early, letting the cool morning air in as she contemplated her latest passion project on the easel. If she couldn't get her mind to quiet down any other way, she could always do it by submersing herself in her craft.

She longed for those days. Without that escape, somedays she struggled to overcome her fears and the oppressing unknowns.

She'd start a list.

Make sure Drew had everything he'd need while he was with her parents.

That thought sent her mind spiraling again. What would the reunion be like? Would her parents welcome her? Would they understand? How could they? She had disappeared without a word, and she still couldn't explain why. Not if she wanted to keep them safe.

She'd been naïve to think disappearing would provide safety—for her, for Drew, for her parents. She'd altered her name and her appearance to protect her family case Emilio suspected more about her disappearance than she thought.

She'd hoped he'd believe she got bored.

Just one more American who didn't know what she wanted.

But she'd always be afraid he'd follow through on this words that he owned her. He'd dressed her, housed her, provided her with art supplies and so much more those last three years. She'd become tired of the fight to survive, and he'd swept in and taken care of her. She'd been relieved and ignored the price. There was always a price.

It was good to not be alone, to not have to prove to her dad that she could take care of herself. That her dream wasn't some crazy pipe dream. He'd told her she'd fail, and for three years she'd thrived.

Only she hadn't.

Not really.

Instead, she'd traded barely existing for sleeping with the enemy.

She'd deceived herself into believing Emilio loved her, but there were always beautiful women around. He didn't need her, but for some reason he'd wanted her. She'd liked being wanted—and she'd appreciated a worry-free life.

She should have probed deeper, should have sought to understand *why* he wanted her. With Emilio there was always a deeper why. She'd allowed herself to believe he'd loved her when he only lusted after what she created with her paintbrush.

Marie—no, *Charlotte* had closed her eyes and held on to the parts of her dream that were beautiful. Walking the streets of Florence, ignoring the shadow Emilio assigned to her. Hours in the Uffizi studying the masters, avoiding the days he wouldn't let her leave the villa in the countryside. She'd been trapped, but too full of pride to admit her father had been right.

She couldn't make her dream come true on her own.

She'd aimed too high.

Yet it had always felt right there. Just beyond her fingertips. She was talented. There was something magical, almost anointed that happened when she painted. A connection, a moment of worship. Yet she'd lost herself, her link with God in those dark days with Emilio. It had taken Drew to find her way back.

There had been a slow holiness in her intense love for her son that had reminded her and wooed her back to her heavenly Father. It was in her love for Drew that she had rediscovered the depth of God's love for her. She prayed that her daddy's love for her went as deep.

He'd set hard boundaries for her growing up.

She'd fought them.

So hard.

It's why she'd kept running to Italy.

The lines hadn't played well with her artistic side, and she'd paid the price for not learning how to comply while being true to who she was. She had to believe there was a way to do both—follow the outlines of the boundaries while also being a creative. But she didn't have that freedom. Not in her current constraints.

Maybe she never would.

But a part of her soul longed for the day she could reclaim that part of herself.

It wasn't entirely necessary, but she would rest . . . breathe . . . having everything arranged and settled.

She wiped tears from her cheeks and started a short list of basics that she didn't really need to write, but it gave her mind a place to focus. She and her mom had exchanged texts over the weekend, and her parents would arrive sometime today. After a minute digging up the best directions, she texted them to her mom along with an outline of directions. By the time she woke Drew and got him out the door for school, she'd created a list that would fill his every need for months instead of days. At the school drop off line, she leaned over and gave him a quick kiss. "See you in a few hours, buddy."

His eyes brightened. "You're picking me up early?"

"Not today. But I'll see you at after care."

He slumped against the seat.

"Come on, drama kid." She leaned over and tickled him before giving him another quick kiss. "You'll have a great day."

He sighed and grabbed his backpack before opening the door and sliding out. "Love you, Mom."

"Love you too." So much, that as she pulled away from the curb, she had to blink back tears. She needed to get to work and do her job, but the thought of not having him near her even for a couple weeks made it hard to breathe as the school appeared in her rearview mirror.

"Focus on getting what Drew needs." She'd think clearer once she wasn't worried about her son. She knew it was true, but it didn't make the coming separation any easier.

Recognizing Rahul seemed like slipping backward to what she'd left in Italy. Leaving had been so hard.

As she drove, she glanced in the rearview mirror. Then she squinted and frowned.

Was that someone behind her?

The same white sedan had driven three cars behind her for a while. At least she thought it was the same one.

"What do I do?" She'd planned to run into the grocery store on the way to work for a quick stop for a few of Drew's favorite snacks. Wasn't it a good idea to stay in public areas? Seemed that's what she saw in movies, so Marie pulled into the Kroger parking lot and found a spot close to the doors. Then she hurried inside and watched for the white car. She couldn't be sure, but a similar car pulled into a spot a couple rows from her car. When an older woman with white hair and an arm full of reusable grocery bags climbed out, Marie deflated, but decided to take some time wandering the aisles to be sure.

She'd just pulled back on to the street when she noted another white sedan. "What do I do?" She spoke the words aloud. "Call the police?"

A voice spoke up. "I'm sorry but I didn't get that."

Marie squeaked then laughed at herself. Just her phone's assistant activating. Thank goodness it hadn't placed the call. If she could get to work, she'd be safe until it was time to pick up Drew. She took the long way, zigzagging across north Indianapolis, and acting like a crazy woman as she looped some traffic circles until she almost made herself dizzy, but no one could follow her around one twice without making themselves conspicuous.

By the time she reached the office she felt certain she'd lost whoever might have followed her.

Soon she'd settled into the normal rhythm of a workday, greeting clients as they arrived and patching calls through to the correct line. Then her phone buzzed. She almost ignored it, but when it buzzed again, she pulled it out to check.

Your son needs to be watched.

The number was unfamiliar, but the effect of the words was like her worst nightmare come to life.

Who sent this?

She clicked around until she could hit the number, and her hands trembled so much she wished she was on her headset.

"Hello?"

"Who is this?" She tried not to shout the words but couldn't keep the sharp edge out of her tone.

"Thayer Jackson."

"Wh-why would you . . . text me?" Her words wobbled.

"Who is this?"

"Marie Montgomery."

"Why would I text you? You called me."

"But I just got a text from this number."

"I didn't text you, Marie."

He sounded sincere, but she wasn't going to fall for old tricks again. "You leave my son alone. Do you understand me?"

He let the silence linger a moment before he spoke. "I didn't text you—and I certainly wouldn't say anything about your son. It's easy to tell you love him very much and would do anything for him."

"Yes." The word was so small and insignificant.

"I'm not at the office, but I'm driving in now. Can we meet?"

"Why?"

"So I can try to figure out if someone spoofed my number."

"How else would I think you called?"

"Let's just meet and talk through this."

"Fine. But don't think I trust you."

As she hung up, her words reverberated through her. Was she making yet another foolish decision?

Chapter Nine

TWENTY MINUTES LATER, THAYER ENTERED THE OFFICES OF Hunter & Associates and didn't pause to throw his bag in his office. Instead, when he reached the reception area, Marie wore a frown in stark contrast to her sunny yellow blouse. "I'm not in the mood."

"Understood." Thayer held out his hand. "Can I see your phone?"

Her gaze darted around as if she sought evidence no one lurked in the shadows before she handed it to him. "Drop it, you buy me a new one. On second thought, go ahead and drop it. I backed it up last week."

"You do have a sense of humor."

"It'll be even better when I understand what's going on." She rubbed her arms as if fighting a chill.

He tried to open the phone, then handed it back. "Can you unlock it?"

"Sorry." A second later, she returned it to him.

"What am I looking for?"

She leaned into his side and slid to a different app. "This message."

"The number looks like mine." He took a moment to read the message and then studied it more carefully. "I didn't text you."

"Then who did?"

"I don't know, but look." He pulled out his phone and showed her his messages. "There's nothing here."

"That doesn't mean anything. You could have sent it and then deleted it."

"But you and I talked." He pulled up his phone app. "Look, the record of our call is here."

"Reaching, Jackson."

"Not as much as you think. I don't have anything to gain by sending that text."

"Other than this." She motioned between them. "We're together now."

"Well, you'll just have to trust me. I didn't do anything." He handed the phone back to her. "I'm going to grab a cup of decent coffee. Would you like one?"

Her phone made some sort of dinging hiccough, and she shook her head. "I'm trying to save my son. Tell Mr. Hunter I'm taking the rest of the day off."

With those cryptic words, she spun and hurried to her desk, pulling a small backpack from under the desk and then leaving him watching as she hurried out the door.

It was clear she didn't trust him. She likely didn't trust anyone.

What could he do to change that narrative in her mind? He'd need to find something because he wasn't gaining any ground with her, and if he didn't start, the FBI might send someone else.

The agency was only as good as its information. Right now, it pointed to her as the crux of the solution. She was going to find herself in the crosshairs between two powerful groups, and she would be too naive to get herself out of it.

~

When Marie reached her bungalow close to lunchtime, she didn't know if she'd have a job or not the next day, but she'd had to escape and think. Should she take Drew and flee, or should she stay and fight while her parents spirited him away?

Which was the right and better course?

As she sat in her little bug feeling small and alone, a silver hybrid SUV pulled in behind her. A glance in the rearview mirror showed it was her parents. She wanted to collapse in relief that they'd found her house based on her text, but instead squared her shoulders and stepped from her car, grateful they had come, but unsure what was coming. It would be best to meet her father head on, so she waited on the sidewalk under the shade of a redbud tree for them, braced for an old-fashioned lecture demanding to know what she had done to get in so much trouble that she needed Andrew anywhere but with her.

There was no way to explain what she didn't understand herself.

Her stomach twisted in knots, and she had moments where she couldn't breathe. It had to get better. Had to. Or she didn't know . . . she stopped the thought. No, she would believe everything could be solved. She noticed a dandelion. Bent to pick it. Blew a long exhale that sent the seeds spiraling in individual streams. Her neighbors might not appreciate the weeds that would pop up in a few weeks, but the breath had slowed her heart rate a bit. Now she could smile as her parents stepped from their car.

A door opened but no one exited.

Then a leg extended, and her mother stepped from the car.

The woman had aged in the thirteen years since Marie had seen her. Her mom had allowed her hair to go fully grey and there was a softness to her hairstyle that had been angled against her jawline before. Still, she moved with ease as if she took time to attend regular slots at a yoga or Pilate's studio. Marie let out a breath, knowing her mother could keep up with Drew.

A moment later her dad stood and rounded the SUV. He had none of the softness, but instead looked more edgy with aviator sunglasses shading his eyes.

Marie stood frozen in place as her mother paused, her gaze colliding with her husband's. Then she closed the gap between them with a gasp and pulled Marie into a tight hug. "Hello, sweetheart."

Her mother had long been a believer in twenty second hugs, but held on longer than usual, as if to assure herself Marie really stood there.

"Hi, Mom." She tried to sink into the hug but couldn't relax. "We're okay, I promise."

Mom let her go and slugged her in the shoulder. "Where have you been? It's been thirteen years, Charlotte. Thirteen years!" She swiped under her eyes. "Do you have any idea what not knowing if you were okay . . . if you were even alive . . . did to us?"

"Allison." Her father's word held warning, but it didn't stop Mom from plowing forward.

"I had your father hire a private investigator so we could at least know you were alive." Her mother's clear blue eyes glistened with tears. "And then to learn we had a grandson. One you never told us about."

Marie stepped back, her mouth open. "You knew?"

"Of course we knew, but we didn't know why you were staying away. It killed me to not come, but your father insisted we give you the space you wanted."

"Allison." Now he growled the word.

"Daddy?" Her heart broke with the syllables. And then she noted the pain etched in the lines of his body. It extended far beyond his face into the taunt way he held his back and neck.

"I knew you were tied in with a bad crowd in Italy, but I couldn't figure out exactly what was happening." His face collapsed and he aged in front of her. "You were so determined to make your own way, and I chased you there by holding on too tightly. It was my fault and now you're in danger."

She approached her father cautiously. "I'm sorry, Daddy."

He removed his sunglasses and opened his arms, and she fell into them. "Me too, Charlotte, me too."

She wanted to collapse into his embrace and lose track of time, but she couldn't, not out here. After a minute, she pushed away. "Let's get inside."

Her father's gaze sharpened. "Are you in danger?"

"I-I don't know."

Her mother shook her head, but reached into the car for her purse, before slamming the door. "If you were safe, you wouldn't have called in a panic yesterday."

"It wasn't a panic."

"We're here." She waved a hand between her and Daddy. "You wouldn't have called if you'd had an option." Then she walked up the sidewalk to the front door. "Come on, Steven. She wants us inside where we'll all be safer."

"That's truth." Dad walked beside Marie up the walk, and she noted the grey at his temples. She wasn't ready to accept this reality. "Your mom stewed the whole drive, convincing herself there's a real problem. I'm not sure she'll relax until you tell her this has nothing to do with that deadbeat boyfriend."

If only she could say that and ignore the increasing sense he was somehow involved. "I don't know. There have just been a few strange things." She sighed. "Let's get you both inside and then we can talk out of the heat." She glanced around but didn't see anyone watching them. "I know you don't know him yet, but if you can take Drew on an adventure, I'll feel better." She unlocked the front door and opened it. "At least one car has followed me and a man I think works for the Italian family is in town."

Mom considered her with her cool blue eyes the color of cornflowers. "All right." She seemed determined to assess all the things Marie didn't know how to explain, then shook her head. "Let Drew meet us and let's see how it goes. If he's okay with it, we can take him. It will be good to spend time with him, but he would be more comfortable if you came too"

"It's not that simple, Mom." Marie wanted to stomp her foot. Maybe even scream. "That would just postpone any resolution. I have to stay here to figure out how to make this go away."

"But isn't that what you're doing by sending Drew with us and staying here?" Mom patted her arm and stepped inside. "If it's as bad as you think, you should leave with us."

"Allison, let's all cool off with some tea." Help coming from Dad? "I'm ready to get out of the sun for a bit."

Marie wished she could believe her dad was on her side and trying to distract her mom, but it didn't work that way. Once they were inside, the two would find a way to coordinate their attack. It was so hard to get everything just right, but her parents believed there was a perfect balance and she had not attained it.

She couldn't win.

She did need to water the flowers in her planters. They drooped under the summer heat, the colors fading. "I should take those inside."

"And bring the bugs in?" Mom tightened her hold as if to prevent Marie from carrying a pot inside that moment. "No, just bring pitchers of water out. They'll recover. I've found watering in the cool of the evening works well."

"She watched you do that for twenty years, Allison. I think she's got your system down if she wants to copy it." Daddy took her arm and led Marie to the couch. "Charlotte, sit and explain everything."

She searched his face, and though he'd aged and there were new lines on his face and questions in his eyes, she sensed his love.

So she did as he asked.

She told him about Emilio finding her. About how he wooed her by wining and dining her. Then the weekends at the family's villa in the Tuscan hills. "It was a fairytale."

And then he started pressuring her to paint more, and she wondered if he loved her or her talent. "It was a crazy thing to wonder, but I did. Still he made me feel cherished, so I stayed."

Until that fateful day when she heard him give the order for a man to be killed. Then she spotted the headline that he had been murdered on the same day that her pregnancy test showed positive. "I got organized, and then I fled, but I was concerned Emilio would try to find me and use you to get to me, so I disappeared. And I've stayed hidden."

"Until now." Her mother whispered the words.

"Yes, until now." She wiped her cheeks, and then took a steadying breath. "I thought we were safe. In fact, I was contemplating coming home."

"But?" Her father's voice echoed as he spoke.

"I saw one of my paintings at a local gallery."

"I see." Her dad spoke again, his words weighted.

Marie nodded. "I left everything in Tuscany behind including some paintings. It would make it too easy to find me if I brought it home, so I gave up passion." She swallowed. "I gave up you."

Momma stood from the couch and sat next to Marie, pulling her into another tight hug. "We never let go of you, praying for you every day. We never let go."

"Never." Daddy's word was soft.

"This man from Italy is here. A colleague heard him telling the gallery owner that he needed to tell someone I'd been found. I have to think that means Emilio is on his way. As far as I know they don't have my name, but I need you to take Drew and leave." She pushed a bit back from her mom. "On my way to the office this morning, I picked up Drew's favorite travel snacks. I still need to double-check his suitcase, or you might be stopping at a store for a toothbrush and underwear."

"Good thing there are stores everywhere." Mom's eyes wore the focused look that Marie well remembered. "I let you pack for vacation when you were seven—and then let you live in a swimsuit for a week. It was a polka-dot one with a big strawberry in the middle of your stomach. So cute but got old after you wore it for a week."

Dad nodded. "I thought it would walk out of the hotel room the last day. It was so chlorinated it was stiff." Then he shifted on the other side of Marie. "Let's pray and then we'll figure out how to tell Drew he's leaving with us."

"Thank you." Ten minutes later when her watch buzzed, Marie was more settled. "It's time to go get Drew. Then y'all can leave."

Mother shook her head. "We've got a lot to cover before we take that boy. He has to feel comfortable with us."

Dad nodded. "We'll work fast." His jaw set in that way that always signaled she was out of room to push.

". . . thank you." She choked on the words. They were showing their love in action by being here today. "I love you."

"Remember you are deeply loved by us and your heavenly Father. Your value comes from him, not anything or anyone else."

Marie nodded because if she tried to squeeze a word around the lump in her throat, she knew she'd collapse. Because what if it was Emilio? And even worse what if it wasn't? What if the threat came from an unknown corner?

"You will get through this because you aren't alone." Mom gave her a quick hug then stepped back. "You go get that boy, and I'll check his suitcase. Your dad will check the house and see what we can do to make it more secure."

Dad gave her a quick hug. "You okay?"

She nodded fiercely. "I will be."

"All right. You aren't alone."

"Thank you." She choked on the words, grateful for their love that showed up in actions. "I love you."

"Love you more."

And the healing thing was she believed him. God had redeemed the pain of their relationship and turned it into something rich, and deep and true. Marie was beyond grateful for that gift. "Thank you. All right, I'm off. I'll be back in forty minutes."

Chapter Ten

As soon as she picked him up, Drew started asking questions about his grandparents. His eagerness to know more warmed Marie's heart. She tried to answer his questions as honestly as she could, but she didn't know her parents anymore. It had been thirteen long years since she'd spent significant time with them. The fact they'd arrived within twenty-four hours of her call gave her hope they were the same people she remembered, but it would take time to repair the relationship breach she had created, despite all the grace they were showing her.

No matter how important the cause of the gulf, she still instigated it.

"Mom." Drew drug out the word with an impatient air.

"What?"

"You didn't answer my question."

"Sorry. I must have gotten lost in my thoughts. I'm ready to listen now."

"Do you think they'll like me?"

"I know they're going to love you." She met his gaze in the rearview mirror with a smile that quickly turned to a frown as she spotted a white sedan behind them. It looked like the one she'd spotted that morning, but maybe her imagination simply noted them everywhere now. Wasn't that

250

common psychology, you saw one white sedan, you saw every white sedan?

"Mom?"

"We're okay, buddy." Then she realized he wouldn't know there was any reason they weren't. "I have a surprise for you at home."

Drew promptly started guessing everything from a baby brother—um, not a chance—to a UFO—equally impossible. She just hoped he'd like the surprise she actually had for him.

She took a long, circuitous route home and only pulled into her neighborhood when the white sedan was no longer behind them. Her parents' SUV was still parked at the curb, and she relaxed her grip on the steering wheel.

When she stopped the car in the driveway, she turned to Drew. "Are you ready to meet your grandparents?"

His eyes got wide, and his chin trembled before he nodded his head so that his hair flopped into his eyes. "Yes."

"All right." She hurried around the car, where he fumbled with the seatbelt when she got to his door, his fingers suddenly too big to work the mechanism. "Here, I've got you." She unlatched it and then put her hands on his shoulders and waited until he stilled and met her gaze. "They will love you, Drew."

"How do you know?"

"Because they are just as nervous about you loving them."

"That's silly. I already do."

"And they already love you too."

A slow smile broke on his face. "Okay. I understand." He held out his hand. "Walk with me?"

"Always." And forever. Whatever it took.

Her Mom and Dad waited in the open front doorway. The hesitant hope on their faces almost broke her. Her choices that had kept her safe had harsh consequences for those she loved. She only hoped Drew and her parents could erase the years they had.

Drew's fingers grasped hers, but he soldiered forward and then grinned up at the two adults. "I'm Drew and you must be Grandma and Grandpa."

"We are." Mom's hands clasped and unclasped. "May I hug you?"

"Yep." And Drew threw himself into her arms.

Mom looked over his head and mouthed *thank you*. Then Dad joined the hug. They were already bridging the gap of years.

Soon Mom had Drew settled at the kitchen table with homemade cookies and milk and they were chattering away. Marie's phone rang and she glanced at the screen.

Thayer.

She ducked out to answer it. "Hello?"

"Hi, do you have a minute?"

"A quick one. What's up?"

"I wanted to follow up on that question I asked the other day."

"I don't remember a question."

"Painting for me."

"I don't paint anymore."

"But you did, and you were good enough to have a painting in the 42nd Street Gallery."

"Maybe. I didn't confirm it was my painting."

"We're trying to figure out what's going on at the Gallery and wondered if you'd create a painting for us."

She pulled her phone from her ear and stared at the screen. What was he talking about? "Who's *we*?"

"I can't really say."

"Then I don't really paint. Haven't in eight years."

"It's just one painting." He hesitated, and she braced for whatever was coming next. "And you'd need to copy a famous painting."

"You're crazy."

"Just trying to catch the bad guys. We can pay you enough to make it worth your time."

"Do you know who you're dealing with?"

"We have an idea."

"Then I think I have a better idea than you do. The answer is no. Good-bye, Thayer." She disconnected the call. The man was insane, and she couldn't let him distract her from what she had to do. That was simple and horribly complicated at the same time. Figure out what Emilio knew and dissuade her from coming after her.

~

Maybe it was a good thing Thayer hadn't tried for the FBI, because the way the phone call went, he would be an abject failure. He couldn't seem to find the levers to get this operation right.

Marie Montgomery.

What a crazy dichotomy of a woman.

She had the bohemian flair of an artist who didn't seem to care what others thought, yet she had also had the iron core of resistance against painting for him. He saw moments where he could tell she missed art deeply, either that, or she was a great actress. But he couldn't find the lever that would get her to cooperate with his request. He might not be a ladies' man, but he also wasn't a slouch with women.

What was he supposed to do now?

Johnson wasn't going to be thrilled that he'd made zero progress. Maybe he needed to spend the rest of the day staring at the data. See progress and results. This pseudo-undercover work was a flop. He should do what he did well that helped keep the world in order. The only thing to do in his next meeting with Johnson? Tell him Thayer would stick to analyzing data to give the real agents the information they needed for their investigations.

White collar tracing was important. Without it, Johnson couldn't locate the evidence he needed for search and arrest warrants. Even so, there were days Thayer's contribution seemed . . . irrelevant.

All he did was stare at a computer all day.

He had all the evidence he needed.

Marie Montgomery didn't trust him.

Maybe she didn't trust men in general, but she definitely wasn't buying what he was trying to sell. But before he gave up once and for all, he would go by her house and maybe face to face, he could explain why they needed her help. He probably should have done it in person anyway rather than over the phone.

He drove his hybrid two-door across town to her small house. Before he climbed out, he glanced around, a flicker of something teasing at his mind.

Movement caught his attention and he squinted to get a better view. Had there been someone at the garage?

A tall man built like a linebacker stalked to the garage.

Thayer glanced around for his phone. When he looked back up, the man had disappeared.

Thayer had to assume he was somewhere around the garage.

Who was he?

Then it hit him. The guy was built like the man who had confronted him at the art gallery.

Rahul, that was his name. The man who'd been plaguing Marie.

Had he somehow led that man here and put Marie in danger? He wasn't trained to know how to handle this. What should he do?

He pulled out his phone and sent Johnson a quick text.

> Man from the gallery here at Marie's. Headed to see if I can hear what's going on.

Then he slid his phone back in his jeans pocket and eased his car door closed and crept toward Marie's house.

He was a fool. He wasn't Jack Bauer or James Bond. He'd most likely get them both killed. But if he'd done anything to bring this man to her door, he had to help her. He owed her that.

Marie raised the garage door and carried the bag of trash to the garage and to throw it into the larger can. She'd wanted to give her parents a moment with Drew and needed a second to collect her thoughts. It had gone well, and she was grateful, so very grateful.

The sound of footsteps startled her, and she glanced around. No one should be out here. "Hello?"

"Marie Montgomery, you are to come with me."

The unexpected voice caused her to scream and spin, a hand covering her thumping heart. "Rahul?"

"Who did you expect? Lover boy?" An ugly expression marred his face, and Marie scanned behind him.

"I don't have a guy."

"That's right, your son is your life. Is he Emilio's?" His expression turned ice cold, and she stilled.

A prayer flitted heavenward that her parents would stay inside with Drew. She didn't need her dad playing hero while Rahul was here. Instead, she had to bluff her way through whatever this was to get him away. "What do you want?"

"Sometimes we come to you." His grin was a threat all its own. "And then you come with us."

"I'm assuming you mean just you,"—she made a show of looking around— "since no one else is here." At least she hoped it was only him. He was intimidating enough. If he'd brought a friend, she'd be powerless to do anything but agree to anything he demanded.

"There is no time for word games. We have an appointment."

"What if I need to leave to get my son?"

"He is here, as are a couple."

"How do you know?"

"I've been watching." His expression tightened, and she knew it was time to comply or his frustration could leech out into violence. "We will leave now."

"All right. Let me leave a quick note." She made a show of pulling out her phone and sending a quick text to her mom. "I just need to grab my purse."

"No, your phone is enough." His tone left her cold.

"All right." She silenced her phone and slid it in her pocket. "What can you tell me about where we're going?"

"It is an important meeting. Someone who has wanted to reconnect with you for a while."

"Reconnect?" She swallowed hard. "It's someone I know?"

"That's what I said."

"You say so much with so few words." She froze, unable to continue because of the reality hinted at by his words. She didn't want to borrow trouble, yet her mind screamed whatever was coming wasn't good.

He tugged her elbow, propelling her down the driveway and then sidewalk away from her home to the next house.

"Get in the truck." Rahul's vehicle dwarfed her, the dually seemed larger and jacked up higher than necessary. It had to guzzle enough gas for four regular vehicles, and the sound was throaty.

She scanned looking for anyone who could help but saw no one in her frantic scan. Her only relief was that her parents had stayed inside as she'd asked in her text. At least she wouldn't be expected to talk to him. Marie's thoughts raced as she tried to anticipate where they were headed. But she couldn't. The crossroads passed in a blur, and her mind couldn't latch on to any of them as they went through roundabout after roundabout farther and farther out of town, disorienting her.

She wanted to check her phone and confirm that this one time her parents had done what she asked without a debate or insisting they knew better. Whatever happened, she needed to know Drew was safe. If he was okay, she could do what was necessary—whatever that was. But if she had to worry about him, then she would be lost. A victim to the demands she was beginning to anticipate but didn't want to acknowledge were possible.

Stop borrowing trouble.

Right now, she had concerns. Thoughts. But no actual knowledge.

Marie clutched her hands in her lap, her throat dry. She wouldn't let Rahul see the tremble that threatened to takeover. Instead, she would press through. Discover what was planned for her. Only then would she know if reality was worse than her fears.

Rahul pulled in front of a house. Set in the trees, the large home was covered in tan stucco. It had a peaked roofline in front and wings on each side, one likely a garage with multiple stalls, leaving an overall impression of wealth and privilege that would make it far outside her reach. Yet the richness couldn't shake the reality that she was here now, out of her element, needing to find a way to survive whatever was coming.

"What am I walking into?"

Rahul exited the truck without a word. Should she follow him or wait? Before she reached a decision, he stood at her door and opened it. "You will follow me."

"Sure." What else could she do? "You're making this awful cloak and dagger."

"Not at all."

She waited for him to elaborate, but he stayed quiet, leading the way up the walk to the front door. Instead of knocking, he hit a couple buttons on the lock and then entered when the door eased open.

"Fancy." She drew out the word, but he ignored her as he held the door.

Marie walked past him and then stopped as she took in the soaring two-story entryway. A wide staircase swept to a landing, and a broad hallway led to open double doorways. Everything about the space screamed spacious, yet everything about her being there yelled secretive. A shiver skittered up her spine, but she held herself steady, only allowing a small smile as she rubbed her arms. "It's chilly in here. Guess I needed a jacket."

"Wait here."

"Sure. No problem. Where would I go?"

Rahul moved down the hall toward what she imagined would be the kitchen area, allowing her time to scan the area. Should she open the front door and run?

What would that accomplish? She didn't know where she was or if anyone was nearby to help her.

Instead, she could send someone a pin of her location. That might work. But who should she send it to? If she sent it to her parents, they might decide to come and find her, but she needed them to take Drew and leave. She sent a quick text.

> Please leave. Take Drew and leave now. I'll call when I can.

Maybe they would do it.

She prayed they would.

She didn't have girlfriends. Couldn't allow herself that luxury when she'd been in hiding for the past eight years. Her brother was in another state.

She pulled up Thayer's information and sent him a pin with a quick note to call her if he didn't hear anything in thirty minutes. If it was more than an hour, he should get help. She might be embarrassed if this turned out to be nothing. Better embarrassed than in real trouble and too proud to admit it.

Marie pivoted, letting her sundress flair around her knees. She might not know who was coming, but she could try to feel in control of something even if it was small and ridiculous. Footsteps interrupted her, mid-twirl.

"This is a lovely home. Quite the showpiece." She finished turning, expecting to see Rahul with someone interesting for her to meet, maybe the gallery owner Julian Bond. She froze. It wasn't Julian.

~

Thayer's phone alerted while he waited for Johnson to get back to him. He'd followed the big truck across town, but it had been harder to stay inconspicuous as they'd moved out of town and into the country. The dually was distinctive, but it would take someone oblivious not to notice him a few cars behind, especially as other cars turned off onto side roads and highways. He'd dropped back, but even that might be conspicuous if it was clear he was trying to stay near but not too close.

At last, he heard the click that Johnson was back.

"What do you want me to do?"

"Nothing."

"Nothing?" That didn't make sense.

"You haven't seen illegal behavior. Make a note of where they go. And then keep going."

"Is that what you would do?"

"Probably. Yes."

Probably. That's what Thayer would latch on to. "I'll play it by ear."

"You aren't equipped to 'play it by ear.'"

"Neither is Marie." Thayer trained his eyes on the truck. "I don't think there's any way she's prepared for organized crime."

"I don't know if that's accurate." Something in Johnson's tone set Thayer on alert.

"What do you mean?"

"We've done some discrete digging. When she was in Italy, she may have gotten involved with less than desirable groups."

"Can you be more specific?"

"There's a chance she was involved with organized crime overseas."

He barely noticed the dually slowing down, as that sentence settled over him. "Why do you think that?"

"There's evidence in her social media that she was close, potentially very close, with the son of a leader of a crime family."

"Why didn't I see that?"

"Because she took steps to remove all of it, but it's not as easy to do as the average person thinks." Johnson sighed and there was a squeak like he was leaning back in his chair. "Look we're not sure, but she may not be as clean as she looks."

"She looks sudsy."

"Not completely. Remember there's a reason you went to that gallery showing." There was an edge to Johnson's voice that pulled Thayer up as he scanned for a place to pull over.

"They just turned into a place that looks like a horse farm."

"There might not be anything wrong."

"She's sending her kid away."

"O-okay." Johnson drew the word out.

"She adores her son."

"So you've said."

"She wouldn't send him away if she wasn't worried." There. A spot he could pull into not too far away while he tried to figure out what to do. His phone pinged again, but he ignored it. "What would you do in my shoes?"

"I'd ask why I was so concerned. A few weeks ago, you didn't know her at all. Now you're willing to go into a potentially dangerous environment without any information." He paused. "I'd ask myself some tough questions about why I wanted to do that. Then I'd remind myself I'm not law enforcement and be really careful."

"I may not be the law, but you are."

"And I'm heavily restricted by the law on what I can and can't do. There's nothing yet to suggest I should do anything other than continue to monitor the situation from a distance. I'd advise you to do the same."

"I don't know if I can."

"Doesn't mean you shouldn't." There was the sound of another voice, and then Johnson came back. "I've gotta run. Don't do anything I wouldn't do."

"I'll try." The better warning would have been to only do the things that he was qualified to do. That would be a much smaller array of options.

Then he pulled out his phone and saw the ping of Marie's location. *Father, what do I do with this?*

~

"Ciao, Charlotte." Her name still sounded like the best gianduiotto chocolate on his lips. She wanted to tear her gaze from his, but instead it betrayed her as it scanned Emilio and proved that he was as swarthy and handsome as he'd been ten years earlier when he'd entered her life and swept her off her feet.

She licked her dry lips. Tried to swallow. "Emilio."

"I wondered when we would see each other again." He smiled, the one that tipped up slightly more on the left side and used to reel her in, but the warmth didn't reach his eyes. They seemed devoid of life as they focused on her. "It is time to come home. We need your skills and will use them well."

"What? No words of love?" She tried to force a tone of teasing into her voice but couldn't quite manage it. Instead, the last word fell flat. So much for the mature woman who had no need of him.

Please don't let him ask about Andrew. She had to keep him away from their son . . . *her* son. The moment he had Drew, she would do anything to protect him. She could only pray her family was on the road, somewhere Emilio couldn't find him.

If that was the case, she'd be fine.

If not?

She couldn't let her thoughts go there.

Chapter Eleven

"IT IS TIME FOR YOU TO BRING YOUR SKILLS BACK TO ITALY. I have been patient long enough."

"What do you mean?" Marie struggled to remain calm. "I left you. I'm not even sure how you found me."

"Come, let us have a conversation." He led the way to one of the rooms off the hallway—an expansive sitting area with a grand piano in front of a bank of windows on one wall and a leather loveseat and matching wing chairs offset near a fireplace. "I knew where you were all the time."

No. It couldn't be.

Marie's thoughts spiraled backward through the hours, days, months, and years since she'd escaped her life with Emilio. What he'd said couldn't be possible. She'd made a clean break. But what if he was telling her the truth? Was the safe life she had created nothing more than a lie?

There were parts of her life no one could manipulate. Drew was innocent. Yes, Emilio was his biological dad, but he'd never spent a moment with him or contributed a cent to his care.

Emilio walked over to a loveseat and sank onto it, a prince over his domain at ease while knowing everyone else waited on edge. He gestured to a wing chair. "Have a seat."

She would wrestle with any truth that might be buried in Emilio's words later. Right now, she had to find a way to survive this . . . this interview and get away. If that meant sitting and conversing with her past, she would do so.

She could not go back to Italy. Not this way. Never.

Marie's phone vibrated and she jumped as her watch echoed the vibration. Had thirty minutes passed already? Unlikely, but whoever was calling, she needed the pause.

A moment to breathe. To think. She pulled out her phone and then realized it might be a mistake to alert Emilio to the fact she had it with her. Too late now. "Hello?"

"Are you okay?" Thayer's voice was laced with both concern and strength.

"I think so."

"I'm nearby. Do you need me to come to you or go get someone?"

"Not right now."

"Do you want me to stay?"

She'd reached out to the right person. Thayer understood she couldn't answer freely.

"That might be nice." She glanced at Emilio and noticed the way he watched her. "Thank you for your call." She hung up, poked a few buttons, and slid her phone into her pocket. "Sorry about that." She took a shallow breath as she settled into the wingback chair. Time to confront her past. She'd be brave for Drew's sake. "Why are you here?"

"Like I said. Time to come home, Charlotte. We have let you play and now my father wants us to get to work."

His words stung. She didn't want to admit it, but they did.

"This has nothing to do with you . . . and me?" She'd always known he didn't care for her, not really, or he wouldn't have let her go. If you loved someone, you didn't let them walk away without trying to change their mind. Their relationship had always been more about lust on his side, and she'd let her imagination fill in the gaps. She'd been all too willing to compensate for what he hadn't given her. The typical stupid woman who believed she could make a man love her.

There was no reason to rehash her mistake. She'd worked too hard to change that narrative. To find a place where she could believe she had independent value.

Drew created more of that by bringing her back into a relationship with God.

She would turn neither her self-worth nor her son over to this man who had used her for his purposes. Yes, back then she'd allowed it, but she wasn't that woman now.

His tone softened. "Don't misunderstand, *cara mia*. You are still special to me."

Too little too late, buddy.

She kept the words inside and gave him a small smile instead. "I need to get home, Emilio, so why don't we get down to the real reason you brought me here."

"You have fine skills, and we are in need of your art. You will create paintings for us that we can buy and sell to clean our money when necessary." Then he waved a dismissive hand in the air. "And without the cute little decoys you used in the past. Yes, we found them."

"You kept my paintings?"

"Of course. We provided for your care when you made them. They were ours. Just like we monitored where you were at all times."

She swallowed against the harsh truth that her life hadn't been a clean escape after all. Both her parents and Emilio had known where she was. "What do you need me to do?"

"Paint what we tell you. Nothing changes. You may live in this terrible city. We fill your bank account and leave you and Drew alone." He settled his hands on his lap. "Ignore us, and well, we have compelling ways to make you comply."

Rahul stepped forward from the shadows, startling Marie. She covered her heart with one hand and blew out a long breath, accepting the large yellow envelope he handed her.

She looked from the envelope to Emilio. "What is this?"

"Open it."

She didn't want to, but it was clear he wasn't going to speak until she did.

She turned it over.

Eased open the flap.

Photos spilled onto her lap.

~

Thayer opened his phone. Clicked it off. Opened it again.

Time was trickling by so slowly he almost wondered if his watch worked or had died altogether.

He couldn't come up with a good reason to go onto the property. Nor had he found a good place to observe what was happening.

It was driving him crazy to think of Marie inside the house and nervous enough to ask him to stay.

Something wasn't right.

But he couldn't fix it without information.

Could he find something in the data based on the little bit Johnson had told him?

There was something about her time in Italy that had tipped the FBI off to a possible connection with a crime family. How did that connect with the woman he was getting to know?

It didn't compute. At all.

She was fierce.

Determined.

Vibrant.

How did that equal someone who was involved with the mob or organized crime or whatever the FBI thought it had found?

There had to be something there though.

The real question was whether they were reading the right story in the data. Data could tell any story you wanted it to. His accounting ethics professor had hammered that truth home over and over during their semester together.

What should he look for?

He'd searched the data. What had he missed? Or maybe the better question was what did the new information allow him to ask now? Was there a way to look through social media and figure out which family she had been affiliated with?

If she'd scrubbed it even at a surface level, then probably not. He didn't have the FBI's toys to go deeper. Had the agency acquired a warrant? If agents had enough evidence for that, wouldn't he have known? Then he shook his head. Of course not. Johnson didn't owe him anything. Thayer was a consultant and nothing more.

He decided to make another pass in front of the estate.

Nothing indicated she'd left, but he couldn't be certain unless he drove by to see the dually still parked at the home. As he pulled out of his spot along the road a half mile down the road, he noticed the gas at a quarter tank. He'd need to fill up, so he could follow the truck for a good distance. His little sedan got decent gas mileage, but he didn't love the idea of not having more in reserve.

A couple miles back, there was one of those sporadic highway intersections with a flashing stoplight, a gas station, and a couple of businesses. If he went now, maybe he could get back before anything happened.

Without turning his head, he noted the dually as he drove by and prayed nothing would happen while he sped down the highway to fill up.

The photos spilling from the envelope were like a kick to her stomach.

All contained Drew. Some looked like they were inside his school. Others were from the playground. All showed her handsome boy grinning at friends, revealing the slight gap between his teeth because he was grinning at friends.

"Leave him alone. Please."

"Then do as I ask." Emilio stared at her, coldness seeping from him. "I have two sons, strapping healthy boys in Italy. I do not need this one. However, I will take him if you do not cooperate."

In that moment Marie had no doubt Emilio meant every word.

She also knew she would escape this man a second time.

And this time she would truly leave him. Even if it meant leaving Drew behind with her parents. Nothing was more important than making sure Emilio had no use for her son.

She didn't know how she'd do it, but she would.

Right now, she'd focus on escaping this moment. But that was only the first step in running. She would go as far away as it took to ensure Drew was safe and protected. For now, she'd play along. And then she would take a risk and ask for help. It didn't make sense, but she thought she knew who to ask.

All these thoughts flitted through her mind like a charm of humming-birds, so she gave a careful nod. What response would Emilio expect? She couldn't cave too fast. "If I do what you ask, you'll leave Andrew alone?"

He didn't blink. "Si."

She flipped through a few photos. "How do I know you didn't photoshop these?"

"Would I need to?"

The answer was no. "You would find a way."

"It is not hard. Dollars cover a multitude of requests."

"And where that doesn't, threats do." She held up the photos as a case in point.

He gave a small nod of acknowledgment. "Only when you insist."

"What will I be paid?" She could only hope the recording app was still working and her phone's battery hadn't drained. If it worked, everything would automatically copy to her iCloud. Even if they took her phone, she'd have a copy. It was all she could think to do as insurance when she'd gotten off the phone with Thayer. Now she needed to get the bribe amount, and then she could go to the FBI. Maybe it would be enough to show conspiracy at least, or something equally harmful that would allow them to arrest Emilio. If not, she'd be good and trapped.

"Fifteen thousand a painting."

She tipped her chin up, trying to convey confidence. "Someone else is offering twenty thousand dollars a painting."

"I would imagine that person has no interest in our child."

His use of the word *our* before "child" froze the air in her lungs. "That . . . that person doesn't know I have to provide for *our* child." Maybe the equal emphasis would make him raise the number.

"I would be happy to raise him for you."

And her heart stopped. "Your offer sounds fine."

"That is what I thought. Rahul here will bring you the information on the first painting, but you will need to convince Julian Bond that you are the answer to his artistic dreams. You will have three weeks to complete the painting. If we find anything that alerts anyone to the fact it is not the original, Drew will disappear." He stood and stalked like a panther to loom over her. "Do you understand, cara mia?"

"Yes." She tried not to shrink back against the chair, but it was impossible.

"Then Rahul will take you home. And remember, we will be watching."

As Rahul led her to his truck and she pulled her phone from her pocket. "Don't want to sit on it."

While he walked around the pick-up, she surreptitiously turned off the recorder app and held it against the door. She'd check later to see if it worked. Right now, she just wanted to go home and shut the door on the last hour. If only she could pretend it hadn't happened—but the photos Emilio had shoved in her hands wouldn't let her forget their conversation. Or his threats.

Thayer screwed on the gas cap as the dually pulled up to the stoplight. He tried to give a casual glance to confirm whether Marie was inside. If she wasn't, he'd head back to the house. No way he would leave her there.

Then he noted her shoulder-length blonde hair through the passenger window and tore the receipt from the machine before jumping into his car. He pulled out and waited for a couple cars to pass before pulling into traffic. The few cars between them should help if the driver even remembered his vehicle—but then again, he drove an easily forgettable older model, navy two-door sedan.

When the dually preceded him through a yellow light, he decided to take the calculated bet the man would drive her back home rather than become conspicuous by pressing his luck and running the red light.

A few minutes later he parked several houses from hers and waited to text her until the oversized pick-up pulled away from the curb.

> Can I come in?

There was a pause, then the three dots appeared.

You're here?

Yes. Is that okay?

Can you come around the back just in case?

Give me a minute to move my car.

After pulling around to the side street, he walked down the alley and found Marie standing in her backyard. She seemed worn out, as if she'd survived an emotional and physical marathon.

On instinct, Thayer opened his arms once he entered the yard. Marie walked into his embrace and nestled against his chest as his arms closed around her. He savored the moment. This was where he was supposed to be—offering comfort to this woman he was still getting to know. He might not understand why, but she needed this.

"Do you want to talk about it?"

"Can we go somewhere else?" She glanced around and then moved to tug the back door of her house closed and headed toward the alley and the direction he had come from.

Moments later, they sat in silence in his car. Thayer asked, "Where do you want to go?"

Marie shook her head. "Can you call your FBI agent friend?"

Her request felt out of left field. "Why?"

"Because I have an audio of my former boyfriend soliciting me to commit art forgery for the purpose of money laundering." She sighed and rubbed her forehead. "At least that's what I would call it. I don't know if that's what they would call it. And I haven't checked the audio to make sure you can actually hear anything. But I tried to record our conversation, and I really hope it worked. If it didn't, I don't know what I'm going to do."

"Let me place a call." As Thayer hit speed dial, Marie nodded without saying a word. "Johnson, where can we meet? You're going to want to hear this."

Twenty minutes later they were at a diner that was closed, but

Johnson knew the owners who didn't mind him meeting folks there after hours if they were still cleaning. "What's up?"

Thayer made the introductions, then motioned for Marie to fill his friend in.

"Eight years ago, I thought I left my boyfriend—my life—behind in Italy. I changed my name. My job. Today he had someone bring me north of Carmel. He claims he's watched me this whole time." She pulled her phone out. "If everything worked, I recorded him asking me to forge paintings for him to launder money."

"What's his leverage?" Johnson seemed engaged, yet skeptical as he leaned back against the booth.

Marie reached in her purse with trembling hands. It took her a couple tries to pull an envelope free. "I'm sorry. I'm just so upset." Then she opened the envelope and let the contents spill onto the table.

Chapter Twelve

THE MOMENT DREW GRINNED UP AT THEM FROM THE photographs on the table, Marie could tell Agent Paarlberg began to believe her. He leaned forward and picked up the top photo. Examined it and then made eye contact with her. "This is your son Andrew?"

"Yes." Then she stopped. "Wait. How did you know his name? I didn't say his name." At least she didn't think she had. Not yet. But her thoughts were a panicked, jumbled mess.

"You must have mentioned it." But then Paarlberg's gaze traveled to Thayer.

"Thayer works for you."

"No. He's not FBI."

He seemed adamant, but something was off. What should she do now? "Remember I've patched your calls through to him for a year. I know you're at least friends and I've guessed Thayer does some sort of work with you." She collected the photos, but Thayer held one, studying it.

"Where was this one taken?"

"They're all at his school. Somehow Emilio got a man inside his school. I have to end this so that Drew and I can be safe."

Agent Paarlberg looked between them. "Where is Drew now?"

"Somewhere with my parents."

"Do you know where?"

"No." She was so thankful she could say that. "What are my options?"

"Let's see what you have first." Agent Paarlberg reached for her phone, but she pulled her hand back.

"I might be a receptionist, but I know to negotiate before I give everything away. If this is what I think it is, what are my options?"

"If all that happened is conspiracy? Not a lot. That alone is a crime, but not one that many prosecutors would pursue on its own. Even if Emilio is part of a crime family, if most of the enterprise happens in Italy, that's outside our jurisdiction."

She tried to think back through all the shows she'd watched. What happened in situations like this? "Can't you work with the Italian equivalent? Or Interpol? What if the family is active here? They're threatening my child."

"Potentially. Or this could be a custody dispute with the child's father."

Thayer's intake of breath let her know she wasn't the only one who felt the coldness of that statement.

"Johnson." Thayer's stiff tone mirrored his posture.

Agent Paarlberg held up his hands in front of him. "I'm not saying I agree, but we have to look at this from all angles. That is an argument the District Attorney's office will definitely consider."

"Understood. But if everything I say is validated, what are my options? Other than a casket." These men did not understand some of the "accidents" she'd seen in Italy. The fact they couldn't all be accidents had propelled her to make the hard decision and leave. She had to before it was too late to protect her unborn child. And now, eight years later, she would do anything to protect that same child.

Agent Paarlberg spoke again. "Depending on what you have and who he is, who he's connected to, it could lead to something big."

"Does the name Accardi mean anything? My former boyfriend is Emilio Accardi."

Paarlberg straightened. "I'll make a call as soon as we listen. This may be Witness Protection caliber."

Marie swallowed against the lump forming in her throat. Now the agent believed her. "That sounds bad."

"Or good depending on how you look at it." Agent Paarlberg made a motion. "Let's see what we've got and then we'll move forward. You said he's in town."

"He gave me the photos of Drew."

"Any idea how long he'll stay?"

Not long she hoped. "He didn't say." She held up her phone. "Can I start this now?"

Agent Paarlberg nodded. Her muscles turned to jelly as she listened to a muffled but clear enough capture of her earlier conversation.

As Thayer listened to the call, he clenched his fists as he heard the suave Italian call Marie *Charlotte*. He glanced at her. Who was she? Did he know her like he thought he did?

The conversation didn't bring clarity, other than make him wonder if he could and should do something. Marie needed help. Help the FBI couldn't necessarily provide yet while they planned and schemed for ways to get her closer to this Emilio guy. Listening to his cold detachment as he talked about what he could do to force her to do as he wished caused a hot rage flash through Thayer.

That was an emotion he wasn't used to.

His world was all about keeping things orderly and smooth. That wasn't possible if he focused on everything that could go wrong where Marie was concerned. There was something about her that wouldn't let him walk away. To stay engaged and make sure she was okay.

But at a fundamental level he was ill equipped to do that.

Johnson looked up from the legal pad where he'd taken notes. "Can you forward that file to me at this email address?"

Marie looked at him blankly. "I don't know."

"Then can I take your phone?" Johnson dropped the words like some kind of challenge

"No." Her eyes flared as she shook her head. "I need it to reach my parents."

"Maybe I can help." Thayer held out his hand. "You can watch me send the file to him."

"Will you keep one copy on my phone?"

"Sure. But why?"

"In the movies they always need some kind of insurance." A small, yet captivating smile tipped the right side of her lips.

Johnson cleared his throat and Thayer grinned.

"I like the idea of insurance." In fact, he uploaded a copy to his cloud drive as a second backup, but without telling either Johnson or Marie. He handed her the phone and glanced at Johnson. "Check your email to confirm the file came through."

"I've got it." Johnson clicked a few buttons on his phone, then slid it back in his pocket. "I'll meet with my boss and the U.S. Attorney. See what they think. And you're certain the man on the file is Emilio Accardi?"

"He's my son's father." Two dots of bright color appeared in her cheeks. "I'm certain."

"Great. I'll be in touch. Until then, stay the course. Delay if you can. Don't pretend to be a hero. Do what you normally would and wait for us to get back to you."

"Awesome. So I should cooperate with the monster I fled eight years ago. I get to be the damsel in distress waiting for the man on a white horse. That's not exactly comforting." She stood, then leaned into the table. "You do understand my parents are somewhere with my son. I intentionally don't know where my parents and Drew are because of the man on that file. I sent Drew away before I know for sure Emilio was here. What do you think I'll do now that I know?"

~

Two weeks later, Marie stood in her garage that she'd turned into a makeshift studio. She'd hastily thrown it together after trips to several art supply stores. Rahul had advanced a down payment on the first piece, so she'd quit her job at Hunter & Associates and plunged back into art. Somehow, she had to quickly transform back into an artist. Prove to Emilio she was all in on his scheme even though she'd never agree to forge art. Yet her emotions were a conflicted jumble reflected on the canvas in front of her.

It was more Edvard Munch than Claude Monet.

More silent scream of desperation than peaceful exploration of light and wonder.

There was a darkness to it that wasn't her. From the color choices to the way she slashed the paint on the canvases rather than playfully dabbed and placed the paint, it wasn't her.

Yet it was.

This was her life right now, and she had to find a way to embrace it while also find a way to change it.

She missed Drew so much.

Her life was flat without the life and joy he brought.

For years, caring and providing for him had been her *why*.

It still was, but without him here? Life felt meaningless.

She sighed and set her brush down again, feeling the emptiness threaten to seep through her onto the painting even more than it already had.

She had stepped so far away from art eight years ago, she couldn't just slide back in—yet she had to for Drew's sake. A paintbrush had to become an extension of her hand and brain, but her emotions swirled like muddied paint on a canvas.

This wasn't a work she'd sell. But it would lead to one—she just needed to produce something faster. Emilio wouldn't give her time to rediscover the wonders of creating. She had to press through and tap into the artist that had begged to be released. She had wanted to explore and test the waters, but not this way. She glanced at the other canvases. She'd barely slept as she tried to rediscover the artist inside her.

She'd started with Impressionists, filling ten or twelve canvases with the quick strokes of light and color. Then she'd returned to the Old Masters that Emilio had her copy when she was in Italy. She was most proud of a copy of a Botticelli she'd left on an easel in a corner as it dried. It wasn't perfect. Wouldn't stand up to inspection yet.

Her phone rang and she reluctantly looked at the screen. Julian. Emilio's guy. Guess she'd better take that one.

"Hi."

"We're here. Open the door."

"Here?"

"I have a buyer."

She stared at her phone and then at the garage door. "I'm not ready."

"You are now. Open the door, Marie."

She wanted to insist he was wrong, but she couldn't. She wasn't in control of her art or any part of her life. While the FBI took its time, she had to keep Emilio and his people placated.

Someone started banging on the door.

"Fine. Give me a minute." She hung up and then bowed her head. *Father, I don't know what to do. Will You be with me and protect me? Give me wisdom?*

She walked to the panel on the wall and hit the button to raise the door. Four men stood in the space between the garage and the alley. She took them in at a glance but froze when she recognized one she hadn't expected.

What was Carter doing here?

Her brother worked in a museum in Atlanta the last time she'd done an internet search on him. While she'd reconciled with her parents, she hadn't talked with Carter. Had her parents contacted him?

With Julian and Rahul here, she wasn't going to give them a bit of ammunition to let them know there was any connection they could use against her.

That was too risky when they already knew about Drew.

When had her life become some convoluted plot in a suspense novel?

She didn't bother to smile as she took in the four men. "What can I help you with?"

Julian was still an unknown to her. He walked in with an edge, strolling the perimeter of the space as if searching for something, distinctly out of place in the July heat in his three-piece suit.

"I've brought a buyer. He's in town for only a day, but is intrigued by your style and thinks your work could be a great addition to his galleries. Stanley Dukes, this is one of my artists that you noticed in the gallery. Marie Montgomery is brilliant." Julian frowned at the dark painting on the easel. "Usually she creates light landscapes of Italy with a Monet styled Impressionist feel, though this one looks like a fresh interpretation."

"You know artists like to play and experiment." Marie intentionally simpered. She wanted them gone—the faster the better. Seeing Rahul here now reinforced she couldn't wait for the FBI to help her disappear. She'd have to create her own way out. Selling paintings to this man would get her a step closer to disappearing without waiting for anyone else to decide she and Drew were worth saving.

Mr. Dukes was a small man with a head of silver hair who walked with a lot of attitude, the classic peacock who puffed up to feel better about himself. He strutted to the easel and then looked around. "This one is interesting but where are your others. I know there must be more."

Marie stifled a sigh. The easiest way to get rid of them would be to show him what he wanted. Julian had mentioned her practice paintings, and she glanced at her brother. "Can you help me?"

"Sure." As Carter followed her away from the others, she nudged closer to him. "What are you doing here?"

"Checking on you." Carter was her younger brother, but so serious and business-like he'd always acted older. "Mom is worried, and I'm still furious. She said you weren't responding to calls and she's worried."

"Is Drew safe?"

"Yes, but what's going on?"

"Is he here because of you?"

"Stanley? Yes, I suggested he check out the work of a rising artist. You can't bounce back into Mom and Dad's life and then disappear with a 'take my son we're in trouble.'"

"Are you two done over there?" Julian sounded impatient. "Rahul, go help them out."

"We're fine." Marie pointed toward a painting. "Take that one. There's no way he'll be interested in that." It was a close copy of one of Botticelli's works and had given her fits as she worked on the intricate details of the young woman's clothing and hair. She was proud of what she'd accomplished, but it had taken hours and days to get the details right. "I'll grab these two." They were more traditional landscapes.

"Give me one more. I want him to spend some of his money on you." He gave her a hard stare. "You owe me an explanation, Charlotte."

"As soon as I can. Grab that still life over there." It was another experiment, this one a pointillism interpretation of a still life of lilies with fruit.

She loved it but didn't need it when she disappeared. She could always paint another.

The thought surprised her, but somehow it had solidified in the time these men had invaded her studio. It was right. Her subconscious must have been working on the idea for a while because now she couldn't think of another approach.

She would disappear—but this time she had to do it right. And that meant she'd change her name and erase everything that could connect her to today and the man who had resurrected the darkest part of her past.

～

Thayer pulled up to the front of Marie's home, surprised to see a couple cars already parked along the road. One was the dually pickup, the other a nice Mercedes sedan. His gut tightened and his muscles primed as if ready for a fight as he hurried around to the back where the garage studio was located.

When he reached the garage, there were four men, along with Marie. She looked so small surrounded by them that he had to do something to let her know she wasn't alone. The sight of the gallery owner plus the muscle was enough to have him on edge. Add two strangers, and he was unclear how much danger existed.

"Marie, do you have my painting?" The words popped out before he could think through what he was saying.

She turned to him, weighted down by paintings in each hand. "Thayer? What are you doing here?"

"Came to pick up my painting." He looked at the ones she and the tall guy carried. Which one looked most likely to be a forged copy? His mind scrambled. He was an accountant, not an art connoisseur, but the one with the woman, that looked right. "There she is." He pointed at the one the young man held. "I'll take that, thanks."

The young man looked at Marie, his voice low. "Char?"

"Tell him to give me my painting."

She blinked a few times as if coming out of a dream. "Um . . ."

Thayer turned to Julian. "That's the one she painted for me. I'm here to retrieve it. Then I'll wire the money to the account as we agreed."

277

The small man licked his lips as if salivating over something he had to have. "Let me take a look at it."

The young man reluctantly set it down on an easel. "Be careful."

"That one's not for sale." There was an edge to Marie's voice. "It's not ready."

"Right." Thayer refused to back down. "Because you painted it for me."

Her expression tightened and she gave a tiny shake of her head. "It's not for sale."

"Right. It's mine." He made his voice firm and his stance aggressive.

The small man seemed giddy as he pulled out his phone and turned on the flashlight before running the light over the painting. "You did this? It's not a restoration?"

"It is not a restoration." Marie's voice was hard. Angry.

"Perfect." The man turned to Julian. "What was he going to pay? I'll double it."

"Wait a minute." Thayer waved his arms. "You can't do that. It's mine. I commissioned it." He hadn't, but Julian wouldn't know that. Not really. The man just wanted money. "We had a contract."

"If he's willing to pay forty thousand dollars, then your contract is void." Julian gave him a tight smile. "Marie will paint something different for you. Or you can raise your bid."

He made a pretense of sputtering and being indigent, but there was no way he could go higher. He couldn't afford the original twenty thousand. Ten minutes later Julian and the little man walked out with the painting, Rahul and the younger man trailing. As soon as they were out of earshot, Marie spun on him.

"What have you done?"

Her anger had him stepping back. "What?"

"That painting doesn't have my little Easter egg on it. Anyone who doesn't scrutinize it could think it's real." She spun on her heel. "You just sold a forgery."

Chapter Thirteen

MARIE SPENT THE NEXT FEW DAYS TRYING TO FIGURE OUT HOW to undo the sale to Stanley Dukes as well as stockpiling enough cash to disappear—and how to do it right so that no one, Emilio included, could find her.

Each day was one more without Drew.

Each day was one more chance for Emilio to determine things had gone on long enough.

Each day was another one without contact from the FBI.

She pulled Agent Paarlberg's card from the slot in her phone case, then tucked it away again.

Could she trust him?

She wanted to, but life had taught her to be very careful who she trusted.

Her circle was very small. Her parents had Drew and she didn't dare contact her brother, so that left no one to help her. Her efforts to disappear eight years earlier had been insufficient. Simply changing her first name and her appearance weren't enough. This time she'd have to do it better. Alter birth certificates and passports. Go deeper into new identities for her and Drew.

Thayer kept showing up.

Did she dare to tell him what she planned to do?

She needed to trust someone.

She had a good reason to reach out to him, since he was why that painting had been sold, with the help of Carter's shenanigans. She still didn't know what to do about that, but she'd figure something out. Even if it meant self-reporting the painting. There had to be someone she could alert to the fact the painting was her copy, not an original. She'd played with adding the craquelure to the paint, but it wouldn't stand up to a professional inspection, not when the pattern of cracks served as fingerprints to a painting.

But right now, she had to address the more immediate problem of getting Emilio to leave her alone permanently. That would require leverage she didn't have yet. Or it would require disappearing so he couldn't find her in the future.

Both required access to cash and protection. She needed a profile that would make her disappearance noticeable. Right now, only a handful of people would even know she was gone, especially since she'd quit her job at Hunter & Associates.

She'd watched Emilio's family manipulate the system in their area in Italy. She had entered the relationship with a certain level of innocence, but she hadn't been blind. She could ignore the truth, but she couldn't pretend she hadn't noticed the people who disappeared after a disagreement. Or the way that certain jobs were expected. The way people approached Emilio's father that didn't simply show deference but reflected fear.

Marie had stayed away from the family's villa as much as possible, but she couldn't all the time.

She'd seen Emilio's father's arrogance born of fear and thinly veiled violence.

And then she'd seen the threads of it in Emilio.

He had told her it was time for her to paint for the family. It had explained the pressure for her to paint but, even more, to copy the paintings in the great museums like the Uffizi.

What had started as encouragement to grow in her art had turned to pressure as her paintings were trotted in front of family "friends" who looked and sounded more like art curators than Sicilian businessmen.

She'd always told herself she'd run because she didn't want her child to be swept into the violence of the family business.

But she hadn't wanted to be manipulated into participating, either.

She wouldn't be the muscle, but they wanted her heart. Her art.

And while she'd given Emilio the first, she couldn't . . . wouldn't give him her art.

And now he was back demanding the second.

Thayer had taken her to the FBI agent so he must have some connections. He was her next best option to figure out another plan to escape and disappear.

Decision made.

She called him and asked him to meet her at a small hole in the wall restaurant on the north side of Indy. It was exactly the kind of place Julian wouldn't visit, so she'd trust Emilio wouldn't either.

That was her hope and prayer as she approached it for her meeting with Thayer.

The diner was a former fire station and had the character of a building that had been filled with purpose for years and had transformed into a gathering place. The food was good in an unexpected way, and it was a place with regulars. The kind where people recognized each other even if they didn't know names. She banked on that providing some protection if Rahul did show up. He would stick out with his off the rack suits and broad build. His intensity would be most out of place with the casual gathering vibe, but many who came had served at the station or in other capacities. They wouldn't put up with the threat of violence.

After Marie stepped inside, she glanced around and moved to the back where Thayer waited at a table. He stood as she approached, then the moment turned awkward as if he wasn't sure whether to shake her hand or pull her into a hug. It unnerved her how much the thought of a hug comforted her. She couldn't afford to rely on someone else like that even if she was here exactly because she needed someone. Her life was a study in contrasts right now, a reality she despised.

She stepped into a side hug and let it settle around her. "Thank you for meeting."

"Sure. How can I help?"

"How did you know I needed help?"

He waited for her to sit on one side of the booth then sank onto his side. "You called."

"Yeah." She rolled her shoulders, trying to release the tension. "Are you serious about buying a painting?"

He looked past her, as if trying to read something behind her. "I don't know. I really wanted that painting of the woman."

She frowned at him as she leaned into the table. "You didn't even know about that painting until you created a bidding war for it. Why did you do that?"

He shrugged. "You needed help."

She had, but how did he know that? It would have taken fine-tuned intuition to clue into that detail. "But why that painting?"

"It looked old." He finally met her gaze. "Look, I don't know anything about paintings, but I know you need help. You're stuck in something that I don't think you understand."

Her blood ran cold. "What do you mean I'm stuck?"

"There's an investigation into the gallery. Add that to Emilio Accardi being here." He grimaced as if he was imagining a future he didn't like, but plowed ahead. "I don't like any of this, but I'm really glad you sent your son away."

"I need this to end so Drew can come home. It's been too long."

"I understand."

"No, you don't. You aren't a parent. You have no idea what it's like to be separated from your child, even though you know it's what's best."

"You're right. I'm sorry." He reached for her hand but stopped short.

She wanted to close the gap, and it scared her. What was she supposed to do with that? Let him closer or push him away? If she did the latter, she would truly be alone. Then where would she be?

He seemed to read her tension and let out a slow breath as the waitress stopped by.

"What can I get y'all?"

"Coffee for me." Thayer looked at her. "Do you want anything to eat?"

"I'll have hot tea if you have it, maybe a slice of wheat toast and some fruit?"

"Is that an order, sweetheart, or a wish?"

Marie tried not to grimace. "An order."

"Would you like butter and jam?"

"Sure." She settled back against the booth.

The waitress turned her attention back on Thayer. "Sure you don't want some sustenance?"

He gave her a flirty grin and patted his stomach. "Had some granola and yogurt at home."

"How about some protein?"

"I'm good." He focused on Marie in a way that politely dismissed the woman. She got the message and headed to the next table. "Where were we?"

"I was deciding how much to trust you."

He put a hand over his heart. "You slay me."

"You know I already trust you or I wouldn't have invited you here. The question is how much to trust you."

"I want to help." He rubbed his hand over his floppy hair, only mussing it more.

She bit her lower lip as the waitress returned with a mug of coffee for Thayer and a mug of hot water and a couple tea bags for Marie. "Thank you."

After the woman wandered off, she looked up from swirling the teabag through the water. "I want to trust you, but if you betray that trust, I'm gone."

He nodded solemnly. "I understand. I don't know enough about Emilio Accardi yet, but it's clear he messed you up."

"That's one way of putting it." She took a breath. It was time to trust Thayer, or she needed to walk out. "I need to find a way to disappear before Emilio forces me to return to his world. I don't want Drew to be part of it. Emilio doesn't care about my son. He informed me that he already has two sons and doesn't need Drew—except as a way control me."

"I heard what he said on the recording." He reached across the table and grasped her hand. "I admire what you did to save your son. I can imagine how hard that was."

"It was." She'd been right to trust Thayer. "I thought I knew how to disappear, but I just fooled myself. And if the FBI won't help me, I'm trapped. If I am, Emilio will win. He'll make me paint for him."

"And then . . ."

"Art is highly unregulated. It's technically bought and sold on the open market, but it doesn't truly have value until someone agrees to purchase it. Think about that canvas in my studio. Sure, it looked like a Sandro Botticelli, but it's just paint and canvas. Probably the materials are worth a few hundred dollars . . . maybe a thousand thanks to the gold leaf." She paused as the waitress brought her food, ignoring the way she focused on Thayer. "But without an interested buyer willing to invest in the product, it's essentially worthless. But then when you and the gallery owner started to compete for it, the value jumped from twenty thousand to forty thousand dollars in a matter of minutes. What had little value now was worth more than many Americans make in a year."

"But lots of products are like that. Until there's an interested buyer, there's no real value."

"Yes, but now think about if I had agreed to create a forgery that could be held out as an actual painting by Botticelli rather than a close copy. Suddenly that painting could be worth millions—and very few people could tell us it isn't actually his." Marie paused. How could she keep this simple yet complex enough to illustrate what was at stake? "If I painted something and then it was held out as a painting by someone the entire world values, then immense value is fabricated overnight."

"And when it's purchased and sold money can be cleaned."

"Maybe. I don't know. I'm the artist, not an accountant."

"But *I'm* the accountant. I know what the money can and can't do." He studied her a moment. "Johnson and I have been investigating the gallery for money laundering. It could be a front for organized crime."

"And the Accardi family could be part of that crime." She speared a piece of pineapple and cut it in pieces before forking a bite into her mouth. It was perfectly ripe and delicious, a sunshine explosion for her taste buds and a brief respite from their serious conversation. "I suppose it makes sense. Especially if they've expanded their network to the United

States, but I'd have no idea about any of that. I'm just an artist turned receptionist. All I want to do is create, and nobody will leave me alone to do that."

"If we're right that art is being used to launder money, how do we prove it?"

"Have you purchased a painting? Isn't that what your angle was?"

"Yes, basically."

"So, are you FBI?"

"No." She arched an eyebrow, and he just grinned at her. "Really, I'm an accountant. I don't even play an FBI agent on TV."

"How can you help?"

"Together I think we can track down the information that gives the FBI the evidence it needs to bring down whatever operation Emilio and the Accardis have in place here."

"This is Indianapolis, Indiana. The crossroads of America. Not exactly a crime hotspot."

"Actually, you'd be surprised. I spend a lot of my time analyzing and untangling financial data for the FBI. It's kind of my superpower."

"I'm glad it's yours because numbers are not my friends." She thought about the sorry state of her bank account. There was money in it, but only because she kept a buffer of three thousand dollars. Then she didn't have to nickel and dime every transaction. She shuddered at the idea of spending her days looking at numbers. "You actually enjoy that?"

"Sure. I'm identifying patterns and, since I know what I'm looking for, the patterns are easier to spot."

"Like what?"

"Big transactions. And patterns in those. Is the same person purchasing multiple paintings? Who is selling the paintings? Is there a tight connection between buyers and sellers?"

"There should be because they're buying and selling the same paintings."

"I'm looking for whether the same person is buying paintings from the gallery regularly. If we could get you close enough to Julian, then we could see if there's a high volume that few could sustain legally." He studied her. "Could that happen?"

"I don't know if Emilio would allow that. It might serve his purpose, but it might take too long." She thought a minute. "Even if I could get positioned, traditionally the artist focuses on the number and price of sales not the who behind the purchase. Anything else might be suspicious. And that could be dangerous."

Where large amounts of money were at stake, people got killed.

She'd seen too much in Italy to pretend this wasn't life or death.

Chapter Fourteen

THAYER FOLLOWED MARIE INTO HER HOME, AN AREA THAT reflected her true personality. The palette was a bright yellow backdrop with pops of primary colors. The wood furniture was all painted black for another bright contrast.

"My laptop is over here." She led the way through the kitchen to a small hallway and then to a small room that served as something of an office with tubs of toys. "When the pandemic hit, I had to get creative as a working mom and needed a workable space for me and Drew. I never moved the toys out." She shrugged, a little pink coloring her cheeks, in the most adorable way.

"I think it's great. Not everyone could make that work, but you have." He glanced at the laptop that was plugged into a larger monitor. "What do you want me to look at?"

"Emilio has connected me with Julian, but I'm not sure how to structure this. What do I need to collect from Julian to get what you need?" She shuddered. "Artist, not bookkeeper."

He couldn't resist a grin that he was sure was silly and lopsided. "Bookkeeper and non-creative." He stepped to the desk. "Show me what you've got."

She sat at the desk and started clicking around with the mouse. After a couple minutes, she leaned back. "It's not much, but maybe it will help."

He grabbed a chair from the kitchen and set it next to hers, leaning close enough that their shoulders touched as he took control of the mouse. "You're right. Nothing's immediately obvious. Can I print these emails?"

"Sure."

He clicked through them, noting while he was at it if there were any that she hadn't shared with him.

She reached over and grabbed the sheets of paper from the printer. After organizing it, she handed it to him. "What now?"

"I'm not sure. What do you think the next step should be?"

"We should look into Julian's business. There have to be records online that we can access. Anything might give us a connection to Emilio."

"I've already done some searching, but we can try together. Maybe we'll see something I missed."

"Or I'm crazy to think that way?"

"No, two sets of eyes are always better than one. Here, let me show you where I searched." He clicked around a bit and then landed on a couple pages. When he pulled each up, she didn't seem very impressed.

"What am I supposed to be looking at?"

"Is there any information here that's wrong?"

"I'm not sure I'd know."

"You're more familiar with the art world than I am."

"I *was* more familiar. That was a lifetime ago. Remember I left it to hide, but that didn't work so well." She took a minute to scan, taking control of the mouse and scrolling down.

"How would he arrange the sales?"

"Each would probably be different. When I was in Italy, I'd get a call from Emilio that someone was interested in a painting. Emilio liked to keep me separate from the buyers. He'd send information on the painting or the artist the buyer was most interested in. Other times, he'd find a collector who was intrigued about an artist I was experimenting on."

"What's a typical time from purchase to delivery?"

"The fastest was probably a couple weeks, but that was when I already had it started. Often at that point, I'm playing with how to make it look old. The only problem comes if I mess it up. Bake it too high or fast."

"You bake a painting?"

"It's a fast way to make the paint crack in a way that replicates age." She clicked over to the National Gallery of Art and then zoomed in on a painting. "See how there are cracks in the paint? That's from exposure to heat and age. I have to try to recreate that if I really want someone to believe my painting is a couple hundred years old."

"And you started playing with this why?"

"Because I was curious." She sighed and leaned back in her chair. "My brother told me about some of the work he was doing in one of his restoration classes, and I thought it would be interesting to test how you add age to a painting rather than remove it." She shrugged and an impish grin quirked her lips. "Emilio encouraged my experimentation, and I was too naïve to question that."

"Huh."

"I don't do it often." She shook her head. "That's not true. At the time I dove deeply into an artist's world as I learned how to paint like them. My brother called me a master mimic. I like to think of it as someone who embodies the artist. Not in a weird way, but in a way that I care about how they lived, what they had available to them when they painted, and how to recreate it as closely as possible. It's also why I incorporated something extra in the paintings, so it's not too close."

"Except for the one I sold."

"Exactly. It wasn't ready."

"If we find the earlier pieces circulating on the art market, you can identify them as your copies?"

"Absolutely."

"How?"

She clamped her lips together in a way that made it clear she wasn't speaking.

"You can trust me with the detail. Who would I tell?"

"That's just it. I have no idea." She crossed her arms over her chest and pivoted slightly away from him. "I can't tell you and have you share it with the wrong people and have that advantage get out."

Her doubt in him made him want to argue, but she was being wise.

There was something smart in being aware of what protected her and maintaining it.

"You do understand if something happens to you, no one knows your mark is on these paintings, or even which paintings to watch for."

"Maybe I've got a list somewhere."

"And when we find the information, then we can go to the FBI and get you and Drew in witness protection."

"As long as Drew is safe, that's what matters to me. I want a backup plan if we can't convince them."

The moment Thayer left, the emptiness settled back over Marie.

She had to do something rather than wait for someone else to save her.

How could she trick Julian into letting her get close to his records?

There had to be a way to make him step into the light and do something that would get the FBI excited. Even better if it involved Emilio.

The question was what that needed to be.

She knew that it had to involve money laundering. It was the only thing that made sense.

There was no other reason she could imagine that Emilio and his family would be interested in her. As she thought about it, it was the only reason it made sense that he would have been involved back then too. She wasn't super model pretty. No, she had more of a Drew Barrymore cuteness to her. Soft and cuddly rather than hard and angular. As she considered the earliest days of Emilio's interest in her, it all cycled back to her work. He'd first approached her at the Uffizi. She hadn't thought anything of it since she'd almost lived there as she'd studied one of the Raphael's there. Then she'd moved onto a fascination with Botticelli's *Primavera*. She could have spent years deciphering all the layers he'd embedded in that one painting. It had always bothered her that the average tourist spent mere minutes in front of the wall-sized painting, and she could spend hours studying the brushstrokes in inches.

What she could never decide was if it indicated a problem with them or her.

Emilio had encouraged her compulsion.

THE ART OF DECEPTION

And she'd been all too willing to let him set her up with an apartment.

She'd ignored that there had to be an additional motivation—besides love—behind his interest.

Initially, the only times he'd been angry with her were when he hadn't thought she'd invested enough hours studying. Then it had been when her copies hadn't looked enough like the originals. She'd interpreted it as wanting her to improve and become a master in her own right.

Now she knew he'd been grooming her to be a forger and she'd been too desperate for love to realize it.

It made her sick to think she had been so blind. So easy.

She wouldn't be this time.

Instead, she could use that knowledge to her advantage.

All she had to do was set the trap for him.

Who had been the artist he had encouraged her to focus on at the time? She flipped through the images she hadn't let herself think about for eight years. There had been good times. Many of them that were interspersed with the explosions of anger that had scared her into fleeing before she became one of the people who disappeared. Emilio had liked whisking her off to a city across Italy for a day to show her one of the museums. It had been a show of power and wealth, but it had also been important to her education and something she never could have accomplished on her own.

There had been the time he'd taken her to Paris for the weekend because he'd wanted to show her the Leonardo da Vincis in the Louvre. He was too famous and had too few paintings to suddenly have a new painting appear on the market, so that wouldn't work.

Maybe a Rembrandt?

He was much more prolific. And with his workshop, it just might work to have a new painting appear that could be attributed to Rembrandt or his workshop. His style was also much easier to imitate. In fact, there had been famous forgers who had forged him so adeptly they fooled experts. One had painted a forgery in the courtroom to prove his level of skill.

That might work. The question would be what subject.

Rembrandt was a master of so many styles. Most probably thought of his portraits or self-portraits. But he also had landscapes, and she could copy one of those with a twist where it could look like a new discovery.

That might work.

And she adored landscapes.

It wouldn't be too much of a stretch to change her color palette from the light Impressionist colors she loved to the darker palette of the Dutch painters in the 1600s. Yes, that could work.

She started sketching out an idea.

As it took shape, she also started composing an email. It would be important to strategically lay the breadcrumbs to get Emilio to bite. She needed him to decide he had to have this painting. If he didn't, then all her planning and scheming would be worthless. The key was getting him to bite. Then she'd get the evidence the FBI needed. That's what had to happen.

Otherwise, everything was wasted effort.

~

Walking away from Marie was hard for Thayer. He found the days ticked by slowly and he missed her colorful presence at Hunter & Associates. More than that though, he didn't like that she spent so much time alone at her home. Without Drew, she was getting ready to do something desperate, so Thayer asked Johnson to meet with him at a park off 96th Street before she went off on her own.

Johnson leaned against Thayer's car in the parking lot. "Is all this cloak and dagger necessary?"

"Maybe not. But I want to make sure we're keeping everyone who doesn't need to know in the dark." Thayer leaned against the car next to his friend and studied the other cars in the lot. "How does Rahul always know where we're going to be?"

"Good question." Johnson shrugged. "It bothers me too, but I don't know what to tell you."

"So, what do we do?"

"You don't do anything. You scan the numbers, and I'll work on a plan. That's my job. Yours is to not mess anything up."

"Thanks for the vote of confidence."

"You need to do what you do best and let other people do what they do best. You could get hurt, man. This is a bad family she's embroiled in, I don't think you understand just how bad, but people routinely vanish from the neighborhood. There one day and gone the next."

"Sounds serious,"

"It is." Johnson turned toward him, and Thayer felt the weight of his attention. "This isn't something you play at and go home if it explodes in your face. Do you get that?"

"Got it." Thayer met Johnson's gaze. "She asked me for a new identity. She's not willing to wait and see if you can protect her."

Johnson stilled. "That's dangerous."

"Yes. But she's unnerved that the boyfriend claims to have known where she was all along. She's determined to really disappear this time." He blew out a breath. "She asked me for help."

"That's not a good idea."

"I know."

"Keep her calm and let us work our process. The marshals are the ones to help her disappear. Not you."

The words felt like a slap even if they were accurate. "Then help me help her. I don't want her to panic and disappear. She's the real deal."

Johnson studied him then nodded. "I hope so for your sake, because you're getting it bad."

"What do you mean?"'

Johnson gave him a crooked smile. "I think you know."

And Thayer did.

Chapter Fifteen

OVER THE NEXT FEW DAYS, THE PAINTING TOOK SHAPE. EMILIO called, but she ignored him. Then Julian called, and she ignored him, too. She needed both men teased into being hungry for whatever she had to offer. She didn't want Rahul to show up without an invitation, but she'd have to risk it for another couple days. She needed to accelerate the timeline, because she desperately missed Drew and it had been almost three weeks. She could only imagine how he wanted to come home, no matter how much fun he was having with her parents, and she needed him with her.

But she needed to stay the course long enough to get Emilio hooked and then she could do what was necessary to bring Drew home and know he was safe. It would be worse to bring him home and then force him to leave again. Her heart wouldn't handle it and she wasn't sure his would either.

The rumble of the mail truck caught her attention, so she walked to the front of her cottage to check for some paint she was waiting for. When she pulled out the envelopes, one caught her attention.

Internet Bank of the Ozarks.

What?

She'd never heard of it, but thought it was probably just wanting her money, so she prepared to rip it up, then decided to open the envelope in case it was something important. When she pulled out the sheet, she froze when she read the word stamped in red at the top. DELINQUENT.

What on earth?

She scanned the notice, her panic rising with each line.

Someone believed she owed this bank thousands of dollars in student loans, but she couldn't. She'd paid off the last of her student loans six years earlier.

How could she owe a bank she'd never heard of anything?

And how could she find out one way or another?

She fumbled with her phone and called Thayer, the fear rising in her. She'd fought so hard, eaten so much mac and cheese, to rise out of the foolishness of all her debt. It had taken hard work to walk a different path. What could have happened?

"Marie, are you okay?"

"I don't know." She heard the jangle of something, maybe car keys.

"Tell me what happened and where you are."

"You don't have to come."

"Already on the way, so you might as well tell me where to come."

She sagged with relief. "Thank you." She wiped at a tear she hadn't noticed trailing down her cheek. "I got a notice from a bank I've never heard of that I owe it money for student loans."

"You've not familiar with it?"

"No."

"Then it's probably a phishing scheme. Was it an email?"

"No, paper, which is what makes it feel so official."

"That is unusual. I'll be there in a few minutes. Assuming you're at home?"

"Yes." After she hung up, she went into the house and pulled out cookie dough from the freezer. She needed to do something but wasn't sure what Thayer would like. After the time they'd spent together working on things she should have a better idea. She needed to do something about that. Learn what he liked so she could have his preferences available. Still, chocolate chip cookies were always a safe choice.

When he walked in a few minutes later, she was sliding a pan of four cookies from the oven.

"You didn't need to make anything for me."

"Just like you didn't need to come here for me. But you did."

"I did." He sat at the small wooden table she'd found at a Goodwill and then distressed. It fit the space but looked tiny with him sitting there. "Do you have the letter?"

She pulled it from her back pocket and slid it across the table. "It doesn't make sense. My loans were with a national bank, and I have the paperwork that shows I paid them."

"Good. That will be important." He picked up the letter and she could tell by his pace he read it line by line, word for word, a fact she appreciated. He also seemed to glaze over the fact it was in her real name. "Have you called the number yet?"

"No." She sat and placed her hands on the table. "I wasn't sure if I should call or ignore it."

"Let's call and put it on speaker."

"All right." Thirty minutes later, Thayer had her convinced someone was messing with her after he had the person who picked up tied in knots with his incisive questions.

"What are you working on?"

"Nope, you can't distract me that easily. I want to know how this letter got in my mailbox." She could still feel the adrenaline coursing through her. "This piece of paper derailed my morning and took at least a year off my life."

"Does it really matter?"

"Yes. What if I get something else like this? What if this is just the first salvo?"

"Then whoever is bothering you needs a life."

She flinched at his words, and Thayer tried to soften his stance and words. "Sorry, it was a late-night working. Who would want to disrupt your life by doing something like this?"

"Other than Emilio? No one."

"Has he done anything like this before?"

"That's the thing." She bit her lower lip, in a way that endeared her to him. She had no idea how charming she was. "Until a couple weeks ago, I thought I had successfully disappeared without a trace." She rubbed her eyes and then yawned as if she hadn't gotten much sleep. "Sorry." She waved a hand in front of her mouth. "I don't sleep well when Drew's not here."

"We'll get him home soon."

"I hope so." She sighed. "But I won't rush it. I've seen what happens when Emilio's family is involved."

"I might have some good news." Johnson had finally come through with a thread he'd pulled. It had taken a long time, but he'd started to tug it free.

"I need good news."

"Johnson gave me the name of a company that is owned by a company that's owned by another company that's owned by Julian and Emilio."

"They own a company together?"

"They do. Equal partners. As far as I can tell by the public records, it's an investment company. Investing in art."

"Really?" She stood and paced her small kitchen. "I didn't expect them to be in cahoots. Emilio gives orders. He's too much like his father to partner with anyone."

"Well, he seems to be changing his role now."

"There has to be a reason."

"Yes." Thayer let himself smile. "Large sums of money are running through this entity."

She cocked her head as she studied him with a furrowed brow.

"It's like you told me at the beginning. They're using the gallery as a front, at least in part. Some of it might be real sales, but at least part of it is for organized crime."

"Then we have to trap them." She nodded and stood. "I've got a plan."

"Of course you do." It shouldn't surprise him that she would be working on something.

"I'm not waiting on the FBI agent to decide what he can or can't do. Follow me." She stood and headed to the back door.

It was follow or get left behind, and part of him was concerned that the muscle would appear at any time again. At least if he was near, he could pretend to help if he showed up. She unlocked the garage and then lead the way to an easel standing under lights. "What do you think?"

Thayer stood next to her and stared at a painting of a landscape with greens and browns with a swirl of clouds and pops of water. "It's a scene."

She looked like she couldn't decide whether to laugh or roll her eyes again. "Why did they pick you to go to an art gallery? I don't think there are many people who could know less about art." She turned to the painting and studied it like it was her favorite painting. "I'd like to introduce you to the latest undiscovered painting by Rembrandt."

"I've heard of him."

Marie turned to him and slugged him playfully in the shoulder. "Of course you have. There's only one Rembrandt and everyone's heard of him just like everybody knows who Beethoven and Shakespeare are."

"Who?" He grinned as she muttered under her breath.

"You really are impossible. Dutch master. Sixteen hundreds." When he pretended to be blank, she shook her head. "Neanderthal."

"Just not as passionate as you. The key is why him?"

"Two reasons. Emilio doesn't own one. At least he didn't and he and his father talked about adding one to their collection. Two, he was a prolific painter, so having a new painting surface won't be beyond what's expected or possible. It wouldn't be the first time it's happened." She crossed her arms and studied what was on the canvas. "He's not finished, but I've done a good job."

"When will it be ready?"

"I need a few more days, and then we can bait the trap. The great thing is if everything you've found about the gallery is true, Julian won't care if it's real. He'll love the idea that it might be real and can be sold for a fortune. Emilio will like the idea that he could own a Rembrandt and either keep it or resell it."

"How would it resell?"

"Either through the gallery in a few years or through an auction house or another gallery. It would be pretty amazing if I did such a good job, they were convinced it was genuine, but I only need to convince Emilio. Just enough to get him to bite that it's a forgery he can pass off to others." She rubbed her arms as if she was suddenly cold. "Then we can go to the

FBI with concrete evidence of the money laundering scheme that goes beyond dry entries in a spreadsheet you broke into."

"Hey those entries work, too."

"Sure, but live testimony is always better in the movies."

Thayer snorted. "Life always lines up with the movies."

"Only more boring."

"Sure." He considered the painting. "So you need a few days to make it look old."

"Yes, but not too many. Then I need you to show up demanding a painting. I'll call Julian about this one, and make sure he knows it's the kind of painting I think you and Emilio would like. Julian will imagine a bidding war which will give him visions of a large deposit in his bank account."

"And then we work on the arrest."

"And Drew comes home." The wistfulness in her voice made him willing to do anything to make this happen as quickly as possible.

"All right. Let's do it. I'll get ready to call and apply some pressure on Julian so he can pass that pressure on to you."

"And I'll get this painting ready for its slow bake." She crossed one arm over her stomach and braced the other elbow on it, nibbling her thumbnail. "This has to work, because I need my son back. Our life back."

He pulled her close and she sank against him. Thayer tried not to become distracted by the reality of how right this felt. She was the perfect fit for him. Where he was over-analytical, she was a free spirit. Where he was black and white, she colored outside the lines with a rainbow. And where he stuck to a routine, she explored what could be.

"I like getting to know you, Marie Montgomery."

"I like you too, Thayer."

As those words settled over him, he hoped they'd have the chance to figure out what might be possible between them. After this was mess was resolved and Drew came home.

Chapter Sixteen

THE NEXT DAY MARIE STOOD IN THE GARAGE IN FRONT OF THE painting. She'd done a good job and now it was time to launch the next phase of her plan. She stared at the phone in her hand. Did she have the courage to do this? If the call didn't go well, all the time she'd invested in the painting sitting on the easel would be wasted and Drew would be no closer to coming home. Her arms were so empty without her boy running into them from for a spontaneous hug only to dash away to whatever caught his fancy next.

The loneliness overwhelmed her—especially at night when she tried to sleep but ended up tossing and turning in her bed in her darkened room.

Thayer had to notice the number of times she called him, each time with a reason that became flimsier with the length of time Drew was gone. At some point he would grow weary of her neediness. But then, he kept bringing her tomato soup with fresh croutons, so he couldn't mind too much. The man was quite good at spoiling her.

Did she want to be spoiled?

Yes. But that was beside the point. She'd let her mind wander from the task at hand. From what she didn't want to do.

She had to call Julian.

Convince him to call Emilio. This painting had to become the bait that pulled Emilio more deeply in. If the recorded call also captured enough information to intrigue the agents, better still.

She blew out a slow breath. Prayed for wisdom.

In her own knowledge she would screw this up. No question.

But with God's help, it might work.

It had to work.

Before she could chicken out again, she dialed Julian's number. When he picked up, she launched into her spiel. "Based on my research of his collection, Emilio will love this painting, Julian."

"You're sure you don't want to be the one to approach him?"

She shuddered at the thought of contact. "Certain."

"I'll be over in an hour to look at it."

And then he hung up.

Maria shivered as she realized she had a chance. She spent that hour second-guessing every stroke of paint. Would anyone believe it was a Rembrandt?

A couple hours later as Marie was about to crawl out of her skin, Julian arrived and marched up to the canvas. He tilted his head one way and then the other, before he turned to look at her. "Why are you so sure he'll want a Rembrandt?"

"It's not hard to figure out what he likes to collect."

"He's Italian. He's not interested in the Dutch masters."

Marie snorted at his arrogance and laziness. "Believe in stereotypes much? Emilio's family is all about status."

"How do you know this? Have you seen their home?"

Actually she had, but she didn't want to admit that if she didn't have to. Julian didn't need that type of powerful information about her. "You told me he wants quality paintings by masters. I dug through auction purchase records. They don't own a Rembrandt."

"That you know."

She motioned to the canvas. "This is what he wants."

"But it's not even a copy."

"That's the brilliant part. It's inspired by several of his landscapes. It's not a copy, but someone could argue he or someone in his workshop painted it. Either way it will have enhanced value."

"So it is a forgery." There was a long pause which made her think he wouldn't bite. Then he suddenly clapped his hands. "I love it." Julian paused. "Why for this guy and now?"

"There's something about him I don't like. He seems dangerous and pushy, and I don't like that combination."

"He is, so be sure you're ready for the push back. You can't change your mind in a couple days. We do this, you're all in."

"I understand." Marie forced her voice to remain strong. "My fee is sixty thousand dollars for this painting if it sells for one hundred to three hundred thousand dollars. Above that, my fee is thirty percent of whatever you're paid."

"That's steep."

She didn't budge. "Without me, you don't have a painting. I can also go directly to him. In fact, that's what you wanted me to do, right?"

"Hold on. It's best if everything goes through me." Julian was all business now. "He'll be at the gallery at four this afternoon to see the painting. You'll need to have it there by three and then disappear."

"What if I want to be there?"

"Probably better that you aren't if we want to sell it as a possible new discovery."

"And what's your cover story?"

"A family discovered it going through Grandpa's estate. Not sure what to make of it but it looks like something that should be worth some money and the family asked for my help facilitating a sale. After all, that is part of what I do as a gallery owner. "

"Would it help if there was some competition?"

"Not always. I'll feel him out and develop a strategy for competition if it's needed. Some people want exclusivity. If that doesn't work, we can always take it more broadly, but this is probably the perfect case for a very tight showing. The fewer people who know about it, the better. Let's remember it is a fake."

He stepped closer and studied her painting, then turned and looked at it from another angle. That's when she knew she had him. Julian was still convincing himself it wasn't a Rembrandt.

If he wasn't sure, then there was a strong chance Emilio would be deceived.

~

When Thayer walked up to Julian's gallery, it was just after four o'clock in the afternoon. Marie had given him strict instructions to be a few minutes late because Emilio was usually early but occasionally right on time. They needed Emilio in place for Tucker's entrance to have the maximum impact.

Johnson had helped him add an app to his phone that would work better than a wire to capture everything that happened around him while also transmitting back to Johnson in his vehicle at the end of the block. Johnson would look like he was reading the news on his tablet, but would keep close tabs on everything Thayer could hear.

That was comforting, but Thayer still felt exposed. He expected to see muscle man Rahul standing in a corner of the room with a frown plastered on his face. The man delighted in intimidating everyone, including Thayer.

Thayer paused outside the windows' view and quickly rolled his shoulders then neck. Then he straightened his spine and opened the door before sauntering inside as if he expected everyone inside to jump to attention now that he'd arrived. "Good, you're here."

Julian turned from the back left corner of the studio where Marie had told Thayer to expect the *Rembrandt* to rest on an ornate easel. She'd suggested he make a show of the easel being too gaudy and clashing with the Rembrandt, so he did. This was her show, and he was a bit player.

"Mr. Thayer? What are you doing here?"

"I'm ready to buy my replacement for the painting you sold out from under me." He gave what he hoped was a cold smile. "That is not how I conduct business, and I expect you to honor your promise." He strode up to the painting as if it had been placed there for his viewing and stopped square in front of it, intentionally blocking Emilio Accardi's access to a clear sightline. "You acquired a Rembrandt and didn't tell me?"

"I didn't know you had an interest."

"Who wouldn't?" He tilted his head one way, then propped his chin on a fist as he examined it from the other side. "*Hmm.*"

Julian stayed silent, and Thayer had to admire the way the man didn't panic or push him out. Instead, he seemed content to see how this would play out.

However, Accardi was not so patient. "Who are you?"

Thayer didn't bother to answer, but instead stayed focused on the painting.

Accardi turned to Julian. "This is unacceptable. Ask this man to leave or I will have my man remove him from the gallery."

"That's not yours to do." Julian puffed up a bit as if he didn't like being told what to do in such direct terms. Good, that was helpful information to file away. Julian turned back to Thayer. "Are you a fan of Rembrandt's work?"

"Who isn't? The man was a master of contrasts. Light and dark. Sun dappling dark landscapes." He took a step forward and made a big show of squinting at the brushstrokes. He reached out as if to touch the paint, but Julian physically restrained him.

"Sir, that painting is four hundred years old."

"Sorry about that. I got carried away being this close to one of his paintings. It's quite different not being restrained by the constraints of a museum."

"You are a collector?"

"Of course. You've seen my letter of credit." It was one the FBI had arranged for him with a local bank, because his bank account wouldn't sustain a purchase of the size this operation would require. He should probably act offended. "I'm ready to offer fifty thousand for the painting. Right now, no questions asked. I'll have my curator examine it once we have a contract." He deigned to look in Emilio's direction. "I'd like a signed contract by the end of tomorrow."

"I was here first and had an arrangement with you." Accardi's accent would probably woo ladies as it had Marie, but annoyed Thayer. Why emphasize he wasn't from here? That didn't make him more worthy of the painting.

"No good, my fellow." What had he just said? "I'm certain my contract predates any arrangement you think you had with Mr. Bond. Correct, Julian?"

"If he thinks fifty thousand is what this painting is worth, I'll agree to sixty."

"Seventy." Marie had told him not to go beyond one hundred thousand dollars but had said nothing about what the intermediate steps should look like.

Julian looked between the two as if he wasn't sure what was happening, but he also didn't mind the bidding war. "I could always allow the two of you to put your best bid in a sealed envelope and accept the best. That works quite well in situations like this."

"For you. It's a good way to make out like a bandit." Thayer crossed his arms. This wasn't even his money. "No, we have a contract, and you must honor it."

"I guarantee I am the more serious of the two of us." Accardi snapped his fingers, and muscle man materialized from the shadows. "Rahul, see Mister—" He turned to him. "What is your name?"

"Thayer."

"Show Mr. Thayer out and remind him not to come back. He wearies me."

Rahul nodded and grabbed Thayer's arm. "This way."

Thayer wanted to come up with some sort of pithy retort, but kept his mouth shut. No need poking the bear more than he already had. As Rahul escorted him to the door and then stood outside as he walked away, he prayed what he'd done was enough.

There was enough fog to keep them in the dark for a while. What he and Marie needed now was clarity and the wisdom to know next steps to take to bring this to an end.

From her perch in the coffee shop across the street, Marie watched Rahul studying Thayer as the man walked from the gallery. When Thayer climbed into his sedan, Rahul didn't reenter the gallery but instead continued to watch him. Or maybe his attention had shifted to her. Was it possible Rahul could see her through the large plate glass window?

She didn't think so, but it was unnerving to think he had spotted her.

Nobody should know she waited, observing with her own agenda.

Then Thayer climbed from his vehicle and approached Rahul.

Her heart stopped.

Their conversation wasn't agitated. In fact, if anything it was friendly, like they knew and liked each other. That couldn't be right, but there was nothing antagonistic in their body language.

She needed to hear the conversation but couldn't and what she saw was impossible to believe. These two were cooperating and on friendly terms. Everything she thought she knew slid out of order.

Had Thayer used her just like everyone else?

She'd been right to not fully trust him.

To come here and observe for herself.

If only she'd been inside to hear what he'd said.

It had looked like Thayer had taken her suggestions by arriving at the right time but maybe it had all been show and this interaction was the real part. Why would he steer her a certain direction? And had he? All of this had been her idea, hadn't it? Her head started throbbing.

What she saw made no sense. Once again, she was all alone, on the outside.

What should she do now?

She had to think.

Learn the truth.

Disappear.

But she couldn't.

She needed the money from the sale of this painting.

But if Thayer worked with Rahul, then Julian and Emilio also knew how desperate she was. They all knew her full plan. They'd probably laughed about it over beers, talking about how naive she was. No different from the young woman who'd shown up in Italy and let herself be swept off her feet by the bad boy Italian pretending he would be her prince while knowing something had to be wrong because she had known. There was no other explanation. She'd been willfully blind about who Emilio really was.

She wouldn't be blind this time.

She was a woman now. A woman with a son. She would show them all that she could protect him. She might not have been willing to do it before for herself, but she would now.

For Drew.

Thayer turned away, and his gaze flicked to the coffee shop, something hardening in his expression. She saw it across the street though she wasn't sure how, and her heart broke. She'd wanted to believe in him and the possibility of them. She'd allowed her heart to soften and her mind to believe even when she'd known it was foolish.

Then he crossed the street and opened the door.

"What are you doing?" She tossed the words at him as he marched across the room to her table. She stood so fast her chair fell to the floor behind her.

"I'm getting you out of here."

Chapter Seventeen

As she backed up, Marie's eyes widened as she stared at him, alight with a fire. She must have seen him with Rahul, but he didn't have time to explain what she thought she'd seen. Not now. "We've got to get you out of here. I don't know how, but Rahul is suspicious. For a muscle-bound mountain of a man, he's got ideas brewing in that mind."

"Ideas you probably put there as you were talking. I saw you!"

"It wasn't what you think, but we don't have time to hash it out. We've got to leave before he comes to test his theory." Thayer grabbed her arm, and though she tried to jerk free, it was a halfhearted effort. That gave him hope she didn't want to be angry. "Let's see if Johnson has anything he can use. Then we can decide what's next."

"Does your friend even work with the FBI or is that part of some elaborate ruse?"

"We can argue about this on the way."

"What if you're leading me right back to Emilio?"

"You'll have to see, I guess." He glanced around. "We'll head out the back."

"Well, we're all cloak and dagger now. Cavorting with the enemy one minute and slipping out the back the next." Her muscles had tensed beneath his hand, and she looked brittle and frightened.

"I'll explain later. We need to leave."

And get to the safety of FBI protection. He wasn't an agent. He couldn't protect her when the muscle-bound monster across the street realized that he wasn't on the side of the bad guys. So right now he would choose Marie not knowing if she could trust him if that's what it took to protect her. "We have to move." He tugged her to the front counter. "Can we slide out your back door?"

The barista gave them a curious look then nodded. "Sure. It's that way."

"Thanks."

"Just don't tell my boss."

"No problem." Then he led Marie out and had Siri call Johnson. When Johnson answered, he asked him to come around and meet them a couple blocks over.

"Already on my way."

"Did you hear my conversation with Rahul?"

"Yep. We've got to get you two out of there."

"That's what I thought. Do you think they know what Marie's up to?"

"Unclear, but we need to regroup ASAP. Let's meet at that diner."

"See you in a minute." He hustled a resistant Marie along the street. "Can you pretend to trust me for a couple more minutes before someone calls the police?"

"I'm not sure I should." She rubbed her forehead with her free hand, and he felt a stab of regret.

"I'm still on your side." He opened the passenger door of his car and she climbed in.

"I wish I believed you." She sighed, and it was a world-weary sound. "I liked not feeling alone for a little bit."

~

Marie regretted the words the moment they slipped out. They revealed too much, something she hadn't wanted to admit to herself, much less to Thayer. She couldn't go down that rabbit trail of emotion. Not when she didn't know what she was being dragged to in this moment. Had Siri called Johnson? Had she listened to one half of a conversation with an FBI agent? Good night! Was Johnson even an agent or had this whole situation been an elaborate charade?

It didn't make sense.

She'd been living her safe, albeit hidden life until she agreed to go to that stupid gallery showing with Thayer. She'd opened her heart—a fundamental mistake. That's what she got for beginning to care about anyone. Well, she'd learned her lesson, again, the hard way.

Stop caring.

He pulled from the curb, and she tried to shake her pessimism. That wasn't the real lesson.

She did care and she always would.

It was woven into the fabric of how she approached life.

She owed it to Thayer to give him a chance to explain what she'd seen.

Then she heard something.

A deep thrum.

"Um, Thayer."

"Yeah."

"That sounds like Rahul's truck."

He glanced over his shoulder. "I see a pickup. But this is Indiana. That doesn't mean anything."

She used the side-view mirror and froze as the large black pickup loomed into view. "That looks like his. What are we going to do?"

"Nothing. You don't know for sure it's his, and I'm not a race car driver. If I did anything crazy, I'd just get us, or someone else, killed."

"But if we don't do something, we might get killed anyway."

"That's a bit melodramatic."

"Don't you watch movies? Read books? The bad guy in the pickup or SUV always rams into the small sedan." She glanced around the small car's interior. "That's us, in case you didn't know. We're the small car that gets crushed."

"Siri, call Johnson."

"You think calling Johnson is going to do anything?" She knew her voice was rising, that she sounded hysterical, but she couldn't do anything to stop it.

"What else do you recommend?"

"Drive fast."

"Not happening."

He turned on his blinker. *Turned on his blinker! Stopped at a light!* With the bad guy behind them.

She could barely breathe. "If he has a gun, we're dead."

"According to your doomsday vision, we're dead anyway."

"You're supposed to tell me I'm wrong."

"Hey, Siri. Wake up and call Johnson."

Calling Johnson.

"Finally." Thayer grumbled.

What's that? I didn't understand.

Marie groaned and reached for his phone. "I should have gotten his number. We really are dead if we have to wait for Artificial Intelligence to place the call."

Have I been insulted?

"The phone is smart enough to know she's been insulted but not smart enough to place the call."

Thayer started laughing as the light's turn arrow turned green and he turned and then immediately turned again into a drive thru.

"What? You're hungry?" Marie wanted to bang her hands on the dashboard.

"I figure he won't do anything stupid if we're in a busy line surrounded by other people and witnesses."

She noted the wisdom of that tentative plan as the pickup hung back. "Okay, so be really slow and ask the drive thru operator to call the police." Her hand shook as she tried to get her call to go through. "I'm not getting anything to work. And your phone is locked up like Siri gave up on you."

"I was thinking of asking them to call the FBI."

"I'm sure that wouldn't terrify the kid." She fought the urge to roll her eyes.

He ordered a couple sodas then inched forward. When he reached the order window, he leaned closer. "Could you do me a favor?"

The young man frowned at him. "Hey, look man. I hand out food and drinks. That's it."

"There's a man who's been following us. I need you to call the police for us."

"Don't you have a cell phone?"

"We do, but it isn't working." Thayer shook his head and waved his hands. "Never mind. Maybe this bought us enough time." He pulled forward and looked at Marie. "Did you reach Johnson?"

She shook her head. "No, it's just ringing."

"Do we go inside and wait awhile?" Thayer set the drinks in the cupholders. "See if he gives up?"

"That doesn't seem like Rahul's MO. But I also don't know why he's here. What does he want?" She closed her eyes and rubbed her forehead. She just wanted to rewind the clock. Erase Emilio from her life. But then she'd not have Drew, and her life was richer and more beautiful because of him.

Thayer pulled into a parking space, powered down his phone, and restarted it.

Suddenly a series of texts pinged across it, each one with an increasing level of urgency from Johnson. "Looks like it got jammed up, but now I can let him know why we're stuck."

He shot a text to Johnson.

> Stuck at a Mickey Ds. Bad guy following us and diverted to a public place until we could contact you. Can you meet us here or give us advice on how to get out of this without dying?

> Overly dramatic?

> Don't think so.

> Probably not a great idea to meet quite so publicly if he's there. How about a park? Send me a pin and I'll find a location nearby.

Marie leaned over to read the texts over his shoulder. "I don't love this idea, but there's a community park near 111th and College that wouldn't

THE ART OF DECEPTION

be a bad idea. With the nice weather, there would be people out and about."

Thayer sent the text and Johnson said he'd meet them there.

"All right, let's go." Thayer slid his car into reverse and backed from the slot. "Do you see the pickup?" He kept his gaze on the road, but scanned as much as he could for the truck,

Nothing.

"Watch out!" Marie braced her arm against the dashboard in a move that he didn't think would end well.

"Don't brace." He swerved the opposite direction praying there wasn't another car nearby. How did he avoid something he couldn't see? The next instant, a pickup loomed over him. "Where did he come from?"

"The alley." She recoiled from the dash right before the pickup slammed into them. The impact reverberating through him, Thayer pressed on the accelerator.

"Hang on!" He swerved, steering the car around until they were headed the other direction. "You okay?"

Marie moaned but nodded. "I will be. Just get us out of here."

"Siri, call 911."

This time the AI managed to place the call.

"I've got a dark pickup truck chasing me. It hit me and is still in pursuit. I need help."

"What is your location?"

"I don't know. Can't you track my location with your computer and my GPS or something?" He could hear his voice raising, but he didn't know how to stop it with the pickup gaining speed behind him. "Marie, he's about to hit us again. Ma'am, I'm driving a little sedan and he's got a huge pickup."

Marie screamed, and it pierced his eardrum.

"There's an officer en route."

"One isn't going to do us much good." They flew past a light as he searched for any landmarks he could register, his mind had hyper-focused on surviving. "Marie, do you know where we are?"

She was quiet a moment. "We're near College Park Baptist Church. Headed toward 465, I think. Maybe on Township. Yes, Township."

Thayer didn't slow down for the next roundabout. The pickup went over the top of it. "I thought he'd have to slow down."

The sound of sirens was a far-off blessing. A slow-moving vehicle pulled in front of him, and he started beating on his horn. "Move! Please, move."

Whoever was driving the little hatchback seemed to slow down in protest to his pleading.

The pickup loomed larger in his rearview mirror and Thayer swerved onto the curb and around the little car, its driver swerving the other direction as the dually went between them.

"Slam on your brakes!"

"What?"

"*Hit your brakes!* Trust me." Marie's voice filled the interior.

He didn't have a better idea. Thayer stomped hard on them, putting the seatbelts to the test. Marie groaned, but the next thing the pickup was a block ahead of them and she was motioning to the turn off.

"Go!"

He pulled onto the off ramp as he stared at her. "How did you know?"

"To do that?" She rubbed at her shoulder and pulled the seatbelt. "Clearly, I watch more superhero movies than you. Every chase scene ever shows all the strategies for escaping."

"Now what?" He'd rely on her ideas even if they came from the big screen because his mind was buzzed with adrenaline.

"We change where we're meeting Johnson." Marie sucked in a breath. "Food court at Keystone and hide."

～

The car chase had felt like something out of the movie *Black Widow*. Now Marie was in the middle of *Captain American: The Winter Soldier* as Black Widow trying to get Captain America away from the Hydra bad guys, only she was no Natasha Romanov. She was just trying to survive. Maybe the food court wasn't a great idea, but there should be a lot of people there, and it was the closest public space her rattled brain could spit out at the moment.

When they arrived, she led Thayer to the bathrooms instead of the

THE ART OF DECEPTION

actual food court, which was on the small side at Keystone. The one at Castleton was larger, but it was also a massive mall with a larger parking lot to get attacked in. Somehow the smaller, upscale space at Keystone seemed more familiar. Safer. She also didn't see Rahul being as aware of it.

She might be crazy, but she hoped she was right.

"Text Johnson that we're back by the mall office down by the bathrooms. The ones by HoiTEA." The good thing was they didn't show up on a map. So unless someone was familiar with the mall, it was hard to know where to search. It was her best theory.

"I think he's getting frustrated."

"When he sees my bruises, he can decide if we're paranoid or not." She was going to be so sore tomorrow. She tried to ignore the throb in her shoulder and the tightness building in her neck. She wanted a long, hot shower—an impossibility at the moment. "I'm definitely going to need some ibuprofen and muscle relaxants."

"Maybe we need to go to an emergency room."

"Not right now." She was still walking, and Rahul was out there. She wouldn't feel safe until they had him. Emilio would send someone else, but if they could get Rahul off their tail that would help. Or maybe it was best to know who to look for, but she almost wanted ignorance right now.

She needed to feel safe even if it was pretend for the moment.

They huddled in the back hall around a protective corner and after ten minutes Johnson hurried up.

He took in their appearance and seemed to reach a quick decision about the veracity of their claims. "I've got an agent calling a tow truck for your car, Thayer. He'll keep an eye on it until the truck arrives."

"Thanks." Thayer sounded like he was still in some sort of shock. He had to be exhausted after all that adrenaline leeched from his body.

"We should have gotten you a sugary drink or caffeine."

"No." He shook his head. "I would have crashed even harder."

She looked at Johnson. "Do you have anything sugary we can give him?"

"No, he's right. We need to get him someplace he can collapse for a bit. Let his body recover for a while." He glanced around. "My car is in the back not very far from here. You can spend the night at my house and then we'll devise a plan to get you out."

"Do you have enough to arrest Emilio?" She had to know, or she couldn't disappear, not yet.

"I'm not sure. I planned to meet a prosecutor in the morning, but at most, I'd guess it's conspiracy. That's not going to be enough to put him away for very long. And that's if a judge and jury buy the argument." He shoved his hands in his khaki pockets and she noted the weary lines in his body. "I'm sorry, Marie, but I can't promise it's enough."

She wanted to rail that she'd done all they'd asked, but she could sense Paarlberg was frustrated too.

Instead, she'd have to find a way to get everything they'd need.

"All right. Then you're going to have to give me a list of everything you need on the drive."

"And what then?"

"I'm going to get it for you."

Because this had to end. And it had to end before Emilio managed to have her killed, because he'd gotten too close to accomplishing exactly that.

Chapter Eighteen

When they reached Johnson's house, a car sat at the curb with a man in the driver's seat watching the street. Another car waited in the driveway. The home was a one story, new construction with minimal landscaping. Basic, but well maintained in a neutral beige with forest green door and shutters. As she reached for the passenger door, Johnson raised a hand. "Wait until I confirm everything's secure."

Marie should feel relieved that the FBI and Johnson were finally taking everything seriously, but instead her muscles tightened. She was exposed in the car, even with the agents in cars on the street and in the house.

She knew the reality of Emilio's reach better than anyone around her. That didn't bring her comfort. She was in the best position to make sure she was protected.

This whole experience was surreal. Thayer turned around from the front passenger seat and met her gaze. In that moment, she wished he was next to her. There would be comfort in his presence right there, solid and real.

"We're going to be okay." He infused the words with intensity, but she knew he couldn't keep them. He didn't have that power.

She'd watched him drive.

He'd been a sitting duck without her calling on what she'd seen in movies.

Neither of them had the skills to navigate this, but she possessed more than he did—thanks to watching action films. That wasn't a comforting reality, but it was truth.

Johnson must have received some signal from his colleagues because he opened his door. "Don't linger, but we're cleared to go in."

A minute later they were up the sidewalk and inside the door. She didn't take time to study the clean lines and blank slate of his home. The largest thing to note was the TV on the wall in the living room, so it appeared that, like many single men, he spent much of his free time in front of the large screen. Doing what wasn't clear because she didn't see a game console nor any sports paraphernalia. She followed him down the small hall to the back and the kitchen where the three of them joined another person at the kitchen table.

The woman was about Marie's age, and wore a navy pantsuit and basic white top, very different from Marie's colorful skirt and t-shirt. "Charlotte Montgomery, I'm Agent Angela Clowery. I work with Johnson and have been using the conversation you recorded to dig deeper into what we know about Emilio Accardi and his family."

Marie tried not to grimace at the use of her actual name. "I go by Marie now. Did you get enough to arrest him?"

"Not yet, but if you give us some time, we can reach the core of how the family is infiltrating the United States and the art market."

Marie collapsed onto a chair and shook her head. "You don't understand. I don't have time. My parents are out there somewhere with my son and have been for three weeks because I can't have Drew anywhere near Emilio."

Johnson leaned forward, attention laser-focused on Marie. "That's a missing piece for us. Why are you so determined to keep them apart? Other than the leverage Drew could provide?"

"He's Emilio's son." How did they not know this? Hadn't she told them? She was so exhausted she couldn't remember. Maybe she hadn't and should have. Maybe they'd forgotten or deemed it unimportant. "What information do you need from the gallery?"

"Why do you want to know?"

"I'll get it for you. But in exchange you protect Drew and me. Otherwise, I'll disappear because I'm done waiting for you to figure this out." She swallowed against the sudden lump in her throat. "I need my son."

Thayer took her hand under the table, his skin warm against hers. The grip of his hand was solid and real. Something she could hold onto in a world ready to collapse.

Marie met Johnson's gaze. "I'm losing everything I've rebuilt in the last eight years. Everything." The ground beneath her feet shifted like quicksand "Tell me what you need. But we have to do it now before Rahul tells Emilio I ran."

～

The tears welling in Marie's eyes blurred the strength she was trying so hard to convey, even as she blinked them away.

"We have the financial records." He looked at Johnson.

"And we have the conversation with Emilio talking about the laundering aspect." Agent Clowery tapped a pen against the stone table. "We need the connection."

Johnson nodded. "We need the contracts or communication connecting Julian and the gallery to the Accardi family and its crimes. It seems farfetched from the outside that an art gallery in the middle of Indianapolis would be used by an Italian crime family to launder money, but we know it's happening. We just can't prove it yet."

"Yes, we have to connect the dots. We don't know that those documents are at the gallery." Agent Clowery studied Marie as if wondering if she had the fortitude to do something.

"They will be." Thayer was certain. "There's a large office that they've tried pretty hard to keep people out of."

Marie stared at the table for a minute. "Can you get me a flash drive? I've got some practice copying hard drives."

Johnson nodded. "I have a blank one in my home office. But how will you get in?"

"I have to." She shrugged. "I'll do some internet research on Julian

Bond and will need someone to impersonate an Uber and drop me off at the gallery before it closes. I'll slip in and hide."

Thayer furrowed his brow. "That seems risky."

"I'll disappear until they leave."

"Without calling or alerting Julian." Agent Clowery shrugged. "If they do . . ."

"I leave without anything." Marie shook her head. "I could ask to see if Emilio sent the contract over. That will at least give us information about whether Julian does things on paper or electronically. He seems rather old school, so I imagine it could be both." She rubbed her forehead and then the back of her neck as if she was tightening up from the impact when Rahul tried to destroy them.

He nudged closer. "Here." And he slowly started running his thumbs in small circles in her shoulders. She moaned and leaned into and away from the motion at the same time. "I guess I've found the right spot."

"Yes, thank you." She glanced at her watch. "The gallery closes at six, so we'll need to leave soon. Can someone make sure Rahul isn't there?"

Agent Clowery stood. "They have no idea who I am since I just transferred from St. Louis. I'll head over and shop for a painting for my parents' anniversary. Anyone I should ask for? Either staff or artist?"

Marie thought about it then shook her head. "Sometimes the best approach is curiosity."

"All right." Agent Clowery turned to Johnson. "I'll call with an all clear."

"Got it. We'll stage close but far enough away to stay clear if there's trouble."

"Do you think you're the best option, Agent Paarlberg?" Marie's question was blunt, pointed.

"Thayer can't because Julian, Rahul, and Emilio have all met him, so that leaves me unless we bring more people specifically into our confidence."

Thayer considered the agents who waited outside. "Don't those agents know who we are?"

"No. I told them they're here for security. They understand the need-to-know basis of the assignment. I'll make a few calls in my office and find that flash drive for you. Will you be okay here?"

Marie nodded, though she wrapped her arms protectively around her stomach.

Johnson left, and Marie leaned into Thayer. He slipped an arm around her, and she relaxed into him. Her words cut off his thoughts "Don't promise everything's going to be okay, because you can't keep that promise."

Much as he wanted to argue with her, Marie was right.

He couldn't make that promise. But he wanted to promise that he'd be right here waiting on the other side of her trip to the gallery. "Can I come with you?"

"No, that would look suspicious."

"You're right." Of course, she was. She had an uncanny ability to anticipate what needed to happen. "I seriously underestimated you."

"What do you mean?" She shifted to look at him, wincing as she did so.

"I thought you were just this beautiful receptionist who brought light to work. But you've proven to have quite a depth to you. You're thinking laps around all of us on how to get what we need to connect all the dots and stop the money laundering."

"I hope so." She worried her lower lip between her teeth. "What if I'm wrong?"

"You aren't." He leaned closer, overwhelmed by the need and desire to comfort her and share the burden she'd taken on. When she didn't move away, he leaned his forehead against hers, feeling the electricity of attraction zinging between them. "You're going to help us bring them down. And then Drew and you will be safe."

"What if I can't do it? Then what?"

"Then we figure out the next step. Even if Emilio has any idea you're on to him, he doesn't know why or how."

"Can I trust you?"

"What do you mean?" He leaned back so he could see her eyes.

"Can I trust you?"

"Yes." He closed the distance between them and pressed his lips against hers, a gentle touch. When she didn't break the connection, he deepened the kiss. He wanted her to know he would do anything for her and, as this deeper soul connection flared to life between them, he hoped his actions conveyed what he didn't know how to express with words. There wasn't an equation or numbers to express this, but it was as real and true as any perfect number sequence.

She sighed and eased back. "I saw you with Rahul."

"But I told you that had nothing to do with you."

"Everything with him has ramifications for me."

"I am here because I would do anything for you."

She nodded but seemed to consider him, as if she could see into his soul and weigh the truth of his words. "Okay. I have something for you." She reached into a pocket in her skirt and then pulled something small out. She considered it, almost as if she wasn't sure she could trust him with it. "Promise you won't lose this."

"What is it?"

"Something I've had for eight years."

He did the quick math. "Wait—"

She put a finger on his mouth and a small smile tipped the lips he'd just kissed. He blinked as he tried to focus on this moment and what she thought was so important she needed to entrust it to him without losing sight of it. "I understand."

"I hope you do. I'm not certain what it is, but I think..." Her words trailed off. "It doesn't matter, other than it's important. But I can't take it with me tonight in case something goes wrong. Promise you won't do anything with it unless I don't come back."

"I won't, because it's Drew's insurance."

She blinked a couple times as she nodded. "Exactly. I need to know that if anyone takes him, we have this to bargain with."

"Got it." He slid his hand to her cheek, and she leaned into his touch. "Be careful, okay? I'll be waiting for you." Then he leaned in for another kiss. He could get addicted to these and he thought that might be okay.

"Thank you." She breathed the words against him then leaned back with a small smile as she pressed something small into his hand. "Don't do anything with it until I get back."

Someone cleared his throat from the doorway, and Thayer looked up.

Johnson watched them from the doorway with a grin. "It you two are done now, we can leave, Marie."

"Thank you, Agent Paarlberg." As she answered, she never took her focused attention from Thayer. Then she lowered her voice. "You promised."

He nodded. "Be safe, you two. While you're gone, I'll dig through Agent Clowery's notes and overlay them with my work from the spreadsheets. See if together anything new pops out."

After Marie followed Johnson back to his car, Thayer went to the laptop Johnson had left for him and logged in. Soon he was flipping through the lines of code and looking for how the new information impacted what they already had. Did the new change anything?

That was always the key.

Could he filter the right information through the best lens to help him understand what he was seeing? If he could, then it would come into focus, and he could tell the story.

First, he needed to identify whether he had made any assumptions that prevented him from making sense of the mess.

He thought back over what he'd seen at the gallery and, even before that, what Johnson and the data had told him. The assumption had been that Julian served as the front.

What would flip that on its head?

What if Emilio wasn't the mastermind?

What if it was really Rahul? Everyone assumed Rahul was doing someone else's bidding, but what if Rahul was only working for himself or leading the crime family? What if he was Emilio's brother or cousin, and Emilio was here because of Marie, and he had nothing to do with the laundering scheme and everything to do with making her nervous and stressed? That made a bit of sense and definitely revealed a bias in the way everyone had approached this situation.

What if Julian wasn't merely someone who served the needs of the crime family, but actually told the family what to do? What if this scheme had been his idea and he was the mastermind rather than the servant?

Thayer tried the idea on for size.

It was startling in the way it pivoted Julian's role. He went from someone who followed orders to someone who organized and directed the enterprise.

Thayer rolled that idea around his mind as he paced the small kitchen Johnson had remodeled the prior year when he recovered from a bad acci-

323

dent on the job. Thayer stopped at the small island and considered the options in the fruit bowl. Could it be all three of his approaches were wrong and there was a fourth option that didn't include Emilio, Rahul, or Julian? Maybe, but if he chased those three down, he'd probably get closer to the truth. He'd only considered Julian as the errand boy. Imagining him the brains might change his perspective, as would looking at Emilio and Rahul.

Maybe.

After he returned to the table and woke up the laptop, he settled down to work. With three new ways to approach the data, he started seeing new threads. Before long, he separated them apart in different ways.

The story began to emerge, and it was different than he'd imagined.

Chapter Nineteen

When he pulled in front of the gallery, Agent Paarlberg slowed to a halt. "Your Uber has arrived. You have my number up and ready in text?"

"Yes. And the app is running, just in case, so you can hear everything."

He checked his phone and nodded. "We're good. Just enter a single X, and I'll come running, if I didn't already hear something."

"Got it."

"That's all you need to do to send an emergency code. Nothing fancy. Just a simple X, lower or upper case."

"I've got it. Simple is good. Thank you."

He reached into his jacket and pulled out a small device. "This can hold one gigabyte of data. That should be more than enough. Don't be a hero. If you can't find it, get out of there. We'll try again another day."

"Understood." He might have time for tactics like that, but she didn't. She needed to get in, take all the information she could, and get out. She reached over the seat as if giving him a tip. "Thank you for the ride." Then she slipped from the backseat of the vehicle and watched as it pulled away.

A young man stood at the door watching her approach.

"We close in thirty minutes, ma'am."

"Thank you. I'll browse quickly." She smiled at him, and then walked by. "I just love looking at art. People are so creative." She made the statement sunny and noted the moment his shoulders relaxed.

"Are you looking for anything in particular?"

"A gift for my parents' anniversary. I'll know it when I see it." She walked away from him toward the art that lined the wall that would lead to the stairs. If she could slip up there when he wasn't looking, she could disappear near the bar.

"Let me know if you need anything." The young man turned as a couple strolled in. A few moments later, several more people wandered in, distracting him, and Marie slipped up the stairs, but froze halfway up as a phone rang and the young man answered. His words drifted up to her.

"Thanks for calling me back. Do you have that code? I'm still learning the ins and outs of this latest security upgrade. Without the code, if I miss the ninety seconds window, I have a mess. I wasn't fast earlier this week. Next thing I knew there were police and private security everywhere."

Private security? She hadn't expected that for such a small gallery. Nothing she'd seen on the walls before seemed worth that expense.

"It was the weirdest overkill when all they had to do was call and check the security cameras to confirm it was the new guy hitting the wrong buttons."

She hurried up the rest of the stairs, praying the young man had forgotten all about her. With all the talk about security upgrades, she'd need to get in and out as fast as she could. Her watch vibrated again, this time a call from Thayer, but he would have to wait. She didn't have time to listen to him tell her to be careful. Not when she had to move before Julian checked to make sure the gallery was put to bed for the night.

Without a car, Thayer didn't like feeling stranded at Johnson's home.

He didn't have any way to get to Marie and warn her who was behind the scheme, and she wasn't answering his call. Yes, she'd given him the small device but maybe she still didn't trust him after all. He knew where she was, but how was he going to get to her?

Should he call Johnson, or was there a leak in the FBI?

Somehow the group seemed to anticipate their plans, and the only one

Marie and he talked to was Johnson. He'd never believe Johnson was involved, so it had to mean that if there was a leak it was someone Johnson trusted.

Could Johnson give Marie an SOS signal?

Was it time to get her out?

How could he know when he was twenty minutes away? She would have barely arrived.

It was crazy how fast once he had an idea what he was looking for he traced the money.

The scheme wasn't that elaborate.

In fact it was pretty basic.

Someone affiliated with the Accardis brought suitcases of money into Indiana. He wasn't sure how, but someone else could figure that out. What he did know is the money arrived, and then was used to purchase paintings. Some were legitimate. A few might be forgeries like the one that Thayer pretended to want to purchase.

And that's what had tipped him off to Julian being the mastermind.

If the family didn't intend to buy forged paintings, then Julian was double-crossing them. And that meant when the Accardis figured out that the painting intended for Thayer wasn't a real Rembrandt, then Emilio and Rahul would go after Julian. At least Thayer thought Rahul worked for Emilio, but that piece wasn't clear.

Then he'd seen something that made his blood run cold. A meeting was set for tonight.

At the 42nd Street Gallery.

He tried Marie again, but she continued to ignore him.

He had to get over there. Had to warn Johnson somehow without tipping anyone else off.

What movie would Marie rely on?

He didn't know, but Thayer hurried out to the driveway, only to find it empty. There were no cars, so he needed a real Uber.

Now.

$\sim$

Finally, the lights went off and Marie heard the door lock. She was growing cramped tucked down behind some boxes in the bar area, but the location had shielded her as the young man had made a cursory circuit of the second floor before deciding everyone was gone. She slipped down the stairs and back toward the office. She didn't have time and had no idea where the security cameras were, so she needed to do what she could, as fast as possible. She set the timer on her watch for three minutes and then set a second for five. At the end of the second, she had to leave. Julian would expect the gallery to be empty and the cameras to show a vacant gallery if he checked them.

At least that's what she would do if she owned it.

When she sat at the computer, she tried the man's birthday and then the date the gallery had opened. That unlocked the computer, and she opened his file finder to see what she could locate, her mind racing as she tried to make sense of the disorganization. He wouldn't call it Italian cleaners or money laundering, so what would he use? She tried to think like him but kept coming up blank. Too much was running through her mind, and she froze with indecision.

"Think!"

She clicked on a folder labeled outlines. It had a subfolder labeled contract and another titled conversations. It looked right, so she popped in the drive Johnson had given her and started copying the files over. Her first alarm vibrated.

Then she heard a sound out front.

No.

No one should be here. The gallery was closed.

She hadn't been here too long.

She'd barely been in the office three minutes.

She yanked out the drive. Then she clicked the button turning off the monitor so it would look like no one was there. Empty as it should be. Now what?

She edged to the office door. Should she go out where the space was wide open, but there was the front door and the back door? Or should she try to hide in the office?

The sound of shoes against the floor had her edging backward and reaching for her phone. In the darkness of the office, turning it on to send a text would be very visible.

Under the desk.

She could slide behind or under it and send the message to Johnson and wait for help to arrive. She slid the flash drive into her zippered pocket. At least she couldn't lose it. Now she could only hope she'd found something helpful.

Then she heard voices and crouched lower as she recognized them.

Why were Emilio and Rahul here?

She cowered lower. If she was found, things would be terrible for her.

She had no valid excuse for being here.

Two minutes on the computer would show she had executed something on it.

She wasn't skilled.

She was an artist playing a spy.

She could never create a cover story that Emilio or Julian would buy, and Emilio had always read her like a book. It had been a terrible burden when they'd dated. She wore her emotions on her sleeve, never bothering to hide them because they were what made her unique ... and misunderstood. So few bothered to see her, and she thought that was what made Emilio distinct from everyone else, but she'd been wrong. Again. He'd played her to get what he wanted.

The emotions rushing through her had an intensity that colored them and demanded a word with fire.

The sounds neared the office and then another came from the other end.

"Who's there?"

She cowered lower at Julian's voice. There wasn't fear in it, which surprised her. The man didn't strike her in their brief interactions as the brave sort, more the get along the path of least resistance sort.

"You might not be aware, but I have a security system and it sends me alerts of after-hours activity. Even though we had set a meeting, you weren't supposed to be in here before I arrived. I do believe you messed up, as we would say." As he spoke the steps drew nearer the office doorway. They were confident and steady. What was this man up to?

"I do not bow to others." Okay, so the other in the space was Emilio.

She bit back a whimper and pressed against the desk. The office was too open. She hadn't noticed a good storage area she could hide. To do that she would somehow have to leave, so if the two men entered the office, she would be visible.

As the lights flickered off in the hallway, she blinked.

Why would someone turn them off?

That had to mean that person anticipated trouble.

Or wanted to create it.

That thought was more terrifying.

She considered what she knew about the room she sat in. Other than the desk, the chair behind it, and the couple of chairs in front of it, it was pretty basic. Then she remembered the small table in the corner with an imitation Greek bust in the corner. If she could lift it, she could use Julian's prize piece as a weapon. It would certainly hurt someone if she had time to bash them over the head with it before they could hurt her. It wasn't much of a plan, but it was better than cowering under the desk waiting to be discovered. In that situation, she was waiting to be killed.

At least this way, she was prepared to do something.

Okay.

She could do this.

If she could get her muscles to cooperate.

Because as she tried to move, she found she couldn't.

It was like her body had gone on strike.

Her brain screamed at her legs to move.

And they refused.

Her arms twitched, but that was it. "Come on." She whispered the two words, but someone must have heard, because a shadow eased toward the doorway.

"Who is there?" It was Emilio's voice.

"You know who." Julian didn't sound very happy. "Why did you break in?"

"I never let the other person get an upper hand, even someone as old as you."

"Cocky one, aren't you?" Julian's voice was ice cold, and it scared her. Maybe he wasn't as harmless as he sounded.

She had to move now.

Suddenly her muscles coiled as if sensing the danger, and she could move.

"You weren't honest with me, you old fool." Emilio's voice was filled with disgust. "You must not know what family you mess with."

"Oh, you mean some crime family from Italy, *blah, blah, blah.*"

Marie cringed as Julian poked the Italian wolf. The man was misreading this situation, but that reality got her moving.

"I'm not afraid of you, you pampered idiot."

"Then you are the fool, old man."

She crawled along the floor until she reached the edge of the desk and then she scuttled to the corner where she squeezed next to the bust. She gripped the bust and clenched her eyes closed, praying she wouldn't need to do anything and that she'd have the strength to move if she did.

"Why did you sell me a fake? Did you think I wouldn't realize?" Emilio's voice was calm. Too calm. "I grew up surrounded by true masterpieces."

"If you somehow think it's not real, then we should sit and have a good conversation. Come into my office."

No, no, no.

She might have a plan, but that didn't mean she could execute it.

Footsteps approached.

Chapter Twenty

THAYER HAD TO GET TO THE GALLERY NOW.

How could so much be happening at such a nondescript location. It wasn't a warehouse. It wasn't an upscale location. It was just another strip mall. A nice one, but still. Thayer tried to relax, but his mind was sending a nonstop fight message to his body. Everything in him screamed he'd be too late. And the fact Marie continued to ignore him didn't help.

Everything was wrong, but he was certain Emilio was not the risk.

He was just a pampered, spoiled Italian, wanna-be playboy. Sure, he had guns at his disposal, but he wasn't the greatest threat. Instead, the brains behind the crimes were Julian.

Thayer still tried to wrap his mind around the idea the stiff man had created the scheme. It looked like, in addition to laundering money for organized crime, he also defrauded the bad guys. If you could help them clean their dirty money, why not lift large amounts for your own benefit along the way? After all, what could they do about it? Take you to court for stealing from them?

Nope.

They had other ways to enforce violations.

Violent ways.

While Emilio might be a pampered, spoiled son, he was the heir of a crime boss. He had tools of extortion and violence at his disposal and was used to executing those weapons.

He probably didn't care that he wasn't in Italy and different laws applied here.

Thayer didn't know if different laws applied, and he couldn't take the time to find out because he didn't think Emilio cared.

The Uber finally pulled up near the gallery—just before Thayer lost his ever-loving mind. Thayer clicked the button for payment and bolted from the backseat. Now that he was here, he wasn't sure what to do next.

Then he heard a low whistle and turned to see Johnson waving him over.

When he reached him, Johnson pulled Thayer over like Johnson was concerned Thayer would run inside. A valid concern. "What do you plan to do? Run through the door?"

"I don't know. Maybe?" He planted his fists on his hips. "What do we do?"

"I've got someone trying to hack into the security system to see if we can see inside."

"Can you do that?"

"Probably not legally, but right now I'm more concerned that I let Marie go in there and we've got at least one bad guy inside." Johnson rubbed a hand down his face, his jaw tight. "I'm so far out on a limb, I'm not sure I'll have a job tomorrow, but I need to protect her."

"You're the agent and governed by all the search and seizure rules. I'm not. Let me go in." Thayer took a deep breath. "I can do that and not jeopardize your job or the evidence."

"What? Then I'm responsible for two civilians? How is that helping?"

Okay, so talking about it would only take longer. "If you hear anything bad, then it's exigent circumstances, right?"

"Ye-es ..." Johnson drew out the word. "Wait a minute. Don't do anything stupid."

Thayer sprinted toward the front door. Better to ask for forgiveness than permission, because if anything happened to Marie, he'd never forgive himself.

❧

So far, she hadn't heard Rahul. If it was truly just Julian and Emilio, then if she dropped the bust on Emilio, she felt pretty good she could outrun Julian and escape. If Rahul was there but silent, he could stop her from leaving. She also knew he would be the last person to enter the office. He always lurked in the back of every room.

Who did he work for in this little party anyway?

It was impossible to know anymore.

She had no choice. She had to stay in the corner and hope she wasn't noticed until she had a better idea of whether Rahul was a part of the situation.

"After you." Julian's voice was a command, not an invitation.

There was a hesitation, as if Emilio noticed the difference. Then he entered and a moment later Julian followed but didn't turn on the light. No motion-controlled lights in the office, so the only light trickled in from the hallway. Charlotte breathed a silent thank you as she squeezed into the shadowed corner, holding her breath, and waited to see if a third person entered. When no one did, she started to relax.

Then Julian pulled a gun from his pocket.

So much for using a prized bust as a weapon.

A bullet would win every time.

~

Thayer opened the front door as little as possible and squeezed through the space before darting into the gallery. The lights were on, and he swept his gaze around the front room looking for anyone. No one—but he didn't want to be surprised.

In the movies, he would have a partner and they would each sweep a side. No such luck, so he chose to sweep along the right side, keeping his back to the wall and paintings. He almost bounced some sort of sculpture-thing off its pedestal before grabbing it in time.

Was he in a spy movie or a comedy?

He set the piece in place and froze. Had anyone else heard?

Voices deeper in the building.

He wanted to rush in that direction, but knew that would be a fool's errand so he continued in his deliberate pattern.

He didn't have a weapon.

All he had was himself and a deep need to protect Marie.

Yep.

He was going to get himself killed.

But he moved ahead anyway.

That's what love did.

Walked into danger, not away from it.

~

"Come out of the corner, Marie." Julian didn't turn her direction.

She had no doubt he would pivot in a second and shoot her. No remorse.

"And you know that bust is a fake. I don't care if you drop it."

She took a step forward, but somehow that simple movement frustrated her former boyfriend.

Emilio rolled his eyes. "Just what I needed. You to make everything more complicated." He waved a hand in her direction. "Why are you even here?"

"It's a good question. Why don't you tell him what you suspect?" Julian still hadn't looked at her, but neither had his gun wavered from Emilio. Maybe that meant he didn't think she was a threat.

"I came to get the evidence I need to put you in jail."

"Seems you made an enemy, my Italian friend."

"What can she do?" Emilio sneered at her. "She's just a woman."

"That is your problem—you underestimate her. A critical mistake. Unfortunately for you, not your most critical one."

Emilio shrugged. "She is just an artist. She paints copies. Nothing too original."

"No, you've been blind to her genius." Julian made the slightest turn toward her, but then quickly snapped his attention back to Emilio. "She has great potential, a way of seeing what isn't visible and calling it into being. Under the right tutelage, my tutelage, it's a gift that she transmits to the canvas. People will pay top dollar for it. And under my direction, she will recreate the great paintings. We will make immense money."

Marie bristled. "I'll never agree to create forgeries."

335

"You haven't yet, but that will change."

Now wasn't the time to argue with him, not when he had a gun.

"Enough of the talking, old man. You're going to return my money because I don't like thieves."

"We didn't steal. You saw the painting before you purchased it. You could have insisted on due diligence ahead of time but chose to buy it without any kind of review. That was a poor choice on your part, but it was your prerogative. Maybe you'll be wiser next time."

Julian was riling Emilio up. Marie cringed and stepped back toward her corner. She couldn't retreat to the door because Julian blocked it. Julian might have a gun, but in hand-to-hand fighting, Emilio would win every time. If Julian got Emilio to explode, then Julian would lose unless he got a shot off first. Was the security camera capturing all this? Or the app Johnson had put on her phone? Was there any chance it was still activated? Did she dare to pull it up—or would she just get herself shot?

She had to do something because if she waited for them to go at each other, she'd get caught in their battle of testosterone. There was no way that would end well.

God, give me wisdom, please.

Noise in the hallway interrupted her prayer. Had Julian heard it, too? He didn't turn, so maybe not.

Then there was a clang—the other two men had to have heard it.

Just in case the calvary was arriving—a woman could hope—Marie wanted Emilio and Julian focused on their battle with each other as they went after whatever was out there. She stomped her foot and then didn't know what to do to keep their attention.

"Emilio, Julian has sent you fakes for a while, but they're terrible. I'm still trying to piece it all together, but he's got a bigger scheme than money laundering."

Julian grinned as he steadied his gun hand with his other arm. "I wondered when you'd start putting it together. What tipped you off?"

"Emilio."

Emilio frowned. "What do you mean?"

"Why come to Indianapolis? There's no reason for you to be here. You let me go eight years ago. If you really had any interest in your son, you would have shown up years earlier. There had to be another reason for your sudden appearance. Unless it wasn't so sudden." Marie considered them both. "You've kept tabs on me for a while. You may have approached Julian with the idea of selling art and that evolved to money laundering. I'm not sure, because that feels fairly altruistic for you."

He slapped a hand over where his heart would be if he had one. "You slay me, cara mia."

"I haven't been your *cara mia* in years, if I ever was." Marie turned to Julian. "But I don't understand why the pressure to start forging paintings. You have a fine gallery." She considered him, wondering if she should tell him her secret. "You do know that any paintings of mine Emilio brought you have a tell."

She had his full attention now and she realized it might be a mistake as Emilio, started to ease forward and the gun was turned on her.

"What do you mean a tell?" Julian aimed the gun at her chest.

"I included a symbol in each painting that would make it clear with little effort to any art expert that the paintings aren't authentic." She noted movement beyond the door, and took a breath, hoping her message would be clear. "The flash drive with the list of paintings, purchasers, and my tell is with a friend. If anything happens to me, he knows what to do with it."

Julian roared as he pulled the trigger.

She felt searing pain in her chest near her right shoulder and dropped the bust. It shattered on the floor as she collapsed, almost covering the sound as Julian turned and fired another shot as Emilio hurled himself at Julian.

Thayer called Johnson as he rushed the few steps into the office. "Call an ambulance and get in here. Shots have been fired."

"Get out of there and wait for us."

"I can't." As he peered around the door, he prayed he wouldn't get shot himself. "Johnson, at least two people have been shot and one is Marie. Hurry."

"We're on our way."

He wanted to run to where Marie lay on the ground groaning, red spreading across her chest and beneath her, but getting killed helped no one. It looked like Emilio had been shot, while Julian sported a blackening eye as he towered over the Italian.

Emilio writhed on the ground, clutching his stomach, his face turned toward the door. "You have to help me." The Italian accent sounded different when spoken between gritted teeth.

Thayer looked from him to Marie. "An ambulance is on the way."

"Help me escape these crazy people before they hurt me." Julian's voice was high pitched and strained, yet he didn't cower.

"They aren't going anywhere, Julian." Thayer wanted to rush to Marie, do anything to slow the flood of blood.

"But I could be. Where's the gun?" The man whimpered, but something wasn't right.

"You're the only one who wasn't shot which means you had the gun at some point." Thayer had to get past him to reach Marie. "Marie, honey, can you hear me?"

She moaned but nodded.

"Help is coming."

"That's too bad." In the moment Thayer's attention had been distracted Julian raised the gun. "Guess you were right to be skeptical." Julian waved the gun to nudge Thayer from the hall. "Let's get you in here with everyone else. You mentioned help on the way. When will they arrive?"

"I don't know." Thayer didn't need to pretend he was scared, because the gun terrified him. "I didn't ask for an ETA."

"It'll be long enough." Julian considered him a moment. "You need to move a little faster."

Thayer couldn't lift his feet, appendages that felt encased in concrete. "I won't stop you."

The man cocked his head. "I don't feel very trusting."

Julian's eyes flared and as he fired, Thayer threw himself to the ground. He grunted as a streak of heat sliced his arm. He heard pounding footsteps but rolled toward Marie. He'd have to trust Johnson's team to track down Julian because he had to help Marie. As he sank to her side, Thayer wasn't sure what to do with so much blood spilling from her side.

He pulled off his polo and pushed it against the wound.

As people rushed into the space, Johnson pulled him away.

"You need to get that arm looked at while we get some photos."

Thayer groaned. "I don't understand, and this is just a scratch." At least he hoped, but what did he know about getting shot?

"I can't explain everything right now." Johnson paused and glanced from Thayer's arm to Marie who was being photographed to an unmoving Emilio. "I'm glad you're okay."

"Me too." *God, let Marie be okay.* Thayer edged back but couldn't stop watching as the photographer seemed to stage her, then snapped what must have been a couple hundred photos. Then paramedics swooped in, and she was on a gurney with a bevy of people working on her.

Another paramedic stepped to his side. "Let's get you checked out."

"I'll be fine."

"You'll be better after we get that cleaned up."

Rather than fight, Thayer cooperated as long as he could still see Marie. Then he followed her gurney to the ambulance and then the hospital for the longest night of his life.

Chapter Twenty-One

THE FOG THAT HAD ENVELOPED MARIE EBBED AND LIFTED enough so she could open her eyes. When she did, a presence was there, and she shifted in that direction. She winced as a shaft of pain lanced her side.

The presence shifted and groaned, then Thayer leaned forward. "Hey."

She swallowed, unable to form a reply.

He seemed to understand and grabbed a cup of water and straw from the side table. After she took a careful sip, he set it back down. "You up for a little company?"

"...y-es..."

He stepped to the hall and said something. A moment later he was back with his friend Johnson.

She swallowed again. "Julian?"

"Captured. He tried to flee but was captured at the airport. The US attorney is preparing the grand jury for charges." Johnson leaned against the wall. "Will you be willing to testify against him?"

She nodded. "Emilio?"

"Didn't make it. Julian tapped him with a gut shot. Turns out he had a congenital heart defect that with the stress and internal damage from the gunshot, he didn't survive."

A flicker of pain shot through her. For his family, not for her own loss. She wouldn't miss him. He'd been selfish. Manipulated her. Drew's life would not be better with him in it.

"We think Rahul is the bigger fish."

She wrinkled her brow letting that sink in. "Rahul?"

"Yes." Johnson nodded. "He's disappeared, but we might have a lead on him. For that reason, we're letting people think you died at the gallery. Think of it as heavy-duty witness protection. If we go to trial, at that point you will come back to life, but until then or until Rahul is arrested, you need to stay dead for your safety."

Her heart clenched. "What about Drew?"

"He is still with your parents, and we haven't told them you're alive."

Her heart ached. "That's not fair."

Johnson's gaze didn't waver "I agree. But until we can guarantee you're not his next target, I think it's the best thing to do. Rahul was already targeting you. This way he thinks the need to do that has lifted and Drew should be safe. Do you want your parents to provide long term care for Drew?"

"No, I would want my brother Carter to be his guardian. My parents can help, but they've already raised their children." She swallowed hard, and Thayer brought the glass back to her lips for her to take another sip. "How long?"

"Getting to trial could take a year, at most two."

"That's a long time."

"But it keeps you alive."

The words landed heavily. What could she do but agree?

∾

Three weeks later, Marie was home—or as close to it as she would have until Drew was back with her.

Her stitches were out, and she could almost imagine everything had been a horrible nightmare if the light hadn't gone from her days. Also there was an angry red scar on the right side of her chest with an identical scar on her back.

She had a small apartment above a garage in a small town in southern Indiana. She had no ties to it, had never visited. Now that her strength was beginning to return Johnson and Agent Clowery drove down to capture her testimony. She wanted to remind them she didn't know much, but then she reminded herself she was all they had now that Emilio was dead.

He hadn't been part of her life for a long time.

Still, every time she looked at Drew, a part of her acknowledged Emilio's impact in her life.

In recent days, she wanted to imagine what could be possible with a certain accountant turned awkward not-quite-an-undercover-agent.

But her whole new life was on hold.

That one kiss might be all they ever had. She wouldn't ask him to wait while she lingered in this netherworld for the trial and what happened after. Her life wasn't *Fifty First Dates*. It was worse because it didn't even get to restart.

She was in limbo.

Today she needed to get dressed because it was the first day that Johnson would be here to take an official transcription of events.

She wasn't sure she was ready for it, but she was willing to try.

This would get her a step closer to Drew and creating a new home.

She had to believe this, or she'd give into despair—and she'd never lived that way. She wouldn't start now. She'd choose to keep trusting God.

Thirty painful minutes later, she wore a flowing maxi dress that she could step into and that buttoned up the bodice. Anything that went over her head was still too painful to wear, so she was grateful for warm weather and sundresses.

She wanted to wait outside but was still hesitant to do that on her own.

What if Rahul waited? He had disappeared, and she didn't think she was a target, but she didn't want to test the theory either.

Her phone pinged with a text, and she glanced at it.

Johnson.

We're at the door.

That wasn't the agreed to phrase, but it had felt a little cloak and dagger to have a phrase to let someone in now that everything was over and settled. The way the apartment was set up, she didn't have a view of the front of the house beyond the window in the door. The windows looked over the side of the garage, which wouldn't help right now. Still, she edged the curtain to the side as if that would help.

Nothing.

She let out a breath, and texted Johnson.

> You okay?

It took a minute, but then a text popped up.

> Yep, gonna open the door?

Still not the right phrase, but what was she supposed to do? Johnson was her contact. She opened it and then squealed.

~

The spitfire punched him in the arm, and it hurt.

That was not the reaction Thayer expected when he asked Johnson if he could be the one to let Marie know they'd arrived.

"You scared me to death." She started crying, and he felt like a heel.

"I'm sorry, I just wanted to surprise you."

"Well, you didn't use the phrase."

He glared at Johnson. "You didn't tell me there was a phrase."

"You didn't give me a chance." The man smirked at him. "You were pretty focused on getting inside." He glanced around. "Which would still be a good idea."

"See? That is exactly why you freaked me out. I'm still not safe, am I?"

"Marie, we have no active reason to think you aren't."

"Ugh!" She stomped her foot, causing her side to ache, and then backed into her apartment. It was so dark and small compared to her home in Indy, the one that was now for sale because everyone thought she was dead, and that was what you did when people died—put the house on the market.

Life wasn't very fair for her. But maybe the news he had for her would make it feel a bit better.

Thayer and Johnson took up all the space, so he eased onto the couch that looked like something his grandpa would have made a hundred years ago.

"I don't think you'll break it, Thayer." She moved to the small galley kitchen. "Why are you here?"

"I have some good news, I think."

"Oh? I could use good news, but how would you have any for me?"

"I'm moving here. So you won't be alone anymore."

"Won't your family think it's weird?"

They did, but it didn't matter as long as she understood why he was doing it. And he prayed she did. Because if she didn't, he'd spent the last three weeks upending his life for no reason. He just needed to do it in a way that didn't put too much extra pressure on her. He knew showing up would be enough on its own. She didn't need him asking her for advice and permission.

"It's a world of remote work now. I'm joining that and relocating to beautiful Brown County. And while I'm here, I'm planning to spend quality time with a woman who has captured my heart and attention."

"Would you like me to step out? Maybe check the perimeter?" Johnson didn't try to hide his laughter.

"You're killing the vibe, dude."

"I think you had that covered all on your own."

Marie went from her jaw hanging open to laughing as they bickered, then she launched herself at Thayer, and he wrapped his arms around her. "Are you sure? It's not too much?"

"I'm certain I'm miserable without you. I'm positive I want to spend hours getting to know you when we aren't running for your life. I even have a replacement vehicle now." He held her away from him, more mindful of her injury than she was. "And I'm sure I need to be near you to make sure you're safe. I can't sleep when I want to call you every fifteen minutes and hear your voice."

She gave him a sideways look. "I'm not letting you move in, buster."

"I don't want to." Not until there was a stunning ring on her finger and vows had been exchanged. "But I can bring you coffee every morning from the Daily Grind. And together we can rediscover your hope while we wait for this to wind up and you can bring Drew home. But best of all we can do this together. That's the part I want most."

"That's what I want too, Thayer." She gave him a small smile, then extended her hand. "Hi. My name's Charlotte Montgomery, and I'm a bit of a mess."

He took her hand like it was made of porcelain and raised it to his lips for a kiss, delighting in the shiver that coursed through her. "I'm Thayer Jackson. The pleasure is mine." He met her gaze. "I look forward to getting to know you, Charlotte."

"Me too, Thayer. Me too." And there was a light that pushed back her sadness.

He ignored Johnson and leaned close to seal the hope of what could come with a kiss. One that was sweet and right and filled with the promise while they lingered in the in between of waiting.

About Cara Putman

Want to Know What Happens Next?

To read what happens next for Drew and Carter, be sure to read *Secrets to Keep*, releasing May 2024 from Kregel Publishing.

Cara C. Putman lives in Indiana with her husband and four children. When she's not writing, Cara lectures at a Big Ten University in law and communications. She has loved reading and writing from a young age and now realizes it was all training for writing books. An honors graduate of the University of Nebraska, George Mason University School of Law, and Krannert School of Management at Purdue, Cara loves bringing stories to life. Learn more about Cara and her writing at caraputman.com.

Podcast: https://www.caraputman.com/podcast/

Website: https://www.caraputman.com/

Books on Website: https://www.caraputman.com/books/

twitter.com/cara_putman

instagram.com/caracputman

bookbub.com/authors/cara-putman

pinterest.com/caraputman

Real Justice

KATY LEE

Thank you to all you readers who have joined us on this fun summer heat collection. We dedicate these stories to you!

Chapter One

MARCUS CARTWRIGHT SWIPED AT HIS BROW AS HE ENTERED his law firm on W. St. Julian Street. The Savannah summer sun, scorching already at 9 a.m. had him wishing for another dress shirt under his suit coat. The historical building stood between Ellis Square and Johnson Square, a block from the riverfront and two blocks from where his friend's body had washed up just a few days ago. Marcus walked up to the black and gold sign behind the reception desk. A gold scale of justice balanced beneath the words *Brodsky & Cartwright, Attorneys at Law*. But now with Reginald Brodsky dead, all that was left of the firm was the Cartwright. Marcus doubted he would ever change it out of respect for his business partner and even longer-time friend.

"Gloria, Diane Brodsky will be here shortly," Marcus said, leaning over the top of the high desk with his palms on the edge. "Please ready a conference room for us. Drinks and...tissues will be needed. And text me when she arrives. I need to make a call in my office. It can't be interrupted."

Gloria's efficient nod while she handled her own multiple tasks assured him that his orders would be carried out perfectly. She had been with the firm for five years, and he hoped that wouldn't change now that he was flying solo. The truth was, Reggie handled the logistics of running the business, while Marcus's talents were utilized in keeping their highest-paying clients happy. That meant most of his time was spent uncovering the dirty deeds of their opponents, details that would close cases in his clients' favor. Any other free moment he had was soaked up by the coalition formed to combat Savannah's organized crime problem—the very call he needed to make right now in private. It was time to summon his resources.

Even if he did it begrudgingly.

Marcus closed the door to his office and sat in the leather chair behind his mahogany desk. He leaned back with his cell phone to his ear to make the call that needed to be on his private line.

"Lucius, I need a favor."

"Hello to you too, brother." His twin's condescending voice grated on Marcus's nerves. But he knew that the irritation was more out of his desperation at having to contact Lucius in the first place. Desperate times called for desperate measures.

"I need to make this quick. Reggie Brodsky is dead. He supposedly drowned in the Savannah River. I don't buy it for a second. He was looking into the Moran family."

Lucius chuckled. "Again with the Morans. Will you ever let it go? Never mind, don't answer that. Why aren't you asking your coalition? Isn't that what they're there for? What happened with your partnership with the DA's Office? I thought you all were going to crack down on racketeering and organized crime." More laughter in his brother's voice came through the line.

"We're all being watched." Marcus glanced around the room, feeling a bit paranoid about someone listening in.

"Anyone could have seen that coming." Lucius sighed. "Fine, what am I looking for?"

"Evidence that the Morans killed him. Or had him killed. I plan to bring a civil case against them. If I can't catch them in the act of their illegal dealings, I'll make sure Reggie's wife Diane is taken care of. Reggie had been getting close to proving their part in selling guns to the gangs. He believed deals were being made at their construction sites. I think they killed him and dumped his body in the river. You need to be discreet about this."

Lucius huffed. "When have I not been?"

"I'm just saying. We look alike. This can't be tied back to me."

"My hair is still black, but it's longer than yours. I'll wear brown contacts to cover the blue. And no one will ever see me in a suit. I doubt people would confuse us never mind think we're related." Lucius's realistic words settled Marcus's paranoia. After high school, Marcus had gone to college, while Lucius went into the Navy. It changed him, physically and personally. He became secretive and lived in the shadows. After the military, Marcus wasn't sure what his older brother by three minutes did with his time. Marcus figured he was now CIA, not that Lucius would ever tell him.

Marcus glanced through the glass window to the waiting room and saw Diane Brodsky had arrived. A moment later, his phone buzzed in his hand. Gloria had texted him as asked. "I need to meet with Reggie's wife. She just arrived. Is there anything you need from me to do this?"

"When did this happen? What did the authorities determine? I'll need details and direction."

Marcus had hoped his brother wouldn't ask. "Reggie went missing last week. His body resurfaced three days later. Deemed an accident. No sign of foul play. He had...well, he and Diane had been in a fight, and he went for a walk."

"And you jump to murder by the Morans? That makes sense." Lucius's sarcasm grated on Marcus as always.

"It does when you know they always have their hand in everything, one way or another."

"Including who their daughter dates."

Of course, his brother went there. "Christina has nothing to do with this. That was twelve years ago. They've probably married her off to some business tycoon who will join them in their crimes. I was too clean for her."

"You mean too good for her." Lucius cut quickly to the heart of the matter. "Truth is you never trusted her just because of her last name."

"I loved her."

"You used her. Don't kid yourself. Just like this coalition partnership with the prosecutor's office. The only focus you have is to get the Morans, in any way possible, whatever the costs, and at anyone's expense."

His phone buzzed again, and he could see Diane pacing the waiting room. She looked broken. Her face seemed paler than usual, her brown ponytail was off-kilter, and her eyes were bloodshot from crying.

Was she also a means to an end? He was about to convince her to bring a wrongful death lawsuit when Reggie wasn't even in the ground yet. Maybe Lucius was right about him, and he was blinded by his mission.

Marcus shook his head, unwilling to cater to such an idea. "Kids are dying on the streets from the guns the Morans are putting in their hands. They might as well be pulling the triggers. You grew up in the same home as me. We lived in the same rough neighborhood. The Moran family was serving the gangs around us then, and they still are. You know it, and I know it."

Lucius didn't respond. Marcus wondered if he had hung up on his tirade.

Then his brother spoke, his voice barely audible. "You know, if you don't let this go, you will be next."

Marcus closed his eyes but quickly opened them to look at the newly widowed woman in the waiting room. "I will never stop. I can't. Fear of retribution never slowed me or Reggie down before. It won't now. If anything, I can add justice for Reggie to the mission. We were in this together, and he wouldn't want me to stop now. Perhaps evidence can be found that will warrant a criminal case for his murder, no matter what the ME report says."

"Would Reggie want you to put your life on the line?"

"He would want me to take care of Diane, and this is the best way I know how."

Lucius clicked his tongue. "Fine. We do this. But once we start, there's no going back. Got it?"

"Absolutely."

"No matter what the Morans throw at us. No matter what obstacles they put in our paths. No matter who they use against us. It will end with us only."

"I'm ready."

Lucius laughed once. "You only think you are, brother. These people will not play fair, and most likely lives will be lost. You're stepping on their turf, and there's no way you will be fully ready for how they retaliate. Sleep with your eyes open. I'll be in touch."

The line went dead, and Marcus put his phone on his desk. He stood and went to the door, opening it to the closest opportunity he'd ever had in taking down the Morans. Not even the coalition came this close to touching them. Not even dating their "little princess" left a mark. Unbeknownst to Reggie, his death would be the path to victory.

"Diane, I'm so grateful for your willingness to come in today and hear what I have to say. Reggie would be so proud of you."

Diane sniffed and swiped at her eyes. She lifted her head high and said, "I'll do whatever you want me to."

Marcus smiled and waved for her to walk ahead of him. "The conference room is the second door on the right."

Ready or not, the takedown had begun. After he was done, the Moran family would be finished, come what may.

Chris knew something was off when she arrived home at her New York City apartment building, and the doorman was not at his post. Donny was a fixture as old as the green awning over the door, the same color that matched his aged uniform. She looked down the dark, empty street, first one way then the other before opening the glass door. She missed the sunrise greeting he always gave her when she returned home from working late nights at the club, but she was more concerned about his absence. It wasn't like him.

Inside, she approached the wall of tiny mailboxes and did a double take when the name tag that typically read *Chris DePalo* on the front of hers was now empty. She inserted her key and breathed a sigh of relief when it opened.

The key still worked, but there was no mail.

Her roommate Sam must have brought it up already. Making her way to the stairwell, Chris took the two flights up and headed down the carpeted hallway to the last apartment door on the right.

The door stood ajar.

Slowly, Chris placed her palm on the wood door and gave it a slight push. The first sight on the other side was her pile of mail strewn about on the floor.

"Samantha?" Her voice hitched before she cleared it. "I know you're new to New York City, but you really shouldn't leave the door open. I'm kind of fond of my things and want to keep them. And that includes you."

The sound of Chris's heels clicked across the wooden floor as she slowly entered and bypassed a few envelopes and junk mail. She decided to leave the door open behind her, as things felt off.

A scan around the apartment didn't set off any warning bells. Other than the mail, everything else seemed to be in its meticulous place. The four chairs were pushed in around the table. Her line of framed photographs from the last twelve years remained in place on top of the baby grand piano that she'd inherited with the apartment when she moved in. The latest picture of her and Sam at Central Park stood front and center. They stood on the bridge and looked more like mother and daughter than roommates. But with fifteen years between them, it wasn't surprising. Chris also saw so much of herself in the young woman, and not because they both were blonde-haired with green eyes. She saw the need to be free.

Chris continued her scan of the apartment for anything out of place or stolen. The peacock blue throw pillows on her white sofa looked untouched. Then, beyond the pristine furniture, her gaze stopped at the white chiffon curtain billowing inward with the warm morning breeze. She didn't remember leaving the window open last night, but the air conditioning had been giving them trouble lately. Perhaps Sam opened it when she returned home from her night-time adventures throughout the city.

Chris turned for the hallway that led to the bedrooms. Passing the galley kitchen, she checked to see it was empty and made her way to the closed doors at the end. She tapped softly on Sam's door, but with no answer, she opened it to find it empty except for the small twin bed and a few belongings draped over open drawers. Typically, Sam slept until noon after her nights crawling across the city pubs. But her bed hadn't been slept in at all. Did Sam not return home last night? But then who got the mail? Who opened the door...and left it open?

358

It wouldn't be Sam's first time being irresponsible, but this went beyond typical laziness.

A sinking concern riled Chris and made her wonder why she took in these dreamers, fresh off the bus with nothing in their purses and stars for fame in their eyes.

Maybe because I was one of them once…before reality set in.

Chris faced the other door. Her own room beckoned as did sleep. Still, she reached for her cell phone and dialed Sam's number. This behavior couldn't happen again if she wanted to continue living with her.

A phone rang instantly from somewhere behind Chris's bedroom door. As she listened to the rings through the phone and through her door, anger ramped up. The household rule was to stay out of each other's rooms.

"You have a lot of nerve after everything I've done for you." Chris rushed toward the door and flung it wide.

She inhaled sharply at the sight before her. The whole room had been tossed.

No, destroyed was more like it.

The phone continued to ring, and Chris located it beneath the disordered bed. Had Sam dropped it while she upended the room?

But why?

The two of them struggled a bit but nothing out of the ordinary. Sam felt more like a little sister to her. Their age difference came through in maturity, but Chris only meant to protect Sam from a city that could eat her alive if she wasn't careful. Sam complained sometimes but never seemed angry enough to destroy her things like this. With Sam's phone left behind, all Chris could do was wait for her to return. As tired as she was after working all night running the club, sleep would have to wait. Not that she could sleep in this room now.

Chris walked back to the living room grateful Sam had left the rest of the apartment intact. The door to the hall was still open, and Chris returned to it and closed it with a soft click.

A knife protruded from the back of the door holding a piece of paper in place.

Chris screamed at the sight and couldn't focus on the message scrawled across it. Backing away, she gripped at her throat as she tried to read the few simple, yet debilitating words left for her.

It's time to come home, Christina. Your family needs you.

Below the knife, her mailbox tag was stuck as well. But the name *Chris Depalo* was written over with the name *Christina Moran* in heavy block letters.

Her real name.

Chris stepped back and mindlessly made her way to the sofa. Dropping to the edge, she wondered when they found her. Or had they always known she was in the city? Had they only been waiting to make their move? For years, she slept with the lights on. At what point had she let her guard down?

And how had they gotten in?

She looked to the opened window and stood on shaking legs. At the ledge, she pushed the curtain aside and saw they came up the fire escape. The ladder had been pulled down, and a glance over showed a swatch of green on the ground in the alleyway.

"Donny?" Chris called and climbed out quickly. She descended the rungs of the ladder until she was by his side. Blood trickled on his temple, and he groaned when she turned him over. "Oh, thank God you're alive. Who did this, Donny? Did you see them?"

Had her father come for her himself, or had he sent her brother or one of his goons?

Donny's eyes opened, and he winced. Then he pushed up abruptly to reach for her. "Chris!"

She pushed him back down. "I'm okay, but Sam is gone. They took her. I need to know what you saw."

"There were three of them. But I only saw two at first. I saw them go down the alley, and I followed them. Then a third jumped out...that's all I remember. I've never seen them before. They wore black clothes. One was bald, the other two had brown and black hair. One had a scar."

"Under his right eye?" she asked, knowing exactly who that man was.

"Yeah, how'd you know?"

"I gave it to him." Tears filled her eyes. How foolish she had been to think her family would leave her alone forever. Her brother had found her.

"You did? You know those men?"

Chris ignored the question. "Did they say anything to you?"

Donny paused and closed his eyes again. He shook his head, then said, "Wait, yeah, the one with the scar. He said something."

"What, Donny? What did he say?"

Donny opened his eyes, and his gaze narrowed on her. "He said this was family business and to stay out of it. Are they really related to you? Those men were dangerous. I need to call the police."

"You can, but they're long gone. And they'll cover their tracks. The police have never been able to catch them before." Chris stood and helped him up.

"You said they have Sam?"

"It looks that way. I have no choice but to go after them."

"Where are you going?"

Chris swallowed hard. "Home."

Chapter Two

"Is this the right place?" The driver of Chris's rideshare car pulled up to the three-story house on Gryphon Street. As far as Chris could tell nothing had changed since she walked out the double front doors and descended the staircase to the cab that had waited for her twelve years ago. The white stucco looked pinker than the last time, but that was typical with the red bricks beneath bleeding through. Her father was behind in touching up the white paint. Not that she cared.

"Yes, this is it. Thank you for the ride."

Chris grabbed the single duffle bag she had thrown together from what she could salvage from her destroyed room back in her apartment and opened the rear door. The hot humidity hit her in the face. She'd forgotten how brutal a Georgia August could be. Stifling, really.

"Nice house," the driver said as she stepped foot on home turf.

"It comes with strings," Chris replied and shut the door without a goodbye.

Staring up at the elaborate structure, she stopped her gaze on the third-story window in the right corner. Her childhood room never looked more like a prison cell until this moment. Would Sam be in there? Would her family make it that easy for her?

Only one way to find out.

She hefted the bag up on her shoulder and ascended the stone steps without using the iron railings. At the double doors, she used her old key, surprised they hadn't changed the locks. But then it was never about keeping her out.

The center table in the foyer held the typical flower arrangement of blossoms as big as a face. The house was still and quiet, and she took the opportunity to make her way to the spiral staircase to her left, glad she wore tennis shoes with soft soles.

At the fifth step, she heard a noise from above. A lift of her head showed her father at the top. Chris halted, her hand clutching the smooth railing for dear life. The formidable Vincent Moran glared down at her. But their standoff couldn't last forever, and she couldn't let him set the stage for her time here.

"Where is Sam?" she asked with as much bravado as she could fake.

His face remained stoic. "I haven't the slightest idea of what you're talking about." He took the first step down.

Chris swallowed through a parched throat. Had she made a mistake in coming here? She had no choice.

"My roommate. The young woman you kidnapped from our apartment. Where is she?"

"I have never been to your apartment." He took two more steps. "But I'm glad to see you understand reason and have come home. Welcome back, Christina. You chose wisely."

"I'm not staying. I'm here for Sam only."

Two more steps. "There is no Sam here." He nodded to something behind her. A quick glance showed two men in suits at the bottom of the stairs.

"I should have known your goons would be waiting." She glared back up at her father, who now was three steps closer. "After what you did to my apartment. Are these the men you sent to toss my place?"

"Your place is here. It has always been here." His hand glided down the same railing her sweating hand gripped tightly. "And no, these are not the men I sent to ask you to come home."

"*Ask?*" she couldn't have heard him correctly. "Don't you mean force?"

Her father looked out the window behind her. "As far as I could see, you came here willingly. I watched you step out of the car. You used your key, which I'm pleased you kept all these years. Somewhere deep inside, you knew this would always be your home."

"A symbol of my time in a prison." She held the key up but still couldn't let it go. Was he right in his thinking? Why couldn't she throw it away?

"I'm sorry you feel that way, my daughter." He stopped five steps from her. A glimpse of pain flickered in his gray-blue eyes, and she dropped her gaze to his black shoes. How quickly he played on her emotions. How quickly she let him. "I was actually quite happy to see you step out of that car. Your mother would have run to meet you in tears of joy. Maybe I should have, but I held back. Do you really not want to be here?"

She lifted her face to his. "No. I am only here for Sam, and then I will be gone forever. And don't call me daughter ever again. I am not part of this family."

After a moment of vacant expression that hid his emotions, he nodded once. "Your brother—I mean *Silas*, went to bring you back. He has not arrived yet. If your Sam is with him, I will find out and have her returned immediately."

"You will?" Another trick up his sleeve, she thought.

"Kidnapping is illegal. I can assure you I had nothing to do with taking your roommate. There must be a misunderstanding. I will make sure she is safe *if* she is even with Silas."

Chris realized she had no proof Sam was kidnapped. Sam might have arrived home and seen Silas and his men in the apartment. She could have dropped the mail and run back out. But why not call the police about a break-in? Or call her at the club? Sam would have no place else to run to. Unless she didn't want to lead the men to Club Creare and to Chris. Had Sam been trying to protect her?

"Until then, I do hope you will make yourself comfortable here."

"I'm not staying in this house." She looked up at the closed doors above. "But if what you say is true, I'm sure you won't mind if I look through the rooms to make sure she's not here."

He glanced at the men behind her. Then he stepped aside and waved her on. "The house is all yours."

Chris hesitated for a moment, half expecting to be grabbed. She quickly headed past her father, bracing for anything he would try.

"The house has always been yours, Christina." He spoke so low, she paused to hear him, her eyes closing to keep from leaning into him. Even knowing the criminal acts her family committed didn't change the fact that they were only family she had ever known. No matter how many young women she invited into her life, they would never be her family.

"I'm not a Moran anymore." Her words were meant more to remind herself and not just her father.

"A hundred name changes cannot erase the blood that flows in your veins. You will always be a Moran."

Chris picked up her pace to race to the top of the stairs and through every room of the house, above and below. When she came up from the basement, she found her father sitting at the dining room table with a letter in front of him. His two guards stood behind him by the curtained window. Her steps slowed for the first time since her search for Sam began.

"As I told you, your friend is not here. But I have talked to Silas."

When he didn't go on, Chris moved closer to the table, reaching for the back of the ornate wooden chair across from him.

"Where is she? Where did he take her?" She tightened her grip on the wood. Her father took notice and sniffed.

"You two have always had it out for each other. I should have put a stop to it early on."

"But you didn't."

He smirked. "Only because Silas was always right about you. He knew you would leave us. So, I have to believe he's right again and knows what it will take for you to help us now."

And there was the catch.

Chris tilted her head, letting her long blonde hair fall off her shoulder. "Of course you want something. I didn't believe for a second you actually wanted me home." She scoffed and shook her head at his deceitfulness. "I'm not helping you with anything."

"Do you want to know where your friend is?"

"How dare you. You have put an innocent young woman in jeopardy all because you want to control me. She's barely eighteen. She's practically a child. I won't hesitate to tell the police you were a part of her kidnapping."

He raised the palms of his hands. "I'm clean. I had nothing to do with it."

"Right. That's your excuse for every dirty deed that transpires around you. I will not join you in them. You can forget it."

"I would never ask you to put yourself in harm's way. Or to break the law. I have other people for that. All I'm asking is that you talk to an old friend and...*convince* him to leave me alone."

Chris bit back the question on her tongue. *Who is this old friend?* As soon as she asked it, she would be sucked back in with no way out. Her father pushed the envelope toward her. The name on the return address stamped in the corner became clear and saved her from asking.

"No," she said, shaking her head. "Just no."

"Mr. Cartwright seems to think I killed his partner."

Chris inhaled sharply. "Reggie's dead? You killed Reggie? How—"

"I did no such thing." Her father stood and leaned over the table. "Brodsky and Cartwright have been a thorn in my side for years. I would be stupid to kill either of them. Seeing the conviction in your eyes proves my point. My own daughter thinks I'm guilty. It won't be hard for Marcus Cartwright to find witnesses to say it in court. This case needs to go away. And you're the only person who can convince him to look elsewhere."

"Me? Have you forgotten how things ended between us? He used me to get to you. I mean nothing to the man."

Her father chuckled. "Then a chat with him should be quick. One conversation with him is all I'm asking."

"Or what?"

He shrugged, and she had her answer. She may never see Sam again.

"There had better not be one hair out of place on Samantha's head." Chris pivoted and headed for the front door. She opened it wide, yearning to breathe the thick humid air over the chokehold of Vincent Moran's death grip.

"Goodbye, daughter." Her father's voice and message carried loud and clear as she stepped outside.

Like it or not, Christina Moran was back.

~

Marcus ran along the riverfront on his typical morning jog, approaching the location where Reggie's body had been found. He had already searched the area for any clues and spent longer than necessary torturing himself with the lack of answers. Still, he turned and let his attention be pulled to where he had watched Reggie's body be zipped up in a body bag and taken away.

Marcus picked up his pace and pushed harder in his run. He had done everything he could. All the pieces were in place for the ultimate take-down. Vincent Moran had been served the litigation documents. He would have his day in court, and Marcus would be ready with ironclad witnesses. When this was all done, Moran would be broke, but hopefully, he would have enough evidence to lead to Moran's arrest in a criminal case. The dynasty would be over.

Marcus found himself smiling, his spirits lifted by a determination for justice. He turned the corner to his townhouse and saw a woman sitting on his stoop. The adjacent live oak with its hanging Spanish moss shadowed her face. But as he slowed his steps and focused, he knew Vincent Moran had counter-served his own surprise.

She stood to her full six feet and met him eye-to-eye at the landing of the stairs.

She was more beautiful than ever. Twelve years of maturity looked good on her.

"I see your father brought out the big guns." Marcus swiped at his brow. "Long time no see, Christina. What have you been up to? Your daddy kept you quite hidden. He must be scared if he's letting you out now."

"I'm not here by choice, but *I* kept myself hidden, not that it worked. I even changed my name."

"To what?"

"Never mind. Listen, I'm just as excited to see you as you are to see me, but my father can be persuasive."

"Save it. I'm not interested in anything he has to say. He's going down. Now, if you'll excuse me, I need to get ready for work." Marcus stepped up the first step.

Christina touched his forearm, halting him cold. Even in the day's rising heat, he shivered at her touch.

"I'm sorry about Reggie," she spoke low with genuine sadness in her large sea-green eyes. "I know how close you were."

He didn't respond but looked over her shoulder to a squirrel scurrying up a tree.

"How is Diane?"

He locked his gaze on her. "She'll be better after your family pays for what they did to her husband."

Christina frowned. "He says he had nothing to do with it, Marcus."

"And I'm supposed to believe a word from his mouth, or rather from the prodigal daughter's mouth."

"I haven't returned home."

"Then why are you here doing your father's bidding once again? If you really escaped as you say, then why would you vouch for him now?"

"I don't agree with my father's business practices, but you're accusing him of murder."

"Wrongful death, actually. But I do hope to have the evidence in place after the lawsuit for a murder charge. Will you come out of the woodwork for that too? I'll be sure to be more presentable next time."

She dropped her hand and smirked. Even a snide smile brought out more of her beauty. "Thank you," she said.

"For what?"

Her wide eyes which always made him catch his breath now cut him down in a different way. "For reminding me you could never be trusted. Have a nice life, Marcus." She turned toward the street corner.

"Hey, at least I got a goodbye this time," he called to her retreating back. "Sort of."

"You get what you deserve," she replied without a backward glance. "Consider yourself warned."

He huffed and headed inside as he mumbled, "Once a Moran, always a Moran."

Chapter Three

THE CADENCE OF CHRIS'S FOOTSTEPS ALONG THE SIDEWALKS of historic Savannah matched the rapidly beating heart in her chest. Why did Marcus Cartwright still have such an effect on her? His cavalier attitude, him acting as though they never meant anything to each other only hurt more. She had once believed she would marry him and spend the rest of her life with him. He was smart and kind. He made her feel special and seen. She didn't care that he didn't come from money, and she didn't care that her father hated him. Perhaps, she loved him more because of those things. In the end, her father had been right about Marcus. He used her to get to him, and everything their relationship stood on fell to pieces. Not one word or vow that came out of his mouth had been true. Not one "I love you" came from his heart. She had been nothing but a means to an end, and she wouldn't forget that ever again.

The phone in her back jeans pocket buzzed. Removing it, she saw it was her business partner at the club. She shot off a text that she would be gone for a few days and couldn't explain. She knew she owed her business partner an explanation for taking off without notice, but no one from her new life knew about her roots. Chris wasn't ready for her worlds to meet. How could she give explanations when she didn't know the answers herself? The idea of moving someplace else and changing her name again crossed her mind, but the fact that her family found her only proved that wasn't the answer. And how many friends could she just keep leaving behind as though they never meant anything to her? Rafe Sinclair and Melody Stiles were a huge part of her present life, but then so was Diane Brodsky from her past one.

Chris found herself two streets over from Diane's house and wondered if subconsciously she meant to go there. Unsure if Diane would even open the door, Chris continued to make her way to her old friend's house. Did she really have a right to knock on the door after leaving Georgia and everyone behind without a goodbye? At the time she believed she was protecting her friends, whether they saw it that way or not.

Chris passed numerous glass storefronts along Wells Street, slowing her steps as she approached the single detached brick home that Diane and Reggie had purchased after they married 15 years ago, two high school sweethearts completely in love. It had been run down and boarded up for years before they moved in and rehabbed it while Reggie went to college and law school. Seeing it now in all its splendor, Chris appreciated the work the couple had put into it. She stood on a street corner unable to force herself to cross over. A horse and buggy full of tourists slowly moved down the street, and she let the clopping of the horse's hooves calm her nerves.

"Are you just going to stand here spying on my home?" A voice from behind caught Chris unaware. A quick turn showed Diane behind her with two bags of groceries.

"You scared me," Chris said, clutching her chest. "I wasn't spying, honest. I...I'm not exactly sure how I ended up here. I went to see Marcus, and I was concerned about you. But I understand if you would rather I left."

Diane lightly shrugged. "There is the fact that I'm suing your family. It's probably best if you're not here."

"I understand." Chris took a step backward.

"But I would like you to come in. I think there are things that need to be said."

"Are you sure?"

Diane pressed her lips together in a moment of indecision. "We won't talk about the case. Deal?"

Chris smiled and stepped back closer, lifting her arms to take a bag. "Deal."

They headed around the back to the rear door, passing through a fenced-in courtyard. Most of the flowers were gone from the trees, leaving lush green leaves and buzzing insects flying about. They walked up the gray stepping stones to the door, and Diane unlocked it with her free hand.

"Pardon the mess. I haven't been up to cleaning since...well, since Reggie went missing."

Chris stepped inside the kitchen and absorbed the feel of the place. A black-and-white checkered floor extended toward a formal living room with ornate, Southern furniture.

"You kept the floor," Chris remarked, toeing one of the blocks.

"Took many hours and a strained back to get them this shiny." Diane put her bag on the counter and reached for Chris's. As she emptied them, Chris continued to walk around the kitchen. She came to the table and chose the chair in the corner to sit in.

"So, what did you want to talk about?" Diane asked without turning around. She opened the refrigerator to load it up with milk and vegetables. The shelves had been empty before she did that.

"Not really sure. I suppose I should tell you where I've been for 12 years."

"That's a start." She kicked the door with her foot to close it and faced Chris expectantly.

"New York City. Silly me thought I could make it on Broadway."

"You can't sing."

Chris smiled. "That did pose a problem. So instead, I went into the restaurant business. I own a restaurant club called Club Creare now. We had some problems the past couple of years after my business partner Melody became a target of a killer."

Diane's eyes widened. "Sounds scary. I've always wanted to go to the big city, but perhaps it wouldn't be wise."

"It's fine. You'd be fine. Her stalker found her in a way that had nothing to do with the location we lived in."

"Is she safe now?"

"Absolutely." Chris smiled reassuringly. "She's married now and living in Connecticut with a great guy. I'm happy for her."

Diane's smile flitted from her face. "I hope it lasts a long time. It's unbelievable how quickly someone can be taken from you."

Chris wanted to stand up and wrap her arms around Diane but wasn't sure an embrace would be well received. She remained seated and took a few moments of quiet to consider her words.

"I'm so sorry about Reggie. He was a good man." What more could Chris say? She had been gone too long to miss him now.

"He was planning to rid the streets of your family," Diane replied matter-of-factly, her eyebrows arched in defiance.

Chris took a moment to clear her throat and hide her surprise at Diane's bluntness. "I would be the first to commend him. My father's business ethics are not my own. I run my club with the utmost respect for the law."

Diane crossed her arms and leaned against the counter. "You expect me to believe you run a club and have no ties to organized crime? Why should I trust you?"

Chris pulled her hands in front of her. Leaning back with a sigh, she said, "All I can say is you knew I was never comfortable here. Why would I start over with a new name and a new life only to tarnish it all by cutting corners?"

"Because that's all you knew. It wasn't until you started dating Marcus that you saw anything wrong with the way your family ran their businesses. When Marcus brought you to dinner that first night we met, I nearly choked on my piece of bread." Diane laughed, throwing back her head and looking at the ceiling. "I thought he had lost his marbles by dating you."

"Gee, thanks." Chris forced a smile. "But it turned out dating me was part of his plan to get to my family, so I guess you were right about us. It wasn't real."

Diane came away from the counter and pulled up a chair. "Then I met you and spent time with you and saw you were nothing like your family."

"And yet, you believe my club is corrupt."

Diane tilted her head and slowly shook it. "No, I don't. I'm just angry,

372

and you're sitting in front of me, the closest connection I will ever have to the Moran family. They killed my Reggie."

Chris clenched her fist before making the decision to reach for Diane's hand. "Why do you think this?"

Diane looked down to where Chris's hand covered hers but didn't push her away. "He was about to expose them for money laundering through their construction business. It was the closest crime he had ever come close to proving, and they killed him before he could."

Telling Diane that she believed her family was innocent of Reggie's murder wouldn't go over well. All Chris wanted to do was let her father know she'd kept to her end of the bargain by asking Marcus to back off. Now, she wanted to get Sam and go home to New York.

Instead, she heard herself say, "I'll look into it."

Diane covered her hand and held tight to it. "You will?" Hope filled her eyes, and Chris knew she couldn't leave just yet.

"I think I owe you that much." She stood, squeezing Diane's hand one last time before letting go. "Give me a few days, and I'll see what I can find out. But I can't promise you anything. I'm not part of this family anymore."

Diane nodded as Chris made her way to the door. "I knew I wasn't wrong about you."

Chris smiled and opened the door. As she turned back, something shiny on the floor by the trashcan caught her attention. "Is that glass?" She took a few steps to pick it up and noticed blood was on the shard.

Diane stood and reached for it, taking it from Chris's hand. She opened the trashcan and tossed it in quickly. "It's nothing. I dropped a bottle and cut myself on it. That must've been a piece that I missed earlier."

Chris gazed into her old friend's eyes, searching for her well-being emotionally, physically, and even mentally. "If you need anything while I'm in town, please call me." She reached for a pen and a sticky note on the counter and jotted down her number, tapping it with the pen before she headed out onto the streets.

A glance back showed Diane chewing her lower lip and holding herself together.

Barely.

Marcus stood waiting for Lucius outside of the Morans' latest build site. Two sets of apartment buildings were halfway completed, but all was quiet on the construction site. Without workers around, he wondered if the build had been halted. He checked his phone for any messages and stayed in the shadow of the adjacent rundown building, also owned by the Morans. The family was involved in building new apartments as well as collecting rents as slumlords; they had their hands in everyone's pockets, one way or another.

A man walked down the street. He had a thick salt-and-pepper beard, a ponytail, and large sunglasses that covered half his face. He walked with a limp and wore dirty blue jeans and an open Hawaiian shirt over a white tank. Marcus's first thought was that he was homeless, but when the man reached him, he paused at the streetlight pole and leaned against it to light a cigarette. After the man took a few puffs, Marcus checked his phone again.

"I will never call or text you with recon," the man said.

Lucius?

Marcus felt his mouth drop in shock. "I had no idea it was you. You look nothing like me. And when did you start smoking?"

Lucius made a cutting sign at his neck with his hand and looked down the street. "Don't blow my cover," he whispered harshly.

Marcus could have kicked himself. "Right. Sorry."

"And next time, lose the suit. Are you looking to get robbed?" Lucius lowered his shades to sneer at Marcus's clothes.

"I can take care of myself. Just tell me what you have."

Lucius glanced down the street again. So far, no one had shown them any interest. A few kids were riding bikes at the far end. Another glided on a skateboard. Two old men sat on milk crates and watched the kids on this hot summer day.

"I saw the medical examiner's notes on Reggie. The notes before the report don't match the final report. A hit to the head was what really killed him, not drowning in polluted water. He was dead before he hit the water."

"Then why deem it an accident or suicide?"

"I still trying to figure that out. Someone could have convinced the ME to leave that detail out."

"By threatening him, you mean?"

Lucius let the cigarette burn as he shifted his stance and faced the unfinished buildings. He tugged on his fake beard. It held tightly to his face. Marcus wondered about the glue he used to keep it in place. Again, he wondered what his brother's line of work was since dressing incognito came naturally to him.

"Something's definitely going on at this apartment site," Lucius said. "Word on the street is the Morans received funding for building this complex for low-income tenants. But the funds aren't all going to the project. The materials are cheap, and the safety measures are being ignored. It's a risk to even walk on the site. The workers have all quit, and building has ceased."

"But I'm sure the Morans have already received the money."

Lucius nodded and scratched his bushy beard. He mumbled, "I hate these things. They make me itch." He dropped his hand and jutted his chin toward the apartments. "The half-built buildings will probably sit unfinished for eternity."

"Care to share your source?"

Lucius chuckled and shook his head. "Never. I protect my sources. Always. I care about this town too and the people in it."

Marcus looked in the other direction at the innocent boys on their bikes again. "Unlike the Morans. They couldn't care less about the people who live here. At what point do some of these kids start using the buildings for a hangout? They could get hurt, or worse." Marcus tapped the side of his fist against the building, restraining his pent-up anger. "Not that the Morans care about the kids in these neighborhoods. They've proven they only care about themselves and their bank accounts."

"Then why send their princess?" Lucius asked.

"What? How did you know Christina came to see me?" Marcus wondered how much his bother knew.

"I wasn't talking about that. But good to know." Lucius pointed at the apartments.

Marcus dragged his attention away from the kids to follow Lucius's line of focus. A glimpse of long blonde hair pulled him from the shadows of the alley. An unmistakable tall woman who seemed to walk on air with her dancer's body entered the unfinished apartment building.

It was the so-called Moran princess that Lucius mentioned.

Christina.

A myriad of emotions hit Marcus all at once. His anger was washed away instantly when fear for Christina's safety took precedence. Panic skyrocketed his heart rate and without a second thought, he rushed into the street. Every step pounded on the pavement and then crunched in the gravel as he neared the fence of the building site at a breakneck speed.

"Christina! Stop! It's not safe!" Marcus rushed toward the building with Lucius right behind him. In the next second, a loud crash from inside the unfinished structure shook the ground beneath his feet and stopped him in his tracks. The continuing rumble sounded like all five floors were caving in on each other. Marcus's stomach dropped just as hard. "Christina!"

Chapter Four

ONE SECOND CHRIS WAS SCANNING THE POSTS AND BEAMS OF the construction site as well as the state of the mess around her. Her father had never been so haphazard in any of his projects. She had walked further into the building when something dark red caught her eye.

Blood. And a lot of it. Someone had been seriously hurt here.

Or killed.

In shock at the sight of the spatter, she had backed up right into a post and heard a loud crack above her head. Running across the unfinished floors to a larger beam, she turned back and noticed the post she had hit was cracked.

Had she caused that?

Chris didn't think she had collided with it that hard. Then she heard someone calling her name, and before she could call out, the ceiling above her came crashing down and all she could do was stay close to the larger beam that held up the floors above her as every other area fell around her.

Plumes of dirt and debris filled the air around her and forced her to keep her eyes closed while she struggled to breathe. Even after the crashing ceased and the dust began to settle, Chris kept her face shielded and her eyes closed. For a moment, she wondered if she was alive, but then she felt something touch her back and knew she had survived.

Without moving from her sheltered position against the beam, she opened her eyes to darkness and realized she was barricaded by fallen debris.

Chris felt the touch on her back again, and she reached her hand behind her, fumbling until she made contact with another hand. Afraid to move one inch and cause another collapse, all she could do was hold tightly to this person.

"Are you all right?" the man asked. It was the same voice that had called out to her before the collapse.

Chris knew instantly it was Marcus, and she let the sound of his voice steady her breathing. She tried to speak, but all she could do was nod and hope he could see her.

"I think I can lift this board," another voice spoke to Marcus. "I'll hold it up while you pull her out. On three."

Chris felt Marcus's hand grip tighter as the other person counted down. As planned on three, sunlight streamed through as the crunch of wood and boards lifted and echoed around her. All at the same time, she felt another arm wrap around her waist and pull her back against Marcus's chest. Suddenly, she was falling and let out a scream. But when she landed, it was Marcus who grunted and took the brunt of the fall. He held her tight with his arms wrapped around her as he cushioned her landing.

Above her, Chris observed the collapse of the building and wondered at her survival. She gripped Marcus's hands which still had her cocooned against him. Her body trembled, and somewhere she heard whimpering.

"Shhh...you're safe." Marcus spoke into her ear from behind. "Thank God you're safe. Shhh...It's okay. I've got you."

That's when Chris realized it was her crying that she heard. "What...happened?"

"Your father happened, that's what," Marcus replied. He suddenly sounded angry.

Chris sobered instantly and tried to pull herself from his arms. "What is that supposed to mean?"

A man with a beard stepped up in front of her and offered her his arm. "This is one of your father's buildings. He's been cutting corners to save a buck. He very nearly lost his daughter today because of it."

Chris reached out and took his hand as Marcus let her go. Soon, the three of them stood on the outskirts of the rubble, staring at each other for their next move.

"I don't understand," she said. "Why would he take such a risk?"

Marcus replied, "I could ask the same question of you. What are you doing here?"

"Why can't I be here? It's my family's property" She looked back at the bearded man and squinted. "Lucius? Is that you? Why are you dressed like that?"

"Nice to see you, too," Lucius said.

"I think we can all admit this isn't a friendly gathering," Chris said, folding her arms. "What are the two of you doing here? This is my father's project."

Marcus replied, "It doesn't look like much is going on. All the workers have walked off. Care to share why?"

"I wouldn't have a clue. I have nothing to do with the build." She looked at the mess. "Or what's left of it."

"Then why are you here?" he asked.

"If you must know, I went and saw Diane. She asked me to look into the project. She believes Reggie's death is related to it. I told her I would check it out. That's all."

Marcus glanced at Lucius. "What do you think?"

Lucius looked over his shoulder and spoke low. "I think you both are asking for trouble. Neither of you should be snooping around here. You might want to take this someplace private. The authorities will be here any moment. Someone is bound to call them. I've stayed too long as well. Christina, welcome back." Lucius turned and slipped out of sight without a sound.

"He's just as sneaky as ever," Chris said.

"I could say the same about you. Let's go." Marcus guided Christina by the elbow out of the area.

"Where are we going?"

"To my office. We're going to have a chat."

"What if I don't want to."

"I have the truth about Reggie's death. Care to hear it?"

Chris glanced back at the rubble, remembering the blood she had seen before the floors collapsed. "Yes, I think I need to."

"Even if your father is responsible?"

If Marcus thought she would protect the man, he was sorely mistaken. "Especially."

~

"Are you sure we can speak freely?" Christina asked as Marcus led her into his office. Being Friday afternoon with no appointments or court appearances, he had given Gloria and the office staff an early weekend.

"Everyone is gone for the day. I sent them home early. But I also had the place swept of electronic ears if that's what you mean."

She took a chair in front of his desk. "It's ridiculous that we have to think that way."

"I'm glad to see you aren't naive to the possibility." Marcus dared her to deny the reach of her family's tentacles. "The question is what are you going to do about it?"

"Me?" Her hands grasped the chair's wooden arms in a death grip. "I didn't come back to Savannah to take over the Morans' business dealings."

"Then why are you here?" Marcus sat on the edge of his desk in front of her. She shrunk back in the chair just enough to show him that she felt her space was being encroached on.

"I'm only here to get something they took from me." She frowned and folded her hands in her lap. She had no plans to elaborate.

Marcus inched closer. "Your family stole from one of their own? I'm shocked."

Christina lifted her face to meet his gaze. "I'm Chris DePalo now. I would appreciate you refraining from calling me a Moran from now on."

"DePalo. Where did that name come from?" Marcus leaned back to give her space to share freely.

"My mother's maiden name."

His tactics worked, and he softened his voice more. "She would have liked that."

Christina dropped her gaze to her lap with a nod. "Unfortunately, it wasn't good enough to keep them out of my life."

Her statement didn't make sense. Had she really fled from her own family? "I want to believe that you separated yourself from the Morans, but I'm struggling with it."

"You mean struggling with the idea of someone leaving their money behind."

Marcus shrugged. "It's a lot of money to say no to."

"Well, I did. I went to New York and started over with nothing but a suitcase and a dream to dance."

Marcus smiled, remembering how dancing had been so important to Christina...*Chris*. "And did you dance?"

"I did a few off-Broadway shows but realized soon that I would make more money in the restaurant business." She smiled so genuinely that Marcus wondered if she had her own tactics to demobilize him. He remembered how her serene smiles and sea-green eyes had a way of making him lose his focus. Was she doing it again? It took him twelve years to get back on track. He couldn't afford another twelve. He finally had the Morans in his clutches.

And they knew it.

"Did your family bring you back here to try and stop me?" he asked, once again leaning forward.

"Yes." Her swift answer took him by surprise. An angry expression flashed on her face just as quickly—anger that felt personally directed at him.

Marcus stood and circled his desk, needing a buffer and a moment to consider his next move. She obviously blamed him for her family tracking her down. He took his chair and leaned back.

"Why do I feel like we've been here before?" he asked.

"Because we have. But that doesn't mean we have to play into their hands this time."

"How do I know you're not playing me right now? I have a legal case that would be destroyed if I trust the wrong person."

"Don't forget you were the one who used me as your pawn last time. If anyone can't be trusted, it's you."

"It wasn't like that," he said, but wasn't able to explain something he didn't understand himself. All Marcus knew was Christina wielded more power than he had believed the day he approached her and asked her out on a date. What started as a play in his mission turned into a conflict of interest the moment that she turned her eyes on him. He'd realized he had met his match.

"Then how was it? Because all I remember is you proving my father right. I was a means to an end for you."

Marcus needed to regain control over this interrogation. She was too close to the truth. "What did your family steal from you?"

She looked away from his face and focused on something on his desk.

He leaned forward but tried not to impose on her space. He was far enough away now. He meant to show sincerity. "You want me to trust you, but you're keeping this from me. How can I believe you?"

"Fine." She paused. "But if I tell you, it remains between us only. It's off the record and can't be used in your case or for any reason. Understand?"

"Okay." This had to be incriminating evidence for her to make such a statement. If it was, he'd find a way to use it without breaking his vow to her now.

She stood and paced his office twice. She folded her arms at her midriff and turned to him. "My brother came to my apartment, but I work nights and wasn't home. My roommate came in and appears to have caught them by surprise. So..." She cleared her throat.

Marcus slowly stood up. "So...what happened, Chris?" He braced for the worst. Was she sharing about a murder? Would she really hide a homicide for her family?

"They took her to get me to come back here. My father knew nothing about Silas's plan, and promised to get her back if..."

Realization settled. Not a homicide but kidnapping for ransom. "Ah, I see. It appears your family is still pulling your strings. That's why you showed up on my stoop. To convince me to drop the suit so you can get your roommate back."

"No one is pulling my strings. I need to rescue Sam. She's got to be petrified. That's all."

"And I need to bring justice for Reggie's death. I won't stop for anyone."

"I understand, but Sam is young."

"I'm sorry about your friend. Though not surprised at Silas's tactics. He belongs in jail."

"Yes, he does." She returned to her seat, and Marcus retook his own to hear her out. "But wouldn't you rather see a criminal case against him?"

"Absolutely. May I call the police and have him picked up right now?"

"He never arrived home. He took Sam to an unknown place and won't return her until you drop the case."

Marcus chuckled. "You're kidding, right? I just told you I won't stop for anyone."

She placed her hands on his desk and stood. "You'll have to if I can prove my family had nothing to do with Reggie's death."

"And after today at the apartment site, I hope you're realizing that you're going to get yourself killed if you keep this up."

"Yes, I thought of that when the floors were falling in around me." Chris closed her eyes and visibly trembled. He knew how she felt. His heart rate had yet to stabilize, and the memory of the sound of the floors crashing still echoed in his head. He wondered how he would live with the traumatic experience but then had to figure it was nothing compared to being in the building.

"And yet, you won't stop?" he asked.

Her eyes opened wide. "I can't. I have no choice. Sam is innocent in all of this. I have to get her back safe and sound. But, Marcus, I really don't believe my family is guilty of killing Reggie."

"Reggie was investigating Moran Construction. And you nearly died on one of their worksites. That's a red flag for me."

"How did Reggie die? You said you had information on his report."

"I have knowledge that it wasn't drowning or suicide. But the medical examiner left it out. Blunt force trauma."

She pressed her lips together and crossed her arms again, this time locked in her thoughts. How he wished he could read minds.

"If I prove someone else killed him, will you drop the case?"

Marcus laughed, thinking she was joking. He sobered at her determined glare. "I can't believe I'm going to say this, but I want to help you prove me wrong."

"You do?" She sounded just as surprised as he felt. "Why would you do that?"

"Because there's already been a death and almost another one today. I'd like to avoid another incident. If that means I consider I'm wrong, then so be it. Either way justice for Reggie will be served. And if someone else is responsible for killing him, then I will make sure they go away for a very long time. But I must ask that if your family is responsible, you won't stand in my way."

Chris reached across the desk for a handshake. Marcus stared at her waiting hand. He wondered why he hesitated to take it. But when he finally made contact, he had his answer.

Christina may have changed her name and address, but the power she had over him remained intact. The fact that he had just agreed to help her disprove his case confirmed it.

Chapter Five

CHRIS STEPPED FOOT OUT OF HER HOTEL AND CROSSED THE street to Forsyth Park. She meandered along the walkways, which were draped with live oaks and Spanish moss. Approaching the white fountain that was filled with statues of marble fish spraying water in arches, she circled around the fenced-in fountain and continued by park benches and street musicians.

A man with a flute played a tune, and she stopped to listen to his talented song. After a moment, she tipped him and continued on her way. The sweltering heat had her lifting her hair. Ahead, she saw the stage theater she had spent many nights in. Bypassing the tables and chairs out front, she went inside and immediately felt at home. The ticket counter to her right stood empty since it was so early in the day. The afternoon matinee wouldn't begin for a few hours.

"May I help you?" a voice spoke from behind.

Chris turned to face the man coming out of the office. He immediately recognized her.

"Christina! Where have you been?" He reached his arms out, and she rushed into them.

"Hello, Freddie. I went to New York City and tried to make it on the stage there.

"Tried? That doesn't sound successful." He stepped back but held her hands.

"I'm now the co-owner of a nightclub and restaurant. It's called Club Creare which means "to create" in Italian. My days on the stage are long gone. But that's okay. I'm happy."

Chris looked ahead at the closed doors that led to the auditorium. "I was hoping you would let me take a peek inside for old time's sake."

Freddie stepped back and waved her forward. "Absolutely. Allow me to open the doors for you."

With a grand flourish, Freddie pulled both doors wide and revealed the red carpet and chairs facing the stage at the front. The large platform on the other side of the auditorium beckoned. So many of her shows took place up on this stage.

Chris headed to the left aisle and made her way slowly down, brushing her fingers along the chairs as she moved closer to her past.

"What was your last show?" Freddie asked from the back.

"*Hello, Dolly!* Right after we closed, I walked home and packed a bag."

"You never said goodbye."

Chris took the first steps to get on the stage. She looked across the auditorium at the man who had given her her start. "Would you have let me go?"

"Never. But after you left, I knew it was for the best. You're not one of them, Christina."

She knew what he was talking about. She never fit in with her family before her mother's death, and it was the start Freddie had given her on this stage that kept her from becoming one of them after.

Chris closed her eyes and pirouetted around the stage, ending with a plie completely from muscle memory.

Freddie clapped slowly. "You still have it, my girl. As graceful as a swan. What can I do to get you to come back?"

"I'm too old now."

"Nonsense! You're just as strong as the last day I saw you."

Chris walked off the stage and retraced her steps to the back of the house to her old friend. "Thank you for that. I hire musicians and bands for the club, and I love finding new talent. But I didn't know how much I missed sharing my own. There's just not that much work for a ballet dancer on Broadway."

"You're a natural. Have you returned to Savannah to stay?"

"No. I need to return to my life in the city."

"What brought you back now?"

"My family managed to find me and pull me back. They have a lawsuit against them."

"I heard." Freddie led her back out into the lobby and closed the door behind them.

"I was wondering, Freddie, if you knew who my father was using as his foreman for the construction business."

"Sure. Jesse Madigan is now the foreman."

"Jesse? That's surprising."

"Why do you say that? I thought he was always a responsible guy."

"Exactly. He was. But yesterday, I went to the construction site for an apartment complex my father is building and was nearly killed when floors caved in around me. I can't see Jesse approving such carelessness."

Freddie glanced at the glass windows and grew agitated. "I don't think we should be having this conversation out in the open."

Chris frowned. "Does my father still have such a hold on you?"

"Your father has supported this business for many years."

"So that's a yes. You feel beholden to him?" Chris didn't hide her disappointment at learning her mentor had strings attached to him.

"Sometimes life requires partnerships."

She hesitated to ask the question she always wanted the answer to but did anyway. "Was I even that good? Or did you feel obligated to put me up there?" She nodded toward the stage.

"That wasn't a lie. You are a beautiful dancer."

Chris forced a smile, still not sure if she still got the truth. She stepped up to Freddie and wrapped him in a hug.

"Take care of yourself," he said.

"You too. I hope you know that if it is ever time to go, you can do it."

"Are you sure about that?"

"I did it."

"And yet, you're here still doing their bidding."

"Not for long." Chris held her head high and walked out the glass doors toward her father's house a block over.

She took the staircase, but this time the door opened for her when she reached the top. One of the men she remembered from the last time held the door for her without a word.

"I'm here to see Vincent," she said.

"You can wait in the dining room. Breakfast is still out if you'd like to help yourself."

With each step, her tennis shoes were silent against the marble floors. She grabbed an apple off the buffet table and took a seat.

"I wasn't expecting you so soon." Her father stepped into the dining room and took his usual seat at the head of the table. "I underestimated your power with Marcus."

"I have no power. I simply made a deal. He's looking into figuring out other possibilities for Reggie's death."

"But the case has not been dropped."

"You know it hasn't. Besides, that wasn't what you asked for. All I had to do was ask him to consider it, and I did. In fact, I went above and beyond by getting him to look elsewhere. Now tell me where Sam is."

Her father folded his hands with his elbows resting on the arms of his chair. He tilted his balding head as he studied her like a specimen under a microscope. The annoying smirk on his face told her he didn't plan to give her any information about Sam as promised. She knew how he played. He liked to dangle carrots and make it sound as though just one more thing would get her to where she wanted to be.

This would be no different. How could she have forgotten his tactics?

What would his "one more" request be this time?

She took a bite of the apple, trying to act nonchalant while she waited. She couldn't let him see her panic, even while everything inside of her was screaming at the injustice.

"I heard about your mishap at the apartment complex," he said with beady eyes on her. "May I ask what you were doing there?"

Chris struggled to swallow her first bite of the apple. She put it down on the table and wiped her fingers as she searched for her excuse.

"I'm okay in case you were wondering. I wasn't hurt. But thanks for asking." Her sarcasm went unnoticed as her father's face remained unchanged. "I was looking..." She wasn't sure what to tell him. And how foolish of her to think her father didn't have eyes on her. Of course, he would know her every move. "I was just interested in what the family businesses were up to. That's all."

Her father's eyebrows raised for a split second. "I'm glad to hear you say that. I had your room freshened up just in case," he said.

Chris's heart stalled in her chest. "Forget it. I'm not staying here."

"I've asked Silas to bring Sam here. Don't you want to be here when she arrives? I think that might be calming for her to have a familiar face... after all that she's been through."

"Been through? I warned you. There had better not be one scratch on her."

Her father narrowed his dark eyes as she had seen him do many times when he grew angry. "You forget your place, Christina."

Chris lowered her gaze to the apple with one bite out of it, now sitting there looking like Snow White's poisoned apple that she dropped after trusting the wrong person. Chris had entered the enemy's den. What had she expected to happen?

She cleared her throat. "When will Sam be here? I'll make sure I'm here to pick her up." A last-ditch effort to free herself from the Moran clutches.

"This wasn't an invitation, Christina," he said. "It's time you came home to take your place in the family business."

Never. "That's not possible. Just tell me where Sam is right now. I did as you asked. We had a deal." Panic choked Chris as she realized she had fallen into her father's clutches as easily as Freddie. By doing one thing he asked her to do, she let him know he knew he controlled her still. She might have thought she cut the strings, but her father just proved to her that she had been living a fantasy.

"I'll call the police." She reached for her cell phone, but before she had it out of her back pocket, the man standing at the door swiped it from her hand and smashed it against the wall over the food buffet.

Chris jumped up in shock at the sound, tipping her chair over. "How dare you!" She turned to her father only to see his angry glare. How could she have forgotten about his capabilities? There was a reason she feared him enough to run away in the first place.

He stood with his hands on the edge of the table. He gripped the white linen tablecloth in bunches. "How dare you, Christina, waltzing back in here as if you own the place, making demands when you have no power here any longer."

"I never had power here. Just like Mama!" Her words slipped from her lips without a thought, and she wished she could pull them back in.

Her father's eyes heated to a boil. Then a smile cracked on his face. "Correct. I'm glad to hear you understand that. It will make your stay here that much easier. Something your mother never understood." He nodded once to the man behind her. "Take her to her bedroom."

"Wait!" Chris shouted with her hands up to ward off the man. "I can't stay here. Please!"

The man grabbed her arm and circled it behind her back. Searing pain shot up her arm, and she feared he was about to dislocate it. She cried out in pain and had no way to fight back. All she could do was go with him out of the dining room and up the curved staircase. At the end of the hall, he shoved her inside her old room and pulled the door closed with a slam. In the next second, the sound of the lock clicking over echoed louder than her smashed phone had.

"No!" Chris raced forward and shook the gold doorknob. How foolish she had been to believe herself free. She turned to the two windows only to find them boarded over on the inside.

There would be no way out for her today, perhaps no way out ever again.

～

Marcus called Chris for the fifth time in two hours. Her phone continued to go to voicemail, and all he could think was she had set him up. Had he shared anything that would lead to his case being thrown out?

Marcus put his phone in the back pocket of his jeans. He grabbed his car keys and headed out of his townhouse. He needed to know if she had betrayed their agreement. Had she gone to her father already? She seemed so believable, but then she always had. Marcus felt like a fool again. The woman still had him wrapped around her little finger.

Once in his car, he found himself driving to the Moran house and staring up at the windows that had been her bedroom when she lived there. Was she up there now, living in the lap of stolen luxury? Marcus opened his door bent on finding out. But before he could step from his car, his cell phone rang. A quick glance showed it was his brother.

"This is not a good time," Marcus said.

"Actually, it's the perfect time. I see you and what you're about to do."

Marcus looked around the square and up and down the streets. You're watching the Moran house? Or are you watching me?"

"Both. I'm stopping you from making a big mistake."

"Can you tell me if she's in there?"

Lucius was quiet for a moment, giving Marcus the answer to his question.

"Don't go jumping to conclusions. She went in a while ago and hasn't come out. She hasn't been staying here. She's been over at the hotel across from Forsythe Park. That makes me wonder what's keeping her so long now. I wouldn't put it past her father to force her to stay."

"No one forces Chris to do anything. I tried that once. It didn't work."

"I would say Vincent Moran's tactics are a little more dangerous than yours."

Marcus glanced up at the bedroom windows again, this time looking carefully. "There's no light or shadows coming from the bedroom. She hasn't been answering her phone either. Something is definitely up."

"Why do you care?"

"I don't. I'm just concerned that she's ruining my case."

"The only person that's about to ruin your case is you if you walk up to those doors. You have to let this one go, brother."

Let her go. Had he ever really let her go? It felt more like a holding pattern that he'd been in these last twelve years.

"How do you suggest I do that?"

"Start your car and get out of here. Go do something to get your mind off of her. Go to the beach. Go see a show."

Marcus scoffed. "Both of those will just remind me of her. She loved the beach. She loved dancing more."

"Man, you have it bad. But I guess I always knew that."

"*Had* is the right word. *Had* not *have*."

"Whatever you say," Lucius mumbled.

Marcus sighed and rubbed his forehead. His hand came away wet. The sweat was from the heat, he told himself. Why did it feel like the temperature had surpassed a hundred degrees in a matter of seconds?

"Look, she mentioned her brother kidnapped her roommate from her New York City apartment. I'm just worried that she's turning on me to get her roommate back. That's all. Don't make more of this than that."

"When were you going to tell me that?"

"I just learned about it yesterday. She told me that's why she returned. And that her father was using it to get her to convince me to drop the case."

She told you this, and you think she's a traitor? I'd say she was looking for someone she could confide in. But you just thought the worst of her. Perhaps she's wrong about you."

Lucius was right. How quickly he put his defenses up. "I'll admit that I still have some anger about her leaving without so much as a goodbye. I thought we meant something to each other."

"So did she. But you used her to get to Moran. You can't deny that. I would have left without a goodbye, too."

"I can't change what I did. Yesterday, I had hoped that by making that deal with her, I was proving that I wanted to make amends. I thought she believed me. I thought we could both put our past to rest. But maybe there's just too much water under that bridge."

Marcus started his car.

"It will take more than making a deal with her to get her to trust you again."

"Like what?"

"Well, what did she come down here for?"

"Her roommate."

"Then I would say start there. And if you can track this girl down and prove it was the Morans who kidnapped her, you'll have your case against them and can put them away for a very long time."

"I could get them on murder and kidnapping." Marcus smiled at the thought. "They may not ever see the light of day again."

"And just think how gracious Christina will be to you."

"Chris. She goes by Chris now."

"I know. I looked into her. She's actually quite successful and has a thriving club in the city. Everything seems legit with the business, too. She cut all ties to her family and made it on her own."

Marcus looked back at the house and wondered why she returned then. Would she risk all her achievements for this young girl? Then he thought of the Christina he always knew and had his answer. Yes, she wouldn't have thought twice about helping her roommate. "Moran has something Christian wants back. He must be using that to suck her back in."

"Or she's being held against her wishes."

The idea of Chris being locked up in the house as a prisoner caused a knot to form in Marcus's stomach. He nearly jumped from the car to barge in and find out. But that most likely would get him killed. He knew there were armed guards inside. He wouldn't make it past the entrance.

"If I don't hear from her by the end of the day I'm coming back," Marcus said.

"I'll join you. Until then, stay clean. Let me do the dirty work."

"I'll do my best. But sometimes I'm blinded by vengeance."

"That's why vengeance doesn't belong to you. It belongs to the Lord. Stay focused."

Marcus was surprised at Lucius's quote from the Bible. He didn't think his brother would ever crack that book. More proof that he really didn't know the man. "Thank you for that reminder, Lucius. God does love justice. And He will get it." Marcus looked up at the window again and put his car in Drive. On a sigh, he said, "I just hope she's alive to see it. And to have faith to believe in me again."

Chapter Six

CHRIS'S JAIL CELL GLEAMED WITH EXPENSIVE GOLDEN DECOR imported from around the world. She knew the white satin feather blanket on the canopy bed was luxurious and comfortable but refused to sit on it. The beauty of her childhood room juxtaposed with the ugliness of her captivity took away all its glamorous appeal. No matter the extravagance, the room was still a jail cell. It always had been, which was why she'd left in the first place.

Chris scanned the space for the cameras that she thought might be around somewhere. Big Brother had to be watching somehow. But perhaps her father just posted a guard outside her door. As sinister as her father acted below, she knew these orders came down from Silas. She cringed at the idea of facing him again but knew it was necessary. For her brother to do this only meant she had something he wanted. He may have even tossed her room for it and now meant to keep her here permanently for it.

But what could she possibly have worth all this trouble?

Chris approached the front window again. No matter how hard she tried to pry the wood away from the frame, it wouldn't budge. Whoever nailed these into the wood made sure to use a hundred nails at least. Even with the right tools, it would take hours to get the boards off. Looking around the room, she saw nothing but frilly pillows and cosmetics.

And her old dancing slippers.

Her pointe shoes with their flat, stiff fronts that kept her on her toes still hung from the mirror of her vanity. As she walked toward them, she caught her reflection in the large mirror and saw the fear in her eyes staring back at her. She reached for the shoes and ran her fingers through the silk ribbons that had seen better days. Frayed at the edges, they resembled her own life. And just as it was with her life, the shoes may look worn, but the construction of them would still help her stand tall.

Chris sat in the chair in front of the mirror and removed her shoes. She slipped her feet into the slippers and tied them up around her ankles tightly.

She wondered why she hadn't taken them with her to New York. Perhaps, ballet reminded her too much of her past—and too much of her mother. When Chris had reached the city, she never tried out for any kind of ballet part. She went after dancing roles in the various casts but couldn't keep up with the other styles of dance. Perhaps she would have made it if she had stuck to ballet, maybe even tried out for Julliard. She was tall with lean muscle, the perfect ballerina body.

Standing in her room, she found her balance on her toes and lifted her arms above her head. Her reflection in the mirror looked more like her mother than it ever had before. She closed her eyes and imagined a slow ballad and swayed to the music in her head. She had forgotten how free she felt on her toes.

But her toes wouldn't rescue her today, just as they never rescued her mother. Whether Celia DePalo Moran had ever been locked up or not, she most definitely had been a prisoner in this house. Chris wondered how long it took her mother to realize she had married into organized crime. Had she known early on? Had she been in denial? When she figured it out, did she try to leave? Would she have taken her daughter with her?

So many questions that Chris would never have answers to. She always wondered why her mother didn't fight harder when she was diagnosed with cancer. Being locked up in the same house, Chris figured Celia Moran didn't have much to fight for. She simply gave up.

"But I'm not my mother," she said to herself in the mirror. "I will never give up."

A knock on the door had her standing still. She didn't respond but waited to see if anyone would walk in.

They knocked again, and Chris responded, "Who is it?"

"Your father says dinner is ready. I'm to bring you down."

"I'm not eating. But thank you, anyway." Gratitude was missing from her tone.

"I'll give you fifteen minutes to get ready. That is all. The next time I won't ask."

Chris heard his footsteps disappear as he walked away from her door. She had fifteen minutes before he would return. She had no choice but to go wherever she was told. Anger welled up inside of her, and she reached for the lamp on the vanity. Hauling it back, she threw it at the mirror and shattered the glass in spider cracks that fell in a tinkling sound against the wood. Only a few pieces of mirror were left that showed parts of her reflection. Stepping up to it, she realized why she looked more like her mother now. The vacant look of hopelessness reflected on her just as it had when she looked at her mother in her final years.

Chris picked up a large shard and held it in her hand. The piece came to a point at the end. Holding it caused a cut in her palm and she watched a thin line of blood trickle down her wrist. Sitting down, she removed her slippers and ripped the satin ribbons from the back heel. Slowly, she wrapped it around the shard of glass and let her hand get comfortable holding a weapon. The question that remained was would she have enough strength to use it against multiple men. She would only have one chance.

But one chance was all she needed.

Lacing her tennis shoes back up, she found a way to slip the sharp glass into the hem of her pants. She cleaned up the remaining glass and hid it under her bed then waited until another knock came on the door. The fact that no one checked on the sound told her maybe she didn't have a guard at the door, after all.

"I'm ready now," she said and watched the door open to reveal the same goon as before. "When did you start working for my father? I don't remember you."

The man stepped back to let her pass through in front of him. He didn't say a word.

"Okay, nice talk," she said and stepped up to walk him by. "I guess there are many of you goons. I can't know you all. Too bad for you that you got stuck babysitting me." The man fell in behind her, and all she heard was his deep, hot breathing on her neck.

Chris cringed with each step. She took the stairs slowly, considering her next move. Timing would be critical, and she wondered if she should make a run for it as she passed by the front door or wait for another moment of opportunity.

With each step down the staircase, Chris prepared to make her escape. Taking a deep breath, she squared her shoulders and on the last step, feigned a fall, letting out a scream as she went down. Except as she fell, she reached in and grabbed the shard of glass from the hem of her pants and rolled away toward the front door.

Large, beefy hands reached for her as she swung around with the shard of glass and sliced the man's hand before he touched her.

Shock covered his face as his blood spilled on the white marble. Anger quickly morphed in his dark eyes, but Chris continued to roll until she reached the door and grabbed the handle to pull.

At the same moment, he wrapped his hands around her neck and yanked her back inside. With his hand on her neck, she couldn't scream... but she could kick. Her long leg bent back and hit his kneecap with a crack, causing him to grunt in pain and loosen his hold. She could see out into the square where freedom beckoned. She reached her arms out to try to get a hold of the door jam.

"Help!" She tried to yell, but the sound of her voice was barely a squeak.

Then she saw Lucius in his disguise running her way across the green. *Hurry!* She wanted to shout, but the words wouldn't form on her lips with the chokehold the man behind her had on her neck. Suddenly, the door slammed shut just as Lucius crossed the street.

"No!" She yelled as she felt herself dragged back up the stairs by her neck and hair. Her attempt to escape had failed. There would be no more chances. Chris wanted to cry from the pain but also from her lack of success.

Then the door flew open, banging against the wall with a crack.

"Let her go!" Lucius shouted with a gun in his hand. He took the stairs two at a time and used the gun to hit the man in the face. Instantly, he caught Chris before she fell and guided her down the stairs as fast as he had entered.

They made it outside before the man and one other who joined him could catch up to them. Chris and Lucius didn't stop running for three blocks. Finally, Lucius guided her into an alley while he stood guard.

"What's going to happen next?" she asked, hearing the desperation in her voice. "I have nowhere to run that they won't find me. I have no one to call who they don't have in their back pocket. All I wanted was to find Sam. Instead, I lost my own freedom."

Lucius hit a few buttons on his cell phone and spoke under his breath. He then pocketed his phone and poked his head out onto the street. "Marcus is on his way. Don't come out until he gets here."

"Where are you going?" Chris realized Lucius was leaving her. "You can't leave me. My father has someone watching me. They'll find me and take me back."

He slipped out without a response, leaving her all alone for whatever happened next, or whoever found her here, cornered with no way out. How could he do such a thing? And how could he think she would remain here like a sitting duck?

~

Marcus zipped up and down the grid of streets that made up old Savannah, trying to track the location on the map that Lucius had sent him. He said Chris was at this place, but so far, it felt like he was searching for a needle in a haystack, albeit a very tall one.

He took another turn and was met with construction. Slamming his hand on the steering wheel, he feared he would never find her. It reminded him of another time when he'd hit a dead-end looking for her and how he hated never knowing what happened to her.

"Not again," he said, clenching his jaw with determination. He pulled his car over to the side of the street and jumped out, leaving it behind. He'd cover more ground on his feet.

Holding his phone with the map in front of him, Marcus watched his path get closer to the blinking pin.

Closer to Chris.

And yet, as often as he circled around and as focused as his eyes were, he couldn't see her. Would she have left the spot? Was she taken again?

Marcus called Lucius but only got his voicemail. "Where are you, brother? And where is Chris?" Marcus spoke under his breath in frustration. "What did you do with her?"

Marcus faced the direction of the Moran mansion and took a few steps toward it. He wasn't sure what he planned to do once he got there, but he had no other choice. As he passed by a bookstore located down under an apartment building, he spotted a woman on the other side of the window. She held a book in front of her face, but not her eyes.

Chris's eyes.

He turned and took the stairs to the lower level and opened the door. A bell rang above his head, and the woman lowered the book more when she saw him. It really was her.

"Oh, thank God," he said and rushed forward.

Chris flung the book to the couch and jumped up to meet his embrace, clinging to him and trembling beneath his hold.

"We can't stay here," she whispered against his ear. "I'm being followed. My father has someone watching me. He knew I was at the apartment complex. He knows I was looking for evidence. He locked me up. If he finds me again...well, I don't want to find out what he'll do."

"Me neither. Let's get out of here." Marcus reached for her hand and held on just as tightly as she did. He led her out of the store and up the stairwell, keeping her close to the brick buildings as he picked up his steps. "My car is a street over. Stay close to me."

They turned the corner, and his car came into view—but so did one of Moran's henchmen.

One man was dressed in a black suit and stood by the driver's door with his hand in his coat pocket, most likely curled around the butt of a gun just waiting to pull it.

Marcus stepped back, pulling Chris with him. "Someone's waiting there. We can't get to it." He racked his brain for another way to get her out of the vicinity. Another man turned the corner and spotted them. He lifted his gun.

"The trolley," she said, jutting her chin toward the end of the street where a trolley tour was stopped at a pick-up station. She pulled him in the other direction and together they ran, waving their hands to hold the car.

Looking back, the henchmen were now turning the corner, running after them. Both of their guns were out.

"Get low!" Marcus shouted and moved to run behind Chris. They reached the trolley just as it was starting to move and jumped aboard.

The driver chuckled. "What's your rush? Don't you know there's always another trolley coming?"

Marcus withdrew his wallet and tossed a couple of twenty dollar bills at the driver.

"Just drive. Fast," he said.

Then Marcus guided Chris down the aisle until two seats were open beside each other. She took the seat, and he fell in next to her with his gaze glued to the open windows. The gunman had stopped running but was on the phone now.

"They won't give up," Chris whispered. "Someone will get us at the next stop."

Marcus peeled his gaze from the direction of the man to see the fear in Chris's eyes. He brushed the back of his fingers against her pale cheek but had no words to comfort her. She was right. There was nowhere to hide that Moran wouldn't find them. They sat still, staring at each other with no answers. He brought his hand back to hers and turned to watch the road ahead. The next stop at the riverfront was three blocks down.

"Follow me," he said, standing and heading back down the aisle. Chris kept up with him, and as they neared the front, he said to the driver, "We changed our minds. We need to get off right now."

"Here? The stop is right up ahead."

"Yes, now." Marcus took out his wallet and threw a fifty dollar bill on the dash.

The driver stopped abruptly. He grabbed the money, shaking his head and muttering something about tourists. "Not that I'm complaining," he said and opened the door for them.

Marcus was already crossing the street to another block to avoid hearing the rest of the man's complaining. Chris ran with him, doing as he asked, and when they reached two blocks over, he took a turn for the water.

"What are we going to do? Swim?" Chris asked while looking over her shoulder. "I don't want to survive being killed by a brute only to die by water contamination. There's dangerous pollution in this water. Not to mention the alligators!"

"Same here," Marcus said, but he really had no plan once they reached the river. He could be leading Chris to another dead end. But when the water came into view, he noticed the *Georgia Queen* riverboat with its towering red, white, and blue paddle wheel.

"The boat!"

Marcus stopped short. "It's going out already. It just left the dock. This is one ride we won't be catching." Marcus circled the front for another idea.

"I know," Chris said, taking off without him.

Marcus raced up to her. "Where are we going?"

She pointed ahead to a small cluster of yachts moored at the docks. "Out to sea." She turned her radiant smile on him and picked up her speed. "In the lap of luxury."

Stunned, Marcus stopped moving forward. "Chris! You can't steal a boat. That's illegal!"

Chapter Seven

THE *PAS DE DEUX* BECKONED CHRIS FROM ITS SLIP ALONG THE river. It lined up with other yachts, most of them much larger, but Chris's heart swelled at the sight of her navy-blue hull and name scrawled across the bow. The boat had belonged to her mother, inherited from her father after he passed when Chris was a baby. Chris wondered if the boat had been taken out at all since her mother's death. Chris had no memory of her father caring about the ship, but someone was tending to it. Perhaps her father had sold it, and she was about to steal it from the new owner. She couldn't just walk on board without people noticing.

Pausing on the docks, she turned to Marcus and said, "There's a small dive platform on the boat's aft. We should be able to board without notice back there. It's low enough and won't require a ladder."

Marcus looked around with obvious concern on his face. "We can't steal a boat, Chris. That will bring in the Navy and who knows who else. I'm not well-versed in maritime law."

"It belonged to my mother. So technically, it's not stealing." She followed his line of focus on the street. At any moment, she expected her father's goons to emerge. She wondered if the person her father had watching her was in the shadows somewhere. "Besides, we don't have much time. Just act like we belong here."

"I've never even driven a boat. If that's even the right term."

"I have. My mother taught me to sail when I was young."

"Like twenty years ago?"

Chris frowned at his reminder of how long it had been since her mother had been part of her life. But his words only strengthened her resolve to take back what belonged to her mother.

What should have been Chris's.

"I hated leaving the *Pas de Deux* behind. It should have been mine in the first place."

"What does it mean? Sorry, I grew up in an underprivileged neighborhood. I never learned French. And law school is all Latin."

"It means a step for two. It's not a big yacht, but it's comfortable for two. Please, Marcus, come with me. And not because I don't want to break the law alone."

His piercing blue eyes studied her. "Then why?"

Chris glanced down the street, suddenly feeling uneasy for a different reason. "I don't know. After what happened to us the last time, I shouldn't trust you at all, and yet..."

He touched her hand with a mere brush of his fingertips. "And yet what?"

Chris shook her head. "I guess I understand why you had to use me to get to my father. I was a means to the end of his crimes. But now, I could use your help in return. Please, come with me. Consider it restitution."

He flashed her a warm smile. "If I didn't know better, I'd say you take after your father more than I thought."

She laughed. "Is that a yes?"

He frowned but sighed with a nod. "I will live to regret this, but lead the way, Captain."

She took his hand in hers. "Right this way, First Mate."

The two of them walked down the dock, hand-in-hand, looking like just a couple of lovebirds taking a leisurely stroll. When they reached the boat's aft, Chris glanced back up to make sure no one was watching. She put her finger to her lips to tell him not to make a sound. In the next second, she leaned over and grabbed the railing of the dive deck, hoisting herself over as smoothly and gracefully as the whipping wind. The landing of her feet barely made a sound or moved the boat. She gave her nod to Marcus for his turn and stepped out of the way for him to take the leap.

He glanced up the dock, and she wondered if he would change his mind. Then he also grabbed the railing and hopped aboard. However, when his feet hit, he stumbled a bit. Chris reached up to hold him steady, and she found her lips mere inches away from his—a result of being the same height as him.

"You're so tall," he whispered with a smirk. Then his eyes dimmed as he looked at her lips. "Not that I'm complaining."

Chris stepped away from him and ran her palms over her thighs. Her fingers tingled where they had held him so close. "There's no fraternizing aboard ship," she said, trying to lighten the situation.

"I thought this was a boat for two. That sure sounds romantic to me." A teasing mischief danced in his blues.

Chris rolled her eyes and pivoted on her tiptoes, heading toward the hatch. She lifted the bar to unlock the entrance and climbed through to the dark interior. Instant memories flooded her as she approached the stairwell that led to the deck above and the helm. This was her mother's happy place, and Chris wondered if that was because it was the closest to freedom Celia could ever get. Perhaps she never set sail to escape because she knew her father's hold was strong and his reach long.

Chris waited for Marcus to stand behind her before climbing the first step. He had stopped at the door to the engine room and peered inside where the 10 x 8 black boxes housed the brains of the ship.

Suddenly, the boat jerked and swayed, nearly knocking them off their feet. Chris grabbed the railing to steady herself while Marcus reached for her as well.

"Maybe a boat went by and jostled us," he said.

Then the roar of the engines started, shocking them into silence. Chris looked up the stairwell with her breath stolen from her lungs.

"Marcus, we're not alone. Someone's above deck. It must be owner."

Marcus turned around to head back to the hatch. When he opened the door wide, Chris could see they were no longer at the dock and were heading down the river and out to sea.

She raced forward, but at the door, he put his arm out to stop her.

"You can't swim in this water. There are too many dangers that will kill you."

Chris shook her head as she watched the riverfront grow further away. "It didn't kill Reggie. He was killed at the apartment complex. I saw the blood myself."

A confused look crossed Marcus's face. "Why didn't you tell me?" Then a dawning expression filled his eyes. "That's right, you had to protect your father. I'm such a fool. Did you lead me out here to steal a boat to discredit me and my case right from the start? So sneaky of you, *Christina*. I'm going to plead my case with the boat's owner above and hopes he sees how I was tricked."

With that, he turned and headed for the stairs.

"You're wrong. I've done none of these things. Wait. Let me explain."

"I need to get this boat turned around. I have a case to solve. I can't believe I let you make me forget that again. After I had promised never again."

Chris watched him take the steps with angry footfalls. She wanted to plead her case, but he wasn't wrong. She had kept the information about the blood spatter to herself to allow her father to explain first. She wondered at her loyalty to her father over Marcus. It had been their demise twelve years ago. But seeing how quickly he accused her only reminded her that she couldn't trust anyone.

And maybe Marcus couldn't trust her, either.

Before she could take one step, a loud crash followed by the sound of someone falling on the deck had her scrambling up the stairs. She stepped out of the stairway only to find Marcus sprawled facedown and unconscious in front of her.

She turned around just as something hard hit her head, and darkness took over.

～

Marcus groaned with pain that radiated from the top of his head to every muscle and joint in his body. Ever so slowly, he lifted his chin through the ache and forced his eyes open. Blinding fluorescent light tortured his throbbing head. He waited for the dizziness to abate then turned to his right to see Chris unconscious beside him. Or at least he hoped she was just unconscious.

Marcus dared not speak aloud until he knew who had knocked them out. The boat was still moving, which meant whoever attacked them was now at the helm. Both he and Chris lay on the floor with their hands tied behind their backs, and Marcus wondered what he had planned for them at sea. Thinking about how Reggie's body had been tossed in the water told Marcus it was probably something similar. The farther they made it out, the less likely either he or Chris would return alive.

Marcus rolled along the deck and used his shoulder to push himself up. He watched for any sign of life from Chris and relaxed a bit when he saw her slow breathing. Shimmying over to her, he brushed his cheek against hers.

"Hey, Chris, wake up," he whispered but to no avail. He regretted his last words to her even though his disappointment in her choice to keep him in the dark hurt. He pressed her cheek harder. "You need to wake up. We have to get out of here."

A groan emitted from her lips, and she jerked back away from him. Dazed and confused, she squinted in his direction and then looked around at their surroundings.

"Where am I?"

"Your mother's boat. We climbed aboard, but someone was above deck and now we are at sea. We have to get off this boat before we're too far from land."

She tried to move her arms and looked down in confusion when she couldn't.

"We're tied up. We're going to have to untie each other. Can you roll over?"

Chris didn't respond for a few moments but then nodded and rolled onto her stomach and then onto her shoulder. Marcus did the same until their backs faced each other.

He found her hands and worked his way to her binds. The ropes were tight, but he managed to loosen one and work it through.

"Ouch," she said.

"Sorry. I didn't mean to pinch you."

"Are you sure about that?" She angled a look over her shoulder as he glanced back at her as well.

"Of course, I didn't." He protested but quickly noticed her teasing eyes. "I guess I deserved that. I'm sorry I got upset with you."

"You should be. Storming off is what put us in this mess."

"True. I should've let you go first." He smiled over his shoulder.

"Ha, ha, very funny."

"But seriously, you should've stayed downstairs," he said.

"I'll remember that the next time I hear you take a fall. Did you see who it was?"

"I was hoping you would tell me." He pulled the last remaining rope from her hands, and she quickly sat up and reached for his.

"All I saw was you spread eagle on the deck. Then nothing but blackness."

A glance over his shoulder showed her trying to work the ropes. "Try to loosen just one. Once you do that, the one next to it should follow."

She bit her lip in concentration and then said, "Finally. I got it." She pulled the long rope free and worked on the next one. Slowly, he felt his hands gain more movement until he broke them apart and rubbed his wrists while he stood up. He pocketed his rope into his pants.

Marcus extended a hand to her to help her to her feet. When she stood in front of him, he reached for her head to feel the bump on the right side. She winced under his touch but let him inspect.

"That's a hefty contusion you got there. I think we have matching ones." He touched his own head as he led the way toward the hatch that would lead to the helm. When he reached it, he put his finger to his lips and motioned that he would open it on the count of three.

At her nod, he used his fingers to count to three, and he pushed it wide for the two of them to run out together.

A man at the controls, quickly let go and put his hands up as he leaned back into the wall. "Don't hurt me!" he said. "I have a right to be here!"

Marcus ran straight for him and grabbed his arms, tossing him into the chair. "Who are you?"

"I'm nobody."

"A squatter?"

"Yeah. That's it." The man nodded his head emphatically.

"You're lying."

Chris stepped up beside Marcus. "I know who he is. I remember you. You're Jesse Madigan. You're the foreman on the apartment complex. What are you doing on this boat?"

"I was told to lay low. Silas said I could use the boat."

"My brother told you to lay low? Does it have something to do with the shutdown of the complex?"

Jesse shrugged and avoided eye contact. "I just follow orders."

Chris stepped closer to the man. She leaned in to capture his attention. "What happened out there?"

The man's jumping eyes flitted between the two of them. "Look, I don't have anything to do with it."

"What happened out there? I saw the blood. You were in charge of the project, so you are involved whether you like it or not." Chris crossed her arms in front of her.

Marcus wanted to ask her how she knew this man was the foreman, but after what happened below deck, he thought it best to let her take the lead and ask the questions.

"I didn't see anything. Honest."

"Stop lying," Marcus said, removing the rope from his pocket. He grabbed the man's arms and brought them around the chair. He noticed the boat was still moving forward with no one at the helm. "Chris, take the wheel. I've got him."

Chris stepped up to the controls and asked, "Where were we going, Jesse? Where were you taking us?"

When the man didn't answer, Marcus pulled the ropes hard to tell him they meant business.

"Okay! We were heading to Tybee Island. I was meeting someone there."

Chris glanced Marcus's way. "Shall we find out who?"

Marcus liked the way she thought, but it could be dangerous. They could be walking into another trap. And yet, they couldn't return to Savannah now. Moran would have his men watching her hotel and Marcus's apartment, as well as his office.

Marcus stepped around the chair to face the man. In his most lethal attorney demeanor, he treated the man as a hostile witness in a cross-examination. "Who are we meeting?"

"You're not meeting anyone. *I* was meeting him. You..." The man swallowed convulsively. "You weren't supposed to make it all the way over. Just her. I was taking you out to sea first."

Marcus caught Chris's shocked expression and knew she understood what Jesse wasn't saying.

The man was going to dump their bodies at sea. Or at least his.

Marcus stood to his full height and towered over the man. "You're not in charge anymore. We are. So tell me, who will be meeting us when we dock?"

Sweat poured from the man's temples, pooling and the collar of his t-shirt. He glanced Chris's way. "I don't want to get involved in any family feud."

Marcus leaned close to the man. "You're already involved. The moment you hit us over the head and tied us up."

The man shook his head. "I didn't know who you were. I thought you were breaking and entering."

"Then why not call the police?"

"No cops." He shook his head emphatically and looked at Chris again. "But I didn't realize it was her until after I had already knocked her out. That's when I knew I had to get her over to the island."

"Because why?" Marcus's tone left no room for negotiation.

"Because...because I knew that's what he would want. And after the mess up with that lawyer, it's what I had to do to make things right again."

"That lawyer? Do you mean Reggie Brodsky?"

"Yeah, I guess so. He was snooping around the complex. I was told to make him go away."

"Who told you to make him go away? And what did you do?" Marcus thought his head would explode. He knew how to keep his cool in a court of law, but this was too personal. Did this man hold the truth about Reggie's death? Was he responsible for it?

Marcus reached for the man's shirt, fisting it and pulling him forward.

"Ow! You're hurting me!"

"Marcus!" Chris called from the wheel. "You of all people should know a confession under duress will not stand up in the court."

"He knows what happened to Reggie. He knows Reggie did not fall into the river, don't you, Madigan? Now I want answers. Who told you to get rid of him? Was it Vincent Moran?"

The man looked at Chris again. He shook his head. "Her brother," he said nervously. "That's who we're going to see right now. Silas is waiting on the island...for her."

Chris let go of the controls. "He's there now? Does he have Sam with him?"

The man shook his head and tried to shrug. "I don't know anything. I've been hiding out on this boat. I sent everyone home at the worksite and closed it up. Just as I was told to. Moran didn't want anyone scoping out the construction site. He told me to shut it down until he could get back here."

"When did he arrive on the island?" Chris asked. "How long has he been here?"

"As far as I know, just the last couple of days. That's when he contacted me. And I don't know who Sam is."

Marcus interrupted, "I still want to know how you got rid of Reggie?"

"I didn't have to. Someone else killed him. I just dumped him in the river. I found his body at the complex. He was already dead. Like I said, I don't know anything."

"But you did throw his body in the river?"

"Yes."

"And you were dumping mine as well," Marcus asked.

"Far out at sea so another body wouldn't turn up. Silas nearly killed me when the lawyer resurfaced."

Marcus looked for Chris's take on Madigan's excuse. But all she did, was face forward at the controls and pick up speed toward Tybee Island. She had her own questions to be answered and a roommate to rescue. Marcus knew no amount of convincing her would get her to turn this boat around now. Not even the possibility of their deaths.

Chapter Eight

CHRIS HAD FOND MEMORIES OF TYBEE ISLAND. IT HAD BEEN A stop for her and her mother when they took the *Pas de Duex* out, but that was long before she became ill. Chris figured maybe she was sixteen years old the last time they had taken the boat over to the peaceful beaches. Her mother had always dreamed of buying one of the beach houses. The fact that Silas had a place on the island only aggravated Chris more. On top of that, now she was having to rescue her kidnapped roommate from this place of fond memories which tarnished her love for the island—another thing Silas ruined for her.

The island itself was more of a barrier island at the end of the Savannah River. It was known for its wide, sandy beaches with a pier, a pavilion, and various historical ruins of past wars. As Chris navigated by Fort Screven, a guarding fort at the mouth of the Savannah River, she remembered crawling around the gun battery that formerly stored projectiles and gunpowder. She wished she had at least one gun before approaching her brother. Going in empty-handed wasn't the best move she'd ever made. She could only hope the element of surprise would give her the upper hand.

"Where to, Madigan?" she called over her shoulder. "I need some direction."

When the man didn't answer, Marcus pulled on his ropes, and that seemed to remind him who was in charge.

"Just past South Beach," Jesse admitted reluctantly. "He's in the large Italian villa."

"Of course, he is," Chris said, growing more irritated. "Nothing but the best for my big brother. He better be treating Sam well, that's all I have to say."

Marcus asked, "Is there a dock for the boat?"

Jesse replied, "Yes, it's right out front of the house."

As Chris made her way around the island toward the South Beach area, she realized how much she missed this place. Leaving her home in Savannah never bothered her, but leaving this island and its beaches behind felt like she lost a part of her childhood and identity. She steered the boat around the bend until the Italian villa that Madigan had mentioned came into view. The three-story, tan structure was open on the bottom to allow for tropical storms. Currently, there were three black cars parked beneath the house. Her brother always did travel with at least two others in his pack. Like father like son. A glance over her shoulder showed Marcus was also speculating about what they were running into. He captured her gaze, but if he meant to deter her, he held his tongue.

Still, the look in his eyes spoke volumes.

"I know what you're thinking," she said, looking back at the house.

"No, you don't," he replied.

She steered toward the dock. Before she spoke, she noticed Jesse staring at the house in obvious fear for what he believed was his fate at her brother's hand. She whispered to Marcus, "You think I'm foolish for facing him without a weapon or backup."

"I'm your backup."

She stole a quick glance at him, needing to know what he meant by those words. She wanted to believe him, but their past carried more weight. "I was never looking for backup." She spoke from the heart. "I was looking for a partner I could believe in."

Marcus averted his gaze, looking out at the shoreline. She wondered if he would deny his part in their failed relationship. She was glad when he didn't. Instead, all three of them remained somber and silent as she docked the boat in the rolling waves.

The slip felt like a threshold not only to a place of her past but a portal to her future—or lack of one. As soon as she disembarked there would be no going back, not to the sweltering heat of her father's Savannah or the façade of freedom in her New York City life.

"What's the plan, Captain?" Marcus asked.

"To break every hold the Moran family has on me, for good," Chris spoke more to herself. Then she turned to Jesse. "But for now, you are going to disembark first. I know you fear my brother, but if you do as I say, I promise you I will do everything I can to get you out of here alive. Are you willing?"

Jesse nodded once.

"Good. You will walk to the middle of the dock and stop. I want you to lure my brother out of the house."

"What are you going to do?" he asked.

Chris wasn't willing to spill her plans to the man. "I'll join you after. Marcus, you stay aboard and listen to the conversation. Get a feel if Silas is alone, or if he has Sam with him. I don't want him knowing I'm aboard."

Marcus said, "I don't like this one bit, but I'll wait here." He pulled Jesse's wrists. "And I'll hear everything you say. Understand?"

Jesse nodded. "I won't say anything about either of you being here. Promise. Just don't let him kill me."

Chris bit her lower lip in indecision but made up her mind to move forward with the plan. "Okay, untie him." As Marcus worked his binds, she glared at Jesse. "Take your time securing the boat to the dock. Understand?"

Jesse appeared nervous with a sheening sweat on his upper lip. He brought his freed hands to his front, rubbing his wrists. "He's going to ask about you. He's expecting you. What do I say?"

She shrugged. "Tell him you threw us both overboard like you did Reggie. Maybe he'll confess to killing him. Then you'll be off the hook for his murder."

"I told you I didn't kill him."

"Prove it." Marcus moved to face the man. "Otherwise, if you manage to make it out alive today, I'll make sure you go down for murder."

Jesse grew more frustrated, swiping at his hair and yanking it back in a

413

fidgeting grip. He looked at Chris. "Fine. I'll tell him you're swimming with the fish. I'll tell him you fought me, and I had no choice."

"Good. Now, give me your cell phone."

Jesse sighed but turned it over without complaint.

"Both of them." She kept her hand out for the second burner phone she knew the goons kept.

Jesse grumbled something about a death wish but retrieved the other phone from his sock and passed it to her.

Chris waved for him to move toward the hatch that led to the top deck and gangway. "Remember, stop in the middle of the dock to bring Silas to us. Keep him there as long as you can. Maybe show some angst for having to do his dirty work."

"Yeah, yeah, I got it." Jesse may have understood, but he didn't seem too sure of the outcome. But then, neither did Chris. Her brother was unpredictable. She just hoped Jesse could keep Silas busy long enough for her to make her way out through the dive platform and into the house unnoticed.

~

"Your plan is to swim under the dock?" Marcus watched Chris remove her shoes and place them in a secure dive bag. She hoisted it onto her back.

"My plan is to swim out toward the beach. I'll slip in with the swimmers and exit to the street. I'll come around the front of the house and enter that way."

"I doubt Jesse will be able to hold Silas that long. And what if he has a guard at the front of the house?"

"I'll cross that dock when I get to it."

"Cute, but I'm being serious right now. I think I should go with you."

"So am I. I need to sneak into that house and look for Sam. She's all I can worry about right now." Chris exited the hatch and stepped out onto the dive platform. "If you're joining me, grab a bag for your shoes." In the next second, she slipped into the rolling waves and disappeared under the water.

Marcus watched her emerge ten feet away but stay low in the waves. She moved toward the crowds and quickly slipped in with them unnoticed. He stepped to the right to risk a glance in the direction of the dock, but Silas had yet to exit the house. Marcus worried that this plan would fail from the get-go. What if he didn't come out to meet Jesse? What if he expected Jesse to come to him? Chris could be walking right into danger. Did he really have a choice but to join her? He couldn't let her go in there alone.

Marcus did as Chris said and grabbed a bag for his shoes. Clothed and all, he entered the ocean and follow the same path she had taken. Water pulled and pushed him closer to the shore, but he did his best to stay low and out of sight. He kept glancing toward the house and still no sign of Silas or his men. Marcus searched for Chris and could no longer see her. Then he caught sight of her making her way to the street. She was already so far ahead of him and heading straight into Silas's clutches.

Marcus picked up his speed, not caring who saw him at this point. When he reached the crowds, he rushed toward the shore and up onto the sand in the direction she went. Cutting through a side path, he reached the street and took a left. The summer crowds made it hard for him to track Chris, but he dodged in and out of tourist groups meandering down the sidewalks until he caught a glimpse of her long, wet hair. He'd yet to put his shoes back on but couldn't risk losing her again.

"Chris! Wait!" Calling her did nothing to slow her down. He picked up his speed and ignored the gawking stares of people watching them both go by fully clothed and drenched. He knew they looked a sight, and the people would never understand the gravity of the situation.

The back of Chris's head came into view again, now closer than she had been before. She was putting her shoes on, and it allowed him to close the gap between them.

"He's not out yet," Marcus said as he neared her. "The plan's not working. He must know something's up."

Chris stood while he put his own shoes on. She glanced up at the house, studying the second and third-floor windows.

"She's up there in one of those rooms. I just know it," she said.

"We should probably call the police and let them go in to look for her."

"I'm not waiting, and Silas would never let them in without a warrant. I'm going with or without you."

Marcus stood. "Of course, you are." He pulled his wet hair out of his face while studying the house on stilts. "Fine. We go in. But through the garage stairs. Not the front door."

Through the open first floor, he could see the yacht and Jesse still on the dock. At some point, Silas would wonder what the man was taking so long for.

Then suddenly the man stepped down from the second-floor deck on the ocean side and walked down the steps to the sand.

Silas wore a pair of tan shorts and an open shirt, whipping in the sea breeze. The wind lifted his shirt just enough to show he had a gun in the back waistband of his shorts. Then two of his men dressed in full black joined him from behind.

"I don't believe it, it's working," Marcus said.

"Let's go. We don't have much time." Chris took off through the first-floor entrance, ducking low alongside the three cars parked beneath the house. She reached the door to the stairwell up into the house, and it opened with ease. "Doesn't look like he's expecting trouble," she whispered.

"Or it's a trap."

She put her finger to her lips and slipped inside, closing the door quietly behind them. Marcus stepped up the stairs first, and when he reached the top, he scanned the open floor plan in a circle. Not a person was in sight, and not a sound could be heard. It appeared they were alone. Nodding to Chris, he ascended the rest of the stairs on careful footing.

Standing beside him, she pointed up to the third floor where the bedrooms must be. The second floor showcased multiple couches and chairs placed in various settings. A large fireplace hearth had two brown leather sofas facing each other in front of it. A large-screen television that took up a whole wall had a sectional sofa set and recliners around it. The television played a movie at a low volume.

Marcus led the way around to the third-floor set of stairs, passing the floor-to-ceiling window that showed Silas and his two men on the dock talking to Jesse. The three men had their arms crossed as Jesse's lips moved fast and his hands moved even faster.

"We don't have much time," he whispered. "Silas doesn't look pleased. And who knows if Jesse isn't telling all."

Chris picked up her pace and took the next set of stairs. At the top, she looked right and then left. She pointed for him to take one way, and she took the other.

Marcus didn't like separating, but he moved to the left side of the house to check the three doors on that side. The first door was a linen closet. The second door was the main bedroom with two walls of windows looking out at the ocean. He caught Silas turning to head back to the house. Marcus ran back to tell Chris it was time to go just as a muffled scream came from the other side of the upstairs.

"Sam, it's okay," Chris shouted. "It's me, Chris. You're okay. You're safe now."

A woman was crying as Marcus ran into a dark bedroom to find Chris struggling to remove a blindfold from Sam's face. The young woman was fighting Chris.

"We have to go right now," he said. "They're coming back inside."

"Wait a minute," Chris said. "Help me untie her feet and hands. Sam, we're here to help you. Don't fight us. And don't make a sound when I take your gag out. Please. They'll kill us all."

Marcus stood at the door, trying to listen for the doors to the deck. "There's no time. Just do her feet. We'll untie her hands outside." Once the men were on the open second floor, there would be no way to escape by them without being seen.

Chris helped the young woman who looked more like a frightened child now. With no time for introductions, Marcus wrapped an arm around her and led her to the stairs at a rapid speed, practically carrying her down the steps. Chris stayed close on his heels, and at the landing, they ran around to the stairs to the first floor just as heavy footfalls and men talking could be heard on the deck.

Marcus took the next stairs with the door to the exit beckoning him to run faster. He glanced back at Chris to see she was still right behind him. They were going to make it. He couldn't believe it.

"Sit down!" Silas's voice demanded, stopping them cold on the stairs. "I'm really disappointed in you, Jesse. You really messed this one up. Your directions were to bring me my sister, not throw her overboard. Now, we're going to have two more bodies washing ashore, and when they're identified, the police will blame my father. We were able to cover up the lawyer and could have made the other lawyer's death be about him being distraught. But my *sister*?" The sound of a gun cocking snapped Chris's eyes wide.

Marcus shook his head as he saw Chris look back up the stairs.

"Go!" she mouthed and waved at the door and turned back.

"No," Marcus whispered, but she was already running back up. Marcus opened the door and whispered to Sam, "Run for the police." He passed her his cell phone and pushed her outside. He slammed the door loudly just as Chris reached the second floor.

"Stop!" she shouted. "Don't shoot him. It's me you want."

But the gun blasted through the house, and all Marcus could see from thirteen steps away was Chris fall backward as though someone had punched her.

No, not someone, but something more powerful—a bullet—had sent her flying to the floor.

Chapter Nine

CHRIS LAY MOTIONLESS, STUNNED BY THE IMPACT THE BULLET made. She knew it had hit her in the arm and could already feel pain pulsating from her left side. She also knew it could have been so much worse if that man in black hadn't jumped in front of Silas and shot him.

That man.

Who was he?

Everything had happened in a blur. One moment she emerged from down below to see Silas aiming the gun at Jesse, ready to kill him at point-blank range. In the next second, when she called out to him to stop, he swung to kill her. Whether she startled him, or he meant to pull the trigger, she would never know.

She would never know because he was also sprawled on the floor, eyes open with a vacant stare that only meant one thing.

Silas Moran was dead.

But dead at the hands of his own man? How was this possible?

Chris tore her gaze from her brother's face just as Marcus appeared over the top of the stairs, his panicked eyes searching her from head to toe.

"I'm okay," she said. "The bullet just nicked my arm. But Silas..." She looked at her brother again, feeling guilty when elation ran through her. She reminded herself that the man would have killed her without a second thought. Had he been angry at Jesse because he had wanted to do the honors himself?

Marcus knelt beside her, holding her arm, pressing on it to stop the blood flow. Was it worse than she thought? Reaching over to a long table, he pulled down the table runner and wrapped it around her upper arm. "I think that should stop the bleeding. It's not that bad."

"Yeah, I know. Someone stopped Silas from killing me." Chris used her other arm to sit up.

Marcus glanced behind him to see Jesse inspecting Silas's body. "Where's the other guy?" he asked the man. "I know there were two of them."

"They both ran out on the deck. But everything happened so fast. I guess he could still be in the house, but I thought he went after the shooter." Jesse looked at Chris, a startled expression on his face.

"Well, we're not staying to find out. Let's go." Marcus helped her to her feet and guided her to the top of the stairs.

Chris had yet to take her eyes off her brother. "Wait. Give me a second."

"Chris, I don't think this is a good idea. We need to call the police."

Chris stepped up beside Jesse and looked down at her brother's dead body. As glad as she was that he couldn't hurt her anymore, the idea that he would not have another opportunity to fix his mistakes sadden her.

"He was going to kill me," Jesse said. "After everything I've done for him." He looked at Chris again. "And you stopped him. I wasn't sure if you meant what you said, but you did."

Marcus put his hand across his back, reminding her that they needed to leave. "It's still not safe here. We need to get the law involved. Sam should've already called the police. Until they get here, we need to get outside."

"Sam?" The mention of her roommate's name pulled Chris away from her brother. "Where is she?"

"I sent her out to call for help."

"She was still bound."

"I'm hoping some locals helped her out with that. Let's go find her."

Chris turned for the stairs, but at the top, she looked back at Jesse.

The man was a shell of himself now. Realizing that everything about his life had been a lie had to be debilitating.

"Don't go anywhere. I'm sure the police will want to ask you some questions. I'm glad you're alive. You'll get a second chance to make amends. I suggest you start by confessing to dumping Reggie's body." With that, she took the lead down the stairs and out into the sunshine of the sweet island of her memories, thankful that the day's situation hadn't ruined those.

On the street, she spotted Sam, her arms now free, talking to a couple of police officers. As soon as she noticed Chris, she took off running, her arms wide and her facial expression full of gratitude. The police followed her and as Chris enveloped her, she let Marcus fill them in on how everything went down.

"I'm so sorry you were taken," Chris said. "You must have been so scared."

"Is he really dead?"

Chris nodded, and Sam cried into Chris's neck, unable to get any words out now that she had found safety. "I want to go home," she finally managed to whisper.

"Going back to your parents' house might be a good idea for a while, maybe permanently."

Sam shook her head and lifted her face to look at Chris. "No, I want to go back to our apartment. That's my home. With you. Can we go now?"

"Finding you was all that mattered to me. But there's more going on than I understood. I don't think going back to the city is a good idea right now."

"Then where will we go?"

"Not we. You. I'm going to arrange for you to be in a safe place while I make sure nothing like this ever happens again."

"Where am I going? Why can't you go with me?" Sam was visibly panicked with trembling shoulders. As the warm sun disappeared over the horizon, the two of them were both freezing. Chris's clothes had yet to dry, but that had nothing to do with the fear chilling her veins. The loss of blood also contributed.

Chris looked around to make sure nobody was listening. "You're going to Mel's house. She and Jeremy will take care of you. And no one will know where you are. As soon as I get to a phone, I'm calling them to come get you."

"Oh, here." Sam passed Marcus's phone to her. "Use this."

Chris took the phone but chose not to make the call from it. "I don't want to leave any trail to Melody. I'll make the call from a private line. But don't worry. They will come for you right away."

Sam relaxed against her and nodded her agreement. Since Chris's old roommate, Melody married her long-time sweetheart, Jeremy, Sam had a few opportunities to get to know the couple. She had even spent the weekend at their Connecticut home, tucked in the peaceful and secluded hills.

Chris was glad to see Sam accept this next step for her. "Good girl. It's the safest place for you right now."

"I know. I just wish you would come with me."

Marcus left the cluster of police and made his way toward them again. Chris whispered, "Don't talk about this to anyone. But I will join you when it's safe."

Sam watched Marcus. "Even him?"

Chris wished she could say Marcus could be trusted, and maybe he could be. But now was not the time to test those waters, and the least amount of people that knew of where they were going the better, for everyone's sake, including his.

Marcus started talking as he approached. "I told the police everything we know, which isn't much. I mentioned Reggie's death, but until the medical examiner deems his death a homicide, there's not too much interest in connecting today's incident to him."

"I'm sorry," Chris said. "The truth will come out. I don't know how, but I know it will. Maybe Jesse will do the right thing."

"I've asked for a ride back to my law firm. We'll be safe there for the night."

Sam looked at Chris with questioning eyes, waiting to take her direction from her. Chris did her best not to give any of her own plans away.

"That's fine. I appreciate the ride. Even though Silas is dead, I don't feel comfortable going to my hotel just yet. There are still too many goons walking around the place, and I don't know who will issue their next order. I can't trust anyone."

Marcus frowned and looked at her wrapped arm. "You can trust me. I mean it, Chris. Seeing you fly back like that—" He swallowed convulsively.

Chris reached to tap his forearm. "I'm okay. Whoever stepped in the way, saved my life. For whatever reason, I'm grateful."

An officer stepped up to them, wearing blue latex gloves. "Did either of you happen to see who else was hurt in the building?"

Marcus shook his head and looked at Chris who shrugged. "As far as I know it's just me, and of course my brother. Why? Is there someone else hurt?"

"Whoever ran out onto the deck had also been hit. There are drops of blood down the stairs and into the sand. I'm thinking they took your bullet first before the projectile exited them and came for you."

The idea that one of Silas's goons took her bullet made her wonder even more who it was. They really had saved her life and may lose their own because of it.

~

Marcus led Chris and Sam into the building of his law firm. He unlocked the first set of doors and then the second set through the vestibule. When he pulled the heavy wooden door open, he saw the lights were on and heard a rustling sound somewhere at the back of the hallway.

"Hello?" he called out.

The rustling sound ceased. In the next second, Gloria peeked her head out from one of the back interview rooms.

"I'm sorry, Marcus. I wasn't expecting you to come in on the weekend."

"Weekend? It's Sunday night. What are you doing here that couldn't wait until morning?"

His receptionist stepped out of the room and made her way down the hallway toward them. Even on the weekend, she dressed efficiently and kept her hair pulled back neatly in a bun.

"Do you ever take a day off?" He made a joke that fell flat. At the moment, he wasn't trusting of anyone, even his most loyal receptionist and assistant.

Gloria walked up behind her desk and took her seat. "I had some filing to get done. You sent us home early on Friday, and I forgot about the Simmons case. You're due in court this week. I hadn't typed up the brief yet."

"Surely that can wait until tomorrow. Go on home." Marcus headed to his office expecting his receptionist to follow orders without question.

Except, she didn't move. In fact, there was obviously something she needed to talk to him about.

"What is it, Gloria?"

She stood slowly and picked an envelope up from her desk. Glancing at Chris and Sam, she said, "I think we need to talk in private."

Marcus looked at Chris and shrugged. "Does this have something to do with a confidential court case?"

She shook her head and shifted her feet nervously. "No, but you may not want this information public."

Chris took Sam by the hand. "We can wait in your office."

As she reached him, he put his hand out and stopped her. "If it's not a confidential case, then just share what you have, Gloria. Whatever you need to say you can say it in front of Chris." He didn't miss the surprise in Chris's eyes at such a remark. But it was the truth, and he needed her to know he never wanted to keep anything from her, not now, not ever.

His receptionist bit her lower lip and then held the envelope out to him. "I didn't open it until this afternoon when I arrived. It was delivered by certified mail on Friday morning, and I completely forgot about it when you sent us home early. I remembered this morning that I never opened it. That's why I came back. It's a registered letter from the county assessor."

"County assessor," Marcus mumbled as he stepped up to retrieve the letter. "Am I being sued by the state?"

Gloria let out a deep breath. "No, sir. You're being foreclosed on. The building is going up for an auction for delinquencies on taxes."

"Delinquencies," Marcus spoke aloud as he read quietly, each word befuddling him further. "I don't understand. Reggie had always assured me the business was taken care of. But this letter claims he hasn't paid taxes for four years?" A glance up at Gloria showed her wringing her hands. "What do you know about this?"

"I've been in the back going through all the internal revenue service forms. There are none for four years. I've looked three times. I tore the place apart." She dropped her gaze to the floor, looking paler than normal. "We have until the end of the month to move out."

"This must be some kind of joke." The words on the page didn't change. No matter how many times Marcus read through them, they reiterated what Gloria said. He had two weeks to move his business elsewhere.

"They're also taking the furniture to offset losses," Gloria said, but he had already read that part. What would he do with a bunch of corporate tables and chairs without a place to put them in?

Marcus felt Chris's hand on his forearm and tore his gaze from the letter. He wasn't sure if he saw sympathy or pity in her eyes.

"Maybe Diane can shed some light on this," Chris said. "She might know if something was going on with her husband."

Marcus agreed and directed Gloria to make the phone call. "Have her come in right away." He turned for his office but looked down the hall toward Reggie's door. He had yet to go in there since his partner's death.

Partner.

The term didn't match his definition of a partner or friend anymore. The man kept secrets from him. Four years of lying to him, telling him that the business was in the black. He never missed a payment of their profit-sharing arrangement, but he missed paying taxes? Did he not realize they would lose this historic building and be left with nothing?

"I need the key to his office," he said without looking at Gloria. He heard her go through her drawer and remove a jingling ring of keys. She walked them to him and placed them in his hand.

Slowly, Marcus moved toward Reggie's office. At the door, he read his friend's name stenciled on the wood. He unlocked it and went in.

The sparse room matched his own with the same filing cabinet against the wall. Marcus opened it and rifled through past cases his partner had tried. Nothing seemed out of the ordinary, and to anyone looking in the window, it all looked on the up and up. He even had multiple files on the Morans just as Marcus did. Reggie was just as passionate about taking down the organized crime in Savannah as he was.

Except, Reggie's hidden choices mirrored unethical business practices.

Was he one of them? All this time, Marcus couldn't make headway in the least. For over twelve years, the Morans stayed one step ahead of him, if not more. Was he never supposed to gain ground in taking them down? Was Reggie putting roadblocks in his way from the beginning of their partnership?

Was Reggie a mole in the office the whole time? Marcus didn't need to worry about electronic ears listening to his every word if the Morans had real-life ears planted within the walls to begin with.

Marcus pulled out three folders on the Moran family. He dropped them on the desk and sat down in Reggie's chair. He flipped open the first file as Chris stepped into the doorway.

"You might not want to be in here," he said. "You might not like what I find in these files. You and Sam can sleep in my office. There are two sofas in there. I'll stay in here."

She stepped up to the desk and took one look before tapping her fingers on the wood. "You think my father was involved in this?"

"Isn't he always?"

"I can go if that would be better."

"It's not safe for you out there until we know what your father is up to. I know he's behind this tax lien auction as well. I'll be up all night going through these."

"I see nothing has changed." Chris tilted her head with a frown. "There are other things more important than my father."

"Like what?" He scanned paper after paper, flipping through to find anything with Moran's name associated with the assessor's office.

"How about the fact that I almost died. Do you have any bandages or a first-aid kit?"

Marcus lifted his gaze to the tablecloth still tied around her arm. Both of them still were in damp clothes with mussed saltwater-filled hair. They needed to get cleaned up, and yet he couldn't take a moment away from figuring out what happened to Reggie.

"I don't have much time. I need..." He dropped his head into his hands and stared blindly at the files in front of him. "Need to know if my friend was a traitor."

Out from the side of his eyes, he watched Chris kneel at the edge of his desk. She met him eye to eye and reached for his hand with her good arm.

"He wasn't a traitor. But something must have made him desperate these last four years. Don't jump to conclusions without talking to Diane. His wife will know if there had been something wrong that might lead to this behavior."

"There could be something here that I missed."

"Poring over his files will not bring you answers. He wouldn't have left evidence behind, no matter who was controlling him. You're only causing yourself distress. Don't deny it. I know what I'm looking at...it's the same look you had twelve years ago. The day I left town."

Marcus dropped his other hand to the desk and covered hers. "I hate that he always wins. No matter what I do, Vincent Moran always wins. He even took you from me."

"I ran away on my own."

"He gave you no choice."

"Neither did you."

Marcus ran out of excuses. All he had left was the truth. "I looked for you. I looked for months." He closed his eyes, remembering the dead ends he met with daily. "Nothing consumed me more, nothing besides..."

Chris pressed her lips together and looked at him with expectant eyes. When he didn't finish his sentence, she finished it for him. "Nothing besides trying to take down my father. Don't shut me out. Let me help you this time."

Slowly, Marcus turned in the swivel chair and pulled her toward him. He watched his own hand tremble in hers. He was losing everything that was important to him. And yet, as she placed her palm against his cheek and leaned in to capture his lips, Marcus inhaled at the powerful feeling of a second chance with Christina Moran, the only woman he had ever loved. Suddenly, he realized he wasn't losing everything.

Marcus wrapped his arm around her good side and deepened their kiss, feeling desperate to never let her go again. When he finally broke away and locked his gaze on hers, a mere inch away, he saw something he had never seen before in her eyes.

"I don't deserve your trust," he whispered. "I never earned it."

She touched his cheek again. "I'm choosing to give it to you. Can you say the same?"

Her words were the crux of their problem. The first moment he laid eyes on her and walked up to her to ask her out, he had never trusted her because of her name. Could he let go of his mission to rid the streets of the Moran name long enough to see the individual woman before him? Could he separate her from any connection she had to Vincent Moran?

"I want to. I really do. But I don't know if it's possible. I don't know how to live my life without this need inside of me to make the Moran name disappear from Savannah forever."

"I'm not a Moran anymore."

Marcus huffed, barely smothering a cynical laugh. "Some might call that denial. You're your father's daughter. He knows it, and you know it. You want me to trust you. Start there."

Chris pulled away, and he dropped his hand away from her arm. She stood to her full height, and even though he sat in the chair, she lifted her chin to look down at him further. Did she not realize how it made her look even more like Vincent Moran?

"I'm sorry to hear you say that," she said with disdain. "I had hoped everything we'd been through these past few days would have proven I am not your enemy. That I never was."

"I didn't say you were my enemy."

"You don't see me as part of your team. That's the same thing." Chris turned for the door just as Gloria stepped up.

Strands of hair had escaped from Gloria's bun, and Marcus didn't think he had ever seen her in such a state.

"What is it, Gloria?" he asked. "Or do I not want to know? I'm not sure how much more I can take today."

"Sir, Diane's not answering her phone. And her voicemail box is full. I took the liberty to call the police for a wellness check, under the circumstances with the tax lien."

"And?" Marcus slowly stood to his feet, expecting to hear something devastating had happened to his friend's wife.

"She's gone. All her personal things as well. The house is vacant."

Chapter Ten

EARLY, THE NEXT MORNING, CHRIS APPROACHED DIANE'S house and met the officer by the back door. Sam stayed with Gloria at the office until Mel could arrive for her. Marcus now followed from a few paces behind but remained silent since they left his office building. She couldn't believe how quickly things had turned for them last night, and yet, what did she expect? Marcus's hatred for her father was deep-rooted and went back a lot longer than the two of them.

Chris entered the house and stood in the middle of the kitchen. She turned in a circle and noticed the same dirty dishes on the table that were there when she visited Diane just a few days ago. A glance at the counter showed the slip of paper with her phone number scrawled across it. Diane had left it behind. Was it on purpose? Or had someone rushed her out against her will?

Marcus had walked through the house and now reentered the kitchen again. "She left in a hurry, but nothing seems like foul play." He took out his business card and gave it to the police officer. "If you track her down, please call me. She's the wife of my business partner, Reggie Brodsky."

The officer looked at the card and then pocketed it in his shirt pocket below his badge. "I heard about him. Something definitely doesn't feel right about any of this, but perhaps, Mrs. Brodsky just needed to get away from everything. I'll put out a BOLO for the nearby departments to be looking, and I'll contact her next of kin to see if they've heard from her. Do you know if she has family she might have decided to visit?"

Chris waited for Marcus to reply, but all he did was shrug. Then he said, "I'm sorry to say, I'm not positive. She and Reggie spent most holidays with his parents. I could run over there and check with them. Maybe she contacted them to tell them her plans."

The officer nodded and walked them out. "I'll be in touch if I find anything out."

"Same," Marcus said. On the street, he said the Chris, "I'm walking over to pick up my car. Then I'm going back to the old neighborhood to see Reggie's parents."

"The old neighborhood? Where is that?"

Marcus smirked. "A place you've never been."

"Can I go with you?" Chris held her breath as myriad emotions crossed his face. "Please?"

"Why, Chris?"

"Because you think you know everything about me because of where I grew up. I think it's only fair that I know where you grew up too."

Marcus shook his head. She didn't think he would agree. "Don't you have someone coming to pick Sam up?"

"Mel and Jeremy won't be here for a few hours. Sam is safe with Gloria. I have time to go downtown."

"Downtown? You make it sound so sweet like we're going shopping or grabbing a slice of pizza. We'll be going west toward Garden City. These are rough neighborhoods, but they're also people's homes. Most of the residents are doing the best they can to live in these areas of gangs and poverty because it's all they have and ever will have. Something I don't expect you to understand, growing up in your mansion with your gold doorknobs."

"That's not fair." Chris crossed her arms, insulted by his lack of faith in her character. "I gave all that up twelve years ago. Everything I have, I have worked hard for. No one handed me anything. You don't want to be judged based on your past, well neither do I. Let me show you a different side of myself, one that has nothing to do with my family name."

Marcus averted his gaze for a moment. She watched his jaw tick in indecision. "I'll probably live to regret this. But I suppose it could be entertaining. All right, Princess, follow me to the car. Just don't get yourself shot."

Chris bit back a retort at such a reference. After all, she did ask for this. Taking a breath of composure, she fell in line with him but did wonder if she was prepared for this excursion into his past.

Things between them may go from bad to worse. And if guns were going off, the probability of another person stepping in front of a bullet for her was nil.

~

Marcus drove west into his childhood neighborhood. Chris remained silent beside him as they passed by graffitied fences and rundown homes. He filled the void in the car by acting as a tour guide. "There are nearly seventy sets of gangs on the streets. Most fall under the two largest organizations. But there's also a few others popping up that are all about making a profit. Trafficking guns, mostly, but drugs and human trafficking as well. Most of the sets of gangs are divided by street posses." He jutted his chin at the intersection in front of them. "Like this street here."

Chris sunk a little in her seat. "How can you tell which gang they belong to?"

"Their tattoos will tell their story. Law enforcement does its best to categorize the markings, so they know something about the members they meet, apprehend...or find dead. But the groups are always changing and growing to stay ahead."

"Do the police know which groups are selling the guns? Can't they just focus on them?"

"There's a coalition now with the DA's office. I'm part of it. We're trying to track down the traffickers, but the distribution goes much higher than the street gangs. The suppliers stay clear of the neighborhoods, so they're protected."

"They should have to come down here and see the people they affect." Chris turned away from him and stared out the window as they passed by a cluster of kids in front of a convenience store. "There are even girls in there. None of them look older than thirteen years old."

431

"They're probably not. And some probably won't make it out of their teens. I pray for them daily." Marcus gripped the steering wheel so tight that his knuckles turned white. "I don't know if God hears me, though. Nothing changes."

Chris turned his way with such sadness in her large eyes. The green in them appeared to liquefy before him. "God hears you, and He sees you too. He sees how you care, and all your efforts don't go unnoticed by Him. But I can understand how you might wonder. When you're in the thick of the darkness, it's hard to not let it affect you." She dropped her gaze to her lap where her hands rested on her knees. "It's hard not to let it consume you and change you."

"Are you speaking from experience?" he asked. "New York City does have its own rough neighborhoods."

"Oh, sure, but that's not what I was talking about. I was able to find an apartment building with a devoted doorman named Donny."

"Devoted doorman named Donny." He laughed. "Sounds humorous."

Chris frowned. "There was nothing humorous about what my brother and his men did to Donny when they came for me and took Samantha. No, I was talking about the darkness of living with my brother here in Georgia."

Marcus took the next turn to the street Reggie grew up on. He pulled up in front of a multifamily home and parked. He shut down the car and considered his response to her insight into living in the Moran household. As poor as Reggie's home life was, on the other side of the front door was nothing but love.

"He can't hurt you anymore," Marcus whispered but had yet to face her. "Your brother is dead."

After a few moments, he heard Chris sniffle, and a glance her way showed her blonde hair shielding her face from his view. Her shoulders trembled, and Marcus realized he'd neglected to ask her how she felt about Silas's death. He'd just assumed she wouldn't be affected by it after all the man had done.

He'd assumed wrong.

"Hey, I'm sorry," Marcus said, reaching for one of her hands to hold. "That was blunt and uncalled for. I'm sure you had hoped someday Silas would change. I think I've seen too much death down here to be cynical about people changing. Those junior high schoolers back there most likely won't. They're in it to the end. Whatever that end happens to be for them. I'm numb to it, but you're not. I should have realized that."

Chris shook her head and lifted her reddened eyes to him. "Silas knew the kind of life he lived. I'm not naïve to why he died by a gun. He lived by the gun. And he almost killed me today because of it. I'm sad because I thought I had escaped this darkness, but I see that darkness pulls you back in if you let your guard down. I let my guard down. When my father hears that Silas is dead, he will be relentless. All he talked about was me returning to take over the family businesses. Marcus, I may never be free again."

So much was on his tongue about some of those Moran businesses. But now was not the time. Right now, he needed to be honest with Chris on a different topic.

"You're stronger than you give yourself credit for," he said. "In fact, if I played any part in causing you to doubt your strength, I am sorry. The truth is I envied you when you were able to walk away from your darkness. I am consumed by mine. It's all I can focus on. It has me in its grip. But not you. I know you're afraid your father will have the power to control you, but I don't see you ever giving that up."

She tilted her head and looked at him with an unconvinced expression. "If it wasn't for your brother, I would still be locked in my room."

Marcus rolled his eyes. "Just great. Now I have another favor I owe him. Will it ever end?"

Chris giggled so sweetly that the sound made him smile. "Well, he did leave me in an alley with a gunman chasing me."

"Right. Never mind. I owe him nothing. Phew."

They shared a laugh that trailed off into silence. Chris looked away to face the house outside of her window.

"So this is where Reggie grew up?"

"Yes, and mine was the house two doors down. The second-floor unit. My parents are not there any longer. I moved them out after I joined the practice."

"But Reggie's family remained here? Why's that?"

"They didn't want to move. Mrs. Brodsky said this neighborhood was all she knew and would never give up hope of seeing it rehabilitated."

Chris hummed. "Talk about a strong woman." She pulled the door handle. "I'm excited to meet her."

"Wait," Marcus said, jumping from his side of the car. He raced around the front and opened her door.

"Marcus, I can open my own door." She stepped out without taking his hand.

He wrapped an arm around her back. "Humor me. I've already seen you take a bullet once this week."

Chris pressed closer to him and glanced over her shoulder. "If you're trying to scare me, it's working."

"If scaring you makes you want to be this close to me, get ready to be terrified constantly."

Marcus felt her shoulders rumble with laughter, but he was glad she didn't pull away. He liked her right where she was. Together they walked up the stoop to the porch of his friend's house. He had just been here to inform them about Reggie's death, and now he was here to ask about Diane's disappearance. How much more bad news could the family take?

He rapped on the door and was greeted by the sound of their German Shepherd barking. Soon, the curtain lifted from the window beside it, and the lock turned over.

Martha Brodsky clapped her hands in delight after opening the door for them. "Come in, Marcus, welcome back." She stood on tippytoes to kiss his cheek. Then she gasped at the sight of Chris. "Christina Moran, I don't believe my eyes. Is this your first time on this side of the tracks?"

"Martha, be nice," Marcus warned, even though he knew the woman was joking. He couldn't really blame her. He never dared bring Chris to his hometown when they were dating.

Martha reached for Chris and gave her a hug. "I'm just kidding. Welcome to my home. You just couldn't stay away from beautiful Savannah, could you? I completely understand."

Chris glanced over Martha's shoulder at him. Her eyes were wide with surprise. "Actually, it wasn't my choice to return, but yes, Savannah will always hold a special place in my heart."

Martha pulled away and patted her cheek. "Follow your heart. You'll never regret it." She led them into the living room. Old but sturdy and well-maintained furniture welcomed them. The rooms were meticulously clean, proving cleanliness was a priority for the Brodsky family. The state of the neighborhood outside didn't affect the inside of their home.

"Can I pour you some sweet tea?" Martha asked, turning toward the stairs to the second floor. "Joe! Marcus is here with his girlfriend! Hurry up and get down here! I'll be right back with your iced tea. Make yourselves comfortable."

Once they were alone, Marcus whispered, "Sorry about that. She means well."

Chris smiled, a slight pink blush on her cheeks. Did she even know how beautiful she was? "I understand she didn't mean anything by calling me your girlfriend. I'm surprised she remembered me at all. I'm embarrassed to say I don't remember meeting her."

"You didn't."

Chris tilted her head in confusion. "Then how does she know me?"

"Everyone knows the famous Moran heir."

Chris frowned as Joe Brodsky trudged down the stairs. "Well, well, look what the ferry boat dragged in. Christina Moran." Joe took her hands and kissed the backs of them, first one then the other. "To what do we own this honor?"

Chris glanced in terror at Marcus, the words "help me" practically on her lips.

Marcus smiled and saved her from any more embarrassment. "Mr. Brodsky, we're here to ask you if you've heard from Diane. It seems she left town recently but didn't tell anyone."

"I don't think so." Joe rubbed his bald head. Just then, Martha stepped into the room with a tray filled with four glasses of sweet tea. Joe continued, "Honey, have you heard from Di?"

"Not in a week. I left her numerous messages. I planned to drive over tomorrow if she didn't return my calls. Why? What's going on? Is she okay? I've been worried about her, no matter how many times she says she's fine. She just lost her husband, *my* son. How can she be fine?"

Martha passed out the teas and took her seat beside Chris on the sofa. She sipped her tea, sweet enjoyment on her lips. Then she noticed the somber look on Chris's face.

"Why isn't anyone drinking their tea? What happened?" Martha straightened in her seat.

Marcus had no other way to say this but to just say it. "The state is taking the law building from me. Apparently, Reggie hadn't been paying the taxes for the last four years. I need to find Diane to see what she knows. Are you sure you don't know where she might have gone?"

Martha sat stunned and silent. Slowly, she put her tea down on the tray. She pursed her lips, and all the warm welcome left her. "Now you sound like Diane. I'll tell you the same thing I told her. My Reggie would never steal. He was honorable."

Marcus leaned in, confused by her words. "What do you mean? Did Diane come to you about this? Did she know about it before Reggie died?"

Joe put his hand on his wife's knee. "Don't raise your blood pressure, dear. Marcus is not the enemy."

Martha stole a quick heated glance at Chris. "Marcus isn't, but she is."

Chris was about to stand up, but Marcus shook his head for her to remain seated. Thankfully, she gave him a moment. "Chris is not our enemy. I promise you that. I wouldn't have brought her here if I thought so. You can trust her. Please, tell us what you know."

Martha released her anger, and after a moment said, "I'm sorry, Christina. That was unfair of me. I shouldn't judge."

"It's okay," Chris said. "Maybe I deserve your criticism. I was a bit clueless when I lived in Georgia. But you can trust me now."

Diane came by a week before Reggie disappeared. She had a foreclosure notice on the house. They were losing it. So, I'm not surprised about the law firm building being taken. I'm sorry, Marcus. This must be killing you."

"That's an understatement," he mumbled and looked at the floor. He felt Chris touch his hand, and he quickly held on. "So Diane knew Reggie was struggling. You knew he wasn't paying the taxes and mortgage on his home. Why wasn't I told? I was his partner. I was his friend."

Martha smiled sadly. "His very best friend, sweetie. He looked up to you and wished he was as brave as you. He let you battle the court cases because he knew he could never do them justice. Not like you." She glanced at her husband and at his nod, she continued, "But Reggie hadn't always been so honorable. He took hush money for a long time. It's how he had the money to buy the house and business in the first place. But when he tried to break free and do the right thing..." She sighed and dropped her head. "Well, they broke *him* instead."

"Who is they?" Chris asked and then inhaled sharply. "On second thought. Don't answer that. I already know the answer." Chris stood and headed for the door. She stopped with her hand on the doorknob. "Marcus, take me home."

"Home?" Marcus asked, slowly gaining his feet.

"Yes, home. I want to see my father's face when I tell him his legacy has come to an end."

Chapter Eleven

MARCUS ENTERED THE HISTORIC SAVANNAH STREETS, DRIVING toward the Moran house. "I don't think you should go in." He spoke his mind, even though he didn't think Chris would listen. Her anger was heavy and seething in the car, and he feared for her safety if she made an irrational move. However, seeing this angry side of her, he also feared *her* a little. Maybe he was underestimating her.

"My father will have been notified about Silas by now."

"I'm sure. He may take his pain out on you. If he locked you up when he wasn't angry, I don't want to imagine what he'll do now."

"He needs to be stopped, and I am the only one left to do it. His reach has touched everyone I have loved and cared about. I'm surprised he has nothing on you."

Marcus reflected on her comment for a moment. He drove in silence as he wondered why Vincent Moran left him alone. He got to Reggie, so why not him?

"Maybe Reggie made a deal with him," he said, thinking aloud. "Maybe my partner sacrificed himself to keep me clean. He knew I was the relentless litigator between us. He was the businessman. Maybe I was part of a transaction."

"Except, Reggie had been delinquent on taxes for four years. If the bribe money to my father stopped four years ago, you would have heard from him by now. So something else kept him from showing up on your doorstep."

"Maybe he couldn't find anything on me. The fact that his only connection to me was you tells me that I'm untouchable to him."

Chris scoffed. "No one is untouchable. We all have skeletons in our closet. Things we have done that we wished we hadn't. He would have dug until he found something on you. Something from your past in your neighborhood, perhaps. Can you honestly tell me you have never done anything wrong? Nobody's perfect. We all fall short. God's word tells us that. So be honest."

The temperature in the car seemed to skyrocket, and it had nothing to do with the summer heat. Marcus drove in silence as a few memories resurfaced from his college days. He had some things he wished he could forget or go back and change.

"Okay, I'll be honest. I broke some rules to get out of my neighborhood. I was a different person then. Law school changed me. But Jesus transformed me. I suppose I don't think of those days anymore because I do my best to walk with God daily now."

Chris smiled softly beside him. "I'm really glad to hear you say that, Marcus."

He glanced away, a little embarrassed at his quick confession of his faith. "Why? Because I'm going to need Him more than ever now?"

"We always need Him." She slapped her hands on her knees. "But yes, if it was Reggie keeping my father at bay, you can expect him to start digging up everything you don't want people to know about you. He may even come in as your rescuer to save your firm."

Marcus felt his jaw drop. "Reggie's not even in the grave yet. That would be cruel."

Chris raised her eyebrows. "Have you met my father?"

"Actually, no, I have never met Vincent Moran. At least not formally. I've hated him my whole life and wouldn't have put myself in a situation where I would have to be in the room with him."

"Why would a boy from the west side care about my father?" Chris's eyes narrowed at him with genuine curiosity.

But could he tell her what he knew?

"Chris, you say I can trust you, right?

She hesitated for a second. "Yes, and I meant that. I will hold your confidence in whatever you have to tell me."

"It's not about holding confidence. It's about me being able to trust that you won't try to interfere. You could get yourself killed with this knowledge."

As Chris sat in contemplative silence, Marcus took the next few turns and parked at the end of the street, choosing to stay clear of the Moran house. When she didn't step out, he wondered if she had changed her mind.

"You don't have to go in," he said.

"Tell me what you know."

"Are you sure? I watched you leave the Brodsky house in a rage of fury. You won't be able to do that with this information. Instead, it will consume you and depress you because it's a battle that can never be won. The coalition tries, but there are even days that I wonder if Moran hasn't already gotten to them."

"Tell me," she said again. But she had yet to look at him. She faced forward with her chin held high, an invisible shield around her as she waited for his words to hit her. She was already braced for impact.

All that was left was his decision to share or not.

As soon as the words were out, there would be no going back. "Give me your hand," he said, holding out his own.

"So you can hold me here. That will make you no different than my father. He kept me locked in my bedroom because he knew I would leave. You either trust me to stay or you don't."

Marcus moved his hand to the steering wheel, wrapping his fingers around it for his own stability. He had to trust that she wouldn't react irrationally and undo all the work that he and the coalition had already done.

"All right, the truth is the Moran family has been supplying guns to the gangs on the Savannah streets."

Chris's eyes grew wide. "What?" She looked straight at him with as much shock in her expression as he had hoped to see. It meant she knew nothing about it and had never been involved in any way. The one good thing Vincent Moran did was protect his daughter from his involvement in his crimes.

"I know it's hard to comprehend. The idea of someone putting guns in kids' hands is too insane to understand and feels like something that only happens in the movies. But this is real life. The gangs get the guns from someone."

"That someone doesn't have to be my father." She glanced at the house, a place full of wealth and prominent status. "How would it benefit him to keep crime up?"

"Crime affects business. It affects real estate prices. Most people would want lower crime and higher real estate. Unless, of course, you're the one looking for cheap land to build slum housing."

Chris leaned back on the headrest and stared at the ceiling. "Of course. He has never been interested in philanthropy unless there was an angle to play. Do you remember Freddie from the theater?"

Marcus wondered about the change of topic but nodded. "Sure, Freddie's been working there for years. Why?"

"I went to see him and realized my father has something on him too. He's just a man who runs a theater. My father doesn't even care about the shows. He never attended any of mine. So why invest in Freddie's business unless he can use Freddie to lift his own business up." She turned to face him. "At the end of the day, it's all about his bottom line. It doesn't matter who had to die that day or go to jail. Loss doesn't matter to him because he has others lined up to take their place. He has a machine so well-oiled that he can sit up in that house and never lift a finger to do any work, dirty or otherwise. And because of that, he's untouchable. It's not fair."

"Life isn't fair, believe me. Laws are put in place to protect people at the same time other laws are created to protect the criminals. Deals are made for lesser sentences for career criminals while those who spend their lives trying to do the right thing get the book thrown at them when they slip up once. I take solace in knowing that there will be a true judgment day someday. Real justice will be served by the One who avenges for us."

Chris closed her eyes. "I just keep seeing those kids from your neighborhood. I have to believe that God will avenge them too."

"He will. He promises that anyone who has caused a child to stumble or harmed them in any way will be punished. That it would be better for them to have a millstone tied around their neck and thrown into the sea."

Chris laughed nervously. "If that would be better for them, I would hate to see what their actual punishment will be." She sighed and now reached for his hand. "I work so hard to keep girls off the street. I can't save them all, but when I see one that needs to believe someone cares about them, I do my best to give them a place to live or give them a job. To think that my father is doing just the opposite kills me. I don't know if I can wait for God's justice to be served to him."

Marcus rubbed her hand with his thumb. "This is why I worried about telling you. You can't do anything or say anything. The coalition is trying its best to catch him. If we can, we will put him away and anyone else who has worked for him. I can't have you alert him. Do you understand?"

"I understand. I don't like it, but I understand. I think it's best if I don't go in there right now. I may not be able to control myself. Just go back to Gloria's. Mel and Jeremy should be arriving soon if they're not already there."

Marcus refrained from showing relief and put the car in Drive. He continued the rest of the way down the street, slowly creeping by the Moran house to his left. Suddenly the front door opened, and he picked up his speed so he wouldn't be seen.

"Wait." Chris grabbed the wheel. "Is that your brother?"

Marcus slammed on the brakes just as Lucius came down the front steps. Lucius also halted, freezing in his spot. This time he wore no disguise. Just a ponytail and a black sport coat and black pants—looking like a Moran henchman.

The two brothers stared at each other, both in shock and horror.

In the next second, Lucius pivoted on a run, but not before Marcus noticed a large bandage on his hand.

Marcus hit the gas, but by the time he made it to the corner, his brother had slipped into the shadows once again.

~

Chris couldn't imagine how Marcus must be feeling. Everything he believed his life was about was coming unglued at the seams. His business was over. His coalition was proving to be useless. Reggie, his friend and business partner, was dead, most likely murdered. And now, his brother, his own twin was working for the enemy.

Lucius Cartwright was one of her father's goons.

As they returned to Gloria's apartment, Marcus pulled up to the door and said, "I'll be back in a little while."

Chris had her hand on the door handle and paused. "Where are you going?"

"I'm not sure. Maybe the firm. I just need a quiet place to process this."

"Are you sure you're not going looking for him? You asked me to refrain from reacting to the information you had about my father. I'm asking the same of you."

Marcus shook his head. "I'm not going after him. He wouldn't tell me anything anyway. I honestly have no idea what my brother does for a living. It's always been a big secret since he got out of the military. But seeing him step so casually out of the Moran house tells me it wasn't his first time going in and out. There was also a day when I was going to meet you there, and he called me before I got out of my car. He was there watching me. I thought he was watching the house, but perhaps he was watching from the house. He hinted that you had been taken but told me to go home. Unreal."

Chris could tell Marcus was struggling to understand this information. "Rehashing every conversation that you've had with Lucius won't help you. The man lives in disguise, and that means his words are just as..."

"It's okay. You can say it. A lie. His words are all lies."

Chris sighed. "That's not what I was going to say. I was going to say fake. I don't think Lucius means to lie to you. He's your brother, and he loves you. That much I know is true. He must have a valid reason for working for my father. If nothing else, he did rescue me from that house. Focus on that. I probably would be dead if he hadn't shown up and burst in. I had just cut the guard with a piece of glass. He was ready to kill me, or at least pummel me. I, for one, want to give him a chance to explain. I owe him that."

443

Marcus blew out a deep breath. "I'll remind myself of that when I see him."

"So that *is* where you're going. You're going to look for Lucius."

"I have to." He nodded to Gloria's apartment. "I want you to stay here with your friends. No one knows you're here, so you'll be safe."

"My brother is dead. There is no one else after me to kill me."

"Still, humor me. Your father may decide to carry out Silas's plan. In fact, you might want to go back with your friends to Connecticut. You'll be even safer there. What could possibly go wrong in a small country town?"

Chris giggled despite the heavy conversation. "Actually, before Jeremy and Mel married, they both had to fight a killer in that small country town. They nearly lost their lives and each other."

"I'm sorry to hear that. Living in the city my whole life, I suppose, I always thought the grass wasn't only greener but sweeter on the other side of the buildings. The attorney in me knows that crime can happen anywhere. But for the most part, it typically is a lot tamer. Maybe someday I'll hang my shingle in a little country town and work on probate cases." He chuckled.

Chris rolled her eyes. "You would be bored out of your mind, and you know it. No, Marcus, God has you here for a reason. You love Savannah, and you will fight for it until your dying breath."

He flashed her his beautiful smile, and she knew she was right. Marcus Cartwright may have lost his building, but he would rebuild his business again right here in Savannah.

"I need this place just as much as it needs me," he said proudly.

Chris opened the door and stepped out. Glancing back inside, she said. "Don't be too long. I would love for you to meet Mel and Jeremy. Mel was the first girl I rescued."

His eyes dimmed as did his smile. "Sounds like New York City needs you too."

Chris agreed wholeheartedly. "I suppose I am a city girl at heart. I've never cared much about the grass. I'll say good night, but I won't say goodbye. Good night, Marcus." She shut the door and headed into Gloria's apartment.

Chris wasn't inside for more than two seconds before she found herself embraced by her best friend of more than ten years. Mel Styles, formally Mel Mesini barely came up to her neck, which was fine, because Chris loved to use her soft, brown curls as a place to rest her chin.

"I need to get you another cell phone. I don't like not being able to call you," Mel said, squeezing her tighter. "Thank God you're safe. Sam filled us in on what has been happening." She pulled back and looked up at Chris. "I had no idea the danger you ran from. You hid it well, my friend, but you shouldn't have."

Jeremy stepped into the kitchen. He wore civilian clothes, but his serious cop expression was in place. His blue eyes held no warmth as he looked at her bandaged arm. "Is it safe for us to be here, Chris?"

Chris let go of his wife and nodded. "For now, but I still want you to take Sam back with you. I'll come for her as soon as I can."

Mel looped her arm through hers. "Please come with us now. There's no reason for you to stay."

A flash of Marcus's face crossed Chris's mind, but she pushed that thought away as ludicrous. She needed to focus on her future, not her past. "I need to end things with my father, or I'll never stop looking over my shoulder. I shouldn't have in the first place. I got too comfortable, lazy even."

Jeremy said, "I'm sorry you're going through this, but you put lives at risk by not being honest. Poor Sam is traumatized." He pulled his wife close to him and kissed her forehead. "It could have been Melody that they kidnapped if your father decided to come for you two years sooner."

Mel shushed her husband. "That's not helping, Jeremy. Chris did what she thought was best."

"She kept you, Rafe, and Sam in the dark."

There was no reason to deny Jeremy's words. "No, Mel, he's right. I put you all at risk. All I wanted was to help you and give you a safe place to fall. You were a runaway just like me. I wanted to give you what I wished someone had given me. I was hurt and broken and scared. I thought if I believed in you and helped you then I was better than the family I came from. I was living a lie."

Mel pulled away from her husband and took Chris's hands. Her liquid brown eyes shimmered with tears. "I have told you before, but I will tell you again. You saved my life. Please, Chris, let me return the favor and take you back with us. We can leave tonight. We don't have to wait until the morning. And you'll never have to come back here again."

"And what, change my name again? Move to another apartment? To another city? I'm tired. I don't want to start over. And..."

"And what?" Mel prodded her to continue.

"You're going to think I'm crazy, but I want to see my father ruined."

Jeremy folded his arms at his chest. "Are you talking about physically harming him? As a police officer, I must counsel you against that."

Chris shook her head. "No, I don't mean violence. That's *his* MO. I mean I want to see him lose everything. His power, his money, his reach. I want to see it all cut off. And if I go back into hiding, he wins and all those things just multiply."

Mel glanced over her shoulder at her husband. Jeremy nodded to her and pulled her close into his chest again. "I'll be praying for you nonstop. You can trust that Sam will be safe with us, and if you change your mind, you know where we are. But you have to promise me something."

"What's that?"

Mel dropped her hand to her belly. "That my little baby will meet her aunt."

Chris inhaled sharply while tears filled her eyes. "You're having a baby?" Her voice squeaked. "Why didn't you tell me sooner?"

"We planned to when we came into the city next week. I wanted to tell you in person. You have to come back to us. Promise me you will."

Chris reached for her friend again. "Of course, I will." But even she detected the lack of surety in her voice. She glanced over Mel's head at Jeremy and mouthed, "Take care of her."

He mouthed back, "Always."

Taking a deep breath, she composed herself and pulled back with the most excited smile she could muster for her friend. "When are you due? Let's go into the living room and talk. You have so much to tell me. So, you're having a girl?"

"Well, it's too soon to know, but we have heard the heartbeat. She's going to be so strong."

Jeremy cleared his throat, sitting across from them in the recliner.

"Okay, maybe he," Mel corrected herself with a wink toward her husband.

"Oh, Jeremy, who are you kidding?" Chris teased. "You would spoil a little girl rotten. And make sure all the boys stayed away until she is eighteen years old."

"True that," he replied without hesitation.

Mel put her finger on her chin. "Speaking of boys, would you care to share about who this Marcus is? He is all Sam is talking about."

Chris waved her hand. "He's just someone I used to know."

Mel's mouth dropped wide. "I don't believe my eyes. The always cool and collected Chris DePalo is blushing. Jeremy, go to bed. Chris and I have important girl things to talk about."

"I said there's nothing to talk about. He's nobody." Chris shifted uneasily on the sofa. As Jeremy stood up to leave, she said, "You don't have to go anywhere. Save me, please, Jeremy!"

Jeremy didn't even look back. He just walked upstairs. Halfway up, he said, "I consider this justice served. Good night, Chris, although for you, I think it's going to be a very long one. Enjoy the hot seat."

Chapter Twelve

MARCUS SAT AT HIS DESK WITH HIS HANDS FOLDED ON TOP. The only light on in the dark building was the small lamp off to his right. He hadn't moved since he arrived over an hour ago. Chris had asked him not to go after Lucius, but she didn't know that no one ever went after Lucius. His brother always came to them. And tonight would be no different.

"How long have you been working both sides?" Marcus asked into the shadows. He couldn't see his brother but knew he was there somewhere, hidden as always.

"Don't ask questions when you're not ready for the answer." The response came slow and smooth. If his brother was ruffled at all, he hid his emotions well.

"I would say at this point I have nothing left to lose. If your plan was to break me as you broke Reggie, then I would say you succeeded." Marcus looked around his office. "I have a matter of days before I must be out of here and have no place to go and no money to start again. My whole career has been a façade. A lie, and you knew it. The least you can do is step into the light to face me."

After a moment of silence, the floor outside his office door creaked.

448

Then Lucius stood in the doorway, still shadowed but out in the open now. Marcus noticed the bandage on his hand again.

"It was you," he said. "You killed Silas and took the bullet meant for Chris. Why?"

"I can't tell you. It's part of—"

"Your job, yes, I've heard that before. Many times. And yet, I have no idea what this job that you do is all about. I have no idea if it even exists outside your head. Who do you work for? And don't say Vincent Moran, because you just killed his son. Does he know it was you?"

"Absolutely not. And you will not tell him, or you will jeopardize something so much bigger than the Moran family. That man is chump change, but even he doesn't realize it. This goes way beyond Savannah, and as I told you last week, if you keep this up, you will be killed."

"Who...do...you *work for?*" Marcus shouted, slamming his fist on the desk.

Lucius looked to the ceiling and then took a step inside the room. First one, then another until he stood fully in the lamplight.

All disguises were gone, and it was like looking in a mirror. This twin of his had cut his hair and lost any sign of the beard, the fake one and the real one.

He even wore a suit.

Marcus smirked. "I thought you wouldn't be caught dead in a suit? Or is the Moran black suit your one exception?"

"You need to leave town...tonight," Lucius said in a low demanding voice. "I'm going to finish this. Don't come back until you hear that Vincent Moran is dead."

Marcus leaned back in his chair. "Are you confessing to me, a man of law, your plan to kill someone? Premeditated murder will get you 25 to life. In case you didn't know capital punishment is a legal penalty in the state of Georgia. With my testimony, you could be looking at the death penalty."

Then the disguise became clear.

He nearly bent over as though his brother physically punched him. Marcus felt his heart pound practically out of his chest. Air seized in his lungs and choked him. Never had he felt so deflated...so disappointed. "You traitor. You want me to leave town so you can frame me for murder.

Of course." Marcus huffed. "And here I thought you were out of disguise, but brother, this getup is your grandest incognito yet. Well done." Marcus slow clapped. "Growing up, I never let my guard down in case someone slipped a knife into my back. I thought moving to historic Savannah would let me relax a little. I forgot you were good with a knife."

"Think what you want as long as you are nowhere near this city tonight."

"No can do. I'm not going anywhere."

"Moran is coming for you. And Christina."

A chill ran up Marcus's spine. "She's safe. I made sure of it."

"If you say so. Personally, I wouldn't want to take such a risk. You should let me handle this."

"And let you frame me? No way."

Lucius's jaw ticked as he stared him down. "Have it your way, but when the dust settles, I can't promise that you won't have blood on your hands. Or your own spilled out. If you own a gun, you might want to have it by your side and loaded up. Everything goes down tonight."

Marcus leaned over to his right side to open his bottom drawer. His gun waited there. He took his eyes off the doorway for one second, but that was all his brother needed to disappear again.

"Now what?" Marcus shouted. "Are there going to be two of us running around this city tonight?"

Somewhere off in the building, Lucius responded in a deep voice. "You better pray that come morning there will still be two of us alive."

The slightest click of a door told Marcus he was alone again. Careless of his brother to let him hear him leave? Probably not. Lucius wanted him to know he was now alone in whatever came his way.

Whatever that was would be happening tonight.

But how was Marcus to fight against a masked enemy? The irony that his brother was now unmasked didn't go unnoticed.

What was he up to?

There was only one way to find out.

Marcus stood and walked to his closet. He removed his gray suit coat, opting for a black sport coat and black pants. He fought his battles in the courtroom but wasn't new to the streets. If that's where he had to return, then so be it.

~

"I cannot believe you never told me about Marcus," Mel said, laying on the opposite end of the sofa. Chris sat cross-legged on the other end with a cup of tea in her hands.

"There wasn't much to tell. Or at least I thought there wasn't. As far as I was concerned, he was out of my life for good."

"But he looked for you." Mel sat up.

"So he says."

"Why would Marcus lie? Now, after becoming a Christian and choosing the straight and narrow life. I say give him another chance."

Chris put her teacup down on the side table. "You haven't even met him. Why would you defend him like this?"

"Because you love him."

Chris sputtered. "I do not. That's absurd."

"Is it? Chris, I have rarely seen you date anyone."

"My life was complicated. I couldn't bring someone into it. Besides, opening Club Creare meant more to me. Not as much as it meant to you, but it kept me busy."

Mel smiled and closed her eyes. "I miss working at the club." Her eyes widened. "But I love my life with Jeremy and could never go back. Rafe is going to blow his top when he hears you aren't coming back either."

"Who said I wasn't going back?" Chris scooted away, feeling affronted by her friend's accusation.

Mel scooted closer, studying Chris intently. "Hear me out. You know I love you, and it's because I love you that I want you to follow your heart."

"Following my heart already proved to be a bad choice. I know you mean well, and going home for you worked out amazingly well, but it won't for me. Savannah can't be my home anymore. And it's the only home that Marcus knows. I could never take him out of it."

"Don't you hear yourself?" Mel grabbed her hands. "I could shake you right now. Stop trying to take care of everyone else and take care of yourself for once. You matter too. You don't have to live a life of sacrifice. You were meant for more."

451

Mel leaned toward the back of the sofa as Chris pondered her words. "You make it sound so easy."

She turned her head toward Chris. "When I almost died because of my stubbornness and addiction you were honest with me. No matter how much it hurt to hear you say I had a problem, you were right. Well, Chris, you have a problem too. You're not living your life."

"I just said I love working at the club."

"But it's not your dream. It was mine. It was always mine, and I had to let it go so I could live again. What's your dream?"

Chris didn't have to think long or hard.

Mel tugged on her hand. "Go ahead, say it. We both know the answer."

Tears filled Chris's eyes. "To...dance." She sniffed and swiped at her eyes with the palm of her hand. "Ballet is all I ever wanted to do. I may not have been good enough to dance the styles for Broadway, but Freddie gave me every opportunity to dance ballet here, even if it was probably because Vincent Moran is my father. Still, aside from leaving Marcus, leaving the theater hurt almost as much."

"I'm glad to hear you admit that leaving Marcus did hurt you."

"Of course, it did. I loved him, even if it wasn't reciprocal. I understand why he had to use me to take down my father. I really understand now. I don't hold it against him anymore."

The soft rap on the back door pulled their attention toward the kitchen.

Chris stretched her legs and stood. "That will be Marcus. Care to meet him?"

Mel clapped her hands giddily. "I wouldn't miss this for the world. In fact, I'll beat you to the door."

Mel raced past Chris, but she caught up with her in the doorway. The two squeezed through, giggling the rest of the way to the back door.

The overhead light glowed a soft yellow and revealed Marcus still in his suit but standing off to the side in the shadows.

Chris opened the door and said, "Come in. I want to introduce you to Mel."

"I really don't have time to meet him right now. It's late." Marcus's words were low almost hushed.

"No. My friend Melody. What is wrong with you? You know who Mel is. I've talked about her many times."

"If you say so. Look, it's late. I'd like you to come back with me where I can keep an eye on you tonight."

Something was wrong. "You don't think I'm safe here? What about everyone else? Jeremy, Sam, Gloria, they're already in bed. Should I wake them up?"

"No. They're fine. It's you I'm worried about." Marcus looked out into the darkness, only raising the hair on the back of her neck more. "We need to go."

"Okay. Let me just say goodbye." Chris reluctantly turned around and opened her arms to Mel. "Take good care of Sam. I'll be there as soon as I can."

Mel studied Marcus's profile in the shadows. She chewed on her lower lip in consternation. Turning away from the door, she whispered, "You like him? He doesn't seem very nice."

Chris had to agree there was something wrong with his behavior. But he had his reasons, and they were valid. "He's going through a rough time right now. Perhaps, you'll have a second chance for a better first impression."

"I'll take your word for it, but I think I might have been wrong in my advice to you. This one I think you should run from again."

Chris pulled Mel in for a hug. "As I said, it's not an easy choice. I'll see you soon."

Chris opened the door wide and stepped out into the night. Marcus was already down the steps out of the light, and she ran up beside him.

"Where are we going?" she asked.

Marcus gave no response but continued walking down the street.

"Where's your car?"

Again, no answer.

"Why aren't you talking? What happened? And why were you so mean to Mel?"

"So many questions," he mumbled. "How does he handle this?"

"How does who handle what? Marcus, you're confusing me. Can we just stop walking and discuss the plan?"

He picked up his pace and walked faster. Chris did her best to keep up and soon found herself in a full run but had no idea where she was running to.

Then the view of the river, sparkling under the lights alerted her to their direction. Marcus stopped and scanned the area. Chris followed his gaze to see what he was looking at but could barely make out anything in the dark. All the restaurants were closed for the night, and the river drifted by silently and peacefully.

Nothing seemed out of the ordinary.

Then a tall figure stepped out from the tree with the outline of a gun by his side. In the next second, Marcus grabbed Chris by the neck and jammed what could only be a gun to the side of her head.

"Drop it, old man or she's dead."

"Let my daughter go." The unmistakable sound of her father's voice carried along the breeze.

But all Chris could focus on was the gun jammed at her temple and his chokehold blocking the air from her lungs. She quickly realized she had fallen for his lies again. "Marcus! What are you doing?" How wrong she had been about him. The moment she let her guard down, he only proved that he was using her to get to her father again. "Why are you doing this?"

"Shut it. I've had enough of your questions. Ask one more and I'll shoot you anyway."

Chris had no choice but to give in and give up.

Chapter Thirteen

MARCUS TAPPED ON THE GLASS WINDOW TO GLORIA'S BACK kitchen door. All the lights inside were off, and he figured Chris had gone to bed for the night. He should just leave her be, but what if danger came knocking during the night? She was safer with him, no matter what.

He tapped again just as a light turned on in the kitchen. A man in plaid shorts and a T-shirt squinted his way.

"Can I help you?" The man held a gun in his hand, and instant panic surged in Marcus.

"Let me in," he demanded.

"Not until you tell me who you are," the strange man said. Was he one of Vincent's henchmen?

"Marcus. Who are you?"

"Jeremy." The man unlocked the door and step back. "What are you doing back? And where's Chris?"

Marcus looked toward the stairs. "She'd better be here. I told her to stay and wait for me."

"Jeremy?" A short woman with curly brown hair stepped off the stairs. "What's going on?"

"Marcus says he came to get Chris. I thought she left."

The woman rushed into the kitchen. "You're not Marcus I mean maybe you look like him, but you're wearing different clothes."

"What? No, no, no...are you telling me Chris went with a man looking like me but wearing a suit?"

"Yes, that's exactly what I'm saying. Are you telling me you're Marcus?"

"I am Marcus Cartwright. The man that Chris went with is my twin, Lucius."

"Oh, thank God," the woman said.

"No, there's nothing to thank God about here. Lucius means trouble. I need to know where he took her."

"Took her? Is Chris in danger?"

"Very much so. Where did they go?"

The woman grabbed at her head. "I could only see them for a little while. But they went to the left. They were walking fast and then disappeared into the dark. I lost them after that. I figured she knew what she was doing by going with him, even though I didn't really like it very much. I was surprised she loved someone like that. He was kind of mean."

"That's being nice about it. And just so you know, I love her too." Marcus turned around to head back out the door.

Jeremy called after him, "Let me go with you."

"No. Stay with the women and keep that gun by your side the whole time. Got it? Don't let anyone in."

"You don't have to tell me twice. We'll be praying you find Chris in time."

"Thank you. Yes, God, keep her safe." Marcus took off in a run and could only hope he was heading in the right direction. He didn't know why Lucius would kidnap Chris by pretending to be him, but it couldn't be good. Impersonating him was one thing, but tricking Chris to go with him crossed the line.

Marcus felt for his gun in the holster at his side. If he had to use it on his brother tonight, he would. He put his hand on the butt and pulled it out. The Glock fit snugly in his hand as he kept it at the ready.

He ran through the grid of streets, hoping he wasn't running in the wrong direction. Every alley he passed, he scanned, and every street he looked up and down for any sign of movement. Every couple strolling around that he passed, he brought his gun to his side and moved closer to identify them.

Savannah had never felt so large and overwhelming.

He stopped in one of the squares just as a gunshot echoed through the night.

"The river," he said aloud and took off in a run again. Four streets over, three streets down, and two more gunshots through the night.

By now, dogs were barking and lights were turning on, but Marcus pushed himself past his limits, denying what he would find when he reached the waterfront.

Suddenly, a voice in the shadows spoke. "Boss says we need to stay out here on the outskirts. Something's going down."

Marcus stumbled to a halt while his chest heaved from exertion. He quickly pushed up against a building and out of the streetlights. "What?" He didn't know who this man was and squinted through the dark to find where he was hiding. "Identify yourself."

"It's me Freddie. What is wrong with you, Lucius?"

Lucius?

Right, Lucius is pretending to be me, he thought to himself. *Freddie thinks I'm Lucius.*

"Slow night at the theater?" Marcus tried to act nonchalant.

"No show tonight. I'm on street duty."

It was no wonder Moran was always three steps ahead of everyone else and could never be caught in his crimes. The man had men lurking in shadows all over the city. "Who's shooting? What's going down?"

"I'm surprised you don't know, being Moran's hidden Ace in the Hole. The boss is getting his daughter back tonight. Man, I wish Christina stayed away. I believed she was free. But I guess we both know freedom is a façade. Moran will always win in the end."

Hidden Ace in the Hole? Marcus did his best not to growl in anger at his brother. Lucius was his mole. Marcus glanced toward the riverfront, needing to be there but also not wanting to alert Freddie to his true identity.

"How long have you worked for Moran?" *Is there anyone in this city who doesn't?*

Freddie grunted. "It must be going on thirty years now, you?"

Marcus didn't have an answer to that question. Had Lucius been involved with Moran's dealings their whole life? Even while they lived on the west side? Even while Lucius was in the military?

"Not sure," Marcus answered truthfully.

Freddie laughed. "I understand. It's not like we're working toward a pension. We're just trying to pay our bills. Moran keeps you in the shadows. You must be pretty important to be the man with no face."

Marcus hated hearing about his brother's honored placement in Moran's business. "Do you know why I took the job?" He couldn't help asking.

Freddie grunted again. "Eh, we don't usually ask. We all have our reasons, but I did hear you were a tribute."

A tribute? As in Lucius took someone's place? *Whose?*

Two more gunshots blasted to the night, jerking Marcus back against the wall. They sounded close.

"I'm going in," he said.

Freddie stepped out of the shadows with his hands up to block him. "Directions were to stand guard and watch for Marcus and apprehend him. Once we have your brother, Toby will go and get Christina. We know where Marcus is hiding her."

Marcus pressed harder against the wall. He couldn't let Freddie see him directly. He would realize he was talking to the real Marcus. In the shadows, he thought through Freddie's statement. The man didn't know that Lucius already had Christina. But why didn't he know? And why had his brother veered from the plan and taken her early but not told Moran's team? Marcus needed to get down to the river ASAP. That's all he did know.

There was only one way to get by Freddie without raising any flags.

"There's been a change of plans. I guess you hadn't heard. Marcus took Christina out of the house. That shooting you're hearing is the boss needing our help. I'm going in."

Freddie huffed and turned toward the river. "Why am I always the last to know?"

Before the man took off, Marcus said, "Freddie, I think you should go home. I got this. Don't you have a wife?"

"Yes, and I love her dearly. Are you sure about this? Moran gave me directions to wait here."

Marcus wanted to tell him that his days of being a henchman were coming to an end, but could he really promise such a thing?

"That was before Lu—*Marcus* got word of the plan. Looks like he rushed things and caught Moran by surprise. And yes, go home. This is what I'm for. The man in the shadows. The Ace in the Hole. The man for the surprises. I'm not married. I have no connections to anyone. If I die, who will miss me?"

Marcus realized instantly what his brother had done tonight.

The tribute...*for him*. It was why Moran left him alone. First Reggie, and then Lucius stood in his place.

As Freddie turned to head home, Marcus said, "Four years. I've been working for Moran for four years...to keep him away from my brother."

Freddie put up his hands. "As I said, we all have our reasons. Be safe out there."

Marcus waited for the sounds of his footsteps to disappear and then took off in a run. He had no idea how many men were waiting and how many had jumped in to help. Judging by the five gunshots he heard, there could be a couple.

He could only hope those bullets had not found their mark.

And he still may never forgive his brother for tricking Chris into going with him. He could only hope he had gotten her to safety before the bullets started flying.

Except, as he reached the riverfront, he immediately saw that wasn't the case.

The site of Lucius holding Chris in a chokehold with the gun to her head nearly brought him to his knees.

Another blast went off, sparking a flash from the trees by the river. The shooter was hidden, and their bullet went up into the night sky. Marcus was glad he wasn't shooting at Chris, but he hated seeing his brother hold her in such a paralyzing position.

"Let her go!" Marcus shouted at the top of his lungs. His feet were practically lifting in the air as he raced into the fray.

"No!" his brother shouted back, but it didn't sound like an order. It sounded desperate. Marcus didn't think he had ever heard Lucius sound so frantic. "Go home, brother. This has nothing to do with you."

A cackle from the trees echoed and rumbled into a burst of deep laughter. "Actually, Marcus, this has everything to do with him. Get my daughter, Lucius, and bring her to me. And while you're at it, put a bullet in your brother's head. He killed my son, and now he will die for it."

The shooter was Vincent Moran....and he thought Marcus was Lucius, his Ace in the Hole, come to do his dirty work.

Marcus stood frozen on what his next move would be. He felt as though he was in the courtroom standing between the DA and the jury. He had one chance to end Moran's authority and persuade Lucius to go along with him.

"I know what you did," Marcus said to his brother. "But you don't have to take care of me anymore. You can walk away right now. Let Christina go and let me finish this."

Lucius tightened his hold on Christina causing her to choke a little. He kept the gun pressed to her temple. "You don't know what you're asking for. You will never be free again. There is no finishing it if he gets what he wants tonight."

"Bring me my daughter, *now*," Moran demanded in a lethal tone. "Kill him!

Marcus moved slowly toward his brother. "You're hurting her. Just let her go. I know you don't want to hurt her. It's part of the act."

Lucius sent him a heated glare. "You're ruining everything," he spoke through gritted teeth.

"No, I'm bringing the truth to light. No more living in the shadows. No more paying tribute to protect me. We're not some kids on the street anymore. We made it out alive, and I am not going to let either of us die tonight."

Moran stepped from the trees. His gun was in his hand at the ready. "You were given directions. Disobey my orders, and I will shoot you right now."

"I'm not killing my brother," Marcus said, turning his head a bit, but keeping Lucius in his view as well. "Take her away, Lucius. This is my fight. It has always been my fight."

Moran lifted his gun and aimed it at him. "Then you have ceased to be valuable to me. Goodbye, Lucius...no, *Marcus*." Moran chuckled with a growing grin as he realized Marcus had given the secret of identities away when he called his brother his real name. "A little game of switching places. How cute. You're right, Marcus, this is our fight. But first." Moran turned his gun quickly on Lucius and shot his gun instantly with no warning.

Lucius flew back, releasing his hold on Chris as he fell back to the ground.

"No!" Marcus ran toward Lucius and Chris. She also fell to the ground in a struggling and gasping heap.

In the next second, three more gunshots blasted through the air. The dirt and cobblestones around Marcus sprayed up where the bullets hit and ricocheted. Marcus scrambled toward Chris, expecting to be hit at any moment. Vincent was out for blood but reaching her was all Marcus cared about. Even if he died beside her. He lifted his own gun as he rolled to Chris and faced Moran. The man took aim and smiled.

"Your hand is shaking, Marcus. You don't have the guts to pull that trigger. Too bad." Moran pulled his and a gun blast louder than any other that night wrenched through the air. Marcus turned his face and waited for the final blow. But then the gunshots stopped, and all went still.

Chris grabbed at her neck and heaved for air while Marcus lay motionless beside her. Her father's shot had found its mark right in his chest. As Lucius reached for Chris, she pushed him away and got on her knees to try and breathe. Air still wouldn't go in.

"Try to breathe slowly," Lucius said, thankfully keeping his distance. Still, she waved him away.

"It's me. It's me Marcus. I promise you. I had nothing to do with this. I didn't use you. I know that's what you're thinking. I love you, Chris. Please, believe me."

Chris sat back, feeling her eyes widen in shock. Then she glanced to the left and couldn't breathe for a whole different reason.

"He's...dead," she said in a raspy voice, looking across the cobblestones toward Moran.

Marcus turned away from her to see her father sprawled in an unnatural position. His eyes were wide and still. His mouth gaped with his last breath never taken.

"But who shot him?" Marcus asked aloud, looking at the gun in his own hand. "Lucius never had a chance to take a shot, and I didn't pull the trigger."

Chris looked between Lucius and the man lying next to her. The man she thought was Marcus. Realization settled within her. "He pretended to be you?"

"Yes," Marcus said. He moved a little closer to her, but she was unsure if she was ready to receive him just yet, and her hands went up to hold him off. "I would never do that to you. He thought he was helping me."

"I was." Lucius suddenly groaned beside her. *The real Lucius.* "I had it all worked out." Lucius elbowed his way up with a grunt. He tore the dress shirt away, popping buttons to reveal his bulletproof vest beneath the suit disguise. "Come out, Diane. It's over."

"Diane?" Chris pushed herself to her feet as Diane Brodsky stepped from behind a trashcan.

Diane held a gun in her hand but not pointed at anyone. It was the evidence that she had been the one to take down Vincent Moran.

"He killed Reggie," she explained with pleading eyes directed at Chris. "When he shot Marcus, I shot him. He would have killed Marcus too. I know what it feels like to lose the man you love. I had no choice but to shoot him. I hope you understand."

"My brother didn't kill Reggie?" Chris asked, taking a step closer to Diane.

She shook her head. "I saw Vincent do it. I followed Reggie to the apartment construction site because I knew he was going to make another deal that would keep us under Vincent's thumb forever. I wanted to stop him."

Diane's lips trembled as she pressed back the tears. "But then, Reggie told Vincent that he had what he needed to put him away. Reggie told him about the misuse of funds and the poor construction. That Vincent was pocketing the allocated money instead. Reggie told him that he would never be under his thumb again. And as my husband turned to leave, Vincent killed him instantly by hitting him over the head with a glass bottle. It shattered in pieces as my husband bled out. I stayed hidden so Vincent didn't know I was there. I watched him cut a beam and run out. I think he meant for the place to cave in on Reggie. I tried to lift Reggie but couldn't. I went to find Lucius, but when we returned the body was gone. After, I tried to keep the bottle pieces in hopes it could be used to convict his murderer. But I didn't know which police I could trust. You found one of the pieces when you were at my house. I must have dropped it when I arrived home that night. I threw it away so your prints wouldn't be found on it."

"It still had blood on it." Chris remembered holding the shard.

"My Reggie's." Tears spilled down Diane's cheeks.

Chris reached Diane and took her into her arms. "I'm so sorry. How scary for you that you thought you had to flee your home in order to be safe. That you couldn't go to the police. That's not right or just."

Diane stared at Chris and touched her face. "I knew you were nothing like him. When you came to see me, I told you what evidence Reggie was gathering on your father, but you said you didn't think he was guilty. I was afraid you would tell him what I said, and I got scared and left town immediately. I was afraid Vincent would come for me next. I feared he might have seen me at the apartment site that night. But then Lucius found me and brought me back to end this forever. I didn't mean to kill him. Lucius's plan was just to get him to confess to murdering Reggie. I was here to tell Vincent what I saw him do. We were going to pretend to bargain you for the confession. You're all he wanted. I guess he cared about you in a weird and twisted way."

Chris shook her head. "He cared about control. I was the last Moran he could control."

"Still, I'm sorry we had to use you."

Chris turned to face Lucius, now on his feet. She glanced at Marcus as well. "Am I the only one who didn't know about this plan? A little notice would have been nice. My heart still hasn't slowed down." She touched her neck. "I can feel my neck already bruising."

Marcus walked to her. "I didn't know, honey. I promise."

Lucius pulled the bulletproof vest away from his chest so he could rub the spot the bullet had hit right over his heart. "That man was a good shot. I'll give him that. Anyway, I couldn't tell either of you. It was too risky."

He waved a hand at Marcus. "You're too much into your head and *the law* to go along with us." He pointed at Chris. "And you, you're a Moran. Why would I tell you?"

Chris huffed and stood tall to face him. "I am a DePalo."

"You may want to reconsider that," Lucius said with a smirk and a chuckle. "You're now a very wealthy woman. Moran never changed his will because he always planned to bring you back, whether you liked it or not. In fact, Silas only went to kill you when he went to New York City, so he could be sure he was the last Moran. He was so jealous of you. For twelve years, all he heard from his father was how you were the better child. You would be dead if you had been at home that night. But now, you are the last Moran, take it or leave it."

Tears of frustration filled her eyes, and she shook her head in denial. "I want nothing to do with his money."

Lucius walked to Diane and took the gun, pocketing it in the suit coat. "No one said you had to keep it. Let's go, Diane. We were never here. I suggest the two of you hightail it out of here too."

Marcus looked around. "Where are the police? And the rest of Moran's goons?"

Lucius had his arm wrapped around Diane and as he passed Marcus, he flashed him a grin. "The police had the night off. And the goons are all probably going home to their families. No boss? No orders to follow. They're free tonight, too. All you have to know is it's over. I'll call the body in."

Marcus stood stunned, shaking his head as he watched his brother disappear into the shadows again. "Who do you work for?" Marcus asked for the third time that night, even knowing he would never get a straight answer.

Suddenly, Chris laughed and covered her lips. He reached for her, and she ran right into his arms.

"It's over," she said against his neck. "I can't believe it's over. I'm finally free."

Marcus glanced Moran's way, and she followed his focus. The man was really dead. Marcus said, "He's not coming back from this one. Let's go."

Marcus wrapped his arm around her and pulled her close. She rested her head on his shoulder as they walked in silence, each processing the night's events.

"I'm so glad you're with me," she said, reaching for his hand. "It seems fitting that we would end this together, after, well, after he stood between us for so long."

Marcus leaned over and kissed her forehead. "I meant what I said. I love you, Chris DePalo. I always have."

Chris smiled against him. "You can call me Christina Moran if you want to. I'm going to change the meaning of the name if it's the last thing I ever do."

Marcus chuckled. "I always knew you were one strong woman, and I know you will do it. You will take Savannah by storm."

"I'm going to start with the kids in the neighborhood. Right after I pay your taxes," she giggled. "I'm going to need an attorney on retainer, and I want nothing but the best. Brodsky and Cartwright, Attorneys at Law. I hear they always win."

Marcus stopped and pulled her into his arms. "I sure feel like a winner tonight." He moved in and claimed her lips, not that she planned to ever withhold them from him again.

Chris lifted her face for only a moment. "I've always loved you too. I wish I had known you looked for me. But I won't hide from you anymore."

Marcus brushed her lips with his thumb and moved his hand to the side of her face. "Then you better not get used to the Moran name, sweetheart. Christina Cartwright does have a nice ring to it too, don't you think?"

Chris laughed as tears pricked her eyes again. "Don't tease me unless you mean it, Marcus Cartwright."

"I have never been more serious, Chris. You are it for me. You always were. You're stuck with me, and if I must debate this further, you should know I have gone eight hours straight in the courtroom without breaking a sweat. And I always make my point."

Chris looked to the skies. "I wish my mother was here to see this. She would have loved you nearly as much as I do." Chris wrapped her arms around him, never wanting to let him go again.

Rejoicing that she didn't have to.

"This feels better than any case I have ever won," he whispered against her ear. "You know why?"

She shook her head and swiped at her tears. "Why?"

"Because we let God have His vengeance and didn't take it into our own hands. He's going to bless us because of this, Chris. He avenged us all tonight, including your mother."

Chris searched the starry sky and smiled. "It's over, Mom." Looking back at Marcus, she took his hand. "Jeremy must be having a fit right now. We should get back and let them know everyone is safe."

As they made their way back to Gloria's, they noticed the lights were all on downstairs, and Chris ran up the steps to be enveloped in a hug by Mel once again.

"Are you okay?" She demanded to know.

Chris nodded and glanced at Jeremy who was fully clothed with his gun in his hand. "He's dead. My father is dead."

Jeremy put the gun away and grabbed a chair at the table. "You girls really know how to age a man," he said. "Are there any other bad guys in your past that I should know about?"

Chris laughed with Mel because he wasn't wrong. "Did we take another ten years off your life, Jeremy?"

"At least. I should've gone with you. I hated sitting here, waiting for trouble to come knocking." He looked at Marcus, "So are you the real Marcus this time?"

Marcus held out his hand to Jeremy. "Yes, I apologize for my brother. He has a flair for the dramatic. You never really know what he's going to be dressed up as."

"Sounds like an interesting fellow."

Mel interrupted, "Well, I'm so glad that you're the real Marcus. Because your brother is not very nice. I was all set to kidnap Chris myself. Speaking of which, would you come back with us tomorrow?"

Chris glanced at Marcus and put her hand out. As soon as he touched her and stepped close, she said, "Actually, I'm staying in the Savannah. Permanently. I have a lot of work I can do here. I'm needed here."

Marcus smiled at her. "By me. I need her. Please don't take her away."

Jeremy laughed, resting an arm on the table. "Oh man, I know exactly how you feel. I'm glad to see you embrace it. So, when's the wedding?"

Chris sputtered. "We haven't gotten that far. We just know we never want to be separated again."

Mel glanced at her husband and nodded. "I understand." She took a deep breath and let out a long sigh. "However, Rafe Sinclair is running the restaurant all by himself now. I don't know if he is going to be as understanding. We need to approach this with a strategic plan, or he will go ballistic."

Chris thought of Rafe's temper, and how he went 0 to 60 in 2.3 seconds. Rafe's good food wasn't the only thing hot in the kitchen. He had a temper to match.

"I hadn't thought about Rafe," Chris said, chewing on her bottom lip. She looked at her future husband with a desperate plea for help.

Marcus flashed her his beautiful smile. "Don't worry, I've been known to take care of my clients very well. I have reason to believe that a well-drawn-up agreement keeps all parties satisfied at the table. And if the man still thinks he's going to keep you, the gloves will come off and I will fight him to the death."

Chris laughed and mock-punched Marcus in the gut. "Rafe will have no idea who he's up against. It would be in his best interest to go along with the agreement, I think."

"I concur. And for the record, October in Savannah is the best time for a wedding. So what do you say, do we have a deal?"

Chris bit her lip and looked at Mel. "Can you get back here that soon?"

"I wouldn't miss it for the world. Say yes to him, or I will say yes for you." Mel beamed a bright smile, full of support and love. Mel may think that Chris saved her life, but Chris knew the rescue was mutual.

Chris faced her future husband, the love of her life. "I say October sounds perfect to become your wife, Marcus. Yes, I will marry you."

Marcus leaned in to kiss her, but a sound on the stairs pulled all their attention. Then Gloria and Sam stepped into the kitchen. They rubbed their eyes from sleep. Sam asked, "What's going on? Why is everyone up in the middle of the night? Is there a problem?"

Chris looked nervously at Marcus, and Marcus looked at Jeremy for help while Mel burst out at the top of her lungs, "They're getting married!"

About Katy Lee

Dear Reader,

Thank you for joining me in Savannah, Georgia for Chris and Marcus's journey back to each other. Even in the sweltering heat of summer, love can be found. If you would like to read Mel and Jeremy's journey, you can check out *Real Virtue* wherever books are sold. Ebooks and Print are also available on my website, KatyLeeBooks.com.

Happy Reading!

Katy Lee

Sign up for my Newsletter and receive a free short story: https://dl.book funnel.com/4p9kuzeuet

Who is Katy Lee:

Best-selling author Katy Lee has written over thirty novels, filled with romance, suspense, and inspiration. She lives in the rugged beauty of the Utah mountains where she is also a special education teacher at a school for international students. Katy has earned a Master's degree in Global Studies and Professional Writing and coaches people worldwide with their writing projects. She is also the Founder and CEO of her non-profit Story

Haven Writers, Inc. Keep up with Katy and her latest novels at KatyLeeBooks.com.

Induction

~∞~

AN AGENCY FILES INTRODUCTORY NOVEL

CHAUTONA HAVIG

To Terry

Your love of the Lord shines in all you do. I'm so grateful for the guidance, mentorship, and example you've set for the church in this town. May God continue to bless you.

Chapter One

Rockland
June 27, 2012
10:52 a.m.

HE'D DODGED BULLETS—LITERAL ONES—FOR YEARS AND without flinching. Much. So why did a stupid interview to secure his next career path... *daunt* him?

After staring at the nondescript building from the sidewalk, Keith Auger inhaled, held it, exhaled slowly, and took the steps at a swift but steady pace. No one would have noticed the half-second hesitation before he gripped the metal door handle and jerked it open. But he felt it and promised himself a stern talking-to about it—later.

A bored receptionist took his name, clattered her ridiculously long fingernails over a keyboard, and reached for a card which she encoded with something. "ID?" Only then did she look up at him. Her attitude shifted just a little as he passed her his driver's license. "Thank you, Mr. Auger. Down the hall to your left. Would you like me to show you?"

Women liked him—they always had. He didn't know if it was due to the obvious military training, the way he *didn't* flirt with them, or if he was as good looking as they seemed to think. He'd never taken the time to examine himself. Call him a coward—and he knew he was in this area—but he didn't want to decide that he came up wanting.

"I think I've got it, but if I find out I'm wrong, I'll be back."

The woman's expression changed, and only then did he realize she'd gone from frustrated to hopeful. The hopeful was obvious. Frustrated... it could have been terrified. She had a difficult face to read. "Well, I'll be here if you need anything."

Keith chose not to reflect on whether the emphasis he thought he heard on "anything" was really there. *You're an attractive woman, but the more you speak, the quicker it fades.* He would have added, "kill the desperation," but he stopped himself in time. He had no right to make that judgment.

His shoes created light echoes across the tile flooring as he crossed the sterile lobby. Fake plants, black and white photos of Rockland landmarks, lots of grays and that weird color that always seemed to be fighting within itself over whether it was gray or brown. It couldn't be a more generic place if it had been designed to be.

At the end of a ridiculously long hallway, a guard requested the pass and after inserting it into the reader, demanded his ID. A call, a few close stares, a couple of questions about who he had come to see and who had given him the pass seemed to reassure her. Awfully tight security for an interview.

Understanding hit him about the time he punched the elevator button. The layout of a Secret Service building would probably be valuable information on some market or another. And he thought the military had written the manual on security.

A woman stood inside the doorway of one of the offices—likely the woman who would decide his fate. Would he become a Secret Service agent? From all he'd been told, he'd know by the end of the day.

She couldn't be more than five-foot-two, although her obscene heels hinted at closer to five-five. Probably a hundred pounds in winter, wearing full ski gear. And a bowling ball. Dark wavy hair and equally dark eyes... Indian for sure. She had that exotic, aristocratic look that some Indian women managed without even trying. Beautiful? An understatement.

Her hand thrust out to grasp his and in the span of a single shake, Keith revised his assessment. She might be as much as a hundred-ten...

sans bowling ball, even. The woman was strong. No, she didn't squeeze the life from his hand, but he'd learned to gauge a person's strength from the way she gripped or the way he moved. Every move this woman made told a story and every one of them impressed him.

Could he take her in a fight? Most likely. He had almost a hundred pounds on her for one thing. Could she do some serious damage before he took her out? Most likely—if he were caught off guard, certainly.

"Hani Kaur. You're..."

Interesting. She didn't make assumptions. Just as he introduced himself, Keith realized. The interview had already begun. "Keith Auger."

"Nice to meet you. Please have a seat."

The office, though on the small side, felt open. The desk that housed a computer monitor and desk pad was narrower than most. Then he saw it —a lift. It had hydraulics to make it a standing desk. That's probably why the chair had been moved aside. In front of that desk sat two smallish armchairs. Round-backed. Probably crazy comfy for her. They'd kill his lumbar region in another ten years... at best.

It seemed ridiculous, but Keith hesitated between the two chairs for half a second before deciding to ask. "Do you have a preference for which chair I sit in?"

"Either is fine."

You're overthinking this, Auger.

When she seated himself in the chair opposite, Keith's throat began to constrict. Something about this didn't feel right. What was she doing?

Without preamble, Ms. Kaur reached for an iPad and began flicking across the screen. All his friends had said those iPad things wouldn't catch on. Clearly, they had here. "You have an impressive service record, Mr. Auger."

How did he respond to that? Implying he didn't would be dishonest, not to mention a great way to hint that someone else might be a better fit. But... A glance at her showed he'd taken too much thinking time already. "No more than a lot of guys. We did our jobs. Some of us were put in situations that required more from us than others faced. Had they been in our shoes..." He let the thought lay there and hoped for the best.

Those eyes widened just a bit. Surprise? Disbelief? It wasn't disgust. That one he'd have been able to detect.

"You're—"

A buzzing sound stopped her. She stared at the door, rising from her seat as she did. After half a second, she pulled her weapon from a back holster and pointed for him to get behind the desk, despite it being useless as a barrier. He'd have protested, but the look she gave him prompted obedience—against every instinct in his body.

She's your commanding officer right now. You listen. It's probably a test.

The door opened just as she reached for it. One second, he peered over the desktop, ready to spring into action and the next, a stinging gas filled his eyes and lungs. He coughed, sputtered, and squeezed his eyes shut before vaulting the desk and bolting from the room. Half a second later, he jumped back inside as a couple of wild shots rang out in the hallway. A second look showed an empty hall. Keith, coughing again, took a look both ways and saw exit signs at each end of the hall.

Perspiration dampened his armpits as he bolted for the one closest to the rear of the building. Even if they'd taken the elevator, they'd have to go out the back. No one would try to drag a woman out the front of the Rockland Secret Service field office in broad daylight.

The door to the stairwell took too long to reach. Ten seconds? It should've been five. He didn't *have* any seconds to waste if they used the elevator. Just as he reached for the handle, Keith hesitated and glanced around. No fire extinguisher. Great. There went that plan.

He dashed into the stairwell and made it down two steps before the red extinguisher registered in his brain. He backtracked, ripped it off the wall, and took the steps two and three at a time. In movies, the hero would've jumped over corners to get down faster, but he'd never done it. Breaking an ankle wouldn't end this nightmare, but it could prevent *him* from stopping it.

Just as he passed the second floor, his footfalls echoing in the stairwell, he heard fumbling and stomping above him. A glance back told him he'd better hurry. They'd gotten off the elevator before the lobby. Smart move. If he'd had time to sit and ponder like a villain in some superhero movie, Keith would likely have allowed himself half a second of a diabolical grin. As it was, he barely got the door shut and himself in position before he heard them coming.

He'd read it in a book once. Well, actually, his mom had played the audio CD on a long car trip to the Grand Canyon when he was fifteen, but he remembered it well. An old lady spy at a compound in Italy and karate chops to the neck, one invader at a time.

With the extinguisher in one hand, ready to brain the guy, and his other hand ready to jerk the jerk out of the way, Keith waited. *Please don't let them push her out first.* He'd do it—conk her over the head with it if she happened to appear first. There wouldn't be time to prevent it. But she'd end up with a concussion. Still, better that than kidnapped.

The door pulled open one centimeter at a time. The guy looked left first and stepped forward just a bit more as his head turned. Their gazes met, but before the guy could call out a warning, Keith slammed the fire extinguisher down on his head and jerked him out of the way.

A new thought hit him just as the door pushed open further. The next one *would* be Ms. Kaur. Great. But it was too late. He pulled his blow as much as possible, but she dropped to the ground with the same, sickening crack of the head as the last guy. *Should've dropped her on him.*

Footfalls on the stairs told him the other guy had taken off. Keith didn't have time to waste.

He hoisted the unconscious woman over his shoulder in a fireman's hold and rushed for the back entrance. Someone called for him to stop, but since he didn't know who that was, he kept going. He'd get her far away, make sure they weren't followed, and then take her to an urgent care —maybe in one of the little towns around the loop.

Too bad he didn't know what they were, how to get there, and which ones had decent medical care.

As he slid her into the back seat of his '39 Packard, Keith winced at her goose egg. *So much for that job.*

~

Hani groaned, opened her eyes, and at the sight of a world that seemed distorted by a psychedelic filter, closed them again. A voice—a familiarish one—said, "Did I see you move your eyelids?"

The recruit. He'd gotten her out. Impressive. "Yes." As much as she hated to admit it, even to herself, saying more than that would probably make her moan. *Never show weakness. Especially when you're half the size of your target.*

The car lurched left and accelerated, only to come to a near stop a moment later. A peek left showed the man clenching his jaw and gripping the steering wheel while attempting to bore holes in the rearview mirror with laser vision or something. *Are they behind us?*

When the light changed, he shot forward and around a car, passing on the right. Impressive. She hadn't thought he'd do that. A moment later, she slammed into his seat.

"Might want to buckle up. I didn't have time."

Never would've guessed. Hani wouldn't have smiled exactly, but feeling her sarcastic side emerge told her she'd be okay. "Why does my head hurt?"

"Conked you with a fire extinguisher." He glanced at her in the rearview mirror before adding, "Sorry. I tried to pull it when I realized they'd push you out next, but it was too late."

"And where are we?" Hani couldn't look out the window. That still did wonky things to her vision and her equilibrium.

"No clue. Don't know the city. So far, I've managed to evade these guys three times, but they always find me again. I kind of have a conspicuous car."

That's when she saw it. Wood trim by her hand hinted at a car from the forties or fifties. Why hadn't she known what he drove? Hani squeezed her eyes in an attempt to clear them. *He'd been driving a rental. Didn't we look to see if he owned a vehicle?* She thought they had. Why couldn't she remember?

"I decided that I needed to get us out of the city, but every time I get near an onramp, I see something that makes me think we're being followed." This time he shot into a parking lot.

Nooo... easy to get boxed in!

But he didn't, he managed to squeeze between two vans and wait. "I think I lost them before I turned in here." The guy (what was his name?) turned to look at her. "Can you look at me? I think you'll probably have a concussion."

Even as he peered into her eyes, his hands fumbled in the glove compartment of a car built when women probably still wore gloves to church on Sundays. He pulled a Garmin from within and plugged it into a cigarette lighter—all without taking his eyes off hers. Hani eventually closed them, needing a steadying moment.

"Yep. Concussion. Sorry. This is good, though. I didn't trust myself to stop driving long enough to try to get my GPS going." He sounded truly apologetic. Interesting. That went on a mental inventory.

"How will a GPS help you evade these guys?"

"It won't. But it'll help me figure out where I am and am going once I do."

Good.

Someone climbed into the van to Hani's right, and the man growled. "Wasn't ready to take off yet, but here goes."

Before he could put the car in reverse, she climbed over the seat and pulled the buckle tight around her. Her stomach clenched, head swam, and her eyes... well, if they ever worked right again, she'd be grateful.

Three empty spaces appeared when the van backed out and drove away. Her rescuer (she really needed to remember his name—or ask!) backed out as well, took off around the back of the building, and flung the car into reverse as he reached the corner. "I don't think they saw me, but there's a car just sitting there. No idea if it's them or not, but not risking it."

"How'd you see them?"

Tires squealed as Keith missed a hatchback by mere centimeters.

"Gas tanker to the right. Reflective." The car swung around, and the driver of the hatchback flung a rude gesture at them and screamed obscenities as they passed.

"He's not happy."

Hani snickered. She couldn't help it.

Back on the streets, she tried to get her bearing, but he changed directions wildly. Someone needed to teach him evasion tactics. As he veered around one corner, sped through an alley, and went right back on the road he'd been driving down, she held on tight. He might just get away with it. Their pursuers would expect someone with skills and try to predict moves based on prior ones. No one could predict this guy. He drove like a taxi driver in a bad movie—skilled and scary.

Throbbing above and to the left of her right temple sent her hand fumbling and prompted a gasp of pain when fingers made contact. Her self-appointed chauffeur hissed a, "Sorry." He broke off what else he might have said and began watching the rearview mirror in earnest. "Might be a different car now or a citizen. It's hard to tell. How many are there? What do they want?"

"Don't know."

Something in her tone must have fired off alarm bells because he slammed on his brakes at a yellow light and stared at her as cars screeched to stops behind him. "Okay... do you know how to get out of the city without using the loop?"

She did... didn't she? With pain still shooting through her, Hani closed her eyes and said, "Don't get off city streets until you know you've lost them. It's harder to take someone out in a crowded area."

"Good point." After a second glance at her, he shot through the light half a second before it turned red. A car that had tried to gun it through a yellow screeched and swerved, nearly colliding with a median.

Hani's head slammed into the window when he swerved to avoid a car pulling out into traffic and saw red, then white, before blackness consumed her again.

Chapter Two

Fairbury
June 27, 2012
1:10 p.m.

"... SUCH A MOUSE. I DON'T GET HOW SHE LANDED HIM. SHE'S just there— no personality, nothing."

Standing near his usual table at Marcello's, Roman Simon listened to his employees discuss their opinion of his wife. He'd heard it all, and it never became easier, but Anna always shook her head, smiled that special smile she reserved only for him, and said, "Who cares what they think? If you love me, that's all that matters."

Maybe he shouldn't, but he did care. Even his mother, the wonderful woman that she was, had asked the night before his wedding, "Are you sure, Roman? Can you be happy with someone so bland?"

At times like this, he wanted to stand on the rooftops and shout his triumph. They had no Anna—no one did. She was his—better than that, he was *hers*—which made him the happiest man alive.

~

Anna Simon had overheard the comments as well and smiled when she saw Roman stiffen. He'd be livid. At least once a week, usually on Wednesday, he came home raving about some perceived injustice against her, but she didn't care. Roman loved her, just as she was, and always would. In her experience, few women ever felt the beauty and security of the knowledge that a man loved them unconditionally. That luxury was reserved for a select few—women like Anna who were patient, chose well, and nurtured their relationships with the care of a gardener in a conservatory.

In the restroom, Anna brushed the wind-tossed curls into perfect waves and adjusted her dress. The temperatures outside soared to miserable heights, but she'd come anyway. It was what she did. Roman managed Marcello's, Fairbury's nicest restaurant, and she supported him in his goal of buying out Philip Marcel. They'd almost reached the goal. Any day now.

Every Wednesday, she walked the four blocks from their small flat, took a seat in the corner of the room, and waited to order until Roman could spare the time to eat with her. Sometimes they ate within minutes of her arrival, the food appearing before her without any idea of what he'd chosen. Other times, she waited an hour or more until the lunch rush was over, and he could sit. On those days, Roman usually gave the table a one-fingered tap as he passed—a signal for, "Order for me; I'll be here soon."

Today, the restaurant was only half-full, so Roman would have ordered by now. She shouldn't keep him waiting. With a last glance at her reflection, Anna decided she looked nice. Her hair was tamed, her dress fit well, and her face clean—just how he liked her.

Roman stood at the table, waiting impatiently. She'd taken too long. She hurried to the chair he held for her and sat down, an apology on her lips before he could reach his own chair. "I'm sorry, Roman."

"Don't."

She played with the plain gold band on her left hand. The server who filled their glasses would take that apology in all the wrong ways. Once the woman left, Anna tried again. "I *am* sorry, Roman. You have so little time, and I wasted it."

"They'll be talking about how I've made you cower for a thirty-second wait."

Her smile never reached her lips. With infinite control, Anna hid her amusement perfectly. Roman would be mortified if he could see how his glowering demeanor made him look like the monster everyone assumed him to be. "Let them. We know better. I made you wait, and I am sorry for it. Their opinion shouldn't change my good manners."

"Next time, apologize at home if you must."

She'd never thought of that, but Anna made a mental note. She offered him *the look*, that one only Roman ever saw as she leaned forward and murmured, "I'll do that."

The room faded into the background as he smiled back at her as if saying, *Message received. I'll hold you to it.* The moment evaporated when he said, "I ordered you the grilled salmon. You need more fish, and it is excellent."

"I may need more fish, but you know I don't like it." She inserted no recrimination into her tone, no complaint— just a simple statement of fact as she waited for their meals to arrive.

Lauren, their server, spun in place and returned to the kitchen with their basket of bread. A glance at Roman showed he hadn't noticed. Good. Anna could just imagine her ranting about his boorish domination of his wife or what a doormat she was.

While those in the kitchen speculated about whether he was physically abusive at home, Anna considered the fish situation. The restaurant staff all knew of her aversion to fish, and he'd just made himself look bad in their eyes. She'd fix that.

Lauren returned with their bread *and* their salmon plates. Roman rebuked her for failing to keep the flow of the meal to the restaurant's standards, and Anna used that opportunity to take a bite of fish. Closing her eyes, she forced a smile onto her lips and said around the mouthful, "This is so good, Roman!"

Her husband's look of incredulity was only slightly overshadowed by the disgust on Lauren's face. "Really?" Roman and Lauren asked in near-perfect unison.

"Definitely. If I knew fish could be this good..." Without finishing her statement, Anna took another bite and closed her eyes again as if enraptured with the flavor of her least favorite food.

Lauren left to refill glasses, present patrons with their checks, and presumably to sneak into the kitchen to share the latest with the staff. Roman waited until they could not be overheard and then asked, "What are you doing?" He took a bite and shook his head. "This is good, but it's not that good."

"No, but now they have nothing to gossip about, do they? They all know I don't like fish."

Comprehension lit a spark in Roman's eyes. He set down his fork and gazed at her. "You are too good to me. I didn't think about that when I ordered it."

"It's fine. I'm thankful that you care enough about me to order what I need." It took a moment of chewing, swallowing, and washing it down before Anna added, "I get what I want almost all the time. Getting what I need is good for me sometimes."

The salmon really was delicious. Roman chewed each bite, savoring flavors and congratulating himself on having one of the best chefs in the Rockland area. Out of habit, he scanned the room, watching for customers who needed attention, others that might cause trouble, servers goofing off or dealing with difficult people. One couple struck him as... out of place. That was the only way to put it. The man would've looked like any businessman out for a business lunch if the woman with him hadn't been a little too perfect and definitely overdressed for the occasion.

Clueless or that full of herself? She's dressed for a cocktail party on a Wednesday afternoon.

A few furtive looks their way told him customers had noticed the awkward moment with the salmon. Roman could've raged at himself for putting both of them in a bad public light— again. How did she do that? How did Anna always know what people thought and how to make him look good? He'd tried. For years, he'd tried to show the world what a treasure he had and what they were missing. The world never appreciated her.

At that thought, Anna looked up at him and smiled. He knew— without any hint of a doubt—that she'd read his thoughts. "Thank you for lunch," she whispered. "It's my favorite hour of the week..." She allowed her lips to turn up slightly before adding, "...days."

And just like that, the meal was over. He held her chair and walked her to the front entrance, kissed her much too briefly, and stood watching her walk away. Hands in his pocket, heart in his throat, he whispered a prayer of thanksgiving to a God he neglected more than served for a wife such as Anna.

A glance at one of the windows showed Lauren watching Anna's trek down toward the market, a scowl on the server's face. He could read her thoughts (he'd heard them vocalized often enough). *That silence was probably some kind of dressing down for daring to hint that his choice of fish wasn't superior.*

What the silly girl—she might think of herself as a *woman,* but she didn't know what the word meant—didn't know is that Anna probably had her head ducked to avoid the wind and lost in thought about what she'd make for their late dinner. It was her way.

Anna dreaded Wednesday nights. He knew it. But this one would be different. Roman fingered the simple, folded piece of paper in his pocket. Tonight... he'd go home without it, and that would change their lives forever. *Roses. I should order roses, too.*

Chapter Three
〜

Rockland
June 27, 2012
11:59 a.m.

THE NEXT WORDS HANI HEARD WERE, "GONNA LOSE YOU THIS time!" She sure hoped so. Her rescuer took a hard right into an alley and circled the block. Excellent instincts.

The people chasing were good, but as she became more aware of her surroundings and of his reactions, Hani began to feel as though he might just get them out of this despite their pursuers' manpower and obvious training. Too bad a wave of nausea sent her scrambling for the manual window roller. "Got a barf bag?"

Even as he reached behind her seat, Keith said, "I didn't think my driving was that bad."

As if to prove him a liar, she hurled her breakfast into the bag as he slammed on his brakes in the middle of a four-lane city street and began reversing. "What...?" She spat out the vile stuff and continued. "Do you think—?" Centrifugal force flung her against the window, causing another wave of nausea. "—you're doing?" They spun backward into an alley, and she heard the distinct sound of metal crunching and glass breaking.

"Other than costing me a fortune, avoiding a roadblock." He reversed the whole way down the alley without hitting another object and pulled onto a side street. Then the guy laughed. "We're near the transportation hub. I'll put this in long-term parking and rent a car. We'll be out in thirty minutes.

Hani said nothing. She waited for him to navigate the crawling traffic near the car rental area, waiting for them to be overtaken and blocked off. Their pursuers would grab her at the first opportunity. Still, even if leaving him behind was in the cards, Hani couldn't have done it. He'd really walloped her. *You'll pay for that one, Auger. Keith! That's your name.* Keith *Auger.*

~

Fairbury
June 27, 2012
3:52 p.m.

Philip Marcel wore an inscrutable expression when Roman stepped into the office. "Got my Florida condo paid for?"

Though grinning inside, Roman just nodded and pulled the check from his pocket. "Last of the down payment. The funding from my loan should be deposited tomorrow, and Renee already started the lease transfer on the building."

"Still plan to buy it?"

"As soon as I pay off this loan."

Philip Marcel filled the office chair, his buttons straining over his stomach. In a month or less, he'd be browning shirtless on a Florida beach somewhere, but until then, humanity was saved from the assault of mealy-white belly.

"With your skills, that'll only take a couple of years. Then you and the wife going to start that family?"

Roman nodded. "I hate making her wait, but our little place isn't anywhere to raise a child. Kids need room—a yard and a safe, quiet street. I can't give them that yet."

"She's a good woman to stick by you. Everyone can see how much she loves children."

He'd heard it a hundred times in nearly as many ways. No other woman would've given up her dreams to put up with a brute like Roman. Marcel wouldn't say it—not yet. But when the papers were signed and finalized, Roman expected a "word of advice." The man actually thought he'd be helping, too. Idiots. Everything he did was to make life easier and better for Anna, and she knew it. A couple more years wouldn't make them too old to be parents, but it would make full-time motherhood a financial possibility. That made all the difference.

Marcel's expression faltered. "Look, Roman. I've got another offer—a better one. And it's cash up front."

"Yet we have a contract." The words blurted out before Roman could consider the wisdom of them. *But really, you get your money tomorrow. Maybe not as much as whatever this offer is, but we have a binding agreement.*

"Right, right. I'm not trying to get out of it. But this offer..." He swallowed hard enough that Roman could see the man's chins wag with the effort. "It's from some tough people. If they don't get this place from me, they'll be hounding you. I just think—"

After a sigh, the man shrugged. "I can't sell this to you without you knowing there's this hanging over it. Wouldn't be right."

Roman glanced around the office that would soon be his. A few things would go—the fake marlin on the wall, the oversized desk that only ensured piles of invoices and receipts didn't need to be filed until the piles began to topple, the ancient computer...

"We have a contract. I've paid as promised, and I expect you to honor it."

Marcel locked his gaze on Roman. A stare down commenced and ended a second later. He looked away. "I'll give back everything if you want out. I bet Hansen over at The Coventry would consider selling with the right offer."

"Send your other offer to him, then. Marcello's is my restaurant now." The weight of what Marcel *hadn't* said prompted Roman to hesitate, but he'd worked too hard not to fight for the business he'd resurrected from near bankruptcy. "If you try to renege on our agreement, I'll sue. Do the people who are pressuring you really want that kind of legal scrutiny?"

A knock sounded on the door, and Roman stepped back. "I'd better go ensure everything is running smoothly in prep for tonight's service. Saw another of those odd couples out there. I need to see if anyone noticed anything unusual."

The almost former owner of Marcello's winced. "Do that."

Overpowering aftershave assaulted Roman as he opened the door. Philip Marcel's antithesis stood there. "I'd like to speak to Marcel."

Go ahead. Just stay away from my dining room, or you'll ruin the flavor of the food. At best. With the constant increase in sensitivities, he'd probably be dealing with an allergic reaction.

The dining room was nearly empty—only Chief Varney and that author, Alexa Hartfield—sat in one corner, Miss Hartfield scribbling notes as the chief described something or another. Outside, a large black Lincoln SUV sat parked across both handicap reserved spaces, and two men stood there, arms folded over their chests. Was it his imagination, or was one wearing a shoulder harness for a pistol?

~

Rockland
June 27, 2012
12:29 p.m.

The cat and mouse game had gone from ridiculous to something altogether more terrifying. At every turn, someone pulled in behind Keith and stuck like glue. All through the maze of Rockland streets with glass-fronted skyscrapers and historic brick buildings mingling in beautiful incongruity, he prayed. What else could he do? The moment he thought he'd shaken one car another took its place. He had to figure something out fast.

A glance at Hani showed her clutching her head and fighting to open her eyes again.

And get her *medical attention.*

That reminder did it for him. Failure wasn't an option. He couldn't do anything about the way his car stuck out like a hillbilly in overalls at the opera, but he could find a way to hide them until— Keith slammed his

491

palm against the steering wheel and gunned it to the next light. A glance left showed the driver's window down and he leaned across to roll down his passenger window. "Hey! Know where the nearest hospital is?"

A blonde turned to sneer at him, hesitated, and then smiled. "Sure. Up two lights, take a left, and follow the signs."

"Thanks!" Keith shot through the light the moment he saw the cross traffic slow for a yellow. Someone gunning it to beat the red nearly sent them crashing into the oncoming traffic, but his bumper only got a brush, and Keith didn't stop. The cars behind him caught up by the second light, but when he gunned it for the hospital entrance and down toward the ambulance bays, they turned.

A paramedic waved him off, yelling at him to get out of the area, but Keith ignored him. He stopped in a no-parking zone and shoved the car into park. If he could've vaulted the car, he would have, but a mad dash around the front got him there at the same time as the irate man.

"Hey, you can't—"

"She's got a concussion—"

"Hardly an excuse for blocking the bays for other emergency vehicles! Get this car out of here!"

Keith shoved Hani into the man's arms, waited to ensure the guy didn't drop her, and hurried back to the driver's seat. "Get her inside and don't let her out of your sight. Someone's been chasing us."

Never had Keith had to reverse down such a narrow space, but he managed. A few laps around the enormous building had him parking in Dr. Gravestone's (could there be a worse name for a doctor?) space. Hopefully, the good doc had the day off, but surely their pursuers wouldn't be trawling the staff parking lot for his car.

Not for the first time that day, Keith rued his decision to purchase the Packard. *I should've bought a Honda Civic. Or a Corolla!*

The sprint back to the ambulance bay left him with a sweat-soaked shirt. Or maybe that had been the last hour of his life. Keith didn't know anymore. The minute he shoved his way through the emergency doors, a security guard grabbed him. "You the one in the bays?"

"Yes. Where'd they take Hani?"

The guy would've begun a dressing down (and a well-deserved one), but Keith didn't have time for that. He shoved past and found the reception desk. Three people stood waiting to hand over clipboards, but he pushed his way to the window and said, "The woman with a head injury —just came in. Should've been brought by a paramedic just ten minutes ago—tops. Is she safe?"

Whatever the woman behind the desk would've said stuck in her throat. "Safe?"

Behind him, someone complained. "Wait your turn."

"Safe," Keith repeated, ignoring the echoes from the others. "I told the paramedic to make sure she got in and stayed with her. *Is. she. safe?*"

The security guard tried leading Keith away, insisting he leave the building. Keith wouldn't budge. He didn't want to overpower the guy, but he'd do it if necessary. "I'll leave the minute I know she's *safe*. That's all I need to know."

A nurse appeared and pointed at him. "You Auger?"

"Yeah."

The guard clamped a hand around Keith's arm. Well, he tried to, but Keith hadn't worked out daily for years for nothing. "This guy has to go. He can't just—"

Ignoring the guard, she beckoned him to follow. "This way. Now."

All hospital sounds and smells converged on him at once as he hurried after her. How did hospitals smell like disinfectant *and* germs all at the same time? How could a place so quiet be so noisy?

Somewhere close, a child screeched protests against whatever medicinal torture awaited her. He passed a cubicle where others whispered— whispers he somehow heard despite the shrieks. The PA system called for Dr. Gravestone, and Keith groaned.

The nurse grinned. "He's a great doctor."

"And I'm hiding in his parking space."

She winced. "If his car isn't there, you could be safe, but if he's late, then you'll be towed."

"After today, I guarantee I'll be towed. Oh, well. As long as Hani's safe."

That earned him a look as she pulled back the curtain on a cubicle. "I thought maybe this was a ploy to avoid the waiting room, but..."

"Not." Keith tried a smile to soften the word, but if the look on the nurse's face meant anything, it came out more like a grimace.

Her eyes widened and she swallowed hard. That's when he realized her gaze wasn't on him but behind him. Before he could react, a quiet, masculine voice said, "Let him see that Hani is secure and then we'll leave her in your care."

"Of course, Mr. Cho."

As Keith turned, he looked past the man behind him and saw only a woman—a doctor on a mission, it seemed—flying past and a tall, muscular, nearly white-blond man with piercing blue eyes and the best natural tan he'd ever seen. *Can't be Cho. Where'd Cho go?*

The man stuck out his hand. "Mark Cho. Very pleased to meet you, Mr. Auger." While Keith gaped like a teen at the random appearance of her celebrity crush, Mr. Cho pointed to the cubicle behind him. "Check on Hani—good instincts there—and then come with me."

Compliance wasn't an option. The security guard had been joined by two more and made their way toward the little group at the end of the Emergency Room hall. He couldn't fight his way out of four men, even if he were willing to leave Hani alone with them. "Yes, sir." The response came naturally, and Keith could've head butted himself for it.

Instead, he stepped into the cubicle and eyed Hani. "You okay?"

Without turning around, the doctor growled at him. "I understand you're responsible for this concussion?"

"Yes."

"Get out of here."

"It's all right," Hani began. The doctor's expression must have been a doozy because she giggled. "He's not my boyfriend. He didn't mean to hit me—" The giggle turned to laughter which made her wince. "Oooh... that hurts and sounds so bad. But seriously, I've never met him before today. He rescued me, okay?"

The man turned and stared at Keith. Now *this* guy looked like a Mark Cho should look. "Do me a favor."

Keith winced but nodded.

"Never rescue me."

Hani laughed... or howled. Both, really. Watching her mirth-induced pain prompted his own wince. "I'll go now. Sorry about the fire extinguisher."

"It put—" she gasped between chortles and whimpers, "—a real damper—" Again, the wincing giggle. "—on our—relation—ship." This time she clutched her head as she gasped out each word, laughing and moaning at the same time.

Keith left.

Mark didn't look amused—not at first. But a second glance at the guy's eyes gave away repressed amusement. *Maybe I'm not dead, then.*

One elevator, four floors, and two long halls later, Mark led him into a small office. He sat at a desk, gestured for Keith to sit down, and pulled a sheet of paper from beneath the desk pad. "Read this. Read it carefully. Then either sign or walk out the door and don't return to the Secret Service office again."

Keith picked up the paper and began reading. Blood drained from his face, his head swam, his eyes blurred, and his lungs threatened a strike. He closed his eyes and prayed harder than he ever had in Afghanistan.

Chapter Four

❧

THE RED GLOWING NUMBERS BURNED INTO HER EYEBALLS until they switched over to 3:00. Anna swallowed down panic that had kept her company for the last three hours and picked up her phone. A sticky note pressed to the nightstand showed the number for Roman's boss. She'd waited as long as was reasonable before calling—far too long, actually. Willing her fingers to remain steady, she punched in the number and waited. Philip Marcel would be asleep. It might take a few—

"'llo?" The drawled-out tone could be sleep-induced, but she thought he sounded drunk.

"Mr. Marcel? I'm sorry to bother you at this hour, but Roman isn't home, and he isn't answering his phone or the restaurant number. I'm concerned."

The man muttered something about going away and disconnected. Anna stared at the phone, swallowing bile, and dialed the number she should've called hours ago.

A monotonal voice answered. "Nine-one-one, what is your emergency?"

She'd practiced what to say for three hours, revising until she sounded reasonable and so that she wouldn't get a "he's not been gone for twenty-four hours, so we can't do anything" response. "I was wondering if an officer is available to do a safety check for my husband. He hasn't returned from work, and with the recent crimes in Fairbury, I'm concerned."

"What is his place of business?"

"Marcello's. He should have left there by midnight—one o'clock at the latest. He'd be walking home about then."

"I'll send Joe round to check on him and then over to your house... Mrs. Simon?"

The wonders of living in a small town where even the emergency dispatchers might know your name. "Yes. Thank you. He's probably fine —phone died or something, but..."

"Doesn't hurt to check. Just give me a minute... there. Joe's on the way. And don't hesitate to call. These guys get bored at night. Gives them something to keep them awake."

"Thanks... Gayle?"

"Yep. See you at St. Michael's on Sunday."

The wait began. She pulled the covers back over her side of the bed and went out to pour another glass of lemon water. She didn't want it. She'd consumed half the pitcher already. But it gave her something to do, and Anna craved activity to keep her mind occupied.

Just as she'd have reached for the dishcloth, Anna stopped herself. She'd already scrubbed the kitchen—the fridge, the stove—all of it. For that matter, she'd scrubbed the tiny bathroom with its delft blue tiles and sunny yellow towels. She'd also vacuumed the furniture in the living room with little care for their neighbors.

Now she walked a path around their entire apartment. Kitchen to living room, bedroom to bath, back to the dining nook—straighten the vase of roses Roman had sent—and back to the kitchen again. A glance at the wall clock showed it was five minutes after three o'clock. It would be at least ten more minutes before she heard anything... wouldn't it? Her pacing resumed with a new stop added. At each pass near her glass, Anna took a sip of lemon water.

A sound out front sent her racing for the door. She threw it open, ready to pounce on Roman for making her worry, only to find that fireman from across the way. What was his name? She couldn't remember. The man blinked at her and turned away. "Might want to rethink going outside dressed like that Mrs. Simon. Goodnight."

The words made no sense... until they did. With a face hot enough to heat the room (unnecessary tonight), Anna slammed the door shut and scurried off to the bedroom to put on something decent in case Officer Joe arrived. What was his last name?

Maybe it was ridiculous, but Anna focused on trying to remember the guy's surname as she stripped off the skimpy nightie she's worn for Roman and pulled on a skirt and T-shirt. "Feldman? Feinstein? Friedman?"

It was no use. Her mind refused to work.

Instead, she resumed her laps around the apartment. The couch pillows got fluffed again. She moved the coasters to the table by Roman's chair so he wouldn't have to get up to get one, and on the next pass moved them back. He didn't like clutter on that table. A bit of grit beneath her foot prompted her to hunt down the broom.

The doorbell zinged, and the dustpan flew from her hand as she stared at the door. Had they always had a doorbell? She couldn't recall. When it zinged again, Anna rushed for it. Her face fell as she opened it to find Officer *Freidan* standing there. *That's his name. Freidan.*

"Mrs. Simon?"

She nodded.

"May I come in?"

It took a moment for the words to register. "Yes, of course. Please. I'm sorry. The doorbell..."

"Did I wake someone?"

"No... no. I—" Anna didn't continue. They probably already thought her crazy enough. She didn't need to admit she'd forgotten the existence of a doorbell that she now remembered wiping down every week, despite the fact no one ever used it. "Did you find Roman? Is he all right?" Dumb question. His presence gave her the answer. "No, of course. What do you know?"

"Maybe you should sit down..."

~

Rockland
June 27, 2012
1:12 p.m.

"Are you telling me that this was all a test?"

Mark smiled and offered Keith his choice of water, coffee, or soda. "Jerm can go get you an energy drink if you like. Something to eat?"

"I'd prefer an answer to my question." It was a bit pushy, but come on! He'd just spent nearly two hours rescuing a woman from her coworkers and risking damage to his Packard.

A bottle of water appeared on the table before him, and Mark seated himself before replying. "Consider it an interview."

"An interview?"

The man's nearly white eyebrows rose and fell like the breathing machines in hospitals. *Odd analogy, but it fits.*

"We used situations as our questions and your reactions were your responses. We liked what we saw and want to hire you."

"Who is we?" Yes, the question sounded weird, but Keith couldn't even figure out why with all the other questions shoving each other out of the way to be next out of his mouth.

The chair Mark leaned back in had to be top of the line. Keith knew because he sat in its twin, and he'd never been cradled by anything so comfortable in his life. *Sorry, Mom. But it's true.*

"I suppose we is me. I own The Agency."

"And what do your... agents?" It seemed a reasonable assumption, and Keith continued after Mark's nod. "What do they do, exactly?"

"We protect people until law enforcement or other government agencies can remove threats against them."

The impressive-sounding words fizzled as Keith translated them. "You're bodyguards."

"Of a sort." Mark templed his fingers under his chin and eyed Keith. "As are some Secret Service agents."

Score one for the glorified bodyguard boss. Keith chose to ignore the jab and wiped a bead of condensation off the teak tabletop. "And you said you work with law enforcement? How?"

But Mark was already shaking his head. "No... I said that we do our job while law enforcement or other government agencies do theirs. Our job is to keep our clients alive. Theirs is to remove the threat."

"And... isn't that something the Marshal Service could handle?"

A flicker of a smile formed. "You would think so, yes. However, not all of our clients would be comfortable trusting their secrets to those agencies."

That took another moment to translate, but when he did, Keith didn't like it. "You protect criminals from other criminals?"

Mark pulled a water bottle from a cooler and cracked the lid, all without rising from his chair. "Sometimes. More often than not, however, we protect people who discover they've been involved in crimes without their knowledge and request our help to extricate themselves from that situation."

When his next question fired off almost without him thinking, Keith couldn't help but wonder who was interviewing who. "So... rich people."

"Sometimes." After a pause, he added, "Again, more often than not, but we do not refuse to help those unable to pay. It's why our fees are... substantial."

"Why have I never heard of 'The Agency'?"

"We don't advertise our existence, Mr. Auger. One reason we are so successful is our anonymity."

It made sense... and it didn't. "If you don't advertise your existence, how do—oh." Keith felt like an idiot. "Those government agencies send you clients?"

"Occasionally, but not generally, no. I'm afraid I can't tell you more about how things work without a legally binding contract."

That made no sense. Keith knew that Mark couldn't be naive enough to think that any contract held up against a barrage of court nonsense these days. All it took was someone to contest some wording, claim verbal agreement, or put forth myriad other nuances, and the costs would rise until one or both parties chose to settle. So what did Mark *really* mean?

Keith tried leaning back in the chair and giving an air of nonchalance as he pondered the idea. In the end, he pulled his chair forward, leaned his elbows on the table, and asked, "What would the job look like?"

It had seemed like a simple, straightforward question. Instead, three hours and a large bag of Chinese takeout later, Keith thought he had a picture of his potential future. On some days. The salary offered was generous but not so over the top that he found it suspicious. Considering possible sleep deprivation, no predictable work hours, and the danger involved, it was only a little on the high end of reasonable.

What he hadn't expected was an appeal to his faith. "I won't pretend that you being a Christian doesn't make you an ideal candidate. We want you for your military experience, your quick reflexes, your critical thinking skills, and a few other things, but I won't pretend your faith didn't play a big part in why we chose you."

First, he didn't know how they knew about his faith, and while he wasn't ashamed of it, the knowledge did unnerve him a bit. Second, he didn't like feeling like a company talisman. "Why?" There. That was direct enough and probably didn't show his unease.

"People find comfort when they can talk about spiritual things—especially when they are in danger. You are known for not pushing your faith onto your fellow Marines but also for being willing to discuss it with those who wish to. That will be valuable for our clients."

So basically, I'm a combat chaplain of sorts.

It was only when he finally spoke the words aloud and Mark grinned that Keith realized he'd agreed to the job.

∼

Fairbury
July 5, 2012
10:23 a.m.

The sun beat down, relentless. With record highs punishing the entire Rockland area, Fairbury residents stayed indoors and tried to keep cool. Anna left the sanctuary of her cool apartment and stepped into the muggy morning. As she'd done every morning over the past week, Anna turned toward the north end of town and the little police station.

Her mind insisted that the trip would be as futile as it had been every other day. The previous night's trip just before the fireworks display had been particularly silly. Like the police would be looking when they had double the population in town for the Fourth of July celebrations.

Despite all that, Anna's heart refused to listen. She'd go. She'd ask. She'd implore them to keep searching, and she'd leave again. Of all the things she'd read on message boards, staying in contact with the police was the best way to ensure that the case didn't go cold.

Walking down the street in the heat of the morning, Anna could only be thankful that the rising temperatures kept most people indoors and far away from her and her from their prying, accusatory eyes. She'd heard the rumors. How Roman had left her for someone less bland, less of a door-mat. Others said she'd killed him, and her daily treks to the police station were required to keep her out of jail until the police found proof—as if that's how things worked.

But in a small-town rumor mill, no one cared about law, procedure, and logic. They cared only for a good story to feed its ravenous appetite. It reminded her of the sacrifices to Molech in the Bible. At what point did people hand over their souls for that kind of garbage?

She pushed open the station door and stepped in. Officer Freidan and Chief Varney were in deep discussion about her case, while Officer Crane tried to WD-40 the squeaks out of a metal cabinet door. Still, even over the screeches and groans of the metal hinges, she heard every word.

"—not right. Marcel says he deposited the check but never got the rest of the funding for the restaurant."

The chief stroked a goatee he didn't possess. "Think he took off with the money?"

"Money's waiting for transfer. It needs Anna's signature. Marcel wants out of here and is ready to sell to the next bidder if something doesn't happen. There's something wonky there, too."

Logic said that following a money trail might lead to whoever had taken her husband. And someone had. She had no doubt about that. But why? The money? Did they want the money and take him the minute they knew the funds would be released? Did they, whoever "they" were, just assume Roman wouldn't have her on the paperwork?

She sighed. Of course, they would. People always assumed the worst of him. Anna let the door slam behind her and stepped forward. "Any news?"

Both men turned toward her. A glance at Officer Crane showed the woman grinning. *You knew I was listening and didn't stop them. Why?*

"We're following leads," Officer Joe said. "We'll—"

"Let me know when you learn anything. Anything like the fact that Roman didn't take any money, no clothes, nothing? Learn that? Learn that anyone who took him wouldn't get anything out of him? Learn that? What haven't you learned? Oh, I know..." Inside Anna screamed each word at them, but she forced her tone to remain calm but firm. "You haven't learned who *took* my husband." Her voice broke on the last word and tears coursed down her cheeks.

Anna could've shot herself. She'd done so well for so long, desperate to keep her grief private, but it refused to be held back any longer. Great, heaving sobs ripped through her, and she collapsed to the floor before any of them could reach her. Her heart screamed, *Find my Roman!* Even as her mind taunted, *He's not coming back.*

Chapter Five

Rockland
July 7, 2012
11:48 a.m.

Of all the things Keith had expected to do once he became a civilian again, occupying a bland room in the most comfortable chair he'd ever sat in and reading fake dossiers, evaluating hypothetical (or so he assumed) situations, and perusing case summaries wouldn't have made the cut. When the words swam together for the dozenth time, he jumped up and dropped to the floor, doing pushups until his arms screamed. The door opened, and he rose. As he acknowledged Mark's entrance, he guzzled water.

"Finding it hard to concentrate?"

So many sarcastic retorts tried to jostle for position as the winner, but Keith squashed them and tried for something remotely intelligent. "I'm just trying to balance being physically and mentally fit. One thing I can't see is how many cases you deal with each..." Something in Mark's expression changed the direction of his sentence. "Year."

"In other words, how much of your job will be like your first day with Hani, and how much will be like this?"

Busted. Keith shrugged and sat back in his chair. "Something like that."

"No way to tell." At his obvious frustration, Mark laughed, but there wasn't much amusement in that laughter. "Look, Keith. You need to know that a significant amount of your job will be out in the field, watching, waiting, moving, hiding, running—doing whatever it takes to keep the client safe. The rest of your time will be sitting around waiting for those moments or training for them."

Keith ignored that last part. He heard the words "significant" and "running," and his thoughts clicked into gear. "So... living on an adrenaline high."

"Much of the time, sure. Except when you're not."

"Are there supplements for it? Something to keep from killing my adrenals? Especially with the interrupted sleep?"

A slow smile spread across Mark's face. "I knew I was right about you. We've got a high-quality cocktail of supplements that we provide."

As much as he wanted to ask for them now, Keith decided not to. Instead, he nodded and went back to studying the case he'd opened before his last push-up drive. Two words stopped him cold. He reread the entire thing, stopping at them again. *Involuntary extraction.*

It couldn't be real. It couldn't be. How did Mark and his agency even know about someone being in danger if they weren't hired to protect that someone? This case had to do with a teenager being groomed by an online predator. One of the agents he hadn't met yet, Anthony, had shown up at the girl's after-school job at an ice cream shop and just tossed her in a van while another agent continued to pretend to be her while the police coordinated a meet up. It only took three days, but that poor kid must have been terrified, not to mention her parents.

Keith rose, determined to talk to Mark about this. It hadn't been in his job description when he'd signed all the non-disclosure forms and received a rundown of what his duties would be. Protecting people was one thing. Doing it against their will and breaking the law to do it was a whole 'nother ball of wax, as his grandmother had been known to say. He froze, pondering. What did that even mean?

His gaze met Mark's before he took a step. The man hadn't moved. He just stood there, watching Keith. *And you didn't even notice. Some agent you'll be.* Keith decided to ignore that part and cut to the chase—so to speak. "Involuntary extraction?"

"Not that common, but it happens sometimes."

"How?" That might make all the difference. He hadn't finished the case notes. Maybe it wasn't what it seemed.

Mark leaned one shoulder against the wall and slid a hand into his pocket. "Elaborate."

"That's what I'm asking you to do." Yeah, it was a bit... another grandmother word popped into his head. *Churlish.* So it was a bit churlish, but who could blame him? "You're asking me to violate someone's personal agency and potentially break the law. I need more than 'it happens sometimes.'"

Mark watched him for a moment. "Did you finish the report?"

Without answering, Keith kept reading. The kid had started off a fighter—certain that *Anthony* was the predator. She'd nearly gotten away twice and had been terrified the whole time. Bile rose in Keith's throat as he read and tried to imagine what a teen girl would think about someone just taking her.

As he flipped the last page to read the client's statement, he found it hard to breathe—hard to read. Each word became a struggle, but there it was in black and white.

I was so afraid when Anthony took me from Nice Cream. Terrified. But he was great, and now that I've read what Billy was really doing with girls like me—now that I've talked to others who weren't so lucky—I just want to thank him and the other agents for making that call. It's not right to take someone against their will. But it's also not right to sit back and let people hurt other people. I wouldn't have listened. If you'd told my parents, I would have just run away.

A statement from the girl's parents followed. Most of it was similar to what she'd said, but the father's final words pierced through chain mail Keith had been assembling all morning. *I guess what I'm trying to say is thank you. If you'd come to us with your concerns, I'd have blown it off or been certain I could deal with it, and Nita might be lost to us forever now. Just make sure you don't choose to take someone because it's easier than convincing them to come because they should. If it isn't life or death, it isn't right.*

"Between you and me, Keith... our first involuntary extraction nearly died because I waited too long to make the decision just to take her. The ex-husband sent an assassin after her."

Maybe scoffing wasn't a good way to impress your new employer, but come on. An assassin?

"I know. It sounds melodramatic, but her death needed to look like it came from a rival organization rather than her husband. He stood to inherit a lot of money and power if she died and lose everything if he walked."

"How'd you know he even existed?"

Mark hesitated as if trying to decide how much to share. "Ultimately, it came down to the assassin saying something he shouldn't have to someone who knew what we do here *and* knew the wife would never believe it. Taking her was the only way to save her life, and waiting cost me one of my best agents."

Keith's heart pounded. "Someone died?"

"Injured trying to get her out when the assassin wasn't looking. He's in a wheelchair now. If Karen hadn't been there to help..."

That should've solved everything—reassured him that these things were necessary sometimes, but Keith just shook his head. "I've got to pray about this."

When Mark stiffened, Keith tried to explain, but Mark didn't give him a chance. "Pray fast. I think we may have a situation, and it could mean your first case kicks off with an IE."

Only once the door had closed and Keith stared at the report again did he realize what IE was. *Involuntary Extraction.*

~

Fairbury
July 8, 2012
1:37 p.m.

Someone had been in her house. No doubt about it. For half a second, Anna had been convinced Roman was home, but then she saw it. The bedroom window raised half an inch. She hadn't left it up, and Roman never would. He abhorred waste of any kind... especially energy waste.

A yowl in the backyard sent her pulse racing as she jumped, hesitated, and raced back out the front door, her purse bouncing on her hip with every step as she bolted from her yard and back toward the town square. But where to go?

She hadn't been to the police that morning, but she'd promised herself she wouldn't—not until tomorrow. Sure, the groups said she needed to keep reminding them that someone was watching and cared. But a small town like Fairbury had a close-knit, almost familial approach to law enforcement. If she kept up the hounding, she'd drive a wedge in there. A couple of days would at least show she respected them, and with the holiday festivities and everything, they'd be busy.

But an intruder...

A car pulled up just a couple of yards ahead of her and a man got out. The way he watched her approach sent shivers down her spine. And then she saw it. What *it* was, she didn't know for certain—only that his clothes didn't fit as they should, and he'd stepped forward as if to speak to her. Anna spun on her heel and dashed up the steps to the apartments there. An older woman lived in the downstairs front apartment, and she'd let Anna in.

Before the guy could follow, Mrs. Ginsberg opened the door and grinned. "Good morning, Anna!"

Without giving the woman the chance to invite her in, Anna stepped around her and pushed the door shut. A moment later, she slid the dead-bolt in place, too. "Sorry—"

"What's going on?"

Anna pointed at the narrow windows that flanked the door. "Out there. That man. I think he has a gun... or maybe a knife. He scared me."

Mrs. Ginsberg peered through the window and jerked back. "He's coming to the door," she hissed.

Get out. She had to get out before the man knocked. "Just answer the door as slowly as possible. I'm leaving."

"But—"

With a quick hug, Anna dashed through the apartment, out the back door, and through the common patio space to the gate that led to the building next door. One by one she dashed through them until she neared the end of the street. There she slipped into the alley and ran as fast as she could down one alley, across a street, and down another. When stepping out by the town square showed the car circling the square, she leaned against a tree and panted.

You were right about the exercise, Roman. I need more. As the car neared, she slipped behind a tall rhododendron and made a mad dash for the street that led to the police station. No doubt about it. Someone was following her.

Twice she had to dive behind a lilac bush as she raced down Center Street. The car never slowed, though, so the men must not have seen her. By the time she arrived at the police station, she was hot, perspiring from more than the heat, and disheveled. *Probably have twigs or leaves in my hair.*

Officer Martinez stepped forward. "Mrs. Simon. We were just on our way to pay you a visit."

"Have you found him? Roman! Is he all right?"

"No..." The officer shot a look back at the chief and officer Freidan. "However, we have found enough evidence in your finances to warrant an arrest." He stepped around the counter and looked a little regretful as he began his speech. "Anna Simon, I'm arresting you..."

It couldn't be happening. She came to the police for protection and this? *You'll be safe from those men in jail, but it wasn't what I had in mind...* Something about the sarcastic thought struck an off-key chord in her heart. *I must be in shock. Why else would I be so ridiculous?*

The experience couldn't have been more surreal—or terrifying. Through every step of the process, Anna watched as if outside herself. The way Judith Crane walked around with pursed lips. She obviously didn't agree with the decision to arrest Anna. The way Joe Freidan showed respect and kindness even as he fingerprinted her and asked her, for what seemed like the millionth time, if anyone could corroborate her story that she hadn't left the apartment the night Roman disappeared.

And then it hit her. "Did you say you were arresting me for... *murder?*"

Joe shook his head, glanced over at the chief, and turned back. "No...

for fraud, although charges may be added if evidence of your involvement in your husband's disappearance is found."

Fraud. That didn't make sense. A lawyer. She needed to ask for a lawyer. But when Anna finally got the words out, Officer Joe just smiled and said she'd be able to do that when they got her to Brunswick. "The questioning will begin again there, so it only makes sense to save your lawyer and us some time."

Something about his words didn't ring true, but Anna just nodded.

Just as they led her out to the cars, she saw the chief pick up a phone.

Chapter Six

Fairbury
July 8, 2012
2:04 p.m.

NEVER HAD KEITH AUGER SAT IN A RESTAURANT WHERE A couple occupied every table. He'd been told to expect women dressed for a cocktail party, despite it being two in the afternoon, but the women all looked ready for a board meeting at a Fortune 500 company. He, on the other hand, sat alone at an intimate table in the corner, squirming. At any moment, a woman would sit at his table and expect him to... what? Flirt? What did men do with hired escorts... aside from the obvious? At least he'd be rescued before that. They said.

His "date" would stand out like a sore thumb when she arrived. Or would she? The moment he'd thought it, one of the women nearest him leaned over and dabbed at the corner of her partner's mouth with a napkin. Her blouse, which had looked so very circumspect half a second before now spilled open and exposed... far more than Keith wanted to see.

His gaze darted left, avoiding the scenic vista and saw something similar occur when another woman dropped her napkin. Throat drying faster than raindrops on cracked desert ground in July, Keith shifted his gaze once more and then it happened. One by one, table after table, the seduction played out as if this weren't a public place. Nauseating.

And it's your turn next.

He'd quit. That's all there was to it. He'd have to quit. Undercover cop hadn't been part of his job description, and he could be seen! Someone could see him with whatever woman showed up next, and there went his reputation. It was the antithesis of what he thought he'd signed up for. *Privacy, secrecy, hiding out...*

Mark's instructions finally broke through the disturbing scene around him. *"Watch for how the staff reacts. Are they comfortable? Are some comfortable and others not? Is anyone acting like staff who clearly isn't?"*

Again, this felt like undercover work, which they supposedly left to actual law enforcement. Obviously not.

And now they've set you up with an escort. Great.

The flash of sapphire blue sparkles appeared in his peripheral vision, but when he looked up, it was gone. *A mirage?* No, weren't those things you *wanted* to see? *A day-mare?*

While he reflected on the waking nightmare he'd predicted, a man, presumably the manager, caught the attention of a server and murmured something to her. The girl... did she swallow hard? By the look on her face when she turned and walked toward him, yes, she had. A second glance at Mr. Manager proved the guy most definitely wasn't the *restaurant* manager. Not unless the latest trend in hospitality was protecting your guests with armed employees.

Whatever was going down here wasn't good. And Keith wasn't trained to deal with it.

A woman entered and sashayed in his direction. It was the first woman he'd actually seen walk, which might explain how he'd been taken in by the others for so long. While most of her hair was up in a bun, a curtain of smooth bangs hung over half her face. "Librarian glasses"—what they were really called he didn't know—stood out in a room of perfect eyebrows and eyelashes so long they couldn't be real.

He rose to greet her, his vocal cords freezing. She giggled and allowed him to hold her chair. *Lord, what am I* doing *here?*

But the moment he resumed his seat and tried to introduce himself, the woman tucked her bangs behind one ear and pulled off her glasses. He blinked. Something about her was familiar.

The server took her drink order—white wine. Great. He didn't do alcohol and wouldn't start now—not even for Mark or this job. She waited until the server was out of earshot before saying, "It's nice to see you again, Agent Auger."

Hani.

In that moment, a dozen little tidbits flashed through his memory. The way Jerm (the guy's real name was Jeremiah, but he went by *Jerm*) couldn't stop smiling that morning. The arrival of a box for Hani just as he was leaving. Hani hadn't been there... or so he thought. A couple of snickers as he passed through the door to Mark's office. The way Mark wouldn't look at him.

Only one thing didn't fit. They'd expected cocktail dresses. Had they not told him or...? "Did you come with a backup dress?"

She grinned. "Good catch. No, I just went into the restroom and turned it inside out. Chewed out their bouncer over there, too. If they're going to call in someone on vacation, the least they could do is update her on the new protocol." She waited until the server approached with a wine glass, took their orders, and disappeared before adding, "I think me chewing him out is what saved me. He was totally suspicious."

Keith shot a glance in the guy's direction. "We might need to play on that sooner rather than later. He seems to be talking to someone on the phone."

Though she didn't actually say it, he could almost hear the expletive explode from her. "Great."

His phone buzzed, and Keith pulled it from his pocket. A simple text read:

> Get out. Leave Hani. Call in now.

Heart thumping, lungs filling as if he'd jump headfirst into icy water, Keith rose. "Got a call from work. Have to go. It was nice to meet you."

With that, he strode from the restaurant, praying bouncer dude (that really was a better description for the guy) didn't take it out on Hani.

Never fear, he heard her scathing comments even as the restaurant door slammed shut behind him.

The Lexus he'd been assigned blipped as he unlocked the door from twenty feet away, and Keith paused only long enough to hit call and speaker before backing out of the parking lot and taking off down Main Street. "What's up, Mark? Oh, and I'll get payback for that little restaurant stunt."

Only half a chuckle came through before Mark spoke words Keith had been waiting for. "We have an extraction."

~

Fairbury
July 8, 2012
2:29 p.m.

The surreality of each second as the officers led her out the door and to the cruiser both distanced Anna from what was happening and imprinted scenes in her mind at the same time. Judith scowling at the chief. Chief Varney speaking low into his phone, his eyes never moving from his officers as they led her from the building. The emptiness of the street as they pulled onto Center Street and headed to the highway that would take them to Brunswick. Joe Freidan's apologetic gaze in the rearview mirror.

Eight miles outside town, the cruiser slowed. Joe frowned as he came to a stop. In seconds, his gun was drawn, and he ordered her to lie down in the seat. "What's wrong?"

"I don't know. Just stay low, or I can't protect you."

Comforting. The police, who were at present taking her to jail, couldn't protect her if she, handcuffed in the back seat of their locked cruiser, didn't lie down and... what? Pray? She'd start there.

Less than a minute later—maybe half a minute—the back door opened and a man peered in. "Want out of there?"

"I don't know..." She sat up and looked at him. "Do I?"

"Well, I would if I were you, but we have to be quick."

Anna shifted her gaze to where Joe spoke to someone on a phone. Despite his calm exterior, she could see the seething below the surface.

This was one unhappy cop. She snapped her attention back to the man. "Who are you?"

"A guy sent to keep you out of jail. Right now, you have a choice. You can come with me or go to jail. Later, that choice will be up to someone else, and you might not like it."

"Go to jail or go with a stranger..." She shook her head. "Such attractive options."

He grinned and offered his hand. Though she still hadn't decided if she'd risk a yes or a no—both seemed equally terrifying—Anna took it in both of hers.

Officer Joe strode over and shoved the phone into her "rescuer's" hand. "I don't like this."

"I don't either," the guy said. "But I like the idea of her being vulnerable even less." He turned to Anna. "We have twenty seconds tops for you to decide. We've blocked the road too long already." As if to prove his assertions, the sound of an approaching vehicle made both men stiffen.

Anna looked at Joe. "Would you go?"

She could see it in the man's eyes. He wanted to say no, but he nodded. "I don't know what's going on, but as much as I don't agree with it, I trust the chief, and he says for you to go."

That's all it took. Anna followed Keith to a silver Lexus and slid into leather seats as soft as butter. Once he'd backed out and waved at Joe, who flipped a ticket book shut and waved the approaching car past, he shot down the highway back toward Fairbury.

"Did he give you a ticket?"

Keith shook his head. "Just creating the illusion that *he* stopped *me*... um, *us*."

"Who are you?"

When the man didn't answer, she shivered. When he turned onto Main Street, ripples of fear began at her toes and worked up her legs. When he drove past Marcello's, Anna decided she'd lost all hope of rescue. She'd been duped.

"Hani's gone, I think. Good."

What that meant, she couldn't say, but the guy just turned around and headed back for the highway. The next forty minutes passed in silence broken only by her unanswered questions. However, everything shifted when he pulled off the road onto the rest area outside Rockland. A woman in cut-off jeans and a graphic tee stood leaning against a blue Miata. She pushed away as her so-called rescuer pulled in beside her.

"How'd your first extraction go, Keith?"

Well, at least she knew his name now.

"Not too bad, although I don't know if Mrs. Simon would agree with that."

"She came. That's good." To Anna the woman said, "Hi. I'm Hani."

Anna shot a look at Keith. "The woman you said was gone—back at the restaurant?"

He nodded, and Hani shot him a look that relaxed into a smile. "Great instincts. I want you covering my back anytime." She turned her attention back to Anna. "Know what he did the day I met him?" Without waiting for the obvious answer, Hani continued. "He conked me over the head and took me off on a wild chase through the city."

The few nerves that had been reckless enough to relax, zinged into overdrive. "What?"

"It's why we hired him."

You people are crazy. And I'm basically your prisoner.

"Let's go!"

Anna held out her hands. "Can I get these things off?"

Keith started to apologize, but Hani shook her head. "When we get to our safe house, I'll be happy to. It's safer if you are handcuffed for now. Sorry."

How do I ask for jail instead? Just put me away.

Chapter Seven

Covedale, Ohio
July 8, 2012
7:14 p.m.

WHILE HANI UNPACKED THE GROCERIES, ANNA WANDERED around the house. The woman didn't show... anything. Didn't say much. In fact, Hani had never met a blander person in her life. What had Roman Simon seen in her? Then again, her dossier said locals thought he was an abusive husband, so there was that. Abusers liked doormats who would take their garbage.

She pushed veggies into crisper drawers, wondering what Anna liked to eat. All they knew was she didn't like a lot of heat and she didn't like fish. Never had she gone into a protection case with so little information on a client.

Hani also wondered what Anna thought of the house. From the outside, it looked like every other seventies suburban tract home that surrounded it. Well, less pristine than a few that had been renovated, but not shabby enough to attract notice.

Inside was a different story. Mark was, one by one, updating all interiors of their "getaways" as he liked to call them. They'd break him of that... someday. This one had comfortable furniture, a casual mix of decor and "personal items," and even photographs (most stock photos, of course) strewn across the mantel.

It also had keypad locks that Anna couldn't operate without a code that Hani would likely never give her. The minute she realized that, Anna might grow a backbone. Clients needed to resist restraints. It was good for their mental stability.

"This is a nice place. Do you come here often?"

As she pulled a bowl down to fill with fruit, Hani shook her head. "Can't tell you. It could be my usual home, or this could be my first actual visit here. It's just not information I can share."

Anna didn't seem bothered by the answer, or rather the *non*-answer. "Are we in Cincy? I thought I recognized The Great American tower just a bit before we turned off."

Not good. She should've insisted on a panel van. They worked best for transport. Clients shouldn't know where they were in case something slipped in a conversation with family. If they found Roman, she'd want to hear his voice, and...

"Hani?" Anna stared while Hani arranged the fruit into some semblance of art. Okay, so it was more like kindergarten finger painting art, but food decor wasn't part of her job description. Before Hani finished, the woman sighed. "Oh. I get it. You can't tell me. Of course. If I know where I am, I could let it slip if I got to talk to Roman or my mom or something."

A wobble on "Roman," belied the woman's calm. She might come off as flat as a fast-food pancake, but that old saying about deep water... or whatever it was. That looked like it might be true.

In an attempt to hide how firmly Anna had nailed the situation, Hani waited until she'd put every bit of fruit in that bowl before she said, "Oh... right. Yes. We're outside Cincy. For now. We probably won't stay more than a few days at most. Hopefully, by then they'll have your husband safe and the guys responsible in jail."

"At least one person doesn't think I killed him anyway."

The words didn't do it. The expressionless tone and features did. Anna couldn't have been more wooden than a John Wayne cutout on an old western set, and it startled Hani into dropping a bottle of olive oil onto the floor. With a crash that echoed through the house, glass and oil mixed as they slid across the ceramic tiles.

Anna jumped and screamed with all the intensity of a woman in labor —or at least a horror movie... or was that the same thing?—just as the back door flung open and a man entered, gun drawn. Before Hani could call out a warning, he dashed forward, headed straight for Anna.

～

Brunswick
July 8, 2012
7:14 p.m.

It was a scene ripped from bad TV. Keith stood next to his trainer in a house in Brunswick and waited for the test run to begin. *I'm so gonna fail this.*

"Remember," his tranq trainer said, "you can't possibly get them all right. It's a lot of calculating in a brief moment. That's why your holster has two guns. Pick the right gun for the situation without getting hit yourself."

Speaking the obvious. Why didn't instructors know that it only made everything *worse*?

When he turned to ask a question, Keith found himself alone armed with one weapon holding empty tranq darts (was he seriously in some alternate *Alias* reality?) and the other, an air soft pistol. His mission? Get Mark out of the building by stealth or neutralization. The only appropriate use of the air soft pistol—if someone pulled his or her weapon.

The enclosed entry porch offered the security of time, but in a real situation, he wouldn't know if his client had that luxury. Keith drew both weapons and prayed he'd use the right one at the right moment. After hesitating, he swapped the pistol to his dominant hand. Better to have dominant for backup if a dart went wide.

He peered through the side of the window and saw one guy in the corner of the living room drinking something and relaxing. Keith would be able to get two darts off on that guy before he even reached for a gun. Tranq there. A shuffle to the other side of the door showed nothing.

And that was the worst of it. There could be one guy in this place or a dozen. He had to be prepared for any and all of it. After a moment of thinking, he opted for recon. Military training doesn't die hard, and preparedness mattered. The extra thirty seconds should be worth it.

Only once he stepped outside the porch and onto the walkway did Keith realize his mistake. He moved like a guy on the prowl. A glance up at a window on the house next door showed a woman moving back and forth. It took a few precious seconds to realize she jostled a crying baby.

Great.

That did it. He strolled as casually as he could to the back door, took the steps in a single bound, and pulled it open. A quick look inside showed no one, so he pretended to wait for someone to tell him to come in—just in case someone was looking.

And yes, he felt like a complete idiot.

A cellphone rang somewhere upstairs, and Keith could hear low voices —more than one. On speakerphone or someone else in the room? Was Mark in there or...? That was the problem. He couldn't be certain.

Keith stepped inside, slipped through the kitchen, and took out the guy in the chair before the man could get out a shout. With a thumbs-up, the guy pulled his ski mask over his face—the one with large white X's over the eye holes to make him look dead. Jerm's doing. Keith would bet dinner for the whole crew on that. The kid had a weird and wicked sense of humor.

A quick scan of the downstairs showed no one else. He took a deep breath and exhaled slowly. Next up... the stairs. Killer zone if ever there was one. In a real scenario, he'd have backup in case he got taken out, but here he was the only thing between life and death for Mark. So to speak.

Keith opted for three steps at a time. Once. The old stairs were high and steep, leaving him more unbalanced than he'd like. Two at a time got him to the landing. He looked up and saw a guy's back to him. *What, are you guys taking it easy on me?*

He fired a tranq dart. With a "Hey!" the guy stumbled, and the second dart sent him reeling. Whatever he mumbled got lost in the conversation and the sound of him falling.

The appearance of someone else in a doorway killed the easy motion.

Keith fired and missed. The guy aimed, fired himself, and then shut the door.

Keeping quiet didn't make sense anymore, so Keith rushed up the steps, jumped over a guy with a (no joke) ski mask embroidered with closed eyes and fluttery eyelashes. He couldn't help but grin. *Jerm needs a raise.*

A gun blast rang out followed by, "Side door near the hinges!"

Keith called back, "Miss. And you're a dead man going for me like that." He shoved the tranq gun into the back waistband of his jeans and winced when it missed the holster. He'd have to confess that one later, but he did take three precious seconds to holster it properly. *How do guys in the movies do it?* Gangbangers just shoved them in the front of their jeans—a quicker draw, but no guy wanted to de-junk that way.

He shuddered—just as another blast hit the door. This time, he knew where it was and called out before the gunman could call out position, "Miss. Even I saw that one coming." As he spoke, he kicked the door open, firing three times in quick succession.

The guy dropped to the floor in a cartoon-like over-dramatized collapse and pulled the X mask over his face. Mark hopped up and ran to him. "Let's go."

Isn't that my line?

But there he was, rushing after his boss like a devoted puppy. At the car, Mark demanded the keys. *Still part of the exercise?* Keith wasn't sure. "Um—"

A few choice words flew out as Mark demanded the keys. Keith tossed them, trying not to wince. Out of the Marines for less than six months, and he'd already gotten used to a curse-free life. Mostly.

The moment they tore out of the development and onto the highway, Mark said the words Keith had been dreading and anticipating since the day he'd signed his contract.

"You have your first assignment."

∼

Covedale
July 8, 2012

7:22 p.m.

A gun pointed right at her. Anna froze, her startled scream cut off by sheer terror. Just as the gun swung left of her head, the man went down with a crunch, a pop, and a yowl that should've signified a cat fight in the alley. Hani snatched up a towel, but instead of using it to strangle the intruder, she dropped it onto the floor near him and leapt onto it. "Saul! You okay?"

"You know him?" Anna's question came at the same time "Saul" demanded a medic team.

"Can't get up. It's gotta be torn." The guy swore. "I'd rather have a break."

A glance at Saul's ballooning, awkwardly-angled knee and the blood pooling on the floor beneath it sent the room spinning. Hani screamed, "Sit down, Anna! Now!"

Anna sat. Right in the middle of the wide-plank flooring. Not even on the area rug.

"Head between your knees."

She looked up to see Hani trying to reach into the freezer. The room spun again, and as Hani scooped several bags of frozen veggies onto the floor, she caught Anna's gaze and shouted, "Now!"

Anna's head dropped between her knees, and she did feel better almost immediately. Doubting that Hani would be able to understand her, Anna asked, "Who is that?"

"Our backup. He probably heard the crash and scream and thought someone came in."

Apparently, the guy's groan was in the affirmative.

"I'll call Mark. He'll have someone here in no time. Meanwhile, I need to clean up enough of this that people can move safely."

That was something she could do. Anna stood, waited for another wave of dizziness, and moved forward when it didn't arrive. "I'm fine now, and I can clean up this mess."

"It'll take forever." Hani might not admit to wailing... but she did.

Anna shook her head. "No...fifteen minutes tops. Where would I find flour?"

Hani shook her head. "Don't have any."

"Salt or baking soda?"

Hani nodded. "Pantry to your left."

A bag of confectioner's sugar stopped her short. What pantry had powdered sugar but no flour? A box of cornmeal called to her, too. *With that, I could almost fry up corn crispies...*

She started with the cornmeal. Some ended up stuck to Saul's leg and Hani's shoes, but Anna flung it over the mess until the box emptied. She moved onto the box of baking soda next. "Got a squeegee?"

Though Hani was busy talking to "Mark," Saul shook his head. Then he froze. "Wait... I think there's one in the shower."

By the time a team arrived to take Saul off for medical evaluation, Anna had cleaned up the kitchen and gotten dinner started—all while Hani protested. Not enough to stop Anna, of course. But she'd protested, nonetheless.

Hani prowled the house, watching her phone, the neighborhood, and security cameras—in that order. When a call came through, Anna only heard snatches of the conversation. Words like, "torn ACL" and "possible dislocation."

Possible? They'd all heard the pop. They'd all seen how Saul couldn't move half an inch without writhing. They'd all seen the way it looked bent out of shape. Sure... it was *possible* that the knee wasn't dislocated just as it was *possible* that Roman had left her for another woman.

Her musings fled when she heard Hani say, "Send Keith. I want him."

The guy who rescued me from a lifetime behind bars? Okay. I can get behind that.

"—know, but he has good instincts, and I can tell Anna trusts him. That's big. I need him ASAP, though. Use the chopper? We've drawn a lot of attention to ourselves. Good call with the ambulance. Bet Mike's guys weren't happy to hand it over, though!" A laugh filled the room, and Anna turned back to the stove. Everything was fine. Just fine. Hani was laughing, dinner was almost done, and Keith would come.

Next, maybe they'll find Roman. Her chest heaved and her throat constricted. *Alive.*

Chapter Eight

Covedale
July 8, 2012
11:14 p.m.

KEITH SHOULD'VE BEEN THERE AN HOUR AGO BY HANI'S calculations. To be fair, those calculations were best-case scenario ones where Keith left from the helipad on the Mayflower Building where The Agency's offices were nestled among actuarial tables and other insurance... things. What did an insurance company need a skyscraper for, anyway?

The security system kept fritzing, forcing her to enter the code every twenty or so minutes. It was enough to string her nerves up and leave her dangling. Anna, unable to take her pacing, watching, and general bad attitude, had given up reading *Moby Dick* and opted to take a shower. Probably to get away from her.

Aaand... that adds another half hour to three hours depending on where Keith actually was and if they brought in a chopper. He'd gone to the Simons' apartment to fill a bag for Anna. Hani didn't even have to send Jerm, the office manager and computer genius, a text to know that. The extraction had been a last-minute thing. No time to grab essentials, so poor Anna had to deal with too small bicycle shorts and a tank top that would probably cover her navel—if she didn't move and kept hunched over. Mark would definitely ensure she had her own things.

With that thought, Hani forced herself to sit. Relax her shoulders. Examine the room again. Something about it was off—not in a "I'm gonna getcha" sort of way but more of a design flaw. She needed to figure it out.

Or rather, she needed the distraction.

Perhaps it was the lack of a lived-in feeling. Hani glanced around the room and nodded. That could be it. After all, no one lived in the house. There weren't half-read magazines on the coffee table—no protein bar wrappers sitting on the end table, waiting for someone to take them to the kitchen garbage. For that matter, there weren't dirty dishes in the kitchen sink or toothpaste splatters on the mirror in the bathroom.

Those were the kinds of things the house *didn't* have that it should. Well, she could fix the toothpaste problem if she brushed her teeth. She could eradicate the stale garlic taste from her mouth and add those spatters in one go.

A glance down the hall still showed a light under Anna's door. She'd been in there for ages. It felt like hours. The woman didn't want to talk. She wouldn't cry. She wouldn't yell or engage at all.

Instead, she'd cleaned up that mess in the kitchen as if she'd made it. Without a word, without complaint. And who knew that throwing stuff on top of oil on the floor would clean it up faster, anyway?

Hani did now.

It felt as though there should be a clock ticking somewhere—one of those obnoxious pendulum things that swung back and forth, growing louder and louder with each pass until she thought she'd go crazy. Isn't that what situations like this were all about? A battle with time until the call came to say all was well. They were safe.

Hani flopped onto the couch and rubbed her eyes. She wanted to sleep. She needed it—eight long, uninterrupted hours of blissful sleep.

After three whole seconds on the couch, Hani hopped up and paced through the living room again, peered through the curtains again, scoured the street for headlights. Again. Nothing. Not even a flickering streetlight.

A shadow shifted on the lawn, sending her senses on high alert. But a second glance showed nothing. The whole scenario couldn't be more ridiculous. Never had she been so skittish.

Headlights appeared and headed straight for the house. Hani tensed, her hands gripping the curtains. *You can't just drive up at this time of night, Keith. People will notice.*

It drove past without even slowing, but Hani saw him. A kid. Probably terrified of getting bawled out by dad when he walked in the door. Poor kid.

When the third yawn followed immediately after the second, Hani dreamed of sleep. She ached to crawl beneath cool sheets and drift into blissful unconsciousness. What was it like to go to sleep without wondering if you'd be jerked awake sixty-one seconds later?

What was it like to dream of something other than scenarios where people chased you with murderous intent—something pleasant. That's what she wanted. But as soon as the thoughts invaded her mind and tried to force her to consider them, Hani pushed them out.

This was her dream job. She made a difference. That's why she'd taken it. And she was good at it. She saved lives. Not every day, but definitely every month, and that mattered. Deep down. Hani knew that mattered.

But at times like this when a dog barked somewhere, when a siren wailed in the distance, when shadows shifted outside where there shouldn't be shadows... She wondered. *Is it really worth it?*

As much as she wanted to go crawl into that bed, and to try to have those happier dreams of crazy road trips with girlfriends (isn't that what normal people did?), as much as she wanted to do that she couldn't. Because down the hall, behind that door, an assignment sat in a room with nothing that belonged to her, with no idea of where her husband had gone, and with no idea what would happen next.

Worse than that, with no idea that her life was in jeopardy. At least, it seemed as though Anna really hadn't figured that out yet. And if Hani had anything to do with it, she wouldn't.

Outside somewhere, a door slammed. Her guess was one belonging to a beat-up, rusty car that probably lost a chunk of its underbelly with that slam. She could hear it even inside the house, even with the AC blasting cold air that warmed almost as quickly as it dropped into the room.

Where did this heatwave come from?

Hani peered out the window between the drapes that hung without a speck of dust, hoping it was Keith (and she'd blast him for being so loud) but saw nothing. Probably some little kid cried for her nighttime lovey left in the back seat, and dad had to go crawl out there to grab it. Mostly because he loved his daughter, but honesty would force him to admit it was also so he might be able to get sleep before work tomorrow.

Need to remind Mark that most people don't keep their drapes vacuumed this thoroughly. The guy tried, but he often forgot that the rest of the world didn't have house cleaners on retainer.

The next time a shadow shifted, her pulse rose. Hani huffed out her exasperation and strode into the kitchen. She'd make cookies. That sounded good.

Finally feeling as if she had purpose, Hani opened the pantry just in time to remember that there was no flour. Essential to delicious cookie baking. Sure, there were flourless cookies, but she didn't know how to make them and probably didn't have those ingredients, either.

Either get a grip on yourself or call out. You're no good to Anna this rattled.

Just as she closed the door, wondering what else she could make or what else she could do to distract herself until Keith got there, she heard the security system blip again. If it did it one more time, she'd take a hammer to it. Mark needed someone out there to fix that thing. Fix it and now.

She moved toward the mudroom ready to figure out how to disconnect or turn it off. Indefinitely. Hani froze next to the fridge and wasted precious moments noting the irony. But then it happened again—a shifting shadow and this time it was inside the house.

Ugh, why did I leave my gun on the coffee table? I know better! Getting careless cost lives, and she'd gotten careless. When was the last time that had happened? *Rookie days. That's when. Get your head in the game!*

~

Covedale
July 8, 2012
11:22 p.m.

. . .

Keith pulled up four doors down from the safe house and sagged before another burst of adrenaline coursed through him. He'd have to learn to control it again. With a large duffel slung over one shoulder, he made his way up the dark, tree-lined sidewalk. Clouds kept the moon from view, which he appreciated—right up to the moment that he tripped over a root growing up through the concrete.

Two steps later, something else tripped him up. A man pulled up in front of the house across the street and dashed over to the garage opposite —the garage Keith had every intention of entering himself. His heart pounded as he slid behind the nearest tree and craned his neck around it.

The man took a few furtive glances around him before vaulting the back fence as if it was a track meet hurdle. Impressive. And dangerous.

Also, Keith decided after failing his own attempt, embarrassing. He scrambled over while ordering himself to practice fence jumping. Who knew it would be a job requirement?

If the intruder hadn't made such a point of not being seen, Keith would've assumed he just had the wrong house. Thankfully, he left the side door to the garage open. It allowed Keith to follow without having to worry about creaking hinges or air movement.

As if he'd been there a million times, the guy entered, paused to disarm the security system, and crept from the garage into the house. Alarm exploded into fury. *Not on my watch.*

Keith dashed around the car and to what should be the mudroom door. Now in action, the floor plans he'd studied ran together in his mind until he wasn't sure he had even entered the right house anymore.

Catching the door as it shut behind the intruder, Keith hesitated long enough to ensure the guy had moved away. Sweat ran in rivulets down his temple, down his back, down his sides. The hardest part came now. Getting around that door blind. Once inside, he'd be able to see what happened, but if the guy were looking behind him when Keith entered, all hope of surprise vanished.

"You're not alone in this." Mark's words came back to him. If Hani were on her game, she'd hear the alarm blip and be on alert. If not, she'd still hear if Keith called out. So as long as he could get a drop on the assassin, they'd be golden. And if he couldn't... well, Hani could keep Anna safe if anything happened to him.

Two are definitely better than one.

An idea popped up just about the time Keith pushed the door open a bit more. Feeling like an idiot, Keith stuck his hand through and waited. Nothing. He stuck his arm through. Again, nothing. With a "here goes nothing" approach, Keith slipped through the door and let it rest against the strike plate.

The intruder moved forward. He might have been cautious, but Keith saw no hesitation, no uncertainty at all. This guy knew what he wanted and would get it. *Not on my—no, our watch.*

As he reached the end of the small hallway, the guy hesitated for the first time. Keith decided that was his chance. He rushed and tackled, pinning the guy against the hard flooring. His knee protested. That'd be a bad bruise.

The man bucked, throwing Keith to one side, but before the guy could get turned around, Keith jabbed an elbow into his temple and pulled the guy's arms back behind him. "Hani!"

"Good one."

The voice was too close. Keith looked up to find her standing there, a knife glittering in one hand. He grinned. "Hi, Hani. I'm home. Got a zip tie or two?"

A groan escaped as the guy's stunned brain reengaged. Keith pulled the tranq from its holster, not as smoothly as he'd have liked, but he did it. With one quick pull of the trigger, the dart hit the guy's shoulder. "One more, right?"

Hani nodded. "Good gauge. I'll call Mark."

"Why?"

"Because you need to get Anna out of here, and Mark needs to be the one who took this guy down."

The "why" almost surfaced again, but instead, the answer came fast and hard. Police would want to check the house. Mark had connections. Keith didn't. "Gotcha. I'll go get Anna."

"Anna is right here. Who is that?"

Keith started to answer that it was someone after her, but Hani broke in. "Looks like some idiot thought this would be a good house to break into. He'll regret that for a very long time."

Wait... burglar? Really? I went through all that for a guy trying to steal a couple of laptops and the cash in the sock drawer? The non-existent cash in the non-existent sock drawer?

As if she didn't know he needed time to process, Hani continued. "You and Keith get out of here. We don't have much time. Glad I didn't go to St. Louis or Louisville."

"She's got something for the Louis, doesn't she?"

Anna grinned down at him. "Ready? I am. I travel light—as in, with nothing."

He couldn't resist. "Not anymore. I filled a duffel with everything I could pack into it from your apartment. Let's go." To Hani he added, "Are you sure you've got this?"

"Totally. Good job, Keith. Really good job."

It was just lucky—or Providential—timing, but I'll take it. "Thanks."

Chapter Nine

Fairbury
July 8, 2012
10:23 p.m.

THE COMPUTER SCREEN FINALLY LOADED, AND PHILIP MARCEL pounded the desk. No funds. Anna hadn't signed yet. He'd left four messages on her phone warning her that he'd return Roman's check. He wouldn't, of course. The contract stipulated that all payments were non-refundable in the event that financing didn't come in by the balloon payment date. He hated to see his restaurant in the hands of the Solari syndicate, but if she didn't come through in time, so be it.

Philip began stuffing thumb drives, external hard drives, financial records, and anything else he might need in a duffel. He had to get out of there before Solari's men returned. That little weasel, Leone would be back to demand he accept the deal, and Philip had no intention of being in the state much less the town.

A knock preceded Marissa's entrance. The new hostess slipped through and leaned back against the door, visibly shaken. "There are guys here. I saw a gun on one. Do I call the police?"

He pounded the desk with his fist to keep it from trembling. Marissa

531

jumped, and Philip relaxed a bit. It wasn't the woman's fault. With a forced smile, he set the duffel on the floor and tried to slide it under the desk without her noticing. "They'll want to see me. They may be taking over the restaurant."

"I thought Rom—" Marissa broke off and turned to go. "I'll let them back."

Did I give something away or did she figure it out? Bet she doesn't show up for work tomorrow.

He sat there, perspiring enough to soak the back of his shirt and, if he were honest, raising his arms wouldn't be a good idea, either. When the knock came, Philip inhaled, exhaled, and mopped his brow with his shirt-tail before calling out, "Yeah?" Might as well pretend he expected an employee.

Leone stepped inside and smiled. The guy could cause heart attacks with that so-called smile. As if to prove the assertion, Philip's heart raced around the man, his two thugs—erm, bodyguards—and out the room. Philip just hoped he could catch up with some shred of dignity (or life, he'd take life) left.

Without preamble or invitation, Leone sat and said without a shred of emotion, "It's taken care of."

Could they see him sweat? Probably. By the glint in the one guy's eye, Philip was next. He had nothing to lose. "Anna Simon's name is still on all the documents. If both of them go missing, it'll look suspicious. You can't do this."

Leone didn't even twitch.

"Where is Anna? I can't get a hold of her." It was suicide, but his tongue apparently had a death wish. "If you've killed her, too..."

There, the smile returned. Philip shivered and swiped some of the perspiration off with the back of his hand. Then Leone asked in a near whisper, "Who said anything about killing?"

What sense of self-preservation he'd retained dashed out the door in search of his heart... and probably his brains. "Don't give me that. I'm not stupid. Of course, you killed him. If you killed her, too, they'll figure it out and I'll be caught up in this mess." He leaned forward and tried to sound menacing. "I'm not going to take the fall for your—"

Leone laughing chilled him in all new ways. Hollow, pointed, and full of that thing his last girlfriend had said he was no good at. What was it again? Perspiration soaked his armpits now. Great. They'd see as it spread toward his chest soon. Stupid knit shirts.

Subtext. That laughter has subtext.

Then Leone said the last thing Philip Marcel would have ever imagined. "We couldn't kill someone who has disappeared. We don't know where she is." If anything, the smile softened. The perspiration poured down his face, and Philip let it. He couldn't hide it anyway.

"Where is she, Mr. Marcel?"

As if his body finally realized it didn't have a beating heart anymore, his chest clenched and constricted. Philip gasped for air, and Leone gave a short jerk of the head. "Help our friend to the car. He needs medical attention." As the first bodyguard came around the desk, Leone added, "Oh, and retrieve the duffel bag from under there. We'll need that."

I'm a dead man. The thought repeated itself on an endless loop as the men "helped" him from the building and into the waiting car.

~

Covedale
July 8, 2012
10:42 p.m.

The moment Mark arrived at the house, he put in a 9-1-1 call stating they'd captured a burglar in the house. "I was concerned for my friend and tackled the guy. Unfortunately, I seem to have knocked him out, but he's coming around now, I think."

Their intruder sat against the wall, slumped against the couch cushion they'd propped up next to him. The guy's eyes opened and fixed on Mark standing above him. "Who are you?"

"Followed you in. Saw you heading for my friend and tackled you."

A siren wailed in the distance.

Their intruder chose to wail in four-letter disharmony. Something about not heading back to prison. About a warrant out for him. About never making it "inside" again. Apparently, it had less to do with the discomforts of prison life and everything to do with having irritated inmates in his likely home for the next eighteen months plus whatever that warrant was for.

In the middle of an impressive string of words, a few of which Mark had never heard, the guy broke off and stared at him. "You didn't knock me down. Your voice is wrong. Arms, too. That guy had dark hair."

Ugh. "Guess you hit your head harder than I thought," Mark said. "Sorry." He raised an arm as if confessing he'd chopped down a cherry tree. "My fault. Must have..." A burst of inspiration hit him. "Seen your own arm as you went down."

Their guy stared at his arm as if he'd never noticed he possessed one. The sirens grew louder. They'd turn onto the street any moment now. That was the great thing about small towns. They usually had less crime, and with everything packed together, they also had shorter distances to travel.

Hani shuffled in an obvious attempt to get Mark's attention. She gave him an exaggerated questioning look. Turning his attention to their unwanted guest, he asked, "What were you hoping to get your hands on?"

"Place has been empty for a few weeks. Been hangin' with a guy across the way and noticed. Thought there might be—" Here the guy stopped. After shaking his head to clear it, he added in a rush, "Someone who needed help. What with the light on in here."

That was interesting... the guy had seen a light and come in anyway. A glance at Hani showed her frowning. That could only mean one thing. There hadn't been a light. Things just got more interesting.

"Who sent you?" A siren screeched up the street.

"Sent... What?" As if he hadn't spoken, the guy wiped confusion off his face and replaced it with a hard edge. "Wouldn't you like to know."

You are actually just a garden variety thief. A few choice expletives begged for the chance to prove themselves, but Mark just turned away and strode to the door to let in the officers. A woman built like a linebacker with twice the ferocity in her features and a scrawny kid who looked like he couldn't be out of the Explorer program were headed up the walk. Mark waved. "He's in here. Tackled him and he hit his head."

The kid—no worries. He probably hadn't been on more than a couple of routine traffic stops. An actual B & E was so far out of his experience that he'd be bragging to his girlfriend for days. Mark gave an apologetic shrug. "Didn't mean to hurt him. Just didn't want him hurting Hani. The guy conked his head on the wall—"

Hani broke in with a huff. "It was the *floor*..." The way she dragged out "floor" made her sound like a SoCal princess who had to point out that Gucci and Prada were vastly different companies.

"Right." Mark offered another shrug. "I was in the process of trying not to get slugged, so I must have made an assumption. Thought it was the wall."

"Floor."

Officer Jefferson glared at her. "We got it. Floor."

Their intruder's name was Jimmy Simmons, not that he offered up the information. Officer Jefferson flashed a grin and shook her head when she got a good look at him. "Well, Jimmy Simmons. My captain is gonna be happy to see you—and the back of you. This just gave you a one-way ticket back to Rockland."

Jimmy looked from her to Mark and back to her again. "I just wanted to check on a friend." He glared at Mark. "And *he* didn't tackle me. It was someone else. The voice is different, and that guy had dark hair. Or his arms did. Don't remember the face. This guy is lying."

Once again, Hani huffed and folded her arms over her chest. "Like your word means anything?" Her nose rose a couple of centimeters and a sniff followed. "You're pathetic."

"What time did this man enter the house?"

"About ten-fif—"

"Ten thirty-two," Hani broke in. When Mark shot her a look, she added with more attitude than he'd ever seen her show, "What? I looked at the clock when I heard a sound." She pointed at the knife. "I was getting that."

"All right," Officer Jefferson said. "So ten-thirty-two..."

"Whatever. I looked at my watch when I got back, and it was ten-fifteen."

Never had he seen a transformation come over anyone with such force. Hani got in his face, pushing against him with her chest and almost screaming at him. "So, you stand out there texting your little side job for fifteen minutes while some guy is trying to break in? That's how you want to play this? You're pathetic! I'm done!"

She started to storm off, but the scrawny cop stopped her. "We still need to get your statement."

"We'll do it out here, because if I stay in there with that cheatin' jerk, I'll reconsider the use of that knife." She gasped. "I didn't mean that. Ugh. What a thing to say to a cop!" And then, with the skills of an A-list actress, she burst into tears.

Even as Mark arranged his features into a sneer, he gave an internal standing ovation. Great deflection. *Bonus on your next check for that one.*

Chapter Ten

THANKS TO THE MOONLESS NIGHT, KEITH NEARLY MISSED where Grand Drive became Birds Nest Road. Anna slept beside him, her body leaning against the window of Hani's Miata. Okay, it belonged to Mark, most likely, but Keith thought of it as hers. *Definitely not mine. A guy needs leg room.*

Half a mile and on the right. Packed in by trees. He couldn't decide if he liked that idea or not. Wide open made it hard for folks to sneak up on you, but it also made it impossible for you to run and hide if they managed it. Still, he'd had about thirty minutes to decide between Kentucky, Tennessee, and Missouri. In the end, he'd decided they needed places to hide. He might miss someone coming through the trees, but at least he had a better shot of getting Anna out safe and hiding her if that happened. So Steelville, Missouri it was—right on the edge of a couple of farms but still nestled in the woods of the southeastern part of the state.

When the trees disappeared and farmland greeted them, Keith slowed

537

and made a three-point turn to head back. He'd missed their drive. Anna stirred. "Are we there?"

"Almost. Can you help look for—oh. There it is."

A "for sale" sign out by the road gave him pause, but the house looked just like its picture. No doubt. It was the right place. *Might have told me about that sign. Would've made finding it easier if someone had been following me and I needed to disappear.*

"We're staying at a listed property? Won't people be coming through to view it?"

Sharp eyes. Keith couldn't answer the question with anything more comforting than, "I'm sure Mark has it covered."

Anna squeaked as if about to protest and stopped herself. "Of course, he does. He knew when to send you to rescue me. He wouldn't send you here if it wasn't safe." Keith wasn't certain, but he thought she added, "I hope the bed is comfortable."

On the off chance there were comfy beds, Keith would be sitting at the table (assuming there was one), not reclining at all. Worst part of his new job? Solo guarding. He hadn't known it until the moment he had to decide if she would stay in the car or come into the house with him. Self-preservation demanded he text Mark or Jerm. Jerm would be better. Why wake his boss and annoy the guy with proof of his incompetence? Pride said he could protect her better if she were with him. That if they faced something inside, he'd give her a chance to bolt while he fought off any attack.

That one. As he parked the car at the front of a small, ranch style house, Keith formulated and troubleshot his plan. He passed Anna the keys and said, "Follow me and stay close. If anything feels off at all, get in that car and drive away."

"How do I know when to come back or where to go? What if something happens and you need help? What do I do then?"

The little intel he'd been given on Anna Simon had hinted at a clueless doormat. Not how he'd describe her. He dug for his cellphone and passed it over. "Only use this in a 100% emergency. You call. You tell whoever answers where to find you, then you remove the SIM card and battery. Got it?"

For the first time, Anna wobbled. She'd been crazy strong, but now... "This is real, isn't it? I'm really running for my life."

He had to get her inside before she fell apart and he had to carry her. "Yes, and you'll be safer if you're out of the way here, so let's get you inside."

As he climbed out of the low-slung car, Keith retrieved the weapon he'd tucked into his seat for easy access. In a case like this, his Glock was the best choice. He wasn't experienced enough to calculate and fire a dart in an ambush, and he'd be taken by surprise—no time for it to work. He might not want to admit it to a group that was so proud of its revolutionary research and development of working tranq pistols, but he definitely felt more comfortable with traditional firearms.

Anna took him at his word. She stayed close enough that he could feel her behind him. The oppressive muggy air promised a downpour. Great for cutting the humidity... terrible for being able to hear anything that sounded off.

A lockbox behind the coiled hose sported a few angry spiders and a combination he nearly forgot. At the third try, it popped open, but nothing would make it shut again. Anna's shiver behind him hinted that perhaps now wasn't the time for dealing with a fussy lock. *When a woman shivers in the heat of a miserable night, you get her inside where AC can comfort her and give her happy shivers of delicious cool air.*

"Once I give the room a once over, you follow me in and stay by the door. If I say run, you go. Don't hesitate. Not even to inhale. Got it?"

Without waiting for an answer, Keith eased the key into the lock and hesitated. A crane of his neck showed curtains closed at the front window. So much for a peek inside first. *Just do it.*

Stealth or surprise? He chose to barrel in with guns blazing—or they would've been if anyone had been in the room. "Safe. Stay here. He moved to the kitchen—nothing but eighties linoleum and oak cabinets, according to his pocket flashlight. The mud porch—empty. The hallway and its closet... clear. So far, so good.

In the bathroom, he nearly jumped out of his skin at an unexpected mirror behind the door. At least he hadn't pulled an Audie Murphy and shot it up. No one but he and the Lord knew he'd spooked himself. The polka-dotted shower curtain ripped aside with the brush of his hand to reveal... mold in the grout but nothing else. *Scrub that tomorrow.*

The first bedroom held only a twin-sized bed, a small dresser doubling as a nightstand, and a tiny bookshelf on the wall by the door. The shelf held a journal collection and teen girl romances. That probably explained the hot pink comforter. Maybe Anna wanted to revisit her younger self. The moment that thought entered his brain, he shoved it out. Anna had probably read Virginia Woolf or Dostoevsky at twelve, though why he thought that was something to ponder at another time.

The next bedroom was the male equivalent but with camo bedding. This bookshelf held a comic book collection and a variety of dystopian and fantasy series. Hopefully, this would be his room. Maybe Hani could have sweet romance and navel gazing.

The last room at the end of the hall must have once been a garage as well. The enormous room served as a combination bedroom, bathroom, closet, and office. No signs of anyone having been there for a while if the fine layer of dust meant anything. Relief relaxed his shoulder muscles, and Keith turned to call out the all-clear when he sensed movement.

He froze, perspiration beading on his forehead as he scanned the room. It couldn't be something outside showing through the window. The darkness didn't allow for shadows. Maybe it wasn't pitch black but...

The beam of his little flashlight swept the room again. Nothing. Had he created a shadow with it? Imagination getting the better of him? He took one step and then another, hoping to recreate the motion to assuage his nerves. Something swished somewhere. He could hear it.

The curtains, you idiot. You didn't check behind the curtains. Not that the room had half a dozen of them or anything. One by one, he advanced, flattened himself against drapes hanging on each side of a window, and then swept them aside. At the ones facing the street, something scurried across his toes, and Keith did a lousy imitation of a highland fling. His feet hopped, his flashlight flew up in the air, crashed to the old Berber carpeting, and rolled to illuminate... glowing eyes. A possum.

"Oh, come on!"

"Everything okay?"

"Know how to get rid of possums without getting bitten and contracting rabies?"

Anna's voice sounded closer. "Can I come down?"

Smart or dumb? A rabid animal could be a problem, but an extra pair of eyes while he tried to figure out how it had gotten in would be good. "Sure... but hold onto the doorknob when you get here. If it charges, pull the door shut."

Keith jumped when she said right behind him, "I don't think possums are prone to rabies."

That threw him. "Really?"

"Something about lower body temperature making it hard for the virus to live."

The threat of rabies mostly neutralized, Keith focused on examining the room. The possum now lay "dead" on the floor. Anna giggled—a bit high pitched not to be on the verge of stress and exhaustion-induced hysteria. "I knew they did that, but I've never seen it."

"Why don't you go choose a bed? I'll just close this door and maybe he'll go away on his own. Then we'll find the hole and plug it—in daylight."

"Can we turn the lights on now?"

It took a full three seconds for Keith to realize why he hadn't in the first place. "Yeah. It's clear, so it's safe."

"Good. Bathroom then bed. Don't suppose there's any food?"

Keith shrugged. "There will be something, but I'm not sure what."

Five minutes later, they sat at the table eating canned ravioli and Pop-Tarts.

≈

St. Clair, Missouri
July 9, 2012
5:47 a.m.

The sky began its slow shift from darkness to the sickly green gray of first light. Strange how sunrises always began so ugly before bursting into glorious color. Well, sometimes they just wiped away the streaky ugliness that filled the small gap between darkness and light, but even that had an impressive effect.

Fifteen minutes from Steelville, Hani pulled off I44 and headed south down North Franklin Street in Cuba, Missouri. First Hardee's then Sonic called to her as she passed, but Hani kept going. She had groceries in the car, and Keith needed sleep. Eventually, North and South Franklin became Highway 19, and the search for Bird's Nest Road began. She'd never used this house. Mark had purchased it months ago and then left the realtor's sign in the yard.

The moment she'd left the Cincinnati area, she'd felt, on and off, as though she were being followed, despite no evidence at all. There'd have to have been a team of a dozen drivers and a couple dozen cars for it to have worked. Impossible.

The feeling returned with a vengeance as she drove through the tree-dense road, past the Meramec River Resort and down toward a large section of farmland. It made no sense. There wasn't a single vehicle on the road, and yet her eyes shifted from rearview mirror to side mirrors and back again. Perspiration beaded on Hani's upper lip, and she shifted in her seat. "It's all in your head," she told herself in the same firm, scolding voice her mother used to use.

Yeah. Bad idea. Saying that aloud after so many hours of silence only made things worse.

A truck idled at the road to a farmhouse, its headlights unnecessary in the now full morning light. That was probably good, wasn't it? Someone trying to hide wouldn't have headlights on when they weren't necessary... would they? Double bluff? Hani begged the truck to turn right.

It pulled out behind her instead.

Ahead, another truck idled at a turnout just before where Hani figured the driveway would be. Her head spun. She couldn't pull in. Even if they'd let her. Sure enough, just seconds before she reached the place where the truck idled, it peeled out onto the road, forcing her to slam on her brakes. Heart racing faster than her engine now, Hani darted a glance at her rearview mirror and saw that truck barreling up on her before coming to a quick slow.

The truck ahead of her shot down the road as if chased by every cop in the county. At the next driveway on her right, she risked slowing and pulling over. Once the truck behind her drove out of sight, she could turn around.

It slowed as it passed and then pulled up, blocking her in. Sure, she could back up, but not in time to avoid whatever would come next. She pulled out her Glock and aimed. Keeping it hidden—not so easy, but she tried to hide all but the muzzle. A man stepped down from his truck with an ease that didn't hint at danger, but the most brutal people she'd ever dealt with approached killing with indifference.

He held up a hand and grinned as he approached. Hani slid the gun down and to her side. She hit the window button and tried not to shake as it slid down in the track. *Stay calm. No one even knows you're not from this state.*

"Hey, you okay? Saw Pete Fikkers pull out and nearly hit you."

She relaxed, but her hand remained on the gun. How did she know this guy actually knew the jerk who now had probably reached the next county? A damsel in distress might be the best option, but if she ran into him again, she'd likely blow that if he caught her off guard—especially with that farm so close to the house. Better be standoffish. "I'm fine. Annoyed, but fine. Thanks for asking." She shot a glare at his truck before turning her attention back to him. "Then again, you've blocked me in, so maybe you're the one I should be worried about."

The grin returned. "Guess that's a fair statement." He held out his hand, "Granger Payne."

A dozen thoughts flitted through her mind as he initiated the handshake. Was it genuine? Just a guy being friendly? Technically, some might consider southern Missouri to be "the South," so it wasn't far out of reason. Was it a ploy to get her to drop the gun? If so, did that mean he knew she had it there, or was he just checking? Something else?

She must have hesitated too long, because Granger put his hands up and took a step back. Or maybe he saw the gun. "Hey... I didn't mean to make you feel uncomfortable." Another step back. "I just saw you slam on your brakes and then pull over. Thought I should check to see that you were okay." This time, he took two steps back and dropped his hands. "I'm sorry for unsettling you."

The guy had an accent—a slight Southern cadence with a hint of twang on a couple of words. And he had a killer smile. It turned up on one side for a full second or two before the other side followed. Crinkles

543

around the eyes. *No, Hani. You're on a job, and your job doesn't allow for guys.* She gave him a weak smile in return. *Not even cute ones like him.*

"No worries. I'm just tired. Long drive. Sorry for being so jumpy."

Granger Payne settled his hands low on his hips for a moment before saying, "As long as you're okay...?" Strange how some people made statements sound like questions and others made questions sound like statements. Another thing to ponder when she had a few months off. At the rate those things piled up, it'd need to be a year soon.

"Fine. And thanks for stopping. I'm glad to know if I had been hurt, I wouldn't be out here with a concussion and no one to help."

"Better get you a cellphone. They don't always work on this stretch of Bird's Nest, but down by my place and up the road there a bit, service is pretty decent."

No need to tell the guy she had a smartphone sans SIM and drained battery in her purse pocket and six burners in her backpack. "I'll have to think about that."

"There's a store in Cuba if you need good service. Tell Homer I sent you."

"Homer." There was one of those statements that really were questions. But really... people were still named "Homer" around here?

"Todd Homer at the CellShack. He'll take care of everything. Granger Payne." He jerked a thumb at his chest. "Just in case you forgot. Homer'll take good care of you if you mention me. He owes me."

She had no business sitting there chatting with a guy while Keith was fighting to stay awake on an adrenaline crash, but Hani couldn't resist asking. "Owes you?"

"I let him date my sister. Owes me big time." And with that, the guy returned to his truck and hopped in. With one arm waving out of the window, he pulled onto the highway and took off down the road. She waited, watching until she couldn't see a hint of his taillights before turning the truck around and easing back to the driveway where "her" Miata stood.

Note to Mark. Don't let us drive such distinctive cars to this one. People will remember it. I'll have to play it up if I see anyone. Make being noticed work in my favor, I guess.

Then again, Granger had seen her in the truck that they would need to pass off as Keith's. He'd be her brother... and she'd have had... something in the back. But what? It couldn't stick out, or Granger would've seen it. So what?

When the curtains twitched, she hauled herself out of the truck and dragged the backpack behind her. She'd figure that out later. The curtain pulled aside more, and Keith waved.

Better yet, you can figure it out. Good training exercise.

Chapter Eleven

Steelville
July 9, 2012
2:53 p.m.

KNOWING THE GUY YOU TRUST IS A ROOKIE WHO DOESN'T know what he's doing can leave your confidence shaken. Not that Anna knew anything about that. As she watched Hani and Keith discuss how to play out their presence there in Steelville, even she could see Hani was training him with every turn of the conversation. Did he realize it?

Hani pulled a phone from her bag, assembled it, and made a call. "Any word?" Her facial expression—unreadable, but Anna saw a slight tensing of her shoulders. Her posture straightened ever so slightly. Even Keith noticed.

They'd be on the move again. Was any of it worth it? Let whoever took Roman have whatever they wanted—even all the money for the restaurant. She'd get a job. They'd pay off the loan and start over.

Disappointment crept in and squeezed at her heart. If that happened, they'd be near forty before they could afford children, but none of this was worth it. Something else tiptoed in behind disappointment and sucker-punched her. Anna gasped.

Keith was on his feet, ready. "What?"

"I just realized. You—both of you. Protecting me. This is going to be expensive. We can't afford this."

A slight smile formed before Hani turned away, but Keith stepped closer. "There won't be a charge."

Her "Ha!" sounded even more hollow aloud than it did in her heart. "No one does this much work with this much expense for free."

Keith answered before Hani could. "Let's just say that my boss charges enough to afford to help someone who can't pay for that help. It's covered. No charge."

And she believed him. The kind of sincerity radiating from him couldn't be faked. Could it? In her peripheral vision, she saw Hani shift again. Something was off. A focused look at Keith showed he'd figured it out, too.

"Um... well, thanks. I don't know how we'd ever pay for this."

Keith gave her a smile and shot a glance over at Hani. His hand rubbed the back of his neck, and in that moment, Anna realized the problem... and the solution. "You don't have to be her boyfriend."

"I'm not going to be your boyfriend or husband. I can't do that."

"You don't have to. You can be her brother—half-brother, most likely but still."

"Who are you then?" Keith raised his eyebrows and shook his head. "You look more like her than I do but three adult siblings? Not likely."

And here would be the genius of the plan... as long as they got rid of that possum. She wasn't afraid of the thing, but neither did she want to cohabitate with it. "I'm not here."

Hani gasped and looked at her. "Duh! We're such idiots. Of course! You're not here. You'll stay in the basement."

As his face turned a sickly green, Keith's eyes bulged, and his words stuck in his throat. Anna gave a short shake of her head, but it did no good. "I... um..." He pulled out his gun and stepped around Anna. "Where is the door to the basement?"

"Auger!" Hani barked, "Bye!" and slammed the phone on the counter. "What? You didn't clear the basement before you let her sleep in this place? What is wrong with you?"

Anna waited for him to remind her of the fact that he was still in training. He didn't. "Clearly my thoroughness for starters. Now where is the door? How did I miss it? I need to go check. Maybe that's where the possum comes through."

"Possum?" Hani's gaze darted from one to the other of them. "You've got a rabid rodent in here, too?"

"Not rabid." She and Keith spoke in unison. A co-conspiratorial glance passed between them before Anna added, "I think running across a critter in the back room probably derailed Keith's investigation or whatever you call it. We're fine, and it's not like you've not been training him the whole time we've been here. Clearly, he's new and still learning, so give the guy who saved me from jail a break, okay?"

Both of her guards stared at her for a moment before Hani smiled. "You've got more moxie than I gave you credit for."

Anna sighed and turned away. "People assume that if you're quiet or forbearing that you're weak. People are fools."

❧

She waited for the squeak of the bedroom door and the soft click of a latch before turning to Keith. "Roman's dead. So's Philip Marcel."

"The guy who owns the restaurant?"

"Yeah. They tried to make Marcel look like he was skipping out after killing Roman, but even small-town cops figured out it was a setup. The restaurant there has paperwork signed for a sale. They have the financials to prove they paid cash for one third of it. This just got worse."

Keith gripped the counter and stared out the kitchen window. He did that a lot. What did he see out there that kept him so riveted? Nothing but trees and the occasional deer. Was he afraid of nature? In love with it? What?

"So we have to tell our client that her husband is dead. Great."

"No."

He turned to face her. "What?"

"Don't tell her. We need to be sure she keeps fighting to get back to him. We'll tell her when this is over."

"Lie?"

And this was where she differed with Mark. The guy's religious scruples would get people killed. She liked Keith. He was good. But his religion thing wouldn't work. Still, she had to try—for everyone's sake. "Yes, Keith. You lie. You say whatever you have to say and do whatever you have to do to keep your client alive. This isn't about self-preservation. It's about Anna's. So you pretend to be my boyfriend. You hold my hand if someone's around. You kiss me anytime you can make it look like you think we're alone when we're not." She eyed him. "And you make it convincing."

"I—"

"Because that is what Anna needs to ensure no one gets suspicious."

He turned away from the window, leaned against the counter, and folded his arms over his chest. "What happened to you being my sister?"

"Sister?" She'd forgotten that. Eying him closer, she shrugged. "We might be able to share one parent."

"We can share both. I look just like Dad. You look just like Mom." He gave her a weak smile. "I can lie about this kind of thing, Hani. But lying to the client? You think that's best?"

Okay, so she'd gone on the wrong tangent. Fine. Hani glanced down the hall before moving to his side and whispering, "Look. Anna is too unreadable. We don't have a solid dossier on her. It's patchy, and what we've seen doesn't jive with it. So she's either in league with the Solaris and we're in danger, or we have inaccurate information from people who don't really know her. Probably the latter, but until we know... we need to keep ourselves safe." After another Anna check, Hani returned and added, "The best way to do that is to ensure she doesn't know about Roman. If she was behind that, knowing it's done could turn things ugly."

"You think we're protecting the kingpin? Really? Her?"

The guy wasn't a fool, but apparently, that didn't keep him from acting like one. "Until we know who is behind this, we assume anyone could be."

"You said Solari took over the restaurant."

"Doesn't mean he's behind it. It probably does, but it could be him taking advantage of the situation."

She pulled pizzas from the fridge. Everything else had been solid in the ice chest, but the pizzas on top had started to defrost. She'd make them now. Hani groaned. And heat up the house. To a questioning Keith, she shook her head and said, "Go check the basement. Make sure it's habitable. Anna not being here is optimal. I feel like an idiot for not thinking of it."

"You arrived during daylight and were seen. You've had less sleep than I have. It's bound to happen."

Hani shook her head. "No... I'm paid for it not to happen. That's how we keep our clients alive, Keith."

Without a word, he went to explore the basement. He hadn't stood up for himself. Hadn't made excuses. Anna had done that for him. Interesting.

Once the oven beeped, she slid the pizzas on the racks and set the timer for ten minutes before hurrying down the hall and into the back room. That would've been the last place he checked, and if he ran into a possum, maybe he didn't check well enough to see the door behind the door. Whoever had decided to turn that back room into a suite hadn't thought through the logistics of the basement access.

She found him standing in a semi-finished basement, hands on hips much like Granger Payne's. Without looking over his shoulder, he said, "If she's going to be down here, we're going to fix it up. It'll be an excuse for me to be visiting. That's why you brought the truck instead of me."

"It is?"

This time he turned. "Yep. You were going to pick up stuff in Sullivan but made better time than you expected. So, your little brother has to go off and do the dirty work." He held out his hand. "Keys?"

"You're serious?"

Keith shrugged and extended his hand a bit further. "We need a reason for me to be here that doesn't make me look like a mooch."

Relief sent a wash of exhaustion over her. He could roll with things. She checked her watch and moved back toward the stairs. "Just be sure you measure once so we don't have to go back to Sullivan twice." At the top of the stairs, she added, "Oh, and go tomorrow. Anna can sleep upstairs for one night.

~

Rockland

INDUCTION

July 9, 2012
8:07 p.m.

When Jeremiah "Jerm" Boyer's computer pinged, he swiveled to scan the player roster for the hundredth time that evening. A glance at the screen's clock showed just past eight o'clock. And there she was. Lauren Humboldt, server at Marcello's. Abandoning the security code he'd been working on, he pulled the other keyboard closer and typed out a greeting.

/hey

The cursor blinked on his end while he waited for some sign of a reply. Nothing. The questions fired at him faster than a warrior charge. Was she spooked? Had he been too aggressive? Too laid-back to take him seriously? As he sat there considering the myriad options before him, her reply appeared.

/hey just got home from work and my apartment is an oven!
/stupid roommate turned off the AC when she left

That he could work with. Jerm hesitated and decided to strike now. Knowing that Roman Simon and Philip Marcel were dead meant they had less time than ever.

/things better tonight?

Of course, they weren't. But he wasn't supposed to know that. Her reply came faster than expected.

/worse. Seriously, things just got creepy
/they found the owner and manager dead and now some weird thugs are taking over
/this guy has been hanging around for the last couple of weeks, and now he and his goons are here all the time
/we're supposed to take orders from him. As if! I'm thinking about quitting

551

Oh, no you don't. You can't do that. We need you in there. After considering a few options, Jerm tried for practical.

/sounds smart
/got a new job lined up?

There... now come on. Think. Tell me the guy's name. She'd mentioned Roman once—what a jerk he was to his doormat wife. If he could get confirmation on Leone, that would give them leverage. They needed leverage. After much too long a wait, her reply came.

/not yet
/asking at Coventry but...

Two seconds later, she fired back,

/oops
/didn't mean to be so specific

He had to relax her.

/no worries
/won't show up anywhere to be all creepy
/probably a million Coventry places in North America alone

Lauren's rapid-fire response told him he'd made the right call.

/yeah
/wish you were close
/you could tell Boris the goon that I'm not one of Leone's escorts and to leave me alone

Even as Jerm zipped off a "what are you talking about?" he pulled his phone out and sent Mark a text message.

Do we know a Boris connected with Leone?
Lauren Humboldt just mentioned him, Leone,
and escorts.

Lauren's response came after a much longer pause than felt comfortable.

/it's like they're using the restaurant as some mixer for businessmen and call girls.
/gross

He'd played up the nice boy next door persona from the get-go, and now Jerm sagged in relief. A nice boy next door might be shocked enough to ask questions to keep her talking. A player would make a crass joke and move on.

/really?
/like in the movies where some guy needs a date and has to pay someone to go out with him?

He chuckled as he waited for her reply. She'd be laughing at him, but whatever did the job.

/no... like someone with too much money hiring a hooker
/just high class
/probably gets tested for stuff all the time to ensure the "product" is "clean"

Another "gross" followed. Jerm hesitated before typing out the obvious question.

/and this Boris thinks he can drag you into that?
/let me at him!

He'd kept flirting to a minimum, but if any time called for it, now was it. She'd laugh and say something about how sweet he was. She always did.

/wish you could
/and no
/he just wants a toy for when he's bored at work
/no thanks!

The buzz of his phone sent him scrambling to read Mark's message.

> Sounds like Leone might be going rogue. Solari won't have anything to do with the Russians. I'll go over there tomorrow. See if you can convince her to take a day off if she has to work tomorrow.

Jerm considered a few things before choosing the easiest route to ensure she didn't go to work.

/maybe you should be sick for a few days

Lauren didn't hesitate in her reply. Only after he reread it did he realize they'd been typing at the same time.

/I'd take off if I could afford to

/can't afford it

Here goes nothing. Come on, Lauren. Bite. I don't want to see you caught in the crossfire.

/I know a firm in Louisville that is looking for data entry from home

She responded in seconds.

/those are all scams

He flexed his fingers and grinned. She was baited, on the hook, and now it was time to reel her in.

/then I like scams
/been making a couple hundred a week after work to save up for a new laptop

While he scrambled to convert one of his established websites to head-quartered in Louisville, Kentucky, Jerm waited for a response.

/are you for real?

Jerm typed out the email address she should use and sent it before adding,

/just make a new lettersbox.com email address if you want to be extra safe

It took more convincing. Lauren was definitely a hard sell, but in the end, the message he'd waited to hear came through.

/all right
/I'll do it
/gonna be sick for the next couple of weeks or until they find who killed the bosses
/thanks
/now, we gonna play or what?

"Bring it on, Lauren. Bring. It. On."

Chapter Twelve

Steelville
July 11, 2012
9:02 a.m.

AFTER A SHORT SHOWER, ANNA DRAGGED THE DUFFEL BAG
Keith had brought down the basement stairs and set about figuring out
what she'd like moved down there. Hani hoped it would be the tutti-frutti
bedroom stuff rather than the camo. The king-sized bed from the large
room was unsafe for them to move down those steps. Normally, she'd call
dibs on that room. The bigger the bed, the easier it was to find a comfortable spot on it. But with a four-legged on-again-off-again roommate, she'd
just share the camo with Keith.

She snorted at that thought. *Need to make sure I say that one aloud
next time the three of us are in the same room. I give him two seconds before
he's redder than a Coke can.*

As she plotted her first shot into a battle Keith didn't know he'd have
to engage in, Hani wandered the house looking for furniture they could
easily move downstairs. The key was to ensure that things could be
rearranged so it didn't look like something was missing. The odds that

someone coming in would even notice were super-slim, but the risk was never worth it. They had an illusion to maintain.

The dining table sat by a corner window set that overlooked a deck and the backyard. It's why Mark bought the house—corner windows instead of a slider. Sliding glass doors and French doors were great for families who liked to barbecue—not great for agents who needed every possible obstacle to getting into a house. Even if that was just having to hoist up a few feet with broken glass instead of plowing through it.

Nestled among a ton of trees, the house had everything she loved. Quick access to a little-traveled highway, a tourist attraction close by, and of course... those trees. Running into trees in a scary movie might be a bad idea, but when you're trying to hide from folks, having dense foliage meant coverage. Climbing trees meant you could get a drop on an assailant—literally. And if two people went in opposite directions, a single assassin couldn't get you both.

She sighed and went to retrieve her hoodies. After a knock to announce her impending arrival, Hani pushed open the basement door and took the steps two at a time, her eyes scanning the area. Just because Anna was supposed to be alone didn't mean she was.

Never had Anna looked more vulnerable than curled up in a beanbag chair in the corner by the washing machine. Hani stood at the bottom of the stairs, watching her. Instinct screamed for her to be alert, but the woman appeared to be out for the count.

Heart thumping, Hani rushed forward and then stopped mid-stride as Anna asked, "Something wrong?" She didn't even open her eyes.

"Brought you a hoodie."

"Because... it's so cold outside today?" Anna opened one eye, the other squished against her palm. "Why a hoodie?"

"Turn down the thermostat as low as you need to, but wear it at all times. If we run, you pull that hood up over your head and try to disappear into it." Hani turned her back on Anna, stripped off her shirt, and pulled the identical one over her before turning around.

Anna nodded. "I see. So we look alike if we're running."

"You're quick."

The woman's weak smile said more than she probably meant it to. "I know people think that I'm not very intelligent. At least Roman appreciates me for more than something to walk over."

Shock followed by fury coursed through Hani's veins until Anna stood and took a step forward. "Here's a hint. He's never once tried to walk all over me. Not once. He is the kindest, gentlest, most dedicated man I could have ever hoped to meet." Another step, and this time her eyes locked on Hani. "And he chose me. The only reason I'm not fighting to get back to Fairbury to find him is that I know he'd want me safe first." She scrutinized Hani before adding, "So, I'm trusting that someone is actually doing their job to find him. For now."

It felt like a dismissal, so Hani nodded and turned to go. *Impressive. And I bet when she turns that on around her husband, he thinks it's totally hot.*

Upstairs, she hesitated before sliding aside the Eat, Pray, Love, sign and punching in the security code. Out the back door and down onto the deck. Heat and humidity engaged in a battle for the miserablest. Heat won by a hair.

The deck's boards were too far apart to safely hide anyone under it. Mark should fix that. Besides, any woman stepping outside in any kind of heel would find herself stuck or pitching forward. Lawsuit waiting to happen.

The yard sort of dissolved into the trees as if the woods around the home were slowly encroaching. It had been mowed, but the closer the yard got to the tree line, the higher the grass. Common for the area or lazy lawn service? She'd have to find out.

Sweat trickled down her spine and pooled in her bra. Gross. Still, Hani pulled the hood over her head and stepped into the trees. One advantage of a hoodie during summer heat? Perfect protection against ticks. *Take that, Lyme disease!*

The trees grew more densely populated than she'd expected. Too bad it wasn't complete coverage. At night, they might have even blocked out a moon. Without night vision goggles... they'd be invisible as long as they could breathe without making a sound. And didn't move. That would definitely be a perfect announcement of their position.

Then we won't breathe or move. Piece of cake.

Thirty yards or so in, she saw the perfect hiding place. It had everything someone could want—great coverage, easy access, and it looked like it might even have another way out. She'd have to warn Anna to stay far away from it.

On the other hand, another ten feet to the right sat a tree with a low enough branch to grab onto. Hani wrapped her hands around it and walked her feet up the side of the tree, listening as she did. Not too bad. Anyone moving couldn't hear it. Anyone standing still would probably assume footsteps on the decaying leaf-strewn ground. Perfect.

Next up—front access. Across the road was the Meramec River, and if someone came in through the back, they'd have to flee from the front. If they didn't have time to get into the car, they'd have to flee across the road. That meant the river.

Hani double-checked that Anna was still doing well before heading out the front door. As she scanned the yard, she realized there was a row of large rhododendrons along the side of the house that ran close to the trees. It only took a minute to explore and immediately, she made the decision. *If we go out front, she goes there and stays if possible.*

The hairs stood on the back of her neck as she crossed the road and entered the trees on the other side. *Something off or...?* Perspiration trickled down her neck and made its way down her spine. *Or sweat. Call it what it is. Sweat.*

Despite reason insisting all was well, she slipped behind a tree and stood still, listening. An indistinct sound unsettled her until it grew a bit louder, and Hani managed to categorize it as an approaching vehicle. The roar told her that someone had vehicle compensation issues or desperately needed a new muffler.

Leaning against the tree, Hani inhaled the scents around her. The musty, decaying leaves and the earth beneath them. Birds twittered overhead as the loud rumbling faded into the distance.

Her footfalls were quieter here. Was it the nearby water? The closer she came to the river, the more her senses went on high alert. Algae and... minerals? Maybe?

A rustle near her sent Hani jumping back. She scanned the area, looking for the source and saw nothing. The rustle returned, louder this time, and when she glanced over her shoulder, her heart stopped.

I'm with you, Indie. Why did it have to be snakes?

A black snake slithered across the path she'd taken less than a minute before. *I hate this part of my job.* It didn't stop, though. It just kept slithering until its tail disappeared into the underbrush.

That's all she needed. Snakes. First, she'd have to remind Anna to be careful. Next, they had to get out and run around to the back if they couldn't get in the car. Period. No way would she swim across a river here. They might have cottonmouths. Or water moccasins. Wait... were those the same thing? Hani suspected they were.

The moment she couldn't hear the snake moving any longer, she dashed for the road. Only once she'd made it halfway across did she see the guy from that morning standing next to his truck, watching her. And the truck blocked her driveway—facing the wrong way.

Hani reached behind her, ready to pull her weapon from its waistband holster. "Hey..."

Granger waved. "Thought I saw you go in there as I drove this way, so I whipped around and stopped. Everything okay?"

"Just checking out the river." Hani couldn't help shuddering as she shoved her hands into the hoodie pocket.

The way his features shifted, she suspected he'd started to warn her and changed his mind at that shudder. Now he grinned. "In case you didn't know, you might want to wear tall boots if you go in there. Snakes."

"I met a black one. Creepy looking thing. I'm hoping it was just a king snake."

"Possibly..." He leaned against his truck and propped one arm up on the bed. "Could be a cottonmouth, too."

Before she could tell herself to stuff it, Hani found herself asking, "Are they and water moccasins the same thing?"

The guy didn't have to answer. She saw it in his eyes. Great. Just what she needed. First a possum in the bedroom and now a nest of vipers (or at least a cottonmouth) across the road. *Oh, and ticks. Great, heaping gobs of Lyme disease-carrying ticks.*

Still... those ticks would give her an out. "Well, I'd better get in and start the tick inspection."

"Where's your truck?" He jerked a thumb at the Miata. "That's not what you came in."

Who did the guy think he was? What business was it of his? Nerves zinging with warnings on every level imaginable, Hani ordered herself to play it calm. Nonchalant. *And then get outta the streets of Dodge and back to the fort. So to speak.*

"My brother drove my car here. I was going to get stuff in Sullivan, but I made better time than I thought, so he went to get it when he got here."

"Stuff?"

Screaming, "I don't owe you an explanation of my choices!" wouldn't do well to ensure he left her alone, so Hani shrugged and started around his truck. "He wants to do some work on the basement."

"So you bought the place?"

"Considering it. Just renting for now. See you later, Payne."

Yes, she used just his last name. Yes, it was juvenile to enjoy it so much. No, she didn't care. Not one bit.

But as she pulled open the door, Hani shot a look back his way and found him leaning over the truck bed, both arms propped against it, watching her. *Men shouldn't be allowed to be that attractive. It's dangerous. And annoying.* To make herself feel better, she marched in, shoved the door shut, and slid the deadbolt all while rephrasing that thought. "No guy should be that pretty."

There. He'd hate it if he heard her. Of that, she had no doubt. Or guilt. No guilt at all.

Chapter Thirteen

Steelville
July 11, 2012
12:01 p.m.

THE MOMENT KEITH STEPPED INSIDE THE DOOR, HE FOUND himself shoved up against the wall and Hani shaking him. "You've got to go check out the farmer down the road."

Keith eyed her, trying to figure out why she sounded so panicked. On alert, his hand went for his weapon. "Why?"

"First, he blocks me in when I get here, then when I come back from checking out possible escape routes, I find him blocking my driveway and watching me. Something's off there. You need to check him out, get his license plate, run it. Have Mark give us everything we can get on whoever this guy is. He calls himself Granger Payne."

Keith snickered.

Hani's angst softened a bit, and she chuckled. "I know right. Granger for a farmer, but then Payne? What were his parents thinking?"

Relaxing a bit, Keith reholstered his weapon and went for a literal response. "They were probably thinking, 'Oh, we'll use our beloved family name. And nobody but nobody would ever think of mocking him for it.'"

Though Hani scowled, Keith stared right back. When she didn't back down, he tried again, "Like no one's ever called you Hannah."

A bit of unease hit him when Keith realized he'd just noticed her hair was dripping wet and she'd changed into a... a hoodie? Before he could suggest turning up the thermostat over adding layers in summer, Hani pounced again. "Whatever. Just check him out. Something's not right. It's driving me crazy."

You need to calm down or you won't be any good for Anna. He wouldn't say it, of course. She was the senior agent here. But still...

"We need to know what the guy is up to."

"Fine. I'll see what I can find out." To himself he added, *Just as soon as I get that stuff out of the truck and into the basement.* Not that he was looking forward to that.

Keith had only managed to carry in three sheets of drywall before Hani pounced again. "What are you doing? I said go check him out. This is your job."

Using his boot to protect the drywall from dings on the floor, Keith peered around the side of it. "I *am* doing my job. First, I'm maintaining our cover story. Second, I'm protecting our boss's investment in these materials, and third, I'm not acting like a freakazoid so the guy doesn't get suspicious."

After a glare and a huff, Hani stormed off to the kitchen. A moment later, Keith heard her pull open the freezer drawer and let it slide shut. A second later, she'd slammed something onto the counter. It was a really good thing that those counters weren't tile.

By the time he'd filled the hallway with lumber and other supplies, the venting in the kitchen had brought Anna up from the basement. She cocked an eyebrow toward the kitchen in a silent question. "There's something wrong," Keith said. "I think it's just nerves. But it's not like I know what I'm talking about."

Anna took a step toward the kitchen, but when a pan slammed against a burner, she retreated, grabbed a two-by-four, and said, "I'll carry these down."

"You don't have to do that. I can take care of it." Keith reached for three of the two-by-fours himself and started down after her.

By the time he got all the supplies down into the basement and himself cleaned up, Keith had figured out what he would do. After calling out his goodbyes, he bolted for the truck and headed out.

At the edge of the drive, as he waited for a car to pass, Keith called Mark and asked for any information they could get on Granger Payne of Steelville, Missouri. Just in case. "Send it to Hani's phone. She's nervous."

Silence reverberated through the airwaves before Mark asked, "Why? Why do you think she's nervous?"

Keith didn't know how to answer, so he described the confrontation at the door. Mark's quick, sharp questions set his nerves afire. "We'll check it out. Hani's got good instincts. If something's off. She'll sense it, and she obviously has. We'll figure out why."

"So I shouldn't go talk to this guy?"

"No, you should. In a case like this, when you're trying to blend in? Definitely. It's the best way to handle it. It's what most people would do when they're looking at an area to move to."

"Gotcha." Keith would've disconnected, but Mark continued.

"Just be cautious. We've got something going on here. There's a chance this will be over soon."

Keith's senses went on high alert "Oh? Did you figure out who's behind it?"

"That's just the thing," Mark said. "We think we did. And if we're right, it's not Solari."

Being new to the underbelly of Rockland crime, Keith didn't have a good understanding of just who Solari was and what his game was in Rockland. Still, he'd figured out enough and been told enough to know that if this Solari guy was involved, things were bad. So why did hearing Mark say that Solari might not be behind the murders sound even worse?

A reply was required, so Keith said, "Well, keep us posted." Sure it sounded pathetic, but what else could he say? He didn't know what was going on.

A minute later, he pulled into the drive leading to the farm that Hani had described and rolled down the lane. A guy came out from a barn several hundred yards away from the house and stood watching him. Keith parked and stepped out of the truck, pocketing his phone. He headed toward the guy. With each step, he considered everything about the man, but nothing seemed off. He looked like a farmer. No, not a cliché. The guy didn't wear overalls or anything. No straw sticking out from between his teeth. No cowboy hat. Instead, the guy wore jeans and a T-shirt. Details flew at him as Keith closed the distance between them. The guy was built. He wore a baseball cap, and sweat stained the front of his shirt.

Keith waved. "Hey, sorry to bother you. I just had a few questions and thought that maybe someone with a farm might actually have some answers."

The man stepped forward, hand outstretched. "Granger Payne."

Without thinking, Keith shook it and said, "Keith Auger." Great. Hani's last name would have to be Auger now. She wouldn't like that.

"You're new around here then."

A dozen questions ricocheted in his brain, but Keith just shrugged. "Just trying to figure out what kind of place this is." The guy just stared at him. "You know... if it's a good area, what kind of property values there are. The kind of neighborhood it is."

Payne chuckled. "Maybe you haven't noticed, but there aren't that many neighbors around here."

He had to admit the guy had him there. "Yeah, well, you know what I mean. Just..." He scrambled to clarify without making himself look like an idiot... and while scanning the property for anything that looked off. "You know, what kind of people there are around here. I mean, are we looking at young families, people who've lived here a long time, meth labs in hidden trailers somewhere? Just trying to get a feel for it all before we make any decisions."

Granger jerked his head toward the house. "There's a house for sale just over there, but someone just moved in. I think they're just renting it, but the woman seemed a little standoffish." The guy grinned at him. "But then you knew that."

Perspiration trickled down his neck. Keith tried to keep his cool. "I don't follow."

"I met her yesterday morning and then again, a while ago. She's... not very friendly. Said you guys were renting but considering buying." When Keith just stared some more, Granger added, "And you're driving her truck. So I'm assuming you're the brother."

The way his neck heated, he'd be dripping with sweat in no time.

Better "come clean" to the guy before he botched the whole job. "Yeah, well. I'll be honest with you. Hani was concerned. She doesn't know who you are, and what you're doing hanging around, so she asked me to check you out."

Granger gave him half a smile. And there it was. This guy wasn't trying to find out if they had Anna. Hani intrigued this guy—probably because she hadn't fallen for his down-home charm.

"Oh, yeah?"

"Well... she just wants to know more about you."

The smile spread across the rest of his face. "How's that?"

"You know how it is. City girl moves to the country, and someone says hi, and the next thing you know, she's convinced that they're an ax murderer waiting to happen."

Granger shoved his hands in his pockets and tried to look all nonchalant, but Keith saw through it. As he removed and replaced his hat, he added, "And she doesn't have a reason to trust me, so I get it. Still...I guess I made an impression." Granger eyed Keith again before adding, "Well, she said you're doing work around there. I stay pretty busy here, but if you need anything, I'm happy to help. I can give you my number."

Keith almost brushed him off and changed his mind. "Sure, great. Let me just put that in my phone." After repeating back the number, Keith said, "Well, I better get back and let her know she hasn't moved in next door to the next Hannibal Lector."

Once more, Granger cracked a smile. Keith had nearly made it to his truck when Granger called out to him. "I gotta know. How are y'all related? She looks Indian or Pakistani or something. You clearly don't."

With half a glance over his shoulder, Keith called back, "That's what happens when you look like your dad, and your sister looks just like your mom. Everyone always thought that we were a blended family. But we weren't."

~

Steelville
July 11, 2012
5:07 p.m.

The whisper of a beep made Hani freeze for half a second. A dash to the curtains showed a familiar truck and Granger not sauntering up the walk —more like storming the citadel. In seconds, she had Anna by the back door and called for Keith. "Get her out, down between the trees and rhododendrons and out to the road. I'll call as soon as I get rid of him."

The doorbell pealed, but Hani waited until she saw Keith's and Anna's shadows disappear from the grass as she watched through the back window. That's when she finally jerked open the door and gazed at him. "You forgot the casserole or potted plant or whatever."

"Huh?"

Good, she'd disarmed him.

"I assume this is the neighborhood welcome wagon?"

"Like I told your brother. This isn't much of a neighborhood."

Hani gave an exaggerated roll of her eyes and said, "Whatever. What can I do for you?"

"You can tell me what's going on."

Steel solidified in her spine as her nerves zinged. Show time. "Care to elaborate?" *I don't have cable, so...*

Granger shoved his phone into her face before she could see it coming. The numbers on the screen were so close they blurred. "Who is this guy?"

Hani snatched the phone and blinked at it. "You tell me. I've never seen that number before."

"Funny... because that's the number out on that FOR SALE sign out there."

Oops. "Well, I didn't call about this place. Keith did."

"Here's another funny thing," Granger said, not stepping back. The close proximity sent her pulse racing. Perspiration trickled down her temples and her back. Then again, it could've been the heat outside combined with her hoodie. She should invite him in before some environmentalist group cited her (and rightfully so) for contributing to global— whatevering it was this week. But she couldn't. Not yet.

"What?" It was the only word Hani could trust herself to speak.

"This number? The first time they answered, it was for some dog walking service."

She'd kill Jerm. Flay him alive. "Weird." What else could she say?

"That's not the weirdest part." Granger leaned his forearm against the doorjamb and kept his eyes fixed on her. Hani tried not to let her own gaze waver until she heard a car approaching. Then she glanced to the side to see a hint of rustle at the corner of the yard. Good. They were out.

Hani made a snap decision and stepped back. Maybe him being in the house would give Keith and Anna more time for escape—and her more weapons to choose from. "Come in. We're gonna get picketed by the Earth Army or whatever for releasing all this AC into the wild."

When Granger hesitated, she relaxed. Someone looking for Anna would be more likely to plow through, not resist. But frugal farmer won out over suspicious spy, and Granger slipped through the open door and pushed it shut. He didn't, however, follow her into the house. "I called back. That's the weirdest part."

"Because it's so freaky to redial a number you got wrong?"

"No... because this time the realtor answered." Granger folded both arms over his chest. "I checked. I called the same number both times. What's going on?"

You jumped from wrong number to something suspicious? Really? Hani left him there while she went to grab her water tumbler. "Thirsty?"

"No... hungry." When she shot him a look, he added, "For answers. It's what you want when you call the same number two times in a row and get two different businesses. I could swear it was the same guy both times, but he did have kind of a weird accent the second time. So what's *going on?*"

His tirade had given her time to down a gulp of cooling water and strategize. Definitely the "who do you think you are" approach. Nothing else would make sense. "I don't know what you mean by 'going on,' but I can give one reason someone might answer the same number with two different business names. Ever hear of an answering service?"

"And a fake accent?" His retort came faster than she'd expected.

She offered a shrug and took another swig of water before offering an explanation. "Don't know about you, but if I'd answered a call with the wrong business name, I'd probably try to disguise my voice if they called back. I'd be embarrassed." Seeing Granger soften a little, she dove in for the kill. "He just probably punched a wrong button the first time. Meanwhile..." Hani stepped closer to him, putting every bit of the threat she could into it without unleashing what she could really do to him. "Who do you think you are coming here and demanding to know what's 'going on' as if you even had a right to know if something... was! Huh?"

The way he watched her wasn't half as unnerving as what those eyes did to a heart she'd disconnected the day she went to work for Mark Cho. Weird analogy, but they were like jumper cables or something. Scary.

"Don't know."

The words rumbled between them, smooth as honey and with just the hint of that southern drawl that she had *not* replayed in her mind a million times. A dozen or two at most. Definitely less than a hundred.

Hani gave herself a mental shake, a sound scolding, and decided on snarky as her response. "That's your problem then. You called. Not me."

Gesturing to the barstools that sat at the end of a counter, he asked if he could sit. "I think I owe you an apology."

"Aaand... you need to sit? It's going to be that taxing?"

Crinkles formed at his eyes before half his mouth tilted to one side. "Something like that. Sorry... The way this place is for sale, but your brother showed up and then you did—then you guys start working on the place... and then the thing with the realtor..." He shrugged and leaned his arms on the counter, never allowing his gaze to waver from hers. "Something felt off, and I figured I owed it to the..." Granger held up air quotes, "'*neighborhood*' to make sure you were who you said you were."

"So what? We're squatters?"

The smile returned—full force this time. "Strangest squatters I've ever heard of if you are." It might have been her imagination, but Hani would've sworn she heard him add, "Prettiest, too."

"I'll let Keith know you think he's pretty."

And just like that, Granger propped his head on his hand and threw her the sappiest look she'd ever seen. "You do that."

Whoa... flirting? Where'd that come from? Something deep inside her mocked her for the question. *Like you don't know.*

"Where's Keith?" Granger's eyes slid toward the hallway as if he knew where the door to the basement was.

How? How does he know? Is this just a diversion to get Keith out of the house so... Heart racing, Hani realized she'd totally been duped. Mark had to pull her from the case. She'd made every mistake in the book on this one. Anna would die, and it would be her fault.

"Asleep." Hani gave an apologetic smile. "All the driving and then the working on the basement—wore him out. I should probably get some work done and hit the hay myself."

"Why do people always say that?" Granger stood as he spoke. "If people knew what it was like to hit hay, they'd never say that. Pokey and hard unless spread out and fluffed—then it's just pokey."

"Pretty sure 'pokey' isn't a word, but I get it. I'd say hit the sack, but you'd probably ask what the sack was full of, and then I'd just have to hit you with it, so..."

He pushed away from the counter and moved toward the door. "So... goodnight. I've been up since five and I'm getting draggy myself." Granger stopped himself at the door. Turning to face her, he offered that same half-smile. "And again—sorry for being so..."

"Demanding? Nosy?"

"Let's go with nosy this time."

She decided to let it go—act like she wasn't ready to tranq him, tie him up, and get Anna out of Steelville. "Maybe it's not so bad...." Oh, help... there she went flirting back at him. "Maybe it's concern for your neighbors and totally understandable." She pulled the door open for him, trying to act as if his proximity didn't rattle her. "Or not... time will tell."

"Got that right." And with those enigmatic words, he left. Only when she could no longer hear the guy's truck speeding away did she send Keith a text to come back.

That done, she called Jerm and told him exactly what she thought of his flub. "If we have to leave here because of you, you're buying me lunch for a week. What were you *thinking*?"

"Sorry... I had to scramble when I realized what happened. There wasn't time to fix the numbers, so I just winged it."

"Well, he just came over here demanding to know what's going on. I think we have to leave, but that might be more suspicious than ever. Oh, and I'm blowing it, so meanwhile, you'll have to pay up sooner than later, because when Mark hears, he's going to pull me off the case."

"Doubt that. Want me to put you through?"

"Yeah… and head's up—I want chicken marsala from Cucina Italiana the day I arrive back."

"Deal. And really. I'm sorry. It's been crazy here, and I didn't test the number when I set it up. My bad. Here's Mark."

Five minutes later she'd been given the biggest dressing down of her career. And told not to be an idiot. To stay put and do her job.

Chapter Fourteen

Rockland
July 11, 2012
10:03 p.m.

WITHOUT SO MUCH AS A KNOCK, THE DOOR SWUNG OPEN AND Jerm appeared. Mark eyed the kid as he strode to the console and snatched up a remote. With a click, the enormous TV screen went from black to blue and finally to a press conference in progress. Reporters clamored for details of the arrest of Jimmy Simmons.

"Why would they care?"

Jerm just jerked the remote at the screen. Three seconds later, a lawyer with all the stereotypical elements from sleazy TV jurisprudence spoke out. "My client was entrapped by unethical officers of the Covedale Police Department, battered, and is seeking protection and damages."

Simmons pushed himself in front of the mic and said, "The guy who took me down and hit me disappeared. He's gone, and some other guy claimed to do it. But it's a lie. He didn't sound the same or look the same as the guy who hit me."

The roar of questions drowned out what the lawyer said next, so the network went back to the news anchor who added, "Simmons' lawyer is claiming the police department either hired someone to set up the trap or used undercover officers for that purpose. Simmons was taken to Western Hills Medical Center for treatment after having been tackled and beaten by someone in the house he allegedly broke into. Aaron Lehman, Simmons' lawyer, asserts that his client entered the home with a security code that proves he did not break any laws. Simmons has a warrant..."

Jerm clicked off the screen. "What do we do?"

Mark leaned back in his chair, spinning a pen as he thought. The bank of windows to his right looked out over the Rockland skyline. Lights blinked off here and there as workaholics finally gave up and left for home. Most unaware that all over their city rival groups grappled for control of an underbelly those same workers wouldn't want to acknowledge existed.

"Mark?"

After only half a second's hesitation, he sighed. "See if you can get me in contact with the Rockland County court commissioner. We need Simmons put into some place where he'll make connections we need."

"So I was right? The wrong people will find that suspicious?"

Though Solari or Leone's men may not make the connection, *someone* would realize something was off, and if that someone took it to the wrong person... "If they hear of it, possibly. But even if Leone doesn't get wind of it, someone connected with or trying to curry favor with him would."

"Got it. One commissioner connection coming up."

Half an hour later, Mark rose, ready to head home, only for Jerm to pop his head in the door. "I have the court commissioner on hold. Barbara Jessop. She's not happy."

Snatching up the phone, Mark gave Jerm a signal for "record this" and turned his attention to the woman he needed in his court. "Hello, Barbara."

"Mark Cho. I know about you."

He swallowed hard. This wasn't good. As much as he hated trying to determine if someone was trustworthy enough to ask a favor of, this was worse. "You know what about me, exactly?"

"We're going to play this game? You want something from me. Just tell me what it is."

And what, you'll miraculously give it to me? Do you think I'm that stupid or are you just that direct?

"Mark, I don't have all night. I'm guessing this is about James Simmons?"

The woman was sharp. Astute. Especially considering it was an out-of-state issue. He could hear it not only in the directness of her questions but in the timbre of her voice as she spoke. This was a woman he wanted on his side.

"You're right. It is. Can I count on your discretion? Lives—well, now we're looking at one life or death and the quality of lives on another scale —are in jeopardy."

He could almost hear the mortar of the wall she'd built around her crack. "It's true then. You protect people."

"I do."

"Why are you so secretive?"

This he didn't answer. Mark just waited. She'd figure it out.

"Of course. Stupid question."

Silence followed. Mark paced. Pivoted, and paced the other direction. He wanted to head down to his car and then home, but the conversation shouldn't be overheard. Twice he checked to see that they hadn't been disconnected. And still he waited.

"I take it you want James Simmons put somewhere specific. Why?"

"He'll ask for help from the right person. He'll talk and talk about how he showed up to do a job and got taken out by one guy and another one claimed to be the one who did it. And that will get back to the people we're trying to find."

The silence became oppressive.

"I thought you were protection detail. I was led to believe you didn't do investigative work."

Mark's throat dried up faster than a raindrop on a Phoenix sidewalk in July. She shouldn't know that much. How? He had to ask. "Before I answer that, I'd like to know where you got that idea."

"One of your... assignments?"

"We like to call them clients."

The woman actually snorted. "Fine. Whatever. One of your *clients* rambled while under anesthesia for an emergency appendectomy last fall. Everyone thought it was funny—all but a nobody nurse who took it to her uncle... who happens to be my husband. I did some digging. Knew I'd struck something when one of your informants informed *me* that I needed to let it go. My congressman agreed. So I did."

Congressman Marchbanks needed a reminder of whose job it was to keep the Agency a secret. Great.

"Look, Mark. I don't like what you do."

Neither do I half the time.

"But I can see value in it. I appreciate that you try to stick within the law and that you protect all people—not just rich ones, not just those deemed 'beneficial to society.' But I can't agree to do something that may endanger a life."

Mark laughed. "Barbara, you're putting a guy in a detention center. That endangers him. I want you to put him somewhere that will ensure his protection *and* a swift resolution to a problem that has already gotten two men killed."

She sucked in her breath. "This is about the Fairbury thing."

"Yes."

"You know they're running an escort service out of that restaurant."

Again, Mark answered with a simple, "Yes."

"You know that the girls go in voluntarily."

"At first."

This time the silence wasn't as ominous. It was... thoughtful. "I might be able to help you. Call me back tomorrow." She rattled off a number. "And Mark?"

"Yeah?"

"Don't make me regret this. You get this pathetic excuse of a human being killed, and I'll take you down."

Love a woman who takes her job seriously.

～

Steelville
July 12, 2012
3:27 p.m.

With the scent of oatmeal cookies infusing the entire upstairs, and the baking dishes drying on towels on the Formica counter tops, Anna piled a few still-warm cookies on a plate, poured a glass of milk, and headed downstairs. She wanted to help, and her marriage to Roman taught her she might need a diplomatic bribe to get her way.

Halfway down the stairs, she saw Keith wrestling an enormous piece of "green board" into place. Though Anna had no intention of ever becoming a DIY aficionado, she now knew that basements, laundry/mud rooms, and bathrooms needed this "moisture resistant" drywall. At least now, any contractor working for her would find it hard to pull one over on her.

"Snack time."

Keith glanced her way, saw the plate of cookies, and nearly dropped the board in his haste to inhale food. "Thanks! These smell amazing."

The guy scarfed down the *five* cookies she'd piled up in little more time than it took Anna to pull the hated hoodie back over her head and move to where the abandoned wallboard lay. "So... why is this going up in the middle of the room?"

"That's just a wall to hide the laundry stuff. Mark can put cabinets in there later. Right now, we're just making the place seem less..." He grinned at her. "Creepy kidnapper and more 'better use of space' so to speak." Keith drained the glass of milk and wiped his mouth with the back of his hand. "And it gives me an excuse for being here."

She moved to the side of the board and when Keith came to hoist it up on top of the lower one, squatted and lifted with him. "I'll stand here and lean against it. You do your thing."

Keith would have protested, but it must have made things easier, because he nodded and screwed the board into the studs. As if she'd proven herself somehow, Keith didn't protest when Anna stood ready to hold up the next piece. And the next. She held corner protectors, screws, measuring tapes, and even the drill as he used an X-Acto knife to trim away a bit of the drywall where his saw had gone a smidge wide.

A tear splashed down her cheek, but Anna managed to wipe it away before he could see. This was almost like being home. With Roman. Putting together a flat-pack bookshelf or desk. They'd already picked out one for the office when Roman took over. Out with the oversized "principal's desk" and in with sleek, Scandinavian-inspired simplicity.

"You'll be home soon. I can't tell you why I think that, but I do."

So much for hiding it from him. Anna tried to stifle a sigh that felt wrung from her anyway. "I just want Roman to be safe—for him to know I'm safe. He is worried about me—wherever he is. He's that kind of man."

"Did he say anything about the restaurant? Anything seem off to him or...?"

Should she tell him? Anna couldn't be certain. Then again, she'd put her life in these people's hands. She'd done it for Roman. If she could trust them with her life, could she trust them with her suspicions?

"I don't know if he saw it, but I did."

"Saw what?"

Though she couldn't meet his gaze, Anna kept her voice strong and steady. Mostly. "Customers. You saw them. Hani pretended to be one. When I saw women dressed for cocktail parties coming in after the *lunch* rush and fawning over the men in completely inappropriate ways, I knew."

"You think whoever was running that would hold him responsible for... what?"

Anna remembered the days she'd walked over just to see how many vehicles were there. The couples leaving. Glances exchanged with some of the men waiting out front. She had to force out the next words in a whisper. "The guns they carried." This time she couldn't stop the tears from streaking down her cheeks. "Would they shoot him? Roman wouldn't do as he was told. He would fight."

"What if they threatened you? Would he cooperate then?"

Relief only added to her tears. "Probably. Roman would do anything to protect me."

The man's expression said he didn't believe her. Anna wouldn't argue. People believed what they liked about her husband, but it didn't make them right.

Keith grabbed the plate and his glass and headed for the stairs. "I think I'll go start getting the burgers ready. They'll need to come to room temperature before I put them on the grill." He grinned at her questioning look. "Learned that from one of the guys in my unit."

It wasn't until he'd gone upstairs, and she slipped behind the protective plastic curtain leading to her "bedroom" that Keith's questions unsettled her. *He knew all about Marcello's. It's why I'm here. So why did he ask?*

Chapter Fifteen

Steelville
July 12, 2012
6:17 p.m.

BURGER IN HAND, HANI EXCUSED HERSELF TO PATROL THE perimeter of the property. At least, that's what she told Anna and Keith, although she suspected neither of them believed her. Keith's (completely silent and discreet) praying sent hackles rising where no woman should have hackles to rise. And she didn't even know why.

Sure, he said things that pointed to a faith that meant something to him. Why shouldn't he? She talked about her favorite TV shows, her political opinions on the garbage going on in Washington, and areas where systemic racism still controlled the narrative of American (probably world) society. No one got worked up about that.

So why did that brief, silent pause before he picked up his burger make her want to throw hers at his face? She hadn't made it to the corner of the mowed yard before she regretted wearing the stupid hoodie. A bite of the burger irritated her even more. The stupid thing was delicious—amazing, even.

Guys like him shouldn't be allowed. He's honest, hardworking, kind, sincere, good-looking, even... and he can cook? It's like some author didn't know when to quit with him. To soothe her zinging nerves, she worked on a list of flaws. *Stubborn... sometimes.* That concession hurt. *That honesty is also a liability in this job. Likes to shave too much. Seriously, what's wrong with a bit of scruff? He'd be even better looking with it.* She nearly did a jig. *So clearly, he doesn't know how to play up to his strengths... Oh, and he's religious. Definite flaw believing in some cosmic creator who abandons his creation into a bizarre sort of* Lord of the Flies *experiment.*

In her estimation, that god of his hadn't had any better luck with his characters than the guy who wrote that time sucker of a story. And that thought prompted another. *Keith would probably capitalize that A in Author—like they do pronouns in the Bible. See, Keith? I've read some of it. I know.*

That thought nearly sent her into combat mode. She ripped off another bite with a tear any wild carnivore could be proud of and tromped down the side yard to the front, taking care to stay between the rhododendrons and the trees on the next property. You really could hide well in there. Kids would love it for hide and seek. She changed her mind about that almost immediately. Everyone would know to go there.

Which meant any assassin worth his salt would know about it, too. *Keep Anna out.*

Crunching gravel to her right sucked the air right out of her lungs. Hani peered through the bushes and saw the silhouette of a man heading up the drive. Slow. Cautious. Determined.

Oh, no you don't! Hani pulled her hoodie up over her head. Just in case.

Getting to him without him seeing her—difficult. But if she could draw fire, Keith could get Anna to safety. *Man... this is gonna hurt if he nails me.* Truth forced her to admit: *And he will.*

Stepping out from behind a tree, she shouted, "Hey!" and ducked back.

The guy turned toward her before whipping his head back around at the sound of something—probably Keith inside. Good. He'd heard her. Hani hadn't seen enough to even begin giving a description, though. About six feet. Caucasian?

Waiting for the next crunch of feet on gravel to determine which direction he'd go? Torture. She heard one. Soft... and then a thump. Had Keith come for him instead of getting Anna out? She'd kill him.

A peek around the tree earned her a glimpse of him treading in a wide swath across the lawn as if going toward the corner of the house. *Going to come through the back, are you? Get there. I dare you.*

He took her up on that dare.

Just as he reached the corner, Hani bolted after him, her shoes making little sound on the spongy grass. With the constant drone of locusts, cicadas, tree frogs, and crickets, she doubted he'd hear her. She'd reach him in five... four...

He turned and darted toward her. The stupid hoodie blocked a good view, but her momentum propelled her forward, even as her feet got the memo to stop. Sidestepping to avoid a collision... failed.

Granger Payne sidestepped, too. Right into her path. And they went down in a tangle of arms and legs.

Hani glared at him as she rolled off and jumped to her feet. Throwing back the hood, she advanced on the guy as he hopped up. "What do you think you're doing?"

"Coming to see how my new neighbor is. I hoped you'd be glad to see me, but wow!"

Her irritation ramped up into suspicion. "Wait... you thought you'd come see us by sneaking around the side of the house? I don't buy it." Hani's hand slid behind her, ready to grab her gun. The tranq, of course. He could do serious damage before it took effect, but it would still slow him down.

"You called out. Remember? When you hid, I thought this was some weird welcoming hide and seek game. I was going to fake you out with a double back, but then you came tearing at me. Nice sidestep. Too bad we didn't go in opposite directions." A half smile grew into a grin. "Or... maybe not."

"I—" She huffed. What could she say? "I didn't recognize you. It's kind of a lonely road out here, so when I saw someone skulking—"

His laughter boomed out. "Skulking? I was walking up the drive, following the scent of grilled beef, if I'm not mistaken, and trying to decide if I should go to the front or walk around back."

Great. She'd overreacted—in his mind, at least—and now had damage control to do. Hani dusted off her knees and hoodie and beckoned him to follow her around back. As slowly as she could, she pretended to hang back, unwilling to share... whatever it was that she'd come up with. *Got it!*

"Look, some guy broke into my house in Cincy." *That's true enough.* "It kind of left me on edge." *Equally true.* "So... I guess I overreacted."

As if they'd been friends for a lifetime, Granger dropped an arm around her shoulder and walked alongside saying nothing until they reached the corner where the garage had once stood. There she called out, "Hey, Keith! Granger—the farmer boy next door..." Hani gave him a sassy grin before finishing. "—is here! Throw on another burger, would you?"

And there he stopped her. Gazing down at her in the twilight, Granger said, "That wasn't an overreaction. That was solid action. Makes me feel better about you being over here by yourself." That tiny bit of a smile formed again. "Kind of hoping you'll stay a while—buy this house. Play hide and seek when my chores are done..."

"Does your mama let you play after dark?" Hani tried to hide her surprise. Where had that come from? It definitely fit into the category of flirting, and Hani Kaur did not flirt. Even with cute guys with scruff (*see, Keith!*) who didn't go all religious on her.

～

Steelville
July 12, 2012
6:23 p.m.

Hani's call sent them on high alert. Anna hopped up from the table, grabbed her plate and cup, and dashed inside. Keith hesitated between meeting them outside, making sure she got downstairs safely, and playing the protective big brother. All seemed valid options to him. Then he saw her napkin sitting by a vacant seat—one with the chair pushed out. Keith snatched it up, saw a bit of ketchup on the tablecloth and in desperation, squirted some from the bottle across the table.

Time for more training. Lie practice. Who knew that would ever be in my job description?

He was mopping up the mess as Hani and Granger came around the back corner of the house. "Hey! I'll toss a burger on in a minute. Hani's screech startled me, and I tried to use a ketchup bottle as a taser or something."

"I don't screech!"

He gave Granger a pointed look before carrying the wad of napkins he held to the back door. "Says the woman who just screeched."

Hani's protests followed him until the door shut behind him. Then, insulation, double-paned glass, and the low hum of appliances and air conditioning drowned her out. It almost caused physical pain to pull a cool (at least it wasn't cold!) patty from the fridge and carry it back outside, but with Hani protesting enough that Shakespeare would point it out, he took a moment to check on Anna.

But the basement was empty. He checked the bathroom, all bedrooms, and even the coat closet. Nothing. Back downstairs, he called out for her. "Anna? I need to know you're safe. You down here?"

She stepped out from behind a shelving unit. The last he'd seen, that thing had been against the wall. "When did you move that?"

"Hani and I did it on your last trip to town. You can't tell unless you squeeze past that patio umbrella there and really look, so we thought maybe if I couldn't get out, I could hide."

She'd have to get out, though. What was Hani thinking? If he could figure out that any intruder could just blow up the house with all of them in it, obviously Hani could, too.

"Keith? What is it? You don't like it?"

Hani must have had a reason. He stuck with the truth. "I hadn't thought of it. Just trying to think through scenarios. That's the problem when you're the rookie. Everything is new." There. Spoke truth and hopefully didn't freak out the client more than necessary.

"I just thought of something on the way down. One of those random things that make you go, 'Wait...'"

Keith needed to get upstairs, but he decided this might be more important. "What's that?"

"If Roman signed papers and gave Philip Marcel the last of the down payment money, I need to sign the final things. Otherwise, all our hard work will go down the drain. Do you think you could get me the paperwork?"

That he could handle. "I'll talk to Mark. If it can be done, he'll make it happen. Mark is big on ensuring people don't lose their jobs, their income, or their property while in protective care. I'm sure he'll find a way, but I can't promise."

"Thanks. And there's no word from Roman?"

Thank you for putting it that way. Keith shook his head. "He'd stay hidden if he got away—so they didn't find both of us. It's how he is. He'd contact the FBI or something if they took him and he escaped."

All Keith could do was nod.

When Anna said nothing more, Keith started back up the stairs, but halfway up, her soft voice reached him as she asked, "Do you think people know when someone they love dies?"

He nearly choked. "What do you mean?"

"You hear people say it all the time. 'I'd know if he was dead. I'd know it.' Sometimes it's the other way around. 'I knew the moment she died. I felt it deep within me.'" Anna stepped closer. "Do you think that's true?"

He shrugged and said what needed to be said. "I suppose it can be, but too many people are shocked when they get word of a death for me to believe it's common."

Tears slid down her cheeks. "That's what I keep holding onto." She flicked away the tears and stared at him as if trying to see into his mind. "Because my brain says the chances of him being alive are nearly nonexistent now, but my heart insists he must be. I want my heart to kick my brain's butt—so to speak."

Before he said something he shouldn't, Keith promised to get word to Mark and apologized for needing to hurry back to grill that burger. Anna didn't seem suspicious, but his relief was short-lived. By the time he reached the top of the stairs, he could hear the sniffles and repressed sobs.

Lord... comfort her? She needs to grieve, but we need her quiet, too.

A scream sent him through the house and out the back door empty handed.

Chapter Sixteen

Steelville
July 12, 2012
6:42 p.m.

GRANGER ADVANCED, HIS INTENT CLEAR. HANI'S THROAT went dry even as she fumbled for anything she could grab to defend herself. The chair closest to her wasn't much of an option, but she held it up in front of her. Granger laughed—a diabolical sound if she'd ever heard one.

"You think that flimsy thing with its wide-open slats will protect you?"

Hani swallowed hard. She had to find a way to get control of the situation and now. Before she could respond, Keith bolted out the back door and straight toward Granger. She opened her mouth to call out a warning and changed her mind.

Sure enough, Granger turned his attention to Keith and went on the offensive. Keith never had a chance. Sweet tea left the pitcher in a graceful arc, and Keith plowed right into the path.

And that's where Granger made his mistake. He forgot to step aside.

Keith's momentum wasn't the slightest bit arrested by the blast of cold, sticky, leaf water, and down they both went.

"Ouch. Twice in one night. I'm sore enough as it is. You'll hurt tomorrow." Hani didn't even try to temper her glee.

Granger once again was on his feet offering assistance after a tackle. "Good thing I played football in high school. Bad thing that I didn't dodge." He shot Keith a confused and somewhat annoyed look. "What was that for?"

"Hani screamed. I came out and she's using a chair for protection? What did you expect?" Keith pulled his tea-soaked shirt away from his body at the same time a drop fell from his hair to his nose.

Any ideas of not laughing (which she'd never entertained anyway) dissolved. A chuckle became a chortle which rapidly evolved into laughter and culminated (much to her mortification) in a series of guffaws. One moment she stood there wheezing, tears streaming down her cheeks as she let loose the tension of the assignment in the ridiculousness of the day's events... and the next she sat on the grass and let go.

Only seconds later, she found herself jerked up from the grass and pushed back onto the deck. "Do you want to itch for the next week? Seriously?"

Behind him, the evening sky turned purple, fuchsia, and coral. Hani tore her gaze from the living oil painting and back to Granger's scowling face. "Huh?"

The scowl disappeared and the smile she'd begun to associate with him formed. "I thought you were from Cincy?"

"So?"

"So anyone with any brains, and I'm sure you've got a few, knows to stay out of the grass during summer. Sooo..."

So she was an idiot. That so. "Ugh. I know better. What was I not thinking?" Hani thought fast. She flashed him a grin and folded her arms over her chest before laughing at him again. "Oh, right. I was thinking how ridiculous you guys looked colliding in a spray of sweet tea."

"I have a bottle in my truck if you want to join us?" He swatted at his neck. "Then again, I wouldn't wish the mosquitoes on anyone—even someone who disses the Razorbacks."

She couldn't resist. "Come on... 'Woo, pig, soooie'? Really?"

"Don't diss the backs, or I'll reconsider the bloodletting by skeeters."

"You won't win this, Hani." Keith appeared and went straight for the grill. "Razorback fans are as loyal as 'Bama any day."

You did not just intimate that I care anything about football, much less make me— But the look on Granger's face was too good to pass up. She cocked her head, planted hands on hips and jutted out her chin. "Roll tide."

"Them's fightin' words."

"Losin' ones for you." Two could play at the drop-the-G game.

"We've beat you."

Keith snickered at that one. When Granger looked over at him, Keith snickered again. "C'mon, when was it? 2000?"

"2006, but who's countin'?"

You must do the G thing when you want to be taken seriously... or maybe when you're nervous? She hadn't noticed it before, anyway. She'd work out why she cared later.

While Keith went back to getting the grill going to make the perfect burger, Hani beckoned Granger to follow her. "Come on, hawg. Let's get you washed up before the winged vampires turn you into one of them."

The guy actually stuck his arms out like a bird, made buzzing sounds, and headed right for her. She should've stood her ground, but instead, she squealed and dashed for the back door. It slammed into his face with a satisfying rattle, but she couldn't get the deadbolt turned before he twisted the knob and pushed her back. Count Dracula would turn in his coffin if he heard the Southern twang attached to the mock Transylvanian accent the guy affected as he said, "I'm going to drink your blood!"

"That's gross."

Granger nodded. "It really is. How did it ever become a popular genre, anyway?"

"Some things, I don't want to know." Hani offered him the sink. "Want a clean shirt? Keith probably has something that'd work."

He started to refuse, but as he turned on the sprayer, it splashed back at him, soaking what few spots on his shirt hadn't gotten wet. "I think that's a definite, 'Yes, please.'"

Keith's open duffel bag showed a few T-shirts. Hani started to grab the top two and stopped. A quick flip showed only a USMC. The rest were plain. With that in one hand and a solid black in the other, she met Granger in the hallway. "Here. I'll take this one to Keith."

The guy didn't move, and Hani silently thanked Mark for rejecting Jerm's recommendation to consider biosensors for all agents. The way her heart raced sent her mind spinning. That was something they'd have noticed and checked on. *No biosensors. Period.* She gazed up at the guy's eyes and swallowed hard. How had she missed the deep blue that also managed to be bright at the same time? There in the dim hallway, she could see them clearly. And they ramped up her heart's workout.

It's just basic attraction to a good-looking guy. Nothing to see here.

Half that smile formed. It did that slight hesitation thing and then evened out, little crinkles appearing around his eyes. "Um... mind if I change in there?" He pointed to the bathroom door which she effectively blocked.

"Sure."

He waited. So did she. Forget her heart (did heart workouts give it jelly legs like squats did?), her lungs protested now. Breathing became something that required thought.

Slow motion never moved so slowly. Hani's breath hitched as Granger's hand rose and rested on her shoulder. He wouldn't... no he wouldn't. She couldn't let him. But...

All need to figure out a way to get out of a much wanted (what? You just met him, idiot!) kiss dissolved as he rotated their positions and disappeared into the bathroom. Hani felt as if he winked at her as the door closed. Except he didn't. And she'd have to deal with whatever that meant as well as get an exterminator out for the wigglers that had taken up residence in her belly.

Keith appeared. "Need a shirt."

Hani whirled to face him, thrust the shirt at him, and hurried into the kitchen to clean up spattered water. And her reactions. Definitely needed a cleanup on reaction aisle four.

～

Rockland
July 16, 2012

8:16 a.m.

The moment the chief of Fairbury police disconnected, Jerm burst into Mark's office. Corey, Anthony, and Karen clustered about the seating area, relaxing and strategizing. Jerm still didn't know how those two things worked together. Before he could say a word, Anthony was on his feet.

"Got a call from Chief Varney in Fairbury. A woman called. They're tracking her down now, but the gist is, she's concerned for Lauren Humboldt and says she thinks they may be moving in underage women. Varney doesn't know if the woman was one of the escorts or one of the servers. He just couldn't tell. Call came from Marcello's."

The steel in Mark's tone was the only thing that gave away his opinion on the matter. "Corey, head over to Lauren's house. We'll update you on what to do before you arrive." He beckoned Jerm closer. "What is the concern for Lauren?"

"She said the 'bosses' are upset that she's not there. She thinks they'll force Lauren back."

"We have to find out if this caller is restaurant or syndicate. Now."

Jerm would've bolted out to call back and get any recordings of the call, but Mark continued. "Get on your game and be ready to convince Lauren to leave with Corey. I don't want an IE if I can avoid it."

Involuntary extraction. Lauren wouldn't like that. Not one bit. "Gotcha. I think I can work this."

"If you get her before you get the call info from Varney, call me in. I'll deal with the chief."

This he could do. His skill set might not include taking down intruders or evading assassins, but without him, the others couldn't do those things. Not that he reminded himself of that fact every day of his life. At least twice.

The audio had already been uploaded to a secure server before Jerm got the chief on the phone. One of his officers had verified the voice as Abby Turner—a food runner. Abby and Lauren were supposedly friends... or at least friendly. That would work. It had to work. Lauren would be seriously ticked off if they just took her, but Mark would insist if he thought her life was in danger.

Karen stepped into the office and smiled at him. "Never get hurt. We couldn't function without you."

Leave it to Karen to make sure he felt appreciated. Someday the world would equate the name Karen with love and encouragement. He knew it. Today he'd just say thanks.

"Headed out to try to lure someone at the restaurant into giving something away. Got a dress I can borrow?"

Jerm told her to dig it out from the closet in the conference room. "It's next to my manicure set." He held up his hands for inspection. "You know... in case I ever decide to explore my inner nail artist side."

"Ugh." Karen looked at her own plain nails and sighed. "I don't suppose you actually know how to use the thing?"

Shaking his head, Jerm recommended that she stop at the nail salon just before the loop on ramp at Westward. "They accept walk ins and will get you in and out in under thirty minutes—or so my neighbor claims."

"Aaaand... there goes my suspicions that I should take that nail artistry bit more seriously. But I can't spend half an hour—"

He broke in. "From what I gather, these women are polished to the hilt. You can't afford not to. Just get a quick simple manicure. Nothing fancy. And get out there." He swallowed hard at the look she gave him. "That's my opinion anyway."

"No..." Her look turned into something less menacing and more thoughtful. "I think you're right. Good call."

Karen would've left the office, but Jerm called her back. "Um... the dress? You need the dress."

That tripped her up. "How do I know it'll fit?"

"It's one of those tuby things. It'd fit my mom or my twelve-year-old cousin." He gave her a grin. "And my mom is what Dad likes to call comfy shaped."

While he waited for some sign of Lauren on the Warcraft site, Jerm considered other options. Perhaps he should call or email once Corey notified him of her arrival. Maybe if he demonstrated that if he could find her, anyone could. Appeal to her concern for others?

He went back through all their chats and finally decided that he needed to talk to her over the phone. Mentioning Abby would help.

Especially if he pointed out that they'd sent someone to take care of Abby, too.

Another call from Chief Varney came through. Jerm scribbled a note and raced into Mark's office and slapped it on the desk before dashing back. Now that he'd pinged her, he needed to be there if Lauren signed into her account. A glance at her data info showed her working, but some people kept a chat going while they worked.

Knew you'd have integrity.

The sound of the shredder alerted him to the open office door. Jerm asked without looking up, "Solari?"

"That's just it. We got Simmons in with Solari's guy. Solari has the info about the Brunswick house. No move that way from anyone. If Solari were behind it, he'd have sent someone out."

"What if Leone goes later?"

Mark leaned against the doorjamb. "Tells me he's on his own. I'm tempted to talk to Solari myself."

"He likes to eat at the Oakes." Jerm watched the data numbers changing on Lauren's account and smiled.

"Get me a reservation for every night this week. It's time to find out his stake in this game." Mark made a point of looking at his watch. "Corey should be arriving soon."

"I'd give her another ten minutes unless she risked getting pulled over."

Jerm couldn't help but ask, "So... going to put the fear of God in Solari?"

"Nah... going to see if he knows a good escort service. I'm tired of women thinking that they own me after a night together."

It took three looks, a couple of blinks, and even more reminders that what Mark did in his private life was none of his business before he got it. "Whoa... good one. I bought it."

"Good. Because if Solari doesn't, I could end up dead on the steps of The Oakes before the valet can even get *to* my car."

Chapter Seventeen

Rockland
July 16, 2012
9:52 a.m.

WHEN COREY CALLED TO SAY SHE WAS PARKED OUTSIDE Lauren's house, Jerm had to concede defeat. Next up—call. This would not go over well. Who wanted to feel as if her life had been manipulated? No woman he'd ever met. And who could blame them? He wouldn't like it either.

He picked up the phone, chose the data processing center line, and called. The first ring didn't faze him. After all, sometimes it didn't actually ring for the other person the first time. The second set his senses on alert. The third made him antsy. His heart sank with the fourth. She didn't recognize—

"Hello?"

"Lauren, my name is Jerm, but you know me as Gnomebody."

The silence could've started a nuclear reaction. "How did you get my number?"

"From your employee file. I kind of run the data center."

"This is creepy. I'm changing my number. And I quit."

He had to stop her. "Someone will be knocking on your door in just a minute. Her name is Corey, and you need to go with her. You're not safe there. The people at the restaurant are dangerous, and they want you back."

For a moment, he thought she'd disconnected, but then the question came. The one he dreaded. "How do you know that if you're not part of it? I'm not stupid, you know."

"Because Abby the food runner told Chief Varney of the Fairbury police. He let us know." As he spoke, Jerm sent the text he'd hoped to avoid.

> IE. She'll fight.

"Abby?"

While she pondered that, Jerm wondered if he should tell Corey to hold off. Then he realized it had been a question. "Maybe you should call her."

"Before or after your friend comes to take me to safety?" A second later, she added, "And in case you didn't hear them dripping from my sarcasm, I've got air quotes around that word 'safety.'"

It wasn't something he liked doing, but Jerm thought he needed the backup. He pressed the button that would call Mark to him. Mark appeared almost as if he'd been eavesdropping from the other side of the door. Covering the phone with one hand, he whispered, "Can I tell her Anna went with us?"

"No."

"She might go—"

"She might also alert someone to that fact. No."

He had to try again before Corey got in there. "Lauren, I know it feels like you're being messed with, but this is serious. You were scared enough to get out of there. Now be scared enough to get away to somewhere safe. We've sent Corey. She's great. She'll take good care of you—no creepy guy trying to get you to be one of his escorts."

"No, just a creepy guy telling me to go with a total stranger. As if!"

And with that, she disconnected.

Jerm sent the final text.

Go.

"Sorry. I know you didn't want that." Mark leaned against the door-jamb. "None of us ever do. But we can't jeopardize what we do to try to avoid the unpleasant. She's dead if she doesn't cooperate. She's a virtual slave if she does. This is the kindest thing."

He knew it was. But knowing that putting a dying animal out of its misery was the kindest thing didn't make the process any easier, and as far as Jerm was concerned, it was an apt analogy.

After nodding his agreement, Jerm went back to the computer screen and sent a message. Silence. She'd probably either put him on ignore or spam or both.

~

Steelville
July 19, 2012
8:42 p.m.

Keith's nerves twitched at a creak. *Just tree branches in the wind. Calm down.* Instinct (or maybe just good, old-fashioned fear) demanded they get out of there. They'd been parked like sitting ducks for a week now. Far too long in his opinion.

Okay, so Mark's call about having to pull an involuntary extraction didn't help. He'd convinced himself that this wouldn't be a common thing—hardly ever. He might be able to avoid it altogether, in fact. Aaah... wishful thinking strikes again.

Hani had grown nearly as antsy as well. Hers, however, had to do with the boy next door, as Keith liked to put it. Anna had gotten into the teasing as well, and the result would have been hilarious if Keith hadn't been so on edge. Or rather, the result was hilarious, but he couldn't appreciate it.

To prove her immunity to the guy's charms, Hani found an excuse to walk the grounds often. If she happened to end up out where the guy was, well... she had to keep an eye on their nosy neighbor, didn't she? That was Anna's kind version of things, anyway. Keith just asked if she'd learned his *real* favorite color yet. So far it had been black, gray, olive green, and rust—the colors Hani had been wearing at the time.

He also asked how long the farm had been in the family (three generations). Siblings (one sister), what church he went to (First Assembly of Christ), and military service (yes). Army, in fact. That's all he could be. When Keith had thrown that barb, Granger had asked if the Marines were still looking for a few good men or if they'd finally found some. Hani just laughed at the idea that he'd been an Army Granger.

And she'd never admit it, even if she ever figured it out, but she'd stared a bit too long at the guy's lips that time.

The front door slammed shut, jarring Keith out of his thoughts. Anna glanced up from her book, ready to ask if all was well (obviously not) and thought the better of it when she saw Hani on a cleaning rampage. Keith exchanged a short shake of the head at Anna's questioning look. No need to add fuel to the attraction fire.

"This place is a pigsty."

"Been around any lately?"

The armful of clothes, socks, magazines, and the hoodie she needed to put back on flew at him. Keith caught most, earning him a cheer from Anna. "Impressive."

Hani whirled on her. "He tore the magazine—not impressive."

"He caught it all, though!"

"Not my shoe."

Keith couldn't let that slide. "Be honest here. Would *you* have wanted to catch that shoe so close to *your* face?"

All the angst leaked out in one enormous tear rolling down her cheek. It must have stunned her as much as it did him because she stormed down the hall and jerked open the basement door. Anna rose to follow, but instinct told him to go. "Stay alert but stay here."

And there was another problem. He didn't know if that was right. Did she have to come with him? Hopefully not. He bumped into an orange-tinged photo of a little girl in pigtails and missing a front tooth and knocked it off the wall as he hurried after Hani. The frame shattered, but the insert had been plexiglass, something Keith imagined all safe houses used. Interesting. He'd have to pay attention to what *had* been added as much as what hadn't.

He found Hani in the incomplete laundry room, gripping the sides of the dryer as if a lifeline. Without even looking his way she said, "I need to get out of here. I'm calling Mark."

"Mark, why?" This time she turned and the grief spilling over her cheeks answered for her. "Granger?"

She nodded. "He asked me out."

"So go." Before she could get her protest past her indignation, Keith added. "Just tell him *yes*, but that you can't while I'm here. You'll be back—"

"You don't get it, do you?" Her head shook almost as fast as a wet dog's. "This job? We don't get to have lives. We choose to serve others at the expense of our relationships with family and friends. Adding in a significant other doesn't work!"

Actually, he could understand that. But he also saw something she'd missed... or ignored. "I get that. I can even respect it. But Hani, this is a *job*. This isn't a life. If a chance with someone you might be able to love comes along, are you really going to give up the possibility of a lifetime with him for a job that you'll probably be too old for in ten years? Really?"

"So if you met Ms. Right, you'd quit?"

Keith shrugged. "I don't know. I'm not really looking for someone. I'm still adapting to life outside the corps, to life inside The Agency, and all that those entail. I'm learning how I can do this job as a Christian— how I can lie to save a life. How I can sit here keeping Roman's death from Anna because it will keep her fighting. Those are all I can manage right now."

Hani wilted further. "I forgot those days. I'm sorry. There's been a lot on you all at once, and I didn't help."

"Stop wallowing."

Her head snapped up, and her eyes flashed. "Get over yourself! I just apologized for not doing my job, and you call me wallowing? Fine. I won't apologize again."

Keith shoved a few pieces of drywall out of the way and came to stand before her. Hands on her shoulders, he searched her face before saying, "Be defensive if it makes you happy, but I have to add this: If once I've settled all the unsettled parts of my life into their respective boxes, if after all that, I meet someone... yeah. I'm choosing a person over a job."

Flicking tears off her face, Hani's features hardened. "But I'm *on* the job. And I'm falling apart over a guy I don't know."

"And one you have the right to get to know. Okay? What would Mark say?"

She winced and laughed at the same time. "Keep my enemies closer but remember that he will never require I sleep with the enemy. That decision's mine."

Keith couldn't prevent the wince before it formed on his face."

That prompted another laugh—a derisive one this time, but a laugh, nonetheless. "I tell you my boss says I don't have to 'go all the way' to securing a client's safety, and you wince. I don't get you."

"Sorry..." Was he? That would have to be examined later. Hani needed an answer now. "I just winced at the idea that someone might think they should despite his acceptance of that boundary."

She wiped the residual tears from her face and squared her shoulders. "If it makes you feel better, the most I've ever heard of was someone kissing a client—well, fake kissing."

"Fake kissing?" He folded his arms over his chest and leaned back against the laundry sink. "Do tell."

"You know... push someone into a corner and make it look like you're making out. That happens now and then. You might remember it if you get caught somewhere with Anna."

"She's married!"

Hani shook her head. "Two things. First, if it might save her life, you pretend. Period. And second..." For the first time he saw how much the job was getting to her even outside her turmoil over Granger. Hani swallowed hard, steadied herself, and said, "She's not married anymore."

Nothing could've kicked his gut harder. He sucked in the air and shook his head. "Hadn't thought of that. Just when you think it can't get any worse."

"Oh, it can. Wait'll one of us or Mark has to tell her about Roman. That'll be the worst."

With those sobering words in his ears, Keith followed Hani upstairs and opened the door to the sounds of heartrending sobs. "Oh, no..."

Chapter Eighteen

Rockland
July 19, 2012
7:35 p.m.

IF AMBIANCE COULD CONJURE A SELF-IMPORTANT MAN LIKE Steven Solari, Mark wouldn't have had to hang around the restaurant several nights in a row. Alone. Something about that thought niggled at him while he nursed the same drink he'd had since he arrived. Then it hit him. Swigging back the rest of the Scotch he'd ordered, he rose.

His server stopped him. "Can I get you something?"

"Still waiting for my date. Third night this week. I'm losing my touch. But... I think I'll go in the club and get a refill. Never know who you might meet."

That would get the waitstaff talking. Now, to get them going at the bar.

In direct contrast to soft piano music in the dining room, the club in the other half of the old mansion-turned-restaurant pulsated with a persistent beat as the doorman admitted him. He scanned the room and tried to ignore the weariness that consumed him at the sight of writhing, gyrating bodies. When had he gotten too old to enjoy the club scene?

A woman chatted with the right-side bartender as he filled orders one after the other. Well, more like chatted *at* the poor guy. That's where he needed to go. He wedged in just a couple of feet from her and waited for the bartender's questioning gaze. "Double Scotch. I'm going to need it."

The man's raised eyebrow gave him the opening he wanted. "Third night this week I've been stood up." The woman inched his way, and Mark realized his mistake. "Well, most likely. Brandie tends to think an hour late is expected, so there's hope, eh?"

In his peripheral vision, the woman seemed conflicted. Approach or keep back? If he weren't here on business, he'd buy her a drink simply to reward someone not moving in for the kill the moment fresh meat entered the waters. Instead, he took the drink the bartender offered, nodded his thanks, gave her a brief smile, and headed back into the restaurant.

Solari had just seated his wife and was headed his way. Mark made a show of hesitation before detaining the man. Solari eyed him with a question rather than speaking it. Mark complied. "Sorry to bother you here, but I'd heard you were the go-to guy for quality entertainment. Something about a restaurant in Fairbury?"

The man shook his head. "I'm afraid you have me confused with someone else. My business interests are all in Rockland, and I don't deal in that sort of commodity."

Without another word, the ruler of the Rockland underworld disappeared into the bar. Mark seated himself at his table, lost in thought. Going with one's gut could get people killed, but so could waiting too long to act. After another few minutes, and a few bites of his lamb chop, Mark decided. He pulled out his phone and sent Jerm the text.

> Notify the chief.

~

Steelville
July 19, 2012
9:27 p.m.

She'd known for days, but knowing and confirmation were two different animals. Keith had given it away the moment he'd learned. He'd grown gentle with her—careful. And then when she'd brought up information about the new people at the restaurant, he hadn't been surprised. *That gave it away.*

And yet she'd hoped. Maybe they got it wrong. Maybe... maybe.

Alone in her room, after wrangling the details out of Keith and Hani, Anna made plans. They had to go back. Roman would want her to—would insist that they not waste the years of sacrifice. He'd remind her of how much money they'd invested. He'd insist that she get their money back somehow—that she used it to start a new life.

Sobs ripped through her again as the obvious screamed itself into her presence. *Alone.*

An old hymn she hadn't heard since she'd been a very little girl sitting on the pew next to her grandmother filled her mind. *"...no, never alone... no, never alone. He promised never to leave me—never to leave me alone."*

She'd have to take God's word for it, because Anna had never felt more alone and abandoned. Never.

When the clock rolled over to midnight and she still hadn't fallen asleep, Anna climbed the stairs to see if they had chamomile tea—anything to make her sleep. She found Keith washing dishes. "What are you doing up?"

He gave her a weak smile. "How are you?"

Nice evasion of the question. Deliberate or just concern? Anna shrugged. "I miss my husband more than ever. When he might be alive, I could look forward to seeing him soon. Now... half my heart has been ripped out."

"I'm so sorry. You shouldn't have found out like that. I was irresponsible."

"Apologize for not telling me information that is my right to know, not for trying to do your job." As hard as she tried to keep from sharpening the edge of her tongue, Anna knew it had to have cut.

Keith turned off the water and dried his hands. He pulled two bottles of water from the fridge and carried them to the table. He also reached for the last of the oatmeal cookies. "Let's talk. I don't know what I'm doing here, but I do know I need to know how to do my job better."

Even over the hum of the air conditioner, she heard tree frogs and crickets serenading one another, and Anna listened. Sometimes she could hear it in their apartment, but usually not. Out here in the countryside, far more critters called the area home, and the din outside proved it. *This isn't the time for training for future clients. This is the time to deal with* my case.

"Anna?"

"We can talk about how that should've been handled some other day. Today we need to think about this case as it is right now. These people who killed my husband? You think they want to kill me, too. That's why we're hiding, correct?"

The guy ate most of a cookie before he responded. "That's the idea."

"Do you really think they'll do it? Kill me?"

"If they can, yes." He reached across and laid a hand on her arm. "Anna, I can't promise you they won't succeed, but I can promise that they'll have to kill me first. I'll do anything I can to protect you. I just wish we'd known in time that we needed to protect him."

How she wished it, too. Shivers rippled over her, and her arms broke out in goosebumps. This was no time for fear, though. Roman trusted her. "Then we need to go back—gather evidence against them."

"Not possible."

Somehow, she needed to convince Keith that her idea wasn't just sound but imperative. "Listen, Keith. I need to go home. I need to fight for the restaurant, or these guys will win." She could see him preparing a protest, but Anna kept talking. "I know I'm in danger there, but if you came, too, you could protect me. I *must* go home and save our investment —for Roman's sake. You can protect me, and everyone except the bad guys wins."

"We're working on taking them down anyway. You don't have to go."

"But I do," she argued. "Listen. It would work." The more she thought, the better the idea became. "See, you go there before me. Hide. Be there to protect me." The idea grew into the sort of plan only movies tried, but she could see it. "Then someone else brings me home. I'm like bait. You catch them."

While outright rejection wouldn't have surprised her, his hesitation did. The guy looked... confused. "What? What's wrong with it?"

Keith wrapped both hands around his water bottle like a half-frozen man grips a coffee mug in winter. Twice he opened his mouth to say something, and both times he clamped it shut. Finally, he shrugged. "I don't know. Something in my gut tells me it won't work, but I can't figure out why yet."

"Can't we figure it out from Fairbury? Then we're in place?"

"It's not safe."

Grief gave courtesy a smackdown and reared its ugly head. "Are you really saying you can't protect me unless we're in the middle of nowhere? Really?"

"No." It came quickly enough, but it didn't sound defensive to her. Keith gave his head a little shake and met her gaze. "No... that's not it. That's not the reason."

He was serious. And the fact that he hadn't just rejected it outright and moved on gave her hope for reconsideration once he figured out whatever that objection was. Time to move on to other topics and go back to bed. Exhaustion had tiptoed into her body and now tried to smother her.

Anna reached out for his arm this time. "Whenever and wherever it happens, I know the time is coming. I can already feel it. I'm going to become angry about all this and I'll probably take it out on you."

"Probably. Mark said most people do."

She acknowledged that with a nod and rose, water bottle in hand. "Well, right now when I'm just hurting, you need to know that I'm grateful for all you've done for us. It didn't turn out like I'd like..." Anna's voice broke. "But I doubt it was the outcome you wanted, either. So thank you for trying. And Roman would thank you for keeping me safe."

Marines probably didn't cry often, but as she opened the door at the end of the hallway, she would have sworn she heard the sounds of strangled sobs. They'd become too close and personal companions of hers not to recognize them.

∼

Steelville
July 20, 2012
12:09 a.m.

When Granger Payne's parents had moved out of the house and over to Sullivan where they bought a wheelchair accessible house after a bad fall off the barn roof, he'd spent six months avoiding moving into his parents' larger bedroom. In fact, while he and Dad went to a Cardinals game one afternoon, his mother had come out and made the move for him.

Lying in that queen-sized bed, his hands slung behind his head, Granger once again thanked his mother for that gift of love and transference. Cool air ruffled the thin sheet pulled over him, so he rolled on his side to pull it taught. Those ripples never did sit well with him. They tickled in all the wrong ways.

Not like Hani's hair tickled his hand as he'd rotated her out of his way in their narrow hallway. His eyes closed of their own accord, and Granger relived that moment. The way she didn't breathe. Did she know he could tell? The inner turmoil over wanting him to kiss her and knowing it wasn't a good idea. She wasn't the kind of woman who kissed men just because she could. He could see that.

Could she see that he knew she fought temptation and disappointment when he moved past her without so much as a thumb caressing her jaw? Could she see his own thoughts reflected in his eyes? He didn't think so but only because she'd been so consumed with her own desires.

The moon slid out behind clouds and its soft light streamed through his windows. Granger sat up and gazed around the room. How many times had he sat in this very spot in the wee hours of the night and held in the clutches of a ridiculous nightmare so real he believed in its power? How many times had his father sat up beside him and pointed to the waving cornstalks and reminded him that if they bowed down, it was because the Lord willed it rather than because they were coming to swallow him whole.

His mother had still never forgiven Brother Branson for telling the story of Joseph in Egypt with such vivid description. For a four-year-old like Granger, it had been fodder for a different kind of famine—somnolence. If he were honest, he'd admit that occasionally the dream returned, and he still woke up with perspiration beading on his forehead. Being stalked by corn in his nightmares kept his life... disturbing.

But he had his suspicions that he wasn't the only resident in Steelville who had "stalkers." His new neighbor was too skittish not to have something off in her life. The question was... what? His first guess would be that stalker. Why else would someone move into a house with only a couple of duffel bags and some building materials? Sure, they could be fitting out the basement. Or... they could be building a panic room or a false wall—anything to give her a place to hide.

And why had her brother come with her? It wasn't that siblings never lived together, but it still seemed... off. And then there was the lack of job. He hadn't asked yet, but anytime he'd been able to sneak off to check on them, Hani had been there.

Unexpected arrival, combined with no moving truck, combined with her brother building something, and adding in no job left one obvious answer. One or both of them were running away from something or someone. If Hani hadn't shown obvious attraction to him, Granger would've suspected they were lying about that sibling thing. But a guy didn't have to be full of himself to recognize interest. Especially interest that she fought to hide.

She didn't seem interested in church, Lord. Because she's ambivalent or resistant to You, or because she's holing up to protect herself?

Granger rolled over, closed his eyes, and prayed he'd go to sleep. Maybe tomorrow was a good day to try to find out.

Chapter Nineteen

〜

Steelville
July 21, 2012
5:31 p.m.

ASKING GRANGER TO JOIN THEM FOR HER FAMOUS LASAGNA—A strategic, tactical solution. Right up to the point where Hani remembered she didn't have a "famous lasagna" recipe. Anna to the rescue. She sent Hani to the store with a list of preferred items, reasonable substitutions, and "barely better than nothing" options if reasonable didn't exist. Now, half an hour before Granger should appear, the garlic bread was about to go into the oven and Anna was ready to disappear down the stairs. "Did you get that book I asked for?"

Hani nodded. "In my purse. It sounds good."

After retrieving Laura Hillenbrand's *Unbroken* from the suitcase-sized purse on the counter, Anna took her mini lasagna and disappeared downstairs. Keith visibly twitched at it. "It's okay. You have to get used to protection being more important than inclusion. If you're putting forth a narrative of someone not existing, then you have to live it."

"I don't have to like it."

"No... but if you are showing discomfort, you'll make the threat nervous, and—"

"Threat?" Keith's laugh didn't sound exactly mirthful. "The guy isn't our enemy. He's just a neighbor."

While she slid the garlic toast into the oven, Hani went into instructor mode. "No... no. That's not the way to think. *Anyone,* including an agent who acts outside Anna's best interests, is a potential threat. Even me." She slammed the door shut and turned to face him. "Seriously, *I* feel more like a threat than an agent right now. I've only done this kind of immersive assignment a couple of times, and with those, I had training and a back-story bible. I wasn't making it up as I went."

"What... you haven't attracted the boy next door on your previous assignments?" Keith grinned at her scowl. "Find that hard to believe."

"I usually take us to places without neighbors. It's kind of why I decided we should stay here. Sure there are "neighbors," but it's not like I can see their houses from mine. If I hadn't run into Granger—"

The doorbell rang.

Keith finished for her, "You wouldn't be having a date with him chaperoned by your big fake brother."

"Little brother."

"Whatever."

All the nonchalance she'd manufactured between oven and front door evaporated the moment she glanced in the mirror to check her hair. Keith snickered. Her cheeks darkened. *Please think it's just from cooking.* A grin appeared. That'd do it. She jerked open the door. "Hey, Granger. Come in. Need to check the garlic bread." As she hustled back to the oven, she called over her shoulder, "You know how it is. That stuff burns if you blink too slowly."

"Far be it from me to interfere with the proper toasting of garlic and butter on yeasty goodness."

She peered into the oven long enough to make her face hot and grinned as she turned back. "A man after my own heart." Only when Granger grinned back and Keith smirked, did she realize what she'd said. "Hey... gotta keep those vampires away, right?"

This time Keith actually laughed.

Her phone buzzed. Hani pulled it out and saw a message from Anna's temporary number.

> I hear something outside the windows. Possum?

She zipped back a reply.

> Probably. I'll figure out a reason to go outside soon.

Only when she'd checked the toast and called it done did she see Keith and Granger watching her. "What?"

Keith smirked again.

Oh, great.

"Everything okay?"

"Sure! Why would you ask that?" Dumb question. Deflect, not engage. This was basic training stuff, and she'd allowed herself to be distracted by a pair of killer eyes and a half smile.

"You just frowned is all. Can I take that?" Granger reached around the cookie sheet and slid his hand over hers to take command of the potholder. To say Hani swooned would be an exaggeration—but not by much.

"Thanks. Let's eat!"

Nerves pinged one after the other, and Hani nearly convinced herself that it was all about a possible intruder. It had nothing to do with Granger's knee so close to hers that she could feel it without even touching him. Nothing to do with the compliments on how great the meal smelled. Nothing to do with her disappointment in realizing she didn't earn those compliments being washed away by his reaching for her hand when Keith offered to pray.

Prayer. That would do it. She could use it as an excuse for needing space for a moment if it came down to it. Keith would back her up on her lack of religious interests. If Granger had any serious ones, they could commiserate while she was outside cooling off.

That thought prompted both a snicker *and* an idea. "Hey, be right back," Hani said as she pushed away from the table. "Gonna go get a hair tie."

Only when she reached the door did Granger ask why she was going outside. "Hair tie."

Keith looked just as confused. "Don't you have several in the bathroom?"

"Not my favorite one."

Granger's, "Favorite one?" nearly undid her, but Hani pulled the door shut behind her as quietly as possible and raced to the Miata. She found a hair tie beneath the front seat and pulled her hair back into it. Then she raced to the corner of the house, peered around it, and dashed to the opposite corner. Nothing. A glance down the row of rhododendrons showed no one back there. Probably that stupid possum.

When she returned, the men still stared at her as if she'd lost all reason. She couldn't blame them. Her hair probably stood out straight like a mohawk stuck to the back of her head. Too bad. She needed an excuse, and she took it. Time for diversion.

"So... who feels like losing a game of gin rummy after we eat?"

~

Steelville
July 21, 2012
11:01 p.m.

Keith would mock her like nobody's business, but Hani didn't care. She stood at the end of the drive, waving as Granger drove away. She relived each moment of him tugging her arm and urging her to walk him out. The way he'd *nearly* held her hand, moving closer when she'd stepped aside to avoid a rock in the drive. Never had such *near* nearness been so invigorating—so... something.

If anyone had asked if she'd ever want to feel like a kid with her first crush again, she'd have said, "no way." Those awkward, embarrassing days were long behind. But something about the way Granger took small, tentative steps toward showing his interest reminded her of someone savoring a long-awaited meal. When had people quit savoring the little moments?

Her heart light enough to ensure she floated away on the sort of romantic daydreams she'd left behind in high school, Hani crept back into the house. Despite knowing she should prepare for a barrage of teasing, she didn't. There were too many moments to relive again and again. The half smile that Granger gave her every time Keith's attention had been diverted from them. The way he pressed his knee against hers until he realized her knee wasn't the table leg... and then kept it there anyway. The mocking, the teasing, the innuendo that didn't turn inappropriate all through the game of rummy that she'd dominated. As promised.

It all added up to one thing. There was a possibility of something special with this guy, and for the first time in her career, she wanted the opportunity to explore it. *Three months off after this assignment? I could stay here and keep up the cover, maybe. See if there's anything to this? If there is, take off the rest of the year?*

As if an answer to her internal questioning, her phone buzzed. She pulled it out and her throat went dry. "Keith!"

Footfalls thundered up the basement steps. The door banged in the hallway as he sprinted toward her. "What?"

"Jimmy Simmons is dead."

"What does that mean, practically speaking?"

"He said too much to the wrong person in jail and he's been silenced. Mark says Leone is working alone. We might have proof. If you're not packed, get packed. The call could come any minute."

~

Steelville
July 21, 2012
11:24 p.m.

Three minutes into Keith's shower, Hani heard it. She'd been just lost in thought enough not to know what "it" was, but she definitely heard... something that sounded manmade. A few seconds later, she thought she heard it again. This time her mind categorized it as keys or maybe loose change. One of those chains some guys used to connect keys to their belt loops?

When it came the third time, Hani bolted down the hallway and into the bathroom. She poked at Keith through the shower curtain. The guy yelped.

She backed out of the room and pulled the door mostly closed. "You okay in there?"

The guy hesitated too long, but then he called back, "Just turned the water too hot. Scalded myself."

She crept in again and spoke as quietly as possible. "I heard someone outside. Get to Anna and be ready to defend or evacuate."

"Leaving." He turned off the water and fumbled for his towel. Hani backed out of the bathroom but didn't shut the door quite all the way.

"Are you sure?" she whispered. "You don't—"

"I've wanted out for days. We'll go as soon as there's no one around."

As much as she wanted to protest, she knew he was right. "Let Mark know where to send me as soon as you know you're safe. Trust your instincts. You're a good agent."

Hani didn't wait for a response. She strode out front and gave her eyes time to adjust to the darkness. Lights glowed in the windows, but no matter how closely she watched, she saw no sign of Keith or Anna. *Good job.*

It really was. She'd have to tell Mark to get him trained fast. He'd be one of their best in no time.

Something shifted in the night—a shadow lengthening or retreating. Whatever it was, she needed to find it and fast. Better yet, she should draw it away from the house long enough to give Keith time for escape.

She sprinted for the tree line in the backyard. Pretending to stumble, Hani let out a squeak in case their invader hadn't noticed her. He would now. Into the trees, over a couple of fallen logs, and around some brambles that she couldn't identify in the dark. Why didn't she remember this?

"Who's there?" Calling out went against every protective instinct she had, but Keith and Anna needed a chance to get away.

A rustle behind her was all it took. She retrieved her gun from its back holster and nearly ran into a tree when the picture of Granger trying to slip his hand around her waist and connecting with that holster presented itself with a mock salute. No man had ever gotten close enough to her to try anything like it since joining The Agency, but she hadn't forgotten the connectedness and swoon-worthiness of that light touch—as good as a kiss when you couldn't actually have one.

No one stepped out of the shadows to confront her. Not one single shadow shifted over by the house. By the time she stepped back onto the grass, whatever had been out there must have gone. A dog? A coyote? That stupid possum? With her luck, it'd be him. Or her. The possum could totally be a her.

By the time she made it back out front to see if Keith and Anna had left, that eerie feeling of being watched returned. Hani scanned the driveway, the road, and finally decided it must have been a critter. Holstering her gun again, she pulled her shirt down over it, closed her eyes, and took in the muggy summer night. The air hung thick and oppressive, but Hani couldn't decide if it was the humidity or the tension of the moment. One of those two things could be cut with the proverbial knife—maybe both.

She heard the crunch behind her just a fraction of a second before a hand clamped around her arm. Hani twisted, wrenched free, and spun in place, foot extended and ready to kick the air out of whoever had tried to grab her. Granger ducked and wove like a boxing pro. Between trying to pull the kick *and* him not being where she expected, Hani went down into the grass. Hard.

Granger had her on her feet in seconds, likely in an attempt to avoid whatever imminent chigger attack he expected. What was with these Missourians and their obsession with chiggers? She'd never seen anything like it.

"Did you see him?"

Hani froze. "Who?"

"Pete Fikkers. I swear I saw him out here. Drove past on my way to get some milk at the Country Mart, and saw his truck parked at the turnout again—empty. He doesn't live around here."

"I saw someone—felt someone watching me when I came out to see what was going on."

"When?" Granger began searching the yard, the bushes and even heading toward the tree line.

"About ten minutes ago? Don't know. I went looking for whoever was out there and ended up stumbling around in the trees."

After scanning the yard again, Granger pushed her toward the house. "If you've been in the trees, you need to go check to be sure you didn't get any stowaways."

"Stowaways?"

"Ticks."

The low rumble of a truck starting up set Granger into motion. He pointed at the door and said, "Get inside. I'll be right there."

"Where are you going?"

But the guy didn't respond. He just took off toward the road. Meanwhile, Hani pulled out her phone and called Keith. No response.

Chapter Twenty

Steelville
July 21, 2012
11:51 p.m.

GRANGER FOLLOWED AS HANI BURST THROUGH THE FRONT door and into the house. "Keith? Keith!"

No answer.

The nervous confidence (weren't those mutually exclusive things?) Hani exuded outside became nearly frantic inside. "Hey, Keith! Where —?" She turned to him, looking mortified. "Of course. He's downstairs working on the basement. It's looking good down there."

Without inviting him to follow, Hani hurried down the hall and disappeared out of sight. Her footfalls on the stairs played a staccato percussion as she raced down to find Keith. Granger waited with little patience. Something about the whole thing was off.

Both Hani and Keith had been a bit strange at times, but they'd been wary, not frantic. They'd been confident in their caution. He still suspected Hani had an obsessive boyfriend—ex, he hoped—she'd chosen to escape. That would explain a lot.

But Keith not being there when he had been just minutes before?

Hani dashing into the woods when she thought she heard someone? That seemed like the definition of a horror movie. And few women her age not only conceal-carried but did it with a waistband holster. Although, he had to admit to himself, at first it had appeared she'd just shoved it in the waistband like some TV gangster.

And yes, he'd felt like a bit of a creeper staring at the back of her waist as long as he had to decide which it was.

Or... a new thought slapped him upside the head and tried to shake some sense into him. *They could be cops—FBI or ATF. Maybe Pete Fikkers is cooking meth, and they're here to take him down. It would explain a lot.*

Feet pounded back up the stairs, and a truly confused Hani burst out of the door. "He's not there! I just left him!"

"Maybe call?"

Hani leaned against the wall, panting. Then she blinked at him and grinned. "Duh!" She pulled out her phone. "Bet he got hungry and went for ice cream or something. Want anything from The Country Mart if he did? I'm going to have him get me a pint of Ben & Jerry's Cheesecake Brownie."

"Something with caramel. Whatever he finds. Oh, and milk." He grinned at her. "Gives me a reason to stick around for a bit."

The woman's gaze fixed on his, and all the tension faded from her features. Just a second later, a new tension formed there, one he recognized. *Why am I so intrigued by this woman? I know nothing about her—not really.* The fact that she seemed antagonistic to anything connecting with faith should've redirected personal interest to discipleship interest. And it did... but in an inclusive way that he would have pounded a little sister for attempting. If he'd had another sister, that is. Well, and if she'd been so stupid.

Hani glanced at her phone. Then she glared at it. "He's not responding."

"You're sure he left?"

This time she gaped at him. "I'm such an idiot." Pushing past him (he'd explore his nearly overpowering desire to grab her and hold fast later), Hani stormed to the front door and jerked it open. After staring outside long enough to ensure heat began to seep into the entryway, she slammed it shut and turned to him.

"Why didn't I notice the truck was gone?"

His own alarm evaporated. "I should've noticed that, too. You're right. He's probably getting ice cream or maybe an energy drink or whatever."

She punched the screen on her phone again. After a moment, she demanded, "Keith. Pick up. Pull the stupid truck over and pick up!"

"He can't hear you if he doesn't do that in the first place." A new thought occurred to Granger. "He never answers while driving?"

Hani stared—glared, really—at her phone for another few seconds before snapping her head up. "What? Oh, no. Keith won't talk or text and drive—not even on speakerphone. He's fanatical about it. But hasn't it been long enough since we met in the yard for him to have arrived?"

"Speeding there? Super-fast inside? Driving back already?" The times were barely possible... maybe. He doubted it.

The woman began pacing again. The nervous energy radiated from her until he found his own fingers twitching. Desperation to calm them both overrode sense, and on her next pass, he pulled her to him. Hani stiffened as he wrapped both arms around her and began praying. That stiffness, however, relaxed the longer he spent asking the Lord for wisdom, for safety for Keith, and for peace in their hearts.

Everything shifted mid prayer as his own heart began reaching out to connect with hers. The prayer trailed off into the cool, refrigerated air. He tucked her head under his chin and inhaled the scent of her soap—clean and slightly fruity. Citrus? It was hard to decide when his senses reeled at the nearness of her.

He'd have to take his distraction up with the Lord later. Repentance was clearly in order, and Granger didn't look forward to having to ask forgiveness for allowing a moment with a beautiful woman to override conversation with a beautiful Savior.

Just as her arms slipped around his waist and everything seemed to be as perfect as it could be, she stiffened and jumped back. Her wide eyes had filled with horror. Not exactly flattering. But her words soothed his pride. A little. "Where *is* he?!"

∼

Steelville
July 22, 2012
12:08 a.m.

Even as Hani babbled about Keith, her mind screamed at her. *What do you think you're doing? If his arms had dropped just a tiny bit, he'd have felt your gun!! Get your head in the game!!!*

The fact that she might be off Anna's case was also a reality she had to deal with. Keith might decide to go dark. If so, only Mark would know where he was. For now. In a few months or years, it could be that he'd not even tell Mark, but she doubted he would consider that an option. Yet.

"Didn't mean to make you uncomfortable, Hani." Granger's thumb caressed her cheek, and to her relief (and her disgust), she leaned into it.

"You didn't." Though her mind called her a liar, she ran with it. "I just don't know why he's not calling me. He *always* calls. Maybe I'll go looking for him."

Something in Granger shifted. He led her to the couch and gave a gentle shove. Hani dropped into it without resistance. Sitting beside her, he took her hand and captured her attention. "Look, does he have any enemies? Do you?"

Hani snatched back her hand and jumped up. She misjudged the distance to the coffee table and whacked her shin on it. "Ow! No. What are you talking about. This is real life, not some TV show. We're talking about Keith here. The most ordinary man on the planet. Everyone loves him. No crazy mob is chasing him. He's not running from a drug dealer..." One by one she ticked off every TV trope she could think of. "Oh, and no, he didn't witness some crime, and I'm not a US Marshal hiding him out here. Or vice versa for that matter."

"And yet..." Granger tugged her down beside him again, dropping his arm around her shoulder when she leaned into him. "Someone was outside—possibly Pete Fikkers. Your brother was here. Now he's gone."

Oh, how she wanted to sit there and revel in his closeness. But she needed to talk to Keith, and leaving fake messages on one of the office lines wasn't getting her any information. She had to convince Granger to leave and soon.

Then I need to examine my head and find out what is going on in there. I'm blowing this job. I'm a liability right now. And I'm better than this!

"Why do you think he's not picking up his phone?"

"I don't know." She pulled out hers again and tapped the screen. As she knew, it went straight to voicemail. "Okay, Keith. This isn't funny anymore. It's..." she glanced at the time. "It's past midnight. Where *are* you?"

When she said midnight, Granger startled. He jumped up and said, "Hey... are you sure you're okay here?"

Please say you're leaving. I need to call a real number! Hani nodded. "Of course. I'm annoyed more than anything."

"I can stay if you need me to, but my buddy got 'stuck'..." the air quotes couldn't have been more exaggerated, "... camping and needs me to take his shift at the manufacturing plant."

"You work shift work at a plant?"

"Security—off and on sometimes. Mostly off except in winter." He brushed hair away from her face, stroked her cheek, squeezed her shoulder. Every look and movement said he didn't want to go. If she'd been taller or he'd been shorter, he'd have pressed their foreheads together like in some sappy movie, she just knew it. "I don't like leaving you like this. I can call out..."

"No... go. I'll let you know if I let Keith live tomorrow—after you've had some sleep."

A few seconds ticked by—ones in which she knew he considered kissing her. Hani spent the time arguing with herself. Did she want him to? Definitely. Did she consider kissing him first? Absolutely. Was it smart not to let it happen? Equally affirmative. Had she lost her ever lovin' mind? Most assuredly.

"Hani..." His jaw went rigid and with one more squeeze to her shoulder, he disappeared out the door.

Disappointment started a hair-pulling match with relief... and won.

She gave herself fifteen seconds to revel in the moment before bolting to the bathroom to retrieve her toothbrush and deodorant. Usually, she'd leave them, but since she had the time, why not grab 'em? As she cleared out everything she could think of, including a blank journal she'd begun to write in, she called Mark.

"Where'd he go?"

"Don't know. He hasn't checked in since I got the 'gone' text. But as soon as he gets somewhere, he'll set up a new phone and let me know. I'll forward that text."

She thought for a moment before sitting down on the bed. The room didn't have enough girlie bits—a collage wall with poetry and maybe a cute actor. She'd have to tell Mark that later. "So... where do you *think* he'll go?"

"He only knows about three getaways, so it'll likely be one of them unless he decides to go out on his own. He has clearance for it, but I doubt he would. He doesn't have the confidence you gain from experience yet."

"This is weird, Mark. I'm not comfortable. I need those locations. I think I'll start toward the one—"

Mark broke in. "No you won't. You need to stay put."

Her heart kicked into warp speed. "Why? What—?"

"Listen to me, Hani. You've invested in a community there. People know you're there and that you're doing work on that house. You need to create a credible reason for Keith leaving and stick around. If Leone's guys reach over that way, and there's a heavy meth production over there, so it's likely—not just possible—they could get wind of people coming in. They'll think you're ATF and they'll warn Leone and probably go after anyone you've had contact with."

Her heart refused to beat at a reasonable rhythm. It squeezed, thumped, flopped, and squeezed again. Anyone could've seen how often Granger's truck had been out front. How often she'd walked or driven over his way. How often they'd stood out in her drive talking... close.

"With the basement work, he could've injured himself. I'll get some blood from a butcher or something."

"Asian market. Pig blood. Might be freeze-dried, but you can reconstitute it."

How he knew these things, Hani never could figure out, but it also never ceased to impress her. "Got it. When I see Granger next, I'll tell him about the blood I found down there, finally found out from his girlfriend that he hurt himself and went to the hospital. He'll be staying with his girlfriend now so she can take care of him."

"He won't thank you for that."

"He deserves it. Trust me. And Mark?"

"Hmmm?"

Hani sighed. "I suspect you've got your best agent ever now. He's good. He's really good. I plan to try to be better, but... I have to admit, this one's got great instincts."

Chapter Twenty-One

East St. Louis, Illinois
July 22, 2012
1:11 a.m.

JUST PAST ONE O'CLOCK, KEITH PULLED INTO A GAS STATION for a fill up and a pit stop. While he filled the tank, Anna went inside. He watched as two other cars pulled in and one pulled out. The one looked like a guy coming off shift work somewhere. Exhaustion exuded from the man's movements, and yawns punctuated each one as well. Without going inside, he paid for his gas, pumped it, and took off.

A banana yellow Camero pulled in behind Keith, and two half-drunk girls spilled out. He watched them long after the pump clicked off. A guy eventually emerged from the driver's seat and began pumping. Another guy shouted drunken obscenities. Probably college kids on a party crawl before they went back to school next month.

Another car sat near the doors, but only an old lady left the vehicle. When another car (what was with this place and people driving around at one in the morning?) appeared, he pulled up to the far left of the door and exited. Anna was taking forever, but then women tended to be in restrooms far longer than men would. Why was that?

A magazine rack near the small hall to the restrooms was the best opportunity for casual observation, so Keith pulled a copy of *Classic Bikes* from the rack and pretended to thumb through it. The drunk duo stumbled past in their killer heels and too short dresses. One tried to flirt but was too out of it to remember how. Never had he had more trouble *not* laughing at someone. He flipped the page in his magazine instead.

"Come *on*, Tami. We need to *gooo*..."

"But he's cute."

"So's Jase. Go kiss up to Jase."

The girl flipped her hair over her shoulder and tried to stand up straight. "Jase is *your* boyfriend."

"Fine. If he's not good enough, go make out with Gabe. I don't care. Just *gooooo*."

After one last look at him, the girl sighed and waved fingers at him as she passed. "Bye pretty boy..."

Keith could've puked. Pretty boy. Whatever. Still, maybe Anna was being smart and not leaving until everyone else had left the restroom. She was much more intelligent than her placid personality implied.

Time ticked past, and he flipped through enough magazines that guilt began to creep in. Between the underdressed females and the "consume the content without paying for it" aspect, it was too much. An older woman appeared and the look she gave him made him wish he could tell her and her husband to get a hotel room for the night. Anyone that terrified needed to be in a safe, locked room until daylight. He tried a smile, but it only earned him a scowl and a hasty retreat.

Two more minutes passed before Keith couldn't take it anymore. Certain that no one else had entered and that everyone else had exited, he barged into the restroom and began a systematic search of every nook and cranny. No one could have crawled through the tiny window. The stalls were empty and there wasn't even a trash can large enough to hide in or behind. She'd vanished.

Keith whipped out his phone and fumbled for his contacts so fast that he forgot to leave the women's restroom until a woman of about forty entered with a little girl in tow. She froze, apologized, and backed out only to glare at him when she saw the sign on the door. Keith bolted outside to search the parking lot and surrounding area. As he searched, he called Hani.

She answered on the first ring. "Where are you?"

At the same time, Keith asked, "Where would she go?"

"What?"

"Anna! Where would she go? She's gone."

Hani broke into his tirade with more questions. "Gone? What? Where?"

"I don't know. She's gone. She went to the bathroom and disappeared. I have to assume that she left because the alternative is horrifying. *Where would she go?*"

Hani swore and Keith winced. It was bad enough hearing it from men. He didn't care if it made him a chauvinist, a Victorian patriarchal jerk, or even a misogynistic pig. Foul language just sounded even worse coming from a woman.

"Fairbury."

Keith refocused on the conversation. "Fairbury?"

"That's where she'd go. I'll call Mark. You go find her."

Keith protested. "It's my fail. I need to make that call. I need to own up to this. I don't know how—"

Hani stopped him. "Keith! Just stop!" He heard the sound of the ice machine dropping ice into the fridge. Hani must be in the kitchen. "You have to remember she is a free human being. She is capable and allowed to make her own decisions and her own mistakes. She's not a child, and you're not responsible for her—" She interrupted his protest. "No, Keith —not in the way you would be for a child. She's most likely fine."

"It's the most likely part that terrifies me," Keith growled as he climbed up into the truck, ready to head out. He'd head across on I-70 to Indy and then over to Rockland. "If Anna didn't take off on her own, she's dead. And that's on me. Gotta go." He disconnected the call, prayed for courage and honesty, and hit the emergency contact number. As he waited for the ring, he zoomed out of the parking lot and toward the interstate on-ramp and back toward Rockland. Back toward Fairbury. Back toward (at least he hoped) the woman who might have just gotten him fired. He'd revisit that thought later.

Jerm's wince came through the airwaves loud and clear as he apologized. "Sorry, Keith. He's in a meeting. You'll have—"

"9-1-1."

At those words, he heard a click. A moment later, Mark's voice boomed out. "Where's Anna?"

"I don't know. I wish I did, but I don't. She just disappeared. Hani thinks she'd try to go home, so that's where I'm headed."

"I just got word from a cop who is under cover in Solari's group. Leone is definitely making a power play, and you've been tracked. You need to throw *everything* you have away, get another vehicle, and start over. That includes socks, shoes, glasses, everything."

Perspiration soaked his shirt just at the thought. "Money?"

"Hand over everything you've got and get change for it. Make sure you destroy any cards—even your driver's license. Where are you?"

"Just drove out of East St. Louis. Heading up to I-70."

After a bit of mumbled conversation, Mark came back. "Okay, get to the Walmart in Collinsville—off I-55. It's open twenty-four hours. There will be a... Come on Jerm. We need—got it. Thanks." Mark rattled off directions and said, "Got it. Black Ford Focus. It'll be parked by the garden center, but you have to enter the store over by the food. Destroy everything and leave in different trash receptacles around the place. There's a Casey's and a Wendy's. Use those, too. Put *nothing* in that car. And get to Anna's in Fairbury. Jerm will text you the address again *after* you text us a new cell phone. This one dies now. Throw it out the window."

"How'd they track me?" Before Mark could answer he knew. "The lunch meeting. So they've known where we were all along?"

"Sort of. It's more like they've had the ability to find out all along. They needed to get close enough to get a signal. According to our source, they got close enough thanks to some idiot meth head in Steelville."

"Probably Pete Fikkers."

Mark's stunned silence was all the proof Keith needed. At least he'd look better for half a second. "Hey, Mark. I blew it. I lost our client. I know this means I'm fired, but I'll get her again and get her safe if someone else doesn't find her first. I'm so sorry."

"Stop. Just listen. I won't pretend that this isn't bad, and I won't pretend that I haven't fired people for less. But there are a couple of things we have to take into consideration."

"Nice of you but—

Mark broke in. "I wasn't done. So listen and shut up. First, you were put on a job before you were fully trained. Second, people have biological needs, and you can't go into a woman's restroom with her."

To himself, Keith protested that he could have just pulled over to the side of the road in the dark. Another part of himself said, *"But as he said, you weren't trained for this."* His throat constricted anyway. If Anna died, it would kill him.

"Third, you're dealing with a grieving woman. They are unpredictable and most likely that is what this is."

"We left because Hani heard someone outside the house. If they followed me..."

The silence that followed became an ominous nod as if Mark wouldn't verbally acknowledge the truth of it.

"So, I'll let you know when I hit Fairbury. She has a head start on me, but—" A car with non-existent taillights loomed up so fast, that he had to jerk over into the left lane, earning him a blared horn from a semi.

"She has a head start, and you have to do a swap out in Collinsville, but you can do a straight shot from there. Ignore speed limits wherever safe. She'll have to rely on someone coming to get her or on strangers she feels she can trust. You'll beat her."

That was true. Then again, he'd lose time if he got pulled over. "Yeah, and if I get a ticket..."

Mark's laughter diffused some of the tension he'd built up. "Expense it! Also, no worries. We'll get it off your record."

There had been allusions to that kind of preferential treatment, but this was the first time it had ever been overtly vocalized. Just how far did Mark's influence reach?

~

Illinois I-70
July 22, 2012
1:43 a.m.

Guilt pummeled Anna from every side. She smiled into the rearview mirror as the little old man, Charles, caught her gaze once more. He gave her a weak smile back and squeezed his wife's hand. Again.

"Are you sure you're all right?"

Anna nodded. "I am now. I just had to get away. Thank you so much for helping me."

CeeCee, his wife, turned around and gave her a sweet smile. "I wish we could take you all the way. But we're stopping just this side of Indianapolis, and it's such a long drive as it is. Charles doesn't drive well in traffic anymore, so we have to travel at night..."

It was only the fifth time the woman had explained. Nerves? Dementia? Were they really escapees from a nursing home somewhere?

Anna realized CeeCee expected a response and shook her head. "No, no, thank you so much. I just had to get away while I had the opportunity."

The woman nodded. "You hear about these things—some poor woman being abducted and sold into all kinds of horrible things. But you never imagine that it'll actually happen to you."

Anna agreed. She knew Charles still wasn't confident that she wasn't lying. That much was obvious. But Anna stuck to it like nobody's business.

Once more his gaze met hers in the rearview mirror, and once more she smiled back. "Are you sure you don't want us to take you to the police? They could still catch the guy if we were fast enough."

Anna pulled a hair from her pocket and held it up. That she'd ripped it from her own head and broken it into a short piece was information he didn't need to know. "I got a hair sample when he grabbed me. I promised myself I'd get away and take it to the police when I was safe again. The police in Rockland can figure out who he was, but I'm getting as far away from him and anyone he is working with as I can."

The man nodded and seemed to relax. Did he believe her now? She'd piled up enough lies on top of each other that Anna wasn't certain she could live with herself. She'd have to confess to Roman. He hated lies. And reality sucker-punched her. Tears poured down her face at the realization that he wouldn't be there—ever. Never again.

Anna heard the man mumble something to his wife. As quickly as she wiped tears away, new ones fell, but in the tiny moments between, she saw a stricken look on Charles' face. CeeCee looked back and began fumbling through her purse. "Oh, honey, it's going to be all right. It really will. They'll find him. They'll stop him so nobody else has to go through what you went through." She turned on the dome light and asked again, "Are you sure you're not hurt. He didn't..." Tears filled the woman's eyes.

"No... no." Rage, pain, grief ripped through her, sending even more tears coursing down her cheeks. Between sobs, she choked out a promise that she hadn't been assaulted. "He didn't have me for long. I don't know where he was taking me, but I doubt it would've been nice."

CeeCee passed back a small packet of tissues and told her to have a good cry. As if Anna could have prevented it. She snoozed, sniffled, and wept her way across Illinois and Indiana until she saw the sign for Indianapolis—thirteen miles. She'd call her friend again. She'd wait at the truck stop. She'd get home, and with any luck and many blessings, Keith would arrive in time to help her set up a trap for the vile, foul, sorry excuses of humanity who took her Roman from her.

Chapter Twenty-Two

Rockland
July 22, 2012
10:43 a.m.

THE EXCESSIVE SHOW OF WEALTH AND POSITION NAUSEATED Mark, but he sat relaxed in the living room of the Roarke Building penthouse exuding a persona that insisted he deserved every creature comfort imaginable. Jerm, dressed in black slacks, black dress shirt, and black tie hovered near the door, waiting for the knock. As long as Jessica stayed in the room until the right moment as instructed, they'd have this thing sewn up in no time.

A soft ding announced the arrival of the private elevator. Jerm had the door open before Steven Solari could knock—if the man would. You never knew with guys like him. Opening first showed respect, anyway.

Another lie. They got to him when he had to work with thugs like Solari. Usually, lies didn't faze him. You said what you had to in order to do the job. But when it meant working with the very people you often protected people from...

Jerm's soft, "Mr. Madsen?" cued his performance.

Mark looked up, made a show of taking in Solari behind Jerm, and rose. "Solari."

The man stood there in a suit jacket, unbuttoned collared shirt, and slacks. The pocket of the jacket bulged with what could only be a pistol. At that small size, Mark guessed a Sig Sauer. Solari examined him before saying, "You look familiar."

This was it. If he ticked off the man now, it might take even longer to take down Leone. And that was the biggest problem. Only rare cases required The Agency to be a part of this kind of investigative process. He preferred none.

"I ran into you at The Oakes a week or so ago. Pretended to be interested in a little personal entertainment." This time he allowed his disgust to show—a gamble, but if it paid off, he'd learn a lot.

"I remember..." When Mark gestured for Solari to be seated, the man hesitated before taking a chair. "You said pretended."

Mark reclined back onto the couch again and gave Jerm a significant look before returning his attention to Solari. "I'd heard that it was your man Leone's business, but I didn't believe it. You don't strike me as someone who allows his men to run a side hustle for extra cash."

"Side hustle?"

"The escort service taking over Marcello's in Fairbury *is* yours then?" Infusing a microscopic inflection on "is" could make or break the interview.

"Not mine, and Leone knows better." The inference that Mark had incorrect information might as well have been blasted with a megaphone.

Jerm appeared and passed the man a manila folder. Solari held it closed and turned steely eyes on Mark. "Madsen, is it?"

Mark nodded. "Mark is fine, though."

"Mark. When I open this folder, I'll find Leone at this restaurant? Maybe a couple of my men there as protection? And then..."

"Crime scene photos of Roman Simon and Philip Marcel. The previous owners of the restaurant who refused to sell to Leone. Simon's wife is in hiding."

The man's forehead furrowed. "What's this to you?"

"Your man, Leone, is hunting down Mrs. Simon. I don't like it when people try to kill my friends."

That did it. Solari flipped through the photos and paused before the most incriminating. Leone sitting at a large, cheap, oversized desk in a small office with a woman dressed in a sharp business suit bent over enough to expose everything a sleazy cocktail dress would. Solari sucked in his breath. "Jessica?"

"She's been forced into his service. She wants out. She's got all the information you need."

"Where is she?"

Without shifting his gaze from Solari's tightening features, Mark said, "Jeremiah?" Jerm nodded and went to retrieve their witness.

Seconds later, the soft snick of a door latch reached him. Solari looked up, and only the twitch of his jaw gave away his fury. "What are you doing here, Jessica?"

"Establishing my loyalty."

"You should've done that before you followed Leone."

Mark wanted to put a stop to things before anything spiraled out of control, but he couldn't risk missing key information. The tension had to snap soon.

"I would have—if I'd known Leone wasn't under orders. I just learned that he's on his own with the escort service." She scowled at Solari. "Steve, I thought *you* made me do this! If you'd admitted it while I was in there, you'd be a dead man."

Solari pulled a gun—the Sig Sauer, of course—from his pocket. "And if you don't convince me that you're not part of some pathetic attempt at a coup, you'll see how that could have played out."

Behind them all, Jerm reached into his pocket. Mark relaxed. It would be okay. They'd get what they needed. Jessica had felt confident that Solari would be angry but would listen to reason. Mark had decided to trust her, and it looked like that would pay off.

"When Leone let it slip that he'd proven what a fool you were to stay out of the entertainment business, I knew what he was doing and decided to take him down. The girls aren't happy. They're barely paid, kept on a very short leash, and many were promised public appearances only and ended up battered and tossed aside. Then they're in trouble for being out of work while they heal."

Solari swore—first with a single expletive puncturing the silence that followed Jessica's revelations. Then in rapid-fire as if a machine gun had let loose four-letter bullets. He pulled out his phone and sent a text. Without even looking at Mark, he addressed Jerm. "Can you get her to my car—safely? Can you *keep her alive* for that long?"

"Yes, sir."

Wide-eyed, Jessica moved toward him. "Steve! What?"

Solari rose and pointed at the door. "Go. If Leone let anything 'slip,' it was deliberate. You're being watched. If they know you're here, they might assume you've come to meet up with a client—a side hustle of your own. But if they saw me come in, you're dead. Dom will get you to the house. Tell Lynn I sent you to her after your boyfriend hit you—for safety."

"She'll never believe—"

Just as Jerm shot Mark a warning, Steve slammed his fist into her face. Jerm stepped behind her to keep her from falling, and they both stumbled backward. As he worked to keep Jessica upright, Jerm grabbed a wad of Kleenex from a box in a nearby table drawer.

"Now she will. Sorry about that. It had to be real."

The words she called Solari as she moved toward the door seemed mild to Mark, but two seconds after it shut behind her, it opened again, and Jessica's tissue-covered, already-swelling face poked through. "Thanks, Steve. I owe you one."

"I just slugged you. We're even."

This time, when the door shut behind her, Solari turned to Mark. "Can he keep her safe?"

"In this building, yes. He's not trained for more than that."

"Great." The sarcasm could've done more damage than Jerm, but Mark wouldn't admit that. Solari eyed him. "If you're telling the truth about your friend, she'll be safe in forty-eight hours. If you're not, get your affairs in order."

The door hadn't closed behind the man before Mark sent a text to Chief Varney.

> Slight chance you can get Solari, too. It'll be fast. Over in forty-eight max.

~

Steelville
July 22, 2012
10:03 a.m.

When Hani got word from Jerm that they still hadn't found Anna, her heart sank. She insisted on returning. But Mark still demanded she remain.

"You have to keep this cover in case Anna did escape by herself. We need to leak your location and that she's there with you. We'll send Leone's men to you, and you will need to be there. Anthony is on his way as backup."

If tearing out her hair would have helped, she'd have been bald. Still, he was right.

"Meanwhile, you need to leave for a few hours, come back, and then go see the boyfriend."

"He's not my boyfriend."

The softening in Mark's tone told her that he was amused even in the middle of this mess. "That's not what Keith says. Or rather, it's not what he says this guy wants." With that, Mark disconnected.

Blood. She needed some. That'd get her out of the house long enough to have visited her brother. According to Google, she'd find an Asian market in Rolla. Maybe that's where Keith lived. Yep. She'd just moved him there. Perfect. Oh, and that girlfriend's name would be Sadie Jo. Yeah... all peaches and cream and Junior League.

As a diversion, Hani spent the entire trip to and from the store creating a backstory for Keith and Sadie Jo worthy of its own romance novel. A total enemies-to-lovers thing where she thought the military was "mean," and he thought she was as pampered as her purse dog. Yeah... His own, precious "Elle Woods" from Dunwoody instead of Beverley Hills.

At the drive, she slammed on her brakes before pulling in. No extra tire tracks in the gravel. Easing forward, she eyed the grass, the dirt—anywhere there could be footprints. *Should've created an entry trigger before I left.* Anyone who was any good at evasion could easily have fooled her, but goons like Leone's probably wouldn't have bothered.

She mixed four parts water to one part blood powder and eyed the result. Clotting. Blood clotted and was thicker than that after a while. She stirred in another half part and grabbed a hairdryer. Downstairs, she dropped a few spatters across the floor and poured the rest of the blood onto a towel. A spray bottle spritzed with it was enough to leave it damp, but it was still pretty red. The hairdryer both dried out and darkened the spatters. She tried it on the towel, and it did make things darker, but it also dried out the towel more than she thought it should be. Oh, well.

She needed to get out to Granger's place and tell her story. If it lured people to the house while she was gone, even better. Meanwhile, she'd tell him she was leaving. Then she'd hide her car, even if she had to park it on the back lawn like a redneck.

As Hani pulled into the neat but sparce driveway area surrounding his farm, the front door opened. An old-fashioned screen door screeched as it pushed out and then slammed shut with a *thwack!* Barefooted, Granger took the porch steps in one bound and met her at the bottom. He gripped her shoulders, gazing into her eyes as if certain he could read something there.

"What's going on?"

"It's Keith. I found blood down there this morning. I missed it last night—rushing, I guess." Hani found herself flushing at the lies she poured forth and ordered herself to get control. Two things became obvious in that moment. First, she wanted a chance with this guy. Second, she'd have to get permission from Mark to bring him into minimal knowledge of her job for that to be a possibility.

"Whoa. We need to find—"

"Oh, I found him," Hani broke in. "He took himself to the Baptist hospital ER, got all stitched up, and now he's home with Sadie Jo looking out for him."

"Sadie Jo?" The guy's eyes actually twinkled at her. Or something. Whatever they did, it sent a swirl of emotions she wasn't ready to deal with coursing through her veins.

Yeah. She had to get out of there—not see him again until she got the green light from Mark, and that couldn't happen until the case was closed.

"Keith's girlfriend. Actually, she's at his house. Bad laceration to the hand, so he won't be back for a while." A thought prompted a snicker which meant Granger demanded an explanation. "He might not come back at all. I ticked him off pretty badly, so..."

Granger leaned against the step railing and folded arms over his chest. "Yeah?" The guy looked skeptical. "You ticked *him* off?"

Hani shoved her hands in her pockets and gave him a slow smile. "Told him he wouldn't have to worry about Sadie Jo's dad coming after him with a shotgun if he'd put a ring on it."

Granger gave a small smile, but his expression hinted that he'd read through more than she was saying. "I'm not sure what you're doing here. I feel like I'm missing the subtext in an important movie scene."

Great way to put it, but Hani ignored that and focused on her job. If Granger even got an inkling that she'd be around and in danger, he'd never leave her alone. The thought stunned her. It was true, and as much as she wanted to convince herself that she didn't know how she felt about that, it was a lie. She knew, and contrary to everything she liked to think about herself she liked it. *Back on track, Hani! Psychoanalyze yourself later. Then remember you don't need a man to be complete.*

"My brother needs me. I need to get there before he does something really stupid while hopped up on painkillers and really does propose. He'd never forgive me. I just didn't want to go without saying goodbye." When she choked up at that, Hani nearly bolted. This was ridiculous. She didn't get choked up at anything—not Hallmark commercials, not funerals, not even *Budweiser* commercials!

In a move that should've felt like an "atta boy" but instead had every romantic overtone romance readers devoured, Granger gripped the back of her head and pulled her into a hug. "Will you be back?" The words held a raspy quality she hadn't heard from him before. Her insides became a puddle.

"Yes. I'll be back, but I have to go now." *And not because I will lose my job if I don't but because I might just lose my head over you.*

How he did it, she'd probably never know (unless she convinced him to show her someday), but that hug shifted the slightest bit, and his lips took over. She'd been kissed before, or so her life record claimed. Third grade. Sixth. A series of lip-locks that punctuated most days or weeks of high school. College? Mostly just one guy she dumped a week after graduation when he decided they'd get married at Christmas. Not asked... decided. A few between then and signing on with Mark. Nothing since The Agency.

And nothing ever like this. How two lips could envelop a person entirely, she didn't know, but Granger's did. Toe curling? Check. Heart-stopping? Check. Insides melting? Check. Swoon-inducing? *Check!*

It wasn't an "I will love you forever" kiss, thankfully, but more of a "This is where I want us to go" declaration. When he finally released her lips (and she finally released his), Granger pulled her back into that same protective hug and said, "You'd better come back."

"Where'd that come from?"

He pulled back just enough to smile that tiny half smile that did ridiculous, girlie things to her insides. "I don't know, but I want to find out."

Chapter Twenty-Three

Fairbury
July 22, 2012
3:43 p.m.

IT TAKEN THE ENTIRE TRIP FROM ROCKLAND TO FAIRBURY TO convince her friend that she needed to go home and be alone. Tears had finally beaten Stephanie down. But as Anna slipped into her apartment, pushing the door closed behind her and locked it, she almost wished she'd waited. Waited until it wasn't the middle of a hot day. Waited until she knew Keith had figured out where she'd go and had time to get there. Waited until she'd gotten good sleep. Waited until she was ready to deal with the emotions that engulfed her the moment she saw the shape of Roman's favorite chair in the little light allowed by their heavy curtains.

With tears streaming down her cheeks, she fumbled for the thermostat before turning toward the bedroom. Three steps in, took a quick turn as her bladder reminded her that it had been a long drive from Indianapolis. After one look at her tear-stained face, Anna shed her clothes and climbed into the shower. She'd cry there—sob out all her heartbreak.

That thought broke her even further. Anna didn't cry often, but when she did, she did a thorough job of it. Almost always in the shower.

And Roman, hearing her, would come into the bathroom, turn off the water, climb in with her, and hold her. He wouldn't do that today. She gripped the small safety bar and held fast as the iron fist of grief strangled her. He wouldn't comfort her ever again.

It's why I did it, Roman. It's why I forced Keith to come here. For you. We'll stop these people. I'll run your restaurant. We'll win. Because I love you.

Talking to a husband who wasn't there, even in her head, hinted at an instability Anna wasn't ready to contemplate. Then again, perhaps it wasn't that unusual. People kept rooms untouched for decades when loved ones died. The rest of their lives were as normal as they could be, even while upstairs, in one small part of a house, a part of the past they didn't ever want to leave stayed exactly the same.

The pile of dirty clothes on the bathroom floor wouldn't do. Anna wrapped a towel around her and used the hand towel to wipe the mirror. A scream gurgled up in her as the sneering face of a man she half recognized reflected back at her. The man raised a hand, his gun now visible. Anna closed her eyes, steeling herself for the blast that would send her out of a world without Roman—back to him. And in the fragment of a second that the thought formed, the blast came, sounding nothing like she'd expected and with no pain.

She heard herself crumple to the floor, though she didn't feel it. She heard grunts and felt the sting of... Anna opened her eyes and found the mirror shattered. Blood streaked across her arms and trickled down her face, her neck, her chest. The yellow towel, half falling off now, held splotches of blood.

Just as she turned toward the sounds at her feet, she found herself flung over a shoulder and propelled through the door. "Are you crazy?"

Keith. Had he been there all along? Probably. "No..." The right answer appeared on her lips without conscious thought. "I just knew I could trust you."

He set her on the bed and told her to put on something that would give him access to her cuts. Before she could reply, pounding on the front door sent him bolting from the room. The rumble of voices told her that other men had arrived—men who weren't there to attack Keith. Near her door, she heard someone say, "Is she in here?"

"Probably not wearing much. She'd just gotten out of the shower when the guy got in. I'd gone to check the back when this guy came in through the front."

Apparently, "this guy" had come to because someone else began swearing revenge and fighting enough to add to the damage in the bathroom. *That'll be expensive. Roman's not going—*

There, with only underwear and a tank top on, Anna's tears began again.

~

Fairbury
July 23, 2012
3:13 a.m.

"How'd they know she was here?" Hani's words burst into the apartment before her body made it to the door.

Keith glanced up from a pad and paper and nodded at her before going back to whatever he was doing. Mark leaned back in a chair and eyed her. "I thought you were maintaining cover."

"When they came after her, there wasn't a need, was there?"

Wedged into a corner of the couch as small as she could make herself, Anna sat wringing her hands in such a near motionless manner, Hani almost missed it. She didn't miss the pain that etched a little deeper around the woman's eyes every time they looked Mark's way.

She doesn't like Mark? Doesn't make sense... Hani examined the scene before realization struck. "Hey, Mark? Can we talk?"

Only when they'd made it as far as the kitchen did Hani realize that this was the first time she'd ever seen Mark in a client's home like this. She set that thought aside and leaned close to whisper, "You're hurting her. I think that chair is where Roman sat."

The sharp intake of breath told her he hadn't had a clue. "I'll handle it. Thanks."

"Now how did they know she was here? Did they? Or did they trace Keith instead?"

"Keith left everything behind when we found out they'd put a tracker on him. We even swapped out vehicles. They couldn't have followed him."

"Could they guess based on where that stuff went dead?"

Mark seemed to waffle. "Maybe... but they'd have to have gotten close enough to use it. From what we discovered, it doesn't have a long range. They have to be within ten to twenty miles at best."

"Unless your guy's intel is wrong."

"About?" Mark watched her.

Hani stared back. "Any of it," she said after a few achingly long seconds. "The range, who they tracked..."

They both turned their gaze to Anna. Hani spoke first. In a whisper she said, "Keith packed a bag for her. They could've tracked anything in it —including whatever she was wearing yesterday."

"Get her out of here!"

Keith bolted from his chair, grabbed Anna's arm, and dragged her to the door. "Hani, run out front as if you're desperate to get away. Mark, chase after her. Hoodie, Hani!" he added as she raced past. Anna stared as Hani did a mid-run about-face and raced for the bedroom. The only thing she could find was one that had to belong to Roman. This would hurt.

All she could do was run and do her best to draw folks away. She'd sprinted down to the street, making sure to stay in the glow of streetlights, and toward her Miata when she remembered that Anna didn't drive. Locals claimed Roman wouldn't allow her to. She sprinted past the car and ignored Mark's calls and footfalls behind her. They just had to give Keith time to sneak Anna out—however that worked.

Why had Mark let her stay? Why hadn't he removed her immediately? It was protocol—*his* protocol.

Three blocks over, she darted around a corner and found a hydrangea bush large enough to hide them both. Mark joined her several seconds later. He had to have been holding back. No way was a fit guy with legs twice as long as hers not able to catch up. Between huge gulps of air Hani asked the obvious question. "Why was she still there?"

"Because I was." Mark barely sounded winded. "I'm not cut out for agent work. I miss things when I'm present. I was in town..." He drew in a long breath and exhaled. "...and came over. It could've gotten her killed. I've fired people for that kind of mistake."

"Well, you're not an agent. An agent would know better. I almost asked in there, but you being the boss..."

Mark tensed. "Never hesitate to call me on dangerous behavior. Period. I don't have the skills in the field. I just don't. It's why I hire people like you. You don't get distracted."

It wasn't the first time he'd hinted that he'd tried to do the job himself and it hadn't gone well. Now wasn't the time to let him think about that. She focused on that last sentence instead. "Yeah... about that. We need to talk."

"The boyfriend?"

"The guy I kissed and might want to be a boyfriend—maybe." Once she'd spoken the words, Hani knew that they were true. She did want it... and maybe all that "it" meant. Her life would change, though. "I need a few months off—just to see."

"Yours. After we know Leone is out of the picture and Anna is safe."

"Deal."

~

Rockland
July 25, 2012
11:13 a.m.

Jerm burst into the room. "They've installed cameras!"

All conversation around the conference table ceased. Keith watched the others. Hani watched Mark, an idea growing. Would he go for it?

Mark spoke first. "Get a hold of Jill and Corey. Make sure Anna and Lauren are all right."

"Are they together?" Hani's pulse ticked up a notch just at the thought.

Jerm shook his head. "No. Paul is on his way to Jill. Corey and Lauren are holed up in the cabin." He winced. "Bet she hates me more than ever now."

"She's safe," Hani reminded him.

"Yeah."

This was her moment. "What if I go in? Dress to show off everything

I've got and hide what I don't. Not have the money to pay an exorbitant bill. See if it gets me dragged into Leone's office?"

"What?" Mark asked. "The modern version of 'washing the dishes'?"

She shrugged. It would work. She knew it. Especially if she wore a certain dress and bra that gave her assets she really didn't possess. "I get in there, I ascertain if Leone is there, and if so, Fairbury moves in. Done."

"Why not send in Fairbury anyway?"

"He'll get out if they see the police coming. You know they will. We need confirmation first."

"How will you get word to us?"

It would be a risk, and Mark would see that, but it was the only thing that would work that didn't look suspicious. "I have a text ready to send. They get me into the office, I apologize profusely and pull out my phone to 'call my friend' to bring me money. Hit send. It will only take a second to do. So even if they try to stop me, they can't—not from sending the text. Only from making the call."

He didn't like it. She saw that. "What'll your boyfriend say if you get shot?"

"He's not my boyfriend," Hani snapped. The thought of Granger's reaction to her protest prompted a grin. She couldn't help it. "Yet."

"I think we have to try. This could be over today." Mark's jaw tightened, turning his face into a sculpted contour of hard angles before he relaxed it just enough to look like himself again. "All right. Get in there. Need cash for something killer to wear?"

"Nope. My cousin had a bachelorette party a couple of months ago. I've got just the thing."

~

Fairbury
July 25, 2012
6:35 p.m.

Planning the perfect takedown? Easy. Preparing for it? Not too bad. Executing the set up... Hani dabbed at her lips with a napkin before taking a drink of her twenty-five-dollar glass of wine. Lovely. Preparing to ask for the check? Hani changed her thoughts before they broke her out in revolting perspiration. She was supposed to attract notice, not repel it.

Hani sat between two cameras. One practically provided an x-ray of her cleavage. The other offered a full view of her face and most of her upper body—possibly the whole table. She had no way of knowing the zoomed in capabilities.

Her server paused and offered to take her plate. "Dessert? We have an excellent crème brulé tonight."

"I'd love it, but I couldn't even finish this." She gave him her best flirtatious smile. "Too bad, though. I'd love to draw this out as long as possible. Wonderful dining experience."

"Your date had something come up?"

This would be good. "Oh, no. I came alone." She leaned forward, as if letting him in on a secret. "Whenever I need a little 'me time,' I take myself out to a good meal. It's the best. No trying to impress anyone but myself. No one expecting me to keep up my end of a conversation or worse..." She leaned back and stopped herself from winking just in time. "Listening to him."

The guy laughed. "I'll get your check."

"Thank you. No rush. I still have a bit of my wine left. Great stuff. People can say what they want, but I think Napa produces the best wines —if you're willing to pay for the right vintage."

"That's what Mr. Simon used to say." The guy gulped and backed away. "I'll be back."

Was the show of emotion out of respect or distaste? She never could tell. Locals didn't think much of Roman Simon—except those few who thought a *lot* of him.

Anna had overheard the description of him as a controlling, abusive Neanderthal and had laughed. A horrible, hollow, pain-riddled laugh that had sent shivers down Hani's spine when she'd viewed the video of it. "Those idiots." It was almost the harshest, ugliest thing she'd ever heard Anna say. "They thought they knew him. They think I'm weak and pathetic because I grieve him. But they're the weak ones—the pathetic ones." Once she'd started, no one could calm her. She'd begun pacing the floor ranting. "My Roman *loved* me. He never raised his voice to me—not once. Never touched me with anything but love and respect. He *adored* me. I was blessed to know and love him. And they... they can keep their ugly opinions to themselves. It's an insult to his memory!"

A love like that... If Hani could have that, she'd give up her career in a heartbeat. But was it real or in Anna's head? And if real, did it happen to people like her? Could it?

A discreet tray slid onto the table beside her. Anna pulled herself out of her thoughts, took a bracing sip of her wine, and paused over it. Wine. Did Keith drink wine? Beer? Whiskey? Did Christians like him do that?

Something about the question bothered her. Hani stared into the glass as she considered it. When understanding broke through her confusion, she nearly gasped. It bothered her because she wanted the answer. She cared about someone's faith—something she'd refused to consider her whole life. She'd avoided people who talked about their gods—any gods. Even the one they spelled with a capital G as if it made him superior somehow.

Keith didn't do that—talk "about" his god. He talked *to* that god. He practiced his faith—whatever that meant—but he didn't intrude into others' lives with any of it. Invited them, sure. Lived whatever he lived naturally. Didn't hide it. But as much as she'd wanted to claim otherwise, not once had he tried to make her take notice.

Another time, Hani. You're on an assignment.

And she couldn't blow this. Mark rarely agreed to any kind of investigation or set up like this. Protect and return. That was their job. But The Agency's motto of "whatever it takes" had worked in her favor.

She pulled out her purse and reached in. Froze. Stared down into the small handbag. Pulled out phone, lipstick, sunglass case, and car keys. Infusing every bit of panic she knew she'd feel if this were real into the equation, piling on the real nerves that came with knowing she'd be in danger in less than a minute, Hani swallowed hard, shoved everything back in her purse, and pulled out that phone. She typed out a text message and hit send. Anyone reading her phone would only see:

> Steph. I'm at Marcello's in Fairbury, and my wallet isn't here! I need money. Fast! Can you call and offer to pay for it over the phone?

The third time the server came, Hani poured every bit of mortification she could into her words as she whispered, "Can you ask the manager to come here. My wallet—it's gone. I asked a friend to bring me money, but she hasn't responded yet. She's probably on her way, I promise. She forgets to reply all the time, but she's good for it. I told her to call..." On and on she babbled, trying to keep the guy there as long as possible in order to ensure the office saw it.

"I—well, let me go ask. Are you sure your friend is coming?"

"Pretty sure. I'll call someone else if she's not here soon. I just don't want everyone converging on me. It's so embarrassing. I'm so sorry." Hani allowed her eyes to fill with forced tears.

The guy gave her a weak smile and promised to come right back. A minute later, a man in black appeared at her shoulder. "Please come with me."

"Sure... Sure. I'm so sorry. I—" A look from the guy stopped her. Dread mingled with confidence. He had to be taking her to Leone.

A few employees gave her nervous glances as the guy led her past the bar, the kitchen, and the restrooms. He marched her down the dim hallway to a door and knocked. "Yes." Goon dude, as Hani had decided to call him, reached around her and opened the door. With a gentle shove, he pushed her inside, stepped in, and closed the door behind her. Hani glanced over her shoulder at him before moving forward.

"Are you the manager? I'm so sorry. I called my friend, and she's probably on the way—"

The picture they had of Leone was too flattering to the man sitting before her. He looked... older. Frail, almost. And as if she were in a cheesy movie, her first thought was, *Do I detect a flicker of fear in your eyes?*

"Enough."

The hard-bit edge to his voice sent her scrambling into her purse for her phone. She flipped it open and hit send, her thumbs fumbling for a couple of seconds after it went as if she were still writing. Just as goon dude reached for it, she pretended to hit send again. "I asked Steph where she is."

Leone didn't look at her. His eyes were riveted to the guy beside her. Goon dude grunted. "A text says she's forgotten her wallet and asks 'Steph' to bring money. The last one asks where she is."

Leone held out his hand for the phone. After reading through her text messages, he thumb-typed out something, hit send, and pocketed it. "You don't send many text messages, do you?"

"Mostly use a work phone for texts. I like calls better." The moment she said it, Hani's throat closed in on itself. If he checked...

"And you expect me to believe you showed up here, ordered an expensive meal and an equally expensive glass of wine and just 'happened' to forget the means to pay for them? How'd you get here?"

Thinking fast, Hani said, "I drove." A second later, she said, "Maybe my wallet fell out of my purse—in the car. It's not really a wallet—more of just a small case that holds my license on one side and a credit card and twenty bucks on the other—for emergencies" She looked up at goon dude. "You could go look? Here's—"

The guy grabbed her wrist before she could put her hand in her purse again. Smart move. If she'd brought a gun and he hadn't, things could've been bad for both of them. *One more way this case is bizarre. He should've taken my purse from me.*

Sonny and Cher belted out "I've Got You Babe" through Hani's phone. She dove across the desk and tackled Leone as Keith and Anthony burst through the door. Leone fought hard for a scrawny little thing, but Hani flipped him, her knee in his back, his arm twisted to the snapping point. "Don't move, you letch."

When he yowled, Keith remarked, "Hmmm... bet he does that when Solari gets a hold of him."

Leone went limp. It took a moment for her to process, prove, and proclaim, "Um... this guy just fainted."

Epilogue

Fairbury
August 5, 2012
1:32 p.m.

ROMAN WOULD NEVER HAVE RECOGNIZED THE OFFICE AT Marcello's. Despite the low VOC of the butter yellow paint she'd chosen, Anna ran an air purifier to clean out the faint traces of fumes that she insisted she smelled. Laminate plank flooring replaced the old, dingy carpeting. A slim desk took up one corner with plenty of room for her to work from. A stack of invoices lay on top, and she entered each one into the software Jerm from The Agency had shown her how to use.

Their wedding photo sat on the very edge of the desk. Next to it, her Bible. She and Roman hadn't been faithful in the last few years. Sure, she'd prayed while she did housework or took walks, but she'd left reading her Bible for holidays and when she needed the encouragement. As if she didn't *always* need encouragement. How arrogant they'd been. They thought they had all the time in the world.

Lauren knocked on the door. "Ms. Simon?" She peered around it. "I've got a guy out here who's ticked off that his 'date' isn't here waiting for him. He 'arranged' that they'd meet here last month." The girl's face burned. "He then informed me that I'd 'do' if necessary. Can I kick him out?"

"No."

The girl's shock turned to daggers inside half a second.

Anna rose and moved forward. "That's one of the perks of *my* job."

Lauren stopped her just as she started through the door. "Aren't you mad that they took you like that—The Agency people?"

The poor girl. She was the only one Lauren could talk to about it. "I'm grateful they kept me alive. If they had to tie me up and gag me until it was safe, I'd have hated every second of it and still be grateful."

Tears filled the girl's eyes. "I guess. Corey was nice enough. But I kept waiting for something really bad to happen. I was sure that guy was just messing with my head."

Anna laid a hand on her arm. "I meant it. If you need a little time off to deal with this, then take it—with pay."

She'd taken two steps down the little hallway before Lauren spoke up again. "You're doing a good job here. Roman would be pleased. I think he loved you in his own way."

Anna turned and gave her a smile, weak though it was. "Roman loved me more than anyone ever knew or could understand. You all thought he was harsh and abusive—controlling."

Lauren nodded.

"Not once. Not ever. The anger and frustration you saw was that no one else thought I was as amazing as he did."

~

Steelville
August 23, 2012
7:25 p.m.

Granger braked hard, reversed, and pulled into the driveway at Hani's place. A black Dodge Charger sat parked there. *What?*

It only took a dozen steps toward the house before someone appeared in the front doorway. *Hani...*

His feet refused to take another step. Glancing over at the car and back up to her, he asked, "What happened to the zippy car? Crash it? Or did Keith pound it instead of you?

Hani stepped out onto the porch wearing a pink sundress that looked made for her. Pink, of all colors. He'd never have imagined her in pink. He'd never forget her in it now, either. "It wasn't my car."

"So, are you back?" Granger's feet decided to cooperate again, and he took a few steps forward. "For good?"

She met him at the bottom of the porch steps, one hand resting on his chest. "For a while, at least." A smile formed. "I needed to come back and see if a certain kiss was as breathtaking as I remembered."

"Breathtaking, huh?" He couldn't help but smile back. "I bet we can arrange that."

The sun dipped behind the trees across the road. As if the wave of a conductor's wand, the drone of tree frogs and cicadas rose to fill the evening air. Hani sighed, and something in him wanted to remove all sighs from her life. *What an idiotic thought.*

"So... I need to understand your faith—I mean, really understand. You and Keith have something I've never seen before."

"Happy to." He pulled her close, his hand wrapped around the back of her head, his chin resting on top. "So happy to."

They stood unmoving until a swarm of tree swallows swooped in on a pin oak on the other side of the rhododendrons. "I've got a job I can't tell you about," she whispered.

Any lingering uncertainties flew off to join the swallows. "Yeah?" When she looked up at him, Granger chuckled. "Duh. Kind of obvious. But whatever. I'm okay with that."

"How?" She stroked his cheek, and Granger covered her hand with his, holding it there and reveling in the moment. "How can you be okay with it?"

Easiest answer ever. But first... he'd waited long enough for that second kiss, and he decided he wasn't waiting any longer. Hani's arms wrapped around his neck as he lifted her closer. That kiss was worth the wait, but it ended (necessarily but unfortunately) all too soon. With her face cupped in his hands, Granger said, "I'm okay with it because I'm okay with *you*."

About Chautona Havig

Want More?

Induction is the introductory novel to The Agency Files series. Grab the next one, *Justified Means*, **HERE**.

About Chautona:

Chautona Havig lives in an oxymoron, escapes into imaginary worlds that look startlingly similar to ours and writes the stories that emerge. An irrepressible optimist, Chautona sees everything through a kaleidoscope of *It's a Wonderful Life* sprinkled with fairy tales. Find her at chautona.com and say howdy—if you can remember how to spell her name.

Or follow her online!

Newsletter (sign up for news of FREE eBook offers): https://chautona.com/news

facebook.com/chautonahavig

instagram.com/ChautonaHavig

goodreads.com/Chautona

bookbub.com/authors/chautona-havig

Made in the USA
Middletown, DE
23 September 2023

39174362R00385